The Oasis Stone

Jack Davidson

Cover, illustrations, and map by John Spencer.
Edited by Shawna Hampton

Published by Teirmond Publishing
PO Box 10
Durham, CT 06422

www.ralvera.com

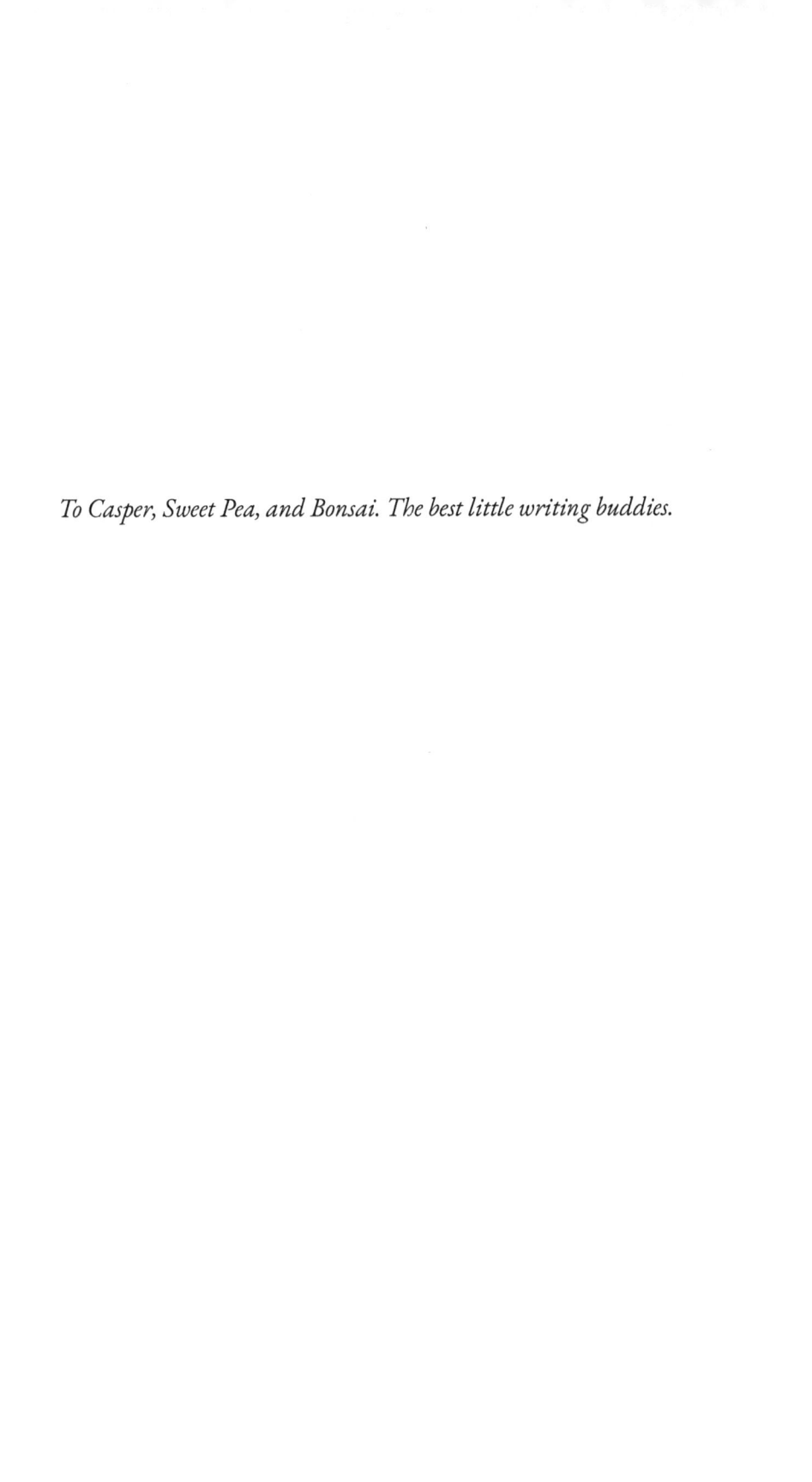

To Casper, Sweet Pea, and Bonsai. The best little writing buddies.

WESTERN FROSTWATERS

THAUMATURN THREE   THAUMATURN FOUR
LOST HOPE

THE SPLINTERED COAST

BIRCHBANE SPINE

THE SEA OF ECHOES

BOREALIS GLEN   THA

AURORA CLIFFS

THE SHATTERING SHELF

BELLITH
GIRREGAN MOUNTAINS

THE DROWNED TUNDRA

HIGHRUIN CLIFFS   THE ANTLE

SAOMMU   BASTION OF PERSEVERANCE   TYRAK PASS   FJORDHEARTH

IELVOST FOREST   THE REMNANT TRAIL

THE VALLEY OF TWILIGHT WATERS   THE WEEPING PEAKS   STAIRS OF RIME   ALGOR HILLOCKS

THE OUTLAWS   FIELD OF RELICS

EKEERA RIVER   THE ASHEN CRESTS

THE MUDWASTES   WALL OF OKANOS   THE BOILING BEND

THE ROOKERY   DEVAROS RIVER

UNFALRETH   TARAKOS   DEVAR

SCORCHRISE

OBSIDIAN LEAP   THE GREAT RALVERA DESERT   YSERA

LEVIATHAN BASIN   CRAG   PORT WENSTN

THE SALT CROWNS   RED EMPIRE   AZRAK MOUNTAINS   LAKE NAWAI   EIGHT KINGS WAY

CASKFELL   GJEROSO PLAINS   SAVIN ACTA

THE CRIMSON TORS   ILJROS

THE KILN ROAD   KHO RIVER   QUYNTR

NOATARA JUNGLE   BASTION OF LIFE   CLESIVE MOOR   REATH

TORUBA SWAMP   AZRAK DELTA   BAY OF TITHES   ERA I

CLESHIRE

NIGHTSAIL SEA   THE TEARDROPS

CARVE   THE WESTSEA STRAIT   THE EAS

CANNONFIRE NARROWS   THE WESTERN EYE

THE STRAYS   THE ABANDONS   SEA OF REFLECTIONS   VULN

THE SHIVERS   ESHRA'S GAMBIT   THE SILENT STEPS

UNEXPLORED ICE

EASTERN FROSTWATERS

ISLAND OF THE LIVING BLIZZARD

VENDOLVELL CASTLE

VRIN

WHITE STRAIT

FIVE'S CRATER

BAY OF PREY

THAUMATURN TWO

WINTER'S FANG

HUNSTMAN DELL

SCULPTURE PASS

SEPULCHER VALE

THE STARVING WOODS

ARCANIST'S GRAVE

HARVEST'S EDGE

HOLLOW CROSSING

TIMBERS

BASTION OF GROWTH

CENORETH FOREST

THE ASHFELL SCAR

MURKSHRINE RIVER

THE GARDEN OF STONE

GLOOMWALL

AMARI BASIN

ROZA'A BADLANDS

DARO SANDS

MONARCH RAVINE

SHORES OF BONE

KATROR

SLOSTIC ESTUARY

HIS SUNDER

THE QUICKSAND SEA

CAVOTROS

THE SANDSCALES

PTREDENORAS

OUTPOST WINDHORN

OAGANSHI

THE QUAKING CLIFFS

THE SPIRE MAZE

OUTPOST SCARSEEK

THE IMPASSABLES

R DESERT

THE GLASSLANDS

STAMPEDING DUNES

THE BEASTBONES

AN MEADOWLANDS

WILDBEAST CROSSING

TANESHRA RIVER

BASTION OF STRENGTH

MAMMOTH CRAGS

HE SAILWAY

SHIPWRECK PILLARS

PHANTOM CROSSWATERS

ICEDUSK STRAIT

FISHOIL ISLAND

WHALER'S CAULDRON

PARLAY ISLAND

SAFE HARBOR

RUNAWAY PASS

AKEN WATCH

KRASILIS

BEHEMOTH TRENCH

RALVERA

"*What are the people of Devar like? First you must ask, what is the Devaros River like? Is it strong? While the River is mighty, there are plenty stronger. Is it lucky? No, for there are many rivers lucky enough to never flow into the desert at all. It is, in fact, defiance that lets the Devaros flow from the Azrak Mountains to the Drowned Tundra. The defiance to avoid evaporation from not one, but three Scorch Vents. The defiance to still gurgle after ceaseless days under the desert sun. The Devaros is defiant, and so is the city built on its shores. Whether sun or sandstorm, flood or famine, Vent beast or Legion sword, Devar will stand defiant. Devar will thrive.*"

—sketch of Devar from aboard a coreskiff, taken from the journal of Oswal Briggin, cavernfolk explorer

Chapter 1

Shortcuts and Promises

Water thundered onto the distant rocks below, drowning out the faint voice in Mayve's head that told her she was in trouble.

Determined to ignore it, she dug her fingers harder into the cliff face, clawing at the rocks slick with condensation. Finding familiar footing, she propelled herself upward, catching an edge and heaving herself up onto an outcrop—nothing more than a bare ledge, jutting from the sheer cliff over a hundred feet of open air.

Mayve pushed her back against the cliff face, feeling the wet stone dig into her through her soaked shirt. Legs dangling over thin air, she paused to catch her breath, letting the burning ache fade from her arms. Far below, the waterfall churned the river into roiling gray clouds, darkened by the shadow of the cliff.

There must have been a storm upriver, the Falls are strong today. Wiping the stinging water out of her green eyes with the damp collar of her sleeveless shirt, Mayve muttered to herself, "All you had to do was look at the Falls before starting your climb. That was *all* you had to do."

The mighty Devaros Falls crashed past her—an entire river, plunging into midair far above. Mayve was in no danger of being swept away by the waters. It was the mist, settling on the rocks like a film of ice, wet and slippery, that would kill her. The roar of the Falls deafened her thoughts, and she doubted anyone would hear her if she called for help. Not that Mayve would ever do so.

She futilely tried to wring out her dark hair before letting it mat over her shoulders again. "Too late now, I suppose." Her words were lost in the roar of the Falls. She usually avoided her shortcuts when the river was this strong.

Peering upward, she searched for the top edge of the cliff through the stinging fog. "About sixty feet to go, looks like. I need to get farther away from the waterfall."

The raging waters had made her favorite path up far too dangerous, but Mayve knew others. She had long since memorized as many ways up the cliff as possible—anything to bypass the long, dry desert road that wound from Darkmist to Silt Row. It was worth any risk, in Mayve's opinion. *Ma would disagree, but she doesn't need to know where I am.* The next path up would hopefully be drier, but it would be a leap through open air to reach the adjacent ledge.

Carefully rising to her feet, one arm on the cliff face and the other keeping her balance, Mayve prepared to jump. She had made farther leaps before, but in the shadow of the cliff, it was impossible to tell if the distant ledge was damp or not.

She took a deep breath and checked that her coin purse was properly secured to her belt. It held just enough coin to buy a few packets of sandpepper seeds, requested by her mother for the garden. *It probably took Ma weeks to save this coin—can't have it going off the cliff.* The leather purse was safely cinched. *The only way that's falling down is if I'm falling with it.*

Mayve had promised her mother she would not take any of her shortcuts today. The worst part about dying here would be her mother finding out she lied through her teeth. Bracing herself, she studied the far ledge, planning each meticulous movement in her mind. The wind chilled her soaked clothes as it whipped across the cliffs, stirring the waterfall mist. The Devaros Falls roared behind her like an endless stampede. She only had room for a half-stride forward—all her strength *needed* to be in one step.

Mayve leapt. For a second, she hung in the air, her arms stretched toward safety. Her palms reached the ledge first, her fingers locking on the rough surface. Dry rock. The friction scraped her skin as the rest of her body slammed into the cliff, turning her sigh of relief into a forced exhale. Catching a foothold, she heaved herself onto the dry ledge, her wet palms gritty with sand and pebbles.

She glanced back at the ledge she leapt from, and was surprised to see just how obscured it was by the waterfall's mist. Mayve made a mental note to take the dreary long way home, and began the final stretch of her climb. The path up the cliff from here was easier, relatively speaking, for Mayve. She could climb the Devaros Falls blindfolded if she wanted to. She almost did before, on a dare from Ingo, but she cheated halfway up.

It was not long before Mayve cleared the top of the cliff and stopped again to catch her breath. Warm, southerly wind filled her lungs. Dry, dusty air, cooled slightly from the river. Mayve was just glad it was free of ash. A northerly or westerly wind was often tainted by ash from the Okanos or Cavotros Vents.

No longer in the shadow of the waterfall, the harsh desert sun offered a brief respite from the chilled mists. Mayve knew in a matter of minutes she would be dry and the glare would become insufferable. Looking downriver, she saw the distant stairs that staggered up the cliff side from Darkmist. From there, a sandy road wound back through the dunes toward the rest of Devar. An uncomfortably long walk, especially in the searing heat.

Beyond thrilled with her shortcut, Mayve put the climb out of mind, quickly forgetting any regrets she may have had about it. With a running start, she bounded up a nearby boulder to see her favorite view of Devar, the greatest city in the Ralveran Desert.

The grand Devaros River, named after the city it flowed through, sprawled out before her, churning sluggishly toward the precipitous cliffside. Mayve only *heard* the water, though. Built across the entire river—like a vast wooden blanket of bridges, stilts, and floating dwellings—was Silt Row, the largest borough of Devar. The wooden sprawl was so dense, the only visible part of the river was in one central canal, bisecting the borough.

Above her, the Devar Arch dominated the sky, a gargantuan mesa arch of reddish-tan sandstone spanning the entire length of the Devaros Falls like a bridge built by gods. Standing beneath it, Mayve could not see the opulent manors and lush gardens of the merchant guild masters and Citadel heirs that adorned the top of the Arch, but she knew well enough what they looked like. She had been up there many times—uninvited, of course—to sneak through their homes and pilfer their extravagant belongings. It was surprisingly easy, *if* you could climb up the Arch from the outside. They never saw her coming, and rightly so. After all, who would be reckless enough to make that climb?

While she could not see the manors, Mayve did see a coreskiff moored off the side of the Arch, swaying in midair with the wind like a boat bobbing over waves at the dock. She rolled her eyes and made a mental note to pay that manor a visit. *If they can afford a coreskiff, they can afford to part ways with some other belongings.*

The blast of horns rumbled over the noise of the Falls, and Mayve quickly forgot her disdain. Far down at the bottom of the Falls, the long silhouette of a boat was pulling into Darkmist Pool, and that meant it was time for the Lockworkers to go to work.

The Locks—a tangled web of ropes and plank bridges that dangled from the underside of the Arch—exploded with activity. Like a wake of vultures descending on a fresh corpse, the Lockworkers spiraled toward their prey from the ropes above, swiftly lowered hundreds of feet by practiced hands.

Each worker landed on the hull of the vessel, six on each side, and attached hefty chains to the special anchor points that all boats traveling on the Devaros were equipped with. Chains secured, a raptor on the hull removed a horn from his belt and sounded the all clear.

The call erupted from the depths of Darkmist, and other horns responded throughout the Locks. As the echoes faded, the Lockworkers yelled out in unison.

"Heave!" The chains snapped taut.

"Heave!" With a groan, the ship lifted from the water, dark figures on board furling sails and stowing oars.

"Heave!" Mayve saw raptors and humans, maybe even some Torn, swinging like jungle monkeys throughout the Locks, attaching ropes to pulleys and pulleys to anchors and anchors to chains.

Slowly and surely, the Lockworkers lifted the ship well above the lip of the waterfall. They swarmed over the hull like spiders, the boat securely tangled in a web of ropes and chains. Even higher, on the underside of the Arch, Lockworkers were carefully attaching the chains to different anchor points, getting ready to swing the boat over the top of the Falls and into the Silt Row canal.

As the boat tilted dangerously forward on its new tethers, several Lockworkers disconnected ropes from the stern of the vessel, and it began to swing with careful precision toward Silt Row. The creaks and groans of the wood always gave Mayve the impression that the boat itself was screaming for help, and now she saw the sailors on the vessel clinging to the railings and ropes for dear life.

An ear-piercing snap, like a tree breaking clean in half, cut through the blaring horns. A faint scream faded to nothing as a Lockworker hurtled down into the depths of Darkmist. One of the chains on the starboard bow had snapped, and the boat was now swinging toward Silt Row at a dangerous angle. Several Lockworkers on the boat scrambled to attach new tethers to the anchor point, but it was too late.

The boat picked up speed, swinging toward the wooden homes at the edge of the waterfall. Warning cries from the boat and screams from Silt Row rang out, followed by the sickening sound of wood splintering against wood. Mayve vaulted off the rock and sprinted between the riverside homes onto the wooden walkways of Silt Row, the river rushing underneath.

Reaching the edge of the canal, Mayve saw the damage was done. The boat was safely righted in the canal, with a fresh gash ripped into the stern, luckily above the waterline. However, the swinging vessel had cleaved through a forest of supporting stilts like a sharp axe, the buildings atop them starting to tilt toward the rushing river.

Buckling on their mangled legs, the houses gave out under their own weight. The occupants, who instinctively evacuated at the first sound of snapping wood, watched helplessly as their dwellings were swept over the edge, the sounds of impact far below mercilessly drowned by the waterfall.

To Mayve's surprise, a single home caught on the edge of the waterfall, digging into the rocky shallows. One support, lodged under a submerged rock in the luckiest, most precise manner, was all that remained between the house and a swift one-way trip into the Darkmist Pool. It vaguely reminded Mayve of how she had been clinging to the side of a cliff not too long ago.

Safely secured against the river's current, the boat was pulled into the docking area of the canal, the Lockworkers unlatching and swinging back into the sky. Pale-faced passengers began to depart, the flow of passengers giving a wide berth to a tall figure at the bottom of the boarding ramp. There, several merchant officials were trying to calm down the enraged boat captain.

Wearing a suit of worn iron plate armor with a tattered, hooded cloak draped over the pauldrons, the captain stood at least a foot taller than the groveling merchants, staring down as one of the dock officials explained—what Mayve could only guess—was extremely unsavory news.

Unfortunately for the official, his decree was cut short as the captain's gauntleted fingers clutched his throat, and he lifted the struggling merchant well off his feet. As the merchant flailed, he desperately grasped at the captain's hood and yanked it down.

A bleached skull, carved with intricate patterns and an inset iron circlet, grimaced in the sun. Glowing red lights set deep in its eye sockets fixated on the merchant.

"Now that I can hear you better, explain to me *again* how *I* am responsible for the damages to my boat." The captain's booming voice carried unnaturally over the crowd, the jaws of his skull moving with no muscles to form the disembodied words.

The dock official's sniveling reply did not carry over the crowd like the skeleton's voice. Mayve took a closer look at the crew, noticing most of the sailors donned similar hooded armor. *They're all Ul'Varin...that must be Captain Vulinor and his Ferrymen!*

To see a lone Ul'Varin on occasion what not unheard of, but to see a vessel full of the fiery skeletons? Only the Ferry boasted such a crew. Mayve had heard plenty of tales of the Ul'Varins' unnatural strength, and the poor merchant who dangled from the captain's grasp like wet laundry was getting a perfect demonstration.

Captain Vulinor's booming voice rang out again. "Perhaps your associates will own up to their mistakes better than you."

With the ease of tossing back a small fish, the captain hurled the merchant upriver. "Kinglor." He motioned to one of his skeletal underlings. "Fish him out. Don't be gentle."

Vulinor turned back to the remaining officials. "We will depart as scheduled in two days, and my boat will be repaired by the end of tomorrow. It is in your *best* interest to not discuss this further." With that, he turned away, cloak billowing as his heavy armored boots thumped up the gangplank of the Ferry.

Mayve wished she could follow him aboard. *Ma and I will take the Ferry one day. Get out to a Verdant city, leave Darkmist and Devar behind.* The Ferry was the only boat that traveled the Devaros that they had any chance of affording.

She took a brief second to plan a route to the Silt Row Market in her mind, avoiding the traffic of the main canal-side pathways, then set out. Confident and sure-footed, Mayve often got lost in her own thoughts as she leapt between bridges and stepped across canals. Navigating the twisting bridges and alleys of Silt Row was second nature for Mayve at this point, and as she traveled she replayed the events of the past hour in her mind's eye, deciding which details were important enough to tell her mother.

The Ul'Varin are always a sight to behold, and her mother would love to know that the Ferry was in town. Travelers and small merchants not affluent enough to afford travel with the merchant guilds usually bought passage on the Ferry. That meant the passengers also lacked the money to rent a good stall in Archtown or Silt Row, and ended up peddling their wares in Darkmist.

The Ferry would be off to Port Wenstnor next, down in the foothills of the Azrak Mountains, then it would pass back through Devar and north to Tyrak Pass. Mayve would move to either in a heartbeat. Cool breezes, lush scenery. The Verdants were entirely different worlds than the massive desert that separated them. *Port Wenstnor might be too posh for us, but perhaps Ma would move to Tyrak Pass.*

The white noise of the river was starting to get drowned out by the endless chatter and yells of the marketplace, now only a few streets away.

She cut into another alleyway and was rudely pulled out of her thoughts by a gruff reptilian voice. "Go on now and empty all those precious coins into this pouch right here."

Mayve's hand shot to her coin purse, but she relaxed as she glanced down the alleyway. Two identical raptors stood side by side, each sporting green scales with a smattering of blood-red feathers. They had cornered a young Oaken Legion soldier against the plank wall of a nearby house, and one had the blade of an axe pressed against the tree's throat.

The Oaken Legion soldier was armored in full timbersteel plate, the jagged edges biting into the plank wall. Greenish-yellow eyes, burning with rage, glared from his bark-clad face. His timbersteel sword and shield were still locked in their sheaths—the poor tree likely had no time to draw his weapons before the raptors ambushed him.

A fully clad Oaken Legion soldier would have been a menacing sight, if it was not for the bloodthirsty raptors that pinned him to the wall. One lizard had a clawed foot pressed onto the tree's chest and an axe at his throat. The other raptor had the tree's head wrenched backward by his hair-like branches, exposing his throat to the blade.

Red blood ran down the soldier's armor, dripping onto the alley's planks—raptor blood, from where the sharp timbersteel armor dug into the lizard's foot. If it bothered the raptor, he did not show it. Instead, he seemed to relish it, tongue hungrily running over his sharp teeth.

The tree spat, "How *dare* you threaten a soldier of the Oaken Legion! I will have my superiors-" The rest of his sentence was expelled with his breath as the second raptor dug his claws into the tree's face and slammed it into the wall.

"Shut your green-cursed mouth and give us the coin. Consider it a travel expense for your stay here in the desert," one of the raptors snarled. The young Oaken Legion soldier looked around for help and locked eyes with Mayve. Both raptors followed his gaze, and suddenly all attention was on her.

She raised both hands and addressed the raptors. "Ingo. Spotch. How is business today?"

The tree's eyes lowered with resignation as he realized no help was coming, and Ingo's mouth widened into the approximation of a human smile, sharp raptor teeth catching the sunlight. "Imayva, how nice to see you out of the Darkmist hole. Funny, Spotch and I were just talking about you."

Spotch ripped the tree's coin purse off his belt and tossed it to Ingo, who jingled it in the air in front of Mayve. "As you can see, the Coinclaws are thriving. You're welcome to join in, of course. Open invitation."

"Can't today, sorry. Helping my mother." Mayve had known Ingo and Spotch for many years. They grew up on the Devar streets together. It was easy—maybe too easy—to make some quick coin running with them, but as they all got older, the twins had grown a little more vicious each year. Still, the money was hard to resist sometimes.

The two brothers turned back to the tree and landed several more vicious blows each, until the unfortunate soldier was on his knees, gasping. Ingo spat into the tree's leaves. "Get out of my face, kindling."

Spotch snarled, "Be sure to thank Imayva here. We were going to kill you, but we'd hate for your pathetic whimpers to sour her morning."

The tree shot one more glance of anger and shame at Mayve, then dropped his gaze and fled the alleyway. Mayve felt a pang of guilt, but she knew better than to get involved with matters involving the raptors and the Oaken Legion, especially with Ingo and Spotch on one side.

She turned to the raptor twins. "Are you offering me a job?"

"Perhaps." Spotch slunk closer, his tail gently swaying side to side like an eerie pendulum. "Would you be interested?"

"Might be. Like I said, I'm busy today." Mayve held her ground. She knew Ingo and Spotch were harmless, at the moment, and refused to let herself be intimidated.

"Nothing out of the usual, other than the pay." Ingo looked around, then stepped in close to form a huddle with Spotch and Mayve. "That tree is part of a larger Oaken Legion convoy. They come through town, rarely, traveling between the Verdants, but this one is different."

Spotch chimed in, "King Coinclaw's informants say that those trees were digging around in the desert, out in some old ruins in the Eastriver Dunes, and we suspect they found something. It's the largest force we've seen pass through in a while, and they've rented out every room in the Hangman's Swing."

"So it's almost certainly something *out of the usual*." Mayve crossed her arms and glared at Ingo, but she was undeniably curious. "How would I play into this, exactly?"

Ingo sheathed his axe and motioned a clawed hand toward Mayve. "We need your particular knack for climbing, and since the Oaken Legion are involved, they'll be immediately suspect of us *scaled scum*." Ingo dropped his voice to mimic the stereotypical, self-righteous attitude of the Oaken Legion. "And less likely to notice a boring human like you."

"Thanks, Ingo, very persuasive of you. What are they even guarding?"

"No idea, but if they've been diving in the ruins, it's probably something very rare and *very* expensive. Buried treasure or a Lost Eon artifact, something Fae maybe. Spotch and I will make sure King Coinclaw gives you a fine cut of the profit."

Imayva shrugged and couldn't help but say, "He's not even a real king."

Both Spotch's and Ingo's smiles dropped away, then Ingo snarled, "And you're a poor wretch from Darkmist. You know, this job alone, you'd make enough to get your mother out of that cave hole you call home. Maybe you won't even need to work with us Coinclaws anymore to get by."

Everyone stood in silence for a moment, each with a struck nerve. Mayve spoke first. "Do you have an actual number for me?" Ingo and Spotch looked at each other, making mute expressions with an occasional hissed word and motions toward Mayve. A language only two close twins could possibly understand.

Eventually they turned back and said, "You'll make five, maybe six hundred teirs easy, if the Legion have something truly valuable."

Mayve failed to hide her shock, and both Ingo and Spotch grinned in unison as they watched her jaw fall open.

"I'll take it you're interested, then," Ingo snarled. Mayve recovered quickly. *Five hundred teirs! What could the trees possibly be carrying that my cut is five hundred teirs?* Mayve knew that was more than enough to take her mother wherever she wanted. It was also enough to get murdered in the street by the Coinclaws, but that voice in her mind was just a faint whisper. She tried to feign calmness. "Fine, I'm interested. Where do I meet?"

The same false smile played across Ingo's maw. "Meet us in the Outer Sands tomorrow at sunset. Three dwellings down and across from the Hangman's Swing, in the direction of the river. Do you have a weapon?" Mayve nodded and revealed her small pocketknife. Both Spotch and Ingo threw their heads back in laughter, feathers ruffling with each breath.

"What about a real weapon? We're going against the Oaken Legion, you've seen their armor." He glanced at Mayve's coin pouch. "That should be enough for a solid dagger."

Mayve grabbed her coin purse and tucked the money out of sight. "How dangerous is this job exactly? I've never needed a weapon before, and I'm not looking to die on a timbersteel blade for your false king."

Spotch finished counting the coin from the Oaken Legion's stolen purse. "If all goes well, you won't have to fight. But it's your funeral if you end up fighting with that butter knife. Think about it. What are you going to do against *timbersteel* with that?"

The way Spotch spat out the word *timbersteel* dripped with utter malice. He scooped a handful of coins and dropped it in Ingo's waiting claws, then flipped a gold teir to Mayve. "Tomorrow. Sunset." The two brothers slunk out of the alley, looked left and right for any sign of trouble, and disappeared into the city.

"Nothing out of the usual..." Mayve mocked the twin's snarls. "Sand-cursed raptors."

Five hundred teirs...Ma and I can go wherever we want. The voice of reason in the back of her mind screamed that something felt off, but she forced it down. *For that kind of money, it's worth it, no matter what the job is.*

Sunset tomorrow, in the Outer Sands, and I need a real weapon. What have I gotten myself into?

Chapter 2

Scales in the Sand

The Outer Sands was nothing more than a neighborhood of dilapidated homes scattered on a sand-eaten main street. Anyone unfortunate to live there scurried as fast as they could between dwellings to avoid the sun, wrapped in whatever rags they could afford. It was where one found all the travelers not welcome in the inner boroughs. Devar was a desert city, and the desert belonged to the raptors. Any Oaken Legion troops desperate enough to pass between the Verdants made their stay in the run-down lodgings of the Outer Sands, along with anyone deemed unfit for common society, and any travelers wishing to keep a low profile.

Despite all that, suspicious eyes still peered out at Srrith as she slithered down the dusty stretch of road toward the Outer Sands' only inn.

This borough was not much different than the desert itself. The unfettered sun kept Srrith's scales uncomfortably hot, and any refreshing breeze from the river was scorched dry long before it reached the dunes. Sand caught in her cloak, grinding against her scales.

In the broken, sand-crusted glass of a nearby window, she caught the first glimpse of herself she had seen in a while. A long hooded cloak kept the sun off her back and hid her face. Underneath, black leather armor matched her black scales, dark as shadow, protecting just her torso.

Making armor for the entire length of her tail was unwieldy, and not pleasant to travel in.

Underneath the cloak, she glimpsed her cobra-like head, scaled hood folded down. Thin yellow eyes peered out, tired but alert. She peeled her parched forked tongue from the roof of her mouth and flexed her jaw, baring her two fangs.

Ahead was the inn. A two-story building made of white sandstone, the inn was the largest building in the whole borough. The crash of the waterfall was easily mistaken for the wind at this distance, and Srrith let out a low hiss, her forked tongue making a brief appearance from the shadow of her cloak.

Her hearing opened. Listening in to the tavern, she now knew the exact occupancy of the taproom, and that there was a table free in the corner.

She slithered toward the saloon-style doors, smoke drifting out the top of the entryway. A skeleton swung from a noose near the entrance —a horrid, four-armed monster from a Scorch Vent, cut down long ago by Ul'Varin. It pivoted in the parched breeze, clutching a wooden sign between its four clawed hands. *The Hangman's Swing.*

Srrith's eyes struggled to distinguish the crudely carved letters in the blinding sun. She shut them and let loose another low hiss, her surroundings painting themselves in her mind's eye. Pushing through the swinging doors, her black scales scraping against the cooler stone floor, she slithered over to the empty table. Several long, central tables were fully occupied by Oaken Legion soldiers, who stared at her from behind timbersteel helmets. A few other travelers at the bar barely spared her a second glance.

Pushing aside the chairs at the empty table, Srrith coiled up, resting on her own body. When her eyes were closed, it was difficult for others to distinguish if she was sleeping or not. Another hiss, and the image of the room sketched itself across the back of her eyelids.

The bartender cautiously approached, giving a polite rap on the table to alert her to his presence. Srrith had watched him walk the whole distance from the bar to her table. Most Ralverans were unaware that the cave tauninaga could echolocate, so she could not fault him. She preferred that they did not know. It made them easier to hunt.

She did him the courtesy of opening her eyes, and ordered a plate of fish. She was here to wait. The Great Seer, Alactashi Sen, had sent her here. Srrith would see her vision through.

Srrith hissed. The tavern and its occupants appeared again. Heartbeats thumped from everybody in the room, betraying their worry. Their *fear*. Tension was brewing here.

Alactashi Sen was never wrong. *Now, I shall wait.* She unsheathed her sickles and placed them on the table in front of her. Srrith knew to stay out of conflict with the Oaken Legion, especially if the raptors knew they were here. There would be conflict soon enough.

She relaxed her coils but kept her mind focused. To any onlooker, she was now asleep. They did not know she was awake, sharp, and studying them through closed eyes. Coiled, she watched, and waited. *I will be ready for the green-eyed girl. The Great Seer says it to be so, and I will not fail her.*

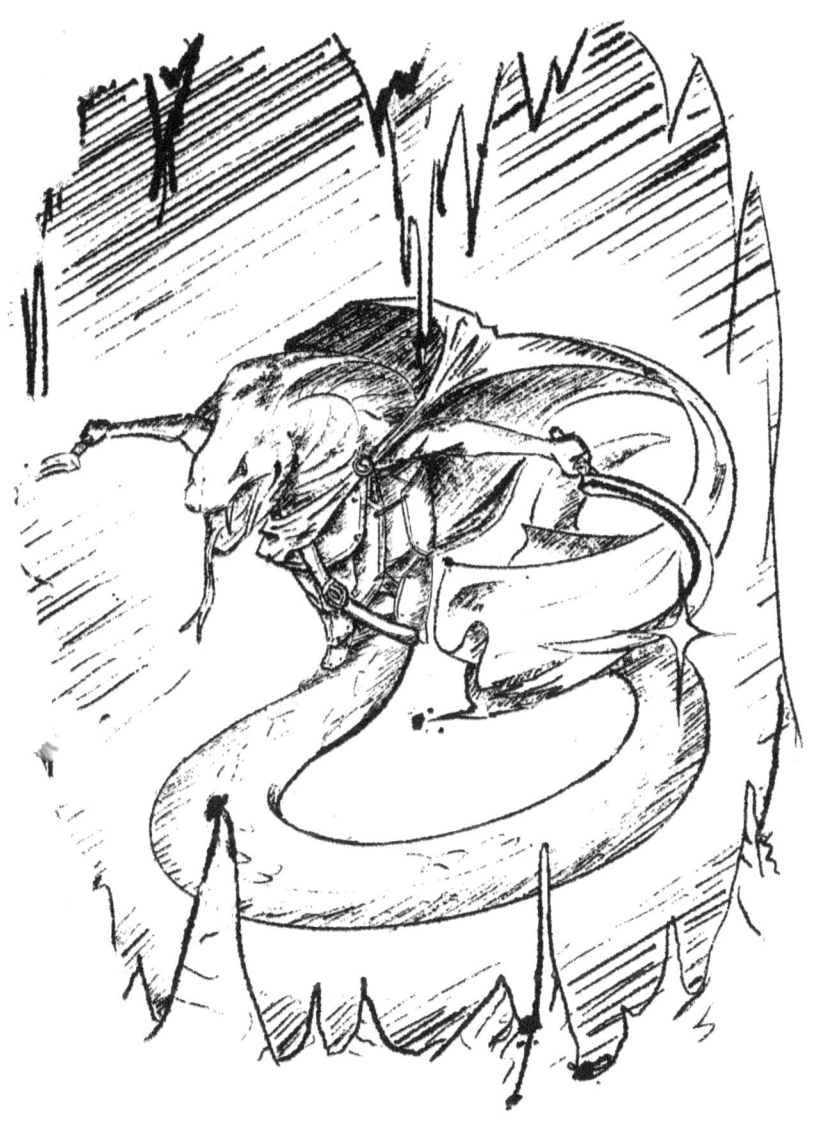

"It does not matter how concealed you think you are. If you can hear them hiss, they know exactly where you're hiding. Run, so you at least feel the wind in your hair before you die."

—common warning given to explorers before venturing into cave tauninagan territory.

Chapter 3

Seeds and Shadow

U nlike the desert, the Silt Row Market was vibrant. Merchants traveled from all over Ralvera to sell their goods at the countless stalls and tents. Mayve stopped for a second to bask in the sights and smells, the cooking foods and exotic spices immediately making her stomach growl.

She approached a green tent where a Twelian, made of shimmering blue energy and dressed in a twisting dress of ornate metal, was tending to a beautiful bonsai tree, their tendril-like metal fingers carefully pruning away leaves. Each branch bore a different kind of fruit, and Mayve pointed to two ripe fruits she had never seen before, flipping the merchant a couple copper dens.

Pocketing one to take home to her mother, she bit into the remaining one. The delicious juice ran down her chin as she continued through the market, looking for a seed merchant. What caught her eye first, however, was a blacksmith. Arranged on the nearby stall were several orange velvet display cases, each with an arsenal of blades. Mayve stopped in her tracks, and immediately felt the weight of the coin purse on her belt.

Ma hates the Coinclaws, but we're not going to earn this coin any other way. If what Ingo and Spotch say is true, then this job will be worth it.

While she doesn't want me working with the Coinclaws, she especially doesn't want me dead. Mayve didn't even realize she had walked right up to the stall, the gruff Oemorg blacksmith staring down at her impatiently.

"That dagger, please." She pointed to a blade near the front of the display that was reflecting the desert sun, with a sturdy hilt decorated with silver inlays. The blade was around three quarters of a foot—almost a sword, but not quite. Fine work, concealable and affordable. *The best I can afford with what's in Ma's purse.*

Silent, the Oemorg reached out his huge, gray hand, his arm covered in red and orange tattoos, motioning for Mayve's coin. She took a deep breath and dropped the whole coin purse into his outstretched palm.

After a minute of counting, the smith dropped a few copper dens back in the purse and tossed it over to Mayve. *This better be worth it, that's weeks of Ma's work gone.* The Oemorg delicately lifted the dagger out of the display case, dwarfing it with his large hands, and slid it in a dark leather sheath before passing it to Mayve. She unsheathed the blade and gave it a few swings, slicing it through the air. *I don't plan on fighting, but if I have to, this can maybe get through a crack in the timbersteel.*

A rare nervousness bubbled inside her. She had never killed anybody, preferring to slip in and out quietly whenever she was not supposed to be somewhere. There was slim chance a fully-plated Oaken Legion soldier would be her first kill, dagger or no dagger.

"It's made for stabbing." The smith grumbled.

"Sure." Maye mumbled back, awkwardly sheathing the blade. *I'm sure it does both just fine.* She peered inside the coin purse at the few dens that remained. Perhaps it would be enough to get a packet of seeds. *Ma will kill me if it's not.*

She attached the sheath to her belt and scanned the market. There was guaranteed to be a seed merchant somewhere here. The difficult part would be finding where.

Mayve wandered between the stalls, taking in the sights. There was a group of Torn selling armor made from the bark of the goliath trees from the Cenoreth Forest. *Seems like a scam.*

A cavernfolk hunter selling furs from the Northern Ice. *This is the wrong place to sell furs, sorry friend*

More food sizzled on grills and turned on spits, making her stomach growl again, and she missed the fruit she just ate. The second fruit she bought was for her mother, who certainly needed it more than she did.

Secretly, she hoped she wouldn't find a seed merchant so she could keep wandering, but finally, she saw what she needed. A yellow tent at the edge of the plaza, set up against a low plank railing, built more to mark a spot where one could fall into the Devaros rather than prevent it from happening.

There was an open awning with many small stands, each with different seeds and gardening equipment. Past a tent flap was a back room of additional storage, and most likely a makeshift office. There was not much need for farming in the desert, but the residents of Archtown keep magnificent gardens. and the occasional peasant, like Mayve's mother, could keep a small plot of specific crops if they had the right place for it.

Mayve strolled up to the stalls, hoping to get a look at the price of sandpeppers without attracting the attention of an overzealous salesman. She clenched her teeth as a voice called out.

"Greetings! Welcome to our humble stall, under the management of the Tyrak-Wenstnor Trade Coalition!" Her worst fear approached, a blonde man wearing a deep purple and sky-blue robe with gold filigree. "You've chosen well! I assure you, we have the finest wares for agricultural needs in all of Devar. What can I help you with today?" Mayve visibly winced, then turned to the overly excited man walking toward her.

"Not looking for much, just sandpepper seeds."

"Of course! We only carry the finest from both Verdants." The merchant bowed low. "You may call me Faldmor, if it pleases you."

Mayve ignored him. There was no reason to give away her name for a simple transaction. Faldmor cleared his throat and motioned to a nearby stall. "Our packets are priced at five hearths."

Phovus, and they call me *a thief. You slimy roach.* "How about three dens?" She countered.

"Oh, that's far too low. I'll settle for three hearths."

"Five dens." *The remainder of my purse*

The merchant did a poor job of hiding a scoff. "If you cannot afford our stock, then I think you should leave."

Mayve rolled her eyes and briefly thought about flipping over one of the stalls, but decided she did not feel like running from the Merchatzi today. Outside the tent, she angrily loitered for a minute, acutely aware of how light the coin purse felt hanging next to her new dagger.

If I head home now, empty-handed except for a shiny new weapon, it will not turn out well. A tempting thought occurred to her. *I don't have to return empty-handed though.*

Mayve sauntered over to the railing between the market plaza and the river below, a good distance upriver from the merchant's tent, and studied the area again. Seated on top of the railing, her feet propped on the second rung below her, she watched the crowds chaotically shift between the stalls. Every so often, a patrolling squad of Merchatzi, each adorned with a different symbol of one of the many merchant guilds and coalitions, muscled through the sea of people as they navigated among the stalls that employed them.

She refilled her canteen from the river below, sipping the cold water as she watched. Soon, Mayve was able to guess within the second when a Merchatzi patrol would appear.

After a few minutes, she decided she had all the information she needed. She watched the latest cohort of guards stomped past, counted an appropriate number of seconds, and tipped backward into the Devaros River.

The river slammed into Mayve like a refreshing brick. She let herself be taken by the murky current, drifting underwater as the hot filth of the desert washed away. Finally, she let her face break the surface as her body naturally floated upward. She tilted an ear out of the water, the muffled rush of the impending rapids replaced with the clamor of the market. No sounds of panic, or anybody rushing to the railing to help. If anyone saw her go over, they must not have cared.

Mayve saw the seed merchant's tent approaching, pressed against the edge of the market plaza above her. Submerging herself, she planted her feet on the sandy riverbed and propelled herself upward with all her might. Breaching the surface, water spraying past her face, she barely grabbed the wooden planks with her outstretched hand.

Pulling herself up was too easy. Mayve was very pleased with how toned her biceps looked as they flexed under the weight of her lean body, glistening with river water. Her face level with the bottom of the merchant tent, she quietly lifted the bottom of the cloth and draped it over her head to look into the tent's back room. The coast was clear. *Faldmor is probably out front, kicking the poor.*

She clambered into the back room of the tent, rolling underneath the cloth wall. The yellow cloth filtered the light into a mustard hue, the scent of earth and dry wood overpowering. Crates of different sizes were stacked in a maze-like formation, and Mayve surreptitiously browsed the wares, paying attention to the tent flap and any noises past it. She vaguely distinguished the sounds of Faldmor greeting a new customer.

Just grab anything. Whatever Ma plants, we'll be long gone by the time the seeds grow. I just need her to not be suspicious for one night. Her eyes fell upon a metal chest in the back corner, secured with a thick padlock, and she thought of how rude Faldmor was. *Although, I might as well grab the expensive stuff.*

Light on her feet, she crept to the chest. The padlock was similar to others she had seen on Coinclaw jobs before. Sturdy, but not well-made, and easily pick-able with a blade thin enough to reach the inner lever.

She rolled the chest onto its back, lock facing upward, and jammed in her pocket knife. Listening carefully as she fiddled the blade back and forth, she heard the tell-tale click, then threw all her weight onto the knife's handle.

The lock clicked and the heavy iron top slammed open, packets of seeds spilling everywhere. The voices outside stopped, and Faldmor threw open the tent flaps, confusion turning to shock as he saw Mayve. He was pushed aside by a second figure, stepping into the tent.

The newcomer had not been there earlier. They wore gold-embroidered black leather armor, and their face was completely hidden behind the combination of a hood and mask. Even in the desert heat, they wore a purple and black long-sleeve tunic, and their hands were covered in black gloves.

Their mask was carved from solid onyx gemstone, night-black and reflective, with amethysts trailing underneath the eyes as if it was streaked with violet tears. The gemstone face bore no expression at all, concealing all the emotions of the strange figure. Despite this, the dark eye-holes watched her curiously—eager to see what she would do next. Chills raced down Mayve's spine, freezing her in place.

Almost frantic, Faldmor shouted, "Stop!" There was fear in his voice, like he was pleading with Mayve rather than commanding her.

The masked figure raised their hand, and the light in the tent darkened. Tendrils of shadow leaked from underneath their armor, coiling up their arm to their outstretched fingertips, pointed right at Mayve.

A spike of terror and adrenaline unfroze Mayve. Grabbing a handful of the seed packets, she bolted for the back of the tent. Hungry shadows erupted from the masked figure's outstretched arm, tendrils streaking around the crates toward Mayve, like eels swimming around rocks toward a cloud of chum.

Leaping for the back of the tent, Mayve rolled sideways underneath the flap, cloth billowing as she tumbled over the edge of the market plaza, splashing into the Devaros. Staying submerged, she swam with the current, praying the shadows did not pierce the water surface like raining arrows and impale through her exposed back.

Eventually, her burning lungs forced her up. She broke the surface with a gasp and frantically looked around, half-expecting the masked figure to be on a nearby bridge, aiming another attack. To her relief, she was alone, and she drifted with the current before grabbing onto a nearby ladder, getting uncomfortably close to the waterfall edge. She shuddered in fear, but not at the waterfall. *Going over the edge would be better than facing whoever that was. A fucking volcomancer, Mayve, your luck today has been something else.*

Utterly exhausted, Mayve pulled herself from the river and took stock of her situation. She had no idea if the merchant and his horrific friend would attempt to look for her, and she did not want to take any chances. Looking downriver, she noted the water was still higher than usual, blocking her shortcut home.

Bunching her sopping wet hair into one thick strand, she lifted it over her shoulder to strain the water out. Her chest sank when she saw the tips of her dark hair were ghost white, where the masked man's shadows just barely scraped her. She wondered what would have happened if the shadows actually hit her, and shuddered. *Depths below, why is a guild merchant associating with that nightmare? A gardening merchant, of all people! There's no way he's with the Merchatzi. Phovus, what a shit day.*

Unsheathing her new dagger, she cut the white tips off her hair with a shaky hand and tossed them in the river before filling her canteen. Mayve was not used to being nervous or afraid, and today forced her to be both. Plotting the least conspicuous route home, she set off for Darkmist.

Mayve had been in two life-threatening situations today, and she could not shake the fear. That masked man had been willing to kill her, or worse, for *seeds*! She took the time to check around corners, paranoid that at every turn that emotionless mask would face her.

She finally left Silt Row with a sigh of relief, rejoining the main road out. Just before Outer Sands, the road curved past the large sandstone stairway that led to Archtown, with a fork leading to the Outer Sands or Darkmist.

After the fork, the road devolved to harsh desert. Mayve unwrapped a shawl she kept on her belt specifically for this journey, and wrapped it around her shoulders to ward off the sun. It was still soaked from her swim and clung refreshingly to her skin, but she knew it would be dry before she was halfway home.

The main road drifted over to hug the cliff's edge overlooking the Devaros River, and eventually, Mayve reached the carved staircase that cut down to Darkmist. At the bottom, the path doubled back along the shadowy riverside toward the Falls. In a better world, this valley would have been bursting with lush vegetation, fed by the nutrient-rich silt of the Devaros. The unnatural aura of the Scorch Vents stifled the growth of nature to only the hardiest plants and the most protected gardens.

Soon enough, Mayve was at the entrance to the Darkmist Tunnels, a gaping hole in the rock at the base of the Devaros Falls. *I would've been here ages ago if I could have used my shortcuts.* She tried to joke with herself, but could not shake the awful fear that had tailed her all the way here.

As she stepped into the cool tunnels, the eternal fog created by the waterfall cooled her skin and dispelled the desert dust. She was safe here.

Only the denizens of Darkmist could find their way around these tunnels, and she had lived here her whole life.

Keeping up a swift pace through the tunnels, she followed her memorized path, cutting through the foggy, rough-hewn pathways. The well-known tunnels were illuminated by torches, sputtering in the mist. The web of less-traveled paths—most of which Mayve knew by heart— were dimly lit through sparse torches, glowing fungi, or nothing at all. Other tunnels sprawled deeper into the vast Ralveran Caverns, and thus were vehemently avoided. The mist from the waterfall was ever-present, filling every tunnel except the deepest caves, slicking every surface with chilled condensation.

Mayve slunk through the sunless tunnels, checking around every corner, looking over her shoulder at every straightaway. She could not shake the feeling that someone was following her. Everywhere she turned, she expected to come face-to-face with the man in the onyx mask, his hand raised, ready to smother her in darkness.

She decided to take no chances and doubled back on her tracks. For a lover of shortcuts, the Darkmist Tunnels were unmatched in secret pathways. Mayve used every path and every trick she knew, doubling back several times, shimmying through crawl spaces and traversing natural chimneys between different tunnels, until there was no possible way anyone could have followed her.

* * *

Once her adrenaline faded, Mayve stopped to rest in a side passage underneath a dim torch, eying the sparse passersby with paranoid scrutiny. Finally able to catch her breath, Mayve pulled the seed packets from her pockets, and took her first real look at them. The simple paper packets, soaked from the river, almost fell to pieces in her hands. Holding them up to the dim light, she spotted a symbol on the soggy parchment. A sword crossed with a blade of wheat. The symbol of Citadel Waldheath.

Must be quality goods if it was going to or from a Citadel. Ma can't see this, though. We certainly can't afford anything like this. She ripped open every packet, emptying all the seeds into her coin purse before shoving the wet paper scraps into cracks in the cave walls. Finally, she untucked her shirt and let it fall over the sheathed dagger on her belt, spending a few seconds to adjust it to be as invisible as possible. Satisfied with her work, Mayve jogged into the shadows toward home.

The quaint household that Imayva shared with her mother was, by every definition, a hole in the wall. Much like every Darkmist residence in the tunnels, the entrance was impossible to search for. The door would often look just like the surrounding wall, forcing visitors—and occasionally the occupants—to search precisely for its location.

Mayve knew exactly where to look, of course, and easily found the wooden door of her home, just down a tight, unlit side passage. The hinges scraped against stone as she pushed the door in, and the small passage instantly filled with the scent of baking bread.

She stepped out of the mist into the clear, warm air of their one and only room. The only light was from a metal hearth in the center of it, which dimly illuminated the dark rock walls. A pipe funneled the smoke through a hole in the ceiling, where it was lost to the caves.

Tending the hearth was Dreva, Imayva's dear mother. She turned to face the door as it scraped open, and her beautiful brown eyes lit up at the sight of Mayve. The light of the hearth rested in the faint wrinkles in her sun-tanned skin that had formed in recent years, and reflected off the few gray streaks that shone in her otherwise dark hair curling just above her shoulders.

Mayve smiled at her mother. Dreva had many good years left in her, and still walked proud and strong, but Mayve could not help but notice the stress of her life taking its toll. *Tomorrow will be the end of it. Five hundred teirs! We'll have a homestead in one of the Verdants, away from the sand and the sun.*

"Good..." Dreva glanced at the sandscale, taking note of the worn notches that indicated the time of day. "...afternoon, my darling girl." Her smile lit the cave more than the hearth did, and she turned back to the bread she was baking. "Took you a while to get to Silt Row and back; did you actually avoid your shortcuts or did you make more trouble on the way?"

Mayve dropped the coin purse with the seeds onto the crude plank table near her mother, and jokingly replied, "A little bit of both, actually."

Dreva rolled her eyes, and plucked the soggy purse from the table. "Imayva, this is dripping! What'd you get into?

"I fell in the river and the seed packets fell to pieces."

"How on earth did you fall in the river?"

"There was a boat crash at the Falls. The Lockworkers didn't check their ropes and the swing knocked some houses out. I was heading past at the time and lost my footing when the impact hit. I'm fine though, Ma, I pulled myself right out, not even a scratch."

"Oh, Imayva, I'm so sorry, that sounds frightening." Dreva pulled Mayve in for a hug, planted a kiss on her forehead, then let go and crossed her arms, pondering for a few long seconds.

"By the Falls, you say? I don't remember ever passing by there on my way to the market." Her eyes fixed upon Mayve with fierce intensity.

Mayve's mind raced to bend the truth. "Don't worry, Ma. I heard the horns of a boat arriving, so I went to watch. Turns out it was the Ferrymen."

Dreva eyed her daughter with the utmost suspicion. Twenty-odd years of Mayve's antics gave her healthy wariness. "Well I'm glad the Ferry is in town; hopefully we'll get some fresh vendors down here."

She did not break her stare, and Mayve turned to avoid her questioning eyes. She felt her mother's gaze boring into the back of her skull as she climbed into the loft she called her bedroom, which was hardly more than a small ledge of rock in the corner of the dwelling.

Her mother called out, "Well, I wouldn't be surprised if these seeds were already starting to grow in this soggy pouch, so I'll go get them in the ground." She shot one last worried glance at Mayve, then exited through the dwelling's back door. Mayve heard the door creak as her mother left for the garden, and waited until she heard it slam shut again. She hated lying to her mother, but she knew it would be worth it when she brought home enough treasure to get them out of Devar. *She'll make a nasty fuss over it all, but at the end of the day we'll be on the Ferry to one of the Verdants and none of it will matter.*

She traced her fingers across the rock wall of her loft, searching for a familiar crevice. Fingers latching around a specific rock, she rolled it out of place to reveal a hidden cache of her most personal belongings. If she wanted to hide something from Dreva, she usually left it outside the dwelling, but some stuff was too precious to her to keep far away.

Fumbling around blind, she picked out items one by one. A wilted flower that a young noble boy had given her from his parents' Archtown garden—she had been in the area to rob his neighbor, but he was cute and she liked the attention. Behind that, a small wooden sword, snapped in half, from when she, Ingo, and Spotch would play pirates, running through Silt Row and nabbing fruit from stalls. Pushing through the trinkets, she felt a crumpled piece of parchment. It crinkled as she carefully unwrapped it, the faded ink only just legible on the yellowed scrap. Written on the parchment was a single sentence.

I would love to meet her one day, if the fates allow.

—A

The rest of the letter had long since been lost to the river. This scrap was all that young Imayva had managed to salvage as Dreva tore the letter apart. She had never met her father, and never really cared to. Her mother still wore his ring on occasion, but he clearly never planned to reunite with either of them.

She still liked to look at the paper every now and then. It was a simple curiosity rather than an obsession. Folding the parchment, she tossed it carelessly back into her cache, placing the dagger gingerly next to it. The dagger cost money; the paper was worthless.

Rolling from her loft, she headed for the back door. The square shape of the door fit oddly in the asymmetrical hole of rock it was fitted over, making the planks scrape as it opened. An earthquake caused by the Okanos Vent almost a decade ago caused several cave-ins throughout Darkmist, but Dreva had been fortunate that fissures opened up in the cave ceiling as a result, large enough to let some daylight deep into the ground. It was here that Dreva built her garden, using the condensation of Darkmist and water fetched from the Devaros to keep the soil watered.

Mayve loved the garden, considering it her personal slice of Verdant hidden in the desert. The smell of moist sand and soil mingled as she swung the wooden door open. Dreva glanced up from where she was kneeling, gently poking the seeds into the earth. She picked up the coin purse and tossed it in front of Mayve. "The rest is for you, strong girl."

Mayve smiled and set to work, gently poking holes in the moist underground soil and dropping seeds in, scraping the displaced earth back into the hole. She continued in silence for a while longer, repeating the simple task, watching her mother out of the corner of her eye.

Dreva was fiddling with the ring on her finger, the one given to her by Mayve's father. She was clearly debating whether or not to pester Mayve about her suspicious activities of the day, but ended up just exhaling a deep sigh.

She left through the wooden door and returned a moment later with bread and water. Dreva and Imayva shared a smile as they stretched out in the dirt and feasted on their dinner. After the desert heat, the just-baked bread was hardly refreshing, but the freezing cave water was delicious.

Mayve noticed that Dreva's portion was tiny compared to her own. She tore off a chunk and offered it to her mother, who held up a hand to politely turn it down. "I'm not hungry, don't worry." She knew her mother was lying, but also knew that any further argument over the matter was useless. Suddenly remembering the fruit she bought earlier, soaking in her pocket, she pulled it out and offered it to her mom. "I bought two of these earlier with some leftover coin and I already had one, so eat it, please."

Dreva took the fruit and bit into it, wiping the yellow-orange juice from her face. "Mmm, where is this from?"

Mayve shrugged. "No idea. A Twelian was selling it from a tree that grew all sorts of things. Probably made with volcomancy."

"Don't be so sure; you can graft plenty of plants together without manifesting." Dreva shook her head in wonder. "Amazing what comes through that market." She happily dug into the fruit. Mayve noticed that her mother's hunger had suddenly returned, even after she'd adamantly declined more bread. *We won't be starved for much longer, Ma. Don't worry.* She wished she could talk about her departure plans, but she needed the gold first.

After eating, they planted the remainder of the seeds. The daylight shining through the fissures in the ceiling grew fainter until Dreva lit a torch and turned to her daughter. "I think that's all we can do today. Looks like we got most of it; I can finish the rest tomorrow. Thank you for your help, dear."

Mayve stood up, dusted the dirt off her knees, and arched her back, trying to get rid of a terrible cramp that had set in. She wrapped an arm around her mother's shoulder and gave it a tight squeeze. "Happy to help, as always."

She went back inside and climbed directly into her loft, collapsing on the hard straw mattress while Dreva began tidying up the cramped space. She called over to Mayve, who was lying on her back, staring at the ceiling. "Are you going to sleep?"

Mayve rolled her head to see her mother. " I think I'll try. Don't worry about making noise if you're going to stay up."

"I'll be done soon. Do you have matches?"

Mayve flailed her left arm blindly underneath her pillow, lazily searching for the crushed matchbox. She tried again with her right arm, and when that failed she sat up and dramatically lifted the pillow to see the matchbox sitting right in the center. There were plenty left inside, perfect for emergency light in the total darkness of the caves. "Plenty."

Dreva lit a candle and snuffed the hearth, dropping the cave into dimmer light. She reset the sandscale and placed the bell at the notch that she best guessed would be closest to dawn. Dreva crawled into her cot, carefully placing the candle nearby, before directing her attention to Mayve's loft. "Any plans tomorrow?"

Mayve was staring at the wall with her back to her mother, running over tomorrow's events in her mind. *Tomorrow. Sunset. Three homes across from the Hangman's Swing, toward the river.* "Not really. I'll be around in the morning, and I'll try to pick up some odd jobs later in the day."

Dreva replied in a half-teasing, half-hopeful tone. "Nothing life-threatening, right?"

Mayve gave a forced laugh and retorted, "That's the plan."

"Alright, dear. I love you, sleep well."

"Love you too, Ma." Mayve made the effort to crane her neck and look behind her as she replied.

Dreva blew out the candle and extinguished all light from the room. Mayve lay alone with her thoughts of raptors and masked volcomancers until she finally drifted to sleep.

Chapter 4

The Legion's Hope

"Explain your failings, Fenmor!"

Raudius Fenmor, soldier of the Bastion of Growth, stood at attention before his superior officer, surrounded by the other soldiers of his quindecis. As ordered, he proclaimed, "I was ambushed by two raptors in the alleyways near the Silt Row Market, sir."

The frutexier of his quindecis, Grenner, was slightly shorter than Raudius but his presence was twice as tall. He stepped in uncomfortably close to Raudius, close enough that he could smell the beer from the inn's taproom on Grenner's breath. "Why were you in the alleys instead of taking the safer route?"

Raudius managed to keep his physical composure even as his stomach flipped. "I took note of the position of the sun and determined myself to be behind schedule. To account for lost time, I made the decision—"

He was cut short with a snap of wood as Grenner headbutted him directly between the eyes. The older tree's gnarled, knotted stump of a forehead smashed into Raudius's bark, and a new crack fissured down his cheek. Oakfire flaring in his eyes, Grenner spat, "You do not *make* decisions! You follow orders, which were to travel the authorized route to the marketplace and acquire supplies."

Grenner paced around Raudius, the plank floor of the Hangman's Swing creaking underneath his timbersteel boots. The other soldiers looked on in tense silence from the outskirts of the common room. *Don't show weakness.*

The frutexier stopped his pacing and glared at Raudius, inviting him to say something. Raudius knew better and kept his mouth shut tight. *It'll be over soon, just weather the storm.*

After a long, uncomfortable silence, Grenner said, "Let me remind you, *Fenmor*, that you are here strictly as a favor to your family. You are nothing but a noble sprout, and a burden to our mission." Grenner stepped in close, his breath in Raudius's ear. "One more mistake, and you're shipping home. This mission is changing the future of the Oaken Legion, and I refuse to let a pampered runt jeopardize everything. Do you understand?"

Raudius kept his eyes forward. "Yes, I understa—" The end of the sentence was expelled out of his mouth as Grenner's gauntlet smashed into his stomach. Raudius's bark crunched under the impact, leaves rustling as he doubled over.

"I did not say you could speak," Grenner snarled. Raudius managed to lift his head and solemnly nod before doubling over and collapsing to his knees.

He heard Grenner mutter to a nearby soldier, and a pile of dirty rags was tossed on the ground in front of him. "I expect to find all the digging equipment spotless tomorrow morning," Grenner snarked. "I wonder who will do it."

Raudius made sure Grenner's footsteps had stomped away before picking up the rags, lest Grenner decide to crush his fingers on a whim. *When my family hears of this ill treatment, it will be the end of his career.*

Bunching the rags in one fist, he stood tall and defiantly glared at the onlooking soldiers. There was an uncomfortable rustling of leaves as the trees returned to their duties. As Raudius turned to leave, several trees broke from the circle and ran up to him, hurriedly checking that Grenner was gone.

His friend Claud, a lanky willow tree, reached him first, offering a shoulder for support. "*Depths below*, Raudius, that's the worst I've seen yet. You'd find better in a raptor camp."

Batia, a short dark oak, and Traticus, a pale birch, approached on either side. Batia produced a clean rag from his pack, handed it to Raudius, and said, "Go clean yourself up, you've got a few cracks that are starting to bleed." Raudius touched the bark on his cheek and felt the specks on green blood on his fingertips.

"What about you draws his ire like that?" Traticus asked.

"You heard him." Claud smirked. "Raudius is a greenling whelp, unfit for the Legion." His bark creaked as he grinned at Raudius, who shot him a glare as jagged as timbersteel. *Claud speaks the truth, though. Grenner has had it out for me since I was assigned here.*

"Careful with your words, unless you're looking for swords," Raudius cautioned, only half-joking.

"What you should do is challenge Grenner to swords." Traticus said. "You're a fine duelist and he could use the beating."

"It's on my mind," Raudius murmured, not wanting to be heard by other soldiers. "But I'm waiting until we're back at the Bastion."

Batia laughed. "With the way he's treating you, you won't make it back."

"Regardless," Raudius grunted, "I could beat him at swords, but he'd just up the challenge to shields, and that would be the end of me."

He remembered what his instructors said, back at the Bastion: *Swords is the gentleman's challenge. Blades only, no shields necessary. You don't need to fully protect yourself because no one is really trying to kill you. You fight to yield, or first blood.*

Shields, on the other hand, is to yield or death. The strong remain, and the Legion marches ever onward, better for it.

He excused himself from his fellow soldiers and headed for the washroom. A squad of soldiers loitered near the door, glaring at him as he pushed past. Each of them bore an insignia carved on their timbersteel pauldrons—an armored fist clutching an oak branch, the same symbol carved on Grenner's armor. *Hope's Gauntlet.*

Raudius did not know what to make of Hope's Gauntlet, or even what to call them. A sect of the army, perhaps? Maybe an unofficial division? Some might even say a cult, but not out loud. That'd be a quick way to get challenged to swords.

They had been around since the Ashen War, but they never had a real structure of command. Many soldiers joined because of the connections offered—if you knew the right people, it was easier to climb the ranks. Especially in times of peace, when feats of bravery and strength were not as common. It was simple to join too. Just a simple oath sworn to the ideals of Hope's Gauntlet, but many soldiers said they found such ideals to be a little *intense* for times of peace.

I've never considered joining. Everyone already knows my name. His grandfather had been a general, and not just any general. *General Arn Fenmor, Conqueror of the Daro Sands, Fifth Elder and Third Praetor of the Bastion of Growth.* Raudius had never needed the comradery of Hope's Gauntlet to rise through the ranks. It made no difference to him if he wore some special symbol on his armor. *We're all the same soldiers, fighting in the same army under the same chain of command. Although, maybe I'll consider joining if it shuts Grenner up.*

In the washroom, he studied himself in the small tavern mirror, leaning on the sink to bring his face into view. Raudius was an oak tree, with regal cheekbones and a thin mouth set on a strong jaw, all clad in light brown bark. The whites of his eyes were light green, while his pupils were a dandelion yellow, flecked with glowing sparks of Oakfire. It still raged in his chest from his humiliating encounter with Grenner, and those *sand-cursed raptor twins*.

Above his head was a tangled mess of branches, crowned with green leaves. He dabbed at the new cracks in his bark with the wet cloth. *Nothing too bad.* Even without their timbersteel armor, the Oaken Legion were sturdy. It unfortunately meant their superiors could be a little rougher with them if they wanted to.

Better get to work before Grenner makes it worse. He headed for the storage closet where the digging equipment from their excavation was kept. It had been grueling work out in the heat, and everyone was ecstatic when the time came to drop the shovels, pack them away, and never look at them again. Hence why they sat untouched and uncleaned. Desert excavation was awful work for anyone, especially a tree of the Oaken Legion. *We stay out of this raptor-ridden, water-starved shithole for a reason.*

As he walked through the inn, he kept his chin up but avoided eye contact from any soldier he passed. They had rented out the entire top floor of a tavern in the Outer Sands—Devar's driest and poorest borough. It had multiple rooms to bunk in and a large common area that they were using for storage and meetings, but it was certainly cramped.

Most of the soldiers spent their day in the taproom downstairs. He was excited to get back to his quarters that he was sharing with Batia, Claud, and Traticus. Right now, it seemed like the only place he was safe from the cutting glares of his fellow soldiers.

As he passed by an open door, a strange noise drew his attention. It was a soft flute-like sound that oscillated quickly between low hums and strange trills, evenly spaced out. Raudius could not help but look, and he saw Grenner hunched over a desk next to a foreign device, hurriedly writing notes on parchment. The contraption looked like a flattened oval cylinder of iridescent metal, punctured with holes. *Is that a core flute? Those are absurdly expensive; it's impossible for Grenner to have one.*

Raudius had seen a brief demonstration of a prototype core flute before he left the Bastion of Growth. It was a miraculous device that allowed communications over long distances by sending vibrations through the Ventix Stratus at a certain frequency able to be detected by other core flutes. Then the message was decoded by the trills and hums that the flute made.

That was the extent of his knowledge. He had left halfway through the presentation to attend dueling practice. From what he heard, the generals had deemed the core flutes to be too unreliable for field use, especially if hostile volcomancers learned how to intercept the messages. *So why does Grenner have one? I doubt he's had it this entire expedition—I surely would have noticed. Some general must have approved it. There's no one else our expedition needs to communicate with that urgently.*

Grenner looked up from translating the message and saw Raudius. With a deathly scowl, he slammed the door to his quarters. *Shit. Stop attracting his wrath, you Vent-cursed fool.* It was not his business anyway. Questioning his commanding officer would not help him in the slight-

est. He hurried to the supply closet where the old digging equipment
was kept.

Raudius cracked open a storage crate and pulled out the first shovel.
The dry rag scraping against the dry shovel did little to remove the layers
of dust and dirt. He set his body to the futile task and let his mind
wander.

He reminded himself why he was here. A soldier must prove
himself, as soon as possible. The Fenmor family had shoved their polit-
ical weight around, and he was lucky enough to be included on a critical
archaeological expedition heading into the forsaken desert. *Very lucky
indeed.* He dug at the caked dirt with a wooden fingernail.

The generals had bought intel from a merchant guild concerning an
important site that potentially contained an artifact of great importance.
*Perhaps an artifact from the Fae, or even the Lost Eon. A centrallion
armed with Lost Eon artifacts would annihilate a horde of raptors.*

Raudius gritted his teeth and heaved the next pickaxe out of the
crate and into his lap, redoubling his efforts at scrubbing the dirt free. *I
will not be sent away like some common soldier. Depths below, I am a
Fenmor.* As much as he hated to admit it, Grenner was the commanding
officer here. If he wanted to send Raudius home, he could. *Or worse.*

He was halfway through the last crate when the door creaked open
behind him. Yuetrix strode into the room and pulled up a stool on the
opposite side of the crate before pulling out one of the remaining shovels. The old soldier's bark was knotted, grizzled with age and scars, and
half the branches on the yew tree's head were wilted or bare. Raudius
welcomed his company though. The old tree had taken Raudius under
his canopy for the expedition, and Raudius was grateful for the guidance he provided.

Raudius hurriedly muttered, "Yuetrix, if Grenner finds you helping
me..." The cracked bark on his head and stomach ached as he raised his
voice.

"Relax," Yuetrix grunted. "He's drinking away the evening in the
taproom with our fellow soldiers. Our passage north does not arrive
until overmorrow, and they don't intend to stay sober in the desert."

He had been a soldier for longer than Raudius had been alive, and
was well acquainted with the hardships of Legion life. Raudius held his

tongue after that, and they sat in silence, diligently at work. Yuetrix eventually dropped a pickaxe into the crate and cleared his throat. Raudius readied himself for some pearls of wisdom, or maybe a scolding.

Yuetrix leaned forward, placing his elbows on his knees, and gestured to a crate that Raudius had already finished with. "Half of these are still dirty. Maybe you are a little green, noble boy."

"Did you come in here to help me or berate me?"

Yuetrix laughed and said, "That is helping you. If you don't fix that crate, Grenner will have words with you." Raudius heaved out an exasperated sigh and tossed his rag to the ground, leaning back in his chair.

Yuetrix looked curiously at Raudius and asked, "Why did you stray from the main road to Silt Row?"

Raudius knew that Yuetrix already knew the answer, but replied anyway. "Because Grenner demanded I return before noon, and there was not enough time to get to the market and back taking the main road. I was merely trying to complete the request made of me."

Yuetrix followed with another question. "Can you control the flow of time? Or when an unreasonable order is given to you?"

Raudius rolled his eyes. "Obviously not."

"So, whose fault would it have been if you had followed orders exactly and arrived back late?"

Raudius, realizing where Yuetrix was leading him, lowered his head and muttered, "Grenner's."

"Excellent," Yuetrix nodded. "The young tree isn't completely green."

Raudius stared defiantly at Yuetrix, ready to poke holes in his logic. "So, then, is your grand pearl of wisdom to blindly follow orders?"

Yuetrix picked up a pickaxe and thwacked Raudius in the head with the haft, the wooden handle making a hollow *thonk* against his oaken forehead. "No, greenling. My pearl of wisdom is that the chain of command is not always your ally. I know many fine trees who get lost amongst the faces of the Legion because their superiors set them up to fail."

Raudius fell into a sullen silence. Yuetrix continued, "Grenner sent you alone, to complete an impossible task, in the middle of *sand-*

cursed Devar. You're damn lucky that all you lost was coin to those raptors."

"Either way I fail, following orders exactly or not," Raudius sulked.

Yuetrix shrugged. "You know that Grenner doesn't want you here. Hands were shook, favors were called in, and that's how you're in the middle of the desert. But when we get home, will you say you failed because of *your* decisions, or because of *Grenner's* decisions."

Raudius's Oakfire flared hot in his chest. "Is that it, then? I have to endure Grenner all the way home to the Bastion of Growth, then pit my word against his?"

"I'm sure you've noticed that there's an even split amongst our quindecis? Hope's Gauntlet actually outnumbers the normal Legion here thirteen to twelve. That's twelve soldiers who will likely vouch for you at the Bastion, not including myself."

Raudius nodded. His mind flashed to the symbol emblazoned on the pauldrons of the Hope's Gauntlet soldiers—the symbol etched in Yuetrix's pauldrons.

"We're all the same soldiers in the same army, aren't we?" Raudius asked.

Yuetrix shrugged. "I used to think so. Hope's Gauntlet has changed since I joined them. Well, maybe they've stayed the same, and I've changed. Too late for me now, though." He stood up, timbersteel armor scraping at the joints. "There used to be a time when your fellow soldiers would die for you without a second thought. I believe that's still the case, but the signs of rot are beginning to show. You'll need to prove yourself to Grenner, or put your faith in your fellow soldiers to vouch for you. Otherwise any grand future you have planned for yourself will put down roots too early."

"So, should I join Hope's Gauntlet, then? Is that your advice?"

Yuetrix laid his armored hand on Raudius's shoulder as he passed, and patted it reassuringly. "I joined Hope's Gauntlet around your age, and I don't know if I would do the same today. The world has changed since then, and is still changing. Turns out, that never stops. But you're a bright sapling, I'm sure you'll figure it out." The door creaked and slammed shut as Yuetrix took his leave.

Raudius begrudgingly set back to work, seething as he scrubbed at the dirt. *If I return home, complaining about my service and rallying other soldiers to testify against my commanding officer...no one will forget that. I'll be the spoiled son of Fenmor who couldn't hack one expedition.*

On the other hand, if I let Grenner push me around and besmirch my name, same outcome.

All that stands in the path of my ambition is one frutexier with an overinflated ego, who could Fell me at the slightest mistake. You have to be unshakable. Infallible. Strong.

"*Strength. Perseverance. Growth. Life. Our Bastions, mighty and unbroken, stand upon these ideals. No matter the foe that encroaches on our Verdant lands, be it Vent beast or raptor or atrocity still unknown, they shall break upon our shields. And while they crumble back to soil, within their forgotten graves, the Legion marches ever onward.*"

    —recorded speech of General Arn Fenmor, 85th year of the Ashen Century

Chapter 5

Consequences of Lies

Mayve woke up to her mother calling from the garden. "Imayva, dear, would you mind stepping out here?" There was a hint of coldness in her voice that gave Mayve pause.

She rolled off her loft onto the cold cave floor. The hearth was lit, giving the cave the same dim lighting as last night. The only indicator that it was a different time of day was the sandscale tipped in the opposite direction.

Mayve threw on a new shirt, which happened to be her only other shirt, and climbed into the same pants as yesterday before stumbling out the back door. Her eyes took a second to adjust to the daylight streaming through the bright cracks in the ceiling, then finally focused on her mother standing in the middle of a flourishing garden.

The garden, freshly planted last evening, was thick with waist-high brambles. Dreva stood in the center of the plot with her hands on her hips, the thorny shrubs up to her chest. "Would you mind explaining this?"

She motioned with outstretched arms to the jungle surrounding her, then plucked a large black flower from one of the bramble strands. Its round petals curved into pointed, droopy ends, unfurling from a mass of dark blue stigmas. "I'm no scholar or botanist, but I'm positive these are *not* sandpeppers."

Mayve, stunned to silence at the explosion of growth overnight, had nothing to say. Under her mother's ireful gaze, she stammered out, "I guess I was sold the wrong plant."

Dreva threw her hands in the air, completely flustered. "No plant I know grows like this overnight, Imayva. You expect me to believe the merchant *accidentally* sold something like this?" Mayve did nothing but look down, ashamed. She saw the brambles growing before her very eyes, twisting toward her feet.

Her mother picked her way out of the bramble mess, thorns snagging on her dress. "I'll have to spend days clearing this out. Days that I *don't have,* and it still might be unsalvageable considering how fast these are growing." A green vine crept across Dreva's shoe and she shook it off. The vine twisted and grasped at the air, looking for another hold to spiral around. "This garden *feeds* us, Imayva, you know this! How much work will I have to miss cleaning this up?"

Mayve swallowed her guilt and tried to show her concern. "I can help, Ma"

Dreva shot her daughter a vicious look and said, "I would hope so. I have half a mind to make you fix this by yourself."

Mayve raised her hands in feigned innocence. "It's not my fault the merchant gave us the wrong crops!" She desperately hoped that her mother would believe her. These sand-cursed seeds had all but ruined her plan to hide her wrongdoings. The onyx mask of that mysterious man flashed through her mind's eye. *That volcomancer is probably behind these seeds. Phovus, give me your luck, because mine has run dry.*

Dreva responded with a withering gaze and absolute silence. Mayve weathered the silence, hoping the lie would hold and Dreva would redirect her anger. The creeping vines around them had completely undermined her deception. As Dreva held the silence, it was clear the game was up.

"Imayva." Her voice was an octave lower and filled with pain. "What's more likely? That a Silt Row merchant *accidentally* gave you seeds that, from what I can tell, grow so fast they *have* to be made with volcomancy. Or, you stole them."

Mayve knew there was nothing up for debate. She hung her head and replied, "I'm sorry." There was a sickly stench from the brambles' black flowers hanging in the air.

Dreva waved her hand down as if smacking the apology away and stifled a sob. "You're not sorry about stealing and lying. You're sorry about getting caught. Imayva, you'll get yourself *killed*."

Mayve had nothing to say. She hated to see her mother this way, but Dreva had seen right through her. She was furious that her plan to conceal this had fallen apart because she accidentally stole *volcomantic seeds*. Somewhere deep down, Mayve felt guilty, but she knew she did what she had to do. *She'll understand when we're aboard passage to Tyrak Pass, free from this hole in the ground. I can give her a real apology then.*

She looked up from her feet to meet Dreva's stare. Tears were running down her mother's cheeks, falling into the garden. The creeping brambles dove greedily into the wet sand, clambering up Dreva's shoes and spiraling around her ankles like green centipedes. She offered Mayve the palm of her hand, demanding an explanation. "Care to tell me what you did with all my money, then?"

Mayve stared back adamantly. "I bought equipment for a job coming up."

Dreva flung her hands up and shouted, "Still not telling the full truth, I see. I'm not even sure I want to know what you're going to do." She tried to step out of the garden and tripped on the vines, crashing into the sand and dirt.

Mayve knelt to help her mother up. As soon as Dreva was back on her feet, she stormed inside, blood welling up from the bramble scratches and falling to the sand in thick droplets. As they hit the ground, the bramble tendrils suddenly shifted, creeping toward the blood-soaked dirt. Mayve followed her mother inside, catching the door before it slammed shut.

Dreva was over by her cot, mindlessly turning her ring around her finger. Her despair seemed inescapable in their cramped home. As Mayve entered, her mother whispered, "Imayva, you know what I have to say on the matter. Lawless ways only end one way. Abruptly. I refuse to lose you."

Mayve wanted to bury her head in the sand. Dreva continued, "I can stomach your climbs. You have always been reckless, and as much as I wish you would reign that in, I know those lessons are best learned the hard way. If climbing injuries were the worst that awaited you, I would sleep soundly. But crossing the Merchatzi, the Coinclaws, or whoever else, you get involved with folk you shouldn't. You invite people into your life who can only cause misery."

She twisted the ring around her finger with more fervor. "I am happy with our life here. If you want more, *need* more, then we can work toward that, *honestly*."

Mayve bit back her rage. "I've always talked about leaving. All I want is to get us both out of here. Why do I get the feeling that I'll be leaving alone?"

"I have a place here. It's not glamorous, but I get by just fine. You want more. I *want* you to have more."

Mayve gestured around their cramped dwelling. "We live in a cave hole. We can *both* live better than this, and I'm doing what *really* needs to be done to make that happen. You want me to *leave* you here? I'd rather hurl myself into a Vent!"

Dreva's voice rose. "There is nothing wrong with how we live."

Mayve matched her mother's volume and then some. "You just mentioned me leaving, so make up your mind. Is there a better life for me? Or should I be grateful for this dark cave room? How many times have you skipped a meal to let me eat? I want *us* to live better, not just me. You've done *so much* for me, and you *never* let me return the favor!"

She reached up to her loft and leaned over the bed, grabbing her new dagger from its hiding place. "Just so you know, I bought this with your money yesterday." She flashed the blade at her mother. "Maybe now I won't have to worry about getting robbed in these tunnels, or dragged down a fissure into the Caverns by some wandering abomination."

Dreva sat down on her cot, head in her hands. Mayve stormed toward the door. "I'll be back tonight with enough money to get us out of here. Pack up our few belongings while I'm gone because we're leaving for a Verdant tomorrow morning, whether you like it or not."

She kicked open the dwelling door and disappeared into the darkness of the caves, trying to ignore her mother's gentle sobs echoing behind her. Her own tears flowed freely down her cheeks and she steeled her resolve. *I'm doing this for both of us, because we deserve better. You deserve better.*

Chapter 6

The Green-Eyed Girl

Mayve had not expected to leave their dwelling so early, and found she had plenty of time to kill before sunset. Stepping out of the Darkmist Tunnels into the shadowy midmorning fog, she found the Devaros Falls were even stronger today. The perpetual torrent churned Darkmist Pool into a fine mist, clouding the air and drenching the rotting wooden docks. The only sign it was morning was the faintest hint of sunlight spilling over the brim of the waterfall, a mere ghost of daylight down in the shadows.

The Falls have only gotten worse today. No shortcuts for me. Mayve begrudgingly started the long walk up to the city, stewing in her thoughts.

Lost in her own head, the parched trek up the desert road passed in the blink of an eye. Anxious to kill time, Mayve loitered toward Silt Row, not wanting to stray far from the river, but not wanting to return home. Her stomach growled with hunger. Stealing a bite to eat or pick-pocketing some coin would be easy enough, but she did not want to risk getting caught right before such a lucrative job. At least her mother would be tending to their garden all day. *Fixing my mistake, as usual.*

Before setting foot in Silt Row Market, she found a perch atop a rickety plank hovel to survey the colorful sea of tents, specifically looking for Faldmor's yellow one. There was plenty of yellow, but none that looked familiar. A green-and-white checkered tent stood where Faldmor's had at the edge of the plaza.

Odd. The Devar Consortium's last merchant rotation was four days ago. If they packed up and left, they missed out on weeks of prime location. Did they move just because of her theft? Maybe those seeds she stole were so expensive, they could not risk another thievery. *Good riddance.*

The seeds had to be made with volcomancy to grow that fast, and of all the crops, why brambles? She wondered what manifestation was needed to create such a thing. Mayve did not know nearly enough about the practice of volcomancy to make any sort of guess. However, just the thought was enough to conjure the image of the masked man, deadly shadows coiling around their outstretched fingertips. *I hope he left town with Faldmor.*

She shivered again at the thought of how close she came to death. The strands of white hair she cut away had been dry and shriveled. *I can only imagine what would have happened if those shadows hit my chest.*

It didn't matter, it was in the past. This evening needed all her focus.

To ease her fears, she navigated through the crowded market to the green-and-white checkered tent. A human manned the new stall, dressed in a sky blue and beige robe—the colors of the Devar Consortium. His back was turned as he unpacked a trunk of books, piling them haphazardly on his single table.

Mayve pretended to look confused and lost—a tactic that worked far too often for her liking. "Excuse me, there was a seed merchant here yesterday? Faldmor, from the Tyrak-Wenstnor Trade Coalition? I was hoping to buy more of his stock."

The merchant turned with a flash of annoyance, realizing she probably was not a paying customer. His gaze turned to pity rather quickly and said, "Sorry, ma'am, I got this spot as a sudden replacement. Faldmor shipped off yesterday to Port Wenstnor, in quite a hurry."

"In a hurry?" Mayve asked, prodding for more.

"Seemed like it. Put in his departure notice with the Consortium right before the guild hall closed." The merchant shrugged, then chuckled. "Selling seeds in the desert must not be as profitable as he thought.

Shame, if he stuck around a day then at least he'd have one more customer!"

Mayve smiled along with the merchant, then thanked him for his time. *I hope Faldmor goes bankrupt.* At least almost getting killed for those sand-cursed seeds had a silver lining.

Out of curiosity and an abundance of time, she checked on the smashed dwelling that the Ferry crushed in yesterday's accident. Despite the river surging around it, the ramshackle house still clung to the edge of the Falls. Mayve fought the urge to throw rocks at the last supporting stilt.

As the sun touched the top of the sandstone hills around Devar, she topped off her canteen from the river. The Devaros was higher than she had seen in years, surging beneath the wooden city. She would not be back to the water until well past nightfall, and when she did, she'd have hundreds of teirs in her coin purse. Leaving the river behind, she took the road for the Outer Sands.

* * *

The road to the Outer Sands was half-eaten by dunes, the slightest breeze swirling the sand into swaying dust devils. The sun was partially obscured by the hills, bathing the desert in an orange glow.

Down in Darkmist, it's probably black as night already. Despite the approaching dusk, the street was alive with denizens, trudging home after a long day away or escaping their homes for the first time as the harsh desert sun disappeared.

Mayve counted three dwellings down and across from the Hangman's Swing, each house dilapidated and dark. Noting the raptor-claw prints in the sand, she approached the door and knocked twice.

It creaked open a hairline crack. The interior was dark, and the dying sun did little to illuminate anything past the door. Ingo's grinning maw materialized out of the shadow. His green scales looked black in the low light, and his dark red feathers looked like freshly pooled blood.

Tongue flicking across his sharp teeth, he hissed in his Raptoran accent. "Was beginning to think you wouldn't show. Come on in." He retreated into the shadows, leaving the door cracked as a silent invitation.

Mayve stepped inside, closing the door behind her. It was uncomfortably warm in the dwelling, which reeked of smoke, cooking meat, and other, more chemical scents that stung her nose. On a nearby crate sat a mortar and pestle, coated in pungent grime. The earthy smells of whatever concoction the raptors were making suffocated the room.

The ground floor of the dwelling was just that—rock, sand, and little else save for some wooden crates piled around the edge of the room. The air was hazy from a small campfire burning in the center, the smoke filtering through smashed holes in the crumbling ceiling. Roasting above the campfire was a spit of skewered fish and desert shrew. Mayve eyed the spit hungrily, reminding herself this was the last time she wouldn't have enough to eat.

Ingo slunk over next to Spotch, who was tending the campfire. Lounging on the crates and by the fire were six other raptors, sharpening knives and ripping into food. They ravaged the meat fresh out of the fire, tearing off strips of rodent and gulping down entire fish. As they ate, Mayve looked around for anyone she recognized. The Coinclaws changed members often. Death played some part in that, but each of these raptors belonged to their own tribes as well, camped out in the dunes.

Ingo and Spotch have a tribe, I think, although they don't leave the city very often. Getting information about their life away was like prying fangs. They'd talked about a third brother before, but never their parents. However, they never asked for her life story either, so she did not pry.

Unfortunately for Mayve, she recognized no one except for the twins. They were also the largest raptors here, except for one hulking fellow with blue scales and no feathers. The other unknown faces were a smattering of different colors and feather patterns, forming a disjointed rainbow around the campfire. It might have been a pretty sight if they were not certainly all cutthroats and murderers.

She settled into a corner out of the way and scanned the room again, this time recognizing a face on second glance. A raptor with brown scales and sand-colored feathers arranged like a lion's mane. His name escaped her, but she gave him a nod across the room, which was curtly returned. Spotch offered her grilled shrew from the fire, which she happily accepted. She tried not to look too desperate as she dug in.

This wasn't her first job with the Coinclaws, but something was different here. Her stomach flipped as she realized what it was. *Look at how well-armed they are. They're dressed for war.* All of them wore full leather armor crafted from the hides of slaughtered animals. Blades made of tooth, bone, and metal were holstered in every conceivable place a blade could be drawn from.

Doubt flooded her. *They're out for blood tonight...Spotch said I wouldn't have to fight; that better be true or I'll wring his feathered neck.* The dagger on her belt looked utterly useless compared to the arsenal each raptor carried. Across the fire, Ingo and Spotch traded their weapons for the other to inspect. Twin axes, with decorated bone hilts, probably carved from the same hunted animal.

They jingled some coin in front of my eyes and now I'm about to walk into battle against the Oaken Legion. Depths below, if I survive this, I'm never telling Ma.

Ingo traded axes back with Spotch, and both stood up to address the circle. Ingo normally spoke with the confidence of a cat toying with its prey. *Being one of the toughest raptors in Devar comes with an unavoidable bravado.* Now, his tone was dead serious. No minced words, no sarcastic, fanged smile. Only grim words that reeked of death.

"Brethren." The room snarled, then fell into hungry silence. "We've gathered you here for more than a simple job. Tonight, we defend our home."

Another chorus of snarls erupted. Mayve did her best to look as excited as the rest of the raptors, but the nervous knot welled in her stomach again.

"The Oaken Legion, in all their laughable arrogance, believe they can exile us to the desert and still safely travel between their precious Verdants? There is debt to be paid. Our blood stains these sands, and so must theirs."

Murder. That's the first thing out of his mouth. Not money, not this treasure the Legion has. Murder. Mayve shifted in her seat as the other raptors broke into malicious grins.

"Now, lucky for us," Ingo snarled, "the Legion have brought a little present into town with them. According to dear King Coinclaw's scouts, the green-cursed trees were digging around in the Eastriver Dunes, and whatever they were looking for, they found."

Spotch unsheathed an obsidian dagger and began sketching the tavern and its surrounding buildings on the sandy floor. As he drew, a raptor with yellow scales and an uneven smattering of teal feathers interjected. He had an unnaturally long tail draped over the crates that flicked back and forth like a drunk rattlesnake. "Tell us what we're looking for. What in the depths dragged the trees all the way out here?" He licked his maw with a long tongue.

Spotch did not respond until he finished drawing. "I'd tell ya if I knew, but I don't. So shut yer trap and listen."

He pointed to the square in the sand that represented the Hangman's Swing, and scratched a line in the dirt directly from the street through the front door. "It's not our usual smash and grab. We all enter the taproom. No commotion yet."

Ingo pointed at Mayve with his axe. "This is Mayve. We've worked together before. She's a passing thief." He flashed her a cheeky grin. "But she can climb the underside of the Arch and sleep there like a bat if she wanted to."

Mayve appreciated the compliment, although she was painfully aware of the eight pairs of raptor eyes fixed on her, flickering in the fire's light. She felt like one of the skewered fish.

Ingo made a single dot in the sand, in the alleyway between the Hangman and its neighboring building. "Mayve will already be here." He traced another line down the alley, branching from the first. "Fevriz will be here."

Fevriz, right. That was the brown-scaled raptor's name. Mayve and Fevriz had worked together breaking into an Archtown manor abandoned by a guild official on a long trip to Carve.

"Szez will stay at the entrance here." The yellow-scaled raptor with the long tail leaned forward, paying closer attention. Spotch continued.

"Every room on the Hangman Swing's top floor has a window, unfortunately for the trees." He spit into the center of the sand drawing. The room hissed with flicking tongues. "Mayve, if she's quiet enough, can climb around the outside and see where they are keeping our prize. Once she —"

Mayve tried to interrupt and ended up coughing. Her throat was bone-dry and clenched shut. She took a swig from her canteen, and restarted her sentence. "If you don't even know what you're looking for, how will I know when I see it?"

Szez spoke up. "It's the Oaken Legion. It will probably be in a grand golden chest covered in beautiful green vines." His laugh sounded like a dying crow.

Ingo affirmed Szez's exaggeration. "You know how it is, Mayve. It will be heavily guarded. I wouldn't even put an extravagant chest out of the question." He turned back to the diagram. "When Mayve spots the target, she will signal Fevriz. Fevriz will signal Szez, and that's when we start the *commotion*." The room echoed with bloodthirsty hisses and the snapping of jaws, twisting Mayve's nervousness into fear.

Depths below, they don't even know what the Legion has. They've just assumed they've found something, and assumed it's valuable. This is all just an excuse. An excuse to kill some fucking trees, and I'm caught in the middle. About to climb up a building searching for a treasure that might not exist.

Spotch raised a dagger and gently lowered it through the air. The volume in the room dropped with it. He pointed the blade at each folk as he mentioned them. "Once the fighting starts, Mayve breaks into the upstairs, takes the treasure, and throws it out the window to Fevriz, who will run for the hideout. Szez, you can join the fight once it begins. As for us, it's every raptor for themselves once the metal clashes. Fight, run, or die. Regroup at the king's palace for your cut, if you survive. The coin will be sent to your tribe if you die. Mayve, all you gotta do is disappear and find us tomorrow."

Mayve felt lightheaded. She tried to focus, but her mind was racing. There was an energy in the room, rising to a fever pitch. The hisses and snaps of the raptors' jaws were constant now. Most were standing. They were ready for more than a standard heist. She was here to steal something, but they were here to kill.

Ingo continued, his voice rising. "Wreck the place. Burn it down if you fancy. Only kill the trees. The owner needs to learn that any price is too high when renting to the Oaken Legion." Mayve felt sick, but she couldn't run. *This is how I earn my way out of this city.*

Spotch reached for a drinking horn that sat next to the mortar and pestle. "Verdant's Bane. Everyone take a swig. Not you, Mayve. This is likely toxic to mammals like you." He uncorked the horn and a wretched smell engulfed the room, like a bonfire of weeds and diseased meat.

Mayve choked back vomit, relieved she was spared drinking whatever foul concoction it was. The raptors licked their scaled lips and gnashed their teeth. One by one they drank from the horn before passing it to the next. When the last was done, they gathered close and huddled together, pressing their heads together. As one, they snarled,

Sand and sail, ice and bone,
Scale thrive where none dare roam.
Oaken sword and Verdant throne,
Claws and fangs defend our home.

Mayve watched anxiously, back against the dwelling's wall. This ritual was not meant for her, and she wanted no more part in this than she already had. The raptors checked their armor and blades one last time, then Ingo looked at Mayve, bloodlust in his eyes. "Ready?"

Mayve could do nothing but nod her head. She swallowed her fear and focused her mind. *I don't need to fight. I'm just climbing and stealing. Nothing out of the usual.* She almost believed her lie.

* * *

Srrith had waited in the tavern all day, so she received her meal in a timely manner. The innkeeper slid a plate of cooked fish in front of her, with a side of eggs. A safe choice. The Hangman's Swing saw a lot of travel; he likely had an eye for discerning what species ate what. Meat was always good for anyone with scales.

He scraped the coins Srrith had laid out off the table and said,

"Thank you, traveler. If I can be of any further service, please let me know." Srrith nodded with no reply. Upstairs, she heard many sets of heavy footsteps thudding against the floorboards.

As Srrith unhinged her jaw and swallowed the fish, the footsteps migrated across the floor to the thin staircase, and the Oaken Legion descended in single file. Timbersteel armor scraped as nearly a dozen soldiers jostled into the room and commandeered the central table.

The innkeeper scurried between them like a bewildered rat in a miniature forest, running back and forth between the table and a large pot of some sort of vegetable stew that simmered behind the bar. Srrith opened up her hearing, hoping to catch snippets of any conversation.

"...unexpected. We're unfortunately stranded here until tomorrow," said a gruff voice emanating from the gnarled tree at the head of the table. The commanding officer, likely.

Another voice. "The boat's arrival is delayed?"

The officer replied, "No. The boat's departure is delayed."

The same other voice countered, with a hint of skepticism, "Are we not their only passengers? We should march to the docks and demand departure. Every minute we spend here is dangerous."

The head soldier smashed his gauntlet into the table. "Shut your hollow! Preparations are clearly not done." The ceramic bowls rattled against the impact. One of the bowls dumped its contents into a soldier's lap, who scrambled to dab it up without drawing attention to himself.

Srrith heard the officer's heart rate elevate. A normal effect of anger. She tilted her head to get a better angle. *No, that is not anger. That is dishonesty.* The two sounded similar, but Srrith knew the subtle differences. The officer was keeping something from the other trees.

She tuned her hearing and heard other elevated heartbeats. Not from every tree, though. *Some of the trees know something that the others do not. It seems the trees never stop fighting, even amongst themselves.*

The officer tree glanced around the room and saw Srrith for the first time. He pushed his chair back, the violent scrape against the stone floor cutting any conversation short. He marched toward Srrith, eyes burning green. *Ah, the oak wishes to change the subject.*

"Snake. This tavern is under Oaken Legion occupation. Get out."

Flicking her forked tongue at him, Srrith replied, "I am a regular." Looking him dead in the eyes, she took another bite of breakfast. The tree reached for her plate.

Srrith pulled it toward her just as his fingers reached it, and he grabbed only air. Under the table, Srrith's tail hooked around the soldier's knee and pulled, bending his leg inward. The soldier immediately lost his balance and slammed hard into the table. To everyone else in the room, it looked like he simply overreached himself.

The tree leapt to his feet and his hand reached for the sword sheathed at his side. Srrith closed her hearing as a cacophony of scraping chairs bombarded her. Every soldier was on their feet, gauntlets on sword hilts. One shouted with concern "Frutexier Grenner— "

Srrith held up her hand. She spoke quickly and firmly this time. "Maybe I will come back with friends."

The taproom froze, every tree holding their breath. Srrith had no friends in Devar, but they did not need to know that. They were simply looking at her scales, trying to guess how many raptors she might know. The soldier named Grenner spoke again. "And if we kill you here and now?"

Srrith shrugged. "Then my friends may come looking here. I am a regular, of course." She looked around with fake curiosity, then locked eyes with Grenner. "I wonder what they will find."

Almost every tree shifted nervously, leaves rustling. *Fear moves like wind through a forest, gentle yet pervasive. Caressing all in its path.* Grenner removed his hand from his sword hilt and stomped back to his chair. The rest of the soldiers slowly returned to their seats and resumed eating in tense silence.

It is in my best interest to leave, before I get a lesson in Oaken Legion combat. She hissed her frustrations away. *Alas, I cannot miss the green-eyed girl, whenever she chooses to arrive.*

As she finished her meal, the dinner rush filtered in, bringing Hangman's Swing near capacity. She ordered more water, then assumed her fake sleeping position, relying on her echolocation to avoid suspicion. Across the room, a flamboyantly dressed performer plucked away at a droning string instrument, every note vibrating through her mind rather unpleasantly.

Srrith thought back to the music of her village, hidden away in the Ralveran Depths. Cave tauninagan music is difficult for outsiders to grasp. If an expert musician were to listen in, they would label the music as discordant and hollow, lacking melody and rhythm. They made the mistake of *listening* to the music instead of *looking* at it. Cave tauninagan music is meant to be seen, not heard. When viewed with echolocation, their music can weave beautiful tapestries and images through their mind's eye.

This music only gave Srrith's mind's eye a splitting headache. She tried to listen elsewhere, to no avail.

Suddenly, the music died. All sound clattered to a halt as six raptors strode into the taproom.

Srrith hissed, relieved she could finally see again. Her mind painted the raptors as they moved. Two slunk to the bar, dangerously close to the Oaken Legion table. Twins, Srrith heard. Painted identical in her mind. The other four spread out around the tavern.

My "friends". Perfect timing. Srrith flicked her tongue in frustration. They might scare away the green-eyed girl.

Each lizard was armed to the teeth. One of the twins at the bar motioned to the minstrel. "Don't stop just for us, please." He flashed his teeth to the room. "It was so lovely."

The music did not start again. At the central table, the Legion were slowly standing up, reaching for their weapons and shields. *Yes, that's right. Look intimidating. Hope the raptors rethink their plans.*

The other twin said, "A round of refreshing water for myself and my comrades." His smile disappeared as he caught the bartender's eye. "It's wonderful to find an inn so welcoming to *everyone*." He emphasized the final word with a malicious stare at the innkeeper, licking his scaled lips.

Srrith heard the innkeeper's heart falter and breath catch in his throat, and he hurried to fill the tankards with shaking hands, as if fixing them drinks would stop what was about to happen.

With the music gone, she opened her hearing even further. The flood of racing heartbeats felt like a stampede of enraged beasts. Except for the raptors'. Their hearts beat calm. *Everyone fears what might happen next, but the raptors are not afraid. They know exactly what will happen next.* Srrith reached for her sickles.

Her hearing picked up a single whisper from the raptor at the door. It was directed at no one, muttered impatiently from the raptor to someone outside. "Hurry up, girl."

She is here. Srrith looked across the crowded taproom and knew she had to get outside somehow.

Several seconds later, the door raptor nodded to the twins at the bar. One of them turned his drink upside-down, gulped down the entire thing, then obliterated the glass tankard over the nearest tree's skull.

The inn erupted into chaos.

* * *

Raudius leapt up as the glass shattered over Otrix's skull. On his left, Uldius stood and drew his sword so fast his elbow knocked into Raudius's face. He sprawled backward, crashing to the tavern floor.

Remember your training, Raudius. Stand up and stand strong. As he struggled for footing, a red-scaled raptor was already leaping at him, a dagger in each hand. *I'm too slow.*

Across the table, Yuetrix pulled his shield off his back and hurled it like a discus. It caught the raptor mid-flight and the lizard crashed into a nearby table, splitting it in half. Raudius scrambled to his feet and drew his sword, looking around frantically for where he could help.

Grenner and a green-scaled raptor were wrestling across the table. The raptor had its maw clamped over Grenner's shoulder, and Grenner was landing hard punches into its leather-clad rib cage. Otrix, with shards of glass in his bark, had drawn his sword and was exchanging blows with a hulking blue raptor. Yuetrix stumbled back from a wild headbutt and slashed his sword across a raptor's throat. A spray of blood covered Uldius, and suddenly he howled in pain as the raptor's blood sizzled and melted his bark.

"Verdant's Bane! Avoid their blood!" shouted Yuetrix. Grenner wrangled his raptor into a headlock and hurled it away. It landed on its back, then somersaulted backward onto all fours, skidding to a stop as its long claws dug into the stone, its tail swaying for balance. Another raptor slammed a hatchet into Potorius's back and kicked him over the bar.

Across the tavern, patrons scrambled for cover, sprinting for the door only to get trampled underfoot by the rolling tide of battle. Yellow-green Oakfire raging up his branches, Grenner yelled out, "For the Verdant!"

The other soldiers, each fighting their own separate battle, shouted in unison, *"For the Legion!"* Raudius bellowed along, head on a swivel as he tried to spot where Claud or Batia were among the chaos. Another scream cut through as a tree burned alive somewhere in the turmoil, covered in sizzling raptor blood.

Yuetrix appeared out of the chaos, grabbing his arm. The older soldier shouted over the sounds of clashing steel. "Upstairs, now! Send Adarias down and replace him on guard duty."

A flash of blue scales caught Raudius's eye. He grabbed Yuetrix's shield from where it lay and muscled past the old tree, raising the shield just in time to catch an axe strike.

The impact slammed him to the tavern floor, reverberating through his whole body. Yuetrix ripped his shield from Raudius's arm and smashed its edge into the raptor's jaw. Teeth clattered across the stone floor.

"Move, soldier!" Yuetrix yelled. Across the room, Grenner was shouting, "Formations! Stand strong!" The Oaken Legion hurried to lock shields as the raptors snarled, leaping at the trees like hunting lions.

Raudius sprinted upstairs, chased by screams. He had no idea if they were from raptors, cut down by Legion timbersteel, or from his friends, splintered by axes and boiled by Verdant's Bane.

He ran to the large common room where they kept the artifact. The chest that held it stood as far away from the entrance as possible, pressed against the window. Adarias was there, clad in full timbersteel armor with his sword drawn and shield raised. He had taken the time to don his helmet when he heard combat erupt. The jagged timbersteel fit perfectly over his branches, crafted by a forgemaster specifically for him.

"I was sent to replace you," Raudius said, out of breath.

Adarias shoved him out of the way, stomping for the stairs. "Useless greenling. You'll be dead anyway if they reach here."

Raudius did not disagree. He took position in front of the chest, hoping his brethren downstairs were managing well. *I was useless. I stood there like a fawn in its first storm.* His sword felt weak in his arms. *That's false. You saved Yuetrix. You held your ground.* He faced the door, planning out what to do if a raptor and not a tree burst through.

Something smashed through the window behind him.

"The savages came from the sand and the snow. Their raiding parties burned our farms to ash and coals. Their starving masses decimated what flora and fauna survived the Paroxysm. But the Legion stood strong. Our roots dig deep into the Verdant earth, and the raptors soon learned we would not be shaken from our home so easily."

—spoken by Corus Treth, Praetor of the Bastion of Perseverance. Except taken from "*The Ashen Century*" historical tome.

Chapter 7

The Price of Greed

Mayve let gravity take her. Her fingers dug into the wooden window frame, fighting her momentum. Her boots shattered the window and the momentum carried her through, her arms shielding her face from the sharp glass fragments. She slammed into the young soldier and they both tumbled to the ground in a crystal hail.

The tree looked up from the ground, dazed, and recognition briefly flashed across his face before Mayve's foot collided with it, bark crunching against her boot. *The tree that Ingo and Spotch mugged. Poor sap.*

She wrenched the soldier's sword from its sheath and hurled it out the open window. Then she drew her pocketknife and knelt in front of the chest to examine the lock. *Could be pickable, but I bet there's a key nearby.*

A rough bear hug pinned her arms to the side. Jagged timbersteel pierced her, slicing open long seams of blood. *Depth's below, he's still conscious?*

A thought occurred to Mayve that trees might, in fact, be different than humans, and that they might not get knocked out the same way.

She slammed the pocket knife into the armored leg. There was a metallic snap and the blade ricocheted across the room. Mayve shouted and pushed her feet off the chest to send both her and the soldier tumbling to the ground. The crash into the floor loosened the tree's grip just enough for Mayve to wriggle out and roll away, timbersteel tearing ribbons from her shirt.

Rolling to her feet, she unsheathed her new dagger. *This doesn't feel much better than the pocketknife.* The soldier fell into a brawler's stance, gauntlets guarding his face, the only unarmored part of his body.

Mayve ducked in and tried an exploratory stab at the soldier, hoping to prod his defenses. With deliberate and precise movements, the tree stepped in past the attack and slammed a gauntlet into her ribs. It was faster than she was ready for, and Mayve twisted at the last second, the punch staggering her backward.

Thanks to her reflexes, the blow merely knocked the wind out of her instead of breaking a rib. She felt warm blood pooling in her shirt as the rough armor cut through the fabric and into her skin.

The rumors she had heard about Oaken Legion combat training appeared to be more than tall tales. She had been in her fair share of fist-fights, but she had never faced someone with such precise movements. *I'll die if I try that again.* Screams rang from downstairs. Time was running out.

The only ideas she had were risky, but that rarely gave Mayve pause. She hurled the dagger at the soldier's face. He raised his forearms and the dagger pinged harmlessly away, but as he lowered his guard again, Mayve was halfway through a dropkick, landing a boot on each shoulder of the soldier. The force of the kick sent the tree toppling backward onto the prized chest. The chest crunched under the sharp armor's impact, splintered fissures cracking down the lid.

Mayve was on her feet as the soldier was still falling. As he tried to stand, she grabbed his legs and wrenched him off-balance. She heaved upward, and as the tree fell, his head hit the edge of the chest with a sharp crack. The soldier went limp, becoming dead weight. *So they can be knocked out the same way. It's just a little more effort.*

The tree groaned and began to rise once more. Mayve grabbed a nearby chair, sent a quick prayer to Phovus that it was heavy enough to put a tree to sleep, then shattered it over the tree's oaken skull. His body collapsed back to the ground, finally still. *A lot more effort. Depths below, you soldiers are hardy.*

She ran to the chest and inspected the lock. She reached for her pocket knife and found it was no longer a knife, just a handle. *Phovus, I won't ask again—where did all my luck go?* She scrambled around for the dagger she threw, and found it underneath a table, but the blade was too thick for the lock. *Come on Mayve, so close. So close to freedom. Just open this Vent-cursed chest.*

Silence fell and Mayve froze. The sounds of combat downstairs were gone. Armored footfalls thundered up the stairs. Panic overtook Mayve and she frantically smashed her heel into the cracked wooden lid over and over, willing the lid to explode into a cloud of dust. *Just need a little more! Break, Phovus, break!*

The incoming footsteps and her frenzied heartbeat were indistinguishable. The door would burst open any split second and she would be impaled on a timbersteel blade.

In a fit of adrenaline, Mayve dug her fingers in the bottom of the heavy chest and struggled to her feet. She heaved it out the window just as the door burst open. Furious shouts in Oakish followed her as she swung herself out the window. Timbersteel gauntlets made a desperate grab for her as she climbed down the wall so fast she was practically falling. Gravity overpowered her grip just before she reached the ground and she slammed into the sands.

The wooden chest was smashed to nothing more than scattered planks and metal bindings around a crater in the sand. Sitting in the debris was a leather pouch, the drawstring loose and unbound. Lying in the sand next to it, slipped from the pouch by the impact, was the most peculiar item Mayve had ever laid eyes on.

It was a perfectly cut oval sapphire, large enough to barely fit in her hand. Brilliant golden etchings, thinner than any jeweler could craft, looped across the gem's surface in intricate foreign patterns. Curiosity drowning her fear of capture, Mayve picked it up. The texture was similar to a rock worn smooth by a river for a thousand years, and sand rolled off the side like water over glass.

The Oakish shouts from within the tavern knocked Mayve out of her trance. She dropped the rock back into its bag and then dropped the bag back in the sand like a hot coal. *Fevriz could have slaughtered me then and there if he thought I was stealing it.* She needed to disappear, fast.

Speaking of Fevriz, he should have been halfway to Archtown with the artifact by now. Yet the treasure lay still at Mayve's feet, no raptors nearby. She heard the tavern's saloon doors slam open, Legion soldiers charging into the night.

Her eyes adjusted to the dark and she saw that a shape knelt in the sand nearby. *That sneaky scalescum, camouflaged and ready to ambush me.* The creature stood up, far taller than Fevriz. Mayve now saw there were two shapes in the shadows. One was Fevriz, lying still in the sand, and whatever was hulking over him.

The Oaken Legion rounded the corner, torches illuminating the alleyway and the creature that stood between them and Mayve. It was drenched in Fevriz's blood, his body lying mangled in crimson sand. The Verdant's Bane in the raptor's blood violently boiled the creature's face, but it was so consumed in draining every ounce from the raptor's mutilated carcass it did not notice, or did not care.

The eldritch monster turned to face Mayve, staring right at her with no eyes. Its body was constructed of tightly woven brambles, molded into a vaguely human shape with four tangled limbs and a mess of thorned vines for a head. Beneath it, she saw several crimson vines snaking through the bloody sand like worms, chasing every droplet of Fevriz's blood. As its vines boiled from the Verdant's Bane, more grew from its body mass, coiling up and replacing the injured tendrils.

Mayve almost threw up as the light caught on something growing from the creature. It was covered in several wilting black flowers. She had seen those same flowers earlier that morning.

This monster—it was made of the same brambles that grew in their garden overnight. It *came from* their garden. A petal as black as night detached and drifted gently into the blood. *The garden my mother is tending alone.*

From a tangled mouth of melting, blood-soaked brambles, the creature screamed and charged.

Chapter 8

Screams in the Night

The unearthly scream echoed off the surrounding dunes as the monstrous bramble creature leapt toward the Oaken Legion. Leaving them behind, Mayve sprinted around the other side of the tavern and broke onto the main road, nausea threatening to overwhelm her.

The raptors had carried the fight outside the inn, engaging the Oaken Legion in scattered bouts around the street. Ingo and Spotch spotted her running by as they hacked a tree into kindling, prying off his timbersteel and digging their axes into his struggling bark. The moonlight illuminated their crazed eyes.

Spotch shouted, "Mayve! Where are you going with *that*?"

Mayve realized she had scooped the treasure out of the sand without realizing it; the leather pouch was clutched tight in her hand. Spotch and Ingo brandished their axes and slunk toward her like wolves on the hunt.

Another unnatural, bloodcurdling scream cut off Mayve's apology, and a second bramble eldritch, also covered in wilting black flowers, charged out of the darkness at the twins. It was dripping with blood from a fresh corpse that lay shredded in the alleyway behind it. It leapt at Ingo with a scream, and Spotch tackled him out of harm's way.

The two brothers rolled apart and into fighting stances, gnashing their maws at the bramble creature before launching at it in a savage fray of blade, fang, and thorn. Mayve did not stay to see the winner, flying across the sands toward Silt Row. More screams erupted in the dark from seemingly every direction. Warning bells rang across the city. *They're everywhere. Please be okay, Ma. Please, Phovus, please make sure she's okay. Please.* Mayve begged the god of luck as she ran, praying he could hear her.

Faldmor and the masked man. They didn't leave town because I stole from them. They left because they knew this would happen. On the far horizon, the Okanos Vent glowed like a crimson sunset. Silhouettes of smoke rose from Silt Row as something caught fire in the wooden city.

As she ran, Mayve tried to count how many seeds she had planted yesterday and shoved the thought out of her mind. *Countless.* The cold desert air bit her lungs, every breath becoming a freezing gasp. She arrived at the top of her shortcut down the Falls and nearly hurled herself over the edge to start her descent. Halfway down, she realized her mistake.

The Devaros River was still surging, and it had only swelled further as night fell. The path she had climbed last morning was completely underneath the raging Falls. Mayve dropped onto a ledge that was dry yesterday and immediately lost her footing. Drenched in moisture from the mist, the rocks were as slippery as ice.

Her vision shook as her shoulder slammed into the hard rock. By instinct, her hands latched onto a groove in the cliff face, fingers burning as her legs dangled over the abyss, her grip barely saving her from a plummet into the afterlife. Pain coursed through her veins like venom as she heaved herself back onto the ledge. Mayve looked for a new path, but there was nowhere to go but back up.

If she climbed back up, she would have the long path into Darkmist. Something stung her side, and she realized her soaked shirt was sticking to the wound there, blood creeping like red mold into the fabric. She would have to deal with it later. Her voice whispered in her head, *You're already out of time. Your mother is out of time.*

Taking the long way wasn't going to happen. Climbing down safely was no longer an option either. The lower Falls had far more fog, it would only get more dangerous. Nighttime was especially dangerous, when the blazing desert sun could not lend a helping hand to disperse the fog and dry the rocks. Mayve pried a loose stone free from the cliff face and thought of a terrible plan.

Peering at the upper lip of the Falls, Mayve saw a void in the sky, blotting out the stars behind it: the old dwelling from the Ferry's crash, still caught on the edge of the Falls. She clenched her jaw to force down the pain in her side, focusing on where she needed to aim. *This might be the dumbest shit I've ever done.* Minding her footing on the slippery ledge, she hurled the rock into the void. If she took too long getting home, though, if her mother died because of her mistakes...

Anything was worth the risk.

A resounding crack pierced the roar of the waterfall, followed by splintering wood and snapping ropes. The ruined dwelling tipped slightly closer to the edge but did not give in to gravity. By some miracle, it clung to life against the push of the raging river and the pull of the abyss.

Her voice drenched in frustration, Mayve screamed into the roar of the Falls. She furiously dug into the cliff until her fingers were raw, tearing another rock free. She was soaked to her bones in mist and blood, her long dark hair strangling her neck. Mayve clenched her jaw again like she was trying to bite through iron and hurled the second rock at the last supports.

Another resounding crack. Ropes and planks snapped as the dwelling finally gave up and leaned into its own demise. With one final creak, the dark mass of wood and shrapnel hurtled down the Falls, revealing the stars in the sky behind it. Mayve's pain disappeared in a surge of adrenaline and she hurled herself into thin air. If the jump was too early, she would be instantly crushed by a falling house. Too late, and she would leap into the Devaros Falls and plunge to her death with the water.

Mayve caught the edge of the house as it plummeted past. The falling dwelling wrenched her downward but she held firm. Water slammed into her like a thousand punches, its icy cold grasp freezing her breath in her chest. She fumbled a free hand around, racing against time to find the sturdiest plank she could grab. Just as the dwelling crashed into Darkmist Pool, she wrapped her arms and legs tightly around a supporting beam and prayed the Falls would let her float away in one piece.

The current ripped the house into splinters immediately. The dwelling shouldered the impact of the fall for Mayve, but it still knocked her breath away right before she was dragged underwater. Opening her eyes, she only saw the inky blackness of Darkmist Pool in every direction.

Up and down blended together as the beam was spun through the watery depths, smashed back underwater over and over by the constant pummeling of the Falls. Mayve's lungs were already on fire, and still the river tossed her mercilessly. The swirling currents swung chunks of debris through the water like a massive spinning flail, battering Mayve with the force of nature. A splinter of wood pierced her wounded side and she screamed in visceral pain, the last precious bubbles erupting from her mouth.

With a thud, the whirlwind of motion crunched to a halt. The waterfall pounded on the surface above like an enraged god smashing their fists against the sky, and the currents raged like a hurricane around her. However, she was no longer a leaf in the wind and instead was a tree weathering the storm. The pillar she hugged had lodged itself in the riverbed like a javelin. Her lifeboat was trapped under the waves.

If Mayve let go, the hurricane of water would whisk her away. She had heard plenty of tales of people falling off the Falls, as is bound to happen when a city is built at the top. Sometimes, it would take weeks for their body to resurface. Sometimes never. The churning vortex beneath the Devaros Falls wrapped its cold tendrils around everything that fell in. Her lungs gasped for air, begging Mayve to inhale the water around her. Even without light, Mayve saw the edges of her vision tunneling to black.

Pushing herself down the pillar of wood, Mayve planted her feet on the riverbed, feeling for the rocks that trapped the beam in its watery grave. Friction gave way and her feet slipped free. The watery hurricane took her without hesitation, her body flailing with the current. Splinters dug into her hands as they gripped the beam, and she fought the waves that desperately tried to pull her into the void.

Dragging herself back to her wooden pillar, she planted her boots on the riverbed again. Her consciousness slipped as the last bit of oxygen in her lungs bled away. More splinters of wood dug into her arms and cheek like mosquitoes. Her pain dwindled to a numb cold, the roar of the Falls fading into a muffled drone. The world went quiet as she pushed with all her might, her body draining everything left into one final burst of adrenaline.

The beam dislodged, and the current instantly swiped her and her precious beam back into the vortex, the water ripping past her, lulling her to sleep. Eternal rest called to her consciousness, inviting her to stay.

The muffled roar of the Falls crashed back to life as her beam breached the surface. Her lungs instinctively gasped, sucking in the sweet Darkmist fog. The wood gently bobbed in Darkmist Pool, meandering downstream, indifferent to the ragged human clinging to life on its back. Mayve's head spun with the sudden inrush of oxygen, her consciousness clawing back from oblivion.

Feelings returned to her extremities, and she realized she was freezing cold. Her trusty beam snagged on an outstretched dock with a benign thud, as if politely informing Mayve that this was where they should part ways. She heaved herself out of Darkmist Pool and collapsed, shivering, onto the planks. Her vision swam with the swirling mists, dizzying her mind.

A scream from somewhere in the Darkmist fog slammed her sense back into her body. As her mind pieced itself back together, it dissected the scream into two screams: the unnatural screech of another bramble eldritch and the dying breath of its prey, a poor Darkmist denizen somewhere in the fog. *Of course the monsters are here. This is where they grew.* With shaky arms, Mayve willed herself to stand and stumbled toward the tunnel entrance.

The rage of the Falls died away as she pushed through the fog into the Darkmist Tunnels. The crash of water used to be a comforting familiarity, shrouding Mayve like a well-worn cloak. Now, the thunderous roar felt suffocating, drowning her mind in visions of the dark, turbulent abyss hidden beneath the waves. Just moments ago, it was nearly her tomb. The echoes pursued her deep into the cave, refusing to release their grasp on Mayve's mind.

She took as many shortcuts as possible to reach their dwelling, grabbing a torch from a nearby sconce to light the way as she left the main path. Every step closer, her heart pounded, threatening to explode out of her chest. Turning down her tunnel with reckless haste, she absentmindedly kicked a plank on the ground, sending it skittering across the rock floor. Wondering where in the depths that came from, her confusion turned to panic as she looked farther into the darkness.

The wooden door of the dwelling was ripped to shreds, scattered all over the tunnel. Mayve saw in her mind's eye a mass of bramble eldritches—twisted together in a screaming, roiling heap—explode from the inside of the dwelling, smashing the door to splinters. Stepping through the decimated entryway, she entered her home with her dagger drawn.

The entire dwelling was in shambles. The back door was obliterated inward from the garden side, proving beyond doubt that the eldritches came from their garden. Scratches marred every surface in the house, eerie signs of the bramble horde that clawed its way through. Soil from the garden swamped the floor, tracked in by the freshly sprouted monsters.

Mayve walked in a trance through her home. Sand and glass from the shattered sandscale scraped underneath her boots. They had pinched dens for months to buy a functional one from Silt Row. *Dreva pinched dens. I helped Ingo scam some Lockworkers.*

The garden looked like an excavated graveyard, Dreva's orderly planting rows churned to nothing. Far above ground, the freezing desert air condensed into a thick fog that drifted through the cracks in the ceiling, dividing the cave with ethereal curtains. Mayve's torch lit upon a hulking mass in the corner, and every emotion drained from her body.

A monster of thorns and vines lifted itself from the ground, uncovering Dreva. Creepers extracted themselves from her body, swollen with blood, leaving crimson pockmarks as the thorns tore at the flesh. Mayve's vision blurred as tears welled up, her face too numb to feel the water streaming down her cheeks. A spark of rage collided with a wave of fear in her chest. Her fight and flight battled for control as she struggled to draw breath.

There was nothing she could do but stand there, petrified, as the blood-soaked plant shrieked and leapt. Steel flashed in the misty torchlight and a black shape crashed into the bramble eldritch.

Chapter 9

The Huntress Strikes

Srrith barreled through the door to the garden and slammed her shoulder into the mass of brambles, hooking its vines with her sickles and wrenching it away from the green-eyed girl.

Thorns scraped against her scales, some finding purchase in the skin beneath with sharp pricks of pain. She and the bramble eldritch tumbled away through the churned garden, leaving the girl startled and frozen. Creepers wrapped around her body and Srrith slashed them away with her sickles as she spun out of reach.

Quickly, she coiled into a striking stance and readied her twin blades. The bramble eldritch roiled and morphed into a humanoid form, hunching over and charging her on all fours.

Blood trickled into her eyes from cuts on her forehead. Srrith closed them, hissing with every breath. Every detail of the room formed in her mind's eye. She saw the creature running forward, heard every step it took. The dirt crunching beneath its bramble hooves told her it was about to leap.

Her serpentine body twisted only as much as needed to avoid the monster, and her steel sang. The sickles spun as she twisted away, slashing through the center mass of the brambles. Dark liquid sprayed the cave wall, far more than brambles should hold. The bramble eldritch stitched itself back together, sealing the deep cut her sickles had just opened.

The tauninaga hissed with every breath, gathering information on the target and the surroundings. She dropped into an evasive stance as the creature charged again. Then, it screamed.

The shriek ripped apart her echolocation and turned her mind to static. Reeling like her head was split open, Srrith focused on where she last saw the creature, and coiled to the left. Her sickles turned her spinning body into a whirlwind of steel and scales, and she felt another spray of warm liquid as her sickles carved through more brambles. Her vision returned with the next hiss, and she saw the shriveled body of another human lying still in the corner. *This monster is engorged with blood.*

Srrith struck from her coiled position as the creature was regaining its footing. Her sickles cut through the vines, blood gushing into the dirt. The wounds quickly knitted themselves back together as quickly as Srrith opened new ones. With each slash, less blood sprayed from the wound. The creature screamed again, blurring Srrith's mind. She opened her eyes and uncoiled backward, launching herself just out of reach from the deadly thorns.

The bramble eldritch, fully enraged, shrieked again and charged. This time at the green-eyed girl.

It needs more blood. Srrith whipped out her tail and caught the creature by its ankle, the thorns digging into her. The creature crashed into the dirt only a foot away from the girl, clawing at the ground before her, reaching for the warm blood inside its prey. On the other side of its body, tendrils of thorns were already worming between Srrith's scales, seeking her fresh blood.

Srrith flexed every muscle in her coils and dragged the writhing brambles back toward her. She swung both her sickles into the bramble's back, burying them deep in the plant. Her hearing picked up a subtle sound that told her everything she needed to know. A crunch of dry, dead, vines deep within its core. *The more I cut it, the more it heals, and the dryer it becomes.*

The bramble eldritch ceased struggling toward the girl and turned on Srrith once more, pushing itself off the ground and leaping at the snake. The turn of momentum was so sudden, Srrith almost pulled the creature on top of her. At the last moment, she twisted and spun, coiling up like a tornado of shadows.

Using the sickles buried in its core and the bramble's own momentum, she flung it away from her. The bramble monster and her sickles crashed into the soil on the other side of the garden, writhing back to its feet.

Srrith turned to the green-eyed girl. "When I say so, use the torch."

The girl nodded, brandishing the torch in one hand and a paltry dagger in the other. Srrith heard the girl's heartbeat and breathing accelerate. *She is afraid, but she is also furious.*

The bramble monster charged, howling like an injured animal. Srrith charged back, twisting her body at the last second and catching the creature in her coils. With practiced movements, she draped her body around the creature, smothering it in a tauninagan death coil. The brambles howled and Srrith felt sharp creepers dig between her scales, searching frantically for the precious blood coursing through her veins. Using the embedded sickles as reins, she lifted the monster off its feet and pried the sickles apart. The creature's chest burst open with a dry crack, vines and creepers flailing like thorny intestines.

She didn't need to say a word. The green-eyed girl wasted no time, sprinting across the garden and ramming the torch into the monster's open chest cavity. The flames caught the dry, dead brambles with a voracious hunger. Srrith uncoiled, vines ripping at her skin, and planted herself between the monster and the girl.

The bramble eldritch stumbled backward, smoke pouring from its core. One last dying scream erupted as flames consumed the plant. It took a few strained steps toward Srrith before the fire ate its legs to ash and it collapsed onto the sand.

Srrith and the girl watched the eldritch burn to a pile of ashen coals, letting the rush of combat fade away. Srrith moved first, slithering toward the burning shrub and pulling her sickles from the ashes. The blades were red-hot, steaming in the cold mist. Without a word, the girl ran to the body of her mother, and Srrith slithered inside to leave the human to her grief.

Chapter 10

An Empty Home

It's all my fault. I'm so sorry, Ma.

Imayva buried Dreva in her garden, in a patch she knew would catch the morning daylight through the ceiling cracks. Before the earth took her, Mayve held her mother and cried until tears refused to flow.

As she pushed the last pile of dirt over the grave, another surge of tears dropped her to her knees. She scraped at the freshly dug soil, desperate to give her mother one last hug again, stopping just short of uncovering the body. Her mother was gone, she was alone, and it was her own Vent-cursed fault. Her quiet sobs wandered through the fog.

When Mayve finally entered the dwelling, she was hoping her mysterious savior would have moved on to rescue others. Unfortunately, the large snake lay coiled in the center of the dwelling, around a small campfire she had lit in the remains of the hearth. A couple short of a dozen feet long, the tauninaga dominated the tiny living space. By the bandages wrapped around their coils, it looked like the massive cobra had already tended their wounds. Now, she was hard at work sharpening their sickles, sparks jumping off a whetstone.

Seeing Mayve, the snake stored the whetstone in a long, flat leather pack that hugged her serpentine back like a wet blanket. Mayve had seen similar packs before, sold by passing merchants. They were meant to carry essentials for underground travel, able to fit through cramped cave tunnels with ease and nearly undetectable when accompanied by a cloak. The merchant had called them a specific name, which escaped her memory at the moment.

Taking a deep breath to compose herself, Mayve spoke first. "Who are you and why are you still here?"

The snake picked up their cloak and draped it over their shoulders. "I am called Srrith. You are the green-eyed girl." The snake had a low, airy voice, and flicked her forked tongue as she spoke, each "s" sound elongated into a hiss.

"I prefer Imayva, or Mayve." *I need this strange creature out of my house.* "Thank you for saving me but it's time you moved on. I'm alright now." Mayve began sifting through the wreckage around her for anything she might need. She didn't know where she was going, but she could not stay here. Strewn with rubble, the once-cozy dwelling felt suffocating and dark.

Srrith hissed, "No, I am here for *you.* You are the girl. The Great Seer is never wrong, and it is my duty to fulfill her wishes so that the future passes best for us all."

Her patience razor-thin, Mayve snapped, "I just lost my mother and my home is destroyed. I'm in no mood to be hissed strange garbage by a stranger snake."

She hated that she was somewhat curious. "How did you even find me?"

The tauninaga sheathed her sickles on her back. "I followed you from the Hangman. Alactashi Sen said you would arrive. She was correct. Tracked you to the waterfall, saw your plunge."

Mayve shuddered, remembering the dark abyss beneath the Devaros waters. She asked, "How did you get down so quickly?"

Srrith opened up her slender cave pack and pulled out a handful of pitons. "Climbing equipment. A necessity for cave life."

Mayve failed to hide the jealousy in her eyes. They were always too poor to afford climbing gear, and anything that made it to Silt Row Market was bought fast by the merchant guilds to use in the Locks.

Srrith continued. "I left a path up the cliff face. You must come with me to see the Seer." She spoke with absolute certainty, as if Mayve would happily agree to this insane notion.

Mayve shook her head in absolute disbelief. "Excuse me? No. What I'm *going* to do is hand this artifact over to the Coinclaws." She patted the hefty pouch on her belt. "I'll collect a healthy cut of teirs, and buy passage out of this sand-cursed city."

Her eyes stung from the last remnants of her tears, and her chest felt numb and hollow. She looked past the garden door to the smoking pile of ash that used to be the bramble eldritch. The tiny voice in her mind tried to scream out, muffled by her rage. *You caused that. It's your fault! If you kept your hands in your pockets, your mother would be alive.* She briefly thought about walking out of Darkmist and stepping into the Falls. The void beneath it would feel less numb than her chest right now.

A single spark of rage lit inside her. *Why should that masked man and Faldmor get to walk away from this unscathed? They made those seeds with no good intentions in mind, even if I stole them.* The cave walls of her destroyed home seemed to constrict closer as her anger grew. *You killed your mother, not them.* She still could not shake the image of that wretched onyx mask from her mind, and she suddenly realized she'd never sleep soundly again as long as he lived.

The tauninaga's yellow snake eyes studied her empathetically, as if she knew Mayve's strife. She shifted in her coiled state, scales scraping, and hissed, "I am sorry for my haste, and I am sorry for your loss. In tauninagan culture, we believe all life persists in our dreams. As long as there is someone to hold you in their sleeping thoughts, you are not truly dead. I hope you dream of her tonight."

Mayve turned to wipe away a tear. As she raised her arm, a stabbing pain shot through her from the wound on her stomach and she doubled over. Srrith uncoiled and slithered next to her. "I did not see the brambles hit you. Why do you bleed?"

Mayve grimaced. "This was a gift from the Oaken Legion." She was unsure if the tauninaga held the same hatred toward the trees that the raptors did.

Srrith let out an amused hiss. "Yes, the trees give such lovely gifts." She scrounged in her pack and pulled out a small vial. "This is made by the mountain tauninaga, their healing *sfa-zrueen* is potent. Please apply."

Mayve cracked open the vial. A fragrance of flowers from far away alpine heights wafted from the bottle. The salve was cool and refreshing on her fingers, and she felt the pain numb as she applied it to the open wound.

"Breathe deep and hold it as you apply," Srrith instructed. "Otherwise it will reopen."

Mayve held her breath, and she saw the paste harden on contact with the air, until the slash marks were sealed, the blood flow trickling to a halt. Srrith hissed, "The wound may hold without stitches. We will fix it on the journey if need be."

Mayve grabbed the sheet from her bed and ripped it up to make a bandage. "Thank you for the help, again, but I'm not traveling with you."

Srrith replied, "The Great Seer is at Savin Actai, in the mountains south of Port Wenstnor. We will get you out of the city, and I will convince you to continue once you're safe."

The masked man and Faldmor went to Port Wenstnor. I can't have this snake looking over my shoulder. Mayve opened her mouth to protest and saw that Srrith's tail was holding the pouch with the stolen artifact. She yelled, "Give that back! I stole it first."

She tried to rise but a sharp pain knocked her down again. She sucked in another breath and applied the last of the salve, glaring at the snake. Her wound was already feeling better, she had to admit. The deeper wound sealed, she wiped the remaining salve up her arms to cover the minor lacerations from the timbersteel armor.

Srrith, holding the pouch with her tail, pulled the drawstrings and extracted the weird gemstone inside. She studied it in the dim light, dropped it back in the pouch, then her tail returned it to Mayve. "This was also in the Great Seer's vision. It is yours. Now, what did you say you were going to do with it?"

Mayve angrily fastened the pouch back to her belt, double-checking it was secure. "I'm giving it to the raptors. I need the money and the Coinclaws will gut me if I don't."

Srrith nodded. "Yes, the raptors. They will gut you anyway for running, no? They all saw it."

Mayve gulped. "I don't think so, we're on friendly terms. I've known some of them for years."

Srrith hissed, "You are a human. Only a notch above the Oaken Legion on the raptor food chain. Except you are made of meat, so they might actually eat you."

Mayve shook her head incredulously, but the tauninaga's words crept through her. She *had* run. It was an easy excuse. They would much rather kill her to get the artifact and keep her share of the coin. *I could try to bargain with them and explain myself. Ingo and Spotch will back me up.*

Would they, though? The way they advanced on her, weapons drawn, when they saw her running. There was not an ounce of friendship in their stares.

I either barter with a gang of raptors, or travel south with this deadly tauninagan stranger.

One thought caught and refused to let go. *What do you have left?*

If she managed to convince the raptors not to gut her and throw her off the Arch, she had no one. Her mother lay in the ground outside. All because of those depth-cursed seeds, sold by that bastard Faldmor and the strange masked volcomancer.

A bubble of red anger burst inside her, the first of many. She knew they were heading toward Port Wenstnor—the same direction that Srrith wished to travel. Right now, Mayve thought of nothing else but stomping Faldmor's head into the cobblestones. Anything was better than this guilt gnawing through her mind.

I could use some protection heading south. At least that gets me closer to my mother's killers, instead of rolling the dice with the raptors. They'll kill me in a heartbeat to save that kind of gold.

Mayve turned to Srrith and lied, "Okay, you're right. I'm not sure what to do, but traveling with you is better than facing the Coinclaws." It wasn't completely false. *In my humble opinion, withholding the truth is better than outright lying.*

Srrith nodded and flared her cobra hood in excitement, then slithered into the darkest corner of the dwelling, by the door. "Gather your things. There is not much time before they look for you." She coiled herself in the darkness and shut her eyes. "I must sleep."

Mayve struggled to a sitting position and wrapped the linen strips of her bedsheet around her waist, cinching them tight. The hardened salve crunched like dried resin, but the skin remained numb and cool. She wondered why the snake needed to nap at such an inopportune time, but it would give her a moment alone with her thoughts.

She called across the room, "The raptors don't know where I live, by the way. We should be safe here."

Srrith hissed back, not opening her eyes, "You don't know that."

The tauninaga was not joking about sleeping. Within a few minutes, she was coiled in the corner, exhaling gentle hisses with each unconscious breath.

Mayve would never admit it, but she felt oddly comforted by the snake's presence. She would be dead if it was not for her. Still, Mayve studied the sleeping serpent, wondering if she was actually safe.

Srrith stirred in her sleep like she knew someone was watching. Mayve quickly turned away and busied herself with packing, like the snake had said to do.

Scraping the debris into tidy piles, she managed to find the last scraps of food that Dreva was saving. Mayve then turned to her side of the dwelling and scrounged for her other clothes. It was a struggle to remove her soaked and shredded shirt without tugging on her bandaged wound. The soft hisses from the dark corner reminded Mayve she was not alone, and she changed into her fresh clothes behind the garden door. *I can't shake the feeling the snake is watching me somehow.* When she returned, she tossed her wet rags onto the floor, where they joined the rubble with a moist squelch.

Next she checked her belt. *Shawl, canteen, dagger, coin purse, artifact.* She found a small satchel that Dreva used to carry to and from the market, and filled it with the scraps of food she found. Getting up onto her bed loft posed a small problem with her wound. Luckily she had learned how to climb up one-handed after a nasty fall from a Silt Row rooftop as a child broke her wrist.

The ledge was untouched, clear of debris and thorn scratches.

Mayve was happy to see not everything had been destroyed. For a brief second, her home felt normal again. Her fingers pried the rock loose.

Inside was preserved. *Thanks Phovus.* Mayve rooted around, deciding what she wanted to take. She knew every object by touch, and knew that most of the items in there had no business coming with her. Gently turning each memento in her hand, she said goodbye to each memory she had stashed. Her hand crumbled around the scrap of her father's letter. After a moment of consideration, she dropped the paper into the satchel with the food. *It doesn't weigh anything and maybe I'll run into the bastard.*

Reaching in one last time, her hand clasped an unfamiliar object. For a second, she was startled. *I swear I know everything that's in here.*

The new object was tiny and smooth, made of metal and cold to the touch. She extracted her hand and found herself holding her mother's ring. *She knew about my hidden stash all along. Of course she did.*

Dreva must have stashed the ring there at some point during the day. Mayve wondered if she was passing the ring down for a reason, or if she just wanted her to have it. It could be a gift, or maybe a subtle jab that she knew where Mayve hid everything from her. *Maybe she was finally going to discuss my father.*

Mayve knew she would never find out, and tears soaked the corners of her eyes as she held the last part of her mother left.

Time was in short supply, so Mayve gathered her wits and slid the ring onto her finger. The cold metal quickly warmed on her skin. Crafted from delicately forged iron, it bore a perfectly round signet, with a cryptic pattern of bumps, lines, and indentations. It was not particularly pretty, or made of expensive material. The only eye-catching detail about the jewelry was the strange pattern on the signet. The more Mayve looked at it, the more she saw how complicated the pattern of bumps and etchings was.

With her mother on her mind, Mayve realized she had forgotten an important task. After some searching, she found a suitable rock out in the cave tunnels and rolled it into the garden. Placing it at the head of her mother's grave, she unsheathed her dagger and etched "Dreva" into the surface.

She paused, unsure if she should add anything else. The makeshift gravestone seemed uncaring and empty with only her mother's name. Yet anything else Mayve thought to add seemed superfluous.

She had wandered through the graveyards in the Outer Sands before, on days when the wind moved the dunes off the tombstones. The longest epitaphs always struck her as disingenuous. Long lists of sentiments and titles that were half-baked lies, never spoken out loud until the deceased was no longer around to hear them. To Mayve, the most sentimental words were spoken aloud, shared only briefly between two souls. Not scratched on a tombstone for any passerby to read.

After solemn deliberation, Mayve carved two words below Dreva's name. *My mother.* She stood and sheathed her dagger. Alone in the garden, in the light of the torch, she broke down, trying to say one last apology through her sobs.

Chapter 11

No Turning Back

Contrary to her normal tactics, Srrith was truly asleep this time. While her body was unconscious, her mind was wrapped in dreams. She was coiled in a grassy, moonlit clearing, surrounded by a dark forest. This was *her* clearing, carefully crafted in her dreaming mind from years of careful practice. Far in the dark forest, she felt the nightmares lurking, but it had been long since they bothered her. The Great Seer had taught her to keep them at bay, and she had not feared her dreams since. For that, she owed the Seer her life.

Breathing in the cold night air, Srrith called the shadows to her, and they flocked from the dark tree line in inky swarms. She reached out, collecting shadows in both hands. She coiled and spun, weaving the shadows around her like a cloak, letting them seep through her scales like midnight oil. Carefully, Srrith braided the shadows in an intricate dance, stitching them together, making them *hers*.

She chose to wake up as the garden door slammed shut. The green-eyed girl—who Srrith now knew was a young lady named Imayva—stood in the doorframe, jaw aghast. Srrith looked down to see if her sfa-zrueen had worked. Real shadows coalesced around her coiled form, just like how she wove them in her dreams. Dripping between her scales, they formed a dark puddle underneath her, small tendrils creeping up her serpentine body. The tip of her tail was invisible, shrouded in the shadowy pool. The darkness disobeyed the torchlight, persisting where the light would normally banish it.

"Do not be afraid," Srrith hissed, and flicked her tail at Mayve. A portion of her shadow broke away and raced across the cave floor toward the human. Mayve stumbled back, stomping futilely at the tendrils. The shadows spun like a whirlpool around Mayve's feet before settling into a solid black circle on the floor beneath her.

Mayve calmed down only a little after seeing the shadows were not immediately dangerous. She tried a few more angry kicks in half-hearted attempts to dispel the darkness, but the shadows only followed the swing of her leg with eager obedience. She glared angrily at the tauni-naga and exclaimed, "What on Phovus's green earth did you do to me?"

Srrith uncoiled her body and calmly replied, "The shadows will keep you hidden."

"Is this volcomancy?"

"It is sfa-zrueen, not volcomancy. I see you are unfamiliar. In Ralveran tongue, it roughly translates to *dreams that wake with you.*"

"So you were manifesting *while* you slept?" Mayve asked skeptically.

Srrith hissed, "It is not volcomancy, but if you want to think of it that way, you may. Most humans do. It is easier than explaining how we weave our dreams into threads of reality."

"I've seen a volcomancer control shadows like this before." Mayve kicked at the pool of shadows around her feet. "So what's going on here, then?" The human tread carefully, as if expecting the shadows to rear up and attack.

Srrith heard the human's heart pounding in her chest. *She is afraid of the shadows, more than I expected.*

She responded, "All tauninaga are able to influence reality with their dreams, in specific ways." Srrith motioned to her black scales and cobra-like hood. "I am a cave tauninaga. Our sfa-zrueen helps us travel unseen, and strikes fear into our prey's hearts."

"Other tauninaga weave their dreams differently?" The human seemed curious, her fear of the shadows settling.

"Yes." Srrith cut her off with a hiss, trying to avoid a lecture. "Are you packed? We have to go."

Mayve patted down her belt and satchel, indicating she was ready. Srrith turned to the dwelling entrance. "The shadows help avert unwanted gazes, but do not make you invisible. Stay out of the light and remain hidden, and we should escape unseen." Srrith opened the door and slithered into the darkness, disappearing entirely. The shadows trailed after her, erasing any trace she was there.

Mayve took one last look at her home and stepped into the darkness. Srrith saw the human peer into the dark, searching for her. The shadows clung to her scales, melding her into the cave's lightless walls.

The huge serpent materialized from the shadows behind her and snuffed out her torch. Before Mayve could protest, she hissed, "No light. There are others down here."

She expected to lead the human through the pitch-blackness, and was relieved to find out Mayve seemed to know the tunnels just as well in the dark as she did in the light. Instead of leading the way, Srrith ended up trailing the human as she crept through the sightless maze. It appeared that both of them had grown up in the Ralveran Caverns, memorizing the twisted passages around their home.

Srrith also took note that Mayve had lied earlier, when she talked about traveling to Port Wenstnor. It was a simple rhythmic change in her breathing and heartbeat, but a clear tell that the human was hiding something. *She is withholding information. That is fair, she does not know me yet. It is my duty to convince her of the Seer's vision.*

She opened up her hearing, each returning hiss drawing a detailed map of the surrounding tunnels in her mind's eye.

As they crept closer to the Falls, Srrith's echolocation blurred. She remembered the sensation when she entered the Darkmist Tunnels, trailing after Mayve. The crash of the Falls had distorted her echolocation, and she barely managed to find Mayve's footfalls and labored breathing afterward. Mayve was painted in her mind's eye now, moving assuredly toward the crashing water. One of Srrith's exploratory hisses returned, bouncing off the rock walls and into her highly sensitive ears. The tunnel ahead was partially blocked. Another hiss returned, painting a slinking figure. It was a raptor.

Srrith inspected the map in her mind for a hiding place, and saw a sizable fissure in the ceiling above. She unsheathed her sickles while wrapping her tail around Mayve, dragging her back. Uncoiling upward, she lodged the points of the sickles into the fissure above. The curved blades were crafted specially for climbing, and the sharp points found purchase in the rock. She hissed at Mayve, "Climb up, now."

She used her coils as footstools for Mayve to vault upward, and the human caught the rock on the bottom of the fissure and climbed up. Srrith followed, slithering upward through the crack. Dust and pebbles rained down and bounced off her serpentine hood as the sickles cut into the rocks above.

A quiet hiss showed her that Mayve was securely wedged between the fissure walls. The girl looked incredibly comfortable, using her legs to press her back into the opposite wall, arms dangling at her sides. Srrith wrapped up her coils, pressing into each wall to cement herself in place. She kept one sickle implanted in the wall and unhooked the other sickle, in case they were discovered and she had to drop down to fight. From experience, she took care to hide her steel where it would not catch in any torchlight.

In the darkness, Mayve whispered, "Why are we hiding?"

"Wait and see," Srrith hissed. The human shifted uncomfortably, a few pebbles raining down.

Soon enough, torchlight crept into the fissure from the path below, and faint voices rose above the distant crash of water. Mayve shot a questioning look at Srrith, wondering how the snake could have possibly known that people were approaching. Srrith ignored her. Cave tauninaga echolocation often seemed supernatural to those who did not know what was happening, and they liked to keep it that way.

Srrith hissed again, hoping to get more detail before the raptors closed in. The tunnel's curves and the waterfall's crash returned mostly static, but even so, she was able to distinguish several figures approaching down the tunnel.

The voices were legible now, speaking in harsh Raptoran. The language was similar enough to Tauninagan that Srrith had a base understanding.

"Are you sure this is the way?" a voice snarled.

"Shut your mouth, I've been this way several times," a second, familiar voice snapped back. One of the green-scaled, red-feathered raptors from the Hangman's Swing slunk into view directly below their fissure. Srrith heard Mayve's heartbeat erupt as she also recognized the raptor in the dim light. Her eyes went wide, coming to the realization that the raptors had known where she lived this entire time.

Srrith commanded her shadows to flood the fissure. Tendrils of abyssal darkness wove around both of them, weaving a comforting blanket between them and the eyes below. In the dim torchlight, they were imperceivable. The raptors continued arguing below.

"This tunnel looks the same as the last one, there's no way you know where we are." The voice came from beyond the fissure's field of vision. Srrith saw Mayve grimace, recognizing this voice as well. Most likely another raptor from Hangman's Swing.

The raptors halted directly below their fissure. The red-green raptor growled back at his insubordinate, "You've been out in the desert for months, and you're going to question me on your first job back in the city? Shut your maw and go where I tell you to go."

A third raptor chimed in. "I don't like Darkmist. What if we accidentally wander deeper into the Caverns? That girl could be anywhere by now."

"You shut your maw as well, I didn't ask for your opinion."

A fourth raptor spoke, their voice deeper and slower "Are we getting paid for this?"

"Is now the time to ask that?"

"It's just, I also don't like Darkmi—"

"Everyone shut up right now!" the red-green raptor snapped. "We don't get the treasure, no one gets paid, so swallow your fear and your *moronic fucking* questions. Keep moving, or I'll gut each of you, one by one."

The red-green raptor pointed down the tunnel with his sword and several large raptor shadows slunk beneath the fissure, heading for Mayve's abandoned dwelling. The red-green raptor lingered for just a few seconds longer. He looked directly up into the fissure, fangs visible in a frustrated grimace. Unknown to him, he made eye contact with

Srrith. Every muscle in her coil tensed, ready to fall down and slash his throat if any flash of discovery crossed his face.

The cloak of shadows did what it was supposed to do. After many heartbeats the raptor slunk after his compatriots. Srrith and Mayve remained frozen still, silently suspended until the last glimmer of torchlight receded down the tunnel and darkness enveloped them once again. Quiet as desert mice, they dropped back onto the tunnel floor. Mayve took the lead again, pretending as if nothing happened.

Srrith could tell from Mayve's heartbeat that she was not as fine as she let on. *Her life is falling apart around her. I must take care to not scare her away before she meets the Great Seer.* The echoes of the Devaros Falls turned to thunder, and Srrith had to close her echolocation before the crashing water scrambled her mind. Soon, her scales were slick with moisture as the mist grew dense, and the crash of the Falls pounded her skull. The noise was impossible to keep out, fraying the edges of her mind.

The mist swelled as they neared the exit. Weak flames sputtered from struggling torches, nearly snuffed out by the fog. The boom of the Falls was suffocating: spikes of pain shot through her temples and reverberated down to the tip of her tail. She did her best to focus on Mayve's silhouette, wavering through the torchlit mist. For a cave creature, her real eyesight was useless in the darkness, and under the Falls her echolocation was trying to split her skull open.

There are few situations where a cave tauninaga is fully blind, and this was the second time today Srrith had walked this Vent-cursed path. The torchlight arrived at an abrupt halt, signaling the end of the tunnel, and the exit to the caves. The mist devoured the torchlight, engulfing Mayve as she stepped through.

Slithering into the curtain of fog, the waterfall felt like thousands of hammers slamming against her head. Her thoughts shook like an earthquake, the images in her mind dancing violently in the Falls' rampaging echoes. Her fingers lightly scraped the dripping wall to keep her bearings, grounding her in the darkness.

Mayve was lost to her. The touch of the cold rock and the scrape of her scales were her only senses not engulfed in darkness and thunder.

The rock disappeared from her reach and the world was lost to her, until the minuscule twinkle of starlight reached her eyes through the fog.

Light filtered from a lone lantern, swinging on a post near the closest dock, faintly illuminating the void of Darkmist Pool. Fighting a splitting headache, Srrith's eyes adjusted just in time to see an obscured figure charging out of the mist toward Mayve.

* * *

Mayve was lost in her own thoughts since their close encounter with Ingo. She traversed the cavern tunnels on muscle memory, twisting through her favorite shortcuts. *They knew where I lived, this entire time. We were never safe.*

Stepping through the waterfall's mist, she realized that this might be her last time in Darkmist Tunnels. *It may be a while before I get to visit Ma, and someone may have found the dwelling by then.* Her mind scrambled to make sense of the last hour of her life. Lost in her subconscious, she almost missed a lanky yellow raptor careening out of the night toward her.

"There you are, thief!" Szez leapt from the mist, obsidian hatchet swinging for her throat. Mayve duck away, the axe slicing the fog apart where her skull had just been.

Without missing a second, Szez cleaved at Mayve again and she scrambled backward. The hatchet glanced off the rock path between her legs, showering the night with sparks that illuminated Szez's fangs. Mayve rolled farther away, her hands scraping on wet planks.

Szez drove her down the dock, step by step toward Darkmist Pool and the raging Falls. He snarled at her with joyous malice, his maw widening into a grin. Any words that rolled off his tongue were lost in the thunder of the Falls. The hatchet sliced down again.

Mayve almost rolled off the side of the dock, feeling the hatchet thud into the soft wood where her body had just been. Half of her torso hung off the side, her fingers scraping the surface of the inky water. Knowing the raptor was right behind her, she pushed herself up and launched herself farther down the dock, every nerve in her body tense and screaming. The hatchet's blade kissed the back of her neck like a hungry mosquito, drawing only a drop of blood.

The Falls' mist made the dock as slippery as ice, and Mayve failed to find her footing as she landed. She crashed hard onto the dock, every nerve acutely aware of the murderous lizard raising their axe for another swing. A sickening thud reverberated through the planks as the heavy blade dropped.

Mayve's eyes focused on Szez, standing frozen a foot away. The hatchet was embedded in the planks behind him, having slipped from his claws at the peak of his swing, and he made no attempt to grab his fallen weapon. She cautiously stood, ready for any sudden movement the raptor might pull. The only movement from Szez was a faint trembling, nearly imperceivable in the night. Only then did she notice the shadows.

Tendrils of shadow curled up the raptor's legs, pouring into his mouth and eyes like feasting worms. Two glowing yellow eyes materialized in the darkness, and the dock shuddered as Srrith's long serpentine body slid out of the mists.

The pure terror in Szez's eyes sent wracking shivers down Mayve's spine. Unlike the shadows that Srrith commanded to pool *around* her, these shadows poured *into* Szez with no mercy. The raptor looked utterly petrified, quaking and frozen. His eyes, as wide as full moons, flicked back and forth in panic, straining to see the tauninaga behind him. He looked unable to turn his head, as if the sight would instantly drive him to insanity.

Srrith slid deliberately low to the ground, stalking her terrified prey. As the slithering scrape of scales on wood grew louder, more shadows pushed into the raptor's mouth and eyes. Szez's shakes grew more violent and he collapsed onto one knee, unable to stand.

Srrith's yellow eyes disappeared, and the sound of her slithering stopped. Mayve was frozen too, watching the spectacle like one shrew watching another get devoured from across a field.

Silence hung in the air. From the mist, Srrith's tail draped over Szez's left shoulder. A whimper escaped Szez's mouth, his eyes straining against the fear, and Srrith's yellow irises opened on his right.

With a monstrous hiss, Srrith's serpentine head lunged out of the fog, fangs bared and cobra hood wide open. The poor raptor screamed.

Srrith reared high above the raptor, grabbing the straps of his leather armor and hoisting him off his feet. Shadows pouring into his maw and eyes, Szez screamed until his whole body dropped limp. Srrith eyed the river, perhaps pondering if she should toss him in, before unceremoniously dumping his body back onto the dock.

She turned to Mayve and sternly hissed, "We must move." Without another word, she slithered away.

Mayve stared slack-jawed at Szez. There was no way to tell if he was alive or dead, although he looked as if the life had been drained from his body. She stepped gingerly over the slumped raptor and chased the tauninaga. "Srrith, did you kill him *with shadows*?" It was eerily similar to the shadows of the masked volcomancer, but they were certainly not a cave tauninaga.

"I know how to stop before their heart does. He will live, although perhaps with slightly more humility."

Mayve jogged a few steps to catch up and said, "It will take a couple hours at least to reach the Silt Row docks from here."

Srrith had no reply, and she suddenly veered off the path toward the cliff face. Mayve continued, exasperated, "We can't climb either, with the river this strong, trust me. Especially at night. The mist will cling to every surface without the sun to burn it away."

Srrith remained silent and plucked a nearby lantern from a post, carrying it to the cliff face. Mayve saw her scanning the rock, hissing at steady intervals, searching for something. Then she saw Srrith grab a thin rope, camouflaged against the rock. It hung limp, suspended in the darkness far above. A perfect climbing pathway to the top.

"Well, you could have told me you had a rope," Mayve grumbled.

Srrith shrugged. "Why waste words when you would find out anyway?" She grabbed the rope. "You can climb, yes? I saw you climb down some of the cliff before you decided to jump."

Mayve remembered the suffocating abyss beneath Devaros Falls and pushed it from her mind. "I'll be fine, I have two more legs than you, and you don't seem worried." She meant it as a joke but the snake showed no signs of humor, instead motioning for Mayve to go first.

She grabbed the rope and gave it a tug. It was wet with condensation but provided a good grip, and it held strong under her pull. It was thinner and lighter than the regular rope she had seen in the Locks, and tightly wound in an unfamiliar pattern. The tauninaga had crafted a perfect rope for climbing. She dropped her whole weight on it to make absolutely sure it was safe, then planted both feet on the cliff and began the climb.

After about fifteen feet, she felt the rope below her go taut as Srrith began her ascent. Curious, Mayve looked down and saw Srrith had partially coiled her body around the rope, while her tail searched for supporting grips on the wall. In each hand were her sickles, the curvature perfect for sticking and latching into the wall. She was gaining faster than Mayve expected, and so Mayve doubled her pace to scale the wall.

Rope made the climb far easier than she was used to, and soon she was high up the cliff, alone with her thoughts. *Tunnelsleeve. That's what the tauninaga's skintight pack is called. A tunnelsleeve.* She and Dreva always saw them at the market, but never bought one. Her mother made very clear that she should never go into any tunnel that she could not turn around in. *At least I listened to that advice. If I'd listened to all of it, maybe she'd be alive.*

Her despair turned to rage. She thought of tossing Faldmor off a tall cliff, and driving a dagger through the eye of the masked volcomancer. *All this, it's their fault, not mine.*

At about a hundred and thirty feet in the air, Mayve heard the sounds of the city that Srrith warned about. The faint ringing of alarm bells clanged across the sands, while the yells of panicked denizens and unnatural screams of bramble eldritches pierced the night as they rampaged through Devar. Her heart pounded.

"Calm yourself," Srrith hissed from below. "There is danger above."

Cave-cursed tauninaga, how does she read me so well?

They breached the edge of the cliff, between the base of the Arch and Silt Row. Sand whipped like arrows in the frigid desert wind, the acrid smell of smoke burning her nostrils. As Srrith wound her rope, Mayve looked for any sign of murderous lizards or rampaging brambles.

Screams echoed from every borough. Mayve peeked around the

corner of a dwelling and saw dark shapes moving through the Outer Sands. She was relieved to see only silhouettes of Devar denizens, wrapped in shawls, running into the dunes to seek refuge from the city.

Srrith hissed again, "Quiet. We move." She slunk into the darkness toward Silt Row, and Mayve followed close behind.

Moving through Silt Row was like plunging through a battlefield. A fire had started somewhere on the far bank, bathing the hazy air in an orange glow. Smoke blew across the borough, chasing the fleeing residents as they ran from the wooden city.

Every so often, Srrith would halt and push Mayve against a wall with her tail, always right before a stampede of fleeing denizens would run past. More than thrice, she would grab Mayve and suddenly change course, a bramble eldritch howling unseen amongst the alleyways. Eventually, they reached the dockyard, escaping conflict.

The Silt Row dockyard was the only place in the borough where the wooden jumble of bridges and dwellings abruptly stopped, leaving space for an expansive boardwalk plaza studded with well-maintained docks, extending south upriver. The river canal cut through the center of the dockyard, with several drawbridges spanning across that could be raised and lowered on a whim if a boat needed access to the Locks. Crates filled with goods from both Verdants were stacked wherever space allowed, forming a maze between them and the fleet of ships that floated on the docks.

While normally bustling with activity, tonight the dockyards were in a state of panic. Fervor gripped a turbulent mob crowding the water's edge, pushing toward the boats. Many vessels had already fled, no more than distant lanterns and silhouettes of sails.

The crowd swelled and pushed against itself, fighting for any available boat space. Captains shouted over the din, trying to maintain a semblance of order between their crew and the mob. A few vessels were half-submerged, only an arm's length from the dock, so overburdened with people that the water overtook them.

The largest river barges sat in the center of the dockyard, closest to the canal, surrounded by the mob. Each barge could have let many people aboard, if they so wished. However, the Merchatzi kept the crowd at bay while their crew loaded whatever goods could be saved onto the boat.

Only one boat was taking denizens aboard in as orderly a fashion as its crew could muster. The Ferrymen, helmed by Captain Vulinor, controlled a steady single file stream of people onto the Ferry. The Ul'Varin captain stood tall at the top of the gangplank, his cloak billowing in the scorched breeze and his plate armor catching the glow of the distant fire.

As he shouted booming orders between his crew and the crowd, the torchlight reflected on his pale, barren skull. Red glowing orbs burned fiercely from his dark eye sockets, and even from this distance Mayve saw flames skittering across his bone face, wreathing his skull in wisps of orange fire. His presence, towering over the common folk, was enough to prevent the Ferry from being overrun by the terrified mob.

"Attention! We are leaving!" Vulinor boomed. "The Ferry is heading south for Port Wenstnor. We will not be returning here for several weeks. If you wish to board, we will drop you in the desert tomorrow morning. Payment will be collected on the journey rather than at boarding. If you are unable to pay, we will leave you within walking distance in the morning." His deep, disembodied voice, calm but commanding, cut across the chaos. On the ship, his skeletal crew were running through their duties with efficient determination, gathering supplies and readying the boat.

Mayve looked at Srrith, who wore what Mayve assumed was a grimace on her snake face. She patted Srrith on the cloaked shoulder to get the serpent's attention, and pointed to the Ferry. "The Ferry is cheaper than most ships, and they're heading south." *Toward Port Wenstnor and those wretched merchants.* Just the thought of them overwhelmed her with guilt, and she forced it down, channeling it into pure rage.

Srrith reared to her full height to look over the crowd, searching for a path through the madness. "I have not met the Ul'Varin before. Are they discreet?"

Trying to focus on her present surroundings, Mayve shrugged. "They don't have tongues, how can they spread rumors?"

Srrith nodded as if Mayve made a good point, and Mayve hoped she had not taken that seriously. *At least they're not run by the merchant guilds; there will be fewer prying eyes.*

Srrith pushed through the crowd, expecting Mayve to follow. She uncoiled as tall as she could, flaring her hood to look as terrifying as possible. The shadows around her looked normal. *Whatever she did to Szez, they look fine now.*

Mayve followed close behind, keeping a short distance behind Srrith so the crowd could not separate them. Suddenly, Srrith was swallowed by the mob as someone grabbed Mayve's shoulder and pulled her backward.

Mayve tried to land a hard elbow on whoever had her, but her arm was deftly caught and she was twisted into a headlock. Rancid breath wafted over the back of her neck as she was marched backward, away from the water. A gruff snarl whispered in her ear, "Trying to jump ship, are ya? I'm not surprised you thought you could run, but leaving your dear mum behind? You're more of a rat than I thought."

Spotch spat the last few words directly into Mayve's ear. Three more raptors slunk out of the crowd. They looked bloodied and bruised from their earlier fight with the Oaken Legion, but were hissing ecstatically over finally catching their fleeing prey. The crowd paid them no heed, intent on getting to the boats. It was not the time to stand between the Coinclaws and their victim. It rarely was.

Spotch ripped the artifact's pouch from her belt, and hurled her to the ground in front of the other raptors. "I'm sorry we have to do this Mayve, but thieves need to be punished. We'll try not to kill you, out of courtesy for our friendship." He shrugged and addressed his raptors. "But if she dies, she dies."

Mayve clambered to her feet and drew her dagger. "Spotch, it's not like that. Those brambles attacked. I had to get home to my mother."

"*Home?* In those cavern-cursed *tunnels?*" Spotch laughed. "You think some monster is going to stumble all the way down to Darkmist and just happen upon your shithole home?"

It's not hard when they're planted in the backyard. "Please, Spotch, I've never betrayed you before."

"The stakes were never this high," Spotch snarled. Mayve realized she had no more good graces with her old friend.

Srrith was still lost in the crowd. Mayve hoped to every god that the tauninaga could see her. The circle of raptors tightened as they slunk toward her, weapons drawn and ready. She knew they were toying with her. Tongues flicked from their maws, caressing their fangs. Their prey was cornered, the hunt was over, the artifact was in their claws. Their last task was to teach the thief a deadly lesson. It did not matter that they had what they came for—an example had to be made of her.

One after another, three sounds burned into Mayve's memory forever.

First, the unholy scream of a bramble eldritch sliced over the dockyards as the hulking monster emerged from the Silt Row woodwork, driving a spike of terror deep into the heart of the mob. A chorus of other howls echoed it—other brambles in the city, alerted to the newly discovered feast.

The screams from the panicking townsfolk followed, like baby mice cornered in their den by a snake, drowning out all other sounds. The crowd, which had been steadily pushing toward the ships, now exploded in every direction. Some ran back to the alleyways, others threw themselves into the water, even more leapt for the ships.

The raptors stopped their advance, unsure what to do, turning their beady eyes to Spotch. The crowd surged, violently slamming one of the raptors toward Mayve.

In that split second of chaos and tension, Mayve rammed her dagger into the stumbling raptor's exposed throat. Amid the screams of denizens and monsters, the blade made no sound and the raptor's scales offered little resistance as momentum carried them onto the blade. In a single instant, the blade disappeared and reemerged covered in blood, and the raptor slumped to the planks, clawed hands clutching their neck. The third sound burned in Mayve's memory was the horrendous gurgle of the lizard as they retched blood onto the docks.

Swept up in the panic of the crowd, Mayve made an escape over the dead raptor's body. She ducked underneath a lunge from the second raptor, but Spotch landed a clawed hand on her shoulder, hauling her back. As Mayve turned to face him, a scaly black tail wrapped around Spotch's neck, pulling him into the crowd.

Mayve did not stop. Weaving and pushing through the mob, she stayed course toward the Ferry, looking for Captain Vulinor over the crowd. Srrith was nowhere to be seen, and the howls of feasting brambles were growing in number.

At the docks, she crashed into an immovable wall of denizens. The crowd was packed so tightly around the gangplanks, not even the smallest fly could have slipped between the ranks. As the bramble eldritches surged from Silt Row into the dockyard, more and more ships tossed their moorings and sailed offshore, with the exception of the Ferry and a few other brave vessels. Despite their strength, the Ul'Varin were struggling to control the crowd. Her escape halted, Mayve had no choice but to turn and face the chaos.

Behind her, the crowd thinned as the bramble eldritches charged through. The foul monsters leapt from victim to victim, their thorny vines sinking into their flesh, leaving their corpses pock-marked and drained on the dockyard planks.

The largest bramble eldritch was horrifically bloated, its vines slick and dripping. With every victim, it shrieked a nightmarish scream, fattening itself drop by drop. Mayve frantically looked for Srrith and Spotch, finding nothing. She caught a brief glance of the other raptors across the dockyard, attacking a smaller bramble eldritch in a pack-like assault, darting in and out, slashing and stabbing at the vines.

Her back pressed against an unbreachable wall of people, Mayve had no idea where to go. The behemoth bramble eldritch extracted all its vines from the husk of its latest meal, gazing at the feast near the dock's edge. A mass of fleshy, blood-filled people, with Mayve right in its path. With a delicious howl, it fell onto all fours and galloped toward her, blood squelching from each footfall.

"*Tarsta-bul* approaching! Rak, *to me!*" Captain Vulinor boomed. Three heavy, metallic thuds shook the ground as Vulinor and two other armor-clad skeletons vaulted off the Ferry and slammed onto the docks. The crowd threw themselves out of the way as the Ul'Varin-Rak charged.

Mayve hurled herself with the crowd. The bramble eldritch leapt, and Vulinor caught the monster in a thunderous shoulder charge, smashing the pauldron of his cloaked plate armor into its thorny chest. They crashed to the ground together, rolling away in a thrashing mess.

The blood-sucking vines tried to find the captain's flesh, and the creature screamed in dismay when it discovered Vulinor had none—only metal and bone.

Vulinor's skull flared with elemental energy and he unleashed a blast of white-hot flame from his mouth. The bramble eldritch shrieked and flailed, throwing the skeleton off him. Vulinor tumbled away and rolled onto his feet, moving far more nimbly than any human could in full plate armor and desert cloak. The other two Ul'Varin charged past him, sword and axe raised. Vulinor himself had no weapon, throwing himself at the creature regardless. Meanwhile, Mayve saw her opportunity and sprinted through the parted crowd straight to the Ferry.

Without Vulinor's intimidating presence holding them back, the crowd swarmed the Ferry, the other Ul'Varin dropping their tasks to stem the tide. Mayve leapt to the hull and swung aboard before they could establish control again. Blending into the crowd on board, relief flooded her; she was finally safe. She turned to watch the chaos unfolding on shore.

Of the remaining raptors, one was dead, mauled by an unlucky blow from the creature's thorny appendage. The bramble eldritch had one foot stomped through the corpse, feasting on its blood, while the other raptor fled into Silt Row.

The Ul'Varin were faring far better against the bloated bramble eldritch. Mayve knew the legends. Living on the Scorch Vents, the Ul'Varin-Rak were the first line of defense against the Vent beasts that crawled from the apocalyptic volcanoes. The fiery skeletons fought in practiced formation, using their unnatural strength to their advantage.

Vulinor charged in, grappling the bramble eldritch while the other Ul'Varin hacked away its twisting limbs. Flailing and screaming, the engorged bramble creature wrenched an arm free and smashed an advancing Ul'Varin in their chest. Steel rang and bones cracked as the armor-clad skeleton tumbled away. Superheating his gauntlets into a white-hot glow, Vulinor pummeled his own fist into the creature's stomach; a hiss of bloody steam and smoke erupted from the vines.

From her vantage point, she finally saw Srrith through the madness. The tauninaga and Spotch were clashing steel, oblivious to the running crowd and rampaging monsters. Sparks flew as Spotch's axe caught her sickles, the raptor weaving through the coiling whirlwind, deflecting blows where he could and dodging the others. His counterattacks were swift and brutal, forcing Srrith to spin away. The screams of the crowd drowned out the ringing of steel. To Mayve, the fight was a silent dance that could end at any blood-drenched second.

I could help. Srrith saved me before, I have the chance to return the favor. Mayve's legs refused to budge.

She only saved me because she believes some other tauninaga saw me in a vision. I don't owe her anything. Spotch caught one of the sickles in a clever parry and disarmed it, sending it spiraling out of Srrith's grasp. Mayve lifted her foot to take a step forward, but froze again.

Srrith will only get in my way. I refuse to make this my problem. Guilt washed over her. *I'm not risking my life for a stranger. I don't care if she saved me.* Spotch disarmed Srrith's other sickle, and the tauninaga collapsed exhausted to the dock planks. The raptor closed in for the kill, his smile wide and vicious.

From her distance, Mayve saw something that Spotch did not. Srrith looked disarmed and tired, but her bottom half was coiled taut. As Spotch leapt forward, snarling with bloodlust, Srrith uncoiled and struck in the blink of an eye.

She caught Spotch's arm mid-swing in one hand, while the other grabbed the underside of his maw. Wrenching his head back, she sank her fangs deep into his exposed neck. Stumbling back, Spotch lost his footing and was wrapped in Srrith's coils before he hit the ground. As they collapsed in a struggling mass, Srrith wrenched Spotch's axe out of his grasp and opened his throat with it.

Depths below, Spotch...I'm so sorry. She tried to tell herself that the raptor who just died wasn't her friend anymore, but it still stung. The lump of numb rage in her stomach grew. *Another dead tonight because of those Vent-cursed seeds. Because of me.*

A horrific scream and the hiss of burning flora ripped Mayve back to reality, as Captain Vulinor grabbed the bramble eldritch's head between his superheated gauntlets. The creature shrieked and thrashed as its face smoldered against the white-hot iron. Flames erupted from Vulinor's glowing eye sockets as he exhaled a blast of fire directly into the bramble's face.

The two other Ul'Varin-Rak hacked the bramble eldritch to pieces as it burned into a writhing pile of ash. Standing from the smoking corpse, Vulinor rushed to support his injured shipmate, shouting commands back to the Ferry in Ventish. The crew mobilized immediately, pulling on rigging and unmooring the vessel, ushering on the last few passengers they could take.

Vulinor staggered onto the vessel and passed the injured Ul'Varin to other shipmates. Then he turned to address the crowd. "Order! We are leaving immediately. Follow the directions of my crew or you will be thrown overboard. Payment and other matters will be discussed once we are a safe distance from Devar."

Mayve felt a hand on her shoulder and whipped around to see Srrith. The tauninaga was looking her over for injuries, and once satisfied, hissed in relief. "I am glad you are safe. That was..." She paused, catching her breath. "...more problematic than I thought. The raptor was a strong fighter."

Mayve nodded back, shocked. She was trying to put on a face that did not betray the guilt she was feeling. Srrith had once again risked her life for her. Her guilt only grew as Srrith dropped the leather pouch with the artifact back into Mayve's hand.

"Why are you giving this back to me?"

Srrith replied, "You are the one who stole it. It is yours." She coiled herself on the deck as the boat pushed off from the dock. "Alactashi Sen saw that you are the one to carry it, and I will respect her wishes. Please be more careful with it."

More talk of seers and visions. I want no part of it. Srrith had saved her life twice now over these seers and visions, and the pit of guilt in her heart deepened. *No, I won't be guilt-tripped into following this strange snake.* It was clear now that she would need the snake's protection in her journey south. Faldmor and that masked man responsible for these monstrous seeds were well on their way to Port Wenstnor, quite aware of what Mayve had unleashed. *I'll see to it they grieve just as much as I have.*

Mayve turned to face her home as they drifted away downriver. Smoke blotted out the stars in the crystal clear desert sky. The Silt Row docks were emptied, and she saw swarms of Merchatzi thundering across them, trying to secure their employers' goods. Even from the safety of the boat, the haunting screams of the monsters carried across the water.

Amongst the chaos, a red-feathered raptor with green scales fell to his knees over the corpse of his brother. Ingo cradled his twin, shaking with rage. *I'm sorry, Ingo. I wish he could have lived. If it wasn't for me and all this chaos, we'd all be okay.*

Chapter 12

Felled

Raudius awoke to a splitting headache and a kick to the ribs. His eyes, refusing to focus, flitted across the blurry shapes of his entire quindecis surrounding him where he lay. The rising desert sun blasted through the smashed window, dancing off the shards of glass scattered on the floor. One of the tree shapes leaned down close, and Raudius's eyes painfully sharpened on Grenner's snarling face.

"Get. Up." The livid frutexier hoisted Raudius to his feet, then slammed him back to the ground with a sucker punch to the jaw. "Get up! That's an order!"

Raudius tried to stumble upright, swaying wildly. As he found his balance, Grenner planted an armored foot on his chest and stomped him back down to the floor.

"Do you see anything wrong here?" The frutexier wrapped his fingers underneath Raudius's chin and jerked his head to the side, forcing Raudius to look at the smashed window and the glaringly empty space where the artifact's chest once stood. The memory of what happened earlier washed through him. *Depths below, I was knocked unconscious by a pathetic human.*

Grenner put all of his weight onto Raudius's face, as if trying to crack the floor beneath him and bury him under the earth. "I asked a question, *greenling*. Do you see anything wrong here?"

"Yes, sir," Raudius stammered, "I failed to defen—"

Grenner punched him hard in the face, his timbersteel gauntlet piercing through the bark on Raudius's jaw. "No need to speak further. You failed! All of us! This entire expedition, every branch snapped, every drop of blood spilled, all for nothing. You don't even know what we could have done with that artifact! Can you even *begin* to grasp the ramifications of your failure?" Grenner screamed, spit flecking his bark chin.

Raudius had nothing to say. Everything Grenner said was correct. Raudius had no idea what was in the chest, but he knew it was important. The failure of the entire quindecis was his burden alone.

"Tell me who took it!" Grenner screamed. "Who defeated the *great* Raudius Fenmor?"

Shame welled in his chest. Raudius hung his head and muttered "...a human."

Grenner shook him, as if hoping more details would fall loose. "That's it? This human hit you so hard that's all you remember?"

Raudius tried to recall anything about his assailant. It all happened so fast. "She had green eyes, dark hair, tan-olive skin. Carried a dagger. Must have been working with the raptors."

Grenner spat in his face. "A Fenmor, knocked unconscious by a common fucking thief. Fucking pathetic." He motioned to a Hope's Gauntlet soldier to write down the description, then dropped Raudius back on the ground. "The artifact is as good as gone if it's in raptor hands."

Raudius stumbled upright, expecting to be knocked back down any second. He looked around the room and saw his fellow soldiers. He saw Claud and Batia averting their gaze. The others looked furious, raging Oakfire illuminating their eyes. All except for Yuetrix. The old tree's bark was somber and expressionless, eyes averted down. *Where's Traticus? Depths below, the sand-cursed raptors.* The attack flooded back to him.

Through a cracked door, Raudius saw several wounded soldiers stretched out on their bunks. The quindecis's medic was tending to them, slathering healing salves onto their bark. One soldier turned his head as the medic approached him, allowing Raudius to catch a glimpse of his face. *Traticus, oh my poor friend.* His bark was sloughing off like wet paper, hideous burns seared across his chest. *Verdant's Bane. Those disgusting, sand-cursed raptors and their sick alchemical creations.* Grenner grabbed Raudius by the chin and forcibly wrenched it back toward him.

"Anything to say in your defense, greenling?" Grenner's eyes and mouth burned with Oakfire.

He wants me to apologize and beg for forgiveness. To grovel and admit that I failed.

Yuetrix stepped forward from the watching ranks. "Grenner, sir, I am the one that ordered Raudius upstairs. I believed that Adarias was needed in the skirmish."

Grenner glared at Yuetrix. "You *gave* an order? Did someone forget to tell me you were promoted recently?"

"It was a prudent battlefield decision."

"I will *not* take tactical advice from a decaying stump like yourself!" Grenner screamed. "I give the orders! If Adarias was guarding the artifact, it would still be in our possession! He could have snapped the human in half over his knee!"

"Sir..."

"Not another word, Yuetrix." Grenner spun back on Raudius. "You accepted false orders from outside the chain of command to flee the battlefield, is that correct?"

Oakfire raged in Raudius's chest. "No, I completely disagree."

"Even after you fled the battlefield, you were *still* defeated in combat, dealing a blow to the entire Legion with your incompetence!"

He's dragging your name through the fucking mud. Challenge him to swords. Depths below, challenge him to shields! Defend your honor!

But he's not wrong. You failed. Bested by a sand-cursed human, who has long since disappeared into the streets of Devar.

"Do you have *anything* to say in your defense? I grant you permission to speak, just this once!" Grenner shouted.

Raudius took a deep breath. "I followed what I believed to be good orders. Everything after that, however, those failings are my own."

"Very well." Seething with rage, Grenner composed his stature to a more officer-like stance. Projecting his voice for the whole regiment to hear, he proclaimed, "Raudius Fenmor, with the absolute power as your commanding officer, I pronounce you Felled from the Oaken Legion. Gather your belongings and leave for home, or die on the road. It is no longer my concern."

Every soldier in the room froze. *Felled.* With his proclamation still hanging in the air, Grenner motioned to his top soldiers and stomped away before Raudius could say another word.

Felled...he can't do this to me. Felled?! Raudius looked at Yuetrix, who stared back with wide, shocked eyes. *This cannot be worth the price of my failure. I can't be Felled. I have to get home. I have to fight. I'm a soldier. Depths below, I'm a fucking soldier!*

Not anymore.

The next few moments passed in a haze. Raudius walked to his bunk in a trance and gathered his pack. He had nothing other than a few days of rations and a handful of dens and hearths. As he left the room, every soldier avoided eye contact. There were no goodbyes or words of condolences. They were not forbidden, but why would they tarnish their reputations like that?

Yuetrix passed by. Raudius tried to make eye contact with the old tree, hoping for a single word of advice or a nod goodbye. He received neither.

As he approached the stairway, his eyes connected with Grenner, who shot a look of murderous anger across the room. Raudius thought he saw a brief smile flash across his hard face before he was lost to view, but he was too numb to feel any rage. Too numb to challenge him to swords. *He'd just challenge me to shields instead and kill me where I stand. Maybe that's better than this. At least I'd die a soldier.*

The taproom looked as if a Vent's earthquake had leveled the building. Splintered tables and shattered glass coated the floor in a sharp carpet. The bar stood strong, but the body of a raptor was slumped unceremoniously across it. The wooden counter had melted inward around the body, disintegrated by the raptor's acidic blood.

On the center table, the bodies of three Oaken Legion soldiers lay side by side, shields and swords placed carefully on their chests. Only one had the Hope's Gauntlet symbol on their pauldron. Raudius stopped a moment to pay his respects to his fallen brethren. *Three more dead soldiers, killed by raptor savages.* Their bark was cold to the touch, the Oakfire within them long extinguished. *Lost so far from home. Their spores will never return to the ancestral graveyard.*

He pulled a still-intact chair out of the rubble and took a seat. He knew he could not stay long, but he was in no rush to face the city of Devar on his own. Last time he took to the streets, he was mugged.

That girl was there. The same one that stole the artifact. She knew the raptors, that's why she was working with them. What was it they called her? Imayva. Depths below, I know her name! I know the thief's name!

As he thought back to that incident, heavy thuds sounded on the stairs and Yuetrix entered the taproom. Raudius looked up at him, trying to be noticed, but Yuetrix kept his gaze averted. He strode to the soldiers' corpses, and stood so his back was to Raudius.

Raudius knew he would get no response, but whispered all the same, "Yuetrix, I'm sorry for my failings. Please accept my thanks for all your support, even if my name no longer holds meaning."

Yuetrix did not acknowledge the sentiment, and placed a hand on one of the fallen soldiers. There was a moment of silence, then Yuetrix spoke in a mournful whisper. "My fallen brethren. You fought bravely, but death claims us all eventually."

He paused for a moment, adjusting the dead soldier's sword. "We will continue fighting to preserve the mission, so that you did not give your life in vain for the Great Legion." He dropped his head and clasped both hands together. "The loss of your life was an injustice, but we will bring redemption. We will seek out the raptors who stole the artifact you gave your life for, and wrest it back into Oaken Legion hands. Wherever your soul is now, I hope you still fight alongside us, to find the artifact and bring great honor to your family."

The last sentence seemed out of place in a eulogy, and Raudius realized Yuetrix was not talking to the corpse. *The soldiers are going after the artifact still, and I have a lead. I know Imayva's name and they don't.* Raudius dropped his voice to the quietest whisper. "Do you think I can be Unfelled if I find the artifact first?"

Yuetrix knelt down and touched the foreheads of each fallen tree, muttering, "I wish you safe passage on your next journey, good soldiers."

Raudius stood up, hoisting his shield onto his back. As he moved to the door, he whispered barely louder than a breath, "Thank you, Yuetrix." Without a word, Yuetrix disappeared from view.

As he stepped into the morning sun, the rising heat of the desert smothered Raudius, the sun blinding him until his eyes adjusted. In front of the door, the Oaken Legion had crafted a makeshift barricade out of broken furniture. As he pushed past the fortifications, Raudius saw two huge, misshapen mounds of brambles sprawled in the sand. They look like they had been shredded to pieces by timbersteel swords, blood still soaking into the sand. *What in the depths are those? Raptor creations or some other monstrosity? My brethren must have defended the tavern the whole night.*

Not only did I lose to a pathetic human and failed to protect the artifact, they fought all night killing these ... things ... while I napped upstairs.

Looking toward Silt Row, Raudius stared in disbelief at the columns of smoke spiraling into the sky. The sound of bells ringing in Archtown rolled across the desert, and the streets of the Outer Sands were empty. It was clear he had missed something very dangerous, and the realization only added to his burden of guilt and shame.

He found his sword sticking out of a dune around the back of the Hangman's Swing, from where Imayva had hurled it. Pulling it from the sand was nearly as shameful as bearing the hateful gaze of his fellow soldiers. Sheathing it, he turned toward the Devar Arch.

There is nothing I can do now. I have a long road to prove myself a soldier again. Raudius took a deep breath. *Finding raptors in Devar will be easy. Finding the raptors who will spill information on the other raptors will be impossible. Luckily, I know someone who might have an idea where to start. I just need to find this Imayva.*

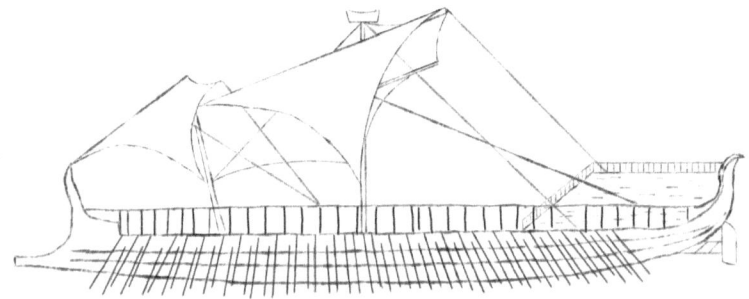

"I've taken the Ferry on many voyages, whenever my coin is low. It happens more often than I care to admit. Do I find the Ul'Varin unnerving? Yes. Traveling aboard a vessel where the entire crew is a reflection of your own mortality can be difficult, putting it mildly."

"Looking back, though, there was always a certain comfort about taking the Ferry that I haven't found elsewhere. Even though I'm sleeping on hard planks in a cramped hold, surrounded by a skeleton crew, I always felt safe."

—sketch of the Ferry from the Devaros Shore, by Megrid, human on the Briggin expedition

Chapter 13

Aboard the Ferry

The creak of timbers and gentle slap of breaking waves lulled Mayve out of a restless sleep. She stretched her limbs to release the aching stored in her sore muscles. Yesterday had been a long day, and sleeping on a hard plank floor had done her no favors.

Sitting upright, she looked around the hold where she had spent the night. Townsfolk and travelers were packed shoulder to shoulder, far more than the Ferry had space for. Some were prepared for a journey, resting comfortably on bedrolls. Others, like Mayve, slept on their arms. She shrugged out the crick in her neck from doing so.

Srrith was coiled in a corner, having no trouble sleeping on her own body. She had her own personal space, a semicircle of empty deck around her. It appeared the other travelers would rather compact together than get too close to the massive snake.

The first fleeting minute of Mayve's morning was blissful, then the fog of sleep faded and every memory of the night before rushed back. Her mother was dead. Spotch was dead. She was wanted by dangerous folk.

The thought of Dreva's grave, alone and hidden, brought tears back to the corners of her eyes. Every minute, she sailed farther away from that still patch of earth. *I wonder if anyone else will know she's gone. Is there anyone else who cares? It might just be me.*

Her eyes dried as rage awoke again within her, only dormant for the night. Faldmor and the masked man invaded her mind's eye. They had plagued her dreams too, wisping on the edges of her consciousness. Minute by minute, they were becoming an obsession.

They created the monstrous seeds for some purpose. They knew what would happen when I planted them and they left anyway, without a single warning. Try as she could, she could not shift the blame from her to them. Last night was her fault, and she had to live with it. But she could do her best to make sure more seeds like that never got planted again. *I am completely alone. My entire life died last night, so I might as well drag down those villains with me.*

She remembered that hideous blast of darkness, manifested from the masked man's outstretched hand. How in the depths would she fight *that?* Mayve had little knowledge of how volcomancy worked. Something about manifesting the power of the Vents. No one had ever bothered to explain it to her, and she had never bothered to seek it out. It had rarely interfered with her life up until now.

Maybe Srrith can teach me. The tauninaga had some sort of power, but she called it sfa-zrueen, not volcomancy. *How different are they really? She controlled shadows, just like the masked man.*

All this for a strange stone I swiped from both the raptors and the Oaken Legion. I should ask Srrith about that as well. If it's so powerful, if so many people want it, maybe I can use it against the masked man.

She reached for the pouch on her belt and grasped nothing but open air. Panic overtook her, then she remembered she had given it to Srrith for the night to avoid pickpockets. Looking at the sleeping tauninaga, she knew the leather pouch was cradled somewhere in her scaled coils, protected from thieving hands.

She decided to let Srrith sleep, not before checking that all the shadows around her were staying where they were supposed to be, and headed for the stairs to the open deck above. *I have the entire boat ride to think of a plan for Port Wenstnor. For now, I'll use Srrith's help to get south.*

The heat of the desert sun battled against the chilled river breeze.

Ul'Varin-Rak scurried across the deck, going about their duties with practiced efficiency. A few early rising travelers milled about under red cloth awnings that cast shade across the Ferry's deck, quietly eating or staring into the desert. Some wounded were being tended to, nursing bruises and a few broken bones caused by the madness of the crowd. The mood was grim. They had left behind a city on fire, unsure of what they might return to.

She looked out over the silty waters to the desert, stretching infinitely outward from both river banks—twin oceans of dunes studded with the occasional rocky outcrop. The smallest, driest shrubbery clung to the riverbank, desperate to not get swallowed by the sea of sand. Downriver, the Devar Arch still dominated the sky. Upriver, a column of gray clouds rose over the horizon. Ash, spewing from the Ysera Vent. A similar plume from the Cavotros Vent rose over the portside horizon, even farther away.

The heavy clank of armor drew Mayve's attention to Captain Vulinor, marching across the deck of his vessel. He stopped in front of a double-doored hatch, large enough for a wagon to drive through. With a swift motion, he unbolted the latch and flung open the heavy wooden doors as if they were made of air. The crack of wood drew everyone's attention. Then, the rustling of feathers and scratch of talons drew everyone's awe as a phoenix clawed its way out of the Ferry's hold.

The huge bird reared up and unfurled the full length of its wingspan, orange-and-red feathers catching the sun. Captain Vulinor removed his gauntlet and scratched the fiery down feathers on the bird's chest, small licks of flame dancing between the feathers and his skeletal fingers. Starting at its head and shaking down to its tail, the phoenix ruffled its feathers in a satisfied, full-body shake, scattering floating embers as it stretched away the cramps of the hold.

It's a phoenix! Mayve stared amazed at the creature before her. She had heard the Ul'Varin-Rak tamed the great fiery birds, riding them into battle against the hideous Vent beasts that crawled from the depths of the volcanoes, but she never thought a Ferryman would have one. This particular phoenix stood nearly twelve feet tall, towering over Vulinor. Its feathers were mostly orange, with speckles of yellow in its down and tail, and brilliant red feathers accenting its spear-like beak.

Vulinor's eye sockets glowed with a warm orange light as he looked at his feathered companion and stroked the smoldering feathers on its head. The phoenix lowered its beak and nuzzled into Vulinor's sandy cloak. The Ul'Varin whispered to the firebird, then pointed toward the port of the ship. The bird stomped to the edge of the vessel, spread its wings, and took to the sky. A gust of uncomfortably hot wind blasted across the deck, rustling the furled sails.

The phoenix flew several wide circles around the vessel, its outstretched tail feathers catching the sun like stained glass. As it flew, it left behind a trail of cinders that flitted in the tailwinds before evaporating. It swung its great wings through the air and landed on the deck near Vulinor in another gust of scorched wind. His cloaked billowed in the wind as he spoke, this time audibly, to the phoenix.

"Screech, please wake up our passengers. I have much to discuss with them." Screech opened their beak and released a geyser of white-hot flame into the air. Mayve felt the heat radiate across the open deck, wondering how well trained this bird had to be, living on a wooden ship.

Screech then let loose the most unholy, earsplitting shriek that Mayve had ever heard, rivaling the screams of the bramble eldritches. Every passenger on deck slammed their hands to their ears, some leaping to their feet, startled. Below deck, a stampede of feet took to the stairs as the horde of rudely awakened travelers scrambled upward to see what the commotion was about.

As the crowd streamed onto the deck, groggy and confused, Captain Vulinor strode to the helm of the Ferry, Screech stomping behind like an obedient, sentient furnace. At the helm of his ship, with a phoenix at his back, Vulinor looked grander than a Citadel Lord.

The familiar boom of his voice carried over the rabble. "As I am sure you all know, we made a hasty exit from Devar last night. I saw the emergency as a fine opportunity to start our journey south. As such, the Ferry will be continuing to Port Wenstnor." He strode back and forth across the raised stern of the vessel, surveying the crowd.

"We are anchored no more than half a day's walk from Devar. We will be docking momentarily to let anyone depart who wishes to. If you stay on the river shore, you will reach the city safely. Be warned, I am unaware of the state of the city. All I can do is pray to Varin that the Merchatzi have regained control."

As he spoke, the Ul'Varin crew were already hustling around the deck, preparing rowboats. Vulinor continued, ignoring the commotion. "Anyone who wishes to continue the journey to Port Wenstnor is welcome to do so. You will pay us the standard fare for the journey, of course. Given the emergency circumstances, we will also allow passengers to cover their fare with work. If there are any complaints, I would first remind you that I have extended a very generous offer here not usually seen on my vessel. If there are complaints after that, I will remove you from the vessel personally. That is all." Screech blasted another explosive scream across the deck and everyone winced in discomfort.

Chains rattled as rowboats splashed into the Devaros. The skeletal crew herded the crowd into two groups—one departing for shore and one staying on the boat. Mayve merged with the flow of people, slipping over to Srrith's side.

The cave tauninaga had her cobra hood closed and her hands pressed tightly against the side of her head. She cautiously dropped them as Mayve approached, keeping a wary eye on Screech, who was happily attempting to catch fish off the side of the boat. Following the snake's gaze, Mayve saw Screech gulp down some sort of river fish, water steaming off its feathers.

"Don't like the phoenix?" Mayve cracked a smile, already knowing the answer. Srrith only glared back.

"Well, I think it's cute." Mayve smirked. Screech screamed again as it tried to eat Vulinor's cloak, making Srrith wince.

The crowd jostled past them, awkwardly carrying them along. They had a lot to talk about, but Srrith almost seemed content to simply let the journey continue onward, the past forgotten. Mayve broached the subject first.

"You killed Spotch."

Srrith hissed, "The raptor? I am sorry if he was a friend."

Mayve pondered the thought. *Used to be, I suppose.* She shrugged. "No, just someone I worked with before." She fiddled with her mother's ring on her finger. "You were right, I'm sure you know. The raptors got the artifact and still tried to kill me."

Srrith nodded. "The raptors have been through generations of hardship. Hardship only breeds contempt, and contempt is predictably savage."

Mayve remembered the visceral hatred that all the raptors held against the Oaken Legion. She said, "Thank you for saving my life. Twice."

Srrith nodded. "No thanks is needed. It is fortunate the fates crossed our paths in such dire timing." She reared above the crowd and looked upriver, the Devaros twisting away between the desert hills. "Last night is only the beginning. If the artifact you hold is as precious as we think, then the killing has only just begun." Mayve thought the tauninaga was being dramatic, but the certainty in her voice was chilling.

I have at least two more bodies in mind. She thought of her prey in Port Wenstnor, possibly preparing to plant more of those seeds in the ground.

Srrith seemed to sense her grim thoughts, and posed a question. "Have you taken a life before?"

Mayve shook her head, then abruptly halted as she remembered the horrendous gurgle of the dying raptor the night before. "Not until last night. One of the raptors. It was more of an accident than a real fight, though. Not like how you handled Spotch."

Srrith hissed empathetically. "I am sorry. It is a jarring experience, your first life, but it must be done sometimes in a world like this." Her long tail tapped the hilt of the dagger sheathed on Mayve's belt. "If you would like, I will teach you how to use this."

I will need to know how to fight if I hope to stand any chance of killing that masked volcomancer. "I would appreciate that, thank you, Srrith. Maybe we can train later tonight if we can find space in the hold."

An Ul'Varin stepped onto a crate of supplies to stand over the crowd. A light female voice—disembodied from within her skull—shouted out, "Form a line! Form a line! If you're in this crowd, you're staying on board the Ferry, and to stay on board the Ferry you need to form a line!"

It took a minute for the crowd to fall in order—this Ul'Varin did not command the same presence as Vulinor. Small wisps of smoke curled off her bare skull, which Mayve took as a sign of frustration. *It's hard to tell what they're thinking without any skin.*

Once the vague resemblance of a line had been formed, another Ul'Varin with a hefty ledger took their place at the front. The first Ul'Varin shouted out again, "When you get in the line, give us your name. In return, I'll tell you mine right now. My name is Oribori, I'm the quartermaster of this ship, this here is Vanite, our scribe." She thumped the book Vanite was carrying, nearly causing the second skeleton to drop it.

"Once you give us your name, we'll write it in this fine ledger here, and then you'll give us five hearths for the passage south. Because of the emergency procedures, if you can't pay then we'll put you to work for the duration of the journey. If you can't work and can't pay for whatever reason, you'll be tossed overboard, nice and quick." Speech over, Oribori stepped off the crate and the line shambled forward.

Srrith pulled a coin purse from her tunnelsleeve and riffled through it, hissing to herself. She turned to Mayve, "How much coin do you carry?"

"I'm flattered you think I have a single den to my name. I was supposed to be rich today, I wasn't saving my money."

Srrith replied, matter-of-factly, "I only have enough for my own passage. I deeply apologize."

Mayve brushed Srrith's apology aside and said, "It's fine, consider my debt for saving my life paid." She pushed the idea of pickpocketing a nearby passenger out of her mind. "I guess I'll do an honest day's work for once." Getting thrown overboard into the desert would not help much.

The rest of the wait was quiet as they shuffled forward in the long queue. The pair were separated when the skeletons graciously accepted Srrith's coin, leaving her to roam the ship at will, while they ushered Mayve into a ragtag group nearby. There she was forced to wait until the line had dwindled to nothing, when Oribori and Vanite could finally talk to them.

One by one, Oribori went through the new workers and assigned everyone a job to do for their stay aboard the Ferry. As she talked, Mayve finally got the chance to look at this skeleton up close. Oribori's face was carved like swirling smoke, and she had a row of tiny rubies inlaid underneath her eyes. Vanite had no carvings but more rubies inset like a constellation on her forehead. Both of them were around Mayve's height—she wondered if they were taller when they were alive, with muscles and skin. They both used to be human, after all, until the Vents brought them back.

Many of the jobs involved helping the Ferry's chef, Bolios, prepare meals in the galley. More able-bodied travelers were assigned to harder labor. Mayve was grouped with the latter, designated to a shift of rowing each day, alongside occasional shifts of keeping watch. Her debrief complete, Oribori informed them that their schedules would commence immediately upon departure, and dismissed them.

An hour later, everyone who was departing the ship was gone, walking through the dunes back to Devar. A column stretched down the riverbank, hugging the lifesaving shoreline. With their heads wrapped in desert shawls to ward off the sun and sand, and a limitless supply of fresh, cold water, their trip back to Devar would be tiring, but safe. *Assuming no Vent beasts or raptors lurk behind the dunes.* Mayve was glad the renowned strength of the Ul'Varin-Rak deterred bandits from attacking the Ferry.

With the anchor hoisted, oars slapped the water and the Ferry gained speed, cutting south through the gentle current toward Port Wenstnor. Mayve found Srrith near the bow of the vessel. The tauni-naga was fiddling with a spool of fishing string, compressed flat from its time in her tunnelsleeve. As Mayve approached, she got the tauninaga's attention with a short wave.

"In a couple hours, I get to row the boat. Lucky me."

Mayve's lighthearted self-deprecation went straight over Srrith's head, who replied in a concerned tone, "I apologize again for not being able to fund your passage. You are making this journey on behalf of the Great Seer; I wish we could do more to accommodate you."

Mayve awkwardly waved away the tauninaga's concern. "I have nothing left in Devar, the raptors have made sure of that. I had no choice but to leave last night."

Srrith continued in her dead serious tone, "That thought has been lurking in my mind, I agree. It is fortunate the Great Seer led me to save your life, but in the chaos of last evening I fear you did not have much say in the matter. Your escape was paramount to both of us. In the midst of such turmoil and grief, it is easy to make decisions you may regret. If you are reconsidering your decision to journey with me to Savin Actai, I urge you to voice your concerns."

Mayve was taken aback by Srrith's considerate forwardness. Srrith seemed to sense her apprehension, and tried to explain further. "If you are not interested, then I will not bother you again. The Great Seer foresaw you carrying the Stone, and in a way, you already have. Perhaps we are meant to part ways already. However, if you do wish to continue our journey, then I will train you in tauninagan combat for the duration of our passage, and do my utmost to make sure you arrive in Savin Actai safely. The Seer stressed to me that the artifact is of great importance, and there will be grave consequences depending on whose hands hold it."

Before she could respond, a voice blasted across the deck. "Tauninaga!" Both she and Srrith spun to face Captain Vulinor, thudding toward them. Screech ambled behind, brilliant orange-and-red feathers reflecting the intense desert sun.

The captain inserted himself into the conversation with the grand importance of someone who can do whatever they want, whenever they want. It was his vessel, and he could interrupt whoever at anytime he pleased. Up close, he was twice as intimidating. Judging from his skeleton, Captain Vulinor clearly used to be a goliath of a man. Adding on the height and bulk of his armor, the skeleton towered over everyone, completely dwarfing Mayve.

The captain gave her the courtesy of a polite nod and extended a gauntlet. "Captain Vulinor, at your service." Mayve tried to hide her apprehension as she shook the armored hand. *He could superheat the metal in an instant and my hand would be reduced to char.* Vulinor shook Srrith's hand and turned his attention toward her.

"I could not help but notice your choice of weapon." He motioned to Srrith's sickles sheathed on her back. "Not only that, but you are dressed like a tauninagan hunter as well. I suspect you know how to use those blades?"

Srrith nodded and remained quiet, waiting for the captain to get to his point. Vulinor continued without pause, "The Ralveran Caverns are rife with terrors, almost as dangerous as the Vents themselves, I reckon."

Srrith shrugged. "They each carry their dangers." Vulinor's skull was unable to smile, but flames danced like jesters in the corners of his jaw. *Almost like a smile. Phovus, they express emotions with the fire and smoke on their skull! I'm going to have to learn how to read them before I offend someone.*

The captain boomed, "Well, as we near Port Wenstnor, the river will carry us past the Ysera Vent. Not dangerously close, but closer than most folk like, which isn't saying much. We don't have encounters with Vent beasts on every journey, but it's not uncommon."

Vulinor looked across the deck, still buzzing with Ul'Varin crew and passengers. "I do not usually ask our esteemed travelers to take up arms, but we have taken on more passengers than usual, and I fear we may have trouble defending every soul should a Vent beast find us."

Srrith nodded again and hissed, "I accept your request. We departed under dire circumstances, and you did a great justice allowing so many to find safety aboard your vessel. My blades are yours."

Captain Vulinor slammed his fists together, showering sparks into the air. His skull radiated with fiery energy, and his voice roared, "Excellent! The might of the Rak welcome your blades! If all goes well, we will have no need of them." Screech matched his excitement with a deafening squawk, making Srrith visibly wince again.

Vulinor noticed and quickly grabbed Screech's pointy beak in a vise grip with his gauntlet. The phoenix cooed through its clamped beak. "My apologies. It has been ages since I ferried a cave tauninaga. I'll make sure Screech keeps her namesake noise to a minimum."

He motioned for the phoenix to fall in line, then bade Mayve and Srrith one last farewell. "Enjoy your travel upon the Ferry." Screech stomped after him with happy trills.

Below deck, a heavy drumbeat quaked the deck and Oribori yelled, "Oarsmen, to your stations!"

The Ferry was setting sail.

Chapter 14

A Wanderer from the North

Called away for her first shift on the Ferry, Mayve left Srrith at the stern of the vessel. Their conversation cut short, she had still never given Srrith a decisive answer on whether she would travel with her or not. Mayve decided it did not matter what she said, as long as she arrived in Port Wenstnor on Faldmor's trail.

She joined another group of passengers, all short on coin, and an Ul'Varin crew member named Kinglor escorted them. He was a large skeleton, but a normal large. Nothing that turned heads like Vulinor. Mayve recognized him as one of the Ul'Varin that had fought the bramble eldritch alongside his captain.

Kinglor led them to the long, recessed alcoves, sunk into the deck along the railings. He pointed at a few rows of empty benches and read off the names. The crew had erected an awning to keep the sun off these specific rows—most folk were not as suited for rowing under the desert sun as the fiery Ul'Varin-Rak.

Mayve's name was read last, meaning she had to sit at a bench that was only half-empty. Sitting on the side closest to the water was a cloaked skeleton. Mayve saw the flash of a white skull under the hood, and his bare skeletal hands grasped the oar.

Mayve slid onto the rough wooden bench, keeping an arm's length between her and the skeleton. Kinglor shouted out, "Hour on, hour off, alternating rows. Follow the drums, and listen for the command to holster oars if the wind is at our backs." With that, he turned heel and disappeared out of view of her oarsmen alcove.

Is that it? Mayve had way more questions, and it was obvious the other travelers did too. They all looked at each other in confusion, some awkwardly standing up to see if Kinglor was coming back.

The Ul'Varin seated next to her spoke up. His voice was calm and steady, lacking the grandiose boom of the other Ul'Varin. "My bench is rowing, everyone count from us to see if you're with us. The instructions from the coxswain are intuitive, but please ask me if you have any questions. The Ul'Varin-Rak will handle the brunt of the rowing so don't push yourselves too hard, but don't tell anyone I said that."

With that, the skeleton slid the oar out of its holster and off the side of the ship, dipping it into the water. Mayve held on and followed his lead. She thought it would be easier with a super strong skeleton at her side, but the water seemed to offer enough resistance that she was putting in her fair share of effort. In no time at all, she was drenched in sweat as the heat of the desert crept through the shaded covering.

The drum, hidden somewhere below deck, was heard clearly through small slits in the deck. The skeleton next to her was correct; it took no time at all for her to find a rhythm of push and pull. The time flew by as fast as the desert landscape around them, and before long a triple beat of the drum signaled it was time to change shifts. Mayve and her skeleton partner slid the oar out of the water, holstering it as the other benches scraped their oars into place.

Mayve reached into the air to catch as much breeze as possible. The rowing was not as strenuous as she thought it would be, but the heat was gnawing away at her and she was drenched in sweat regardless. The Ul'Varin-Rak oarsmen shouldered the brunt of the physical labor, an inadvertent side effect of their unnatural strength.

The Ul'Varin next to her spoke up, "If you don't mind, allow me."

Mayve looked to see him place his hands together and drop his head in concentration. With a cracking sound, crystals of ice formed on his hands, and Mayve saw the skeleton's eye sockets glow with blue light. A lattice of frost crept across his skull like a frozen spider web, and the temperature around them plummeted. Despite the desert heat, a layer of rime grew across the ship's deck. Within seconds, Mayve was pleasantly cool, almost freezing. It was reminiscent of the fog of the Devaros Falls washing through the Darkmist Tunnels on a windy day, but a hundred-fold colder.

Stunned, Mayve let the cold air catch in her sweat and send goose-bumps down her skin. When the last trace of freezing rime dissipated, and the heat of the desert rushed back in, she faced the Ul'Varin and exclaimed, "You're not an Ul'Varin-Rak, you're one of the Ul'Varin from the Frost Vents! An Ul'Varin..." She searched for the correct suffix, but could not remember it.

The Ul'Varin laughed. "Ul'Varin-Zul. Yes, I'm from Rulnevrin, on the Northern Frost Vent. My name is Eiklo."

He extended a bony hand, dripping with water as the ice melted. Mayve shook the skinless hand, his bones freezing cold. Her hand returned wet with chilled water, and she wondered if it was polite to wipe it on her forehead to cool herself down, ultimately deciding against it.

"I'm Mayve." She wiped the condensation onto her pants, then mimicked the Ul'Varin-Zul's hand motions he used to drop the temper-ature. "Can you do that often?"

"It's a simple manifestation, not too taxing. Although the more ice I make, the wetter my clothing gets as it melts, which isn't too comfortable."

"Wet clothes are nice in the desert, I thought. It always helps keep me cool."

"Unfortunately, I'm always cold."

That makes sense. Don't make a fool of yourself, Mayve. "Certainly an odd place for an Ul'Varin-Zul to be, how did you end up here?"

Eiklo shrugged. "I left Rulnevrin a few years ago to see the world, traveled south for a bit and got passage on the Ferry. Ended up enjoying my time here, and the Ul'Varin-Rak find me useful so I've stuck with them for a bit."

"Sounds like I've lucked out with the seating arrangement if I'm working with an ice skeleton with Ul'Varin strength."

"Actually the Ul'Varin-Zul don't have the unnatural strength that the Rak do. That's why I'm seated over here with you all."

"Oh. I take it back, then, you're pretty useless."

"I'll start charging you coin for my frost volcomancy. You won't have a problem with that, will you?"

They laughed together. Cold fog spilled from Eiklo's expressionless jaw, giving him an unsettling visage, but the laugh emanating from his bare skull was youthful and filled with energy.

Eiklo removed his hood, exposing his bare skull to the open air. A circlet of foreign runes were etched into the bone, just above his brow, and a blue sapphire was inset right above his nose, between where his eyebrows would be if he were alive. As he spoke, tiny creepings of rime danced and evaporated around his eye sockets, which glowed with orbs of dark blue light.

"Why are you traveling south?" Eiklo asked. "Is Port Wenstnor your destination or just a stop on the journey?"

"I've got business there."

"How vague."

"I just met you."

"Well, just so you know, your business sounds illegal when you phrase it like that."

Mayve sighed, and Eiklo had a short, mischievous laugh at her expense. Her brain raced for a quick lie to tell but Eiklo continued first. "Don't worry, I don't mean to pry. I saw you traveling with the cave tauninaga. They're all infamously secretive, especially the cave ones. I'm sure this is no different. Must be exciting, though, I'm quite curious."

Mayve jumped on the opportunity for an excuse. "You're right. It's important tauninagan business. Discretion is key." She held a finger to her mouth to mime a shush. Eiklo mimicked the action; his bony finger and skeleton mouth crackled with tiny veins of blue elemental energy. Without facial expressions, it was incredibly difficult to read the skeleton's emotions. The little flares of frost and subtle elemental effects around the skull *had* to be how the Ul'Varin showed their feelings.

I hope that particular expression is humor, and not suspicion. Mayve resolved to figure out more before the journey ended.

A new expression appeared on his skull. The blue orbs of light in his sockets glowed with focused intensity, and wisps of rime crisscrossed his brow. "If you get the chance, you should ask the cave tauninaga about their echolocation. I've been immensely curious how it works."

"Their what?"

"Echolocation. It's the cave tauninagan adaptation for underground life. They can see with sound."

Suddenly, so many of Srrith's odd tendencies made perfect sense. Mayve was stunned with realization. "Eiklo, thank you so much for letting me know that."

Mist drifted off the Ul'Varin-Zul's bleached skull. "Glad to help. Sorry for assuming you knew."

"Is that common knowledge?"

"No, certainly not. The cave tauninaga prefer people not to know, because it gives them a distinct advantage in almost everything, combat and otherwise. Along with a disastrous weakness to loud noises, like from our good friend Screech over there." Eiklo pointed a bony digit at the phoenix, who was drilling her beak repeatedly into the central mast like a hellish woodpecker.

The Ul'Varin-Zul seemed like a font of knowledge, and Mayve wanted to pick through his mind even more. She tilted her head curiously and wondered, "You seem more educated than the usual lot I've met."

"I spent a year at Thaumaturn Six on my travels south. The Northern Ice raptors lectured me in volcomancy, as well as some basic history and biology of the Ralveran folk. There's plenty I don't know, though, and I wanted to experience more of it with my own eyes, not through books. Although, that's harder than it sounds. Books aren't as dangerous as the real world."

As he spoke, Eiklo had the same intense blue glow in his eyes, with rime dancing across his brow. Mayve realized that this look must be an expression of curiosity. *He's intelligent. Maybe he knows a few things about the artifact. Phovus, stop thinking about it. Unless it can help you kill the masked man, it will only get you tangled up with tauninagan bullshit.* "You know volcomancy? Did the Northern raptors have any powerful artifacts stored up there in the ice?"

Eiklo shook his head. "I'm sure they do, but everything like that was kept far away from me. Artifacts from the Lost Eon, before the Paroxysm, are very powerful and closely guarded. Anything built after the Paroxysm is most likely Fae in origin, and they've long since left this world. The Northern raptors can create some volcomantic items, but nothing as close in power to the Fae, or what came before."

Mayve wondered if her strange stone was from the Fae or the Lost Eon. Either would make the artifact in her pocket immensely valuable. She wanted to show it to Eiklo, but decided that was a terrible idea. For now.

Thinking of the Oaken Legion reminded her of the soldier she fought in the Hangman's Swing, and she suddenly remembered the gash inflicted on her side from his jagged timbersteel armor. Her hands leapt to her side, expecting the wound to be open after all the rowing, but she felt only dry fabric.

Rolling her shirt up, she inspected her flank and found only a thick pink scar, still coated in residue from the paste Srrith gave her. Eiklo tilted his head—an easy way to convey confusion. "Looks like a nasty wound."

"It was. Yesterday. My tauninaga friend gave me some healing salve from the mountains and it seems to have fixed everything overnight."

Eiklo nodded. "The mountain tauninaga are renowned for their healing abilities."

Mayve furrowed her brow. "So I'm told. They have a healing sfa-zrueen, whatever that is. Is that like volcomancy?"

"Not really, as far as I can tell. I don't know too much about it," Eiklo said, watching the other rowers. "I could talk at length about volcomancy, and the next rowing shift is about to start."

Mayve sighed and clambered to her feet. She waved her canteen to Eiklo. "I need more water. Is it rude to assume you don't?"

Freezing mist poured from underneath his skull. *That must be the expression for amused.* "I'm fine, thanks. No organs or blood."

Mayve took some time finding her way to the galley amongst the general bustle of the top deck, and made it back to the bench just in time. The series of triple taps on the drum beneath deck signaled it was time to switch rowers. She and Eiklo slid the oar from its resting place, dipping it into the silty waters of the Devaros, ready for another round of labor.

The desert shoreline soon blurred together as it passed, the dunes seeming to repeat themselves as the Ferry surged upriver. Even Mayve, who often found beauty in the vast emptiness of the desert, soon grew tired of the monotony, and turned instead to watch the Ferry's passengers mill about the deck. She only turned her attention back to the desert when a crowd gathered on the starboard bow, pressed up to the railing and the edge of her rowing alcove, eyes locked on the horizon.

There, framed between two hill-sized dunes, was a Citadel, hovering high above the desert sands. Through the mirage of desert heat, it looked like little more than an ink blot smeared across the blue sky. Even so, its grandeur was not lost. A flying island, suspended among the clouds, no doubt carrying its esteemed Citadel Lord to their next destination.

As soon as it appeared, it was gone, obscured by another mountain of a dune. Mayve turned to Eiklo and asked, "Which Citadel do you think that was?"

"Couldn't tell from this distance. Seemed a little flat on top, so maybe Citadel Marcrest? What was the most recent one to travel through Devar?"

"It's been many months. I don't pay too much attention to whichever rich lord is blocking out the sun above my city, but I vaguely remember it was Ashfell."

"Hmm. Whoever it is, it seems like they're heading to the Tarakos Vent to reheat their core."

Mayve thought about asking Eiklo how in the depths the Citadels flew—it seemed like he knew, but she did not care much for the answer. At the end of the day, she was the one rowing upriver while they got to drift through the skies, and she bet they knew just as little as she did about how their islands flew. *Those lords and ladies certainly aren't doing the maintenance themselves.*

The rest of the rowing shift passed quickly. With slow currents and gracious winds, it ended up being good exercise for Mayve, and she appreciated the activity. She suspected she was not allowed to climb the main mast, and did not want to get restless on the journey.

As the drum sounded a series of quintuple beats, signaling a major change in shift, she bid farewell to Eiklo and hurried to find Srrith. She had much to discuss with her about their journey, and it was time to learn how to wield the dagger sheathed on her hip. Her business in Port Wenstnor would require it.

Chapter 15

The Lies of the Wounded

T he girl was hiding something from her. This Srrith knew for sure.

The rhythm of her heartbeat betrayed her whenever she spoke of traveling to Savin Actai. Srrith could not fault her for her attempt at deception. Mayve had suffered more than most in the past twenty-four hours. Despite this, the young woman did not seem lost—like those stricken with grief often are—and instead spoke with purpose, as though she had a plan she was determined to carry out.

Srrith knew Mayve had been involved with unsavory people. The human was a thief, first and foremost. She certainly knew that the artifact she held was worth a substantial amount of coin to the right buyer. *If she would tell me what plagues her mind, I would help. Yet she seems determined to keep her secrets.*

If Mayve wanted to part ways, so be it. The visions of Alactashi Sen were not always exact premonitions. The sfa-zrueen that the forest tauninaga used to glimpse the future was not a precise art, although the Great Seer was the best at it by far. She was rarely wrong, but it was not unheard of. Especially a vision of this grand scale.

It was something else that tore at Srrith's conscience. If Mayve decided to go her separate way, through honesty or subterfuge, and did not hand over the artifact, Srrith would have to take the artifact by force —an option Srrith absolutely dreaded. She was here to guide Mayve, not attack her. Alactashi Sen said the girl was important, but it was more so necessary that the Stone not fall into the wrong hands.

Srrith hated the thought of choosing between Mayve and the Stone, but she hated the thought of disappointing Alactashi even more. She had taught Srrith to control her nightmares, and Srrith owed her everything for that.

Her fishing line tugged, the silvery thread pulling taut, and Srrith tensed. She carefully wrapped the cord in her fist, ready. Once again the line pulled, and Srrith yanked back. The water thrashed downriver as the hook caught, and Srrith began the long fight to tire out the creature on the other end. After a fierce but short-lived battle, Srrith hauled a fine-looking Nawai salmon overboard. Its scales shimmered with an iridescent beige, camouflaging it in the overwhelming sand color of the Ralveran Desert. As it traveled back upriver to Lake Nawai for spawning season, its scales would transition to a shade of beautiful green.

Srrith unhooked the wriggling fish and sank one of her fangs behind its eye. The wriggling abruptly turned to dead weight, and she laid the fresh kill down on the deck while she packed the fishing line back in her tunnelsleeve, taking care to flatten the spool. She was not going back underground anytime soon, but she would not carelessly toss aside her habits while traveling sunside.

She filleted the catch with a few precise cuts from her sickles, and gulped one of the slices down raw. Cooked fish was better, sometimes, but she did not want to bother with the ship's galley.

Feeling the familiar sense of being watched, she scanned the deck until she saw Screech. The phoenix was staring at her from across the ship, eyes locked on the fish Srrith caught. Just the thought of Screech's horrible, mind-rending cries gave Srrith a splitting headache. She held eye contact with the phoenix as she gulped down the rest of her dinner, then slithered below deck for a nap.

The chatter of passengers and the stomping from the deck above worked their way into her dreams, creating strange, dancing patterns as her echolocation messed with her sleeping mind. Every so often, she would wake up and let out a short hiss to gauge the room and check her

surroundings—a habit she picked up from her many days alone in the
caves and on the road. After several hours, one of these echolocation
checks painted a strange picture in her mind. Across the hold, a young
woman was crouched over, waving directly at her.

Srrith's eyes shot open to see Mayve, who was trying to silently get
her attention from the other side of the room. As soon as she spotted
the tauninaga's eyes open, she jogged across the room with a grin on her
face.

The human cheerfully asked, "Could you see me? Or hear me? I
don't know how it works." Srrith unwound and stretched away the
drowsiness, not ready to offer her any explanation.

"I sensed you. Who told you about the cave tauninagan
adaptation?"

"An Ul'Varin I met while rowing. He was quite knowledgeable."

Srrith sighed. "I thought all the knowledgeable Rak stayed on the
Vents."

Mayve grinned. "This one is an Ul'Varin-Zul. Pretty neat, huh? So,
is there anything else you can do besides weaving shadows and seeing
with your ears?"

"That's it."

"Shame. Any chance you can teach me any of that?"

"No. Only how to wield that dagger."

"Shame again. I'll take it, though."

Srrith groggily unclasped her sickles and turned her back to Mayve,
unsheathing the blades. "Are you ready for training, then?"

Mayve unsheathed her dagger. "I think so. We should have some
time—" The wind was knocked out of her as Srrith's tail snapped
around her ankles and pulled her legs out from underneath her.

"Excellent. Awareness is your first lesson." Srrith slashed her two
sickles against each other, a shower of sparks dissipating into the air.
"Sheathe your blade."

Mayve, rolling onto her feet, grunted, "Don't I need my blade?"

"Not for today. I doubt a dagger will be your weapon of choice
forever. It is a difficult weapon to fight with. You will be easily
outmatched by any competent opponent wielding a real weapon.

Against a volcomancer or roaming Vent beast, you would stand no chance."

Srrith swiped at Mayve's ankle with her tail again. The human jumped to avoid the strike and Srrith stepped in quickly, slamming Mayve midair with a sickle hilt. The human crashed to the deck once again, the dagger clattering away. As she scrambled for the hilt, Srrith's long tail shot out and swiped it from her, then the tauninaga leveled a sickle at the prone girl's throat.

"Never jump straight up. Don't jump at all if you can avoid it. You cannot change direction midair. Now stand and try again. Keep your feet and your center of balance controlled so you can move in any direction with no hindrance."

Srrith slithered away and coiled her lower half. Mayve picked herself up and pulled a splinter out of her hand with her teeth, spitting it onto the floor. She assumed a fighting stance, shifting her balance between the balls of her feet.

Srrith uncoiled and struck in the blink of an eye, headbutting Mayve in the chest. The poor human stumbled backward, tripping on Srrith's tail and slamming into the ground for the third time. As soon as she gathered her wits, she rolled away and jumped to her feet. Srrith could tell from her lack of breathing that she had the wind knocked out of her.

Srrith coiled again, and was pleased to see Mayve react, taking several steps back to keep out of range. She reached into her tunnelsleeve, hidden beneath her cloak, and grabbed the spool of fishing line. The tauninaga launched forward again, this time feigning a full strike. Mayve took a long step backward, and Srrith whipped the spool out and chucked it. It whacked harmlessly off Mayve's forehead, and she froze with a confused look.

"If that was a throwing dagger, you'd be dead. Perhaps I am actually a forest tauninaga, and I just spit venom in your eyes. Now you're blind."

Mayve crossed her arms in protest. "It was a spool of fishing line! I'm not going to dodge that."

"You did not dodge it because you *could* not dodge it. Because you were not ready. What is the lesson I am trying to teach you here?"

"That everyone has tricks up their sleeve?"

Srrith grasped both sickles in one hand and raised the other, motioning for Mayve to toss her fishing line back, which she did begrudgingly. "Not precisely. Those were not tricks. This is how I fight, along with many tauninaga. You simply did not know."

Srrith continued, slithering a wide circle around Mayve. She was not going to attack, but watching the human warily track her movements was amusing. "Do you know how many different folk in Ralvera there are?"

Mayve started to count and Srrith cut her off. "It does not matter. Maybe you will fight them all one day, but whether it is raptor, Oemorg, or tauninaga, you will not learn the quirks and subtleties of all their fighting styles for many years. Maybe never in the course of a human life. That does not even account for the Ralveran wildlife, the infinite spew of monstrosities from the Vents, or that anyone you meet could be a master volcomancer. Most of your fights will begin shrouded in uncertainty, with you unaware of what deadly abilities your opponents have."

Srrith suddenly clashed her sickles together, creating another shower of sparks. Mayve leaped back, on edge and ready for a strike, and the tauninaga let loose a long hiss of amusement. She continued, "This is why awareness and evasiveness are the key to survival. Your opponent cannot surprise you if they can never hit you. This is how we will train."

She reared to full height, baring her fangs. Her forked tongue flicked rapidly, tasking the air, and her sickles gleamed in the dim light below deck. "When I am no longer able to hit you, then you may unsheathe your dagger."

* * *

The dinner bell rang, echoing into the hold. It mingled with the thuds of the rowing drum, merging into an ominous chorus of thuds and clangs. The drummer executed a long drum roll, punctuated by a rattling chain as the Ferry's anchor was dropped overboard into the silty riverbed. The sun painted the crests of the desert dunes, the sky lit on fire with red-and-orange glows. Srrith decided this was an opportune time to stop Mayve's training.

Mayve muttered some beleaguered thanks to Srrith, and staggered toward the stairs. Srrith took a minute to inspect her sickles and properly repack her tunnelsleeve—she had thrown a few more items in the course of the training.

The human had shown decent improvement over the last several hours. By the end, she had established better footing and had even made a few dodges that left Srrith mildly impressed. There was still much room for improvement, and it was clear she was battling exhaustion near the end. *The girl is headstrong, but admirably persistent. She is determined, driven toward something. Whatever is driving her may be the source of her dishonesty. I must find out more.*

The temperature was dropping fast outside, and the refreshing evening air mingled with an overpowering smell of stew and spice. The galley crew were ladling out portions for the travelers lined up. Next to the stew was a selection of dried fruits and vegetables, heaped in overflowing baskets.

"Srrith, here!" Mayve waved to her spot in line. The gentleman behind her turned to protest against anyone cutting in front of him, but quickly lowered his gaze to his boots as he saw the pitch-black tauninaga winding toward them.

At the front of the line, Mayve grabbed a bowl of stew and some fruit. Srrith was not too hungry after her fish earlier, but took a small portion of stew, skipping the vegetables.

Mayve walked over to a rowing alcove on the starboard bow and jumped in to sit on one of the benches, taking care not to spill her stew. Srrith coiled nearby, drooping her long tail into the alcove. They ate in silence, enjoying the cool evening air.

Srrith expected Mayve to scarf down her food, as one would expect from a starving Devarian street urchin, but the human ate at a surprisingly reasonable pace. However, Srrith caught Mayve sneaking glances her way out of the corner of her eye, and she wondered if the human was secretly coveting her food. She decided that the girl needed it more than she did, after such rigorous training today, and offered the half-eaten bowl of stew to her.

"Would you like to finish it? I am not as hungry as I thought I was."

Mayve's mouth was full, and she held up a finger to Srrith and a fist to her mouth as she choked down the bite before responding, "Nope, I'm good with this. Thanks for offering, though."

The woman's heartbeat showed no signs of deception, but Srrith knew for certain she had been eying her food. Srrith held the bowl closer and hissed, "There is no problem. I saw your eyes wander toward it many times. You must be hungry."

Expecting a defensive response, Srrith was surprised to see a sheepish look cross Mayve's face. She mumbled, "Sorry, it's just an old habit." The sound of her heartbeat gave away that she was not telling the whole truth.

Srrith hissed, "In the wilderness, you can live off the land if you lack wealth. A city does not allow such privilege. You live and die by the coins in your pocket. If you want my food, please take it."

Mayve glared at the tauninaga. "I'm not looking for your pity or your scraps." The tauninaga tightened her coils and held her tongue, not wanting to upset anyone.

After a pause and a sigh, Mayve spoke. "My mother would always lie about how hungry she was and pass her food to me. When I got older, I got used to watching her eat to make sure she took her fair share."

Deeply embarrassed at how she had interpreted Mayve's behavior, Srrith bowed her head and hissed, "Please accept my apology. I did not mean to unearth such conversation."

Mayve had her knees wrapped in a hug, staring off into the desert. An Ul'Varin sailor trudged around the deck, lighting lanterns with their super-heated fingertips. The torchlight reflected off Mayve's green eyes, pooling in a forming tear.

The wind picked up, colder than the breezes before it. The night air was settling in, and the Ferry rocked gently back and forth in the waves. Deep from within the dunes, a pack of gorgonwolves howled, the echoes carrying across the river. Elsewhere on deck, laughter erupted from a group of passengers and Ul'Varin betting on dice. In a lull between sounds, Srrith softly hissed, "Your mother sounds like an excellent caregiver. You were lucky to have each other."

"I was lucky to have her. She was burdened with me." Mayve did not take her eyes off the desert horizon, the blue sky deepening into a black expanse.

Srrith replied, "No, she did everything for you and loved every minute of it. When parents do not want their child, nothing is more clear." Srrith thought of the last time she saw her mother, through the crack in a slamming door. *That was made perfectly clear to me.*

Holding up her fingers a hairsbreadth apart, Mayve said, "I was this close to getting her the life she deserved. If those sand-cursed brambles hadn't erupted from the earth, this purse would be filled with teirs instead of this strange rock. My mother and I would be sailing in the opposite direction, to start a new life in Tyrak Pass."

Srrith hissed a long, solemn sigh. She sensed a deep wound in Mayve's voice, something she would only open further the more she talked. Instead, she quietly changed the subject. "Speaking of sailing in a direction you do not want to go, have you given any more thought to traveling to the Great Seer? To avoid bribing you, I promise to continue your combat training for our entire trip on the Devaros, at the very least. Whether you accompany me to Savin Actai or not."

Mayve pondered for a moment, mindlessly spinning her mother's iron ring around her finger. "Say I come with you, through Port Wenstnor, all the way to this mountain city. I deliver this to the Great Seer, as she predicted." She patted the leather bag on her belt. "What then?"

"It is for the Seer to decide. But she does not waste her time or others' on matters that are not important."

"How do I know I won't be sacrificed in some archaic snake ritual?"

"You have my word and my blades that no harm will befall you."

"As if you'd tell me." Mayve managed a half-hearted smile.

Srrith sighed in frustration and was about to continue arguing when Mayve laughed and said, "I have a lot to think through, but for now, consider me a traveling companion. If I'm already lost, then I might as well wander."

Relieved, Srrith nodded her thanks. Mayve leaned toward Srrith and pulled the leather pouch off her belt, loosening the drawstrings so both of them could see the artifact nestled inside. Even in the near darkness, the smooth surface of the enormous sapphire captured the starlight from above and refracted it into a brilliant snowfall of lights within the gem. The golden-etched traces not only reflected the torchlight, but seemed to collect it, glowing like a warm hearth.

"What do you think it does?" Mayve asked. She did not take her eyes off the beautiful gem, pinpricks of starlight shimmering in her eyes.

Srrith replied, "I have no knowledge of what it does. Alactashi Sen's vision was cryptic, to say the least."

She recalled the exact wording that she committed to memory before leaving Savin Actai, repeating it out loud to Mayve. "*A green-eyed girl drifts through an ocean of sand. Gallows swing from an arch of sandstone overhead. The green-eyed girl holds a stone as blue as the deep sea. Without it, we are all lost, for it is worth life itself.*"

Mayve sat silent. Srrith hissed, "Whatever this artifact does, Alactashi Sen will surely know. She did give it a name, however. The Oasis Stone."

"The Oasis Stone," Mayve repeated in a hushed whisper. "It must do something powerful, if both the Oaken Legion and the raptors want it this terribly."

"We will find out," Srrith hissed. "For now, we must keep it safe from prying eyes, and keep ourselves away from the centuries-long war between the trees and lizards, and anyone else who wants the Stone, for that matter."

Mayve cinched the drawstring tight and secured the pouch. "The Ul'Varin-Zul I met today—Eiklo. It seems he and I will be rowing partners for the journey. He was very knowledgeable, in a scholarly way. Perhaps he's heard of the Oasis Stone before. He studied briefly with the Northern Ice raptors."

Srrith shook her head. "No one can know. We will get all the answers we need at Savin Actai."

"It would not hurt to get more information where we can. The skeleton could offer a more academic perspective, instead of your..." The human searched for the right word, aware of Srrith's offended glare. "...more mystical approach."

Srrith's glare intensified, her yellow eyes like miniature suns against the night sky. "We don't know who is looking for this, or who the Zul might tell." She took a deep breath. *Let her walk her own path. Guide her, not direct her.* "However, if you think he can be trusted, then perhaps pry for information."

"We shall see. Better safe than sorry, I suppose." Mayve climbed from the rowing alcove and strolled back toward the hold. "I'm going to pass out, today has exhausted me. Good night, Srrith."

"Excellent, it is good to be well rested. We will train more tomorrow once you are done with your duties."

Srrith thought of one more thing to add as Mayve walked away. "Your mother would be overjoyed to know you are safe. I will honor her memory with your protection."

Mayve motioned to the ship around her and jingled the artifact's pouch. "I doubt she would approve of any of this." She continued away without another word.

The tauninaga watched her disappear below deck. There was a steady stream of travelers breaking away from dinner, heading below deck to rest, as well as a horde of skeletons disappearing into the crew's hold to rest before their shifts. The crew quarters were separated completely from the travelers' hold, with a separate entrance on the top deck. It was most likely for crew safety and privacy, but Srrith doubted any paying passengers would feel comfortable sleeping alongside a host of dead.

Screech sliced through the night with an ear-piercing shriek. A split-ting headache erupted from behind Srrith's eyes and chaotic images exploded in her mind as the phoenix circled the boat, aloft on a burning wind. Their gorgeous red-and-orange plumage, wreathed in flame, looked like a smoldering comet against the dark blue sky, and the embers drifting off its feathers mingled with the twilight stars to create a shower of twinkling lights.

Vulinor strode toward the large double-doored hatch that Screech used to get below deck and called to Srrith, "My apologies, tauninaga. I've been keeping her quiet but she can't hold it in all day. Screech, to me!" He held up a skeletal fist and ignited it in a ball of flame, waving it back and forth to signal to the bird. *How does Vulinor know about our cave tauninagan echolocation? He must be a well-traveled skeleton. Everyone seems to know these days; perhaps the secret is finally out.* Srrith sometimes hated how fast the world was changing.

Screech flew low to the water, her fiery reflection shimmering along the waves, and dipped her beak below the surface. A cloud of steam cloaked the bird as fire met water, then the phoenix slammed onto the deck with a sizable salmon in her beak. The bird raised her beak to the sky, fish wriggling, and let loose a stream of flame, the heat almost unbearable even at Srrith's distance. Screech then gulped down the freshly-cooked fish and happily trudged beneath deck. Vulinor gave his phoenix a few loving pats before slamming the doors. *Good riddance.*

The top deck was quickly emptying. A few travelers were still up, partaking in a drinking game that had gone on longer than their livers could handle. A skeleton crew wandered the perimeter of the ship, keeping watch and sustaining the torches. In the quiet, Srrith pondered her conversation with her traveling companion.

When Mayve said she was lost, Srrith heard a distinct lie. The perceptible change in heart rate and slight catch in her breath all but confirmed Srrith's earlier suspicions that the human had other plans. But she had sounded truthful in her statement of joining Srrith's quest. *The girl must have business in Port Wenstnor, business that she thinks she can accomplish simply passing through the town.* The nature of this business perplexed Srrith.

The girl had let slip other important information. *The bramble eldritches erupted from the earth.* It could have been an educated guess. They *were* plants, after all, but the human spoke with no uncertainty. She had some knowledge of where they came from.

Srrith remembered fighting the bramble eldritch in Mayve's dwelling. The churned earth of the back room where her mother was found dead, and the destruction of the interior. She had not thought much of it at the time. One monster could have caused it all, but now she was unsure. *The girl knows far more than she lets on. Much more.* How did a bramble eldritch find its way through the Darkmist Tunnels to that specific dwelling? *Unless that's where it came from.*

Their journey was in peril if Mayve was in any way connected to the monstrous attack on Devar. *I have the rest of the passage to consider this information. If she is in true danger, I wish she would not hide it. My blades are hers, but I cannot protect her from what I do not know.*

Whatever the human's ulterior motives, Srrith would have to confront her as they neared Port Wenstnor.

The tauninaga made her way below deck to rest. The corner she slept in the previous night was completely clear, courtesy of all the frightened passengers. Srrith was used to such behavior from all folk, including her own. As she slithered over to the corner, Srrith heard the heartbeats increase of every traveler she slid by, swelling and ebbing as she passed.

She carefully wound herself into a sleeping coil, clutching her belongings in the center of her mass. Amid the breathing and rustling of the sleeping passengers, she caught Mayve's heartbeat, lying closest to her in the crowded hold. Her heartbeat and breathing melded into a pattern that was all too familiar to Srrith, as the sleeping human fought off a nightmare.

Chapter 16

The Lost Soldier

The tepid Devaros breeze rustled through Raudius's leaves as he gazed upriver, one hand on the rudder while the other lazily skimmed the water. The vessel he rented passage aboard only rose a couple feet above the surface, and the sail provided meager shade from the glaring sun. A cloth awning covered half the boat, stretched over a rickety wooden frame. He could have taken shelter from the sun in the tiny cabin, but at the moment it was filled with a small pile of fish, freshly caught and ripe smelling.

A cavernfolk fisherman squatted inside, skinning and preparing the fish before stringing them over a small mechanical box that was spewing out smoke. A second cavernfolk, sitting next to the box with a fishing rod in hand, adjusted a knob on the contraption, sending different-sized plumes of smoke into the sky. She hummed to herself as the line gently bobbed in the water, the hook trailing far behind the boat.

Raudius hated the trail of smoke billowing into the air. It was a clear signal to anything in the surrounding desert that someone was there. The cavernfolk couple did not seem worried in the slightest, happily going about their chores. He sighed, leaning on the rudder. It had been difficult enough to find such inexpensive passage south—this cavernfolk pair had been gracious enough to let him on the boat, so he held his tongue.

The wind at their backs, they were making good time toward Port Wenstnor. Toward the girl named Imayva—the artifact thief. He pored over the past thirty-six hours in his mind, searching for any detail he might have missed in his investigation.

With only a name to start with, it had been no easy task finding where to start. Devar was in chaos, recovering from the monstrous attack that Raudius had slept through—albeit, not by choice. He started at the Silt Row Market, but found many of the stalls deserted. Those still there did not recognize the name Imayva, or simply did not care to help an Oaken Legion soldier. When he saw Grenner and a host of soldiers enter the market, he made a hasty exit. He did not want to take any chances, lest Grenner decide that exile was too light a punishment.

Leaving Silt Row with no leads, he found himself wandering aimlessly through the wooden shacks on the riverside. In a flash of recognition, Raudius realized he was standing in the alleyway where the two raptors had relieved him of his coin. Shuddering at the memory, he recalled the girl arriving at the scene. She had rounded the corner at the north end of the alley. He distinctly remembered a look of relief on her face when she saw it was him getting mugged and not her.

Why anyone would decide to ally with robbers and thieves, much less the vile scalescum, is beyond me. Raudius fervently glanced up and down the alley, half expecting the blood-feathered twins to appear on either end with swords drawn. *Both of them were at the Hangman's Swing last night! I should have recognized them; I knew the human was friends with them.* Ingo and Spotch. That's what Imayva addressed them as.

He headed in the direction that Imayva had come from, leaving the alleyway behind. This area of Silt Row was light on foot traffic, blanketed in the shadow of the mesa arch, and Raudius found himself picking through tight corridors and traversing makeshift bridges as he held the direction steady. Before long, he found himself at the edge of the Falls, the river rushing past and cascading into mist. Peering over the edge, he saw the pinprick lights of lanterns speckling the dark fog like lost fireflies.

There is a borough down there, from what I recall from the briefing on the city. The slums of Darkmist. It made perfect sense that a rat like Imayva would call that place home.

For a moment, he stared at the grand height of the Falls, lost in awe at the spectacle of nature. *A shame that a natural monument so grand has to be hidden in the midst of this accursed sand.* Even more bewildering was that he believed Imayva had climbed the waterfall. *She climbed up the outside of the tavern and crashed through the window. It's not impossible.* He peeked once more over the edge and his eyes swam with vertigo. *Still, only fools would climb this.*

Before he left the river, he filled both his canteens and dunked his head beneath the surface as an added measure to keep himself cool. To keep up his energy, he photosynthesized as he walked, but soon the water on his branches evaporated and the desert heat ate away at the water in his body.

The road down to Darkmist was long, but the borough was a pleasant change from the glaring sun. As he reached the bottom of the carved cliffside steps, he breathed in a refreshing gasp of foggy air, then retched away the fetid smell it carried.

He wandered along the road that led back upriver. Ramshackle stalls of soggy wood and protruding nails lined the path, more than Raudius had seen at Silt Row Market earlier. The denizens of Darkmist did not have the luxury of halting business for personal safety—teirs had to change hands or they would not eat that night.

One by one, Raudius approached each stall. Most would shoo him away immediately upon seeing his timbersteel armor. Others would entertain him long enough for him to ask about the girl, then they would wave him away once they realized he had no intention of buying their wares.

The Falls grew ever closer as he neared the end of the road, his frustration swelling with the roar of water. The fog soaked through his cloak, condensation on his armor seeping between the joints onto his bark. It would have been welcome in the desert sun, but down in the fog-soaked shadows, it only fouled his mood further. Raudius marched, damp and discouraged, to the next market stall nestled between two dilapidated docks, half-eaten by the river.

Flies buzzed around the wooden table slick with water and blood. Laid out in unorganized rows were the merchant's catches—blind cave rats of varying size, some skinned, others covered in mangy fur. Several were mangled into indistinguishable clumps of meat, clearly plucked from a trap and thumped right onto the table. Every possible state of decay was arranged here, and Raudius tried not to grimace as he approached the leathery human sitting behind the stall.

"Greetings, merchant. I'm looking for some help."

The merchant passed a hand, missing a couple fingers, over his haul. "Take your pick. Rotten bits are half off."

Raudius refused to glance down at the rancid stock, pressing his investigation. "I am looking for a human, a girl named Imayva. Do you know where I could find her, or perhaps a relation?"

The merchant, if one could even call him that, picked up a juicy, decapitated rat and dangled it before Raudius. Flecks of blood dripped from the stump. "This one is only four dens! That'll fill you right up. Only reasonable prices here."

Raudius snapped back, "I'm not here to buy anything, I am just looking for the simple answer to a simple question. Do me that courtesy."

"Well, I might be more inclined to do that courtesy of yours if you buy something." It was subtle, but Raudius detected a hint of mockery in the merchant's voice that only fueled his frustration further.

"The Oaken Legion doesn't eat meat."

"Then we don't have answers for ya. Sorry, tree."

Raudius desperately wanted to walk away, but this was the first person who had not shooed him away. Infuriated, he dug out the meager handful of coins he had to his name and slammed one den onto the counter, pointing at the most rotten, disgusting slab of meat he saw.

The merchant did not move a muscle, except to jangle the fresh rat corpse in front of Raudius. The tree looked in his coin purse to see only four dens and a couple hearths left. Seething, he fished out another three dens and dropped them on the table, then snatched the squishy rat corpse out of the merchant's fingers. Without hesitation, he hurled it far into the mists, where it disappeared with a distant splash.

He slammed his gauntlets into the stall, the jagged timbersteel knuckles burying into the soggy planks. "Glad we reached a deal. Now tell me where Imayva is!"

The merchant shrugged and chuckled, "Never heard of her."

Raudius flung the stall to the side, the meat scattering across the rocks and splashing into the river. The merchant took a startled step backward and Raudius caught his collar in an armored fist. His other hand clenched around the merchant's throat, the timbersteel drawing blood as it dug into his flesh. "Tell me where Imayva is, and then give me back my money."

Terrified, the merchant pried at Raudius's gauntlet, cutting his fingers on the rough armor. Trying to keep his neck still, he managed to stammer out, "You just threw your money into the river." The coins had been sitting on the stall when Raudius flipped it. "I don't have any more, I'm sorry" The tree opened his mouth to respond when something squelched against the back of his helmet.

Still holding the merchant, he turned to see a small circle of Darkmist merchants gathering around him. Another mushy object hit his chest, an overripe fruit splatting across him. He felt the juices running down the grooves in his bark and dripping off his branches. Jeers flew from the crowd, some pleading him to drop the man and leave, others slinging more heinous threats.

"Stop bothering him and leave!"

"Go back to your precious Verdant, barklicker!"

"Drop him or we'll call the raptors!"

The fruit was quickly replaced by rocks from the crowd, pinging off his armor. He ducked a few that were aimed dangerously high and released the merchant's throat to shield his own face, keeping a strong grip on the merchant's shirt collar. The yelling intensified and the mob closed in.

Raudius drew his sword, the hideous scraping silencing the crowd in an instant, and planted the blade firmly on the merchant's neck. "Someone here knows Imayva. Someone has to! Speak now, or the river will run red as this pathetic thief floats down it. Now!"

The crowd stopped in their tracks. The merchant at Raudius's blade clenched his eyes tightly shut and muttered a prayer. "Phovus, grant me your luck if you have some to spare." His hands clawed to no avail at the timbersteel armor, blood running down the gauntlet. The deadly silence was drowned by the crash of the Falls. Raudius yelled above the noise, "I won't ask a third time! Imayva, now!" Trails of blood dribbled down the meat merchant's throat.

"That's Dreva's girl." The crowd parted to reveal an old lady. She was meek in stance, but stared at Raudius with heated intensity. "Strong young woman. Green eyes and dark hair. The climber." Several folk in the crowd nodded in recognition, finally attaching a name to a face.

Raudius growled angrily, "Where is she?"

"She and her mother live in the tunnels there. Good luck finding them." The old woman spat at Raudius, who retaliated by forcing the merchant to his knees and placing the point of his sword on the back of the man's neck. "I'm going to need more information than that, you hag. Hurry."

Another voice stammered above the crowd, this time from a small Torn with a molting carapace. Its chitinous mandibles buzzed together as it forced out the syllables in Ralveran. "I saw the girl at the docks. Last night, very late. She was leaving with a tauninaga, fighting with raptors and such. Boarded the Ferry, they did."

Raudius glared at the bug, wondering if they were speaking the truth. This changed a lot. *The girl fought the raptors; did one of them betray the other? The raptors probably turned on the girl like the honorless shits they are. But where did the tauninaga come from? Could it be the one that was sleeping in the tavern every day?*

There were too many questions racing through his mind, but at least the path forward was clear. The human had left town, otherwise she would be raptor dinner. And unlike a human girl, tauninagas stuck out from crowds like Scorch Vents from the desert sand. A much easier target to track.

Raudius shook the merchant. "Get back! Everyone!" He dragged the human toward the edge of the crowd, which parted cautiously before him. As his escape route cleared, Raudius dropped the man and took off at a sprint toward the Darkmist cliff pathway, leaving the merchant on the soaked rock pathway clutching his bleeding throat.

* * *

"Wer gunna be stopping ashore just a couple bends downriver, good tree." The homely voice of the cavernfolk fisherman snapped Raudius back to the present.

Wuilge was his name, if Raudius remembered correctly. The four-foot-tall gray creature called out to him, their eyes hidden behind huge tinted goggles. They carried an armful of filleted fish to their partner at the smokebox. "One of the best fishing spots, the missus and I reckon. We stop every journey up and down."

The missus, Oraine, shook her head. "Only you reckon that, darling." She turned to Raudius, hand held between her mouth and Wuilge in mock secrecy. "I like to humor him, though."

"Bah, you'll eat yer words when I catch anotha record salmon here, I'll tell ya that." He snapped his fingers in Raudius's face and ambled off to check the sails. "Don't be dozing away at the rudder there, good sir. No good fer business being wrecked in the sands."

Raudius kept a straight face, fuming internally. Every stop they made, Imayva disappeared farther downriver. He had no grounds to protest, though. Wuilge and Oraine were transporting him for mere pennies compared to the normal price of travel upriver.

Oakfire raged in his chest. He tried to quell it, but the mystical force that breathed life into the Legion's bark had a stranglehold on his emotions. He wanted to sail all night and all day, maybe even catch the Ferry before reaching Port Wenstnor. Run his sword through Imayva and whoever gets in his way, retrieve the artifact and return victorious, honorable and Unfelled. These cave-cursed cavernfolk were far too lazy.

"Just up 'ere, by those rocks." Wuilge's voice pulled Raudius's attention again, the cavernfolk pointing to a rocky outcropping on the river side. "Wait till you see this, young tree, the shade of these boulders attracts the largest swimmers you'll ever see."

Raudius hid his scowl and angled the craft toward shore. Wuilge and Oraine scurried about, securing ropes and lowering the sails, then Wuilge grabbed a pair of oars stowed away beneath a bench and began paddling. The rocky outcrop formed a small cove that they carefully maneuvered the boat into. Wuilge prodded the rocks with the oar to adjust the vessel and they hit the shoreline with a hollow bump.

Oraine stepped into the shallow water and secured the boat to the rocks with a few ropes. "Hop to it, Wuilge. We've got a passenger this trip, we can't dillydally all day like we usually do."

Raudius gave Oraine an appreciative look and she smiled back, her eyes hidden behind her goggles. Cavernfolk eyes function terribly in direct sunlight, forcing any who spend their time above ground to wear the tinted goggles. Although, the goggles had several extraneous lenses built into them that made Raudius think the cavernfolk often saw more than they let on.

Wading through the shallows to shore, he collapsed into the nearby shade of a large rocky outcropping to escape the sun, and lazily watched the cavernfolk work. Oraine had hefted the smokebox off the ship and was letting the smoke billow at maximum strength, several fish laid on top. It was probably visible for miles, but they did not seem to care. *They only have fish and a few coin, and I suppose cavernfolk are too small to be worth eating. However, everything is hungry in the desert.*

Raudius had spent his last hearth buying passage aboard their boat. He had been laughed away by several larger merchant vessels, many of which employed a few raptors and were not willing to risk any conflict aboard. He finally asked the small fishing ship at the end of the dock, where Wuilge and Oraine had agreed to transport him for only a hearth. It was an outrageously generous offer, and although he had to do a bit of steering, they had not asked much of him on the journey.

Overall, it had been a successful couple of days. Raudius was confident he was well ahead of his old quindecis in resecuring the artifact. They were most likely still hunting and interrogating raptors in the area, and would soon be forced to retreat downriver or face a full attack from a nearby tribe. Meanwhile, Raudius had a strong lead and was lounging in the shade. *I will make sure Grenner knows the mistake he made in Felling me.* He watched Wuilge attach a chunk of bread to his hook and plunk it into the cove pool, whistling a simple cavernfolk tune.

Oraine caught his attention with a wave and yelled, "Raudius, could I trouble you to take a brief look for some wanderweed? The smokebox could use a bit of fuel."

"Of course, I am at your service." *Better hurry up and get this done so we can get back on the water.* "Do you specifically need wanderweed?"

Raudius trudged into the sand. Oraine called after him, "Anything dry will do. Don't go far, it's not too important."

His boots sinking in the sand, Raudius scrambled on his hands and knees up a nearby dune. It would provide a solid vantage point to see any nearby shrubbery not eaten away by the sun or the Vents. The sand eroded beneath his weight, and he cursed as it sneaked between the cracks in his armor. *I will need to remove it all for thorough maintenance on the boat tonight.*

He breached the top of the dune and locked eyes with a grinning raptor, lying in wait on the other side.

Raudius reached for his sword, but the raptor was faster. They leapt up and kicked Raudius square in the chest, sending him tumbling down all the way down the slope in a cloud of sand. Raudius rolled to his feet at the bottom, sand spilling off his armor, and drew his sword while he called out, "Oraine, Wuilge, ready the boat!"

He turned to face the raptor, who was sliding gracefully down the dune, axe carving a path through the sand. More colors dotted the surrounding dunes. An entire raiding party of raptors, bows drawn and spears ready, all aimed directly at Raudius. Several leapt over the dunes with snarling laughter, prowling toward their trapped prey.

"Drop your weapon, barkscum." The voice snarled from behind Raudius, and he spun to see a gray-feathered raptor slinking out of the rocks toward the cavernfolk couple, sword drawn. Wuilge and Oraine were in the midst of untying the vessel. "Those arrows are coated in Verdant's Bane." The raptor pointed their scimitar at the surrounding archers and Raudius heard the ache of bowstrings growing taunt.

Raudius yelled, "We don't have anything but fish, and I'm not part of the Legion. You're wasting your time."

The gray raptor strode over to Wuilge and dropped a hefty purse into his outstretched palm. Raudius heard the clink of coins even from this distance.

"Pleasure doin' business with ya, Lairro." Wuilge chuckled, then jingled the pouch in Raudius's direction. "I told yer, young tree, this fishing spot always delivers." He shook the raptor's hand and said, "Glad you got our signals, it's always a pleasure doing business." *The smokebox. I should have seen it. I did see it. Raudius, you fucking fool.* The cavernfolk boarded the ship and set off, leaving Raudius to his fate without a second glance.

Raudius let his sword fall as the boat drifted away from shore and the raptors closed in around him. His hopelessness melted to grim resolve.

If I am to die here, I will take as many sand-cursed lizards as I can with me. He hoisted his sword and yelled, "For the Verdant!" As he charged the gray raptor named Lairro, a chorus of bowstrings twanged and he felt a rain of arrows snap against his armor.

He almost reached Lairro when an arrow buried itself in a joint of his armor. A sharp, excruciating pain traveled up his neck and raced through his branches. His legs lost all support and he collapsed in the sand, completely paralyzed. Sand spilled into his mouth, and the sensation of the grains on his tongue faded away as everything went numb.

This isn't Verdant's Bane—my veins would be sludge by now. It's a different poison. They're taking me prisoner. His mind felt as numb as his body.

The raptors wasted no time ripping his timbersteel armor off, hurling it into the river along with his sword. At the angle he lay, he heard the splash, muffled by whatever toxin was coursing through his veins. Then, he was bound and trussed like hunted game, carried over the dunes to a herd of waiting animals. Thrown over the back of some pack animal he did not recognize, his eyes were buried in the creature's fur and everything went dark.

Chapter 17

Bark and Claw

Raudius was dumped like a sack of grain into a tent, from what he could tell. He'd lost control of his eyes on the journey here, which only made him more nauseous. A few branches snapped off as he hit the ground at an odd angle. It should have hurt, but he felt only a numb void. After a minute, he was rolled onto his side and found himself staring at a young raptor, with burnt orange scales and full plumage of bright orange feathers. The raptor looked a handful of years younger than Ingo, some feathers still not fully formed in his adolescence.

The raptor inspected Raudius, muttering to itself. It wrapped one of its hands in cloth, then disappeared from view. Its claws numbly scraped the back of Raudius's head, and he felt a dull prick as something was yanked out of his neck. The orange raptor dropped an arrowhead into a small clay bowl nearby, and sat down cross-legged in Raudius's field of view.

For the first time in an hour or two, Raudius's vision focused. Slowly, the numb mumbling of the raptor turned into coherent Ralveran sentences. "...a nasty toxin for all species really, and fairly rare so we can't make enough for full warfare, but it works wonders for small targets like you."

The orange raptor noticed Raudius's eyes lift, and snapped his fingers back and forth to see if his vision followed. "You're coming back! Good thing you only got hit by one arrow. I'm not sure what would have happened if several got you. Next time I'd surrender quietly."

The raptor rolled Raudius onto his back. "You'll regain your senses first, then your muscles. Don't bother struggling, you're tied up well and the whole tribe is outside waiting." They picked up some of Raudius's broken branches and held them in front of his eyes. "Can I have these?"

Raudius couldn't even grunt. The orange raptor shrugged and said, "I'm gonna take them. Might make good ingredients for something."

It took every ounce of willpower to move his eyes, fighting against every nerve in his body. He was in a tall, circular tent. The floor was sand, covered in a few blankets, with various pots and jugs lining the rim. The raptor noticed him straining and said, "You're recovering quickly. Very interesting. I'd brace yourself, your sense of pain should return any moment."

As if on cue, the wound from the arrow in his bark and his snapped branch stubs exploded in pain. He grimaced and arched his back, straining against his bindings. The burning pain raced down every nerve in his body. The raptor leaned over and crushed some bluish-green leaves into Raudius's mouth. The taste was sweet and acidic. He felt the pain recede slightly as his body absorbed the juices. The raptor shook a claw at him, "Don't tell anyone I gave you that."

Moving his jaw felt like he was biting through a lump of molasses. As it loosened, Raudius spat out, "I thought...the arrows...Verdant's Bane."

The raptor chuckled. "Ah no, no, they just say that to get you to come quietly. Don't tell them I told you that either." In a more serious tone, the raptor whispered, "Although I bet they'll use that later when they torture you for information. Sorry." The small raptor winced, baring his sharp teeth apologetically.

Raudius rolled over and spat at the raptor, "Untie me, you fucking sand-cursed wretch. I'll give you nothing so you might as well kill me."

The raptor sighed, his orange feathers ruffled. "They'll probably end up doing that. It's a whole event when we catch one of you. Everyone's lost someone to the Legion, so everyone wants to get a few punches in."

The cloth tent flap opened and Lairro slunk in. The gray-feathered raptor was not the tallest Raudius had seen, but was certainly larger than the orange-raptor. They spoke to each other in low, guttural Raptoran, both gesturing to the incapacitated tree. Then the orange one turned back to Raudius and said in Ralveran, "He's asking if you're well enough to walk. Do you think that's possible?"

Raudius tried to move his legs. Each movement felt as if he were waist deep in a thick bog. Lairro leaned over Raudius and asked, "Can it talk?"

"Eat shit and die," Raudius spat.

"That's good enough for me." The gray raptor picked up Raudius's limp body and dragged him out the tent.

Having regained control of his face, Raudius was finally able to look around the encampment after his eyes adjusted to the blinding sunlight. They were amidst a clutter of sand-swept tents of all shapes and sizes, each one colored in patterns of reds, yellows, and blues stitched onto beige cloth. The stench of animals hung ripe in the air between gusts of arid wind. It was taught in all Legion training that the raptors possessed the unnatural ability to bend animals to their will, especially the desert raptors. The sight of it was far more unsettling than the books described, as a large sabertooth cat prowled by.

Raptors were scattered around the entire camp, tending to animals and preparing food. As Raudius was dragged out, they all stopped what they were doing and slunk over to watch the spectacle, snarling with excitement. Lairro threw him onto the ground in the center of the encampment. He crashed into the sand and tried to stand, screaming at his nerves to react, but the best he could do was slowly bend his knees and turn his head to see the sabertooth plodding toward him, fangs bared.

The massive cat reared down, its haunches tightening into a hunter's pose, ready to pounce. A voice called out in Raptoran, in the distinct tone of command, and the cat froze. The voice sounded chillingly familiar to Raudius, and a raptor with blood-red feathers strode out of the crowd.

The sabertooth lowered its head for Ingo as he gave it a few scratches behind its ears and tossed a chunk of meat into its mouth. Ingo slunk over to Raudius and placed his clawed foot on his chest, both him and the cat staring down with gleeful hatred. The raptor's claws dug into Raudius's bark through his white linen shirt, painfully reminding him that his timbersteel armor was long gone.

"I recognize this one," Ingo growled. "He was with the Legion in Devar. Long way from your pack, aren't you, greenling?" He stomped hard on Raudius's chest, causing his bark to creak under the stress.

Raudius strained under the pressure and spat out, "You and your scum killed three good soldiers. We were just passing through."

"A small price to pay for all the innocent lives lost to your pathetic Legion. I hope their deaths were slow and painful."

"Shut your maw, you animal-bred wretch."

"I see you met Wuilge and Oraine. Pleasant folks." Ingo hoisted his bone-hilt axe, and placed the edge on Raudius's throat. An identical axe hung at his side. The fervent hiss of excitement from the onlooking crowd chilled Raudius's spine. "What are you doing traveling all by yourself? Seems dangerous to me."

Raudius noted the second axe at the raptor's waist and grinned. "What are *you* doing all by yourself? I thought you had a twin."

Any trace of clever smugness drained from Ingo's face. His smile faded into a grimace and his eyes drowned in rage. Raudius knew well enough what that meant. He smiled as wide as he could and whispered, "I hope it was the Legion that got him."

Ingo roared and collapsed onto Raudius, pummeling the tree's face with the hilt of his axe. Raudius was too paralyzed to do anything but meekly struggle. He felt the bark splintering, and blinding pain cracked through his skull on every hit.

The crowd of raptors were cheering, but Lairro and the orange raptor ran forward and pulled Ingo off Raudius. The gray one shouted, "Hold your rage, Ingo, we need to know more."

Ingo shook away from his tribesmen and leaned against his sabertooth, which nuzzled against him with a comforting purr. He turned and shouted at Raudius, pointing his axe at the tree. "Your green-cursed Legion never touched Spotch, and they never could! He was killed by a tauninaga, lucky you, 'cause he could have killed all of you if he had the chance!"

Despite the pain crashing through his skull, a lifeline of a plan formed in Raudius's mind. He managed to stammer out, "He was decapitated at the docks, yes?"

Ingo froze in his tracks. "How in the depths do you know that?"

Raudius strained every muscle in his core to pull himself to a sitting position. He sat in the sand, hands bound behind his back, and told the bravest lie he ever would. "I know where that tauninaga is, and if you let me live then I'll take you to them."

To the chagrin of the bloodthirsty mob, Ingo dragged Raudius by the branches into a nearby tent, larger than the healer's hut he had been in before, and threw him onto the sandy ground. Lairro slunk in behind, tying the flap doors closed behind him to muffle the snarls of the waiting crowd. Ingo grabbed a fistful of Raudius's branches, snapping some in the process, and wrenched Raudius to his knees, holding his axe to Raudius's throat with the other.

"Talk, greenling!" Ingo snarled, the axe blade biting into his bark. "Tell us where the tauninaga is, and I'll let you die a swift and painless death."

Raudius thought about spitting a mouthful of blood into Ingo's face, barely deciding not to. "That's not what I said, Ingo. I said I'd *take* you there, not give away the location. That's the only thing keeping me alive right now."

Ingo raised a fist to strike, frothing at the maw in rage, but Lairro caught his wrist, snarling in Raptoran at him. Ingo yelled back, the guttural growls of the raptor's barbaric language grating on Raudius's ears. From the back and forth, it was difficult to see who was in charge here.

The yelling match ended with Lairro pushing Ingo away, who released Raudius and backed away to the dimly lit perimeter of the tent, his yellow eyes piercing the darkness like two hellish moons. Lairro drew his own weapon—a straight iron sword with a hilt adorned with beige feathers—and leveled it at Raudius. "This tauninaga...what else do you know about them?"

The raptors must know that the snake is traveling with Imayva. Ingo may be blinded by revenge, but this gray raptor might know the worth of my words, and what the girl carries. Raudius spit out green blood to clear his mouth, intentionally aiming for a rug instead of the sand floor. "The tauninaga travels with a human. A girl named Imayva. Ingo knows her as well, I believe."

Lairro glanced at Ingo, who returned a nod. *I need to convince them of my worth. If I don't, I'm dead.* Raudius continued, "This girl stole something of significant importance from the Oaken Legion. If she was working with the raptors who attacked the Hangman's Swing, then you may be interested in what she stole as well."

Lairro and Ingo snarled at each other in hushed Raptoran before turning back to Raudius. Lairro snarled, "So, let's say we chase after this snake and this girl, and we make it all the way south to Port Wenstnor. How exactly are you finding the snake?"

"The tauninaga like to remain hidden, but they keep a watchful eye on any Verdant cities that could potentially threaten their clans," Raudius said. "What they don't know is that the Oaken Legion keeps a watchful eye on them as well. The snakes have a hideout in Port Wenstnor that the tauninaga will seek refuge in, and I know exactly where to find it. I'm a native of the South Verdant, after all, from the Bastion of Life. I've got contacts all over the South Verdant."

Raudius held his gaze, still and unwavering, hoping the raptors didn't pry much more into what he said. His words about the tauninaga were true...in the *North* Verdant, where he was actually from. Everything else he said were outright lies. Raudius had never set foot in the South Verdant before, and was from the Bastion of Growth. He specifically chose the Bastion of Life because it was the most isolated, and historically had less conflicts with the raptors than the other three Bastions. *Which isn't saying much.*

Luckily, Ingo moved the conversation along with an impatient snarl. "Why are you traveling all on your own?"

Raudius had to tell the truth here. For the raptors to trust him, he had to show some vulnerability. "I was Felled, for my disastrous failures during the fight at Hangman's Swing." The truth stung to say out loud.

"What's Felled? Is that exiled?"

Raudius nodded. "Yes."

"Then just say exiled, barkscum."

The gray raptor interjected. "What kind of *failure*?"

Raudius tried to look as ashamed as he could—it was not hard, he was deeply ashamed, but he needed the raptors to know it. It was best that the raptors thought he was weaker than he was. "I was the one guarding the artifact when Imayva stole it. She knocked me out cold."

Ingo doubled over, cackling with laughter. The gray raptor remained cold-faced, but Raudius thought he saw a twitch of a fanged smile in the corners of his maw. The smile disappeared, though, as he studied Raudius with dangerously distrusting eyes.

As Ingo's laughter died, he and Lairro stared at each other for what seemed like an eon. Finally, Lairro spoke. "Fine, barkscum. Here is what this will look like. You will travel as our prisoner into the South Verdant, to Port Wenstnor. There, you help us find the girl and the artifact."

"And the filthy cave-crawling snake that murdered Spotch," Ingo cut in, his temper shifting quickly from laughing to deathly serious.

The gray raptor continued, "My name is Lairro, if you have not heard already. I am the chief of our tribe. You'll have your protection guaranteed on our journey together, as long as you behave."

He sheathed his sword, finally, and Raudius exhaled a sigh of relief. Lairro snarled, "If you deliver us the artifact"— he looked at Ingo— "and the tauninaga, we'll set you free unharmed. However, if you deliver us neither, then take comfort knowing you'll die on Verdant ground."

Lairro grabbed Raudius by his bindings and said, "I'll take care of the prisoner. Ingo, prepare a war party. We leave at dusk."

Ingo snarled with excitement and snapped his maw at Raudius. "Congratulations, soldier, you may be the first tree in history to betray the Oaken Legion." He laughed as he slunk out of the tent.

At least I'm alive and heading south toward the artifact. Raudius thought. Now, instead of minutes to live, he had until he got to Port Wenstnor to figure out how to survive his own lies.

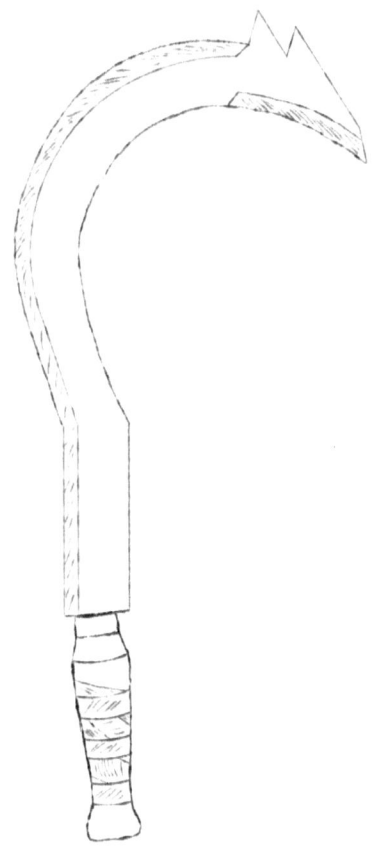

"*The combat sickle is the favored weapon among many tauninaga, especially the cave and jungle clans. Versatile and deadly, the curved blade also doubles as a climbing implement, helping the snakes navigate their challenging home environments. While it's true that the weapon is more like a scimitar than a sickle, due to the blade's location on the outside edge of the curve, the tauninaga have long since given up on correcting outsiders. It doesn't help that they do, in fact, use the weapon to harvest their crops every now and then.*"

—Excerpt from the *Treatise on Tauninagan Tactics,* written by Crottus Gelm from the Bastion of Life

Chapter 18

Up the Devaros

As the journey dragged on, Mayve established a routine aboard the Ferry. Each day began with a quick meal, dished out by Bolios at the galley, then she would laze around the ship before her shift on the oars. The most enjoyable part of the labor was working with Eiklo, who was an excellent conversationalist and was overjoyed to dive into long lectures on whatever Mayve asked about. She was still pondering whether or not to ask him about the Oasis Stone, against Srrith's wishes. Eiklo seemed like a trustworthy font of knowledge, but Srrith's warning of secrecy nagged at her, so she withheld for now.

After rowing, but before dinner, she and Srrith would train below deck. Srrith told her that she was improving every session, yet she always ended up bruised and sore, knocked flat on her back. They were half a week from Port Wenstnor, not nearly enough time to become as proficient a fighter as Srrith was. But still, Mayve felt far more prepared for what awaited her upriver.

Some days she pushed it from her mind, and others she thought of nothing else. Bringing down Faldmor would be easy. If anything, he was simply a lackey of the masked man. With Srrith's training, she was confident she could. The masked volcomancer was a different question. In the sheltered rage of her mind, it was easy to imagine driving her dagger through the eyehole of that dreaded mask. In practice, it would not be as easy.

The two had left Devar the day before the bramble attack. Chances were they were still on the river, just a day or two ahead of them, and the Ferry moved quickly with Ul'Varin-Rak strength at the oars. Mayve often found herself staring upriver, waiting for sails to appear around each bend, wondering what she'd do if she passed them on the river.

I will find Faldmor first. He will know where the volcomancer is, and I'll go from there. It was quite possible that neither would stay in Port Wenstnor, or even go their separate ways, if they had not already. In that case, she would catch their trail, then part ways with Srrith.

The Oasis Stone hung from her belt, a stark reminder of her last night in Devar. *I can barter this for any information I want.* Guilt lingered at the back of her mind, but she quickly stifled it. She had no need for it; it would only stop her from delivering justice. Whatever they planned on using those seeds for, no good would come of it.

The Great Seer said I was supposed to carry it. Why me? What does the Oasis Stone do that makes everyone want it? She gritted her teeth and focused on the masked man in her mind's eye. *Maybe if all goes well, I'll continue up to Savin Actai with Srrith, but I can't plan on it.*

The Ferry bustled with morning activity. A shriek echoed from somewhere far amongst the dunes as Screech explored the desert. The Ul'Varin-Rak clambered through the rigging, adjusting the sails back and forth. The wind was against them, forcing the skeletons to tack upriver and rely heavily on their oarsmen. Yesterday's shift had been especially grueling to Mayve and she was not looking forward to today.

The mood on board was souring. The passengers were getting sick of the river and the food, and the Ul'Varin-Rak were growing more reclusive by the day. Whispers ran through the ship. They were approaching the Devaros Cataracts, a maze of canyons and swift currents, and the closest point of the river to the Ysera Scorch Vent. Not too close, where the rivers run dry and the sky chokes on ash, but close enough that a far-wandering Vent beast would not be a surprise to see.

Usually loud and hot-tempered, Bolios grumbled under his breath as he dished out bowls of warm oatmeal. By the main mast, Kinglor and

Vanite were checking the ship's armory, inspecting the weapons and counting crossbow bolts. At the helm, Oribori and Vulinor were talking in hushed tones. Rumor had it they were not traveling as fast as they wanted to. It was best to get through the Cataracts without delay. The longer you lingered, the higher chance you'd be found.

The rhythmic thumping of the drum below deck signaled a shift change soon. Mayve scarfed down her meal and headed for her alcove. As she stopped at a water barrel for a quick drink before rowing, she noticed her reflection. Her long dark hair was too greasy for her liking. She would have to wash it in the river when she got the chance—it was considered poor manners to wash from the drinking barrel. However, her shoulders caught her eye as well. The passing days of intense rowing and training, along with the constant dehydration of the desert, had only made her lean, muscular build that much more prominent.

A polite cough behind her told her to stop admiring herself and move along. Embarrassed and almost late, she jogged to her rowing post and nearly bumped into Eiklo, walking in the opposite direction. She tapped his bony arm and said, "C'mon, the drums are about to sound."

Eiklo looked at her but didn't stop walking away. "Sorry, Mayve, you'll be with a different rower for the next few days. They need me elsewhere as we go through the Cataracts. It's closest to the Ysera Vent, so it's not uncommon we encounter a stray Vent beast."

"What? That's bullshit. What are you doing instead?"

"Find me later and I'll explain. Apologies again, I think you're with Drai. Not much of a talker." Eiklo hurried away, and Mayve saw him start the climb into the Ferry's crow's nest.

Sitting in Eiklo's usual spot was a stout Ul'Varin-Rak, wide-shouldered and strong-jawed, dressed in a sailor's white tunic, the edges of the cloth singed. Mayve slid onto the bench next to him and said, "Eiklo said your name is Drai. I'm Mayve, it's nice to meet you."

Drai stared back, silent, embers smoldering from the corners of his jaw. Mayve decided to give up on the pleasantries.

Rowing was beyond easy with Drai at the bench. The Ul'Varin-Rak, with his Ventish strength, moved the entire oar himself, leaving Mayve to simply hold on. As nice as Eiklo was, she was likely stronger than he was. The same could not be said for the Ul'Varin of the Scorch Vents.

As soon as the drum sounded the closing shift, Mayve scurried off the rowing bench without a word in case the Ul'Varin had anything to say about the one-sided workload. Drai remained perfectly quiet.

She had no time to find Eiklo and talk with him. Srrith was waiting in the hold for their daily training. As she stomped down the coarse, wooden stairs into the hold, the tauninaga hissed a greeting and tossed something at Mayve. Upon catching it, she discovered it was a wooden stick.

Srrith hissed, "That stick is about the length of the blade you carry. Seeing as there may be danger ahead, I see fit to move your lessons forward to accommodate your dagger."

Mayve swished the stick through the air. She imagined Faldmor on the other end of the knife, gurgling like the raptor she killed at the docks. Srrith reared to full height and bared her sickles. "Let's begin."

The tauninaga struck hard and fast, but Mayve was ready. It was a common opening that Srrith did, looking to end the fight before it began. She sidestepped the snake's fangs, then ducked underneath the following sickle slice.

Srrith spun around, swinging the other sickle at Mayve's head. Mayve raised the stick to parry the blow and successfully caught the outer blade of the sickle on the wood. Blow parried, Srrith relaxed her grip on the sickle just enough so it swiveled in her palm. In an instant, the sickle was now a hook curved around Mayve's weapon. She flicked her wrist and wrenched the stick out of Mayve's grasp, sending it skittering across the hold.

Mayve winced, ready for the scolding. There was no hesitation from Srrith. "Why did you parry that strike?"

Shrugging, Mayve said, "To stop your blade?"

"If you do not know, then say so. Doing otherwise will get you killed. There is no need to parry when you can evade entirely. Go get your blade."

Mayve trudged across the hold and returned with her dumb stick. "So when do I parry, then? Why give me this noble blade if I'm not supposed to use it?"

"When you put your blade between your flesh and their metal, you entrust your life entirely to your weapon, and a weapon is only as strong as the person who wields it. You must reserve your parries for two scenarios only. First, if you have no other choice. Backed into a corner, your blade may be your only defense. Second, if you have a plan to follow that parry with. If you bet your life on your blade, then you better follow with a killing blow."

The rest of the lesson consisted of slow, deliberate repetition of these parries, and a brief spar at the end that left Mayve utterly humiliated and peppered with splinters from the plank floor. At the end of it all, the dinner bell was a welcome relief.

* * *

The dinner line was long, so Mayve went to find Eiklo first. Not only was she curious about what he had been assigned to instead of rowing, she also wanted his opinion on what she might expect to face in Port Wenstnor. If anyone on board knew about strange plant monsters and shadowy volcomancy, it was likely Eiklo.

The Ul'Varin-Zul was nowhere to be found on deck. She worried that he was down in the Ul'Varin quarters—where passengers were forbidden—but remembered she saw him climb to the crow's nest. *He can't still be up there, though, it's been all day.*

She peered up at the crow's nest, but it was impossible to see in the fading twilight. However, it would be an easy climb up to check. That was something she deeply missed about living on the Ferry—she had no time to climb. She grabbed hold of the metal rungs hammered into the mast but only got a few feet off the ground before someone yelled after her.

Kinglor pushed over, waving her down. "Mayve! Off the mast! No passengers up the rigging."

Mayve faked a humble face and said, "Sorry, I just want to talk with Eiklo. Is he still up there?"

"He is, but you're not allowed. We can't have our passengers just crawling up the masts whenever they want. Someone's bound to lose their grip."

"I'm a good climber."

"Many people think they are."

Bolios called out from the galley, "Let her climb! It will be one less mouth to feed when she falls!"

"That's a great point," Mayve said, "Can I climb up if I promise to throw myself down?"

Kinglor looked unamused, his red orbs narrowing and a puff of flame curling from his jaw. Oribori cackled from nearby. "Let her climb, Kinglor. Eiklo's shift is almost done anyway."

Her skeletal jaws clamped shut as Vulinor approached. His voice rumbled like a quaking Vent. "I'll make the final call on who can climb my ship or not." He loomed over Mayve, flames licking his skull. "I've seen you training with Srrith. It's not often that a tauninaga trains a human how to fight like they do."

Mayve nodded, wondering why he was bringing it up. She decided to be polite about it. "Srrith is a deadly hunter. It's an honor to learn from her."

"In this shattered world, everyone should know how to wield a blade. As we approach the Devaros Cataracts, my fine vessel may be attacked by Vent beasts. Are you confident enough with your skills to come to the defense of my ship?"

Srrith would say no. "Absolutely."

Vulinor turned and walked away, waving over his shoulder. "Then climb away. Anyone willingly to put their life on the line for the Ferry can go where they please."

Mayve called after him, "Thank you, Captain! Don't worry, Kinglor, I'll be safe."

Kinglor grunted and shrugged. Oribori grinned, fire spreading up her bone jaw, which was more unsettling than friendly. Without wasting further time, Mayve clambered up the mast.

High above, the wind was stronger, and the sway of the ship was vastly more noticeable. Mayve's fingers clamped around the iron rungs as she rocked across the sky. *I could name a hundred dangerous things about climbing the Devaros Falls, but at least they never fucking moved.* Despite it, she was thrilled to be off the ground again, relishing the exhilarating feeling.

Reaching a trapdoor, she decided to climb up the outside of the crow's nest on a whim. At the very least, she'd scare the shit out of

Kinglor below if he was watching. Hooking her grip onto the metal frame of the crow's nest, she dangled in midair by her fingertips for a brief second before she hauled herself up and over the crow's nest wall.

A hooded figure sat cross-legged in the middle of the nest, not even watching the surrounding desert. As she fell into the crow's nest, they jolted up with a yell and scrambled away, nearly throwing themselves over the edge.

Underneath the hood, Mayve saw Eiklo's familiar skull, blue orbs in his eye sockets piercing the night. They were large and dim, flickering in intensity. A new Ul'Varin emotion that Mayve decided was fear or panic.

She put a finger to her lips and lied, "Shut up! I'm not supposed to be up here."

Eiklo's glowing blue orbs shrank in recognition, and he whispered back, "I know you're not supposed to be up here! By Varin's scroll, if I still had a heart you would've stopped it. Climb down now and maybe Vulinor won't throw you overboard."

"I need to talk to you, and it doesn't look like you're doing much up here."

"I'm on watch! What *else* would I be doing up here?"

"You're clearly shit at your job. You can't even see out of the nest, sitting like that."

"I'll explain if it will shut you up." Eiklo's panicked blue orbs were now focused into frustrated points, ice crystallizing over the sapphire embedded in his forehead.

Mayve sat down, legs crossed, and waved at him to go on. Despite the teasing, she was genuinely interested in learning.

Eiklo sighed and spoke in his lecturing tone. "Ul'Varin-Rak are incredibly strong, yes? It helps them survive on the Scorch Vents. Well, the Vent beasts that spawn from the Frost Vents are true leviathans, so much more gargantuan than anything that crawls from the Scorch Vents. The Ul'Varin-Zul have no chance of fighting them, even if we had the Rak's unnatural strength. So, we avoid them instead."

Eiklo resumed his meditative stance, closing his eyes. With no skin or eyelids, it simply looked like his blue orbs got snuffed out like candles. "If we focus, we can sense the presence of any creature created by a Vent, even from miles away. Captain Vulinor puts me up here whenever we go past the Ysera or Okanos Vents, just as a precaution. The Rak like to have a Zul around because it gives them an early warning of an attack."

Mayve raised her eyebrows, trying to wrap her head about what Eiklo said. "You know where Vent beasts are at all times?"

Eiklo opened one eye to look at Mayve again, one azure glow reappearing suddenly in his left eye socket. "It's more vague than that. It's a practiced skill and I don't practice very often, so it takes a lot of concentration to pinpoint the creatures. But I can sense them for several miles if I have plenty of time to focus. The most practiced Zul can use their powers not just to find Vent beasts but also calm them, even putting them to sleep. I'm nowhere close to that level of practice."

A thought occurred to Mayve. "Were you able to sense the bramble eldritches that attacked Devar?"

Eiklo responded, "I tried, but no. That means something else made them, which I think is even more terrifying."

Mayve took a deep breath, mentally preparing herself. "That's actually why I climbed up here to talk to you. I know more about the bramble eldritches than I think most people do, and I'd appreciate your scholarly opinion on the matter."

Frost crept across Eiklo's brow, as if he furrowed it. He cautiously leaned away but his eyes glowed with intense curiosity. "What do you mean?"

"I know where the brambles came from. I'm the one who planted them in the ground." Mayve leaned forward and clamped a hand over Eiklo's mouth before he could make any exclamation. His skull was freezing cold to the touch. "It's not what you think."

Eiklo lowered Mayve's hand and whispered, "It sure sounds like you caused the attack."

"*Depths below,* yes, I did, but it was an accident, I swear. If you haven't noticed already, I'm not wealthy, and that's not a recent change. I stole some seeds from this merchant, and my mother planted them in her garden. That was the night before the attack. Those creatures grew out of the garden in less than a day."

"This merchant just had enchanted, deadly seeds lying around for sale?" Eiklo pondered out loud, fishing for more information.

"No, no, no," Mayve waved his stupid question. "I stole them from a locked chest in the back of his tent. That's not important. Right now, I'm just curious about what they are and how they were made."

Eiklo still had more questions. "So are you some sort of fugitive, running from the law?"

"Maybe? It's more complicated than that, and I'm not going to tell you more."

"What does your mother think of all this?"

Cold sorrow rushed through her, and Mayve wondered if she wanted to say anything at all. She struggled to get the words out. "My mother didn't survive that night." Just saying the words out loud caused a flash of anger to ignite in her gut.

The words hung for a moment in the air, then Eiklo whispered, "I'm so sorry, Mayve. My mouth moves faster than my thoughts when I'm curious."

Mayve slouched against the opposite wall of the crow's nest, flustered and embarrassed. They sat in silence for a few seconds longer as Mayve gathered herself. "It's fine, you didn't know. Can you please tell me what you think is going on with those seeds?"

Eiklo thought for a moment. "The sad part of the world we live in is that there are plenty of things that could have made those seeds, but my most likely guess is volcomancy. There are infinite possibilities for someone's Natural Manifestation."

"There's more," Mayve said. "I was caught in the middle of the theft by the merchant, and someone else. *Something* else. Probably human by the shape of the body, but they wore a hood and a mask so I truly have no idea. Could even be an Ul'Varin. When they saw me stealing the seeds, shadows burst from their fingertips and chased me from the tent. They nearly hit me, and after I escaped, I saw the ends of my hair were stark white, like I was ninety years old."

Eiklo was stunned, streaks of rime curling from his eye sockets. Mayve prodded him with her boot. "Any thoughts on that?"

Eiklo shook his head in bewilderment. "Some sort of disease or death-based Natural Manifestation. Might even be an Innatural Manifestation if they're a powerful enough volcomancer. If they can twist the power of the Vents to cause that sort of harm, they are very dangerous. I'd run away from Devar too if I were you."

The skeleton was clearly trying to pick Mayve's brain to see if that's why she fled the city. She held her tongue.

Falling back into his train of thought, Eiklo said, "If their Natural Manifestation are these strange shadows, like you mentioned, then it's not out of the realm of possibility that they could have created the seeds. Like I said, everyone manifests the power of the Vents uniquely. This masked man may have a very powerful manifestation that allows him to kill people with shadows and create monstrous, flesh-seeking bramble eldritches. Perhaps they've mastered an Innatural Manifestation, and are combining it with their own Natural one."

Even if I had a more battle-worthy blade than this dagger, killing the masked volcomancer sounds near impossible. I'll have to catch him by surprise, or...

"Have you ever taught someone else volcomancy, Eiklo?"

The skeleton looked curious. "I haven't, but I suppose I could. Are you interested?"

"I'm considering it." Mayve thought about blasting a scorching hole through the masked man's chest with a bolt of lightning, or picking him off the ground and crushing him with unseen telekinetic force, his mask crunching along with his bones.

"Well, we don't have much time together, and a ship on open water is not the best place to learn. Perhaps we'll have a few days in Port Wenstnor where I can show you the basics. Ideally outside of town."

We'll have to see when we get there. I may be gone by then. "I might take you up on that, thanks, Eiklo. Appreciate all the information, it's helpful having a smart friend. It's an interesting change of pace than what I was used to in Devar."

"Glad I could help, even if it's all wild speculation. I hope it satisfied your curiosity." Eiklo stared at her inquisitively, blue orbs narrowed and ice creeping across his brow. "Is curiosity your only reason for asking?"

"Just curiosity. The memories of that night still cling to me. I just wanted some answers." Mayve didn't want to tell him the real reason. She was on her way to kill the masked volcomancer, and it sounded like she'd have to do it with a dagger through the back of his throat.

Eiklo peered over the edge of the crow's nest at his shipmates below. "Again, I'm happy to help, and I wish we could talk more, but I should get back to my watch and you should get back down before you're discovered."

"It's fine. They said I could come up here." Mayve grinned and lifted the trapdoor, swinging her boots back onto the iron rungs. "Bye, Eiklo."

"Varin's scrolls, you're such a pest." Eiklo settled back into his meditative stance. "Get out of here."

Mayve dropped back down the main mast. So far above the deck, with the wind and waves, it was impossible for anyone below to hear their conversation. *Anyone except the cave tauninaga.*

She swallowed a lump in her throat when she saw Srrith coiled on the deck. The snake was eating alone, rummaging in her tunnelsleeve, seemingly unaware of Mayve up in the rigging. *She loves to pretend to be oblivious. Phovus, I hope the wind and other passengers were loud enough to hide our conversation from her. If she heard any of that, what would she do?*

After all the training under Srrith's blades, the thought of facing the tauninaga as a true foe was just as terrifying as facing the masked volcomancer, and pure fear twisted her stomach.

She's here to protect me, she's made that clear. Will she still do so if she knows what I did?

Chapter 19

Across the Desert

Raudius breached the top of the dune, and was pulled into a stumbling descent down the sandy slope. Rope bound his wrists together, the bark beneath scraped smooth after days of travel. A long lead trailed in front of him, keeping him attached to a great pack beast.

The sand eroded beneath each step and he leaned backward to try and slow his descent, but the rope was too short for him to catch his balance. His shaky descent turned into a full tumble as the beast pulled him faster than his legs could manage. Cascading in a plume of sand, he slid to a halt next to the beast, partially buried in a sand-slide. The frigid night air soaked into the ground, the sand cold as snow on his bark.

Raudius wished he could sink deeper, that the dune would collapse behind him and entomb him forever beneath the desert. The rope snapped taut and the pack beast dragged him forward. He struggled to his feet, spitting out the globs of sand that ground between his teeth, and was met with uproarious laughter from the raptor war party. At least the starry sky greeted him each time he fell on his back. Without the canopies of the Verdant forests to hide them, the constellations of the desert stretched for eternity.

The raptor on the pack beast looked over their shoulder with a malicious smile, then leaned over in their saddle to whisper in the beast's ear. The beast let out a low bellow and quickened its pace. Raudius was forced into a jog to keep his footing, eventually tripping on the uneven sand and crashing down once again amidst more howls of laughter.

Despite his poor situation, Raudius held on to his determination. Although this travel was far less luxurious than taking a fishing boat trip upriver, he was still making his way to Port Wenstnor, toward Imayva and the artifact. So far, Lairro's promise of safe passage had held true. Ingo had pleaded to torture him, as expected of desert scum, but Lairro decided that they needed Raudius to be healthy. Port Wenstnor, even on the edge of the South Verdant, was not hospitable to raptors in the slightest.

Luckily for Raudius, neither had pressed for further information. He had never been to Port Wenstnor, and had never even set foot in the South Verdant. But the raptors did not need to know that. When he arrived in Port Wenstnor, he would ditch the raptors at his earliest convenience and continue his hunt for Imayva.

I doubt the raptors will let me simply look around freely, but they'll be in Legion territory. A few well-placed words to the right officials, and I'll be the hero who survived the raptors and warned the town. Worst case, I simply run for it and disappear into the Verdant.

The raptors must have some plan to stop him from running. *I'll simply have to adapt when I get there.*

"Tash, stop running the prisoner ragged! We're making good time, I refuse to stop and take care of a green-cursed tree because you couldn't control yourself," Ingo called back to the gold-scaled, maroon-feathered raptor sitting on the pack beast.

Tash snapped back, "C'mon Ingo, I think it's hungry. It keeps falling over to eat sand." She looked back at Raudius and ran her tongue over her sharp teeth.

Fuck these cretins. Still, it was a terrifying sight for Raudius to walk alongside a war party. How many times had a group just like this stepped from sand into forest, raiding the Verdant and slaughtering the Legion?

Ingo and Lairro rode at the front of the pack, Ingo upon his saber-tooth and Lairro upon a dust-colored, four-legged bird with a long neck. The orange raptor from the healer's hut was there too, walking in the middle of the pack.

There were nine raptors total, including Tash. Some rode animals while others walked on the outskirts, treading across the tops of the dunes and keeping vigilant watch of the surrounding desert. From what Raudius gathered, every raptor had their own animal to look after, from huge pack beasts to tiny birds. One even had a little mouse that sat on their shoulder. The only unpaired animal was a lone sabertooth, plodding by itself on the outskirts of the war party. On the horizon, a void of deep black marked the Scorch Vent of Ysera, its ashen column hiding the stars.

Someone cleared their throat next to him, interrupting his thoughts. He looked to see the orange raptor, holding out a waterskin. He wore a leather cuirass with a bandolier full of stoppered vials and glass bottles, along with several pouches on his belt that overflowed with strands of plants and herbs. Remembering the toxic arrowhead, Raudius eyed the orange raptor suspiciously before tentatively accepting. "This won't paralyze me again, will it?"

"Nope, just water. We need you in good health if we're gonna make good time to Port Wenstnor." The raptor seemed to be studying Raudius. "Speaking of that, though, have you noticed any lasting side effects of the paralysis?"

Disgruntled, Raudius muttered, "Like what?"

The lizard shrugged. "I don't know, that's why I ask. Numbness, blurry vision, lingering paralysis?"

Raudius grunted. "A side effect of your paralysis poison is lingering paralysis? That's just the main effect."

"Some people experience it in waves afterward. But I see your point. I'll take that as a no for side effects." The raptor looked quite pleased with himself, orange feathers on his nape fluffed up.

Raudius gulped down the warm water. He hadn't realized how much he needed it until the water touched his parched bark, then suddenly he couldn't stop himself. He upended the waterskin, making sure to gulp as much as possible before the raptor demanded it back. The more water he drank, the less there would be for the raptors.

Thankfully, the raptor made no attempts to take the waterskin from him.

"If you need more, try to get my attention. We should have plenty for our journey. We each have our own waterskin, and Tash's courg here is carrying a full barrel." He patted the courg on its rough, beige hide, and the huge creature let out a snort.

Raudius pointed his bound hands at the lone sabertooth prowling the outskirts. "That one's not carrying anything and no one's riding it. Why keep it around?"

The raptor sighed. "That was Spotch's bond. Poor cat doesn't know what to do with itself. It's heartbreaking, but I reckon it'll be dead in a couple days. Bonded animals don't last long after their raptor dies."

They pointed to the front of the caravan. "It's actually from the same litter as Ingo's. He and Spotch did their Bonding Hunt together and found the cubs out in the Quaking Cliffs. It's just sticking with its pack for now."

Nothing the raptor said made any sense to Raudius. Tash yelled off the top of her courg, "Getting awfully chatty with the tree, Cindri."

The orange raptor yelled back, "Relax, Tash, just trying to cure my boredom." Finally learning the raptor's name, Raudius addressed him as such. "You know Ingo and Spotch well, Cindri?"

Cindri replied, "I would hope so, I'm their younger brother." His eyes drifted to the lone sabertooth, prowling across the top of a dune several hundred feet away. Its distinct shape was silhouetted against the endless expanse of stars. "I was, I mean. I still am, but...you know."

Raudius almost let words for sympathy slip out of his mouth, but caught them on his tongue at the last minute. *Good riddance.* He remembered the smell of Spotch's rancid breath when the lizard held a knife to his throat and relieved him of his coin, and how the raptor twins hacked away at his fellow soldiers in the Hangman's Swing, Verdant's Bane coursing through their veins in a bloody frenzy. *These raptors are savages and nothing more.*

He had never met a raptor as talkative as Cindri however. If he survived this ordeal, then he could bring any information he learned back to the Legion. They would hail him as an intrepid scholar, gathering new knowledge behind enemy lines. He asked Cindri, "Is Ingo the leader here?"

"Lairro is the chief. The title might have gone to Ingo or Spotch, but they spend too much time in Devar. Besides, they're twins. You gonna make one of them chief and not the other? Or have two chiefs that argue all the time? Lairro was the better choice."

Ingo yelled something in Raptoran to the whole party and Cindri cut himself off. "Gotta go. Keep an eye out for side effects. I'll check in later, I've been put in charge of your well-being. Here." He uncorked a vial from his bandolier and extended it to Raudius.

Raudius reached to grab it and at the last second Cindri yanked the vial away, narrowing his eyes at Raudius. They traded suspicious glances, and Cindri said, "This tincture mitigates water loss, when drunk by raptors. I don't actually know if it works on trees. Could be deadly. You can have it if you want, though."

Raudius frowned and shook his head. "I'll pass."

Cindri shrugged and gingerly pressed the vial back in its holster, then ran off to help Ingo with whatever he called for, leaving Raudius alone with Tash and her courg once again.

It was hours more of walking before they made camp. Not once did the raptors stop. As the dark blue sky slowly transformed to light blue, and the stars twinkled out one by one, the caravan stopped and Lairro started snarling commands. Raudius silently wished that he had been taught the language at some point in his early life. It would have made this situation slightly more bearable. *Unfortunately I don't think any of my teachers foresaw I would end up here.*

Nestled in the valley between dunes, the raptors hustled at break-neck speed, pitching tents and stowing supplies. Raudius noticed that no one was tending to the animals. Not only that, no one even bothered to secure them so that they could not escape.

The only creature that was properly secured was Raudius, whose lead remained firmly attached to the courg. As Tash dismounted, she patted the courg and snarled at Raudius, wearing a shit-eating grin, "If you so much as touch Borgo, he'll stomp you to a pulp."

Raudius replied as calmly as possible, "Borgo is a stupid name."

Tash growled and took a step toward Raudius, stopping when

Lairro yelled an order at her. The maroon raptor shot a death glare at the tree, then began unloading supplies from Borgo's back.

Borgo. Raudius seethed. *I'm bound to Borgo the fucking courg.*

Within a few minutes, a massive awning was constructed against a dune's slope, the sand-patterned cloth blending perfectly to its surroundings. Unlike the colorful tents at the tribe's main camp, the war party used exclusively rock- and sand-colored tones on their shelters.

In almost no time at all, and with even less communication, the raptors constructed a perfect camp, hidden in the dunes. As a soldier, Raudius recognized the clear chain of command going through the group. Lairro and Ingo barked orders at their warriors while carrying out their own tasks, but orders were minimal as each raptor did their work with militaristic efficiency. Lairro clearly trusted Ingo's judgment enough that he was fine letting Ingo give orders, yet Ingo never questioned a direct order from Lairro or shouted anything contradictory.

Raudius hated that he was impressed. He never expected these desert savages to rival the coordination of the Oaken Legion.

Soon after the camp was set, the raptors gathered around Cindri, who dispensed vials and precise portions of herbs to each lizard. Another raptor opened a sack that Borgo had been carrying and tossed small carcasses to each raptor. As the sun peeked above the dunes, the raptors devoured their dinner. The snarling conversation and ripping of meat was entirely different from the camp sounds Raudius was used to, but it invoked the same feeling. *Comradery.* Something the tree missed more by the minute.

Much to his surprise, the animals gathered around the raptors too. Ingo threw his sabertooth a carcass and scratched it behind the ears as it tore its dinner to pieces. Lairro's strange bird creature and Borgo shared a bag of thorny desert plants. A mouse scurried out of one raptor's bag, standing upright on the raptor's shoulder and squeaking in their ear. A bird perched on another raptor's shoulder, its throat bulging as it gulped down a desert shrew. Each animal here was family to these raptors, and also to each other?

That hawk should be eating that mouse. Ingo's sabertooth should be hunting Tash's courg. Cindri mentioned something called bonding—is this an effect of that? I'll have to find out more for my return to the Legion.

Raudius was dragged unwillingly closer to the gathering by Borgo, and did his best to keep his distance. The raptors ignored him. None so much as spared a glance in his direction, except for Cindri, who made brief eye contact but no signs of acknowledgment. As the raptors and their animals shared dinner, Raudius lay in the cold sand, hungry and exhausted. The first hint of the sun's heat drifted onto him like a silken blanket, and he knew sleep would be in short supply today.

As fast as they set up camp, the raptors disappeared into their tents. The animals not sleeping inside wandered to find their own beds for the day, most retreating to the awning that the raptors had set up. It provided a comfortable blanket of shade for the larger creatures like Borgo, who led Raudius across the sands to the awning and thudded onto the sand with a grunt.

The dumb creature towered above Raudius, standing nearly eight feet tall at the highest arch in its back. Its beige, wrinkly skin was weathered by the sun, naked except for a line of thick fur that ran along its spine from head to tail. Its four thick feet crushed the sand beneath it, and sail-like ears flanked a row of sharp horns that ran down its snout. Raudius toyed with the idea of trying to ride Borgo away, but after seeing how connected the animals were to their raptors, he had no doubt that Borgo would trample him to pulp if he so much as touched him.

As the sun rose, Cindri prowled over from the main camp, carrying something familiar: Raudius's old pack, brown cloth and silver buckles with elk-leather straps, which Raudius believed had been thrown into the river with the rest of his equipment. He tossed it to Raudius and said, "We kept this in-case you were carrying anything valuable. Turns out you're as poor as a beggar, but you do have plenty of rations in there."

Raudius ripped open his bag, digging hungrily into the dried vegetables and stale bread. He had not eaten since leaving the boat, and the exhausting hike through the desert had only deepened his starvation. Also inside were his deflated coin purse and canteen, still full.

As he tore into his meal, Cindri kept talking. "I took a look at your food. Lots of plants I haven't seen before in there. I'm only really familiar with desert plants, and a few that live on the border between the

desert and the Verdants, so I'm not sure I can find a substitute. Can you
ration yourself so we don't have to find you more food out here? Lucky
for you, there might be enough in there to make it to the Verdant."

Raudius chose to stuff his face with more food instead of responding. Cindri sat in the sand across from him, giving Borgo a firm pat on
his rump. Despite not receiving an answer, Cindri asked, "Are there any
plants that the Legion eats to help sleep or stay awake? What about
anything that stops water evaporation? That last one might be wishful
thinking."

Raudius swallowed his food and took another mouthful. Cindri
kept talking. "I ask because the desert heat can make it very difficult to
sleep, so when we're out in the open desert like this we take pinches of
sandroot pulp and rock's blood to lower our body temperature. Helps
us keep cool. It's highly poisonous in large doses but just the right
amount and it works wonders. If you know of any concoctions that are
safe for the Legion, I'll prepare some for you."

The tree muttered through his food, "None of that sounds familiar,
but boiled night clovers are good for sleep. Doubt you have it."

Cindri sighed. "You're right, I don't have any of that. If you want to
be the first ever soldier of the Oaken Legion to try sandroot pulp, be my
guest."

"No." Raudius rolled on his side and turned his back to Cindri,
clutching his pack to his chest to keep it from thieving claws. He felt
Cindri's presence linger for a moment, then heard the crunch of sand as
the raptor turned and slunk back to their camp. A breeze rushed
through, unclogging the stench of animal from his nose. The wind was
tepid and warm, and Raudius knew the desert heat would soon crash
upon him like a tidal wave. He needed to fall asleep before it came, but
his anger kept him anchored awake.

Alone in the desert, surrounded by savages and their beasts. If he did
not escape in Port Wenstnor, they'd kill him. Chances were high they'd
kill him long before that, and no one was coming to save him. Tossing in
the sand, Raudius made himself a promise. *I'll die like a soldier, no
matter what. I will snap their bones with my bare hands as they hack me
down. Felled or not, they will know the fury of the Legion.*

Somewhere in the dunes, the roar of a lone sabertooth carried over the sand, calling for a companion that would never answer.

Chapter 20

The Cataracts

S rrith had not lost control of her dreams in many years. When she wove her sfa-zrueen, she commanded her subconscious to grasp the edges of reality and weave them together. She chose when to dream, opening her mind in the depths of unconsciousness.

It was the uncontrollable dreams that Srrith avoided. The dreams that lurked in the dark forest of her consciousness. The ones that flitted in and out of her sleeping mind, leaving images and emotions both unwanted, that wrangled her subconscious and swept her away on grand, incomprehensible journeys.

Srrith did not dream those dreams anymore. She had long since steeled her mind against unwanted intruders. It was a necessity for Srrith. Since she was a young snake, the only dreams that hunted for her in the dark hours of the night were nightmares. She had learned to listen to her sleeping mind, to evade the nightmares before they found her. For those who could weave their dreams into reality, nightmares could be deadly, and not just for the sleeping snake.

This particular nightmare struck with ferocity, arriving so suddenly and without warning that it scattered her practiced defenses. Heart-racing terror condensed into a single scene, dissipating the void of sleep. She found herself lost in a dark forest, no horizon or clearing in sight. The trees pressed in, scraping her scales as she slithered between the thin trunks. Her sickles dripped with blood. The hideous screams of a thousand bramble eldritches shattered her hearing like glass.

Srrith snapped awake, breath trapped in her throat. The nightmare lingered in her mind, deeply unsettling. Was it the start of more to come? Such dreams used to be a nightly occurrence for a young Srrith. *I thought I had them under control. Omaea's scales, I must make haste back to Alactashi Sen, lest these nightmares grow. She will know what to do.* Almost frantic, she looked around the hold for any shadows stretching into places they should not be.

Satisfied her nightmare had not leaked into reality, she let go of her held breathe and started her day, checking her gear and adjusting the tight packing of her tunnelsleeve—an important habit to keep, even this far above the Ralveran Caverns.

As the nightmare faded away, she remembered her troubles in the waking world—she had heard every word of Mayve's conversation with Eiklo the night before. *The attack on Devar. It was all Mayve's fault.*

She should have seen it. She *had* seen it. The destroyed dwelling, the churned soil in the garden behind it, the fact alone that a bramble eldritch somehow found its way through the Darkmist Tunnels to Mayve's dwelling. *I am being too harsh. It is not Mayve's fault. The human did not know what she was doing when she stole those seeds. Then why does she still withhold the truth?* Srrith found she was clenching her jaw, and flexed away the anxiety, fangs bared. *I must protect her, but how can I do so when she hides such secrets?*

Monstrous seeds, and a masked volcomancer with a manifestation eerily similar to my sfa-zrueen, responsible for it all. Srrith remembered the spike of fear in Mayve's heart rate when the human first saw her shadows. *I believed her to be afraid of me, as many are. But it was not so. She was afraid of who she saw use the shadows before.*

Srrith hissed a long sigh, instinctively flaring her hood. *Mayve speaks of this masked volcomancer as if they are not part of her past, but part of her future. I must confront her, before she puts us in grave danger.*

Shouts rang out from above deck. Grabbing her sickles, Srrith slung the sheaths over her back and slithered up into the morning sun. It was close to noon already. Oversleeping was not something Srrith did often, and this troubled her even more.

A tide of passengers heading for the hold met her at the top of the stairs and she pushed through to the main deck. The oarsmen were carrying the vessel forward at full speed, while any Ul'Varin-Rak not on the oars were rushing to Oribori. The quartermaster was distributing weapons from below deck—spears, axes, swords, all far larger than normal weapons, having been forged with the strength of the Ul'Varin-Rak in mind.

Despite the crew on full oars, the boat was not moving very quickly. They were rowing through a desert canyon, with red-and-white sandstone walls towering on either side. The water was deep, dark blue, opaque and waveless as it funneled through the canyon. The sunlight's reflection off the river danced along the rock walls, and the cliffs were high enough that the crew in the rigging could see over the canyon wall, but anyone on the deck was blind to what was happening above.

She reared over the crowd, searching for Captain Vulinor, and spotted the skeleton steering the boat at the helm with Screech perched next to him, staring at the horizon. Slithering to the helm, she waited with tense patience for his attention. Whatever was happening, he would have orders for her. Deep down, she had a sinking suspicion, seeing the eternal smoke of Ysera Vent rise over the edge of the canyon, like ink spilled across the blue sky.

Vulinor finished speaking with Kinglor and handed the helm over to him to steer, then finally turned his attention to the tauninaga. He spoke firmly and to the point. "Srrith, our luck has run out. The Devaros Cataracts are fast-moving and treacherous, dangerous enough in their own right. I thought we had a chance to get through without incident, but reports have informed me that a Vent beast has changed course, and is heading this way. It must have seen our sails from some distance." He turned to a skeleton who was seated at the aft of the ship and intensely concentrating on the horizon. "Eiklo, no changes?"

The skeleton did not raise its head, but Srrith recognized the voice as the Ul'Varin-Zul who Mayve was talking to last night. The knot of anxiety twisted harder in Srrith's chest just thinking about their conversation.

"One *aer* still, sir, fast approaching," Eiklo said. "It'll be over the canyon in a few minutes."

"There you have it," Vulinor stated, fire dancing across his skull. "Ready your weapons. Eiklo said this creature is twice the size of Screech or more; it will scuttle the Ferry if we don't stop it."

Oribori arrived carrying a saddle of unfamiliar design. Vulinor hoisted it from her and said, "I must prepare. Srrith, may your blades find glory! Screech, to me!" The phoenix flattened itself on the deck and Vulinor strapped the saddle to her back. Srrith hurried away. She needed to find Mayve.

The deck was in chaos. Passengers scrambled to get below deck. If the ship sank in these treacherous waters, that hold would quickly become their tomb, but if they stayed on deck, they could be ripped apart by a Vent beast. Srrith could not decide which was worse.

Mayve was still nowhere to be seen. Knowing the human, there was no way she had retreated to the safety of the lower decks. *Sand-cursed girl. The Great Seer should have foreseen a well-mannered girl or a calm girl, instead of the green-eyed, reckless one.*

A roar sounded from overhead, above the lip of the canyon wall. The Ferry reverberated with the roar, the noise shuddering across the deck and through the crowd. Vanite, high in the crow's nest, shouted down, "*Aer*, a hundred yards!" Srrith heard the beating of leathery wings long before anyone else did.

The last of the passengers disappeared into the hold and the visibility on deck cleared. The oarsmen were surging full speed ahead, hoping to get the Ferry to a less treacherous stretch of the Cataracts. Srrith searched for Mayve amongst the ranks, but it looked to be only skeletons manning the oars. The Ferry needed to move as fast as possible and that meant filling every rowing alcove with Raks.

The rest of the Ul'Varin were readying their weapons on deck. Most were outfitted with crossbows, aimed in all directions at the sky. All were armed with a blade, in case the beast got close enough to cut. They held an arsenal of axes and swords, as well as spears and glaives to keep the Vent beasts at bay.

Another roar drowned out the clamor, much closer this time. Srrith scanned frantically for Mayve and finally saw the human standing amongst the Ul'Varin ranks holding a crossbow. *Vent-cursed girl is going to kill herself.* The tauninaga hurried across the deck, weaving through the Ul'Varin soldiers, and grabbed Mayve on the shoulder.

"Get below deck, now. I will not ask again."

Mayve pushed the tauninaga's hand off her shoulder. "Why? I need to know how to fight, what better way than this?"

"There's a difference between learning to swim and diving into a hurricane!" Srrith's hood flared and she towered over Mayve, exerting her presence.

"No. I *need* to learn to fight. This is how I do that." Mayve held her gaze defiantly.

Srrith dropped her voice to a furious hiss and leaned in close to whisper in the human's ear. "Then give me the Oasis Stone so I don't have to pry it off your corpse."

Mayve whispered back, "After this fight, I'll skip the Stone into the river. If you want it, you can fish for it later."

The tauninaga reared over Mayve and bared her fangs. For a split second, she saw a sliver of fear break the human's stare, and she instantly regretted her words. Then a roar blasted across the ship like a battle horn. A gale of wind swept downriver and boulders crumbled off the walls as an enormous Vent beast landed on the cliff's edge.

Talons as large as swords dug into the rock as the Vent beast perched above the Ferry. Bat-like leathery wings spanned nearly half the length of the Ferry, and the beast was clad neck-down in soot-soaked burgundy scales. A mane of tangled brown fur grew from the back of its disfigured head, vaguely reminiscent of a horse but with the long mouth of a crocodile. A twisted mess of crimson antlers grew from behind its ears, wrapping like vines around a pair of devilish horns that sprouted from the top of its skull. At the end of a long, fleshy tail was a maul of sturdy, pale bone, lethal spikes protruding in every direction.

The Vent beast slammed its tail into the ground, sending a shower of rubble down onto the boat, and it let loose another roar that blasted through the canyon like a shock-wave, pounding in Srrith's skull.

Depths below...that one is huge. Srrith had only fought a few Vent beasts in her years, but never anything this large. These were the creatures that brought the apocalypse.

"Fire!" Vulinor's booming order matched the roar of the Vent beast, and a chorus of crossbow bolts whistled into the air. Most deflected harmlessly off the Vent beast's scales, but some found purchase in its fleshy neck and many more punctured through its leathery wings.

The beast propelled itself into the air with one gust of its gargantuan wings and was engulfed in flame as it rose, Screech exhaling a plume of white-hot flame as she chased it upward. Vulinor, riding high in Screech's saddle, held her reins with one hand and wielded a long spear in the other.

Her shriek piercing Srrith's ears, Screech unleashed another stream of white-hot fire into the beast's face. As it was blinded, Vulinor struck. The heavy spearhead glanced off the beast's thick skull with a resounding crack. Screech and Vulinor tore away into the sky as the beast's jaws snapped shut around empty air.

"Fire!" Vulinor's order echoed down like a god's command. Srrith glanced at Mayve, who was still clumsily reloading her crossbow, studying the other Ul'Varin as they deftly reloaded their bolts. A second chorus of deadly whistles cut toward the beast. The bolts turned to black specks in the blue sky, then the Vent beast faltered midair as its wings were shredded once again. Srrith closed her hearing as tight as she could. The sounds of battle were smashing against her mind, trying to force their way through her skull.

Vulinor and the monster fought ferociously high above the canyon. He and Screech twisted and dove around the Vent beast, Vulinor prodding the monster with his spear, embers trailing from Screech's wings. One snap from its jaws or slash from its talons would spell certain death for either of them, but Screech always seemed to bank just out of the beast's reach. When the crossbows were loaded for another volley, Vulinor piloted Screech away in a wide arc, shouting the command to fire. The timing was so precise it was clear to Srrith he knew by instinct exactly how long it took his crew to reload. The bolts would disappear into the blue sky, desperately finding purchase in the creature's hide, then Vulinor would charge again.

The dance in the sky only continued for so long. The beast spun unexpectedly, slamming Screech with an outstretched wing. Screech and Vulinor tumbled away in a spiral of embers, disappearing from the canyon's narrow field of view. The Vent beast roared and dove toward the boat.

The Ul'Varin let loose another volley but the bolts did nothing to stop the beast's descent. "Draw blades!" Oribori yelled, answered by the singing of steel and scraping of iron. Srrith drew her sickles and coiled, ready to spring in any direction needed. Mayve drew her dagger and gripped it with white knuckles, nervous resolve painted across her face. The Vent beast tucked its wings and opened its talons, ready to crash into the Ferry at a meteoric speed.

A flash of red-and-orange fire slammed into the Vent beast just before it fell below the canyon cliffs. Vulinor and Screech, soaring low across the ground, shot into view and crashed into the beast with a scream. The Vent beast's murderous dive was diverted into the canyon wall, sending another avalanche of rubble down onto the vessel. The Ferry rocked violently to its port side as Screech and the Vent beast, locked in a fiery spiral, crash-landed on the deck, beak and crocodile maw snapping at each other with primal fury.

As they fell, Vulinor leapt from Screech's back, thudding to the deck and rolling to his feet. The mainmast splintered and snapped as the entwined beasts thrashed into it, Ul'Varin in the rigging leaping for safety.

With a blood-curdling roar, the Vent beast pinned Screech beneath its talons, and clamped its crocodilian jaws around Screech's neck. The phoenix struggled wildly, thrashing and breathing fire to no avail. With a crunch, Screech's body went limp, her feathers smoldering to ash. Like dry parchment catching a spark, Screech burned away into a flash fire of embers and ash.

Fire licked the deck, creeping around the feet of the Vent beast. Its teeth smoked as Screech's blood sizzled away, and it eyed the crew hungrily. Vulinor was already planted between his crew and the Vent beast, booming more orders. His spear was tossed aside, his gauntlets starting to glow with heat. "Contain! Keep it encircled. Eiklo, put it to sleep!"

Eiklo stammered, "I don't think I can, it's too—"

Vulinor punched his gauntlets together, the metal heating from red-hot to bright white. "That's an order! Everyone, forward!"

"For Varin's glory!" the Ul'Varin-Rak yelled in unison, charging forward. The Vent beast stampeded to meet them, snapping its jaws around one skeleton and hurling them into their crewmates, while its spiky maul of a tail slammed another skeleton into the deck, crunching their bones into shards.

Mayve charged forward and Srrith caught her with her tail. *She won't run for safety, but hopefully she'll listen to other reason.* "Do not interfere with Ul'Varin tactics. You will only hinder them, as will I. We wait as backup." Mayve relented and hung back with the tauninaga, dagger ready and pointed at the beast, keeping her balance as the ship rocked.

The Ul'Varin circled the Vent beast. When it attacked at one side of the circle, those skeletons would back away while the others advanced, landing opportunistic strikes on its exposed flanks. The monsters spun wildly, forcing a swath of the Ul'Varin to hit the deck to avoid its maul tail. In the chaos, Vulinor ran forward and slid underneath the thrashing beast. Instead of delivering a blow to the hard scales of its underside, he grabbed a faint glowing object from Screech's ashes and leapt to safety as its tail splintered the deck where he was.

Eiklo stood on the outskirts of the formation, hands outstretched toward the beast with no weapon, his head bowed in concentration. Vulinor yelled from the flank, "Put it down, Eiklo! Soon!"

Eiklo pushed his empty palms toward the creature, exerting an unseen force through the air. The creature lunged and caught an Ul'Varin crew member by the leg, dragging them out of formation. With a whip of its neck, it flung the Ul'Varin into the nearby oarsmen alcove, where the skeleton crashed in an explosion of wooden splinters.

Eiklo gripped his skull in one hand and reached for the Vent beast with his other palm. He gritted his teeth together, huge crystals of frost growing from his skull as he pushed his will against the beast's. Mid-lunge, the creature froze. It calmly looked over the shoulders of the Ul'Varin crew and locked eyes with Eiklo. Its breathing steadied, its muscles relaxed. Its rage and malice melted away, jaw closing and tail lowering to the deck, at peace with its surroundings. With unspoken coordination, Vulinor charged for the creature's exposed, pacified neck.

With an exhausted cry, the ice crystals on Eiklo's bones shattered and he collapsed. In an instant, anger rushed back to the Vent beast's eyes. It burst upward with a furious roar, its wings knocking the Ul'Varin back. Lowering its antler-horns, it rammed the Ul'Varin front-lines. The horns pierced an unfortunate sailor, and it whipped its head back, throwing the skeleton into the rigging, where they hit the foremast with a sickening crack of timber and bone.

Furious, the Vent beast set its sights on the skeleton who invaded its mind, and sprinted at Eiklo in a hellish gallop, its crocodile-horse snout foaming with rage. Eiklo stumbled upright as the beast leapt, then its jaws snapped shut around empty air. Gone from Srrith's side, Mayve tackled Eiklo out of harm's way. Together they hit the deck hard, tumbling away from the Vent beast's gnarled teeth.

Before the beast could turn upon them, Srrith rushed in. She coiled and struck toward the creature's wing, planting her sickles' razor sharp points into the thin, leathery flesh and dragging downward. With a horrendous ripping sound, the tauninaga opened two long slashes in the beast's wing.

The beast screamed in pain and spun on her. Mayve, who had just rolled back onto her feet, flattened herself on the deck to avoid the tail as it rushed overhead. Another Ul'Varin getting back on their feet was not so lucky. The maul at the end of the tail caught them full force, scattering them in an explosion of bone shards.

Srrith leapt backward as the Vent beast's jaws snapped shut in the air where she just was. Spinning as she retreated, she always kept a slashing blade between her and the Vent beast. The Ul'Varin attacked from either flank, trying to break through its hard scales. Sparks flew as their weapons smashed into the Vent beast's hide with the strength of ten men, blood spilling onto the deck. The Vent beast whipped around, thrashing wildly to rid itself of the pests surrounding it.

Suddenly, its head was slammed into the deck as Captain Vulinor dropped from the rigging onto the back of its neck. He grasped its horns with his white-hot gauntlets, smoke hissing from his grasp. With a roar of his own, he twisted the Vent beast's head, holding on for dear life as the monsters flailed. The captain swung his legs over the creature's neck and used every ounce of his strength to slam the creature's head to the floor.

Srrith saw her opportunity and leapt forward to strike at the beast's incapacitated head. Out of the corner of her vision, she saw Mayve running forward as well. The creature's maul tail thrashed wildly and its wings pummeled the deck, but the young human wove through the chaos like a wraith. She somersaulted over the tail as it swung low, then slid underneath the base of the creature's wing as it slammed to the deck. Dagger raised, she drove it toward the creature's eye. It was then Srrith heard something before everyone else. A subtle but sickening crack—one of the beast's horns snapped in half and Vulinor lost his grip.

With terrifying speed, the beast whipped toward Mayve and snapped its jaws shut. Srrith uncoiled the instant before, slamming her shoulder into Mayve, sending the human tumbling away. She heard the wind get knocked out of Mayve's lungs, and then heard the crunch of her own bones as the Vent beast sunk its fangs deep into her flesh.

Blinding pain smashed all her senses to pieces and she screamed. Then she was sailing through the air, bouncing across the Ferry's deck, her left arm limp and useless. Something heavy crashed next to her, almost crushing her.

Srrith tried to stand, coiling her lower half and pushing up with her right arm. Her left arm felt like it was on fire, unresponsive nerves screaming in agony. Someone wrenched her to her feet and she saw Vulinor through blurry vision. "Up, Srrith! Get up! Move!"

Her eyes focused on the Vent beast. The constant attacks of the Ul'Varin had shredded its bat wings to bloody tatters, and one of its wings looked completely broken. The only way it was getting off the boat was as a corpse, and it was taking as many of them with it as possible.

She saw Eiklo pulling Mayve to her feet, the human bruised but unharmed. *Thank Omaea's scales.* More pain shot through her arm, blood pouring from deep fang marks in her shoulder—a sacrifice for saving Mayve's life once again.

The Vent beast roared, dragging its maul tail down an entire row of oarsmen, the Ul'Varin flattening into the alcove to avoid evisceration. Srrith watched helplessly as both Mayve and Eiklo were caught by the midsection of the tail and flung off the back of the Ferry. The swift canyon currents swallowed them in an instant.

Srrith had no time to think. She couldn't think. The boat listed dangerously starboard, drifting closer to the cliff face. Kinglor, at the helm of the vessel, shouted to the remaining oarsmen, correcting their path. Despite the rampaging Vent beast, they rowed with unwavering determination. If the boat sank against the canyon wall, every passenger would perish.

Vulinor looked at Srrith and asked, "Can you still fight?"

Srrith lifted a sickle in the one arm that could carry it and pointed it at the monster. "Follow two paces behind me, Captain. I will get you an opening."

The Ferry barreled closer and closer to the canyon wall. As the rocks loomed, Vulinor shouted, "For Varin! For glory!" The war cry erupted from the skeletons, and Srrith charged with them.

Screaming at the beast, she flashed her sickle in the air. The Vent beast charged forward, its powerful jaws snapping shut inches from her as the tauninaga coiled and sprang backward, staying tactically outside the creature's reach. Its breath was utterly rancid, and its maw was so dangerously close she saw her own blood coating its fangs. Enraged, the beast turned and swung its tail maul at Srrith. Stepping into the swing, Srrith coiled down and met it with her blade.

The honed steel sliced through the Vent beast's fleshy tail at the base of the maul. The bone maul crashed to the deck behind her, splintering the wood beneath it, and the Vent beast screamed as its tail whipped around like a decapitated eel. Srrith collapsed to the deck, vision fading to black as she quickly lost blood.

Without hesitation, Vulinor ran forward and hoisted the maul with both gauntlets. As the beast whirled around and lunged at Srrith, eyes bloodshot with Vent-like rage, Vulinor brought the maul over his head and slammed it down on the beast's skull. The Vent beast was crushed to the deck, blood spurting from between its broken scales, and it tried to rise with a terrifying scream. The Ul'Varin crew leapt onto the beast, pinning it down, and Vulinor brought the maul down again and again, until the Vent beast's skull was crushed to pulp and its thrashing body fell limp.

Srrith was in a daze. The chaos subsided around her, skeletons running back and forth like ghosts in fog. The burning pain in her arm crept past her shoulder and up her neck, blurring her vision and tearing through her head. As the fervor of battle faded away, she finally realized how much blood she was losing, bubbling from the fang wounds. Her vision quickly tunneled, and she slithered to the aft of the ship to stare into the dark blue canyon waters.

The current was swift and the oarsmen had done their job diligently, stopping for nothing. Behind the boat, Mayve, Eiklo, and the Oasis Stone were gone, swallowed by the deep river. Her strength gave way, and unconsciousness arrived with a snap as her head hit the Ferry's deck.

"*Personally, I don't find the Ventwalkers as unsettling as folks say I should. It's probably because I'm not human, and will never share their fate. To me, they're just Ralverans who happen to look like dead humans.*

"*Megrid, a young human on my expedition, is having quite the opposite reaction. He can hardly look the Raks in their glowing sockets. The poor man must be burdened with the knowledge that if we die out here on the slopes of the Vent, set upon by a rock slide, lava flow, or Vent beast, he'll likely rise again one day, an amnesiac husk.*

"*If I was concerned about death, I wouldn't be here to begin with. My largest grievance here is the damned food. Even though we're sleeping in bunks, in a civilized monastery with a library, chapel, and stables, we've had to pack two weeks of rations as if we're camping in the desert. Vent-cursed skeletons and their lack of stomachs.*"

—from the journal of Oswal Briggin, cavernfolk explorer. Expedition to the Tarakos Vent, circa 44 SR.

Chapter 21

The Axe Forgets

Raudius could not decide which was worse—the nighttime travel, freezing and surrounded by raptors, or the heat of day and the struggle to sleep. He lay outstretched in the sand, the shade from the awning providing meager respite. He could usually get a little bit of sleep early in the morning, before the sun rose to its noon apex, but sleeping through the afternoon was impossible without perfectly crafted shelter or the aid of herbs.

Not to mention that he was forced to share his shade with a menagerie of stinking beasts, any of which would crush him if they wanted to sleep where he was. So, Raudius spent his afternoons trying to exert as little energy as possible, retreating into his mind to analyze the mission before him.

He was beginning to taste his freedom. If Ingo wanted any information at all about the tauninaga that killed his brother, he would have to let Raudius go into town on his own. The raptors surely had a plan for when they arrived in Port Wenstnor, but no amount of planning was infallible.

Raudius knew for a fact that it would be impossible for them to lead a war party through the town. Maybe one of them would be able to accompany them, but even that was a stretch. Port Wenstnor was not an

Oaken Legion Bastion, but it was flush with merchants and wealthy patrons who would rather draw swords against raptors than risk losing their coin to a raid. *No matter what tricks they try to pull, I will have my freedom there.*

Picking himself out of the warm sand, he shuffled to a barrel of water that the raptors laid out for the animals. His lead, attached to a sleeping Borgo, was almost too short to reach. Cupping his hands, he drank enough to sate his thirst, swallowing his disgust at all the animals he saw slobber over this bucket in the last hour alone. Warm water rushed down his throat and absorbed through the bark on his hands. He remembered the cool forest streams near the Bastion of Growth. Crystal clear and perfectly clean, gurgling between mossy rocks amongst the youthful trees of his home forest.

He *would* return there victorious, and Grenner would be forced to award him with the highest honors. Despite his situation, he knew he must be leagues ahead of his quindecis in pursuit of the artifact, and that gave him hope.

As the days burned away, the raptors ignored him more and more, giving him ample time to study them. Raudius deduced many of them were chosen for the skills they had, or the skills their paired animals had.

Tash, the gold-scaled, maroon-feathered raptor was here because Borgo could carry much of their tents and supplies. Presh, an older raptor with dark blue feathers and gray scales, was bonded with a hawk that often flew away with messages clutched in its talons. Cindri had no bonded animal, but was clearly very needed as the war party's herbalist. Lairro and Ingo were the leaders, but their bonds also looked ready for a fight—Ingo's sabertooth and Lairro's enormous bird-horse each had a primal ferocity in their eyes.

There was also Haro, Baritri, and the twins Emba and Ersh. Their bonds were a lanky wolf-like creature, a sparrow, and two mice. Raudius found most of those animals utterly useless, but the war party needed a fighting force, and he suspected if they each brought a massive animal, they'd also have to carry more food and supplies for each one. He suspected those four raptors were here for their fighting prowess.

The only raptor who did not ignore him was Cindri, Ingo's orange younger brother, who made regular check-ins throughout the day.

Raudius was pleased by this—it gave him more opportunities to learn. He had amassed a great deal of knowledge about the raptors from Cindri, more than he was taught in any of his schooling and training. In return, he had been opening up about life in the Bastions. Nothing tactically important that could be used against them, but enough to grease the conversation and keep the raptor talking. *Depths below, that raptor can talk forever about anything, and also somehow nothing.*

Maybe he doesn't care about leaking this information, or maybe he knows I'll never make it back to tell the tale. Cindri seemed too naive for the latter to be true.

One animal was missing. Spotch's lone sabertooth had disappeared a few days ago. The last trace of it was one last sorrowful note, howled at the setting sun. Since then, he had seen neither hide nor tail of it. Cindri was less talkative that day, his sentences trailing and lost, and Ingo had marched far ahead of the war party, retreating to his tent quickly at the end of the day. It reminded Raudius of seeing his fellow soldiers fall in battle, and he felt a piercing of empathy for the savage lizards. *Steel yourself, Raudius. You might be joining that sabertooth soon.*

Amidst his thoughts, his consciousness drifted away and he awoke sometime later as the sun touched the dunes in the west. As if on signal, the raptor camp awoke, quickly disassembled their tents and rallied the pack animals. Raudius rolled out of the sand and ate a quick breakfast from his rations, then waited patiently by the courg. He grunted to the massive animal, "Good evening, Borgo. Shall I carry everything today, or do you want to?"

Borgo grunted and used his tongue to clean his eyeballs.

"Excellent, I'll just walk behind you as usual, then." He muttered under his breath, "Wretched beast." The courg eyed him with disapproval as if he understood.

Tash walked over from the main campground and spat at his feet. "Ready for another march, shitbark?"

Raudius replied, "One day closer to never seeing your ugly face again."

"You think you can just speak freely? Perhaps we've been making you too comfortable." Tash grabbed the bindings on Raudius's wrists and cinched them tighter, the rope digging deeper into his bark. Then she cut the lead in half and tied it back to Borgo. The distance Raudius trailed behind Borgo was now unbearably short, so much so that Raudius had to lean back or duck with every step or risk getting clobbered by the courg's thick tail.

Raudius protested, "I can't travel like this, you scaled shit. I had no idea that Borgo was the smart one between you two."

Without hesitation, Tash picked up her axe and smashed Raudius in the head with its blunt back. He careened into the sand, sharp pain etched from his temple to his forehead above his left eye. As he struggled to his feet, moisture oozed into his right eye. Feeling the cut, his fingers came back stained with his own green blood.

"I will not be spoken to by some pompous Oaken Legion grunt! Shut your mouth unless I speak to you first, and just walk."

In the organized chaos of packing up the camp, no one noticed their little altercation. The animals were running around eating and helping their bonds. The raptors were packing and dismantling their structures. If anyone saw what happened, they didn't show it. Raudius tried to stumble to the water barrel to clean his wound, but his new lead was too short. He felt sand grating inside the cut every time he wiped the blood from his eyes. The wound was tender, and any attempt to get the sand out only put more sand in.

Why would they help him anyway? He would have to persevere. There was no other choice.

The temperature dropped rapidly as the sun disappeared beneath the horizon, and the sky exploded with stars. Raudius loved to stargaze as he marched. Cindri told him that the raptors used the stars to navigate between important landmarks. The Devaros River was an important landmark, as well as all the Scorch Vents—provided you did not stray too close. Over the past week, Raudius passed time by creating his own constellations to mark the directions they were going.

Now, as he tilted his head back to see the stars, blood poured into his eyes. He was forced to march head down, letting the blood drip into the sand, doing his best to avoid Borgo's tail. A splitting headache grew from his temple outward, turning each step into a struggle to keep his balance. He worried if he fell forward, he may get crushed underfoot by Borgo's tree-trunk hind legs.

Raudius let the blood run, the flow drying to his face and welding his eye shut. He was tied so close to the courg that his field of vision was limited exclusively to the beast's ass and the maroon feathers on the back of Tash's head. He scanned the horizon looking for any flanking raptor scouts he could signal too, but his vision doubled, his steps dragging in the sand. *Do not get their attention. There will be no pity. They will join in and add injuries of their own.*

Finally, he heard a voice. "Raudius, I have good news!" Cindri appeared in the moonlight from around the courg's flank. "Why are you walking so close to Borgo?"

Raudius tried to form words, but his tongue was numb. Luckily, Cindri saw his new, shorter bindings and yelled up to Tash, "Tash! What did you do to Raudius's lead? Why is it so short?"

Tash did not bother looking back and snorted, "I thought the tree had too much room to roam; now he's nice and close."

Cindri yelled back, "It was fine where he was. He's way too close to Borgo, he could get hurt."

"What a shame that would be, huh?"

The moonlight fell on Raudius's face, and Cindri finally saw his injury. The look on the raptor's face was foreign to Raudius, something he never thought he'd see on a raptor—disgust, and shame.

"Oh no, oh no no, Raudius, *depths below*, you need attention right now. How did this happen? Did Borgo hit you somehow?" Cindri uncorked a vial and scooped out a ripe-smelling salve from inside. He almost smeared it on Raudius's forehead but pulled his hand back at the last second. "*Depths below*, I don't know if this is poisonous to you or not. We need to get you to the healing tent."

Raudius mumbled, "It smells familiar, if that helps." His speech was slow and his words slurred together. It was impossible to tell if words were really leaving his mouth. His short lead snapped to its maximum length as Borgo plodded onward, tugging him off his weak feet. He managed only two stumbling steps before crashing into the sand.

Cindri slid next to him, unsheathing an obsidian knife. With a bit of sawing, he cut through the rope before the beast could drag Raudius farther. The snapping rope caught Tash's attention and she finally turned in her saddle. When she saw Raudius clambering to his feet with his lead limp in the sand, she shouted in rage.

"*Taru's rain!* What are you doing?" She steered Borgo to face them. The courg lowered its gargantuan horns at Raudius and let out a low, hostile grunt, mimicking its rider's anger.

Cindri shouted, "He's injured, you idiot. Borgo must've struck him somehow."

"He'll try to escape, or worse. Tie him back up or I will." Tash bared her fangs, and her courg pawed at the sand.

Raudius spat out blood and mustered enough energy to mutter, "Where will I go? I'm in the middle of the Vent-cursed fucking desert, surrounded by nothing but sand and savages!" His vision spun wildly as he spat out the last word, forcing him onto one knee.

The rest of the raptors noticed the commotion, circling their animals around them. Cindri planted himself firmly between Borgo and Raudius to ward off a charge from the agitated courg. Tash swung out of the saddle and prowled toward them, drawing her axe from her belt. As she slunk closer, her axe dragged in the sand, leaving a sharp, winding trail.

"Why are we letting a tree from the blood-soaked Legion walk amongst us? Do you not want to watch him scream, after everything they've done to us? After everything they've done to *your* family? He should be thanking us for our mercy with every breath!" Tash was nearing striking distance.

Cindri looked at Tash's axe and looked at Raudius's wound with wide eyes. "You did this to him?" The feathers on the back of his neck rose in anger. "You could have killed him!"

"It serves him right, and I'll do it again. Get out of my way, Cindri. He needs to be restrained and punished."

"He needs help, that's what."

"He doesn't deserve it!" Tash struck, trying to leap over Cindri and land a blow on Raudius. To Raudius, each movement from the raptors blurred together with the dark night, the stars spiraling overhead. His own movements felt like he was neck-deep in a swift river. He was absolutely powerless to stop the axe cleaving toward him.

Cindri leapt forward and tackled Tash. The two raptors rolled through the sand, snarling and biting like wild animals. The ball of feathers and fangs separated with Tash on top, axe lost in the sand. Cindri slapped Tash across the face with an open palm. It seemed like an ineffective strike, barely causing Tash to flinch.

She snarled in anger, then suddenly screamed in pain, throwing herself off Cindri and rolling manically in the sand. Cindri scrambled backward, dropping something back into his herb pouch as he did.

Tash lurched to her feet, clawing at her face. She was struggling to keep her eyes open, and Raudius thought he saw tears streaming down her scales. Tash screamed at Cindri. "You little fucking *rat*, how can you *possibly* defend a Legion soldier?" She leapt at Cindri, and a huge dark shape slammed into her, sending her tumbling away in a cloud of sand.

Ingo and his sabertooth prowled a circle around Tash. The huge cat bared its dagger-like fangs, its low growl sending a shiver down Raudius's spine. Ingo had his twin axes drawn, held outward like razor-sharp wings sprouting from the sabertooth's back. He deftly spun out of the saddle, facing Cindri, and patted his sabertooth, commanding it with a seething snarl, "Keep her there."

The sabertooth bounded through the sand with a feline howl, planting its jaws around Tash before she had the chance to stand. It tossed her back and forth like shaking the dust from a crumpled tent, then it dumped her on the ground and placed a massive clawed paw on her back, pressing the lizard into the sand.

Borgo bellowed and charged, faltering when the sabertooth turned and roared. The courg pawed at the sand, snorting and shaking as Tash held out a hand for it to halt.

Ingo yanked his younger brother to his feet and snarled, "Are you hurt?"

Lairro climbed off the back of his bird creature and barked a single order. "Explain."

Cindri dusted himself off and pointed at Raudius. "Tash hurt Raudius. Badly. Who knows how long ago, but he needs healing, imme-diately." He knelt down and picked up the lead to Raudius's wrist bind-ings. "She also shortened his lead; he could've been hurt far worse if he fell under Borgo."

Ingo grabbed Cindri by the maw and inspected him in the moonlight, snarling again, "Are *you* hurt?"

Cindri shook his head, which seemed to satisfy Ingo. The red-feathered raptor whistled and his sabertooth released Tash, plodding back to its master's side. Lairro slunk over to inspect Raudius. One look at his bloody face verified Cindri's words.

"How did she hurt you?" Lairro asked. Raudius tried to focus on the gray raptor, but clamped his eyes shut as he started seeing double. He managed to whisper, "With the blunt side of her axe."

Lairro picked Tash's axe out of the sand where it lay and inspected the weapon. It was a stone axe, set into sturdy wood gathered from an oasis somewhere in the vast desert. Wrapped around the handle was a grip made of Borgo's shed fur. He turned the axe around in his hand and strode toward Tash, who was pushing herself out of the sand. Borgo thumped over and scooped Tash to her feet with his horn, braying softly. Tash used the courg's horn to pull herself to her feet. She steadied herself on Borgo's snout, gasping back all the air the sabertooth had crushed out of her lungs.

Lairro stopped just short of Tash, silently waiting for her to compose herself. Tash spoke first, speaking between gasps, "Why, Chief? He's from the green-cursed Oaken Legion, yet he shares our water. How can you make us walk with this filth?"

"We gave our word that he would live, that's how." Lairro motioned at Borgo, and two raptors, Presh and Haro, flanked the beast and led him away by the reins. Lairro's bird-horse pecked at the great beast's heels, helping to drive it backward.

Tash pleaded, "But he is still alive, our word is kept! How can we let him walk away unscathed? The Legion will think we are soft. They will come for us like they have many times before. You would trust this sniveling brat to not turn on us?"

"I have said *nothing* about trust," Lairro snarled, "But if you were captured by the Legion, and they promised you could live, would you find this treatment just? Would you walk away satisfied they kept their promise?" For once, Tash held her tongue. Lairro continued, "I thought not. Now stand and face retribution."

Tash stood straight, eyes closed. Lairro spoke calmly, but his voice betrayed a hint of guilt. "A blow for a blow." Then he struck Tash with the blunt side of her axe, right in the scales above her eye. She screeched in pain and doubled over. Lairro tossed the axe into the sand and said, "That is your punishment for abusing a prisoner in our care. However, your punishment for attacking Cindri, a member of our tribe, is still unresolved."

Cindri quickly interjected, "Lairro, I hit her in the eyes with sand-pepper dust. Seeing as I'm unharmed, that's punishment enough. If I may say so, I would hate to see her punished further. It is a strange journey for all of us."

Lairro looked long and hard at Tash, who was still blinking away a river of tears that now mixed with the blood pouring from the gash above her eye. "Fine. Cindri, tend to Tash and then the tree. Tash, remember your sand-cursed place, and thank Cindri not just for his healing, but also his mercy." He shouted to the rest of the camp, "The sun rises soon. We will set up camp early so the wounded can be treated."

Sunrise already? Raudius's thoughts blurred as he struggled to remember the night. Barks of approval and the squawks of animals resounded as the raptors began their efficient camp setup, unloading and constructing the tents. Cindri led Tash and Raudius to the center of the under-construction camp and left them standing there while he pitched his own tent, which Raudius assumed doubled as the medical tent.

A rough hand clasped his shoulder and claws dug into his bark. Raudius saw Tash's spine straighten in fear as a matching hand wrapped around her shoulder as well. Ingo's blood-red maw appeared in the corner of Raudius's vision as the raptor stepped between him and Tash. His breath smelled of rancid meat, and some sort of strong alcohol.

The last time Raudius was this close to Ingo, he was in the midst of getting robbed by him and his twin. Faced with only Ingo now, there was something starkly different. There were no frivolous insults, no malicious banter. Ingo's face was cold, but his eyes were manic with hate. He snarled through his fangs, teeth bared, "If either of you lays a hand on my brother again, you best pray to your favorite god that I am long dead."

The raptor's claws dug in harder, a dull ache in Raudius's shoulder rising as his bark held strong. On Tash's shoulder, pinpricks of blood formed as Ingo's claws pushed through her scales. She winced and gritted her teeth, trying her best to maintain her dignity despite the blood pouring down her face.

Despite his hatred of her, Raudius felt a shred of empathy. Here they were, suffering the same raptor, identical scars slashed across their faces. Then the empathy disappeared as his head was wracked with pain from the wound Tash had caused with her cruelty.

Ingo relaxed his grip and spoke directly to Tash, turning away from Raudius. He jabbed a pointed claw at her chest. "We are here to avenge Spotch, and get that artifact. For both of those to happen, I need that tree alive and well. Don't forget it. If you've had a change of heart, then pack your tent and ride home."

He turned and slunk away, his tail flicking behind him. The tent door flapped open with a crunch of dry leather and Cindri motioned for them to enter. When they stepped inside, it felt no different than the surrounding desert, other than the starry expanse was replaced with dark leather. The tent lacked any floor, using a flattened circle of desert sand as its base. A torch burned in the middle, illuminating the bland inside, the smoke pouring out a hole in the top from which dangled a thin drawstring used to cinch it closed once the sun rose.

In one corner, Cindri had laid out a blanket of thin fabric on the sand to sleep on. Arranged around the outskirts of the interior were numerous pouches, pots, and baskets, all carrying bountiful quantities of the herbs needed for the raptors' journey. Cindri had hung several more bandoliers of vials and bouquets of herbs from the tent's structural poles, including the bandolier that he wore daily. One odd decoration was a thick wooden stick in the corner that looked like it was regularly chewed on. Raudius wondered if it was some sort of special wood that secreted an important medicine. The orange raptor paid little attention to his patients as he ran around looking for the ingredients he needed, while Raudius and Tash sat across from each other

Cindri approached Tash first, as Lairro had instructed. He applied a poultice to her head wound, then turned her face back and forth to inspect her eyes. "It looks like your injury goes only as deep as the flesh, lucky you. It will need stitches, however, and I'll get you something for your eyes. I don't usually carry the cures for the concoctions I hurl at people."

The raptor grabbed a different vial from a hanging bandolier and carefully applied two drops to each of Tash's eyes. The maroon raptor breathed a sigh of intense relief and tilted her head forward, letting her tears flush out the burning powder.

Cindri then set to work with stitches. Before he started, he grabbed the odd stick that Raudius had noticed before, and handed it to Tash. Tash took it and placed it in her mouth, biting down hard as the needle pierced the thin scales above her eye. *Ah. That's what it's for.* The biting stick had apparently seen lots of use.

Tash held stoically for several dreadfully long minutes, then Cindri finally pulled the needle away and inspected his work. He asked, "When was the last time you shed your scales up here?"

Tash pulled the biting stick out of her mouth and handed it back to Cindri, trying to remember. "It wasn't recently, perhaps six moons ago."

"Good," Cindri said, "You won't have to carry these stitches long, then. I suspect you'll regrow them in the next moon or so; everything will fall off then. Just be wary of infection."

Tash climbed to her feet and took a few steps to the door before pausing in stride. She turned to Cindri, head hung, and spoke a few words in Raptoran to him. He replied in Ralveran, "No apology necessary, Tash. You were an excellent test subject for my latest sandpepper-dust recipe." She nodded appreciatively, then said a few more words in Raptoran. Raudius wished he could understand. Only a few scholars in the Oaken Legion knew the language these days. The raptors and the Legion did not cross paths, or swords, as much as they used to in the Ashen Century.

As Tash left, Cindri approached Raudius, eyes sparkling with curiosity. "Okay, Raudius, let's get done what should've happened hours ago. Still awake? I'll need all of your attention, as I have no idea what to do with you."

His head reverberated with every word Cindri spoke. He had never wanted anything more than to lie down and drift away into the void of slumber. Cindri snapped his fingers in front of Raudius's eyes. "First off, your wound. Your bark doesn't look like it will agree with any stitches. How does the Legion usually treat these?"

Remembering how his body worked felt like recalling poetry he read months ago. Slowly, he muttered, "We grow everything back on our own, but slowly. I'll get very green bark to fill in the wound in a few days, then it will eventually grow to fresh, strong bark. The scar will be visible for years, though. The best we do is keep it clean and well watered. In a pinch, you can graft different wood into the wound if you have a piece of living tree cut to the right shape."

Cindri thought for a moment as he cleaned the wound, and asked, "Can your body reject a graft?"

Raudius nodded. "It's not harmful, it will just keep the wound open longer. If it does work, though, I'll heal far quicker, but I'll have a strange-looking piece of bark in my skull." Raudius managed to crack a smile. "I haven't seen any living trees out here, and I assume a cactus will not work."

The raptor was already rummaging through his belongings. He rustled through a large clay pot, lifting out fistfuls of strange plants and dried herbs, finally finding what he was looking for at the very bottom. Hefting an opaque glass jar, he yanked out the old cork. From within, he pulled out a thick branch of smooth red wood, dripping wet. Twirling his obsidian knife from his belt, he cut away a sliver of bark, revealing green inside.

"Ah!" Cindri's excitement burst over. "We *must* try this, just to see what happens."

Raudius's thoughts were sluggish. He could do nothing but motion to the red log and mouth the word *"Where?"*

Cindri must've understood, or he was simply about to tell Raudius anyway. "This is Oaganshi pine. It's not a real pine tree like what you have in the Verdants, but it has enough needles that whoever named it didn't care. It can hold water for centuries, they say, and both the raptors and the oasis tauninaga consider it sacred. We're carrying this sapling to plant at a new oasis, but I consider this a planting, of a sort. No one will find out until it's in your skull. Do you even have a skull?"

He used a damp cloth to wipe the last of the grit from the tree's wound, then handed the cloth to Raudius. "Press this to the wound while I cut this to shape."

Raudius complied, feeling his wound soaking up the water slowly but voraciously. Cindri continued to talk while he whittled away at the dark red lumber. "You're showing strong symptoms of wound fatigue. Slurred speech, dazed movement. I assume that means you have a brain?"

Raudius looked at the raptor quizzically. He realized that the raptor was keeping him talking to prevent him from falling asleep. He responded, "I'm not sure what you speak of. I assume no, or perhaps we refer to it as something else. I never heard the term from my anatomy lessons."

"It's what the scholars call a lump of meat inside our skulls. Humans and Oemorgs have them as well. The Torn have several, apparently." Cindri lifted Raudius's hand off the wound to take a look, and held up his work to inspect the shape, then pressed the cloth back and kept whittling. "The Northern Ice raptors have done much research on it. Lots of dissections, I hear. They have many books on the matter from a Lost Eon library that Citadel Teirmond found."

Raudius wondered out loud, "How do you contact them?" Not as tactful as he would have liked, but that was the best he could do in his current condition. If the Legion knew how the desert raptors communicated with the ice raptors, they could isolate them from each other more easily.

Cindri shrugged. "We have many ways. You Legionfolk keep the Verdant secure but you'll never stop us from talking with our brethren in the Ice."

Raudius groaned, dropping the subject. "We have no lumps of meat in our body, as far as I know. The Oakfire burns deep in our chest, where our bark is thickest. That is what gives us life." He knocked a fist on his solid exterior to show where. "The raptors surely know this already."

"I've heard the war stories, yeah. If you somehow drive a spear through a Legion soldier's chest, they are consumed in green fire. The warriors say it is a glorious sight." Cindri absentmindedly held his whittling work up to the torchlight, then looked at Raudius shamefully.

"Sorry. In poor company for that talk. If you have no brain, then why are you experiencing the same symptoms as us flesh-and-blood creatures do with a head wound?"

Raudius divided his attention between keeping his eyes open and forming words. "The Oakfire flows through our veins, if you can call them that, like your blood. It connects all our organs together." Raudius waved his free hand in front of his face. "There's a lot going on up here. Eyes, ears, mouth, which means there are more of these pathways for the Oakfire. Tash severed a good many with her attack."

"Ah, a decentralized nervous system. Very intriguing. That regrows too?" asked Cindri.

"Yes. We heal slowly, but we heal well. A soldier can recover from nearly any wound, even a decapitation. But that's an extreme rarity; the graft of head to body has to be perfect and they have to be sustained by the best healers for the entire duration. A soldier who loses their head on the battlefield is as good as dead." Raudius paused, then forced himself to keep talking as his vision drifted. "We can even regrow limbs, but that takes years."

Cindri removed the cloth again and gently paced the carved Oaganshi pine into the wound. Raudius felt the wound tingle uncomfortably at the touch, the exposed skin incredibly sensitive with the bark cut away.

"Just a few more adjustments," Cindri said. "Tash hit you far harder than Lairro hit Tash. Her cut was far more superficial than this one."

Raudius grimaced. "I'm not surprised."

"She lost both her parents to the Legion, and our people are not even at war anymore. Neither of us agree with what she did, but you must be able to understand it."

"Her parents were soldiers?"

"Shepherds."

Silence took the tent. Cindri finished whittling quietly. "That should do it. After this is in, I'll bandage it tightly. Then we'll make sure to keep everything damp and check it once we reach Port Wenstnor. All that sound agreeable?"

Raudius nodded, and Cindri removed the damp cloth from above his eye. As the freshly cut timber was pressed into the wound, the sensitive flesh buzzed as if a hive of bees nested in his skull, vibrating and stinging. He braced himself, trying to regain his senses. Cindri grabbed his branches and held his head upright, quickly wrapping damp bandages around his forehead. The raptor cinched them tighter, fully pressing the new bark into Raudius's skull. His vision exploded in bright white, then faded to black.

* * *

The crunch of sand woke him some time later. The torch was out, and the tent was pitch-black. The heat was stifling, but still much more comfortable than sleeping with the animals. Raudius saw an outline of red sunlight bordering the tent flap, so thin that a flea would lose its limbs squeezing through. The raptors carefully constructed their tents to let as little light in as possible. Let in too much light and temperature inside would be nigh unlivable. The raptors piled sand around the outside of the tent to keep the sand inside from heating up, leaving a cool bed for the raptors to sleep on, despite the air inside growing stuffier with each passing hour.

His head was aching terribly, but his thoughts were finally clear. Cindri was quietly shuffling around the tent, grabbing materials and mashing them together in a pestle and mortar. He saw Raudius stir and said, "Ah, you're awake! Feeling better?"

Shrugging, Raudius mumbled, "Yes and no."

"That sounds like progress to me. The sun is setting, go outside and dampen your bandages. I'll talk to Lairro about getting better sleeping arrangements; we can't have sand getting under that bandage."

As Raudius climbed to his feet, Cindri exclaimed, "Oh! The good news I had for you, before I was rudely interrupted by your injury! Presh's hawk arrived with news from Devar. He said that your tribe boarded a vessel out of the city, safe and sound."

Raudius furrowed his brow and stared at Cindri intensely, his interest immediately grabbed. "Did Presh say which direction? North or south? I need to know."

Cindri pondered. "North, toward Tyrak Pass. It's a bit of a flight for Presh's hawk. That information is almost several days old I reckon."

This was excellent news to Raudius. His Oakfire flared, fed by fresh hope. He was so far ahead of the Legion in his investigation—they were going the completely wrong direction, or better yet, had given up entirely. All he had to do was survive this trial with the raptors and he would be in an excellent spot to regain his ranking in the army. He envisioned himself traveling back to the Bastion of Growth with the artifact in his possession and presenting it to the elders with the smuggest look on his face. It would by no means be easy, but at least he had the Legion out of his way.

In a moment of strange elation, he clasped Cindri on the shoulder. Scales scraped against his bark underneath a layer of soft feathers. "Thank you, Cindri, that has brightened my day immensely."

Cindri nodded suspiciously. "Glad to be the bearer of good news." He undid the tent flap and pushed it open, stepping out into the dying light. Lukewarm but fresh air rushed into the tent.

The awakening raptors slunk one by one to Cindri, taking pinches of herb from Cindri's bowl. Some sort of stimulant, to evaporate the sluggish drugs they took to sleep. It had a bitter and pungent smell that filled the tent. Even the smell of it sharpened Raudius's senses, and he wondered if it was safe for Legionfolk.

The lump of crimson desert wood in his skull felt like a numb scar underneath the bandage. He secretly hoped the graft would fail so he could regrow his own bark to cover the wound, but he knew he might need the faster healing for what may lay ahead.

Cindri was certainly kinder than the rest of his tribe, but that would only cost him as they entered the Verdant. Raudius was grateful for the healing, but he knew what he might have to do as they approached Port Wenstnor. He splashed the uncomfortably warm water onto his face and scanned the war party, wondering which raptors he might have to kill to gain his freedom in Port Wenstnor.

Chapter 22

Washed Ashore

T he impact of the Vent beast's tail was certainly unpleasant, but not as dangerous as it looked. The fleshy appendage had simply scooped Mayve and Eiklo off the deck and flung them downriver, as if letting go a caught fish, too small to eat. The fight for their lives started when they hit the water and the current ripped them apart.

In the canyon, the river flowed deceptively fast and treacherously deep. Mayve tumbled and bashed against the stone walls, not knowing up from down. Below the surface, the eroded rock curved the river in mysterious ways, directing the unseen currents to pull her in every direction.

Whenever Mayve clawed her way to the surface for a gasp of precious air, a sudden drop of depth would rip her back into the abyss. It was the same helpless power she felt trapped beneath the Devaros Falls, yet this time there was no plank of wood to cling to. Only the twisting and terrifying void.

Beneath the waves, she felt a freezing-cold presence push against her. A hard surface rose beneath her, slippery and cold, heaving her upward. As she broke the surface and wiped the water from her eyes, she finally saw what caught her. A rough disk of ice, drenched in water and bobbing in the waves, cradling Mayve on its freezing surface. She was at the edge of the canyon with the current slamming her new iceberg into the rock wall, splinters of ice cracking away at each impact.

In the center of the river, a similar disk of ice held a cloaked figure, slumped unconscious on its surface. Eiklo. Between trying to calm a rabid Vent beast and fighting the river, he had used his last remaining scraps of consciousness to pull Mayve out of the depths with well-placed volcomancy.

Mayve pushed off the canyon wall, careful to not tip her icy raft. The current on the surface was nowhere as brutal as the riptides hidden below, and with some difficulty she was able to paddle over to Eiklo's raft, which was drifting aimlessly in the center of the river. Unable to pull him over to her raft without tipping either one, Mayve lay flat and held the sleeve of Eiklo's cloak, keeping their icebergs locked together.

Her respite was short-lived. Ice does not last long in the desert. As they were swept downriver, their rafts thinned. The melting ice was slippery, the smallest jolt from the river threatening to slide either person effortlessly into the river. The biting frost burned her fingers, forcing her to change her grip dangerously often. As the canyon walls lowered and transformed gradually into desert riverbank, the ice floats succumbed to the river, sinking in the depths. Mayve and Eiklo were ever so gently left to the river's whims as the ice fell away from beneath them.

That is how Mayve found herself dragging Eiklo through the river, floundering under the dead weight. With the last of her energy, her boots sinking into the silt, she heaved herself and Eiklo onto shore.

The blistering sand ate hungrily at the water dripping from Mayve's body. Below her knees, her legs still floated in the river, the Devaros tugging at her boots. As she lay face-down in the sand, it seared her soaked clothes, clinging like superheated barnacles to her cheek, but she was far too exhausted to move. She sank into the soft riverbank, her lungs gasping mouthfuls of dry air.

To her left, Eiklo lay on his back, soaked to the literal bone. His clothing stuck to his skeletal frame as if he were melting in the sun. Mayve felt a jolt of panic when she realized he wasn't breathing, then remembered he was already dead. She wouldn't know if he was truly dead until he woke up. *He can't drown, can he? If anyone should be dead after that, it's me. If I survived, surely he did.*

Her muscles gave in to the warmth of the sun and sand, refusing any and all commands. However, the desert does not take kindly to those who linger. As the last droplets of water evaporated from her tanned skin, the pleasant warmth gave way to harsh burning, the hot sand that drove away the frigid temperatures of ice and water beginning to scald her face. Mayve forced herself to rise to a sitting position and slid down the riverbank back into the shallows, submersing herself again. The shallows were perfectly cold, and the light filtering through the water danced beautiful patterns on her closed eyes. A bony finger tapped her shoulder, and Mayve reemerged to greet Eiklo.

Once, Mayve watched a fish merchant toss a cat into the Devaros that was trying to pilfer her wares. When the cat clambered out downriver, its fur was comically drenched, clinging to its skin like an ill-fitting coat. Eiklo reminded her of that cat, and she couldn't help but burst out laughing at the sight of the skeleton. Despite his emotionless skull, the poor Ul'Varin-Zul wore an utterly dreary expression, soaked and hunched over on the riverbank.

As she calmed down, Eiklo was staring at her, unamused. Streams of mist huffed out of his skeletal nose holes, and he said dryly, "From all those breaths you're taking, it seems I saved your life?"

Mayve stifled one last giggle at the skeleton's appearance and said, "After I saved yours. Shall we call it even?"

"You know, the Ul'Varin don't need to breathe. I could have been washed all the way back to Devar."

"Then go on, wade back in and let the current smash you open on the rocks."

Eiklo made a sighing noise. Even though he did not have to breathe, the reflex of a good exasperated sigh is forever ingrained in a human, long past death. "Well, I'm glad to see we're alive. I passed out in the middle of forming your ice float. We're lucky it caught you."

"Looked less like luck and more like skill to me. Thank you." She smiled and Eiklo perked up at the sincere compliment. Looking upriver, Mayve asked, "Do you think the Ferry is still floating?"

Holding up a finger to give her pause, Eiklo dropped into medita-

tion. Mayve stifled a laugh again, not wanting to break his concentration. He looked dreadfully shriveled when his head bowed and legs
crossed.

A moment passed and Eiklo said, "We may be too far away, or
perhaps I am too exhausted, but I cannot sense the *aerstab-bourl*
anymore. I pray to Varin that is because they managed to kill it."

Mayve climbed out of the river and sat next to Eiklo. "What now? I
suppose there's not much to do but set off upriver."

Eiklo shook his head. "Traveling during the day is dangerous in the
open desert. You'll suffer quickly, and I'd prefer traveling at night as well.
The environment isn't dangerous to me here, but it's uncomfortable
nonetheless." Eiklo stood up and surveyed the landscape as he spoke,
turning in a slow circle. "However, without any shelter here, perhaps a
slow trek is best. Then at least we may find some shelter to wait the rest
of the day in."

To the south, the Devaros disappeared into the canyon. Beyond
that, the green peaks of the Azrak Mountains seemed like a mirage above
the mirage. Mayve grimaced as she realized this was the last place she'd
be able to safely access the water without having to climb down the
canyon wall—something she would certainly try if she had to, but
would not be pleased about. The climbing would be enjoyable. Falling
back into the Devaros Cataracts, on the other hand, sent a shiver down
her spine.

To the north, the Devaros carved a gorgeous blue path through
dunes. The dry brown shrubbery usually common along the river was
absent here. It was too close to the Ysera Vent for plant life to flourish. A
Scorch Vent's unnatural presence stifled plant growth for hundreds of
miles around each one.

East and west stretched endless desert, as far as Mayve could see.
Where the dunes swept against each other like a petrified ocean, a
wanderweed tediously climbed up a distant slope. The ball of dried
branches was covered in spiky brown leaves that dug into the sand as it
rolled. Once it turned over, the leaves would unfurl and catch wind
before rolling over again. Plants could not grow here, but the wanderweed didn't care. It grew somewhere else long ago.

On the western horizon, ash spewed from the Ysera Vent, creating a long trail of clouds that stretched wherever the wind took it that day. Tiny flares of light dotted its blackened slopes—eruptions of molten lava, bursting out and pouring down the obsidian rock.

Mayve pointed at the Vent in the far distance. "Should we cross the river, to at least be farther from that?"

Eiklo shook his head. "If a Vent beast wants to eat us, I doubt it will care about a little water."

A jolt of a thought hit Mayve, and her hands leapt to her belt. She sighed with relief when she felt everything was still there. Her shawl and canteen were both securely fastened, along with the pouch that carried the Oasis Stone. She gripped the soaked leather of the pouch, the Oasis Stone's solid heft weighing down the palm of her hand. She unwrapped her shawl and submerged it in the river, then covered her upper half with the cloth, relishing the wet fabric on her bare arms.

Looking south, she knew Port Wenstnor was nestled in the foothills of the Azraks, somewhere over that horizon. "You don't think they'll turn the boat around for us, do you?"

Eiklo shook his head. "Not for several days. The Cataracts are all narrow canyons and fast-moving currents. It will prevent them from turning around until they reach safer waters. Then they may need to stop at Port Wenstnor to replenish their supplies and drop off the passengers. After all that is done, Vulinor will certainly come looking. I'm sure it's troubling him greatly."

Mayve nodded, expecting such an answer. "Then I suppose we start walking."

With an affirming nod from Eiklo, the pair began their trek upriver.

* * *

They skirted the canyon edge, its height growing more and more treacherous as the river fell farther away. Mayve walked with her head down, watching her footing and keeping the sun off her face. The shawl kept the worst of the sun from her neck and arms, yet the heat still soaked through the fabric, almost certainly amplified by the Ysera Vent's proximity. Whenever the breeze shifted to blow from the west, it reeked of ash and sulfur. Even though the Vent was still a hundred miles away, Mayve balked at how hot it must be on the Vent's slopes.

As the canyon's edge meandered with the river, her concentration on the trek broke when she found herself dangerously close to the edge. Maybe thirty, perhaps thirty-five feet below, the river was a silent blue scar running through the red sandstone. Mayve did not fear the height. It was the end of the fall that terrified her. She might survive the impact, but the momentum from the fall would plunge her deep into the river, into the dark riptides that whirled around the smooth canyon walls and stone floor. Without Eiklo, she would be trapped in the currents until her last breath was knocked away.

Mayve quickly sidestepped away from the edge and looked back at Eiklo, simply to give him a glance of utmost displeasure. The Ul'Varin-Zul was trudging behind her by several paces. Considering he needed neither food nor water, he was handling the desert much better than she was, but the blistering heat still took its toll on him. Ul'Varin-Rak were born on the fiery slopes of the Scorch Vents, clawing their way out of embers and ash to start their new undead life. They were accustomed to heat far more suffocating than the Great Ralveran Desert. Eiklo was granted his undeath in the freezing cold of the Northern Ice, and was ill-equipped for open desert travel. The heat gnawed at him, replacing energy with fatigue as his elementally charged skeleton struggled to keep cool.

When the sun was at its peak in the crystal clear blue sky, the traveling pair were graced with a pleasant sight: a huge jagged boulder, tilted over a depression in the sand, casting just enough shade for two weary travelers. They hustled to the boulder and practically dove beneath it, the shade providing immediate respite from the glaring light.

Sighing with relief, Mayve lay back in the cooler sand and unwound her shawl, airing out her neck and arms from the stifling caress of hot cloth. Eiklo removed his hood, baring his skull to the desert air, the embedded sapphire reflecting the desert.

Mayve uncapped her canteen and took a long draw. She swished the remaining water around, gauging how much she had left. *About half.* Walking even one hour like this was dangerous, and several was foolhardy without a proper water supply. Now that they could wait till nightfall, she was confident she could make the latter half of the canteen last a little longer before they had to attempt filling it from the Devaros.

Ideally, we can make it to a safer section of the canyon before I have to descend for more water. With a shorter climb and safer currents. Mayve was utterly fed up with nearly drowning, and was pissed it happened so often, despite living her entire life in the desert.

Eiklo spoke up, exhaustion heavy in his voice. "How much do you have left?"

"Half," Mayve replied. "I wish it was more but we'll have to make do."

The skeleton sat up and said, "Hold it still, let's see if this works." He cupped his hands about an inch above the mouth of the canteen and his eye orbs flared from sapphire blue to a winter white. The temperature around him plummeted as he concentrated his manifestation on the space between his palms. After a few seconds, several drops of water fell from his cupped hands and plinked into Mayve's canteen.

Eiklo leaned back against the boulder, disappointed. "I thought I'd get more than that, with the river right there. It's as dry as a Scorch Vent out here."

"I appreciate the effort." Mayve raised her canteen to him as a toast, then took one last drink before securing it on her belt.

"One day I'll be able to craft pillars of ice out of nothing, like the masters of the Zul cathedrals. Even in this heat, they could raise a wall of ice out of the sand as if they were standing in the ocean, no water required. I'm not as practiced as that yet."

Mayve pondered for a moment, then asked, "Since we have some time before sunset, could you teach me?"

"Teach you volcomancy?" Eiklo shrugged. "If you're interested, I'll try."

"Might as well. Nothing ventured, nothing gained. If it doesn't work for me then that's that. I'm curious more than anything."

"Well, the scholars say that everyone in Ralvera has the potential to be a volcomancer," Eiklo said. "Most simply don't know how. Some never can, and for some it comes so easily they wield the Vents' power every day in subtle ways, never aware what they're doing." He stood up, careful to not leave the comfort of the shade.

"The Vents, Frost and Scorch, exude a powerful unseen force throughout Ralvera, like an infinite, invisible lake covering everything beneath it. It's called many names. The Torn call it 'the Humming,' the Northern Ice raptors call it '*Arcaish Aquoa*,' which translates from Raptoran into 'the Arcane Tide.' Its most common name comes from the human scholars. The *Ventix Stratus.*"

Eiklo waved away all those names as if they were meaningless. "The Ul'Varin call it the 'Du'ul Immortanus.' The blood of the Calamity Hydra, slain by Varin at the beginning of the Paroxysm. Just some Ul'Varin mythology for you." Eiklo shrugged, as if nothing he said was true. "Not even the smartest scholars know what this force is, so most turn to myth and legend. The fact remains, however, that the Du'ul flows through all creatures. The closer you are to a Vent, the stronger it is."

Eiklo held up a bony finger, still lecturing. "It's helpful to know, since you happen to be traveling with one, that tauninagan sfa-zrueen does not come from the Vents. It was taught to the tauninaga by the Fae long ago." He motioned for Mayve to stand up. "Volcomancy comes in three steps. Just watch for now."

The glowing blue orbs in the skeleton's eye sockets disappeared as he closed his eyes, pressing his hands together. He spoke, softly and meditatively. "The Du'ul is already flowing through you. It flows through every blade of grass, every rock on every mountain peak. Insect, raptor, leviathan. The Du'ul is like a river, not flowing around you, but *through* you, and it is content to do so. You first have to feel that power. Feel the Du'ul Immortanus crashing through you, connecting you to the world around you.

"Next, you must trap the Du'ul within you. When you capture it, it will rage to escape. It will thrash like a gale on the Southern Ice. It wants to rejoin the Du'ul around it, screams for it. This is the most dangerous part of volcomancy. You have built a dam in the river, trapping the pure, violent energy of the Vents, and if you do not release it properly, then the dam will burst. Trust me, it's never good."

Eiklo fell silent, concentrating. Mayve watched intently, waiting for something to happen. After a moment, Eiklo seemed to stiffen, the sapphire in his skull glowing a bright blue. He opened his eyes, his glowing orbs reappearing white instead of blue, like the sunlight reflecting off a lake of ice. As he spoke, there was noticeable strain in his voice, as if he were struggling to lift the boulder that shaded them. "After you trap the Du'ul, you manifest it. You decide how you release the energy back to the river. Weave it from your fingertips, exhale it like a geyser, or clench your fist and smash the energy back into the void!"

Eiklo stepped forward and punched the air. The temperature plummeted, Mayve's breath condensing into a faint mist. A hurricane of freezing air blasted across the sands, picking up the particles in a spiral of wind. Snowflakes whirled forth, catching the sunlight like a tornado of diamonds before the heat ate them to nothing. Mayve's hair whipped around her face and Eiklo's hood was blown clean off his carved skull.

As the wind died down and the temperature crept back to its normal, insufferable heat, Eiklo replaced his hood and turned to Mayve to finish his demonstration. "When the Du'ul exits your body, it will manifest itself in the physical world in strange, unpredictable ways. How it manifests is different for everyone, and it's called your Natural Manifestation. For some races, it is extremely predictable. Almost every Ul'Varin-Rak has the Du'ul manifest as fire, and every Ul'Varin-Zul has it manifest as ice. For humans, however, it seems entirely random. We won't know what your Natural Manifestation is until you manage to do it."

Eiklo locked eyes with Mayve, his piercing blue orbs unwavering. "This is why it's important to have a plan for when you finally trap the Du'ul. It is a disastrous power to contain. I use the Ul'Varin phrasing of 'Du'ul Immortanus' not just because I am Ul'Varin, but because I believe it most aptly describes the ferocity of bending the Vent's energy to your will. The blood of a Calamity Hydra is flowing through you, and it will rip you to pieces if you are careless. When you finally trap it, stay calm and direct the flow where you intend."

Lying down in the sand, the skeleton sighed. "From my year with the Northern Ice raptors, I heard many horrible tales of volcomancers in training capturing the Arcaish Aquoa for their first time and panicking. Releasing that much uncontrolled energy has violent, if not gruesome, consequences. If you're intent on learning, work on sensing the Du'ul first."

Standing up in the shade, Mayve awkwardly spaced out her legs and squared her stance, dropping into a confused fighting pose. She looked more prepared to throw a punch than anything else. Eiklo did not seem to mind, saying, "It may take a while. This part of volcomancy is mentally taxing. You have to conceptualize it in a way that works for you. I'm gonna try and sleep the day away, but wake me if you have questions, and please don't try to trap it."

As Eiklo settled into the sand, falling silent, Mayve stayed standing. She pondered how best she could connect with the Du'ul. It was certainly not as simple as resting your hand in the Devaros and letting the current swirl through your fingers.

An infinite river of apocalyptic energy, all around me. She sat down into a cross-legged position so the ache of her sore muscles wouldn't interfere with her concentration. Then she stood back up with a grumble. *If I do get the chance to wield this energy, it won't be useful if I'm sitting down.*

Ignoring her aching muscles, she closed her eyes, but could not figure out what to focus on. The rush of the river, echoing off the canyon walls? The wind whispering through the sand? Her own breathing? *How do I connect to everything at once?*

She should have asked more questions, but did not want to disturb Eiklo. Being well rested for the journey was more important than her own curiosity. There was more at stake, though. The masked volcomancer, responsible for creating the monstrous bramble eldritches, was able to wield the Du'ul. Not only that, but his Natural Manifestation was powerful. He twisted the Du'ul in horrifying ways, wielding deadly shadows at his whim. If she could wield it herself, any fight with him would tilt more in her favor, even if only slightly.

She decided she would focus on the river analogy that Eiklo used. Removing her boots, she buried her feet in the shaded sand. Eyes closed, she pictured herself standing just a single step into the river, the Devaros swirling around her ankles. An infinite Devaros, as long as it is wide, flowing across the entire desert. She imagined how this infinite river would flow down one side of the canyon and up the other, defying the laws of nature. How it would crash and swirl around the rock that sheltered them. A breeze kicked up, and Mayve added it to her meditation, picturing how the wind would ripple across this imaginary river. The sounds of wind and water were indistinguishable, so similar in many ways. Her breath joined the chorus. It was also wind, in a way. Another note in the chord.

She stepped further into the unnatural river she was creating in her mind's eye. The cold feeling of the sand spread upward to her knees. Wading in the infinite expanse, the chorus of wind and water blended into one single noise, rushing over the world. She imagined she was the rock that sheltered her, comfortably cool on one side and scorching hot on the other. Her back warmed at the thought. She focused on Eiklo. His body was irradiating an ice-cold energy, sending glittering snowflakes adrift in the infinite river as it flowed over him.

Distant thunder boomed as the Ysera Vent shot a plume of lava into the air. It should have been inaudible at this distance, yet Mayve felt it collide with her chest. She did not know if she was in control of her mind's eye anymore. It felt too real. A shock wave from the Ysera Vent rippled through the infinite river, a tide of Du'ul rushing across the desert.

The wave crashed into her. All noise disappeared in an instant, drowned away. She was floating. Terror overtook her. It was all too familiar to the watery abyss under the Devaros Falls, to the dark riptides of the canyon. The current was not swirling around her, it was punching straight through her. She was in the infinite river, but she was no obstacle. The energy flowed through her, as it flowed through the boulder and the sand and Eiklo. Her body hummed as the immense power of the Vents overwhelmed her senses.

She wrenched her eyes open. The gentle whisper of the winds was distinguishable from the running water once again. As it blew across her skin, Mayve realized she had broken out in a cold sweat, which the wind was delicately wisping off her body. A tiny flash of light from far in the distance signaled another explosion of lava from the Ysera Vent.

She had sensed the Du'ul, she was sure of it. Now she knew the terrifying power that coursed unseen from the volcanoes. A shiver ran down her spine. *Am I scared? Or am I feeling the ripples in the Du'ul Immortanus?* She *had* to talk with Eiklo again. The amount of raw power that burst through every inch of her body just then—the thought she would have to trap even a fraction of that was daunting.

But if she could, that masked volcomancer would stand no chance. Mayve collapsed into the sand, staring into the cloudless blue sky.

* * *

Between the heat and her own overactive mind, finding sleep was difficult. It must have found her at some point, though, as Eiklo prodded her awake. His eyes shone like two blue lanterns against the orange sky behind him. Mayve silently added "being shaken awake by a skeleton" to the short list of things that unsettled her, then pushed herself upright.

Eiklo whispered as if she was still sleeping, "Sun is setting. Best we be on our way." She groaned and nodded, her mouth already dry.

The next few minutes were spent in silence, both collecting their thoughts. Mayve's stomach grumbled. Her appetite had been quelled by the copious adrenaline pumped through her by the morning's events. It was eerie to think they had fought a Vent beast just that morning, not to mention almost drowning. Now that sleep had calmed her body, hunger had returned in full force.

"Keep an eye out for food," Mayve said groggily, her head resting tiredly on the boulder. "Edible desert plants, small rodents, or fish down below. Not that we have the means to catch any."

Eiklo paused, then gave a deep nod like an old man hearing the name of a childhood best friend. It was obvious he had forgotten that Mayve needed to eat to survive. "We may have to be creative to keep you sustained."

Mayve snorted. "Creative, or desperate?"

"They are the same, more often than not."

"Do you miss eating and drinking?" Mayve realized after the words left her mouth that the Ul'Varin might find them rude. Eiklo was always cordial in entertaining her curiosity; she would hate to trespass.

Luckily, it seemed like a normal question that Eiklo had fielded before, perhaps from many different strangers. He shook his head and said, "Ul'Varin remember nothing about who they were. We wake up knowing only our name. As the elder monks say, one's name can only be forgotten by others."

Mayve leaned in, curious as ever. "So you were once a human named Eiklo? That's all you know?"

"I was once a human, that's all I actually know. No skeleton has ever proven if the name they remember was truly their name in their past life. It's just an assumption," Eiklo said.

He stared contemplatively at the Ysera Vent on the horizon. "It's all a mystery. How long ago did I live? Why did I die on a Vent? Is the sound of my voice the same as it was, or do I speak a new voice in undeath? All good questions pondered by the Ul'Varin-Rak and Zul alike." The skeleton chuckled to himself. "One of my mentors at Rulnevrin kept notes on all outsiders who visited the cathedral, on the not unlikely chance they died on the Vent and were later resurrected."

Mayve laughed. "Well, it's a minor comfort that if I somehow die on the slopes of a Vent, I may be given a second chance." She paused. "Even if I may not be the same person."

Streaks of rime crept down Eiklo's skull and into his eye sockets. "I can still feel the person I used to be. Memories, if you can call them that, skitter at the edge of my consciousness, forever out of reach. All Ul'Varin feel them. Several have skills that they were good at in life. For example, I excel at reading maps, despite never being taught how."

He looked at Mayve and his blue eyes flared, wisps of condensation spiraling up from the corners of his mouth. The Ul'Varin-Zul equivalent of a shit-eating grin. "Captain Vulinor is a breathtaking basket weaver. We ferried a merchant a couple years ago who was plying his craft on the deck. Vulinor sat down next to him and picked up a handful of reeds, and proceeded to braid a basket that was far better than anything the merchant was selling. The best part is, the captain had the most confused expression the whole time, as if he could not believe what he was doing as well." Eiklo finally took his eyes off the distant Vent and leaned back to look at the infinite blue sky. "If I remember correctly, the merchant sold that basket in Tyrak Pass for more coin than he usually sees."

The thought of Dreva as a skeleton pushed through Mayve's mind. Her mother's simple beauty and kind wrinkles, reduced to white bone with burning red eyes. *What is the point of returning if you cannot remember the ones you loved.* She looked at Eiklo and grew unbearably sad. *He must have had a family and friends. Folks who loved him, perhaps even still alive today. He died young, a gruesome death on the Northern Frost Vent no less, and now knows no one who used to care for him.*

Mayve grimaced. She did not need to die on a Vent to be alone in this world; she was accomplishing that already with no trouble. "I've reconsidered. I would like to stay dead when I die."

Eiklo had a tinge of sadness in his voice. "I think we all would prefer that. It would be better if I remembered nothing. If I crawled out of the ice with no name and no muffled voice in the back of my mind. It would be no different than a new life. Instead, I feel who I was, buried away in an impenetrable coffin. It's like looking in a cloudy mirror, with too much grime to see who you really are."

The skeleton's depression hung in the air. After a pause, Eiklo stood and dusted the sand from his robes. "Luckily for you, you're not going to die on a Vent. You're going to die out here in the desert unless we find you some food and water. Out here, you can only get resurrected as vulture dung."

Mayve gave a half-hearted laugh, warding away her dark thoughts, and fell to silence as they stepped from the rock for the next leg of their desert trek. With a half-filled canteen and an empty stomach, the threat of death in the sand-drowned wilderness was all too present on Mayve's mind.

Chapter 23

Hunted

The setting sun painted the endless sky in fiery oranges and soft pinks, but the dunes were dark, bathed in the shadows of their neighboring dunes. Far below, the river was nothing more than the echo of waves lapping against rock, the shadow of the canyon obscuring the bottom. Even the gurgle of the river put a pit of fear in Mayve's stomach.

Travel was far more comfortable in the cooling air. The pair trekked across the sandy rock, revitalized by the dwindling temperature. Mayve knew it would be unpleasantly cold soon, but she preferred that over the deadly heat. If she wrapped her shawl tight and kept moving, she'd be fine. At least the Ysera Vent, far away as it was, would prevent the temperature from becoming deathly cold.

The initial fear of her first contact with the Du'ul wearing off, Mayve wanted Eiklo's opinion. Minding her step near the canyon edge, she called back over her shoulder, "I think I was able to feel the Du'ul Immortanus while you were asleep."

"Already?" The skeleton sounded shocked. "*Varin's scrolls,* I don't believe you. It takes two weeks of thrice-daily meditation for most new students to feel the Du'ul."

"Perhaps I am an incredibly talented individual."

"Or you have no idea what you're talking about," Eiklo taunted. "Describe the sensation for me, then."

A sprout of terror formed in Mayve's gut as she remembered the experience. She knew the Du'ul could not hurt her unless she trapped it within her, however the sensation of the Vent's power crashing through her was so akin to drowning that she dreaded reliving it. She took a deep breath and tried to capture the sensation in words.

"I pictured myself standing in a river, unseen but everywhere, flowing across the landscape. I think it was cold? Or maybe that was just the sand in the shade. The sounds around me blended together. The river, the wind, my breathing and heartbeat." This part of the experience had been interesting to her, pleasant even. It was what followed that made her pause.

Eiklo's boots crunched in the sand behind her. "Hmm, from my opinion you had a deep meditative experience, but there are no markers of feeling the Du'ul Immortanus."

"Will you hold on? I thought I was the impatient one." Mayve continued her retelling. "As I was wading in this river I created in my mind, there was a boom from the Ysera Vent. I shouldn't have been able to hear it from this distance, but I did."

Mayve paused, trying to find the right words for what happened next. "I know I imagined the river myself. I think you chose a good metaphor to help me visualize the Du'ul. The Vent's eruption...it created a tidal wave. Despite it being my own imagination, I had no control over it. The wave hit me and I was plunged beneath the surface. It felt like standing in front of a searing oven and an icy wind at the same time, just a raw force of nature exhaling through me."

Eiklo stopped in his tracks several paces behind her, skeletal jaw agape. Trails of rime encircled his eye sockets. Most likely the Ul'Varin-Zul's expression for surprise. Mayve laughed at the flabbergasted skeleton. "Is that recollection more to your liking? What do you think of that?"

Eiklo shook his head. "I did, true, although I figured you would only experience some calm mediation." He looked at Mayve with a cold seriousness. "What you described is quite certainly the Du'ul

Immortanus. You're either a natural volcomancer or you're lying to me."

Mayve shrugged. "I'd know if I felt it before. I've never felt anything like it."

"Then perhaps we will try trapping it soon. Although I would recommend becoming more comfortable connecting with it. You look rattled just from recalling the experience. Remember, the Du'ul is a destructive force. It will rip you apart from the inside out if you can't control it. It is raw, apocalyptic energy from the Vents themselves. Some scholars even theorize the Du'ul is what prevents plants from growing in the Vents' auras."

She did feel rattled, but did not realize she was outwardly showing it. Eiklo was right. She had to get used to sensing the Du'ul before she tried trapping it.

A cacophony of howls interrupted their conversation, echoing from somewhere far out in the dunes, northwest. "Gorgonwolves." Eiklo said, matter-of-factly. His voice was calm but his face betrayed him. Each eye socket had three arcs of rime, curving away like tears in a strong wind. The Zul emotion for nervousness. Mayve had seen it the morning before the Vent beast attacked the ship.

"They sound comfortably far away," Mayve said. Their howls were common in the hills around Devar; Mayve had almost grown accustomed to the sound. However, hearing them with her boots in the sand, miles from civilization, was far more unnerving. "Can you track them with your Ul'Varin-Zul sense?"

"No, only by their howls. Gorgonwolves are not Vent beasts, just regular animals. The Ul'Varin-Zul sense only works on monsters created in the Vents." Eiklo pushed past Mayve and resumed the hike, this time with a more fervent pace. "They have an excellent sense of smell. Almost supernatural, I've read. We have to keep moving and hope the wind stays in the right direction."

The Devaros River rushed below, only one harrowing climb away. *The water would easily take our scent, but it might take us with it.* The canyon walls were sheer and the Devaros dangerously fast. Even if it was feasible, she had no idea how she would help Eiklo up and down the cliff. Maybe it was presumptuous, but she did not fancy him a good climber.

She held a hand above her head to catch the breeze. The cold, dry wind drifted across the canyon, silently racing toward the Ysera Vent. "The wind is westerly. Not ideal, but we're not directly upwind." Jogging up to Eiklo to walk side by side, she patted his bony frame through his cloak. "Focus on helping me find food. I won't make a good meal for the gorgonwolves if I can't eat something myself. Come to think of it, you won't make a great meal for them either."

"I'm sure they'll have no qualms ripping me to pieces and gnawing on my bones for fun," Eiklo muttered.

He was taking their situation far more seriously, clearly anxious. Whether it stemmed from general pessimism or an abundance of caution, Mayve did not know. She decided the latter was more pleasant.

* * *

The orange sky faded to a deep, inky blue. As the sun finally disappeared past the dunes, pulling the light of day with it, the sky burst with stars, as if the gods had smashed a diamond into dust and scattered it to the wind.

The howls of the gorgonwolves never ceased. They never heard them in the same place twice, as the animals prowled the dunes with terrifying speed. Often, they heard the howls from different directions, the gorgonwolves starting an eerie call and response across the sands. In all cases, the howls emanated still from behind them, although they were creeping more westerly instead of northwest, signaling the pack was moving into the dunes and not following the river gorge.

Eiklo stopped and listened at every sound, trying to pinpoint the pack's location. It quickly grew on Mayve's nerves—if he stopped every time to listen, then they only fell closer to the gorgonwolves. The closer they were, the higher chance the creatures would catch their scent. They had to keep moving.

Pulling her canteen off her belt, Mayve was unpleasantly surprised with how light it was. Swishing it around, she judged it was a little less than a quarter full. Enough to get her to the next morning, if she was conservative with it, but not through tomorrow. *Out here, being stingy with your water is just as deadly as gulping it down.* She ignored the hunger that gnawed at her insides. *I'll die of thirst a thousand times before I die of starvation out here.*

"Hold here," she called to Eiklo. "I need to climb down and refill my canteen."

The skeleton looked nervously over his shoulder at where they last heard the howls. "Now? Are you sure?"

"I'd rather try now while I still have some water. The cliff here looks climbable and we're not sure what's up ahead. Especially if we don't find suitable shelter to wait out the sun soon."

Ice furrowed across the skeleton's brow. Ul'Varin-Zul displeasure. "Make it quick, we can't stay here long." He looked over the edge of the gorge and said, "But also be very careful."

"I'll climb quickly and make no mistakes while doing so. Genius, thanks Eiklo." Mayve sat down and dangled her legs over the edge, looking down at the shadow-drenched river. Her heart palpitated, thumping with excitement. The last climb she had done was up the rigging to visit Eiklo on his watch. The boat and flat desert provided meager opportunities for it otherwise. She missed clinging to a face of rock in the open air, held aloft by just her strength.

She swung over the edge and her feet found purchase in the rocks. Climbing down was always harder than climbing up for her. When ascending, she could see the path ahead, changing her handholds to footholds as she clambered upward. Descending, it was difficult to see past her boots while hugging the rock wall so closely. Especially in the darkness of the gorge, Mayve found herself searching for footholds almost blindly, testing each crevice to see if it could support her weight before taking another step down. The air in the gorge was substantially colder, numbing her fingers as she gripped the cold stone.

Mayve loved every second. It felt all too similar to scaling the Devar cliffs, adjacent to the crashing Falls. The silence of the river below was especially eerie, flowing deceptively quiet for such a dangerous current. Most rapids have white-capped waves and sharp rocks to dissuade entry; this gorge had no such warnings.

Halfway down the cliff, the howls began.

They rushed through the gorge, reverberating off the rock walls. The howls before were long, drawn-out notes. A single crescendo meant to carry across the dunes. There was a fervor to these new howls. A chorus of barks and roars, filled with purpose and hunger. The gorgonwolves were hunting.

Mayve strained her neck upward. The silhouette of Eiklo's skull peeked over the edge of the ravine. His eyes were wide with worry, the blue lights expanding in the empty sockets.

He called down, his voice wracked with anxiety, "They have our scent."

She needed more water. If she didn't, she'd start to deteriorate fast. She scrambled to find another foothold below her, searching blindly along the rock with the toe of her boot.

"Mayve, get back up here! We need to go!" Eiklo shouted. The howls were at a fever pitch, the echoes in the gorge making it impossible to tell how far away they were.

She shouted back, "We can use your ice to cross the river!"

Eiklo looked over his shoulder, frantically searching for anything bearing down on them. "Are you insane? I can't do that!"

"Why not!"

"I can't concentrate enough to make an ice raft while clinging to the side of a cliff! Besides, we'll just get swept downriver!"

"It will work! We'll climb up the other side!"

"No, we won't!" The howls intensified, harbingers of their feral demise. Eiklo's skull disappeared from view. Mayve heard some muffled swearing in Ventish, then his skull appeared again, framed in starlight. "Mayve!"

Her plan *would* work if Eiklo would take a sand-cursed risk. A simple ice raft, if they were cautious, could get them across. Eiklo would have to do some climbing, but she had confidence in him

If anything went wrong, however, they would be swept downriver. At worst, they would be battered to death in the currents. At best, they would lose all their progress, washing up downriver of the Devaros Cataracts, most likely still chased by gorgonwolves.

Phovus, where is your fucking luck? If Eiklo was unwilling to risk a river crossing, then there was nothing she could do. She hoped he had a better plan other than running for their lives and started the climb back up, the river and its precious water receding beneath her.

Ascending was easier than descending. She flew up the cliff face, reaching the top in a quarter of the time it took to get down. Eiklo extended a skeletal hand to assist, but Mayve ignored it, pushing past him. Clambering back to the top of the gorge, she found herself on the edge of a desert with only a few mouthfuls of water and a hungry pack of gorgonwolves on her trail.

As soon as her boots were on horizontal rock, she and Eiklo tore away along the gorge edge. Not a full sprint—they would have to reserve their energy if, or when, the wolves caught up—but a brisk pace nonetheless. Mayve's lungs soon pained as she gasped in the cold dry air.

The edge of the gorge snaked parallel to their footsteps, sometimes dangerously close, enticing them to misplace a foot and tumble into the shadows. The braying of the hounds intensified, calling across the dunes that they had found a meal.

Through measured breaths, Mayve asked Eiklo, "What's your plan then?" Condensation misted her every exhale, her water disappearing.

"Can't run forever. We have to find shelter." Eiklo looked over his shoulder, once again trying to see their pursuers amongst the dunes. Keeping pace with her, the skeleton showed no signs of stress except for a strain in his voice. His breathless mouth left no condensation in the air. "We'll just need to survive until dawn."

We can still ford the river, we might have time. The adrenaline rush sharpened her instincts yet made it impossible to tell if the howls were louder than they were before. If she did manage to get Eiklo down to water level, and the skeleton was able to manifest stable ice while clinging to the rock face, it could all be undone if the wolves arrived and one decided to risk a jump. She had no idea how intelligent these beasts were, or if they were starved enough to do anything to get to them.

She checked her pouch containing the Oasis Stone. It bounced securely on her waist, knocking against her hip bone on every step. Her canteen clanked next to it, the meager water sloshing around inside. If they survived the night, she hoped there would be a few mouthfuls left for the next morning.

Up ahead, the gorge meandered through a field of boulders, the remnants of what was once a mighty mountain, weathered to a fraction of its former glory by the sand-swept winds. Mayve jumped from rock to rock, sure of her footing, while Eiklo picked his way between the boulders, watching his step on the rubble between. Every second was precious lost ground as the wolves hurried after them.

We can't just blindly wander, hoping to stumble upon shelter. Find the wolves, find shelter, survive. It almost felt like Srrith was slithering alongside them. *Awareness, then evasion. That's what she taught me. We can't evade the wolves if we have no idea where they are, much less ourselves.*

She surveyed the boulder field and took off toward the tallest one— a massive shard of rock that slanted out of the sands, forming a natural ramp into the stars. Scrambling up, the surrounding desert was splayed in a grand panorama. The ocean of dunes glowed a luminescent white as they caught the moonlight, casting gray shadows across the smaller dunes. The starlit sky swept from horizon to horizon, dwarfing the vast desert with its endlessness. To the west, the dunes grew larger and larger, obscuring the horizon behind a mountainous wall of sand.

On rare evenings, Dreva and Mayve used to walk up the great Devar Arch to watch the setting sun. Even on a perch far less grand, the view of the desert night never failed to take Mayve's breath away. She'd be happy to spend a few hours with her back on the cold rock, but the howls reminded her she did not have that luxury.

She looked for the wolves first, facing the howls. High above the dunes, it was easier to pinpoint their direction. North by northwest. The gorgonwolves were out in the desert, pursuing them over the sand instead of along the gorge. Emanating from the vast expanse of sand, the starving howls were deeply unsettling. *Likely talking about how best to eat us.*

Despite the noise, she saw no shadows racing amongst the dunes. *They're still not that close. We have some breathing room, for now.* Sighing in relief, she looked for any potential shelter. The edge of the gorge had barely any sand. With nothing to hold the dunes, any westerly or easterly winds simply blew the sand into the Devaros to be whisked away. Combined with the flat landscape and the gradual upward incline as the river curved toward the Azrak Mountains, Mayve saw for miles downriver.

There was nothing. No rocks large enough to take shelter on, no sails from a ship or smoke from a traveler's campfire. Just an expanse of barren land. If they continued upriver, they would find no refuge from the hunt.

Eiklo paced at the bottom, running his hand across his skull to sweep non-existent hair from his eyes, and looked up at the sky. The body language for exasperation transcended death, it seemed. Mayve slid down the rock face with the grim news and relayed everything she saw.

The skeleton looked crestfallen. "So, the wolves will catch us upriver or downriver."

"Seems that way."

"What else is there?"

Mayve could not believe her ears. "We cross the river! There's nothing else!"

"I'm telling you, we can't do that!"

"You've already made an ice raft!"

"I fell unconscious doing so!"

"Last time, you were getting tossed by river currents! Surely it will be easier now."

A round of howls joined their argument. As they yelled at each other, the real danger was sprinting closer.

"Were you able to see anything west or southwest?" Eiklo asked, forcing calm.

"No, the dunes grew too large."

Both she and Eiklo looked west, toward the endless sand and away from the one source of drinking water for many miles. Eiklo pondered, "There might be shelter that way."

"I know you don't need to eat or drink, but I do," Mayve said. "I don't have much water left, and you're suggesting to run into the desert on the chance we find something?"

"Probable death is better than certain death."

"Please, try the river first. If that doesn't work, then we're as good as dead anyway."

Eiklo paused. If he still had lungs, Mayve could picture him taking a deep breath to calm his nerves. She waited for him to mull over their options. They did not have many.

"Alright, I'll do what I can." He sat down on the gorge's edge. "I'm not sure if you were joking earlier, but I absolutely cannot manifest while clinging to the side of a cliff, so I'll have to do it from here. Please watch the dunes."

Good enough. The skeleton was too cautious for his own good, and hers. Eiklo closed his eyes and focused on the dark water below. "I'll have to grow the ice out from the wall, so the current doesn't take it before we get on."

The cracking of ice echoed off the rock walls. The canyon was drenched in too much shadow to see much of anything. Eiklo had to manifest it blind.

Mayve had little to do but pace and watch the desert. Each time the wolves howled, Eiklo flinched, and whatever progress he made snapped away into the swift currents. The howls only grew closer, and the skeleton's work only grew more rushed, his blue orbs intensely alight as he strained to freeze even a fraction of the mighty river.

Mayve looked over the cliff, the fast Devaros currents churning where the sheer rock dropped right into the water. It stretched like this for miles in each direction, a blue scar slicing through solid rock. Where the river met the cliff was dark, but another snap of ice echoed up, and she saw Eiklo's latest failure drift away into the moonlit center of the river.

"Come on, Eiklo," Mayve whispered, her voice flush with urgency, half expecting the gorgonwolves to leap over the closest dune at any moment. *If you can't do it, I very well might be dead.* She couldn't say that part out loud.

"*Varin's sword*, Mayve, I'm trying, I swear." The wolves howled again, and Eiklo stumbled on his own feet, swaying under the exertion of his volcomancy. Mayve knew it was a lost cause. *At this rate, he won't even be able to run from the wolves.* She pulled him back from the edge and said, "We have to go."

Eiklo fell to his knees and muttered faintly, "I'm sorry. I've doomed us."

"Not yet. Probable death is better than certain death, right?" She put on a brave face through the grim dread settling in her chest. "Seems like we have one option left."

"In the desert, there *could* be something, over those dunes." Eiklo picked himself up, steadying himself on Mayve's shoulder. The Du'ul had taken its toll on his energy. "We need to head southwest. That will put us farthest into the desert before the wolves reach us. With any luck, they won't know we changed directions until they pick up our scent again here."

Mayve's mouth was already feeling dry. This wasn't her first brush with death, but it seemed like the first one that she could see coming. A loose rock high up a cliff or a raptor's blade flashing within a crowd, those were reactionary, instant moments. As she stared into the dunes with only a few mouthfuls of water left in her canteen, she knew right then she had a long way to go, and she might not make it back.

The Great Ralveran Desert. A land as harsh and deadly as the Vents themselves. Spurred by the ravenous howls, she stepped into the sand.

Chapter 24

The Ocean Dry

Eiklo sank into the sand as he rolled over the ridge of the massive dune. Ahead of him, Mayve stepped with graceful style down the slope, her footing perfectly sound on the crumbling sands. The Ul'Varin studied the human's movements. *Slide, small jump, angle the landing to soften the impact and avoid falling into a tumble.* His descent was more of an uncontrolled slide, eroding the dune behind him as he pushed into the sand with both his hands and legs.

They had no time to waste on careful descents, or even to pick a path between the dunes. It was up and over each one. Each wasted step put them closer to the gorgonwolves, and they needed each vantage point to look for shelter.

Mayve's climbing skills had beyond impressed him. He was stunned when she had practically thrown herself over the edge of the canyon to try and fill her canteen. It seemed so reckless, but she made it look so simple. *If she ever came back as an Ul'Varin, I bet she'd remember how to climb.*

The howls of the gorgonwolves were in blistering pursuit. Each howl sounded like it was just a dune or two behind them, but it was impossible to tell. The gorgonwolves' calls carried for miles across the desert. They had not seen the wolves yet, but they also had not found any shelter.

Each dune they crested held the promise of salvation, yet they were always met with more dunes. He tried to mimic Mayve's graceful tumbling. *Slide, small jump, angle the landing—*

He grossly misjudged how far a small jump took him off the side of the steep slope. Hitting the sand hard, he pitched too far forward, skull over heels down the dune.

In a cloud of sand and dust, Eiklo accomplished his goal of reaching the bottom of the slope faster, so well that he beat Mayve to the bottom. The human gracefully slid to where the sand flattened out and pulled him out of the sand like a disgruntled buried treasure.

"Are you okay?" she asked, setting him on his feet.

"I'm fine, I'm fine." Embarrassed, he resumed their fast-paced jog, awkwardly trying to shake sand from his cloak as they ran.

"Take very tiny hops. Gravity does a lot of the work, just focus on the landing." Mayve pulled ahead of him, picking up some speed to take on the next dune that was already rapidly approaching. The human hit the ascent hard, taking a few long strides until falling into a four-limbed scramble. Eiklo did the same, digging his bony fingers into the cold sand as the dune became too steep to climb without them. Hopefully the massive slopes were hindering the gorgonwolves as well. He had a sinking feeling they were not.

Halfway up the dune, a wanderweed clung to the slope like a barnacle, the dark brown thorns on its sail-like leaves anchored in the sand. The round leaves on top of its tangled branches were extended, waiting to catch any breeze that wisped over the desert. Eiklo and Mayve tore past it, leaving it to its meandering journey. They breached the lip of the dune, precipice-like drops on either side, and began another frantic but hopeful survey of the desert.

The dunes were only growing in size as they pushed farther west, obstructing their view ahead. Behind them, their footprints were easily visible on the moonlit slopes, disappearing into the shadowed valleys between the mountainous piles of sand.

Still no gorgonwolves or shelter. Only empty sand before and behind them, but the distant howls reminded them of the coming threat. Food was scarce enough in the desert that the pack would not stop for anything less than a second Paroxysm.

Eiklo glanced at Mayve, framed in the stars. The silvery moonlight reflected through the condensation on her breath. It was steady—the human was as fit as possible—but Eiklo could tell she was growing slightly more ragged with each dune. The wisps of condensation on each exhale were growing larger, and he had not seen her drink any more of her water since they left the river, almost certainly conserving it for later. They would have to travel during the day to escape the gorgonwolves, over the very same dunes most likely. The rising sun would bring a day of brutal torture, even for a thirstless skeleton. The icy energy pulsing through his bones did not agree with the heat, and his once-human mind was still frightfully uneasy at the idea of traversing a desert with no water, even if he needed none.

He himself was beginning to wear down. Ul'Varin needed rest to recharge their natural energy, much like being alive. Just like the living, the longer he stayed awake, the more sluggish he would become. Prolonged physical exertion did him no favors either.

"Nothing again." Mayve sighed. "More sand, as far as the eye can see. At this point, I'd chance meeting a murderous raptor tribe." She held her hands above her head, resting her palms in her dark hair.

Eiklo said nothing, looking over the edge. *Tiny hops, let gravity do the work and focus on the landing.* To his left, Mayve stepped gracefully off the precipice. She fell a short way before her boots hit the soft sand. With amazing agility, she surfed through the sand downward, falling in short increments and letting the sand catch her at the perfect time each step.

Eiklo stepped off the dune. Wind rushed over his cloak and through his bare skull. Feeling air pass through your eye sockets and out your ear holes was something you never got used to as a skeleton. He hit the sand and nearly pitched forward into another disastrous tumble, but threw himself backward so his whole body caught the slope. It slowed him just enough to regain his footing, and he took another step, trying to keep pace with the indents that Mayve had left in the slope. Before he knew it, the slope was curving flat and he caught himself with a running stop, streams of sand washing over his boots. Looking to see if Mayve saw his well-executed descent, he instead spotted her already a third of the way up the next dune.

"Varin's sword, she never stops," he groaned, His boots pounded against the soft ground as he jogged across the sandy valley and up the next slope. At least he was a quick learner. Both his mentor at Rulnevrin and the Northern Ice raptors had said so. *Don't fall behind, Eiklo, you're the reason Mayve is out in the desert and not safely across the river.*

Three dunes later, they saw the wolves.

Atop the dune's crest, Eiklo saw a pack of black specks descending a dune after their old tracks. From so far away, they looked like ants caught in an ocean wave. Six of them, loping at a terrifying pace, disappearing into the valley between. Eiklo always knew they would see the gorgonwolves eventually, but it did nothing to stop the terror that gurgled up his ribcage like bile.

Perhaps my eyes are playing tricks on me in the dim light? He waited with bated breath. Six specks appeared, one dune closer. They had scaled the dune with blinding speed.

Mayve whispered, "Run." Eiklo needed no further encouragement.

He and Mayve all but fell down the slope, throwing caution to the wind. His bones jarred on each impact, not slowing down. They needed to get as much distance as they could before the pack arrived, which would not be long judging by the speed with which they saw them moving. As the slope evened to flat land, they flew across the valley and hit the next dune at a full sprint. Mayve reached the top first, scrambling up the slope at a near-inhuman speed that Eiklo could never match. As he reached the top, he threw himself over the crest without looking and tumbled down the other side.

His bones ached as he sprinted across the next valley and up the accompanying slope. He desperately needed a rest. Judging by the clouds of condensation on Mayve's breath, she needed the same, although her pace never slowed an inch. As he neared the top of the next dune, Mayve reached down and pulled him up the last few feet. There was still nothing. No shelter, no salvation, only sand and the wolves.

The blue orbs in his skull narrowed as he strained his vision against the contrasting bright moonlight and dark shadows. Dune after dune lay before them, all the same gargantuan size. "Anything can be hidden behind these dunes. Until they catch us, we run and we pray."

He looked east, searching in the moonlight for the gorgonwolves. They crested several dunes behind them, close enough that Eiklo distinguished their lanky shapes and long strides in the night. One of the wolves paused at the crest—a lean, fierce beast, posed before the sprawling starry sky—and unleashed a long howl. The hunt was coming to a close.

Eiklo and Mayve leapt off the edge, tumbling in a spray of dust. Eiklo rolled to his feet as soon as his momentum would allow and took off toward the next dune, vision still spinning from the tumble. Mayve was far ahead of him, already charging up the slope. At full speed, she completely outclassed him, the distance between them growing. *I hope she doesn't forget about me in her haste.*

She should though. She's leaving you behind. If there's shelter after the fourth dune, and you can only climb three before the wolves get you, then you're dead. Don't drag her with you.

Eiklo breached the next dune, hurling himself over and letting gravity take him. The brays of the pack rang in his skull and his vision disintegrated into a jumble of spinning stars and sand. Rolling to a nauseating stop, he stumbled to his feet and broke into another sprint, growing faint. If he still had lungs, he would be gasping for breath.

Boots sinking into the sand, he raced across the valley. At the top of the upcoming dune, he saw Mayve's silhouette blocking out a small section of the stars, and he heard a shriek of pure joy.

She called down, out of breath but excited, "Hurry Eiklo! We'll be okay, just hurry!" The prospect of safety filled the skeleton with renewed vigor. He charged up the dune in a fury, sand cascading from every footfall and handhold.

Looking over the edge, he saw a rough plateau of hard rock jutting out of the sand at the lowest point in the valley. As the winds swept the dunes along, inch by inch, the rock was likely buried quite often. It was dumb luck that they had encountered it when it was between the dunes, instead of underneath them. *Whether dumb luck or fate, Varin has answered my prayers.*

It was tall enough that he'd have to climb it. Whether it was tall enough to stop a hungry gorgonwolf was something they would have to find out the unpleasant way.

Mayve was already down the slope, dashing like the wind across the open sand. Leaping off the edge of the dune, Eiklo glanced over his shoulder, locking eyes with the ravenous gaze of a gorgonwolf on the dune behind them. The creature was eerily lanky, like a forest wolf stretched thin. Its long limbs held up a lean body, coated in mangy, matted fur. What terrified Eiklo the most was its hideously long snout. Nearly three times the length of a normal dog's snout and lined with sharp teeth, the jaw peeled open as the beast snarled, a spindly thin tongue licking the air. The gorgonwolf unleashed a long, victorious howl as the rest of its pack leapt over the edge, racing down the opposite side of the valley.

Vision blurring, Eiklo flew for the plateau, his cloak billowing behind him. The sand compressed beneath his boots, swallowing every step. Mayve was almost there, the rock looming overhead. Using Mayve for scale, Eiklo estimated it to be about twenty feet high, perhaps twenty-five. Should be perfect for shelter, if they could climb it.

If I can climb it. Mayve hit the rock wall with no hesitation, using her momentum to vertically run up a good portion, catching a hand-hold as gravity clawed at her. As naturally as a spider, she clambered to the top with ease, her practiced eye finding handholds in the rock as easily as picking wares from a market stall.

She turned and cupped her hands around her mouth, yelling back, "Hurry, Eiklo! This spot, right here!" She pointed down at a section of rock near where she had just scaled. The best place for Eiklo to scale the wall, in her opinion. He made the educated decision to trust her judgment. Mayve clearly had no faith that Eiklo could perform the same climb that she did. *A correct assumption.*

The growling of the gorgonwolves was suddenly far too close, no longer muffled by the dunes. Eiklo could not resist glancing behind him, even though he knew exactly what he'd see. Six shadows, gliding down the slope with a deadly grace. Eiklo summoned the last bit of energy he had left, bolting toward the butte. His ribcage ached, his legs ached, his skull pounded with fatigue. Any second, the jaws of a gorgonwolf would clamp over his neck and thrash him into the sand.

Mayve screamed at him, frantically waving her arms, goading him on. His head was pounding too hard to hear if she was saying words. As he approached, she flattened herself on the edge and leaned out as far as she dared.

Eiklo slammed into the rock, skeletal fingers grasping for purchase. Small fragments of Mayve's urgent yells punctured his rapidly deteriorating mind. "Right there...grab....move your foot up." The instructions were almost useless, he had no time to think. His boots kicked the rock over and over, blindly scraping until he found a foothold. All he could think of were jaws clamping over his leg, dragging him from the rock to be eviscerated and devoured.

Mayve directed him from above, her torso dangling. "Push with your right foot....left hand reaches....far as possible." Eiklo launched upward, following her instructions. He stretched his reach as best he could, and his fingers snagged in a crack in the rock. Following where she was pointing, he found a new handhold each time. Her green eyes looked over his shoulder with increasing worry, locked on the beasts closing in.

Mayve stopped pointing at handholds and reached directly for him. "...jump...jump, Eiklo...jump!" Her eyes looked directly at him now. Or maybe she was looking at something directly underneath him.

"Jump, Eiklo! Now! Right now!"

He leapt upward, boots pushing off the meager footholds he had, his hand reaching for Mayve. Their palms touched, and he was yanked upward as jaws snapped shut mere inches away, biting air. With a desperate heave from Mayve, he crashed on solid rock.

Trying to rise, Eiklo found he had no strength left. All he could do was listen to the howls and hungry scrabbling of claws on stone, and pray they were safe for the night.

Chapter 25

Trapped

E iklo awoke to fading stars and a hint of sunrise on the horizon. As his vision focused, he saw Mayve relaxing on the other side of the plateau. *We're both alive, thank Varin. I must have passed out.* The sun peeked over the dunes into their basin, and glinted off something in Mayve's hand. Her canteen?

No, the sunlight was reflecting *through* the object. *A gemstone of some sort, and a sizable one at that. A sapphire?*

Not wanting to alert Mayve that he had awoken, he lay still and focused on the object out of the corner of his eye. It looked like a huge cut gemstone, but completely smooth, as if it was worn down in a river for a thousand years instead of cut by a jeweler. In the first auras of dawn, he thought he saw ornate golden etchings and other foreign runes covering its translucent surface.

Varin's scrolls, what does Mayve have? Had that been hiding on her belt for their entire journey? She did have a leather pouch of a similar shape. He had never thought to ask what was inside. Their past couple days had been hectic, putting it mildly.

He had no idea if Mayve meant trouble yet. *Besides being accidentally responsible for the bramble eldritches terrorizing Devar after stealing some seeds, she's in possession of, at the very least, the most expensive piece of jewelry ever made, if not more. She has to be a thief on the run.*

Mayve stared at the jewel like she was deeply curious, not like a burglar admiring a stolen bounty. Eiklo burst with questions.

He decided to ask her about it once they were safe. Admittedly, he too was very curious about the object, especially if it was stolen. Mayve grew more mysterious the more he learned about her. There was always some sort of far away frustration brewing in her gaze. *A human who climbs like a mountain tauninaga and can sense the Du'ul after an hour of meditation, with a penchant for stealing incredible things.* How much of what she told him was lies? Maybe she already knew volcomancy and it was all a trick.

Pretending to toss and turn a few times to get her attention, Eiklo sat up. A wave of nausea hit him and his muscles ached. His groan of pain was echoed by a low growl from somewhere below the plateau. *They're waiting for us down there.* He rested his agonized skull in his hands. *Thank Varin we're safe.* They would have been ripped to pieces in the night if the gorgonwolves could scale the cliff.

The butte was rough, reddish-beige stone around twenty feet in diameter. It had a gentle slope to it, with one side rising about twenty-five feet above the sand and the other only around twenty. They had climbed up the higher side on their dash for safety. The entire butte jutted up dead center from a ring of towering dunes, obscuring all vision of the horizon. The only sign of which direction they'd come from was their footprints, leading back toward the Devaros and trampled by paw prints.

Mayve stirred as Eiklo did, raising a tired hand in greeting. She was seated with her arms wrapped around her knees, blanketed by her shawl. The strange jewel was hidden away, although now Eiklo was acutely aware of the round pouch safely secured to her belt.

She looked relieved to see Eiklo awake, and breathed a sigh of relief. "Thank Phovus, I was really hoping you weren't dead."

Eiklo spun to face her. "What made you think that?"

"You don't breathe and you have no heartbeat! The only way I know you're alive is the blue orbs in your eyes." Mayve pointed at his eye sockets. "The minute I hauled you up, you collapsed and the lights went out."

"I'm alive. Still deciding which one I'd prefer. Everything hurts."

"At least your *only* problem is the wolves." She stood to face him with her hands on her hips. "What now? We're safe here but I only have a mouthful of water left."

Eiklo jabbed a skeletal thumb toward the plateau edge. "We still have company, I see? They haven't given up yet?"

"You didn't see, because you took an impromptu nap. They were uncomfortably close to getting up here earlier." Mayve pointed to the shorter side of the butte. "One of the beasts almost climbed up, not even half an hour ago. It made several attempts, each better than the last, and even managed to scrape the top half of its body up here, but its hind legs could not find any purchase."

Eiklo's blue orbs were wide with worry. "You should have woken me!"

"I figured if one got up here, you'd appreciate dying in your sleep."

He shot Mayve a cold look.

"...or perhaps they would think you were already dead and leave you be."

Rime crystals crept across Eiklo's brow, expressing frustration. "Luckily we won't be here for long, we can leave as soon as the sun rises."

"The gorgonwolves are certainly not going anywhere."

"Do you know much about gorgonwolves?"

"Not particularly."

"You'll see. It's actually quite a remarkable phenomenon."

Mayve looked at him, skeptical, but pressed on to her next burning question. "If that's so, say we have all day to put distance between us and them. What do we do? They'll follow our trail anywhere, and now we're half a day's walk from the river, which we know has nothing safe around it."

It's true. This rock is really our only safety. But we need to get back to the Devaros and get Mayve more water. She already has far less than enough. Could we get to the Devaros, refill our water, then get back to this rock? They'd be safe, but it would accomplish nothing. Especially if the gorgonwolves were ambitious enough to keep trying to climb the short side of the butte. They may eventually succeed.

There was only one way to survive and he was dreading it.

Mayve seemed to read his mind. "We have to cross the river. I'm not dying on this rock, and I'm done stumbling blindly through the desert. Thank Phovus we had his luck with us."

Eiklo hung his head. "I know, I panicked and now we're here. If you die, it's my fault, and I won't let that happen."

Mayve looked caught off guard, like she was expecting an argument, and uncrossed her arms. "Your plan *did* work, even if it needed a bit of luck."

"I would *not* call it a plan. It was a mad, desperate gamble."

"Yeah, I was being nice."

"I thought it was our only choice."

"It was. You couldn't do it, and I can't cross that river without you."

That's right. You couldn't do it. It's all your fault. She'll die out here without you. She may die out here because of you.

"For what it's worth," Mayve said, "I know you *can* do it. Depths below, you've already done it before, even if it knocked you unconscious. I'll help in any way I can."

Eiklo's eyes glowed a lighter blue. A subtle sign of appreciation. He hoped she truly meant it. The situation for her was far more dire than it was for him. "I'm not used to this."

"All of this? I have to say, it doesn't happen to me very often either."

"No, no, stop it. I'm not used to being in danger."

Mayve eyed him curiously. "You traveled all the way here from the Northern Frost Vent, surely you've been in danger before. That's not an easy trek."

Eiklo thought about his journey south. "There was, on occasion, but it was never up to me. I've been protected by the strongest Ul'Varin-Zul, and the most powerful volcomancers in the Northern Ice, and then Captain Vulinor and the Ferrymen. I've always been protected, not protecting. Depths below, you saw me try to subdue the *aerstab-bourl* on the Ferry. Great lot of good I did there."

Faint mist pooled on the lower rims of his eye sockets. "I left to see the world. Turns out, the world is too dangerous to see on your own. That's why I've been working on the Ferry."

Mayve shrugged. "You've seen more than I have. I've never left Devar and have had to dance around death nonetheless. Maybe if you stayed in Rulnevrin, you'd be leviathan food."

"What a comforting thought. Instead of becoming leviathan food, I'll be gorgonwolf food." He looked at the brightening sky. "Alright. As soon as the sun's up, we trek back to the river. It should take half a day, if we trek carefully and conserve our strength. There, you climb down and get your water, and I'll work on forming a raft of ice before I climb down. I'd appreciate your help climbing down, like earlier. I didn't realize how at home you are on the side of a cliff."

Mayve gave a small nod as thanks, but Eiklo saw a smile hidden in the corners of her mouth. He continued, "We'll take the time to do it right and minimize our risk of capsizing. You can help by climbing down and acting as my eyes."

"Any ideas on how to paddle ourselves across the river?"

Eiklo shook his head. "Not a clue. I suppose we'll have to use our hands, and by we, I mean you. I'll have to spend my time manifesting to keep the raft from melting. We'll lose a lot of ground downriver, but at least we'll be rid of the wolves."

"Speaking of, when can we head out?"

Eiklo stared at the rising sun. With no eyeballs to damage, he could look at it all day long if he chose to, although it was rather bland. A strange perk of being a skeleton, although the overwhelming brightness obscured any interesting details it might have. The fiery ball was just beginning to peek over the dunes that encircled their tiny plateau.

"We might be able to leave now." He peaked over the edge at the beasts—who were lying in a pack near the cliff—and kicked a pebble down. It thudded into the sand with no reaction. "Excellent, looks like we're all set. How about you climb down first so you can direct me if I botch the descent?"

Mayve peeked over the edge. "You're insane, they're waiting right there."

"Trust me, you'll be safe. As long as you don't touch them." Eiklo sat on the edge and threw another rock into the sand. It formed a tiny crater next to the largest wolf's head before bouncing farther away.

Mayve glared at Eiklo, then spun off the cliff. Her boots slammed into the rock and she picked her way down the wall foot by foot. Eiklo saw her gingerly step into the sand by the gorgonwolves and whisper, "Phovus, what the depths happened to it?"

Eiklo grinned, cold rime spreading from the corners of his mouth. He did not remember what smiling felt like, but he figured it did not feel at all like streaks of ice freezing across his face. He peered over the edge and called, "How are they looking?"

Mayve stood in the middle of the pack, staring at the beasts in awe. Five gorgonwolf statues, entombed in stunning detail, stood around her in different poses. Some were curled up sleeping, others stood with their mouths open, mid-breath, stone tongues dangling between their gray teeth. She whispered, "Are they dead? I can never tell when something is dead anymore."

Eiklo called to mind the exact passage from the study of a book on desert fauna he read in the Thaumaturn Six library. "Gorgonwolves, in order to prevent loss of water due to perspiration during the intense heat of daylight hours, undergo a process of self-petrification. During this time, the outer dermis and other extremities transform into a hard substance with all the properties of stone. Further tests are necessary to deduce whether this stimulus is based on heat or light."

Mayve waved a hand in front of the closest gorgonwolf's stone eyes, satisfied with its lack of reaction. "They can't see or hear me?"

"According to accounts given to the Northern Ice raptors by the desert raptors, the only sense that remains is direct touch, so they can un-petrify in case of emergencies."

Mayve grunted in mild curiosity, then wrapped her shawl around her head and shoulders to ward off the incoming sun. She did not have the luxury of turning to stone to keep her dwindling water. "Get down here. It will be a tough trek. The more we cover before the midday sun, the better we'll be for the river crossing." She set off into the sands, following their last set of footprints.

"Let's put some distance between us and these godforsaken beasts." Eiklo carefully dangled off the ledge, blindly kicking for footholds. He looked past his boots at the five petrified animals, excited to study them up close.

He froze, bones running cold. *There were six of them last night.*

A low, guttural snarl rolled across the plateau.

Chapter 26

The Desert Sun

The snarl turned to a starving roar as loping footfalls raced around the plateau. Eiklo screamed at Mayve out in the sands, "Mayve! It's awake! Run!"

She spun around, startled. He frantically waved, pointing to where he heard the growls, hoping she'd understand. Without hesitation, she took off in a dead sprint back toward the plateau.

A chilling howl echoed off every dune as the gorgonwolf rounded the edge of the plateau and saw its prey hightailing for safety. The dark, lanky shadow launched into a terrifying gait, charging toward the meal it had waited so long for. Its long jaws opened wide as it bore down on Mayve.

She's not going to make it. The gorgonwolf sprinted alongside the cliff face, aiming to cut Mayve off. It would catch Mayve as she reached the wall, and the tie would not end in her favor.

Mayve's boots hit the rock wall as the gorgonwolf leapt, mouth wide and teeth bared. In a moment of mindless panic, Eiklo trapped the Du'ul and channeled it through his skeletal fist. The Du'ul manifested outward in a wintery explosion, sending him flying back from the edge.

A hailstone, three times the size of his fist, slammed into the gorgonwolf's head and burst into slivers of icy shrapnel. The creature's leap was diverted right before it clamped its jaws around Mayve, its long muzzle knocked to the side. Its teeth snapped on empty air as Mayve shot up the wall with inhuman speed and over the lip of the plateau.

Eiklo and Mayve lay on the rock, each gasping for breath. Finally, Mayve spoke. "That was..." She gasped for more air. "Fuck that."

The gorgonwolf howled from below and she crawled farther away from the edge, then rolled onto her back. The rising sun glinted off the sweat dripping down her brow. More precious water, lost. "Eiklo, why is that sand-cursed creature still awake?"

Eiklo tried to push himself up and grimaced in pain as he put weight on the hand he'd manifested from. He shifted his weight and used his other arm. "They're smart, that's all I can say. It knew we would try to escape with the sun."

The gorgonwolf howled again, this time from the southern edge. "It's circling us," Mayve groaned. "Did you know they can choose to not petrify themselves?"

"It must be delaying its petrification in hopes that it can catch us. Surely it will have to at some point, just like how we all need sleep," Eiklo pondered. He removed his glove to study his damaged hand. The bones were latticed with hairline cracks, glowing with bright white light, like a cracked vase filled with coals. The fissures were slowly dimming as the elemental energy within him knit the bone back together, but it would hurt for the day, and be sore for several after.

He peered over the edge at the gorgonwolf. It prowled alongside the rock wall, meeting his gaze with hungry eyes. Its spindly tongue licked the dry air, panting. A shiver ran down Eiklo's spine, and he retreated to the center of their safe rock.

Mayve sat down, looking utterly defeated. She noticed Eiklo's glowing hand as he re-gloved it. "What happened to you?"

"I manifested an unhealthy amount of Du'ul and hit the wolf with a big chunk of ice," Eiklo said. "Before you ask, I'm not sure how I did it. I've never done that before, and it was very painful."

Mayve leaned against her knees. "Any chance you can make another one?" The warmth of the sun was quickly burning away the chill of the desert night.

He trapped the Du'ul, feeling the surge of energy as the immense power of the Vents swelled in his chest. Channeling the energy to his uninjured fist, he manifested as much as he possibly could without risking any further damage. A gust of freezing wind blasted the rock face and a flurry of tiny snowflakes followed. Mayve cupped her hands, trying to catch as many as she could. Most evaporated into nothing the instant they landed. She tilted her hands up and shook loose a few measly drops. The skeleton slumped back, head swimming. He would have to completely exhaust himself to give Mayve even a thimble's worth of water.

Eiklo wondered out loud, "It must have been a gut reaction to your impending death. Creating ice from nothing is considered a significant milestone for an ice volcomancer, although I don't think this counts since I can't replicate the results. If it makes you feel better, the ball of ice shattered into a million pieces, so the gorgonwolf doesn't get to drink either."

"Well, congratulations on your volcomantic accomplishment, and thank you for saving my life."

"No need to apologize; we're stuck on this rock because of me, and I'll make sure we survive." Eiklo said.

They sat and stared at the brightening sky like a sentenced man gazing at the gallows, their meager rock already warming under the blistering sun. Finally, Mayve stood up and asked, "Since we have the time, how about another lesson in volcomancy?"

"I don't see why not, not much else to do up here." Eiklo shuffled into a meditative stance. "From what you were telling me yesterday, it sounds like you did, in fact, sense the Du'ul. On your first try, impressively, which is promising for future training. If you're not too exhausted, how about you try to trap it?"

Mayve sat facing Eiklo, legs crossed. "Alright, then, tell me how. Maybe my Natural Manifestation is creating water and all my problems will go away."

Eiklo laughed. He appreciated that Mayve kept her spirits high even when starved and parched on a desert rock, surrounded by voracious beasts. It helped quench his anxiety, if only marginally. "Sense, trap, then manifest. You've got the first part down, so do that again. Once you feel it, let me know."

Mayve closed her eyes, legs crossed, with her hands on her knees. Her breathing slowed, deep and steady. After a minute, he saw her face scrunch and her hands clench, knuckles turning white. Sensing the Du'ul was unnerving to many people. Several of Eiklo's fellow students at Thaumaturn Six had ceased their studies after their first encounter with it.

He had not known Mayve for long, but it was clear she was rarely stopped from doing what she wanted. *It's a miracle I convinced her to plod into the desert at all. She should've thrown me in the river. Maybe I'd make an ice raft then.*

The human spoke tentatively, her mind focused elsewhere. "Okay... I'm in the Du'ul. It's crashing against our rock here, flowing around it and over it...and directly through it. Through me and through you as well."

Eiklo tried to remember how his mentors had taught him, recalling their exact words. "What does it feel like to you?" This was an important question. The Du'ul was perceived in many ways, different for every volcomancer.

Mayve's brow furrowed, trying to describe the experience as she lived it. "Like I'm submerged in the Devaros, but instead of being battered by the current, it's passing through me as if I'm not there."

"Familiarize yourself with it. It can't hurt you until you trap it. Remember that it's always there, always passing through you, even when you're not looking for it." To Eiklo, sensing and trapping the Du'ul had become second nature. If Mayve continued her studies, it would be the same for her.

Eiklo watched Mayve take a deep breath, trying to acclimate to the Du'ul. After a minute, he said, "Remember, once you capture it, you *must* hold it and release it in a controlled manner. If you panic and release all the trapped Du'ul at once, it will go *very* poorly. A dam can control the flow of water, but when it bursts, people die. I can't stress enough how dangerous it is, not just for you, but for me as well, depending on your Natural Manifestation."

Mayve nodded. Her hands fidgeted nervously, but her face was determined. "Tell me how."

Eiklo recalled his past teachings. "Trapping the Du'ul is another mental process, requiring the wielder to visualize themselves from a metaphysical perspective, in order to capture an unseen energy. The most common method, that works for the vast majority of students, is to imagine your skin as a barrier, forming instantly and trapping the Du'ul that's passing through you. Many students find it helpful to imagine the barrier as a material they are familiar with, such as ice, stone, or bark. I knew one master volcomancer who envisioned his skin as a net without holes. He used to be a fisherman, and it worked well for him." He asked Mayve, "Did you understand that?"

She nodded, brow furrowed with intense concentration. "Imagine my skin instantly turning into some solid material, trapping any Du'ul that is flowing through me. Makes sense."

Several quiet minutes followed. Eiklo meditated himself, curiously checking on the Vent beast, now miles away, while also trying to relax and recuperate some energy from the toiling day they just had.

Mayve opened her eyes and fell backward, stretching out on the rock. "Phovus, this is difficult. My head hurts."

"It takes some students months of intense meditation to grasp it. You're doing exceedingly well so far. Both sensing and trapping are both very mentally taxing."

Mayve asked, "How long did it take you to trap the Du'ul?"

"A few weeks," Eiklo said. "However, Ul'Varin are more connected to the Vents. It's not a fair comparison. They brought us back to life, after all."

The human sat up and reseated herself in her cross-legged pose. She closed her eyes and asked, "How will I know when I trap it?"

Eiklo chuckled. "You'll definitely know."

"Why are you always so cryptic?"

"I find discovery to be one of the greatest joys in life, it's always better to see something for yourself than have someone else tell you what they saw."

"Is that why you left the academics behind?"

"In a nutshell."

Mayve sighed in annoyance and resumed her meditation. *She seems to be innately gifted with the Du'ul. It won't be long before we see results.*

He had no idea how fast he would be proven correct.

Mayve's eyes shot wide open and she gasped. "*What the fuck*...this is....Eiklo! I can't...what do I do?" She leapt to her feet, breathing frantic, deep breaths, trying to control what looked like a mixture of excitement, awe, and panic.

Eiklo jumped up too, his blue eyes focused and intense. "You did it! You trapped it! Don't worry, it's not going anywhere, just keep your barriers strong. What does it feel like?" He remembered his first time trapping the Du'ul, the raw hurricane of energy invigorating his every sense.

Mayve stammered between huge breaths, her hands shaking. "Awake! More awake than I've ever been...Phovus, it feels like I swallowed fire!"

"The Du'ul wants to break free, to return to its flow across Ralvera. Your body is the barrier that is preventing it from doing so. It's up to you to control it."

Mayve nodded frantically, eyes wide and buzzing.

"Focus on your fist, or one of your fingers. Imagine the barrier there weakening, slowly cracking. That is how you direct the Du'ul to manifest where you want."

Mayve formed a fist and reared her arm back.

Eiklo dove for cover, covering his face reflexively. "*Varin's sword*, face away from me!"

"Sorry!" Mayve turned her back to the skeleton and punched the air. Nothing happened.

Eiklo's blue eyes focused inquisitively. "Did you do anything?"

Mayve punched the air again. Then she opened her palm and tried twisting her hand. Still nothing. Then she tried flicking her fingers one by one, then pushing with both open palms like throwing open a heavy door. Each time, nothing.

She collapsed back onto the ground. "Is that normal? I'm exhausted."

Eiklo tilted his skull in curiosity. "If you're exhausted, then you've used up all your Du'ul. Which means you did, in fact, manifest it. I suppose we just don't know how."

"Everything hurts." Mayve fell limp on the rock face.

Eiklo regurgitated more of his mentor's teachings. "Sensing and trapping the Du'ul is mentally taxing. Manifesting it, on the other hand, is physically taxing. Holding and directing the Du'ul requires solid physical strength. All of it gets easier with practice, like working out a muscle. The more you practice, the more you can trap, and the stronger your manifestations become." He wondered out loud, "Very strange that we did not see anything. The Du'ul *has* to manifest into something as it leaves your body and returns to the world."

Mayve struggled back to her feet. "Let me try again."

Eiklo quickly interjected, "You should rest. Volcomancy will easily tire you out, and we need our strength."

Mayve sighed. "That rush of power. It was *beyond* exhilarating, like I drank five coffees, ate a basket of sandpeppers, and leapt off the Devaros Falls. That happens every time?"

"Every time. As much as we hate them, the Vents are powerful. Capturing just a fraction of their energy is often more than we can comprehend." Eiklo knew exactly what Mayve was feeling. He remembered it all too well, trapping for the first time. But when he had punched the air, a tornado of cold air froze all of Master Refno's feathers. *Mayve has to have done something. The Du'ul has to manifest.* Still, nothing seemed out of place on their little plateau.

"Phovus, I feel like I climbed the Arch." The exhaustion of manifesting was hitting Mayve hard. "Wake me when we can leave." She wrapped herself in her shawl as a makeshift blanket and lay down as the sun crept across the sky. Sleeping away the day in makeshift shade was her best chance at conserving water and energy.

Eiklo sat motionless, listening attentively for any sounds from the prowling gorgonwolf. The minute it petrified itself, they had to leave. The more daylight burned away, the less time they had to get to the river before sunset.

If I was in Mayve's position...I doubt I'd be alive. The human was strong and recklessly endurant. But, everyone had their limits. He prayed that Mayve was far from approaching her own. If the gorgonwolf remained unpetrified until sunset, they were beyond dead. If Mayve did not waste away by then, the sun and heat would sap her strength to nothing. All assuming the gorgonwolves did not claw their way up onto the plateau in a starving fervor.

Hours passed and the sun climbed higher. With the blazing sun at its apex in the pristine blue sky, there was nothing Eiklo could do but sit and wait, listening to the hungry growls and padding footsteps of the gorgonwolf as it circled their rock. The sun beat voraciously against his cloak, the hood pulled as far over his skull as possible to keep his bleached face in the shade. As uncomfortable as he was, he could not imagine the personal hell that Mayve was experiencing. The human was motionless underneath her shawl, and had been since the morning. The imperceptible flutter of her shawl moving with her breaths was Eiklo's only indicator she was still living.

It was late afternoon when Eiklo heard the faint crunch of stone. He perked up at the sound, and crept to the edge to look at the gorgonwolf pack. Traumatized by the beginning of the day, he counted them multiple times to confirm their numbers.

Six. The final gorgonwolf was encased in perfectly detailed gray stone, every stand of hair immaculately petrified. The beast was frozen mid-lope. *An interesting stance. Makes me think it was resisting petrification, much like an exhausted human can only resist sleep for so long before succumbing against its will.*

Eiklo stared at the beast for several minutes, just to be sure this was not another clever trick. He would never underestimate gorgonwolves again. Once he was sure, he rushed to Mayve and shook her awake, whispering, "Wake up. We're safe."

Mayve slowly unwrapped the shawl from her face, blinking groggily. Her lips were cracked and dry. She pressed her fingers to her temples, which told Eiklo that she had a crushing headache from the dehydration. "Our persistent friend is finally asleep?"

"Finally," Eiklo said. "Let's get going."

Mayve squinted west, where the sun hovered uncomfortably close to the horizon. "We don't have much time until sunset. If we make it to the river, will you have enough time to form an ice raft before the gorgonwolves catch us?"

"We'll just have to find out."

"Spoken like a reckless Devarian street rat. I like it." Mayve pushed a faint smile through her cracked lips. Without wasting a second more, she checked her belt, finished her last sip of water, and climbed down the plateau.

Mayve would survive this, he would make sure of it. He thought about the explosive manifestation that saved her from the gorgonwolf that morning. *I punched the wolf away with a massive hailstone. I didn't know I could do that, but I did. Maybe I can get us across the river.*

Worst-case scenario, if the gorgonwolves catch us, I'll get to see what happens when I manifest the energy through my whole body. One final experiment, to allow Mayve to escape. She will survive this ordeal I created.

He climbed down after Mayve, boots sinking into the sand as he stepped away from their lifesaving rock and toward the dunes. There would be no returning here, he would make sure of that. Determination pushed back the doubts in his mind, but he could not quell all his fears. The faintest whisper of fear in his mind called out to him, as the sun plummeted toward the horizon.

In the dying sun, the wolves will awaken. When the light dies, you will die with it.

"*Imagine a community where there is no strife or conflict. Everyone is given purpose. Everyone is connected in ways we'd find incomprehensible. Now imagine all that is ripped away. That is what it means to be Torn.*"

"*But, are they not free now? With the Queens gone, are they not able to live whatever life they choose?*"

"*Say you lost everything you have right now, everything you know and love, but gain the ultimate freedom to do whatever your heart desires. Would you take that deal?*"

"*I don't know. I suppose not.*"

"*The Torn were not given that choice.*"

—recorded conversation between Master Ebo and his student, Akra. Thaumaturn Two, circa. 37 FR

Chapter 27

Crimson Scars

Raudius opened his right eye for the first time in several days. The bark creaked softly as he blinked several times, the uncovered eye adjusting to the dim light of Cindri's hut.

The orange raptor tossed aside the old bandage and held up a candle to inspect the wound closer.

Raudius grunted, "You know what doesn't sit well with us Oaken Legion folk?"

The raptor snarled, "Not at all, tell me."

"Open flame."

Cindri looked at the candle dancing near the leaves on Raudius's head. "Ah." He quickly repositioned it so he could still see the wound from relative safety.

His reptilian pupils dilated, inspecting the cut above Raudius's eye. It had been several days since they put the carved sliver of red Oaganshi pine into the wound. "You'll need to help me here. How do I know if the graft took hold?"

"That's a good question, I'm no healer myself. Is anything leaking from it? Any blood?"

"It's wet from the bandage, but that looks like it." Cindri peered closer. His fanged maw was directly in front of Raudius's eyes.

He strained to look up at Cindri without moving his head. "Is it flush with the rest of my bark?"

Cindri studied it for several seconds. "Looks like it. I don't see any gaps." He stepped back and rummaged through a nearby satchel, his scaly tail flicking back and forth. "If it worked, the graft should be part of you now. See if you feel anything when you touch it. Maybe try to move it or pull it out?"

Reaching up, Raudius gingerly brushed his fingertips on the graft. It felt like his own forehead. His new skin tingled at his own touch. Unlike the rest of his bark, which was rough oak, the Oaganshi pine was smooth, almost like beech. Cindri told him that the Oaganshi pines were smooth so that sand wouldn't find purchase in its bark. Something Raudius was all too accustomed to, sleeping outside with the animals.

Running his fingers from his oaken bark to the Oaganshi pine, he felt no difference between the two other than the texture. He poked the grafted wood, feeling the pressure on his forehead. Then he grabbed a small carving knife from a nearby sheath and gently scratched the bark. A tiny prick of pain told him that the grafted wood was now fully a part of him.

He quickly returned the knife to its sheath and set it down. Cindri didn't bat an eye, but if Ingo saw him with it, he would assuredly be dragged into the center of camp and beaten senseless.

Cindri turned around, holding a roughly crafted mirror, barely more than a shard of glass. He blew a coating of dust from it—which did very little to improve the quality of the reflection—before handing it over.

Raudius tilted the mirror to catch the torchlight and see the wound simultaneously. He grimaced at the sight of himself. Sand was lodged in every crevice in his bark, and many of his leaves were wilting away, turning as brown as the sand.

His exhaustion was set deep in his eyes. Above his right eye, the smooth red graft showed the extent of the wound Tash had inflicted. It extended from his right temple almost to the center of his forehead. If it wasn't for the graft, he would have needed weeks of healing, maybe even suffered permanent injury. Cindri had done an excellent job carving the Oaganshi pine to fit the cut perfectly.

To his honest surprise, he admired his new bark. He liked the look of it, and it would be an exciting story to add to his adventure. *What will they call me? General Raudius, the Crimson. Or perhaps, Raudius the Bloodied. Praetor Raudius, Fire Eye, or maybe Elder Raudius the Scarred.*

Cindri's orange maw poked around the edge of the mirror, studying him. "Medically speaking, it's fascinating. The Oaganshi pine is only found in the middle of the Sandscales, where no Oaken Legion soldiers have ever set foot. It's not native to the North *or* South Verdants, and now it's fully grafted to your skull."

Raudius grunted, "Strange, indeed. Thank you, Cindri. You've saved me from a grueling recovery."

Cindri took the mirror back and reached for fresh bandages. "I'm glad you've healed properly. Let's re-bandage the wound, before anyone sees I've carved up a sacred plant and stuffed it into a Legion soldier—"

The tent flap swept open and Ingo slunk in, yellow eyes burning from behind matted, blood-red feathers. He looked even more exhausted than Raudius.

His eyes alighted on Raudius's new graft. He bared his maw, lined with sharp fangs, and snarled at Cindri, "Is that a chunk of sacred pine in the tree's skull?"

Cindri looked petrified. He whispered, "Perhaps."

There was terror in his voice, but not for himself. Raudius already knew that Ingo would never lay a claw on Cindri. The orange raptor was terrified of what might happen to Raudius.

Ingo exhaled a low snarl, and motioned with a flick of his maw for Cindri to continue bandaging. "If it helps the tree survive to Port Wenstnor, then I don't care. Cover it. The others might take poorly to it." Ingo scared the Oakfire out of Raudius. There was violence in the raptor's eyes, and Raudius was eternally grateful that a tauninaga in Port Wenstnor was the target of his fury.

When I eventually escape in Port Wenstnor, I better hope I get far away from Ingo in particular, lest I find myself under his blade.

Cindri rushed forward with the bandages, wrapping them around Raudius's head. He left both Raudius's eyes open this time, just covering the bark. The wound was nearly healed; there was no reason to restrict his eyesight anymore.

Ingo snarled, "Presh's hawk arrived with another message. The Oaken Legion we fought in Devar arrived back, with only half their original numbers. It looks like they ran into trouble traveling north and were forced back to the city." Ingo growled the news to Cindri. However, he spoke in Ralveran instead of Raptoran, clearly expecting Raudius to listen in.

Ambushed! By who? In the desert, it could be anybody. A raptor tribe or a roving group of bandits? Sailing north to Tyrak Pass, they would have passed through the Boiling Bend and the Wall of Okanos. The Ul'Varin-Rak held a near impenetrable line of defense, protecting the Devaros River from the Okanos Vent, but it was not unheard of for the most ferocious Vent beasts to break through. *No one but a Vent beast would dare attack a fully armored Oaken Legion quindecis, right?* His stomach sank as he remembered Ingo had done just that at the Hangman's Swing.

Ingo locked his hateful yellow gaze on Raudius and snarled, "Here's what I find especially intriguing. They left Devar quickly, but this time, they're heading south."

Raudius's look of surprise must have intrigued Ingo. The raptor grabbed the collar of Raudius's shirt in his claws and pulled the tree upward toward his maw. Raudius was tall for a soldier, but Ingo was a hulk of a raptor, matching his height and then some. Unlike Cindri, who smelled like an exotic concoction of medicinal herbs, Ingo carried the burning stench of meat and alcohol.

He coated Raudius in this stench as he snarled into the tree's face, tilting his head in feigned curiosity. "What's that look on your face, barkscum? Is that genuine shock, or have you been hiding something? Because we now have an Oaken Legion force sailing to Port Wenstnor, where *you* were so eager to go."

Raudius was too lost in his own fears to attempt any amount of sarcasm or trickery. He stammered out, "I have no idea what their intentions are, I swear on the Verdant! I haven't contacted them since I left Devar! How would I even do that?"

Ingo's tongue flicked in and out as he studied the young tree's expression. "No ideas at all? They were your tribe, after all. You are clue-less to their movements?"

"I swear on the green roots of Verdancias, the last plan I knew about was to travel to the Bastion of Growth. In the North Verdant." Raudius quickly added the last clarification in case the raptors didn't know the Four Bastions. He almost said *return to* instead of *travel to*—he could not let slip that he was from the North Verdant and not the South.

His groveling seemed to convince the raptor. "Strange that such pitiful creatures bring such pain to our people." Ingo spat the words at Raudius. "I hope you're lying, so I can cut off your head later. Regardless, word by hawk travels slowly. The Legion will arrive in Port Wenstnor a day or two after us, I reckon. We should have everything we need by then." He snarled a string of fast-spoken Raptoran at Cindri, his tone suggesting a combination of scolding and confidentiality, likely about the Oaganshi pine sliver. His brother nodded along, eyes staring at the sandy floor of the tent.

Ingo left through the tent flap, long tail curling after him. As he did, he paused to hiss at both of them in Ralveran. "Better keep that bandage on. If any other raptor sees that scar, I can't save you."

Alone again, Cindri and Raudius sat in silence while Cindri finished wrapping the bandage around the tree's head, waiting for the sickening tension of Ingo's presence to die down. Raudius could tell from Cindri's flattened feathers and quieted demeanor that the raptor was worried about his older brother.

For whatever strange reason, he decided to level his inner thoughts with Cindri. "Your brother scares the Oakfire out of me." *Why in the depths did I say that? Show no fear, you incompetent greenling!*

Another voice in his head countered, *Cindri would never use that information against you.* Raudius was not so sure. If he attacked the tribe, Cindri would not hesitate to kill him, surely.

Cindri let out a meek chuckle, feathers ruffling. "He has always been rather intense. Spotch kept him in check, in some ways, and he checked Spotch in others. They were inseparable."

"You seem to be handling his death better than Ingo," Raudius said. "You're not looking for revenge yourself?"

Cindri shook his head. "We all grieve in different ways, and Ingo was undeniably closer to Spotch than I was. He was my protective older brother, but he was Ingo's twin. It's impossible to match that bond."

"Hence, all of...this." Raudius waved a hand to the door. "An entire raptor war party on the hunt for one tauninaga."

Cindri shrugged. "And some artifact that was stolen from us, after we stole it from you."

"Do you even know what it does?" Raudius asked. "I don't, and I'm not sure anyone in my quindecis does either. Maybe Grenner, our ranking officer, but if he did, he never shared."

Cindri replied, "It has to be important if the Oaken Legion were willing to send a 'quindecis,' or whatever you called it, into the desert. If it's important to the Legion, then we have to make sure you don't have it."

"Would Lairro or a raptor in Devar know?"

"Maybe King Coinclaw would know, but if they do then I haven't heard anything. He's not a real king anyway."

Raudius opened his mouth to push further, but Cindri cut him off, tightening the bandage into its final place. "That will hold for a few days at least, until we arrive at Port Wenstnor. Then we'll remove the bandages before you enter the city." He held open the tent flap. "Come find me if the graft takes an unexpected turn for the worst."

The tree took an uncertain step into the center of camp. "I will. Appreciate it, Cindri." The raptor nodded and sealed the tent behind him. The sun was rising and the camp was barren. The beige-patterned tents blended perfectly into the dunes, almost tricking Raudius into thinking he was alone in the vast desert.

He walked back to the open-air shelter, enjoying the illusion of freedom. The raptors did not care about leashing him to Borgo anymore. What would he do? Run into the desert with no water or protection, leaving a perfect set of footprints for them to follow at their leisure?

The pack animals were settling into the sand, going through their usual morning grunts and bites, establishing sleeping space with the other creatures. It still amazed Raudius that these animals stayed nearby, coexisting without any sort of restraints or supervision. The raptors must hold some truly remarkable connection with the beasts.

Lying in the sand, he stewed in his own thoughts. He knew he should attempt to fall asleep before the heat of day took over—he was certainly exhausted enough after a night of walking—but a growing sense of dread kept him awake.

The Oaken Legion marches south. Even if what Ingo said was true, and they lost half their number, that still meant around twelve to fourteen trained Legion soldiers were heading to Port Wenstnor. *They must have found some sort of lead. But after heading north and after getting ambushed? It simply does not make sense.*

He thought of the core flute he saw Grenner using, that day in the tavern. *He could have gotten information from anyone, anywhere. Someone contacted them and spurred them south.*

He could still find the artifact before them. They would arrive a day or two behind them. If winds were favorable, it could be sooner. Either way, Raudius's mission now had a deadline. If he did not recover the artifact before the Legion, he would still be Felled, and the full Ralveran Desert would be between him and home.

Claud, Batia, Traticus. I hope they're safe. I hope Yuetrix is safe. His heart fell for any soldier lost, but he truly hoped his friends were okay. Yuetrix especially had always shown him such kindness and mentorship. Of anyone in his quindecis, he knew that Yuetrix was on his side. He hoped Grenner was amongst the slain, but he knew it was unlikely. Every soldier in that quindecis, him included, would die to shield their commanding officer from harm.

His chance of recovering the artifact—from under the maws of the raptors *and* before the Oaken Legion arrived—were growing increasingly slim. *I can still walk away with my life, if I simply point them to where the tauninaga and the artifact are. Which I don't actually know.*

If the raptors found out he lied? *Death.* If he tried to steal the artifact and they caught him? *Death.* If he acted like a good hostage and walked away from it all after? *Felled.* Forever exiled from the Legion and its Bastions.

Raudius found no sleep that night. As he rose with the sunset, each step took him closer to the bleak and uncertain fate that awaited him in the South Verdant.

Chapter 28

A Moment from Death

T he sun was killing them, step by step. Without the aid of night and the cold temperatures that accompanied it, ascending each dune was grueling torture. Eiklo climbed up each slope of burning dust, the sand scalding every step, praying to see the river on the other side.

While the cold sand of the night felt soothing to Eiklo's freezing bones, the heat sapped his strength and drained his energy. He found himself longing for the frigid halls of the Rulnevrin Cathedral, buried in the glaciers of the Northern Frost Vent. *This is what I get for wanting to see the world.*

While unpleasant, his undeath granted him the strength to persevere in such horrid conditions. He needed no water or food, so he kept a close eye on Mayve, still bound in a mortal body that needed both. Her strength during last night's sprint was gone, and the girl was lagging behind farther and farther. She was out of water, and it had been a couple days since she had eaten. At the crest of the next dune, he trapped the Du'ul Immortanus in his bones and manifested a blast of icy wind.

Mayve stretched her arms and let the wind carry through her shawl, wrapped loosely around her face and shoulders. She was flushed with fatigue.

She took a deep breath of the freezing air. "Reminds me of Darkmist, just before dawn. Sometimes, the mist will ice up the tunnels and you can pretend like you're deep in a Frost Vent."

The human had a far away look in her eyes. Eiklo had been through Devar several times now, on his travels up and down the river. Had they crossed paths before? The vastness of the world still awed Eiklo. So many folk, just in Devar alone, whose lives almost brushed his, and now he was trapped in the desert with one of them.

Curious, he asked, "Have you ever left the desert?"

Mayve shook her head gently, careful not to displace the shawl wrapped around her upper body. "Never. If we make it to Port Wenstnor, it will be my first time in a Verdant."

"You'll be pleased to know that Lake Nawai is frigid, year-round. It's fed by alpine waters from the Azraks."

He saw a twinkle of excitement in her eyes, hardly dampened by their dire situation. Mayve replied absentmindedly, lost in her thoughts, "Mmm. Endless, freezing-cold water..."

The Du'ul inside him faded away as he manifested the last ounce, the freezing wind petering to nothing. Mayve clenched her shawl tighter, hoping to capture the cold for a moment longer, and stepped off the edge of the dune, descending the slope in her graceful, controlled fall. Eiklo followed suit.

Dune after dune, the sun crept lower in the sky. Soon, the temperature would plummet, but the gorgonwolves would awaken. Eiklo used the Du'ul sparingly, whenever he saw Mayve particularly struggling with the heat. At one point, he tried to freeze water in the air to drink, but only managed to condense a few measly drops from far too much effort. He had to save his energy for the river crossing.

Out of an abundance of caution, Eiklo decided to check for Vent beasts. The blue lights in his eye sockets blinked out as he closed them, focusing on a strange feeling in his chest. With proper meditation and a focused mental state, an Ul'Varin-Zul could discern significant information about any nearby Vent creatures.

The grim feeling in his chest focused as he did, slowly shrinking from a broad shiver to a single pinprick of energy pointing out into the desert, as if a long thread connected him to a Vent beast through the dunes and air.

By focusing on the intensity of pinprick, Eiklo could decipher which direction the monster was traveling by how the intensity waxed and waned. If he had the comfort of a calm, safe environment—like the crow's nest of the Ferry—he could have determined much more information about his target. Unfortunately, pressed against the side of a sand dune, exhausted and on edge, did little to improve his concentration. Judging by the height of the thread, it was an *aer*—a flying Vent beast, per Ul'Varin-Rak nomenclature. Judging by the intensity of the thread, it was several miles away over open desert, not in their path to the river. *One less worry.*

The sun soon morphed into a deep red orb set into a blazing orange sky, like an Ul'Varin-Rak eye staring down from the heavens. The bottom half was obscured by the horizon, silhouetting the jagged Ysera Scorch Vent in the wavering heat of the horizon.

The fear in Eiklo's mind whispered away. *Enjoy this sunset. It is your last.* He closed his eyes and blocked out the thoughts. Turning to Mayve, he asked, "How are you holding up?"

Mayve shrugged. "Fine. My tongue is so dry and my head feels like it's splitting apart. We're making good time, though."

"We certainly are. I think we can hit the river before gorgonwolves reach us, but it may be unpleasantly close." Eiklo stared at the setting sun, in the direction of the sleeping beasts. "They'll be waking any minute now."

"If only we were as fast as them," Mayve said. "We'd be in Port Wenstnor by now."

"I'd like to turn to stone while I sleep, it seems peaceful," Eiklo said. "No distractions, nothing to harm you."

Mayve laughed. "You're a volcomancer. One day, you'll be able to encase yourself in ice each night."

"Oh, it's not the same." Eiklo scoffed. "You know, one naturalist at Thaumaturn Six—I think Feshraz was his name. He was originally from a desert tribe, snuck across the Northern Verdant at some point—theorized that a gorgonwolf never dies of old age. As they grow old, they eventually become too weak to break out of the stone each morning, and remain petrified until they starve."

"Why didn't you say this earlier? We could have stayed on the rock until they all died of old age?" Mayve grinned through cracked lips.

They laughed together as the sun fell farther beneath the horizon. A cold breeze carried over the dune, wisping streams of sand over their hands as they clawed up the next dune. Ever so slowly, the dunes were moving, shifting the landscape around them in inches every day.

Eiklo stood up at the edge, looking down at the next valley to cross. He wished they could weave around each dune instead of clambering over them, but they lacked the precious time to do so. He tried to bolster Mayve's spirits. "You're doing well for being severely dehydrated."

"Well, it's good it looks like that, because I am not." Mayve stood beside him and breathed in deeply. "For the sake of honesty, I've been trapping the Du'ul as we walk. The rush of energy you get from holding it in, it's exhilarating and keeps me going."

Eiklo stared at her in astonishment. "You're trapping as you walk? You only just learned to trap yesterday. How are you manifesting it?"

Mayve shrugged. "I remembered how awake and energized I felt, and thought it would help the trek. When I hold it, it clears my headache and the dizziness disappears. As for how I'm manifesting it..." She shrugged, "I'm just letting it dissipate out of me, slowly releasing from all over my body. I haven't seen anything happen yet."

"Neither have I." Eiklo said. "Your Natural Manifestation is perplexing. It can't be nothing." *Can't it, though? The Du'ul can manifest as anything, therefore, it could manifest as nothing.* "Perhaps your Natural Manifestation heals you?"

"The headaches and pains I have return almost immediately once I've run out of Du'ul." Mayve said. "I'm not convinced that's it."

"You're not manifesting away your dehydration, you're just not feeling the effects." Eiklo shrugged. "As long as you're not exhausting yourself, keep going. If it's helping us escape the gorgonwolves, it can't be detrimental, and it's good practice."

The sun fell below the dunes. The inky black sky encroached on the fading remnants of the orange horizon.

As if scared to wake the beasts, Mayve whispered, "We should pick up the pace."

"We'll make it."

It's not enough. It won't be enough. The beasts awaken.

As they crested the next dune, the howls began, fervent and hungry.

Without any further hesitation, they charged across the sands as if the fiery heads of Immortanus were biting at their heels. They were closing in on the river, but Eiklo had no idea if they had enough of a head start to reach it before the gorgonwolves closed in.

Knowing now that Mayve was actively trapping and manifesting the Du'ul, he kept a much closer eye on her as they ran. The human would take a deep breath before each ascension, then charge ahead up the slope with her newfound energy. He had never thought of using the Du'ul as a stimulant before. Trapping it was certainly invigorating. Enticingly so. But manifesting it uncontrolled could cause any number of problems, depending on the caster's Natural Manifestation.

Mayve must have a Natural Manifestation of some sort. She can't have none, the Du'ul has to manifest. We simply don't know its effects yet, or they are completely undetectable. This is why she's able to use the Du'ul as a stimulant, manifesting it without consequences. If Eiklo tried to do the same, he would either plummet the air around him to subzero temperatures, or perhaps freeze himself solid. He wasn't particularly interested in testing it. *Does the Du'ul have to manifest?* All previous studies of the matter pointed to yes.

She could not keep trapping and manifesting like this forever, though. If she did not collapse from physical exhaustion before the night was over, she'd suffer the consequences tomorrow.

"Yes!" Mayve raised both fists to the sky in victory, standing on the top of the dune a few feet above Eiklo. He clambered up next to her and she pointed over the top of the dunes. Several dunes away, the tall slanted rock that Mayve stood on the night before was just visible.

Looking over his shoulder, the gorgonwolves were not in sight yet, but the howls were unsettlingly loud. The dunes were taller heading west. They could be right on the other side and they'd have no idea.

The nasty voice in the back of his mind whispered louder. *You don't have enough time. You're dead either way. Ripped to pieces by savage beasts, or smashed against uncaring rocks by an uncaring river.*

He shoved the thoughts away as he ran. The plan was to trap the Du'ul and freeze a square of the river close to the cliff. It had to be thick enough to support him and Mayve, but he would make it thin enough near the cliff that Mayve would be able to chip it free with her dagger once they were safely aboard.

Boarding would be especially tricky. The river was most dangerous closest to the cliff. If the raft did not hold, or they were unable to safely board, they would be swept into the river along the rocks.

Lost in thought, Eiklo was jarred back to reality as his boots hit solid rock. They had reached the rock field. Ahead, Mayve leapt from boulder to boulder, dashing for the river. Before he could get close, Mayve slid over the edge, disappearing into the gorge.

Eiklo peered over to check, but there was no need. She was already flying down, not missing a single foothold or handhold. Within a minute, she was at the bottom of the cliff, her heels skimming the water-line. The dark river rushed below her, the shadows concealing the swift current.

Keeping her boots on the same footholds, the human carefully chose descending handholds, lowering herself until she was in a crouched position, sitting barely above the waterline. Then she undid the canteen from her belt and unrolled the leather strap. Holding the strap with a free hand, she dropped the canteen into the river. It disappeared under the abyssal waters, the strap growing taunt as the current grabbed in.

Convinced she was safe, Eiklo looked over his shoulder into the desert. Somewhere over those dunes was a pack of vicious gorgonwolves, swiftly closing in.

A few seconds later, Mayve was climbing back up, not bothering to reattach the canteen to her belt. She simply climbed with the strap in hand, the canteen lifting out of the river. It dangled behind her, sloshing excess water from the opening. As soon as she was back on solid land, she upended the canteen, river water gushing into her mouth and spilling over her face and clothes as she drank with abandon.

She didn't stop until the entire canteen was empty. Smiling with relief as water dripped from her nose and chin, exhaustion crashed into her. The many desert treks, her continuous trapping of the Du'ul, and her frantic race to the water appeared to hit her all at once. After a few dizzying steps side to side, Mayve collapsed into a sitting position on the ground, breathing heavily and shivering as her wet clothes soaked in the freezing desert air.

Eiklo started over to her, but she raised a hand to stop him. Between breaths, she gasped, "I'm...okay. Get us across the river." He wanted to help, but Mayve was right—there was no time to delay.

Standing on the edge of the gorge, the river silently coursing beneath him, Eiklo trapped as much Du'ul as his body would allow. The energy of the Vents crescendoed within him, a blizzard raging in his empty chest, obliterating the fatigue of the day. Needing precise control of his manifestation, he curled his skeletal fingers and channeled the Du'ul through each one. They hummed with icy power as he manifested the Du'ul at the river below.

It was near impossible to see what was happening. The waters below were blanketed in the shadow of the cliff, just out of reach of the moonlight. Still, the hollow echoes of cracking ice bounced from the gorge. He had to precisely freeze the running water against the cliff face, growing an iceberg out from the rock. Icicles grew heavy from his jaw as he put every ounce of focus into controlling the Du'ul.

There was a loud crack. A blob of darkness raced downriver, the newly formed raft grabbed by the waters. He needed to strengthen its connection to the wall before he built it outward. He trapped more Du'ul, refilling his body with the vigorous energy, then this time blasted the rock itself with freezing temperatures instead of the water.

Down below, Eiklo saw a dark mass slowly forming outward from the cliff face. The river buffeted against this new obstacle, the inky void-like waters flowing over and under it, determined to wrench it from the canyon wall. He refocused his volcomancy, freezing the water flowing over it to build the raft even higher.

"Eiklo!" Mayve called from some distance away. He looked in her direction to see her standing sentry on a large boulder in the rock field. *She's probably trapping even more Du'ul to stay standing.* "Our friends are here." She pointed into the dunes, where he saw six black specks leap over the top of the farthest dune and disappear down.

Your friends are here. Hurry. The voice of doubt shouted in his mind. There was a flash of pain in his right hand as his volcomancy injury from the morning flared to life. Glowing white fissures raced across his fingers, latticing down the back of his hand.

With another sharp crack, the ice broke away from the cliff face again, swept away. Several more impacts sounded downriver as the iceberg smashed into rocks, splintering to nothing. Eiklo yelled in frustration, "*Ice-cursed fucking river*, hold! Mayve, how much time do we have?"

"A minute or two. They're four dunes away." Mayve rushed to the gorge edge. "How can I help?"

Eiklo trapped even more Du'ul, his blue eyes burning like dying stars, mist pouring from his skull. "I need eyes down there. It keeps breaking away from the cliff and I can barely see what I'm manifesting."

Mayve understood, vaulting over the edge. Eiklo channeled all the Du'ul he could through his arms, manifesting blind into the darkness. He started with the cliff face again, dropping the rock and the nearby water to subzero temperatures. The cracks of the ice mixed with the howls of the impending beasts.

"It needs to be thicker! Don't build into the river yet!" Mayve's voice carried up from the void. Twisting his fingers, he froze the water above and below where he was initially aiming. Another yell came from below: "Keep going! Now build outwards!" He shifted his focus of freezing energy. A new sound echoed from the river. Waves breaking against ice.

The worry in his head screamed. *Look out behind you.* Eiklo couldn't help but glance over his shoulder. The gorgonwolves were descending the final dune, sprinting toward the rock field in complete bloodlust. Their spindly legs covered an ungodly amount of distance in each stride.

He lost concentration, and a final snap of ice echoed from the canyon, the raft breaking free one last time. His soul sank in his chest. The braying of the gorgonwolves closed in. He trapped as much Du'ul as he could, each rib vibrating as if it wanted to shake loose. At least he could take the gorgonwolves with him.

"I caught it! Keep going!" Mayve called from the depths.

Renewed hope surged through Eiklo, and he let down the barrier of his trapped Du'ul, manifesting a massive wave of ice at the float below. The sound of crackling frost filled the night. Mayve shouted below, "That's it! I'm standing on it! Just climb!"

The last bit of Du'ul left his body and exhaustion crashed into him. So focused on the task at hand, he had ignored his other senses. The first thing he heard was rapidly approaching panting, mere feet behind him.

Just like a reckless Devarian street rat. Eiklo jumped.

Jaws snapped shut behind him. A gorgonwolf yelped as its momentum almost carried it over the edge. Wind rushed through his ice-cold skull. His legs hit something solid and buckled, crashing onto smooth ice.

Eiklo's impact pushed the entire float underwater. In the swift current and utter darkness, it was impossible to find a handhold on the slippery surface. Desperately clawing at the raft, he felt himself slide away into the river.

A hand grabbed his cloak and pulled him against the ice. The float burst above the river surface. In his chest, he felt his phantom lungs gasp for air, panicking for breath it didn't need. A long-lost feeling from his past life of flesh and blood. Mayve lay flat against the ice, soaked to the bone. Her dark hair clung to her face in long, amorphous strands. She had one hand grasped on his cloak, and the other clinging for dear life to the handle of her dagger, the blade frozen in the ice up to the hilt. *She placed it there while I was freezing the water. Varin's scrolls, she's clever. And now I owe her my life.*

The ice float rocked back and forth, regaining equilibrium in the river, then moonlight washed over them as they floated out of the cliff's shadow. Eiklo's impact on the ice had knocked them away from the cliff, sending them drifting into the middle of the river.

On the shore, five hungry gorgonwolves howled at the edge of the gorge. They followed the ice raft downriver, snarling and howling in outrage at their meal once again escaping. Luckily, none of them were foolish enough to follow them off the edge of the gorge.

Mayve and Eiklo locked eyes, in utter shock and relief, then both burst out laughing. Eiklo stuttered, "We did it. Holy shit, we did it."

Mayve rolled over and stared up at the stars, exhausted and smiling, as Eiklo rested his skull on the cool ice. They would need to start paddling across the river soon, but the freezing night temperatures would keep the ice from melting.

Up on the canyon edge, the gorgonwolves still prowled after them, following the raft downriver. Mayve groaned, "We need to climb up the other side. If we drift too far, they'll cross the river when we do."

Eiklo didn't have the energy to respond. The thought of climbing up a canyon wall felt beyond his reach. Suddenly, the gorgonwolves stopped their snarling as the beating of wings cut through the night.

A scream from high in the clouds shattered the silence. Eiklo's ribs froze in terror, fusing to his wet cloak. *No, not like this. We were so close. Varin, I checked for Vent beasts, I checked! There were none...*

The night sky ignited into an orange inferno, a raging ball of fire descending from the clouds. Spinning out of a sharp dive, Screech unleashed hellfire onto the gorgonwolves. Whimpers mingled with the crackling of fire as two turned tail, running toward the dunes. Four instantly petrified themselves to escape the flames, frozen in stone mid-howl. Then the phoenix banked sharply over the river, shrieking down at the drifting raft.

Eiklo felt all his fear evaporate. Mayve, still grabbing his cloak, shook him excitedly. He waved at the huge fiery bird, and Screech twisted in midair, falling embers trailing behind her like shooting stars. She swooped low across the water toward their raft, plucking them from the ice with her talons. In a flurry of beating wings, the ice melted below them in a storm of heated air, and suddenly they were soaring, the Devaros falling away into a blue scar beneath them.

Eiklo held on to the rough skin on Screech's feet as she flew them upriver. The heat of her feathers was different from the blistering heat of the desert. It felt more like a fresh hearth, cozy and inviting. The phoenix cut through the clouds, soaring south.

Over the rushing wind, Eiklo called to Mayve, "We survived! Screech or not, we were going to make it!"

Mayve smiled, clutched in Screech's other talon. She held the phoenix's foot with one hand, and her dagger in the other, pulled from the ice as they lifted away. As Screech screamed her own victory into the night, Eiklo and Mayve basked in their shared glory.

Chapter 29

Port Wenstnor

Leaning against the railing of the Ferry, Srrith watched the docks bustle with merchants and workers alike. Below, Vulinor's skeletal crew unloaded empty crates and piled fresh supplies near the boat, while Bolios haggled loudly with the shipwright over the price of repairs.

The dockyard was alive with trade, every prominent merchant guild working in tandem to fuel the small but affluent town of Port Wenstnor. Crunched against the Devaros River by the foothills of the Azraks, the picturesque city was the perfect place for the merchant guilds to hoard their wealth.

The Azrak Mountains loomed to the south, stoically guarding Lake Nawai—more akin to an inland sea—which fed the Devaros River. It was futile to sail farther up the Devaros past Port Wenstnor. Several miles south were the Nawai Falls, which brought the waters of Lake Nawai down from the mountains to the desert. Incredible to see, but impossible to ascend. Nestled far above the lake was the tauninagan city of Savin Actai, and the small hut that Srrith tentatively called home.

Here, protected by the mountains, the South Verdant was able to creep into the Ralveran Desert, reclaiming territory from the Ysera Scorch Vent. The surrounding hills were a hardy mixture of gray rocks and green grass, fed by southern rains and kept short by hot desert winds. Protected by the hills, leafy shrubbery and dense forest thickets grew along the riverbank and through the thin, winding valleys— creeping vestiges of the vast tropical rainforest that blanketed the Azraks.

The Devaros River flowed at a snail's pace northward, its waves lapping at the Ferry's hull. Srrith shifted her weight to her right arm and winced as sharp pain shot up through her shoulder, still ruined from the Vent beast's savage mauling. She luckily escaped with no broken bones, but the puncture wounds from the beast's fangs left her arm almost immobile. Her leather armor, tattered with fang marks, had protected her chest from any lethal wounds.

The Ul'Varin-Rak did what they could, but their treatment was little more than patchwork. Srrith expected nothing better from folk with no blood, muscles, or organs. She had passed out after the Vent beast fell and, according to Vulinor, slept for nearly a day and a half. Since then, she had applied the rest of the mountain tauninagan healing salve to her wounds, but it was not enough. Once she arrived at Savin Actai, the mountain tauninaga would have little trouble restoring her with their sfa-zrueen. Until then, she would have to suffer through it and stay out of trouble.

Whether she left for Savin Actai anytime soon was still a mystery. Mayve was gone, along with the Oasis Stone. Knocked overboard by the Vent beast into the Devaros Cataracts. If the girl survived, she would be miles downstream, struggling through the desert. Srrith desperately wanted to turn back, but she was in no condition to venture out on her own.

The thud of heavy plate mail and growing heat on her back signaled the captain's approach. Vulinor leaned on the rail beside her, gauntlets clasped together. Even while talking at a normal volume, his voice carried a deep gravitas. "May I join you in your watch, tauninaga?"

"Please," Srrith said. She had not talked with the captain since Screech's resurrection, where he informed her that the phoenix would be sent to look for Mayve and Eiklo. Since then, Vulinor was preoccupied every minute, piloting his vessel, mourning the loss of those felled in battle, and bringing his beloved phoenix back from the dead.

The latter was a true spectacle. Once they were free from the Devaros Cataracts, Vulinor anchored the ship at the first sighting of trees and ordered a massive bonfire to be built on the shore. At the peak of the raging flames, Vulinor placed a single golden-red feather, glowing like the hot coals, into the flames. He had rescued the feather from Screech's ashes in the middle of fighting the Vent beast. Shortly after, the phoenix erupted from the bonfire in a glorious blaze, spiraling into the sky with an earth-shattering scream.

Next to her, embers ignited on Vulinor's skull, drifting aimlessly into the air before snuffing out. The red orbs in his eye sockets glowed with immense elemental energy. "Unless my eyes deceive me, you appear to be recovering well. The strength of Varin's spirit must flow through your bones. I must apologize, in all the matters I attend to, I have not expressed my gratitude for your bravery in defending my vessel. Your blades heralded our victory, and you sacrificed much for my crew."

Srrith bowed her head in respect. "I appreciate your words, Captain, but think nothing of it. I was fighting to defend my life as well. It is the grandest honor to fight alongside the Ul'Varin-Rak."

Appreciative fire roared around Vulinor's bone jaw, and he asked, "Where is your journey taking you now, if I may ask? If you are looking for passage back north, I'll offer it for no charge." Srrith knew it was a polite way of asking if she was going to look for Mayve.

"As you may have guessed, my journey is stalled until I learn of Mayve's fate." Srrith hissed. "If your phoenix does not return them by the time your vessel is repaired, I will have no choice but to accept your offer and discover their fate myself."

Flames licked across Vulinor's brow, and the red orbs in his eye sockets narrowed. The Ul'Varin-Rak expression for concern. "I do not doubt your tracking skills, great snake. However, it will be over a week by the time we repair the vessel, board new passengers, and reach the Cataracts again. Footsteps in the desert do not last long before the sands devour them."

"I share your concerns, Captain. If they survived the waters, then they will be traveling along the river south and your phoenix will find them soon. Every other outcome is rather grim, I fear, but I am compelled to try nonetheless." Srrith patted her bandaged arm. "I would leave sooner if I could. I lack the coin to purchase any other means of travel, and I lack the strength to set out on my own."

"It is best that you heal. If you do not, you may carry those injuries for the rest of your life. I doubt you will cross paths with a mountain tauninaga in the desert," Vulinor said. "The ship will be repaired in three days at least, four days at most. I shall ask nothing of you in that time other than for you to rest."

"I accept, Vulinor, most graciously." A silence lulled between them. At the end of the dock, Bolios's argument with the shipwright drifted through the noise. "Two hundred teirs to repair the main mast? Varin's scrolls, you'll kill me a second time! You'll get seventy-five teirs and not a den more."

Vulinor chuckled, wisps of flame curling from the hole where his nose should be. "I'm afraid I will be called away to assist in...*negotiations*, soon. The shipwrights here count our passengers, and raise the price accordingly." He flexed his gauntlets and formed them into fists, the iron palms glowing red-hot. "Is there anything else I can assist you with before I take my leave?"

Srrith flicked her tongue in amusement. "Before you leave on your *diplomatic* excursion, Captain, can you tell me about the Ul'Varin with the blue eyes that was swept overboard with Mayve?"

"He is Eiklo. A youth of recent resurrection, perhaps two decades ago, give or take? All the way from Rulnevrin." As Vulinor spoke, Srrith noted both concern and perhaps a hint of pride in his voice. The captain was glad to have this skeleton in his crew. Speaking with Ul'Varin helped Srrith train her ears to recognize the emotions behind words. While she could normally listen for the beat of the heart or the rhythm of their breath, the Ul'Varin provided a unique challenge as they lacked both.

She carefully interrupted, "My apologies, Captain, is Rulnevrin on the Northern or Southern Frost Vent?"

"Northern. On his way south, Eiklo studied with the Northern Ice raptors at Thaumaturn...Two or Six, it escapes my memory. He is exceptionally bright, as well as a growing volcmancer, and his Ul'Varin-Zul sense provides excellent support on our journeys along the river. I doubt he is accustomed to survival situations like the one he is in now, but he is a logical thinker and will certainly find ways to make his abilities useful to your traveling companion, if the river did not sweep them apart."

"Excellent," Srrith said. "This gives some ease to my mind, thank you."

"And Mayve? What is she like? From our short interactions, I wager she is not one to die quietly from a tumble into a river," the captain asked.

Mayve holds many secrets, and one of the most sought-after artifacts in Ralvera. Out loud, she said, "Mayve is headstrong and reckless, but also determined to a fault. I also suspect she is nigh unkillable by anything other than divine intervention."

Vulinor laughed, flames dancing across his expressionless skull. "I sensed the strength of Varin in her. This is good news, I have high hopes for our lost friends, then. Eiklo needs a bit more recklessness in his bones."

On the docks, Bolios yelled, "Excellent, what amazing news! I will tell the esteemed Captain Vulinor of the *reasonable* price you have set. If it is as reasonable as you claim, I am sure he will have no qualms." The skeleton stormed down the dock toward the Ferry.

Vulinor groaned and said, "I am being summoned. Thank you for your time, Srrith, and enjoy yourself in Port Wenstnor. I will pray to Varin for Screech's success, and your swift recovery." With that, he vaulted over the railing of the Ferry and landed on the dock with a sturdy crash, grabbing the attention of everyone in the vicinity. Standing at least a foot and a half taller than every merchant and skeleton around, he strode calmly toward the shipwright's hut, flames leaking from beneath his scorched hood.

Is Mayve my friend? She is certainly my ward, but she has not been very forthcoming with me. The girl unknowingly stole corrupted seeds, presumably to feed her household. Seeds that spawned a monstrous rampage, taking the life of her mother. Srrith wondered what she would do in that situation.

The realization sickened her. *I would hunt those responsible.*

If Mayve was after revenge, then she would have followed the trail of the merchant and the masked volcomancer. *This is no unknown question. She is following the trail.* This merchant must be in Port Wenstnor.

What was Mayve planning to do? Kill him? Srrith had met cold-blooded killers before; Mayve was not one of them, although rage was how they were born. *Many think rage is like fire. In truth, it is cold and simmering, lurking always beneath the waking mind.*

Somewhere in town, a bell tower clanged several times, the ringing putting pressure on Srrith's sensitive hearing. Arm still in pain, she took Captain Vulinor's advice and went for a rest, slithering below deck into the shadows of the hold. Coiled in her usual corner, she drifted into sleep, and also into dreaming.

She arrived in the shadowed forest clearing, the place she always went in her dreams, where she was safe from nightmares. Grasping the sfa-zrueen of the cave tauninagas, she wove the shadows of the forest clearing around her. At the same time, the real shadows in the Ferry's hold crept toward her, stitching themselves into her scales.

Perhaps because Mayve was fresh on her mind, Srrith found her thoughts wandering to her own training, when her father taught her to wield the cave sfa-zrueen. He was a long, gruff cobra, his scales growing silver with age, his eyesight long gone from his years beneath the surface. He did not need it, down in the dark. His echolocation worked far better.

"Our sfa-zrueen was given to us by the Fae," her father said, as they were both coiled around a campfire at the edge of a subterranean lake. "In the midst of the Paroxysm, as the Vents sundered the land and their beasts roamed far, the Fae and the tauninaga held strong together, and so the Fae granted us a portion of their power. To master sfa-zrueen, your waking mind and your dreaming mind must work together, weaving sleeping thought into reality. Sleep, and draw upon the nature around you, just like the Fae."

Srrith did what he said, sleeping on the shores of that dark cavern lake. She excelled, the shadows bending to any whim she dreamed.

As it always was, with dreams came nightmares. Her father said she was cursed. He told her to leave and never return, and she never did. Even when Alactashi Sen taught her to control her nightmares, she still kept far away from her old home.

The nightmares still roamed the shadowed woods of her dreams, always ready to pounce, but she kept this clearing safe and tidy. This is where Alactashi Sen taught her to weave her sfa-zrueen in safety. Sfa-zrueen rippling down her scales, she wreathed her body in shadow.

* * *

Srrith awoke later to the metallic clangs of the same bell tower. The last thing she remembered was weaving her sfa-zrueen, then darkness. Too distracted by the thoughts of her past, she had let her waking mind slip away.

Looking around the hold, she noticed nothing out of place—other than the braids of shadow slithering in between her black scales. That was to be expected. It was the shadows *not* under her control that she had to be wary of. But they were not here, thankfully. She rubbed her eyes and hissed disapprovingly at herself.

The light from above deck was tinted a dim orange. *I slept for several hours, Akthoru be damned.* She could not pretend that she wasn't injured. The wounds from the Vent beast still throbbed, the pain returning as she woke up. The more she ignored it, the longer it would cling to her. She needed proper rest.

Slithering above deck, she saw the sun had long since fallen below the mountains. The sky was still orange, but Port Wenstnor was bathed in the shadows of the foothills, the waters of the Devaros murky in the darkness. On the Ferry, the Ul'Varin were hard at work preparing for the upcoming repairs, as they sawed away the remnant stub of the main mast that was shattered by the Vent beast.

Something was missing. It was dinnertime, but Bolios was gone and the galley was dark. *No more passengers, no more food.* The skeletons did not need it, and neither did Srrith. She had business in town. If Mayve was alive, she would seek out the merchant. Srrith would find them first.

Her scaled underbelly scraped down the gangplank, then across the dock onto neat cobblestones. The shadows followed her in impercep-tible motions, woven into her scales. Her dreaming mind had willed them to her command. The sfa-zrueen of the cave tauninaga had far little uses than the healing sfa-zrueen of the mountain tauninaga, or the illusionary sfa-zrueen of the swamp tauninaga. Her shadows did not heal her wounds or make her invisible. They hid her in the dark, and spread terror to those they touched.

It was good for one thing, and one thing only. Hunting.

The dockyard calmed as night fell, but a night shift of workers still mulled around, preparing shipments for the morning. Past the dock-yard, tidy cobblestone streets were laid in perfect rows between blocks of townhomes.

Srrith had been here before, in her travels to and from Savin Actai, and was pleased to see the streets had not changed. Ahead was the central market, organized on a wide cobblestone plaza around a feature-less obelisk of gray granite. She veered down a side alley just before the road opened into the square. Glancing behind her to check for observers, Srrith swept her bound shadows into a cloak around her, disappearing into the darkness.

The main roads were lit well with lanterns, but the alleyways only held sparse torches, far enough apart to let darkness linger between them. Hugging the darkness, Srrith snuck around the market square, unseen and watching. Unlike the Silt Row Market, most of the shops here were permanent structures—stone and mortar storefronts with frosted-glass windows and sturdy, dark oak doors.

Srrith did not bother watching those stores. Her target, if her suspi-cions about Mayve's intentions were correct, would be a tent from Devar. That is, assuming her target set up their stall at all—perhaps they were lying low, avoiding the public eye after their monsters ran red the streets of Devar. On the far side of the plaza, two rows of colorful tents stood back-to-back. It would cost a heavy purse of teirs to rent one of those spaces.

A Merchatzi patrolman turned the corner just ahead of her. Anyone else would have been spotted immediately, but Srrith heard the guard approaching before he even made the decision to turn, and she pressed herself into a recessed doorway. The shadows coiled around her, sheathing her black scales. The guard muttered to himself about lighting a lantern and trudged past, blissfully unaware he was within blade's reach of a cave tauninaga, yellow eyes tracking his every step.

The guard stopped, digging into his pocket. Srrith heard him whisper under his breath, "Tyberia's breath, did I leave my matchbook behind?"

Srrith rolled her eyes and sent a sliver of shadow to hasten the poor guard. Nothing dangerous, just enough to give him a chill. The thin tendril of darkness raced across the cobblestone and spiraled up the guard's leg, fading through his trousers into his body. Srrith heard the man's heartbeat amplify and his breath stop hard in his chest. Nearly jumping out of his skin, the guard rushed to the end of the alley, slowing to a fast walk as he entered the plaza in a sorry attempt to maintain some composure.

Humans and their poor fear of the dark. Srrith emerged from the shadows and continued to the far side of the market, gliding around corners and between side streets. *They are right to be afraid, though.*

She was looking for an agricultural merchant of some sort. They would sell seeds, certainly, but maybe other wares as well. The more she thought, the more she realized there was no reason for the merchant to avoid the market. *Monsters sprouting from seeds? Only a madman would think of that. People will blame the Vents first, and the Caverns second. No one would suspect a simple merchant.* A merchant missing a chance to make some profit? Now that was unbelievable.

There were only four tents on the market strip, each the size of a small hut with an overhang to shield their wares from the sun. In the light of day, they would be a vibrant display, but the fading twilight muted their colors into dull greens, reds, and yellows.

She opened her hearing and focused on the first tent. A disgruntled whisper drifted over the evening plaza. *"...four teirs? How about four dens? These apples look like you rolled them all the way from Reath."*

A fruit vendor, or a farmer selling their harvest. Not quite what I'm looking for, but promising. She focused on the next tent. A female voice spoke, coming from a hulking Oemorg. The torchlight glinted off the large opal horns erupting from her gray skull. *"I almost love this dress, but I'm afraid these frills on the shoulders are too much for my taste. How much would you charge to alter? I'll add..."* Srrith stopped listening and turned her hearing on the third tent.

"...are very hardy, they'll thrive best in half sun, half shade, then full sun in a year when their canopy grows in." A human male, speaking in a

salesman's tone to a curious shopper, also human. Srrith uncoiled slightly to lean in closer, trying to direct her hearing on that specific tent. *"If you're looking to sneak in some additional crops this season, though, look no further than these Cenoreth-strand beans, cultivated near Outpost Windhorn. Fast growers, certainly, you can plant them tomorrow and see profits come harvest."*

Srrith allowed a small hiss of satisfaction. This merchant sold seeds, but did he come from Devar? Did he sell the seeds of death? If he did have them, Port Wenstnor could be in grave danger if he planned to plant them. *Maybe he already did. Mayve told Eiklo they took less than a day to grow.*

She decided to wait and watch. There was more to gain by following the merchant back to wherever he was lodging. Settling back into the shadows, Srrith waited only minutes before she saw a figure, escorted by five Merchatzi, striding with purpose toward the seed merchant's tent. Four of the guards were dressed in gleaming chainmail emblazoned with the purple, blue, and gold livery of a prominent merchant guild. Srrith wished she knew which one. She never cared to learn them.

The fifth guard—a human with pale skin and light brown, close-shaved hair—was dressed in intricate armor made of interlocking pieces of leather, carefully padded at each joint with white fur. Normally, Srrith would hear leather armor scrunch and crinkle as it moved, but this set was deathly silent, crafted for perfect, noiseless movement, as if it was made with a cave tauninaga's hearing in mind.

Dual scimitars were sheathed on his back, longer and more traditionally curved than Srrith's sickle-style blades. This style of armor and selection of weapon was dangerously familiar. Srrith shifted in the shadows uncomfortably. That man was a Dreaming Blade.

She shifted focus to whom the guards were escorting. In the stillness of night, Srrith's perceptive hisses sounded like nothing more than a whisper of a breeze. Her echolocation painted the leader in her mind's eye. A tall, thin human-shaped folk. She heard the crunch of his black leather armor, and heard the cloth of the cloak's hood over his head rustle. His face was strange, slightly bulkier than it should be for a man of his stature, almost protruding from the cloak's hood.

A shiver ran down Srrith's tail as she realized it was a mask.

There is no doubt, these are the people who Mayve stole from. As the masked volcomancer approached the tent, Srrith heard the merchant's heartbeat accelerate and his breath snag in his throat—common symptoms of pure terror.

He stammered to the shopper he was attending to, "Excuse me, I must apologize but the stall is closing for the evening. I implore you to return tomorrow and we will finalize a lucrative deal for you."

"But...are we not almost done here?" the customer said, "I'm ready to purchase—"

"No, unfortunately no, I am quite sorry." The merchant nearly shoved the customer out of the tent's overhang and into the street as the volcomancer and his escort grew near. His heartbeat sounded like an army in thunderous retreat. "Please, come back tomorrow. A quarter off your purchase—no, half! Half off! Have a good evening and come back soon!"

The customer trudged away, jaded and perplexed. The merchant hastily adjusted his robes and clasped his hands together, bowing as the masked man arrived.

"Good evening, sir, everything is running smoothly here. We turned a profit an hour past noon today—"

The masked man raised a gloved hand and the merchant clamped his mouth shut. Srrith opened her hearing as far as she could to catch every word from behind the mask. The man spoke in a calm, direct manner. His voice was smooth and refined, methodical, with a cadence of flowing gold.

"The last of us arrived this afternoon. Will you accompany me to the gathering?" The masked man beckoned to his guards, two of whom stepped forward to flank the merchant. Although posed as a question, it was clearly an order he could not refuse. As they left the tent, the Dreaming Blade fell in behind them, while the final two guards stepped into the back of the tent.

I see they've increased security since Mayve's thievery. Srrith backed into the shadows, tailing her new prey from the alleyways. The masked man had no qualms walking in public, it seemed, despite his odd appearance. Srrith kept her distance, using the natural shadows for cover. She still had shadows under her control from her sfa-zrueen, but she kept them in reserve. The more she used her shadows, the less she had until she wove more in her sleep. Chances were high she would need them later.

The merchant's heartbeat was still racing. The guards were calm, but alert, and the masked man...had no heartbeat. This did not surprise Srrith. Ul'Varin and Twelians both had no heartbeat, and Oaken Legion soldiers had the Oakfire, which Srrith could hear crackle and spark as they talked. So, the masked man could be either of the first two. Nevertheless, it left her feeling uneasy.

A Twelian would not fit in such human clothes. They must be Ul'Varin, then. But why wear a mask?

She hoped he was Ul'Varin-Zul. She did not want to fight a volcomancer with Rak strength.

The Dreaming Blade concerned her even more. *They would never jaunt in public like this, nor follow the commands of a merchant guild. This man must no longer be a true Dreaming Blade. An exile, perhaps, or someone who killed one and took their armor.* Both were equally terrible. A man with all the skills of a Dreaming Blade assassin, but with nothing to guide him except the coin flowing into his pockets.

As they moved toward the north side of Port Wenstnor, the quaint townhouses grew larger and grander. Farther up the street, Srrith saw the townhouses divide into spacious manors, surrounded by walled courtyards and gardens.

Merchatzi patrolled in small droves past the manors of their benefactors, paying little heed to the masked volcomancer and his escort. Srrith, on the other hand, was forced to take several precautions, slithering from alley to alley, while her prey steadily gained distance. Ahead, the streets opened up as the houses grew farther and farther apart, leaving little space for a lurking tauninaga to hide. The shadows of her sfazrueen coiled tightly around her tail, as if the darkness itself anticipated its use.

Ahead on the street, another group of figures approached the masked man. To Srrith's surprise, both groups cut sharply down a side street, just before reaching the larger manors, and stopped at a gorgeous chalet townhouse. The building was three stories of beautiful limestone masonry with a lumber frame. Lanterns floated above each door in the row, suspended by wrought-iron hooks, invisible in the dark night.

The two parties faced each other as the masked man's guards knocked on the townhouse door. Srrith slithered down the adjacent street, then cut into a dark alleyway perpendicular to her prey. At the end, she saw the silhouette of the masked man, standing straight with his hands clasped behind his back, addressing the leader of the other group. They wore what looked like a large flowing headdress, shaped almost like a fountain. As the figure nodded their head, the headdress moved in individual strands, and Srrith heard the rustling of leaves, the creak of bark, and the infamous scraping of timbersteel armor.

The Oaken Legion. There had been Legion in Devar as well, but Srrith remembered the bramble eldritches attacking the trees. Perhaps the Legion here were traitors, or perhaps the bramble eldritches were not smart enough to recognize their own allies. She opened her hearing as far as she could.

"...much to report. We must discuss the *altercation* in Devar, if I may use that word." The Oaken Legion tree spoke in a deep, hoarse creak. The escorting soldiers stood at rapt attention behind him, also clad in full timbersteel. Srrith had never seen an Oaken Legion soldier in anything else.

"That is why we are here, Eborius," the masked man said. "Although I would prefer we hold our tongues until we are off the street, away from prying eyes and ears." His tone was calm but his words cold. He held his volume just above a cautious whisper, but nothing was quiet enough to escape a cave tauninaga's hearing.

The Oaken Legion officer, Eborius, seemed less concerned with such things, speaking again at a normal volume. "Yes, yes, I could not agree more. This should prove to be a productive gathering if everyone is present."

"They are indeed." The masked man said. "I expect to make good use of our brief time together." The door to the townhouse cracked open, spilling light onto the front stoop. A guard dressed in identical livery to the others stood in the frame, beckoning entry. The masked man bowed and extended an arm toward the townhouse. "Please, after you."

The Oaken Legion soldiers marched up the steps behind Eborius, followed by the masked man. Through the door, Srrith saw the shapes of other folk flitting back and forth inside. She had to get closer. Even some brief snippets of conversation from the open doorway would provide invaluable information, and the alleyway leading closer was blanketed in beautiful darkness.

Rounding the corner, Srrith hugged the ground, racing toward the closing door. She called upon her sfa-zrueen, the shadows leaping from her scales and cocooning around her, silencing the scrape of her scales and cloaking her in night.

The volcomancer froze, then turned. The mask's lifeless eyes stared directly at Srrith.

Now Srrith froze, her good arm falling to her sickle hilt. This had never happened before. She *should* be hidden, wrapped in shadow, but there was no doubt. The mask was looking directly at her.

"Inside, please," the masked man commanded. The seed merchant was shouldered through by his two guards, his heart shivering in terror. "Vrato, we have a guest in the alleyway. A tauninaga."

The Dreaming Blade exile drew his scimitars and sprinted toward the alley. Srrith spun and ran. With one working arm, she was in no condition to fight a Dreaming Blade. Turning quickly, she almost ran full speed into a brick wall. The alleyway was a dead end, the side she entered on blocked by an impassable stone wall.

Her eyes lied to her, but her echolocation told her the truth. Illusions cannot reflect sound. The normal alleyway painted itself in her mind, showing the path was clear. The pause it gave her was enough, though, and the Dreaming Blade assassin fell upon her.

Srrith saw his shape and his falling swords painted in her mind before she turned, unsheathing her sickle and slashing the blades out of their deadly path. Steel rang against steel, sparks erupting as the scimitars were knocked away. She bared her fangs and hissed, drawing her second sickle even though her right arm screamed in pain. Vrato spun with his momentum, the twin scimitars carving the darkness, the blades passing a hairsbreadth from Srrith as she coiled away.

Suddenly, Vrato glowed a deep purple, his body transforming into a magenta silhouette. From the silhouette sprang two assassins, one spinning left as the other spun right. A single hiss told Srrith which one was real, and she used her working right arm to parry the true blade as she pretended to parry the illusionary one with her bad arm. She paid life-saving attention to her echolocation as Vrato feigned back and forth, sending fake copies of himself in every direction, raining down multiple fake blows, each illusion just as deadly looking as the real blade. She took care with her movements to not reveal her echolocation—a Dreaming Blade would certainly know about the cave tauninaga, but he might not know he was fighting one in the darkness of the alley.

He will see I am not easily fooled. No matter how many illusions he summoned, he was nothing but a lone swordsman to Srrith. She let herself be driven backward, dodging both illusionary and real steel. With the fake stone wall at her back, she feigned that she was captured, ceasing her retreat. Vrato spawned a second copy of himself, and all three assassins launched at Srrith, six blades swinging in different arcs. A second before the blades fell, Srrith retreated backward through the fake wall, parrying the scimitar and wrapping her tail around Vrato's neck. With a flick, she slammed the assassin into a very real stone wall, and he went down with a sharp crack.

Behind the crumpled assassin, the masked man walked down the alley, calm and composed. Srrith's tail coiled around the hilt of a scimitar and she pulled it toward her. With her good arm, she twisted down, grabbed the sword, and hurled it at the masked man in one fluid motion. With breathless ease, he tilted just enough for the blade to sing past him, missing him by a hairsbreadth and clattering down the alley behind him.

Still advancing, the volcomancer placed a gloved hand on each wall of the alleyway. At his fingertips, the shadows writhed, boiling off the walls. The darkness, blacker than night, spread toward Srrith like a rising tide. Behind the masked man, the shadows rose like a tidal wave, ascending the townhouses and snuffing out lanterns like matches in a hurricane.

There was no outrunning them. As the shadows hit Srrith, she felt terror unlike anything she had felt in years, back when the nightmares used to plague her sleep, when she used to wake screaming every night.

Her mind panicked, twisting and sundering as unseen monsters made of her own shadows turned against her.

Stifling a scream, she sheathed her sickles and ran. The alleyway grew faster than she could move, stretching incomprehensibly long before her. Looking behind her, she saw Vrato, on the ground but awake, with a fist clenched in concentration, magenta illusions racing along the walls.

Omaea save me. She slammed into a wall, hoping it was an illusion. *Real.* The masked man drew closer. She tried another wall, recoiling from the impact. *Real.* She tried to echolocate, but terror clouded her mind. Up and down blended together as darkness hid her eyes. *Real.* The masked man was striding toward her, arms outstretched, the shadows flowing from him.

My shadows have betrayed me. What horrid manifestation does this man have, to steal my shadows from me?! I will not die this way! I am the master of the shadows! Unsheathing her sickles, she reared to full height, fangs bared, hood flaring. As she brought her sickles down, the masked man summoned the shadows from the ground in a geyser of darkness, and pure terror shattered her mind.

Chapter 30

Quiet Rage

The Du'ul radiated through Mayve like heat from a blazing wood stove. She pictured herself sitting next to Dreva's ramshackle oven, the chill of the mist-strewn tunnels melting away. The delicious smell of fresh-baked bread filled the dwelling as her mother opened the oven door, blasting Mayve with warmth. Once she started thinking of the Du'ul as heat rather than a river, it became easier for her to sense it.

As she felt the Ventish heat in her body swell, she imagined her skin transforming into the iron of the oven, capturing the heat within. Instantly, she felt an overwhelming surge of energy as she trapped the Du'ul.

Mayve was no stranger to adrenaline. It fueled her every climb, every frantic sprint from the Merchatzi, every quiet breath as she snuck through a nobleman's home. The burst of energy she got when trapping the Du'ul made everything feel relaxing in comparison.

Inside her chest, it felt like an infinite waterfall crashing onto an unquenchable wildfire, unleashing a raging inferno of steam. Opening her eyes with a gasp, Mayve leapt to her feet and manifested the Du'ul through her fist, punching the air toward an unlit campfire in front of her.

Nothing happened. The inferno within her lessened as some of the Du'ul dissipated, manifested back into the world through her fist. Mayve channeled more Du'ul through her fingers, trying to twist the air, then she threw her arms wide, trying to fling the unlit logs in every direction. Still nothing.

With her last sliver of Du'ul, she picked up a gnarled log and held it in her hands; manifesting through her fingers again, she tried to send the Du'ul through the wood, hoping to see it change color, or catch fire, or disappear. Anything at all that would help her understand her seemingly-useless power. The log stayed defiantly unchanged.

Drained and frustrated, Mayve tossed the log back into the campfire pile. Pointing at the unlit bonfire, she sighed, "Fine, go ahead."

"Caw!" Screech exhaled a plume of flame, igniting the logs and dissipating the gloom of the evening twilight. The crackling fire cast dancing shadows on the surrounding trees, glowing in the sapphires embedded in Eiklo's gleaming skull.

He took a seat next to the new flame. "Honestly, I'm baffled. After learning to trap the Du'ul, it rarely takes more than a day to figure out what your Natural Manifestation is."

Mayve collapsed into the grass by the fire and said, "Maybe I don't have a Natural Manifestation. Is that possible? The Du'ul doesn't manifest, it just leaves me and disappears without a trace."

"I suppose so," Eiklo pondered. "As far as I know, it's never been recorded before, but it doesn't sound impossible. The Northern Ice raptors pretend to know a lot, but there are plenty of mysteries still out there." He paused. "Sorry, they *do* know a lot, they *pretend* to know everything, "

Thinking of the masked volcomancer, Mayve asked, "Have you ever had to fight a volcomancer before?"

Eiklo shook his head. "A few training spars at the Thaumaturn. Enough to learn how to trap the Du'ul while under pressure. Many people can't do it. It's hard enough to trap and manifest while peacefully meditating. Why do you ask?"

"Just trying to be prepared for anything."

"Well, no need to worry about it for now. We're in the Verdant, volcomancy is weaker here. The farther you are from the Vents, the less

Du'ul there is. That might be why your manifestation isn't appearing. It's weak here."

"That's great. If someone shoots lightning at me, I'll just remind myself that they're weaker, and they could be shooting *more* lightning."

"Maybe your Natural Manifestation is being rude as fuck."

"Come on, give me a real answer."

"There is no real answer. It's rare, but anyone can do it. Just assume everyone you fight could *maybe* shoot lightning. If you're rich, buy yourself some Cavotros iron, but that's just as rare as volcomancers, and likely out of your price range."

"Cavotros iron?" Mayve had heard of it maybe once before, but never quite realized what it was used for.

"It's a special metal with anti-volcomantic properties. If you have trapped Du'ul inside you, don't get cut by a Cavotros blade. Don't even let one touch your manifestations—the feedback of the Du'ul being destroyed will knock you unconscious *at best.*"

Could I find Cavotros iron before finding the masked volcomancer? It may be expensive, but so is the Oasis Stone, and Port Wenstnor is a wealthy town. He'll be weaker in the Verdant too. Her plan slowly took a more concrete shape.

If only her manifestation did anything at all. "Nothing happened in the desert either, when we were closer to the Ysera Vent. Are you saying I might have to get to the slopes of a Vent before I can manifest?"

"I hope not. But perhaps."

Mayve sat up with an exasperated grunt. Unsheathing her dagger, she grabbed the salmon that Screech caught earlier, laid it on the ground in front of her, and began prepping it. She cut through it with practiced motions. Dreva had taught her how long ago, when Mayve would catch fish from Darkmist Pool when there wasn't enough coin to buy a meal that night.

She saw her mother in everything she did. The truth was, her mother had taught her everything she knew. In return, Mayve got her killed.

The dagger sliced through the meat, her knuckles clenched around the blade. *Tomorrow, we reach Port Wenstnor.* She thought of driving the knife through the masked man's neck, and was reminded of the dying gurgles of the Coinclaw raptor, gasping for breath at the Silt Row docks. Could she really do that again? *Srrith said I would have to kill again on this journey. She did not know I was seeking it out. I can't let this man roam free, not just for my own sake but also my mother's and everyone else's he might hurt.*

He knew what he had in that chest. Pure destruction, waiting to be planted. He knew how dangerous those seeds were, and left town without a word to anyone. No one was ready for that attack, not even the wealthiest guild masters. I heard the Archtown bells ringing that night, along with all the other boroughs'.

I know it's my fault, and that leaves it to me to make this right. I'm the only one who knows what he did. If he had issued a single warning, my mother might still be alive. She almost muttered out loud, her mouth silently forming the words in disbelief. *They wanted to see what would happen.*

Her mother was in the ground, punctured and drained by vampiric brambles. Death was less than Faldmor and that cursed volcomancer deserved. Her eyes fell on her dagger, lying sheathed on the ground next to the fire. As they closed in on Port Wenstnor, she had been sleeping worse and worse, plagued with nightmares of her last night in Devar. *I will bring the consequences back to him, no matter how far he runs.*

She became aware of a large beak inching into her peripheral vision. Screech leaned over her shoulder, making hungry coos at the salmon.

"Hey now, I'm almost done! Hold on." Mayve said. She filleted a strip of meat for herself and set it aside, then tossed the rest to Screech. The phoenix caught it in her beak, then blasted a pillar of fire into the air, charring the fish to near ash before gulping it down whole. The bird let out a satisfied scream and a series of trilled coos before settling down in a pile of singed grass.

"You overcook your food, Screech," Mayve said, "That's why I have to cook mine separately, I've told you this." Screech responded with a caw and ruffled her feathers to cover her talons. Mayve stood to find a suitable stick for roasting her fish. She pointed at the phoenix, then pointed to her portion of the fish and said, "Not for you."

Mayve was still in complete and utter awe of how many trees were in the foothills of the Azraks. Just the foothills! When she asked Eiklo about it, he had laughed and said, "These clumps of trees barely count as woods. You should see Cenoreth Forest, or Noatara Jungle. Vast beyond belief." She struggled to comprehend what that even looked like. The color green was rare in Devar, and now it was the only thing she could see.

She found a fine branch with no trouble at all. Back at camp, Eiklo was still sitting motionless by the fire, lost in thought, cold mist drifting from the intricate carvings in his skull.

"Still pondering my Natural Manifestation?" Mayve asked. She knew he was, but wanted to hear his thoughts spoken out loud.

He nodded. "The Northern Ice raptors have a well-thought process for determining a person's Natural Manifestation. It starts with simply manifesting the Du'ul directly in front of you with a punching or throwing motion. This tells you, quite instantly, if you have some sort of elemental-based manifestation, like throwing fire or hurling a gust of wind." He chuckled to himself and said, "Because I manifest the Du'ul as ice, that's as far into the process as I got."

"So I won't be throwing any bolts of lightning. That's disappointing."

"Most likely not, sorry. That brings us to the second class of manifestations, the ones that don't create anything but alter what's already around them. Manifestations that shape earth, change substances alchemically, raise the dead, those sorts of things. Considering we've been surrounded by rocks, dirt, and dead fish, we would've seen something happen by now."

He looked up curiously, "Have you tried manifesting out of your ears or mouth? I've heard that's how some volcomancers communicate with trees and animals."

Mayve trapped a small portion of Du'ul and channeled it through her tongue and ears. She turned to the phoenix. "Hello, Screech, how was the fish?"

"*Rraaaa!*"

"That's a hard no, Eiklo," Mayve said.

"Any words from the plants, maybe?"

"The grass you're sitting on says you're too cold and it's very unpleasant."

Rime crept across Eiklo's brow as he rolled the blue lights in his eye sockets. One of the few expressions that the Ul'Varin keep in undeath, luckily for everyone. "Good thing you can't hear them—the trees probably hate you for taking one of their arms and spearing it through a fish."

"They have plenty and they'll grow more." Mayve turned her skewered dinner over the fire. "So, I can't do anything you've said. What's next?"

Eiklo rubbed his temples in ancient habit, even though there were no longer any muscles to massage. "This is where it gets tricky. The only manifestations left are those that defy the laws of the natural world, things that no race in Ralvera can really conceptualize, except maybe a few species of tauninaga. Things like creating illusions, teleportation, divination, flight."

"With any of those, I feel like we would have seen something, even if I couldn't control it," Mayve said.

"Probably, but not necessarily. Those manifestations require very precise channeling, or nothing will happen. If you have an illusion manifestation, maybe you're simply making an exact illusion of an object overlaid on the real item, ostensibly creating nothing."

"Ugh." Mayve inspected her skewered fish, then stuck it back in the flame.

"Your tauninagan friend...Srrith, right? She might be able to help. Weaving sfa-zrueen is quite intricate, supposedly, and they do it in their sleep. It's not volcomancy, but her insight may help."

Mayve stared into the orange flames. She had pushed away any thoughts of Srrith since falling off the Ferry. Her last words to Srrith had been deeply unpleasant, and Mayve had been bottling up the guilt she felt. Would she even see the snake again? Anything could happen at Port Wenstnor; Mayve wasn't even sure what she herself was going to do.

"Mayve? Did you hear me?"

"Hmm? Yes, sorry, just thinking everything over. Srrith might be able to help. Her sfa-zrueen is certainly strange." Mayve didn't look up at the skeleton, pretending to focus on the fire and her dinner.

"Using sfa-zrueen is completely different than the Du'ul." Eiklo talked out his thoughts aloud. "But both require very specific ways of thinking. Volcomancers and tauninaga could learn from each other, I bet."

Mayve simply muttered her agreement, her mood quickly fouling. *Srrith has been nothing but kind to you, even saving your life, and this is how you're going to repay her? You were seen by the Great Seer. There could be more for you out there, instead of rotting in a jail cell for murder.* The tiny voice of reason in Mayve's mind told her she wouldn't escape this foolish endeavor unscathed.

Fish cooked, she ate in silence, and Eiklo went to check Screech's saddle for the flight tomorrow. Lying down with her back to the fire and her front to Screech, Mayve closed her eyes, trying to drift away in the cozy warmth. Still, she clung to a hollow feeling in her chest, knowing finding sleep would be difficult. *If I change course, and leave for the mountains with Srrith, will sleep get easier? Or will I never sleep again until I put that masked volcomancer deep into the ground?*

Death might not be too bad either, if he gets me. She'd get to see her mother again. To embrace her tightly and apologize to her. Maybe if she could provoke the masked man in a public space, he would end her swiftly and expose himself as a monster in the process.

She turned her mother's ring around and around on her finger, the smooth iron still warm from its proximity to the fire. Maybe in the after-life, her mother would be less tight-lipped about her father. *Chances are, he's there too. We could have a family reunion.*

Srrith crossed her mind again. The tauninaga had saved her life over and over, just so Mayve could get herself killed by a strange volco-mancer? She was not in debt. If the tauninaga wanted to live her life in service to some *Great Seer*, traveling the land in pursuit of some strange prophecy, then by all means, she could. All the more lucky for Mayve she got to be saved.

Still, guilt sat in her stomach like a lump of iron in the coals of a forge. Srrith had done so much for her, for nothing in return. She could not dismiss the tauninaga so callously, but there was nothing Srrith could do to stop her either. Her last words to Srrith before the Vent beast attacked turned over and over in her mind. The tauninaga deserved a better companion. All she wanted to do was keep Mayve safe.

Subconsciously, she found her hand clasped around the Oasis

Stone's pouch. She had been staring at it more and more recently, wondering what it did. It offered another path—a chance to forget about Devar and her mother, and start something new. *But I would need to let the masked man go. Can I do that?*

Mayve came to a decision as the fire dwindled and the shadows of the forest crept in, although sleep would not arrive until there was nothing left but smoldering coals.

Chapter 31

Goodbyes

Far below, the Devaros River sliced through the South Verdant,
green mountains on either side. Farther south, the mountains
rose even higher, standing majestic guard around the shores of
the gargantuan inland sea that was Lake Nawai, nestled shimmering and
resplendent.

The foliage grew and grew as they flew farther south, the green
flora truly staggering to a girl who had never left the desert. While the
forest captured her eyes, the mountains captured her breath. Mayve
used to think the Devar Arch was tall, but these were incomparable. *I
could climb them if I wanted to, if I follow Srrith. If I let the masked
man go.*

The wind whipped past as Screech banked over the river, hugging
the eastern shore. The peaks themselves were bare rock, colored green
with short grass. The narrow valleys, barely wide enough for a single
horse, overflowed with dense foliage, running like verdant tributaries
between the hills.

Eiklo steered Screech with a set of long reins that looped around the
base of her beak. Mayve sat behind him, one hand on Eiklo's shoulder
and the other on the saddle. Riding the phoenix was utterly exhilarating.
It reminded her of swinging through the Locks underneath the Devar

Arch. Similar to climbing, but free and unfettered, beyond the confines of the cliff face.

She tapped Eiklo's bony shoulder. "Let me steer!"

"Absolutely not!" he yelled back over the rushing air. "I'm not even steering myself. Screech seems to know where to go."

"If you're not even steering, then it shouldn't matter if I hold the reins."

"Look me in the eyes and tell me you wouldn't attempt some crazy aerial trick." Eiklo craned his neck to look behind him at Mayve, who grinned madly. He muttered, "That's what I thought."

The wind was freezing, but the saddle was kept pleasantly warm by Screech's body. Mayve ran her fingers through the phoenix's bright feathers until they got too hot, pulling her hand back before it burned. The great bird's orange-and-red plumage captured the sun's rays, a dancing rainbow of fiery colors. Screech caught an updraft and let out an earsplitting shriek as they gusted higher and higher. The screech echoed through the mountains, and Mayve hoped the noise would not forecast their arrival to Srrith and the Ferrymen.

Port Wenstnor was nestled somewhere in the peaks along the eastern bank. Docked ships, including the Ferry, would be the first sighting of civilization they would see, and Mayve did not want to be seen first.

She tapped Eiklo on the shoulder again, and he tilted his skull to better hear her over the wind. "Are we almost there?"

Eiklo nodded. "I believe so. Varin's sword and scrolls, I'll be glad to sleep in my own bunk tonight. I've had enough of dirt and rocks."

"I'm sure Vulinor is worried sick about you, sending his phoenix to look for us."

"I'm flattered; he and Screech are inseparable." Eiklo reached out a hand and scratched the feathers on Screech's neck, which elicited another happy shriek from the phoenix.

"Can you land Screech outside the city, instead of at the Ferry?" Mayve asked. "I need to talk to you about something, before we're surrounded by Srrith and your crew."

Eiklo paused. "I think I can tell Screech to do that," he said, confused. "You can't tell me up here while we're traveling?"

Mayve shook her head and said, "I'd prefer not to. I have something to show you as well, something that's rather important. Can't do that up here."

"Okay, if it's that important, I'll land us in the forest when we get close." His voice was concerned, but the curls of frost forming on his skull betrayed his curiosity. Mayve hoped she was making the right choice, but even if it was the wrong one, at least Eiklo was the perfect person for it.

* * *

Ahead, the river curved around a green peak and the first glimpse of ships came into view, docked along stone moorings. Eiklo tugged on Screech's reins, urging her to fly down to the tree line on the other side of the hills from the village. The phoenix reluctantly agreed, letting loose one last shriek before complying with Eiklo's absurd request.

Mayve winced, knowing everyone along the dockyard heard the phoenix's call, announcing her return. Her stomach dropped as she thought of Srrith looking into the sky, waiting.

Her stomach dropped further as Screech tucked her wings and fell into a rapid descent, swooping low over the river, then up over the trees. Eiklo brought them down above the tree line, just a short hike from Port Wenstnor's north side.

Mayve swung off the phoenix first, running through what she wanted to say over and over in her mind. Even though she had the whole flight to think, the right words still evaded her; there was nothing she could do about it now.

Eiklo dismounted Screech, holding her reins and reaching up to scratch her feathers. He comforted the phoenix with a whisper. "There, there, Screech, it's a brief stop. We'll be on our way soon enough."

Screech replied with a frustrated, raspy "Raaaaa."

The Ul'Varin turned to Mayve, still holding the reins. "Screech will have to listen in, she knows we're close to Vulinor and she's restless." Rime danced in the corners of his mouth—an amused Ul'Varin-Zul smile—but his eyes were wide with curiosity. Mayve wished she could waste some time with their usual banter, but she felt a dark pressure growing inside her. It was time to cut ties and do what she had to do.

Reaching down to her belt, Mayve removed the Oasis Stone and held it out to Eiklo.

The noon sun filled the strange sapphire with glittering light. The gold etchings seemed to shift and spin as the Stone captured different angles of daylight. Eiklo's eyes grew huge, then shrank to blue pinpoints as he took the Oasis Stone and held it up for examination.

"Varin's scroll...it's more beautiful than I thought."

Mayve heart jumped and she yelled, "You've seen this before?"

Ice raced up the corners of Eiklo's expressionless mouth as he grinned. "Only when you took it out of that pouch back on Gorgonwolf Rock."

Mayve rolled her eyes and crossed her arms. "*Phovus's luck*, for a second I thought you might have real answers for me."

Eiklo laughed and said, "I was hoping you'd ask for my opinion on it eventually."

"You really love handing out your opinion, how could I pass on such an opportunity?"

"Well, I'm afraid to say that my opinion might be worthless here." Eiklo traced a bone finger over the Stone. "These etchings are completely foreign to me. Frankly, I'm not even sure this is a sapphire, considering I have several in my skull and they don't look half as spectacular as this one." Holding it up to the sun, he said, "Look how the light refracts and amplifies inside it. It's like ten thousand mirrors, collapsed into what might be the largest gemstone in Ralvera. Phenomenal."

"It really is gorgeous," Mayve said. "And I have no clue what it does, and neither does Srrith." The dark pressure grew a little more in her chest as she thought of the tauninaga.

"What makes you think it does anything?" Eiklo asked. "It's certainly worth the Ferry's weight in gold, if you find the right seller."

Mayve said, "It has to be used for something. Too many are after it to be just about coin."

"Too many?"

"Keeping it short, I helped the raptors steal it from the Oaken Legion, and not even an hour later, Srrith showed up and said the tauninagas need it," Mayve said. "In hindsight, I doubt the raptors knew what they were stealing, other than it was a treasure in Legion hands.

The perfect excuse to make some money and kill some trees along the way."

Eiklo nodded, gaze stuck to the Stone. He rolled it around in his alabaster palms, looking over every inch. "The Oaken Legion would never venture into the desert just for an expensive object. I'm surprised Srrith didn't kill you for it. Why did she let you keep it?"

"Some Great Seer divined that I must carry it," Mayve snarked. "Who am I to stand in the way of such powerful visions?"

"Seems like a self-fulfilling prophecy too if they never try to take it away from you," Eiklo said. Ice crept across his forehead as he furrowed a brow that no longer existed. "It's strange, actually. I swear on Varin's scrolls that I've seen this Stone before, or at least something similar, but I cannot place where for the life of me."

The skeleton finally pried his eyes off the Oasis Stone and handed it back to Mayve. "If I had more time to study it, perhaps I'd remember."

The dark pressure grew even more in Mayve's chest. This was the part of the conversation that she had been dreading. "You'll have a bit more time with it, actually. I need you to bring it to Srrith."

Eiklo's eyes narrowed. "Me? Are you not prophesied to carry it?"

Reach out. Take the Stone. Forget about the masked man and run. She thought of her mother's grave, deep beneath Devar. *Is that who you want to be? The person who killed their mother and ran away? She did everything for you, and that's how you'll repay her?*

Mayve looked at the ground, not wanting to meet Eiklo's gaze. "I'm not going back to the Ferry. I have some personal business to take care of in town, and I don't know where I'll be after that. It will save Srrith a lot of trouble if you bring the Stone to her."

"Why not come to the Ferry first?" Eiklo asked, arm still extended, offering her the Stone back.

"Because Srrith will try to stop me, or you'll try to stop me, and this is not something I can let go." She finally met Eiklo's gaze, her green eyes meeting blue orbs. "I'm sorry for being so vague, but I can't keep the Stone, and I can't let it fall into other hands."

She took a few steps back, unwrapping her shawl and draping it over her head. "Besides, we were about to go our separate ways anyway. I'll be off into the mountains, and you'll be sailing back downriver. We're just saying our goodbyes a little early."

Eiklo's arm fell limp, and he cupped the Oasis Stone with both hands, staring into it to avoid eye contact with Mayve. "I suppose. What do I tell Srrith?" Frost crept like shadow across the underside of his eye sockets, his blue orbs wide with confusion.

"Tell Srrith this is payment for her kindness, and I hope she makes it to the Great Seer safely. Give her my apologies, and give my thanks to Vulinor for the passage." Mayve took a few more steps down the slope, wishing she could either linger forever or take off running. But she had to say goodbye at some point. "Thanks for saving my life, Eiklo, you were a lovely friend. Safe travels and take care."

"You too, Mayve. Thanks for saving mine." He held up the Oasis Stone. "And thank you for trusting me. I hope our paths cross again." A hopeful smile of ice appeared only for a second before fading into mist.

Mayve responded with half a smile and a curt nod, then turned away and began her trek downhill. As she reached the tree line, she felt a hot gust of wind and a shriek as Screech took off, her shadows racing across the forest canopy, carrying Eiklo and the Oasis Stone to safety.

She drew the shawl around her head. Srrith might start looking for her as soon as they landed, so she had to move quickly and carefully. She used to have such a clear vision of what she needed to do—Faldmor and the masked man had to pay. Now, she only felt a dark cloud of anxiety, and she could not stop looking over her shoulder at where Eiklo stood. She hurried downhill toward Port Wenstnor before she could change her mind.

Chapter 32

Revenge

The town bustled with the natural energy that a clear noon sky always brings. After mucking through the dense valley forests, Mayve entered on the wealthy north side of town, hurrying past large estates, strolling nobles, and patrolling Merchatzi. She recognized many of their symbols from Devar—the orange arch of the Devar Consortium, the purple, blue, and gold handshake of the Tyrak-Wenstnor Coalition, the twisting otters of the River Runners. Occasionally a group of guards would pass bearing an unknown symbol, like a gold heron with a pyramid background or a gray book pierced by a dark blue sword. Symbols of far-off South Verdant cities that she may or may not ever see.

The wonder of the new sights almost distracted Mayve from her task at hand. A city made of gray stone and wood, dominated by green mountains, was unrecognizable from her sandstone-beige, dusty home. Her breath caught as she passed by a fountain, gurgling crystal-clear water. Just the sight made her take a habitual swig from her canteen.

Even though the sun was high in the sky, she was the only one wearing a shawl. Cohorts of noblewomen passed by, dressed in airy gowns adorned with flowers. Were they not concerned about the scorching sun? As if waking from a dream, Mayve realized it was simply not that hot. The streets were pleasant and habitable, not superheated like the sandy roads around Devar.

Still, she kept her shawl wrapped around her. Around every corner, she expected to come face-to-face with a furious tauninaga. *You returned the Oasis Stone, surely she will not come looking. She may be disappointed, but she said herself I did not have to follow her.*

Mayve could no longer trade the Stone for a Cavotros iron blade now, if she happened across one, but at least she had partially returned the favor to Srrith. The tauninaga had done so much for her, after all. Part of her was more disappointed that she gave up the Stone at all. *I was foreseen to carry it, and I threw it away, for what?*

She had repaid Srrith, but now she had to repay her mother for what she did to her. No more shortcuts or running away. Still, the two decisions wrestled in her mind, and she forced the Oasis Stone out. *Faldmor comes first. He will tell me where the masked volcomancer is, and I will plan from there.* It seemed like wishful thinking. She barely had a plan for Faldmor, but her best plans were always made in the moment.

Leaving the north-side manors behind, Mayve entered the center of town, with long rows of stone townhouses and well-maintained streets interlaced with tight alleys. In some ways, it reminded her of Silt Row. *If I lived here, I'd find a good many shortcuts to sprint around this city.*

With still no signs of Srrith or the Ferrymen, Mayve scurried through the alleyways looking for any sort of market. It seemed like the best place to start, to find a merchant. She allowed herself to be carried with the flow of the crowd, picking the busiest streets that pointed her toward the center. It was simple to align herself in this city. She could tell the borders of the town easily from the half circle of surrounding mountains. Soon enough, she stumbled upon the market.

Permanent storefronts circled the plaza, enticing shoppers with colorful window displays and carefully arranged platters of delicacies. An obelisk of gray stone towered above the buildings, dividing the cobblestone plaza in half.

Before the obelisk was open space, kept clear for the denizens of Port Wenstnor to enjoy. Several gatherings of townsfolk milled around, catching up on the day's affairs and greeting passing friends. Past the obelisk lay a long row of colorful tents placed back to back, forming a double-sided line of traveling vendors selling their foreign wares. A pale comparison to the Silt Row Market, but it stung Mayve nonetheless to see a slice of her old home so far away. Her jaw clenched hard when she saw a familiar yellow tent, with stalls of seedlings set up underneath the shady overhang, exactly how they were in Devar. *After all these weeks, here you are. Open for business as if nothing happened.*

Breaking from the crowd, Mayve drifted into a side alley with a good view of the tents. She tried to nonchalantly lean on the alley wall as if waiting for someone, but found herself unable to sit still, shifting in tense discomfort. Nausea swept over her and her legs felt numb, and she felt a sharp pain in the palm of her hand. Looking down, she realized she was gripping the hilt of her dagger with such force that her knuckles were white and her fingernails were close to drawing blood from her own hand.

She crossed her arms across her chest and surveyed the tent as best she could through the moving crowd. Through the tide of shoppers, Mayve caught a glimpse of the merchant. His back was turned, but his blond hair and Coalition robes were all too recognizable—Faldmor, the pawn of the masked man who left Devar

Faced with one of the men who had haunted her every conscious second recently, Mayve's uncertainty disappeared. This was how she would right her wrongs—by making sure what happened to her mother would never happen again, no matter the consequences. Her hand fell to her dagger again, and this time she left it there. Her nausea faded away, leaving only raging adrenaline.

She stepped into the crowd, not heading directly for the tent but instead drifting by it, circling like a shark. Underneath the tent's awning, a modestly dressed man and woman talked amongst themselves, patiently browsing while they waited for Faldmor's attention. Faldmor himself was obscured from Mayve's view by a second customer—a hulking, gray-skinned Oemorg dressed in a grubby workman's tunic—but Mayve still caught glances of the merchant's purple-blue robe and greasy hair.

To Mayve's surprise, and relief, it did not look like he had hired any additional security after her last theft. It was a crowded marketplace after all—it would be a lot more difficult for a thief like her to go unnoticed.

A bell in the city rang out, twelve chimes to signal noon. The brazen sound reverberated over the chatter of the market square, and Mayve turned toward the tent. She had no plan yet, but Mayve knew this feeling in her gut. Her body and mind understood what she wanted to do, even if her thoughts had not caught up yet.

She stepped up to the seed stalls, so tantalizingly close to her prey, and pretended to browse, keeping watch on Faldmor and the Oemorg out of the corner of her eye. *As soon as they're done talking, I'll intercept Faldmor before he can approach the other shoppers.*

Glancing down at the stall, she saw small packets of seeds arranged in tidy rows, with a painted wooden sign above them that read *sandpeppers*. The price was painted on—thirteen silver dens. More than twice the price of what he had charged in Devar. Mayve added price gouging to the list of Faldmor's punishable offenses. Her chest burned with anticipation. Everywhere she looked, she saw the symbol of Citadel Waldheath—a blade of wheat crossed with a blade of steel. The same symbol that was on the bramble seeds. This tent could be full of them, and the poor citizens of Port Wenstnor had no idea. *Depths below, he could be selling them away right now.*

I'll walk forward, dagger out of sight. He turns to greet me, I push him into the tent and get my answers. She saw it play out in her mind's eye. *I can't stop. I'll run into the back of the tent and roll underneath it like I did in Devar. If I'm fast, I can get out of the tent on the other side and disappear into the crowd before he raises the alarm.*

Do I let him raise the alarm? Stab him. Let him bleed like your mother did.

He's just a merchant, a servant of the masked man. You don't have to kill him.

He'll tell them that you're here, that you're coming for him. You can't let him live. This is what you're here for, what every one of your nightmares has been about. Put him in the ground!

Forget this! This used to be your only path, now you have others! You can move on!

To her left, coins clinked as the Oemorg counted out a full palm of hearths and dens, dropping them into Faldmor's outstretched hands. The Oemorg paused to pick their newly purchased seeds from the nearby stall, then lumbered away. Mayve turned as he passed, hand on her dagger. *The same dagger I bought with money that should have been used for sandpeppers.*

Faldmor had not turned yet, counting the Oemorg's money one more time and sorting the teirs, hearths, and dens into different pouches. Mayve's steps quickened, fire in her eyes, and the dagger slipped from its sheath. He turned to meet his next customer, eyes connecting with Mayve's, a smile of eerie cheerfulness stuck to his face. "Hello! Welcome to our humble stall, under management of the Tyrak-Wenstnor Trade Coalition." Mayve grabbed Faldmor by the collar of his robe and raised the dagger.

Then she froze. It was not Faldmor.

This merchant wore the same robes and had similar hair, but the face—a slightly longer nose, less chin, dull bluish-gray eyes—this was not the face that haunted her. She had a merchant she had never met before at dagger point.

The merchant's smile evaporated. He opened his mouth to scream and Mayve clamped a hand over his mouth, pushing him through the tent flaps into the back room before anyone saw what was happening. Pressing the dagger to his gut, she whispered, "Call for guards and you'll meet your gods early. Understand?" Uttering the threat felt like speaking a foreign language.

The merchant nodded meekly and stammered, "Take the money, please, those three pouches on my belt. They're all yours."

"I don't want money, I want *him*, the other merchant. I want *Faldmor*," Mayve hissed, struggling to find the right words.

"Fa...Faldmor? You want Faldmor?" The merchant held a mix of fear, confusion, and relief on his face.

"Yes, there you go. Faldmor. Tell me where he is. I'm not after *you*, I'm not after *coin*, I just want *him*."

"I can't..." the merchant stammered. "Why...what do you want him for? Maybe I can help?"

"The seeds, you must know about the seeds." Mayve shook the poor merchant harder and he winced as her dagger pierced his robes and drew blood, deep red pooling in the cloth. "The monstrous bramble seeds, you must know. You *have* to know. Where is Faldmor? *Where is he?*"

The merchant was breathing so fast, he could barely form words. "Please, please don't hurt me." He took a deep breath and cried, "Faldmor closed the tent last night, I got word this morning that he's left town on emergency business. I don't know where he is."

"*Phovus's fucking luck,*" Mayve swore. Everything was falling apart quickly—she needed to run. This merchant knew nothing, or was at least a very good actor. She couldn't kill him. That's not why she was here. But now he knew her face.

She pressed the dagger to the merchant's throat and asked, "What about the masked man? Do you know him?"

"The masked man...Zeteph? Yes, I know of him. Please, just sheathe your blade."

Her stomach dropped. "Who is he? Tell me everything and you'll live, I promise." Mayve looked over her shoulder at the tent flap, catching glimpses of the passing townsfolk just a stone's throw away.

"He holds a fine position in the Tyrak-Wenstnor Coalition. I've only seen him in passing. Used to be a scholar of some sort. He excels at finding archaeological dig sites for the Coalition to fund expeditions to."

Mayve furrowed her brow. "Why does the Coalition want that?"

"I don't know, more money I guess!" the merchant stammered. "You can find all sorts of treasures at those places—Lost Eon relics, Fae treasures, trinkets from the Ashen Century—all can fetch a high price to the right sellers, but are hard to find."

Something dripped on her boot. Blood from the merchant's wound, soaking his robes and running down his leg. She must have accidentally stabbed him deeper than she thought. His face was turning pale, beads of sweat running down his cheeks. *Fuck me, he can't die. I'm not here to kill innocent men.*

"I'm sorry, okay, I'm so sorry, I promise you'll be okay," Mayve pleaded. "Please, tell me where the masked man is? Is he here in town?"

The merchant nodded, and Mayve broke out in a cold sweat. As soon as she left, they would know she was looking for them. She had to find the masked man and Faldmor immediately. The merchant opened his mouth to speak, but someone behind them spoke first.

"Excuse me, my wife and I have been waiting for quite some time!" A shrill voice sounded from on the other side of the tent flap. The waiting man barged through the tent opening, wife in tow. "Now I'm sorry to interrupt, but we were next in line—"

His eyes grew wide as he absorbed the scene: Mayve standing with her dagger to the throat of a merchant covered in blood, more pooling on the stones around his feet. The man hurled his wife toward the street and yelled, "Merchatzi! Guards! There's a thief, a murderer! Help!"

The market erupted in clamor outside, and Mayve heard the clanking of running armor. She threw the merchant away and sprinted for the back of the tent. Grabbing the bottom roll of cloth, she instead grabbed a metal rod, inserted through a stitched loop in the tent wall and attached to the corner frames. *Phovus, they did increase security. Mayve, you fucking idiot. You reckless fucking idiot.* The cloth walls of the tent were now anchored to the frame. Impossible to lift without lifting the whole tent itself.

She stabbed her dagger into the cloth and tried to cut downward, but the heavy, weather-resistant cloth did not slice cleanly. Wrenching downward, she only ripped a few inches each time, and never in a straight line. *Might as well be cutting through metal.* Mayve remembered what the Oemorg smith who sold her the dagger told her. *It's made for stabbing.* There was no easy escape. So she sheathed her dagger and ran.

A glint of steel caught her eye through the tent flap. Mayve leapt at the opening feet first, crashing into the guard on the other side and landing on her back. He stumbled backward into the Merchatzi behind him in a cacophony of metal.

Mayve sprang to her feet in one fluid motion and barreled through the tent flap, using the chest plate of the downed guard to leap on top of the wooden stalls. A third guard, wearing the unknown heron symbol, drew her sword and slashed at Mayve's legs, trying to trip her. Mayve stepped on the flat of the blade as it passed underneath her, trapping it under her weight, then she planted a hard kick on the guard's throat, who reeled backward and smashed through a stall on the other side of the tent, wooden splinters and potted soil flying in the air.

Mayve tumbled off the stall, landing on one of the guards who was trying to climb to his feet, then vaulted over the next one into the crowd. The townsfolk parted from her path, depriving Mayve of any cover for her escape. A hand grabbed her shawl from behind, so she spun quickly, grabbing the arm of the guard and twisting hard. Before he could counterattack, her fist broke his nose, then she hurled him into the crowd.

She turned blindly, running headfirst into another Merchatzi wearing Devar colors leaping from a side alley. He grabbed her by the wrist, and as she reared back to throw a punch, her other arm was caught by a guard behind her.

Arms restrained, Mayve kicked wildly, thrashing against her assailants. In a panic, she tried to trap the Du'ul, hoping the burst of energy would help her escape, but in the chaos of the fight she found herself unable to focus on such a mentally difficult task.

Her struggle ended as a third guard wrapped in her a bear hug and threw her to the ground. Immediately, all three guards piled on, pinning her to the cobblestones and clamping a set of irons around her wrists. One of them yelled to the crowd, "Stand back! Everyone move along, the situation is handled!" while the other guards hoisted Mayve to her feet, dragging her away from the market square.

Still struggling against the irons, her legs and torso thrashing, she cried out to the onlooking crowd, "He's here! You're all in danger, please listen! He wears a mask, he's a volcomancer!"

The Oemorg who just bought seeds was there, standing above the shorter folk. She screamed at him, "Don't plant the seeds! It can't happen again! Please!" One of the guards shoved a ball of cloth in her mouth, shouting, "Shut your mouth! You're disturbing the peace."

Mayve could do nothing but look at the townsfolk, tears pouring. All she saw were looks of pity and confusion. *They think I'm insane. Please, listen to me.* Many turned away to continue their business around the market, shaking their heads and pushing her from their minds.

Maybe I am insane. What have I done? The crowd gasped as the seed merchant stumbled from the tent, hand slick with blood as he clutched his wound. He tried to steady himself on a stall, but only pulled it down with him, collapsing to the cobblestone with a crash. *Please live. You have to live. It wasn't supposed to happen like this.*

She told herself she was willing to accept the consequences, whatever they were, but this...she had burned bridges and stabbed an innocent man, all for nothing.

Faldmor and the masked volcomancer were still out there, and she was captured. It was all over. The path of vengeance and the path of the Oasis Stone, both closed. Mayve was truly alone.

Chapter 33

The Verdant's Bane

Something nibbled on Raudius's bark, snapping him out of meager sleep. He jolted upright, and a plump rat skittered away into the darkness. Water dripped from the ceiling, hitting his leaves like rain in a forest. From the decaying walls, he heard the pitter-patter of tiny paws and incessant squeaks from the hordes of rodents that called this decrepit pit their home.

They arrived in Port Wenstnor under the cover of darkness. Raudius assumed that they would camp outside in the surrounding forest, but Ingo had other plans. Hidden in the underbrush just outside of town was an abandoned root cellar, overgrown and crumbling. An open crevasse in the back delved into the earth. From there, they had clambered through a maze of desolate ruins and sunken buildings, finally setting up camp in the driest room they could find.

According to Cindri, the locals called this place "Old Wenstnor" - what the town used to be before it was destroyed in the Great Nawai Flood. Port Wenstnor, as it stood now, was built atop these ruins, while Old Wenstnor lurked below, festering and forgotten, a haven for thieves, vagrants, and invading raptors looking to move about the city unimpeded.

The walls and ceiling were old brick, all partially collapsed, with water dripping from eroded mortar. Fissures in the walls exposed sodden passageways that crawled through other sunken buildings. Raudius had no idea how this buried building was still standing, and wagered none of it was structurally sound.

Sleeping here was worse than in the desert. The raptors had left their tents behind with their larger animals, sequestered in the forest with Presh as their caretaker. Crammed into the sunken home, Raudius had slept uncomfortably close to several bloodthirsty lizards, with his hands tied to a rotting post in the corner of the room. He did not want to admit it, but he preferred sleeping next to Borgo. If one of the raptors wanted to slit his throat in the night, now would be the time. He knew Tash was certainly interested.

Luckily, he had survived the night. Today, they were in Port Wenstnor, and he would have his freedom.

Around him, the raptors stirred, lighting meager torches and groggily awaking one by one. With Presh watching the animals, the war party focused only on preparing for battle. Raudius watched in curiosity —the preparations of a raptor war party would be invaluable knowledge to bring home.

In the corner, Ingo sat sullenly, sharpening his axes—one of them his, one of them Spotch's—no doubt envisioning his upcoming fight with the tauninaga. Lairro moved from raptor to raptor, checking in. With the room too damp to light a fire, Tash, Haro, and Baritri ate their cold provisions in silence. Emba and Ersh whispered amongst themselves in the corner, protecting their bonded mice from the lurking rats.

Cindri was still with them, although he didn't look like he would be fighting. While others sharpened their weapons and cleaned their leather armor, Cindri dug through his supplies for different plants. Ingo was too overprotective to allow him in any real combat. He seemed to be here for medical needs only—the orange raptor was already hard at work smashing several different herbs together in a mortar and pestle.

The small abode started to clamor with activity. The raptors were restless, a bloodthirsty tension growing thick like fog in the room. Lairro and Ingo whispered alone, then Lairro slunk to the center of the room, tail twitching back and forth. He raised his claws and spoke in Ralveran, "Duneclaws, lend me your ears." A chorus of hisses and snapping jaws followed, and then the room fell silent, save for the dripping water and chittering of rodents.

He spared Raudius one glance, then switched to Raptoran, speaking to everyone but the tree in a series of fast, guttural snarls. His tribe nodded in agreement, almost all of them throwing glances in Raudius's direction. Raudius felt the Oakfire sputter with dread in his chest. Never had he wished he spoke Raptoran more in his life. *Right in front of me. They're sharing information right in front of me that could save my life if I knew it, and I cannot understand a sand-cursed thing.*

With a final snarl, the raptors growled in agreement, then Lairro switched back to Ralveran. "Our Legion friend knows how to find the tauninaga. He will go above ground, find them, and report their location back."

Raudius tried to hide his excitement. The raptors were sending him into town on his own? There had to be a catch, this was too good to be true.

Tash mirrored his hidden joy with outward disgust. "You're letting him walk free? Might as well try to catch sand after throwing it in the wind! He's not coming back."

Ingo growled, "Keep your maw *shut*, Tash. You think one of us should go with him? Open your eyes. We're in the Verdant now. If we pass one patrol of Oaken Legion up there, we're finished."

How right you are. The Oakfire warmed his chest. This was his territory.

Lairro snarled, "Don't think for a second that we trust this tree. He'll come crawling back to us with the information we need. Until then, we will scout as many exits from Old Wenstnor as we can. We'll only get one chance, and we will strike like the lightning that turns dunes into glass." He pointed at different pairs of raptors. "Ingo and Cindri will go west, Tash and I will explore the riverside, Haro and Baritri will take the north. Emba and Ersh, that leaves you two with the south. Wherever the tauninaga is, we need a close exit we can disappear into once the blood stops flowing."

Lairro looked at Ingo. "Ingo, you already know some of the layout from your last visit here?"

"Some," Ingo growled. "Spotch was more careful with the navigation than I was."

"Check whatever you can remember to see if they're still viable pathways."

Ingo nodded silently. Lairro continued. "We'll regroup here at noon, the tree included, and finalize our plans."

Snarls echoed around the room. Lairro unsheathed his sword—a dull iron blade with a hilt made of ivory, adorned with feathers from his bonded animal. The war party followed his lead; spears, axes, and jagged swords rang out as the raptors held their weapons aloft, their voices growling in unison.

Sand and sail, ice and bone,
Scale thrive where none dare roam.
Oaken sword and Verdant throne,
Claws and fangs defend our home.

A shiver ran down Raudius's bark, gross despair bubbling in his stomach. How many times had the raptors sung those lines right before an Oaken Legion town was razed to ash? Countless, he imagined.

"Go forth, my tribe. As swift as the wind through the dunes and as quiet as the hunting sabertooth," Lairro growled. Snarls and barks filled the room, and each pair of raptors prowled away, slinking through the fissures in the walls into darkness. "Ingo, Cindri, and Tash, hold here for just a minute. We must care for our hostage first."

Each raptor pair carried a torch with them, so the room dimmed as half the war party evaporated into Old Wenstnor. In a matter of seconds, the sounds of the retreating raptors were masked by the drip of water, leaving Raudius alone with the remaining four raptors.

Lairro asked Cindri, "Is it ready?"

Cindri nodded, and grabbed a small brown pellet about the size of an acorn from the mortar. Raudius realized that none of the raptors had taken any herbs today—Cindri had been making something specifically for him.

The orange raptor gave Raudius an apologetic look, his maw shut tightly. Ingo and Tash looked on with wide grins. The torchlight reflecting off their teeth in the dim light made it seem as if their fanged smiles were floating in the darkness.

Cindri handed the pellet to Raudius. "Swallow this whole. Don't bite down or you'll regret it." Ingo slunk behind him and roughly cut Raudius's bindings away, intentionally nicking some of the bark on his wrists with the axe.

Raudius cautiously plucked the pellet from Cindri's claws. It felt coarse and a little flaky, and looked to be made of dried mud and plant fibers. He glared at the raptors and asked, "What is this?"

Ingo growled and brandished his axe. "Doesn't matter what it is. You're eating it."

Raudius took a step back, feeling the crumbling brick wall against his bark. "Remember, you need me to find the tauninaga. I'm not eating this without some answers."

Lairro stepped in. He spoke calmly, but his gaze was cold and unyielding, his gray feathers flattened menacingly. The gaze of a leader with people to protect. "This is not a negotiation, tree. You eat this, or we kill you right now and deal with the consequences ourselves."

With nauseating acceptance, Raudius gingerly placed the pellet in the back of his mouth, past his teeth, and swallowed, the coarse texture grinding against his throat as he forced it down. Ingo pushed Cindri forward, who inspected his mouth under the torchlight and muttered, "It's done. He swallowed it."

Raudius tensed, waiting for some adverse effect to grip his body, but nothing happened. His senses were on high alert, overthinking every single tick and ache that shot through him. Lairro spoke, snarling instructions to him. "Listen, tree, here is your part of the plan. Deviate at all, and you will die. Understand?" Raudius nodded.

"Good. Ingo and Cindri will escort you above ground. Remember it well, because you will have to make it back there on your own." Lairro held up a leather pouch and procured from it a glittering white pebble. "We mark our trails through Old Wenstnor with these. They reflect torchlight well, so you should have no issues returning to this room here when you're done. Watch where Cindri and Ingo place them if you need to. We'll leave you a torch at the entrance; don't light yourself on fire with it."

Ingo snarled, "Once above ground, you'll find the tauninaga and the girl. We want to know where in the city they are, what kind of guards are nearby, and how busy the area is."

Raudius interjected, "And once I return with your information, you'll set me free?"

"Not quite, tree. We'll need assurances that you're not leading us into a trap. You'll lead us to the exact location. If we don't like what we see, we'll kill you. Once the snake is dead and we have the Stone, you'll be free to go. After you receive the antidote, of course."

Raudius felt numb. He already knew the answer, but asked anyway. "The antidote?" He wished he could throw up, but Oaken Legion soldiers were not able to. The Oakfire burned away most toxins and ill food. Only the raptors knew how to poison the trees, learned from decades of experience.

"Cindri will explain." Lairro stepped back and motioned to Cindri.

Cindri slunk forward with his tail drooped. "The shell of what you ate is made of ground bark and cactus fibers, mashed into a paste and wrapped around a shell of dried mud. A very fibrous ball that will take you hours to digest. Inside is Verdant's Bane." He tapped a bloodied bandage wrapped around his arm, from where he had drawn his own blood for the recipe.

Raudius felt sick, his Oakfire sputtering. *Damn them. Damn these filthy, Vent-cursed, sand-breathing mongrels!* Memories flashed through his mind of the burned corpses of his comrades, dead on the bar top of the Hangman's Swing. Now he had that same horrid poison sitting inside him, waiting to melt him from the inside out.

His face betrayed his shock, and Tash broke out laughing. "Well done, Cindri! Oh, oh, what if he accidentally bit into it? I bet his jaw would've turned to sludge."

Cindri hastily interjected and said, "I have the neutralizing agent ready, of course. If everything goes to plan, you'll survive with no lasting side effects. I suspect you have around four to eight hours before your digestive system eats through the outer shell."

Raudius glowed with futile anger. He was so close to freedom, but even walking alone he was still under the raptors' claws. Looking at Cindri specifically, knowing he would be less likely to lie, Raudius asked, "How do you know that the antidote works on Oaken Legion? Is there a chance that I do your bidding, then still die a horrific death after all?"

Cindri looked a little sick himself, his feathers flattened against his scales. He replied, "This particular method is reliable. It went through *a lot* of testing in the Ashen War."

Raudius spat back, "I wonder how many good trees had to die to perfect your little trick." Cindri said nothing and Ingo snarled, "Not enough."

"It's time to go," Lairro said. "The tree is running out of time." With a flick of his claw, the gray raptor motioned for Tash to follow and slunk out of the room like a ghost. Tash flicked her forked tongue at Raudius with a fanged grin before disappearing on the chief's heels.

Ingo snarled, "This way." He prowled into the ruins without another word. Cindri and Raudius were close behind, hurriedly stepping to stay in the light of the torch, lest the sunken ruins of Old Wenstnor swallow them into the earth.

The pathway Ingo chose wove through a maze of buried dwellings. Old Wenstnor had sunk to different heights in different places, meaning that Raudius would often shimmy through a half-broken wall only to find himself crawling through a window on the second floor of a townhouse, engulfed deeper into the earth than the building next to it. Then he would follow the raptors up a set of rotting stairs and out a gap in the roof, just to find the front door of an old shop. Very soon, Raudius lost track of how far they traveled, winding their way through the entombed homes. As they went, Ingo left the white stones in the cleverest spots— pushed into rotting supports or wedged between old bricks, placed in such a way that they were always able to see the previous trail-marker, no matter how well hidden.

The most terrifying leg of the journey was a stone tower fallen sideways in the earth, acting like a long tunnel. The windows, which once looked out upon the South Verdant, were now dangerous pitfalls in the floor, staring into the void. Far below was the sound of rushing water— an underground river fed by the mighty Devaros, certain to carry any poor soul who fell in deep into the Ralveran Caverns. All the while, their footsteps echoed through the empty stone as if ghosts mocked their every step.

Some ways past that, they climbed into the third-floor window of a dilapidated but roomy manor, the whole building tilted at an odd angle. Tapestries and paintings—remnants of ancient luxury—sagged off the walls, thick with rot. Through a cracked bedroom door, Raudius saw a skeletal arm hanging limp from underneath a collapsed canopy bed frame. Clambering upward, they arrived at a buried widow's walk, now just a cave beneath the earth. Cut into the earth at shoulder height was a narrow chute, angled upward, so thin that Raudius was skeptical he would even fit.

"Here you go, barkscum," Ingo said. "Up this passage, you'll be at the town's edge, north side. Hopefully this chute hasn't changed much, I would hate for you to get stuck." Ingo's tone of voice heavily implied he couldn't care less if Raudius died, if it wasn't for the fact that Raudius needed to bring him to his brother's killer. He tossed a torch and some flint on the ground near the entrance of the hole. "This is for your return trip."

Raudius tried not to think about getting trapped in the rocks, waiting for the Verdant's Bane to melt his stomach. He tried to ignore Ingo, who was already slinking back into the sunken manor, and turned to Cindri. "How long do you think I have again?"

"At least four hours, at most eight," Cindri said. "Remember, they won't let me give you the antidote until they confirm you're not leading them into a trap, so get what you need to get done and save some time for a couple trips back and forth to where the tauninaga is."

From the manor, Ingo shouted, "Come on, Cindri! We don't have much time."

Cindri shouted back, "On my way!" He turned to Raudius. "I imagine all the raptors will be grouped up at the meeting place again in two hours—that would be a good time to return. Gives you plenty of time to survive." With that, he scampered after his older brother back into the depths of Old Wenstnor.

Raudius checked the torch Ingo left him, confirming it was dry enough to hold flame when he returned. It seemed sufficient, so he turned to the chasm leading up out of the earth. Taking a deep breath to steady his nerves, he stuck in his head and pulled himself into the narrow passageway, his branches scraping on the rock and soil.

Pulling himself hand over fist at this angle was exerting, but the tunnel ended up not being as narrow as he thought. In a pinch, he might actually be able to slide down it going the other way. Soon enough, he tasted fresh air, eyes slowly adjusting to the meager daylight filtering from an opening ahead.

His fingers gripped the edge of the entrance and he pushed his head into the daylight. A cloud of dust emerged with him, and he waved the air clear with a free hand before opening his eyes. Above him, gorgeous Verdant foliage caught the sun's golden rays, fluttering gracefully in the morning breeze. Seeing he was in a secluded forest clearing, Raudius deemed it safe to exit without fear of prying eyes, and clawed his way fully out of the ground.

Even after leaving the desert, the raptors had still traveled exclusively at night to avoid the chances of crossing paths with anyone else. Staring up at the bright green, sunlit leaves, Raudius swelled at the sight. He breathed the scent of the forest, taking a brief moment to appreciate that he was finally back in the Verdant. Not quite his actual home in the North Verdant, but good enough for now. He was back in Legion territory.

Studying his surroundings, Raudius saw he was in a small thicket of trees. Between the trunks, he saw several fine manors lining a wide street. All the humans used stone here as their primary building material. It was the best they could do, considering they did not know how to forge timbersteel, and leagues better than the hovels they had stayed at in the desert.

The wind rustled his branches, and he realized he still had the bandage on, hiding his red-bark graft. He tore it off and stowed it beside the underground entrance. It was best he did not look injured, but he would have to reapply the bandage before returning to the raptors.

Checking for any patrol of Merchatzi and seeing none, Raudius picked his way out of the thicket onto the street, and started off toward the center of town. Seeing Port Wenstnor laid before him was daunting, but if he could follow Imayva's trail in a city as large as Devar, then he could do it again here.

Raudius reminded himself it would not be as easy. *In Devar, you had the name of a local woman and as much time as you needed. Here, you have the name of a stranger from downriver, and very few hours until you melt from the inside out.*

He also had no idea where to find the tauninaga, but he assumed they'd be with Imayva. *If Ingo knew I was wandering around blind, I'd be gutted so fast.* Luckily for him, tauninaga stand out like a tree in a desert wherever they go. A few well-placed questions, and Raudius was confident he would make some headway. This was the South Verdant. Port Wenstnor might be a human town, but Oaken Legion influence was felt through all the Verdant lands—it was impossible to say no to the largest military in Ralvera. This was *their* land.

Thinking about the Oaken Legion, Raudius hoped that his old quindecis had not arrived yet. Supposedly, they were still one or two days behind, but that time could disappear with a few days of fair wind and fast rowing, especially on the Devaros. If he encountered Grenner here, his plans would fall apart very quickly.

If only I could vomit this death pellet into Grenner's mouth and watch him melt instead. An entertaining idea, but not one that would help him get Unfelled.

Lost in thought, Raudius finally noticed the looks he was garnishing from passersby. In this posh neighborhood, the streets were filled mostly by Merchatzi and packs of noblemen with their servants. It dawned on Raudius that after weeks of traveling through the desert, sleeping with animals, and crawling through the underground, he must look like absolute filth.

For the first time in a long while, he looked down and really took stock of the clothes he was wearing. At this point, the finer clothing he had worn upon leaving Devar was merely rags, caked in dust, dirt, and blood—far from the imposing timbersteel armor he was used to flaunting. Ashamed beyond belief, Raudius quickened his pace and hurried for the center of town, where he would go less noticed. *I look like a starving fucking peasant, not an Oaken Legion soldier. Vent-cursed fucking everyone, look how I've fallen.*

Escaping the richer neighborhood, he found some relief in the anonymity of the town center. Shouldering through the crowd, he kept an eye out for a market or public gathering place where he could ask questions. *If the raptors could see me now, wandering around a city that*

I've supposedly been to before. He had to act fast, before the Verdant's Bane turned his insides to slush.

Begrudgingly, he tapped on the shoulder of a young human walking alongside him. The boy was covered in soot, wearing grimy linens and carrying a bag of tools. Raudius saw a hammer and a large pair of blacksmith tongs poking out the top. Probably a blacksmith's apprentice, late for work. The boy's eyes grew wide as he turned and saw Raudius looking down at him. He put on his best authoritative Oaken Legion voice. "Tell me where the market is, human."

The boy stammered out, "Ah, umm, yes sir, take a right ahead, then walk until you see the obelisk over the buildings. It's easy to find from there, sir."

Raudius gave his thanks with a curt nod, and the boy hurried away, nearly spilling his tools in his rush. Raudius smiled. He had missed the inherent power that the Oaken Legion held in the Verdants. If he asked for directions in Devar, that kid would have told him to eat sand and then snitched his location to the raptors.

Taking the next right, Raudius followed this wider street, passing rows of townhouses and storefronts. He stopped in a few general stores to ask about the tauninaga, again putting on his best impression of a commanding Oaken Legion officer. No one had seen the snake, but who knows if they were telling the truth. Of course, these were loyal, honest Verdant folk, but his impersonation of a soldier felt hollow without his timbersteel armor and weapons. He hurried along, ever wary of the death pellet sitting in his gut.

Using the tip of the gray obelisk to orient himself, he finally found the market. If the tauninaga and Imayva were in town, they would have assuredly stopped here. If he still uncovered nothing, he'd try the dockyard. After that...he didn't want to think about it. Hopefully the raptors would just kill him. Maybe they'd tie him up and leave him in the dark until the Verdant's Bane did its job. No point dulling their blades on the dying.

Entering the market square, he watched the throngs of townsfolk drift from store to store and chat around the obelisk. It was not as colorful as the Silt Row Market, but just as lively. This was something that the human cities did right. None of the Bastions had anything as vibrant.

The tree muscled through the crowd, again looking for shops that might cater to a pair of travelers. A general store for provisions, or maybe a blacksmith. He should have asked that apprentice where his shop was. He hurried past a cobbler shop without a second glance. Some shops weren't even worth looking at when pursuing a tauninaga.

On the far side of the market, he passed a double row of merchant tents—a sliver of Devar in the Verdant, a reminder of the desert city's massive influence along its namesake river. *If the Oaken Legion ever conquers the desert—not that we'd want such a lizard-infested hellhole —Devar will be the greatest addition to our empire.* He was wrenched out of his thoughts by a yell from one of the tents. "Merchatzi! Guards! There's a thief, a murderer! Help!"

The crowd swelled as half the townsfolk pushed toward the yelling to see what was happening, while the other half pushed away. Meanwhile, Merchatzi slammed their way through the crowd, using the bulk of their armor to shove people aside. Raudius found himself jostled to the side of the market square, pushed against the pavilion edge alongside a heavy set Ul'Varin with fiery red eyes. The Ventwalkers never failed to creep him out, so he hastily stepped back onto the front stoop of the store to get a better vantage point over the crowd, just in time to see Imayva herself smash out of a yellow tent and slam a guard into the ground.

It's her! I found her! Sand-cursed fool, what is she doing? He watched in panic as she fought off the guards, obliterating the shop in the process. *She's a scrappy fighter, I'll give her that.* He was brutally reminded how she had swiftly dispatched him the night she stole the artifact. Imayva's efforts were in vain, though. Raudius saw several more guards closing in through the crowd toward her.

Sure enough, the human was subdued after a brief struggle, and the guards dragged her away while she kicked and screamed. This sudden turn of events did not bode well for Raudius. If Imayva had the artifact, the guards would assuredly confiscate it upon searching her. Artifact aside, the tauninaga was nowhere in sight. *They may not be traveling together anymore.* If he delivered only the girl, would Ingo still gut him?

He followed the guards, watching their pointed helmets over the crowd at a good distance. Her escort was a smattering of Merchatzi from different guilds. One in green-and-red livery, one in all blue, and one in a combination of blue, purple, and gold. Ahead, the purple-and-gold Merchatzi called out and waved over a passing patrol that matched his colors. Raudius was too far away to hear the exchange, but the other two guards gave a few nods of agreement and passed Imayva to the Merchatzi in purple and gold.

The new escort dragged Imayva in a different direction, back toward the more affluent neighborhoods. Right as the rows of townhouses thinned and gave way to courtyard-enclosed manors, the guards pushed Imayva into a long industrial building of red bricks, with large double doors made of iron and dark oak, and a bell tower that threw a long shadow over the nearby townhouses. Cast-iron letters hung over the entryway, spelling out *Tyrak-Wenstnor Trade Coalition*.

As the oak doors slammed shut on Imayva, Raudius breathed a sigh of relief, his Oakfire calming. He found one of them. Verdancias's green roots, he found Imayva! At least he had something to report to the raptors.

Should he go back, though? The raptors wanted the tauninaga or the artifact. He had found neither, although the argument could be made that the Tyrak-Wenstnor Trade Coalition had the artifact now, since Imayva was likely carrying it.

Time was against him. His body was hard at work digesting the death pellet, unknowingly killing itself. He had two options—spend more of his precious time trying to locate the tauninaga, or return to the raptors and hope that the information he had was enough to satisfy them.

If the artifact is in that building, then a fight between the Merchatzi and the raptors might be the perfect cover to steal it. He was going to have to risk it if he wanted any chance at rejoining the Oaken Legion.

With that in mind, he picked himself off the cobblestones and took off north toward the entrance to Old Wenstnor, every second counting down to his death.

* * *

After replacing his bandage to hide his red scar, Raudius hurried through the buried town, sprinting as fast as he could through underground hallways, slowing down only while crossing the broken tower over the subterranean river. The white stones glittered like tiny crystal fireflies against his torchlight, marking a path through the twisting maze of earth and ruins.

Finally, light caught his eye from far down a corridor, and he heard snarling Raptoran echoing from the room ahead. As he entered, the conversation died and eight pairs of yellow lizard eyes bore into him. The worst nightmare of an Oaken Legion soldier, and here Raudius was, once again ready to lie right to their maws.

Silence hung like thick fog, and Raudius realized that they were all waiting for him to speak. Ingo hissed impatiently, "So, tree? Spill it. Where did you find the tauninaga?"

Raudius stood up straight like a proud soldier, as if he were the raptor's commanding officer. Maybe portraying an air of confidence would make them hate him more, but if he were to die here, he'd rather die with a modicum of dignity instead of groveling at the raptor's claws. With militaristic candor, he stated, "No. I failed to locate the tauninaga."

Furious growls resounded around the dark space, and Ingo unsheathed his axes with a menacing step forward. Raudius's dignity caved just a little and he quickly spoke to save himself from an axe swing. "*However,* I found Imayva, who will know the tauninaga's location."

Lairro raised a hand to halt Ingo's predatory advance. "And the artifact?" That is what the rest of them wanted, after all, not Ingo's revenge.

"Imayva was arrested by a prominent trading guild. If she has it on her, then the guild has it now. If she didn't, then she'll know where it is." Raudius hoped this information was enough. He *needed* it to be enough or Ingo was about to gut him.

Bloodthirsty snarls rose as Lairro stood. "Where in the town is this guild's headquarters?"

Raudius swallowed his fear. "I'll tell you after I get the Verdant's Bane antidote."

Lairro's maw twisted with anger. "That's not what I remember telling you."

"I did what you asked," Raudius argued. "If the battle goes poorly, I want to be able to escape with my life."

In an instant, Lairro bared his fangs and leapt at Raudius, grabbing him and slamming him into the crumbling brick wall. "Courgshit, tree. You think I don't *know* what you want? A poor, exiled soldier, who just happened to be traveling south, *and* just happens to know exactly where the tauninaga we want is? You're fucking *pathetic*. You want the artifact so you can end your exile, and I'd rather spill my blood down a dune and get ripped apart by gorgonwolves than risk even a *sliver* of a chance that you'll grab the artifact in the chaos and escape."

Raudius trembled, shaking in Lairro's grip. There were no more tricks, no more secret plans. He was not a shrewd negotiator, conning the savages to save himself and surviving the odds. He was a mere pawn, surrounded by the most cunning, sharpest folk in Ralvera, born in the coldest ice and harshest deserts. He was a fool for thinking he ever stood a chance.

Lairro held the tree up, his fangs glistening in the torchlight, his eyes glaring at Raudius with pure contempt. "You lied to us, ate with us, and journeyed with us. If we die, you'll do that with us too. Tell me where the girl is, *right now*, or I kill you here."

Defeated, Raudius whispered, "On the edge of the richer borough, with all the manors. North of the center of town. The Tyrak-Wenstnor Coalition guild hall." *Stay strong, Raudius. It's not over yet.* No matter what he told himself, it felt over.

"That's your area, Ingo," Lairro said, "Any exits in that area?"

Ingo nodded. "We found a way into the sewers near there. Tunnels should lead very close, maybe even inside."

"Good work. Everyone prepare yourselves. We strike fast. Secure the artifact first, the human second if we can't find it, then back to the sewers. Ingo, lead the way. Cindri—"

"Is staying here," Ingo commanded.

"Yes, good," Lairro agreed. "Prepare as many painkillers, healing salves, and bandages as you can while we're gone."

Cindri is staying here. A flash of hope. In the worst case, he could sprint back here and Cindri would give him the antidote. *He said he already prepared it. That means I can take it from him by force, if I need to.* Lairro and all his raptors be damned. Who cares if they saw through his little plan. He barely had a plan to begin with, so why change now? *Grab the artifact, force the antidote out of Cindri, then run for my Vent-cursed life.*

Unsheathing his sword, Lairro snarled, "Raptors, to war!"

"To war!" the room echoed him.

"To war," Raudius thought. It did not matter if he was alone. He was the Oaken Legion, and for them, all marches led to war.

Chapter 34

A Concerning Return

The dock workers of Port Wenstnor froze in fear as a shrieking ball of incendiary feathers skimmed the waters of the Devaros River, swooping like a falling sun over the wooden ships floating just offshore. In a hurricane of heated air, Screech cooled her feathers and landed on the deck of the Ferry, calling for Captain Vulinor with earsplitting cries.

Eiklo dismounted and stumbled clear of the flaming bird as she stomped toward the helm of the Ferry, eager to find Vulinor. He was caught by Kinglor, who shouted, "Ayy! The Zul! He survived!"

He hoisted Eiklo in triumph, as easy as picking up an empty bag. The rest of the Ul'Varin-Rak on deck cheered, their red eyes shrunk to flaming pinpricks in excitement.

Oribori pulled Eiklo away from Kinglor and shouted, "The Zul is back! I knew you'd survive. We had many a pessimist on the crew but I told them nay, he'll be back."

"Shut up, Ori, no one doubted Eiklo for a second." Vanite slapped Oribori upside her skull with a hollow crack. "I see the human did not survive, though. How sad. She was a lively girl."

"It's easy to forget how fragile the living are," Kinglor said. He bowed his head, and blue flames licked beneath his eyes. "What killed her? The *aerstab-bourl's* tail? The river? The desert?"

"No, no, no." Eiklo waved his hands to cut the gabble. "The human is fine. We journeyed together until recently. She left for the town." He did not want to talk about Mayve any more than he had to. Even though he knew that she was merely a passenger on the Ferry, destined to leave them behind, he thought he had made a good friend. *Varin's scrolls, after all we survived, she dumps a wanted artifact into my hands and leaves with a curt goodbye.*

More than anything, though, Eiklo was concerned—maybe even afraid—for Mayve's safety. Something was wrong as they parted ways. She seemed less like a traveler seeing the world, and more like a prisoner on their last walk to the gallows.

I should have done more. He had wracked his mind on the brief flight here, thinking of every possible reason she did what she did, and he had arrived at some unsavory conclusions that he had to share with Vulinor.

"Even more good news!" Oribori exclaimed. "She must return to the ship tonight so we can hear all about your escapades through the sands."

Vanite scoffed, "They probably just sat around until Screech found them." She elbowed Eiklo in the ribs. "None of us were there, though, so feel free to embellish for a good story. Add a Vent beast or two in there."

"Oh, oh, and a ferocious raptor tribe, or some hungry animals!" Kinglor shouted.

Eiklo smirked, ice curling in the corners of his skeletal jaw. "Actually, we encountered one of those, but you'll have to wait to hear which ones. I need to talk to Vulinor first."

The crew laughed, relieved that Eiklo was healthy, just as he was happy to see they were fine, and several pairs of fiery hands clapped Eiklo on the back, shoving him toward the helm of the Ferry.

I'll have to see what Srrith and Vulinor think of Mayve's situation. They could tell him to forget it. Mayve was the type of person who did whatever she wanted, and she was kind enough to return the Oasis Stone to Srrith before doing so. Speaking of the tauninaga, Eiklo was surprised that she was not here to greet the phoenix. *She must be away in town.*

Ahead at the helm, Screech was purring like a cat, letting out strings of gentle coos, feathers completely fluffed in comfort, as Vulinor scratched up and down her neck. As Eiklo approached, he heard Vulinor whispering, "Who's a good phoenix? Who's a very good bird? Screech is, yes she is." The captain looked up and saw Eiklo, switching back to his normal booming voice. "Eiklo! Welcome back to the Ferry, how glad I am to see you well!"

Eiklo gave a quick salute. "Captain. Thank you for sending Screech. She arrived at a perfect time."

"It was the best I could do given the circumstances. I'm thrilled she found you, although I had faith in you from the moment you went overboard." Vulinor clasped Eiklo on the shoulder, then looked around, flames dancing across his brow, his burning eyes intensifying. With deep concern in his voice, he asked, "I see you've arrived without Imayva."

Nodding, Eiklo said, "She is alive, and here in town, as a matter of fact. But I don't think she's okay. I need to talk with you and Srrith, if you have the time."

"Srrith went into town last evening and has not returned yet. Perhaps she and Mayve are meeting as we speak."

"I'm not so sure about that, Captain." Eiklo said. "Can we speak in your quarters?"

Vulinor saw the concerned frost creeping across Eiklo's forehead and nodded, striding off without a word but expecting Eiklo to follow. Screech stomped along behind them, cooing and cawing at every Ul'Varin-Rak they passed.

They descended into the Ferry's crew quarters—a separate hold of the ship cut off from where the passengers and cargo were kept. It was always far too warm for Eiklo down here, but he did his best to pretend it was cozy instead of uncomfortable. The fiery bodies of an entire skeletal crew and a phoenix kept the hold at an unpleasantly high temperature for anything not born on a Scorch Vent.

Hammocks lined the walls, stacked in pairs above each other, with wooden chests underneath for the crew's personal items. In the center of the room was a twisted jumble of burnt tree branches, hammocks, and scorched rocks—Screech's nest, which the phoenix stomped into, settling in and fluffing up like a chicken about to lay an egg.

Eiklo accompanied Vulinor to a separate room set apart from the bunks. The captain's quarters were far nicer than the crew quarters, holding a large bed with red silk sheets and an ornate iron chest for Vulinor's personal belongings at the foot. On the other side sat a sturdy oak desk, stacked with papers drawn up by Bolios and Vanite about the ship's expenses, cargo, and recent occupants. In the corner was a stand for Vulinor's armor, currently empty because Vulinor rarely left his quarters unequipped. Most of the crew simply assumed he slept in it, and Vulinor never confirmed or denied it.

Last, a weapon rack mounted to the wall held Vulinor's weapons for easy access, although he much preferred superheating his gauntlets unless riding on Screech. Holstered on the wall were a long glaive, a massive claymore broadsword that Eiklo doubted anyone but Vulinor could lift, and smaller mace made of a dark, iridescent metal.

Lighting a lantern swinging overhead with a touch from his finger, Vulinor pulled over a simple wooden chair for Eiklo to sit on, then took his own seat behind the desk. The captain kicked back in his chair and swung his armored boots up to rest on the corner of the desk, the heels fitting perfectly into existing scorch marks. Eiklo had been in here only a couple times during his tenure aboard the Ferry. It was rare that Vulinor had anything to say that couldn't be said in front of his loyal crew.

"So tell me, young Ul'Varin," Vulinor declared, "you and Imayva were both able to survive the Ralveran Desert—a noble feat regardless if you are flesh or bone. Why are you concerned despite your triumphant return?"

Eiklo calmed his mind, trying to decide where was the best place to start. "Well, Captain, surprisingly enough my concern does not come from my time in the desert. It's today's events that have left me confused."

Vulinor said nothing, waiting for Eiklo to continue, but Eiklo could see his red orbs grow just a fraction out of curiosity. "Just before we arrived, Mayve had us land outside the city so she could set off on her own. It seemed like she had no intention of returning, and she told me to carry her apologies to Srrith, and her thanks to you, of course."

Vulinor mulled over Eiklo's words before he spoke, embers drifting to nothing from his skull. "The human has her reasons, I'm sure, but there's nothing any of us can do if she wants to travel alone." Vulinor scratched his ivory chin with his ironclad hand, perplexed. "We must have misjudged her, taking advantage of Srrith's hospitality and training on the way to Port Wenstnor. The tauninaga will be most displeased. She seemed quite worried about the human's safety while you both were away."

"It's Mayve's demeanor that worries me the most," Eiklo said. "She seemed distraught, said that she had personal business to take care of, and she couldn't stop at the Ferry beforehand because Srrith would try to stop her. I think she's going to do something dangerous. Granted, I've seen her do plenty of dangerous things in our short adventure together, but this was different. She faces danger head-on, with full confidence that she'll live. This time, she looked so unsure. That's what is concerning me."

"And?" Vulinor asked. "What would you do if you knew she was in danger right now?"

"I would rush to help, in whatever way I could," Eiklo said with confidence.

"And if I ordered you not to? What if I told you the Ferry was departing right now? Would you still go?"

Eiklo paused, mulling it over, before saying, "Yes, I'd still go. Friend or not, I don't think I could sail away with my mind at peace."

Orange flames grew from the corners of Vulinor's mouth into a fiery smile. "Excellent!" he boomed. "Then what are we waiting for? Come, we will scour the town for our forlorn traveler. You are a Ferryman, and a friend of yours is a friend of the crew's."

He rose to his feet and paused, confused when Eiklo did not do the same. Vulinor was not brash by any means, but he was a man of action at heart.

"There's more," Eiklo said. Vulinor sat back down and leaned his elbows on the desk, resting his ivory chin in his gauntlets with his flaming red eyes fixed on Eiklo.

"There are two very important things that you should know before we rush to help Mayve." Eiklo paused, trying to collect his ricocheting thoughts. "First and foremost, Mayve confided in me some troubling things, before the Vent beast attack. I'm only breaking this confidence now because I fear the crew could be in more danger than we think if we involve ourselves with Mayve."

As best he could remember, Eiklo relayed to Vulinor everything that Mayve had told him in the crow's nest that night, about how she stole and planted seeds that grew overnight into the eldritch brambles that terrorized Devar and killed her mother, and how she even met the person most likely responsible for creating these seeds; someone with a powerful manifestation who hid their face behind a mask.

Vulinor sat quiet through the whole story, and when Eiklo finished he leaned back in his chair and crossed his arms. "I don't fault her for leaving Devar. If I were her, I would never return. But all that happened downriver, yes?"

Eiklo nodded. "Yes. I have no proof that anything of that sort found its way upriver, but it's not out of the question. If the events of Devar are related in some way to whatever Mayve is doing, we should be cautious."

Vulinor nodded, clearly deep in thought. Eiklo knew that he was already planning the best way to keep the Ferrymen safe if the bramble eldritches appeared again, perhaps internally weighing if he should help Mayve at all.

"Moving to my second point," Eiklo said. "If Mayve's actions are not related to the incident in Devar, they very well could be related to this." He placed the Oasis Stone on the table.

Even in the dim light of the cabin, the Oasis Stone still caught every ray of light possible. Purple streaks refracted through the blue gemstone as Vulinor's red eyes intensified, the reflections of the captain's flames making the artifact flicker like a sapphire bonfire.

Vulinor picked up the Oasis Stone and held it up to the light, perhaps inspecting the cryptic golden runes or simply marveling at its beauty. Finally, he laid it gently on the table, and spoke. "What is this, and where did you get such a thing?"

"I was hoping you could offer some insight into that, Captain," Eiklo said. "Although it looks as if you're laying eyes upon it for the first time."

"That I am. Did you find this curio in the desert?"

"Find? No, I was given it by Mayve just this morning."

Vulinor's red orbs widened in shock and flames smoldered in his temples. "*Given?* Mayve just gave away this gemstone? Did you not just inform me that she was a thief?" He slammed one of his palms on the desk with a thud, while the other hand reached up to his skull and swept back nonexistent hair; a forgotten habit of shock from when he was alive. "We could trade this gem for a second Ferry. Varin's scrolls, maybe two Ferries and start a whole fleet, and the thief just gave it away?"

He leaned back in his chair, his usual stoic demeanor reeling from Eiklo's punch after punch of information. He shook his head incredulously, and said, "You disappear into the desert for several days and this is what you come back with. I take it you have even more to say?" Eiklo nodded, and Vulinor expelled a cloud of embers out of his mouth in exasperation. Sweeping them away from the papers, he leaned back, regained his composure, and motioned for Eiklo to continue.

Eiklo picked up the Stone, and prepared to lecture. "Apparently, this artifact is not just expensive jewelry. Mayve stole it in Devar from the Oaken Legion, while working for the raptors. She gave it to me to return to Srrith, who calls it the Oasis Stone."

"It is highly sought after, as it should be," Vulinor said.

"Very highly sought after. It's expensive, for sure, but expensive enough for the Oaken Legion to venture into the desert? Valuable enough for the raptors and tauninaga to draw blades for it? It *has* to be something more."

Vulinor contemplated, skull resting on his gauntlets. "As a scholarly man yourself, I'm surprised you have not figured out its purpose yet."

Eiklo swelled with pride and tried to keep it from reaching his ego. "I appreciate that, Captain, although I'm hardly an expert on arcane artifacts and the like. By hardly, I mean not at all."

"In which case, you best hide it away until an expert can be found," Vulinor said, showing the rarest hint of anxiety. "If that artifact is Lost Eon or Fae in origin, then it may be unpredictable, and often beyond our comprehension. The less you interact with it the better, until you learn what it's for."

Eiklo hastily slipped the Stone back into its leather drawstring bag and cinched it tight. "Either way, it won't be our problem for long. Once Srrith returns, I'll pass the Stone onto her. I'm only showing you because it's relevant to us saving Mayve." He quickly clarified, "That sounds like I often hide things from you. I certainly never do. Well, not often. It's just not our artifact, it's Mayve's, and now Srrith's."

Vulinor eyed Eiklo in mock suspicion. He was all too familiar with how Eiklo would often talk himself into a corner. *I'm very lucky the captain has boundless patience. Imagine if Oribori or Bolios was captain.* Eiklo shuddered at the thought.

The captain stood without a word and strode over to the weapon rack on the wall. From it, he plucked the mace from its mounting hooks and laid it between him and Eiklo with a thud. It was simple but well crafted, the smith not bothering with any flashy adornments or ornate decorations. Certainly created by an Ul'Varin-Rak, who made weapons for one purpose only—to slay any monstrosities that crawled out of the Vent. The head of the mace was a heavy ball outfitted with eight spiky flanges.

It was much darker than steel, yet it held the metallic sheen of a finely forged weapon. As Eiklo moved his eyes across it, he saw an unnatural iridescent glimmer to the weapon, like oil floating on water. With a stark realization, Eiklo deduced he was looking at Cavotros iron.

"Pick it up," Vulinor said. As Eiklo did, the black metal numbed his hand wherever he touched it. The mace was balanced well. Not heavy enough to be unwieldy, but enough to carry a punch of momentum with each swing. Still, the weapon felt clumsy in Eiklo's hands. He had never wielded anything remotely like it.

"Speaking of expensive items, is this what I think it is?" Eiklo held the weapon like it was made of glass.

"Astute eye, as always," Vulinor said. "That is Cavotros iron. I received this weapon when I was a fresher skeleton, after bringing down a particularly ferocious *tarmor-mourl* on the Valkatror Vent."

"They just gave you this? It might be just as expensive as the Oasis Stone."

"That's where the Cavotros iron is forged; they are less stingy with it than most. That aside, it was a gift, for an act of exceptional bravery or stupidity, depending on which witness you ask." Vulinor shrugged. "A story for another time though. You're lucky that I'm gifting it to you—I don't think you have the coin to buy it from me."

"Gifting?" Eiklo couldn't believe he was being handed another absurdly expensive item today. *If my moral compass was just a little broken, I'd sell both and be drowning in teirs.*

Vulinor gave him a stern look. "You're a smart skeleton, you know what Cavotros iron is used for. If this masked volcomancer you speak of is involved in whatever Imayva has gotten herself into, then this will be invaluable against their manifestations."

"You know, I don't know how to use this." Eiklo held the mace like he was picking up silverware, gesturing to the spiked ball of iridescent black metal.

"It's fairly simple. You swing it at people who want to hurt you," Vulinor said. "It's weighted for normal folk, so I don't use it very often." Ul'Varin-Rak's unnatural strength meant that their smiths forged their weapons larger and heavier, unusable to anyone but the strongest Oemorg. All the better for cleaving through Vent beasts.

There was no arguing with Vulinor. The weapon felt clumsy to Eiklo, but at least he was armed. "Thank you, Captain." Eiklo bowed his head, then saluted. "I'll make sure to return it in impeccable condition." It did feel comforting to know he had Cavotros iron sheathed at his side, in the event some insane masked volcomancer who imbued shadows into brambles was involved.

Vulinor scoffed. "Don't tell me that. I expect to receive it back battered and bruised. Maybe Srrith can train you with it; she's already training Imayva."

Eiklo stopped, confused, and said, "I'm only using the mace for today, though. If everything goes to plan, then Srrith will continue into the Azraks and Mayve will...I don't know, but I'm not keeping this for long enough to train with it."

Vulinor chuckled, as if Eiklo had just said something laughably stupid. "You're pretty dense for such a smart lad, you know that?"

What did I miss? He riffled through the past ten seconds of the conversation, trying to understand what Vulinor meant. "I'm sorry, Captain, I don't understand?"

"You're probably not coming back to the Ferry, my lad."

"What do you mean?" Eiklo said. "Of course I am."

"We'll see, but I doubt it. I'm rarely wrong when I see that look on my crew's skulls," Vulinor said. "I've known for a while that you'd leave us eventually. Your talents are wasted here, and you'd see that soon enough if you stayed."

Eiklo stammered, "But where would I go if not back here?"

"*Varin's scrolls,* Eiklo, with Srrith, or with Imayva. Maybe both. Maybe Srrith and Imayva have gone their separate ways, and you're stuck with the Oasis Stone.. You would just toss that with your belongings and never think about it again? Or would you travel back north to the Thaumaturns, or down to the Grand Library of Quyntrell in search of answers? I know what you would do."

Eiklo looked at his boots, a little ashamed that Vulinor had seen it before him. Everything the captain was saying had utterly piqued his interest. But what about the crew? All of his friends? Would he set off alone if he had to?

Vulinor opened a drawer on his desk and riffled through some papers until he found a specific sheet he was looking for. He studied it for a second, then flipped it around for Eiklo to take a look. It was a service contract for the Ferry, detailing duties, pay, and term length. A dotted line at the bottom was adorned with Eiklo's chicken-scratch signature.

"This yours?" Vulinor pointed to the dotted line. At Eiklo's nod, the contract evaporated to ashes in a burst of flame from Vulinor's fingers. "I release you from your duties here. Thank you for a job well served, Eiklo. I'll re-enlist you at sunset if you so choose, but whatever happens today, know you have my full support."

Vulinor extended his hand, and Eiklo met it over the table with a firm shake, the captain's grip almost crushing his fingers to bonemeal.

"Now," Vulinor boomed, "let's go see if we can help our good friend Imayva, and perhaps find our elusive snake friend on the way."

He opened the quarters' door to find Bolios waiting, nervously stroking Screech's plumage. Screech was cooing softly, perhaps comforting the anxious cook or simply enjoying the attention. Seeing Eiklo and Vulinor, Bolios hurried over and snapped into a rapt salute.

"Eiklo, good to see you looking well. Captain, sir." Eiklo had no idea how a skeleton could look plump, but somehow, Bolios was. The skeleton stood at attention, waiting for permission to speak. His foot tapped anxiously, and embers flitted from the corners of his mouth like tiny fairies.

"Bolios." Vulinor saluted back. "Out with it, you look like you're about to disintegrate."

"Yes, sir," Bolios stammered. "I was at the market, looking for a better deal on foodstuffs than what the rats at the dockyard were giving us, and I saw something peculiar. The crew on deck thought that you and Eiklo would find it interesting."

"*Varin's scroll*, Bolios, just tell us," Vulinor boomed.

"Our old passenger, Imayva, sir." As Bolios said the name, Eiklo's chest overturned in worry. "I saw her in the market. She was fighting the Merchatzi. I only caught snippets. It looked like she was stealing, but someone was screaming about a murder!"

Vulinor's red orbs flared with heat. "Where is she now?"

"Arrested, Captain sir. I tailed them for a bit, out of curiosity. Strange thing is, they didn't go to the town jail—they dragged her to the Tyrak-Wenstnor Coalition guild hall."

The captain looked at Eiklo. "Imayva...would she murder someone?"

Eiklo tried to think clearly, still reeling from the information Bolios had laid out. He slowly started to shake his head. "I don't think so. At least, I *didn't* think so. She seemed in a lot of pain when I last saw her. Even if she did, she's not that kind of person. She's saved my life. A person like that can't kill, can they?"

Firmly and directly, Vulinor spoke. "Make the call, Eiklo. I will not risk the lives or the reputation of my crew for a murderer. If you think there's more to this, then the Ferrymen will go ashore."

"There has to be more than this," Eiklo said. "I'm going to see myself, Ferrymen or not."

"Then the crew comes with you." Vulinor turned to Bolios. "Tell Vanite to prepare my best for a fight. Armed, but not dangerous enough that we can't walk through town without suspicion." Bolios saluted and ran off, scrambling up the hold's steps.

"The Tyrak-Wenstnor Coalition won't be happy about a group of Ul'Varin barging in."

"It's called intimidation, young skeleton, and it's something I'm very good at." Vulinor smirked, spirals of fire twisting from his jaw. "The cowardly merchants talk big, but bend like reeds when a flaming skeleton is shouting in their faces. It's one of undeath's simple pleasures."

He tossed Eiklo a belt with a metal loop sewn on—perfect for carrying a mace on the hip. Eiklo hurriedly buckled it and slid the mace into the loop with an abundance of caution, making sure the spiky mace head was unable to prick him. He would hate to be cut by Cavotros iron mid-manifestation. The Northern Ice raptors warned him long ago that the metal's anti-Du'ul was deadly to volcomancers.

"First and foremost, we're going to ask some questions," Vulinor said, as they marched together up the stairs to the deck. "See what Imayva did and if it warrants our intervention. Perhaps speak with the young woman ourselves, get her side of the story. It's hard to refuse anything to a group of armed Ul'Varin."

"What if we don't like the answers? If it's all somehow related to the Oasis Stone or, Varin forbid, the bramble eldritches? They might lie through their teeth to keep her there."

Vulinor looked over his shoulder right at Eiklo. His red orbs ignited with crimson fire. "That's why we're going armed."

Chapter 35

The Masked Man

Mayve stopped struggling shortly after losing sight of the market square. Any fighting was fruitless, and the pitiful stares of the onlookers had shunned her into silence. They only saw her as some berserk animal, cornered and caught by the courageous Merchatzi. Or worse, a crazed murderer.

Head limp, she watched the cobblestones pass as she stumbled to keep up with the guards' brisk pace. In what seemed like a blink of an eye, she was dragged into a building and dumped unceremoniously into a cell. The door slammed shut, a heavy lock clicked into place, and boots stomped away down the hall.

It was a long while before Mayve rose to a sitting position. Her vision was blurry, and she realized she was too numb to feel she was crying. Letting the tears fall onto the cell floor, she remained motionless until her eyes finally dried.

Any chance of avenging her mother was gone. Dreva's killers still roamed the city, living free as if they had never ended others with their twisted creations, while Mayve was trapped, destined for a prison or worse. It wasn't just her mother. She had made friends. There were others who cared for her, Eiklo and Srrith, and she'd pushed them away, all for nothing. She might rot in this cell for a long time. Maybe they'd kill her tonight. Perhaps a passing Citadel would take all the prisoners for a fee and dump them into the Outcasts, where she would die on a desert rock.

Mayve had already almost died on a desert rock. Surviving the first time had been difficult, but she had something to push for, something to make it back to. If she had felt this way back then, she would have walked into the waiting jaws of the gorgonwolves.

She slumped onto her back. The ceiling of her cell was just iron bars, allowing her to look up at the rafters of a tall room. The floor was made of rough stone, and the door itself was made of thick oak with a small window of iron bars. The remaining four walls were maroon brick. The absence of a bed, or anywhere to relieve herself, told Mayve that this housing was likely temporary.

Mind wandering, Mayve remembered her first time behind bars. Years ago, when Dreva was finally allowing her to roam Devar on her own, Spotch dared her to sneak into the yard of an Archtown manor and steal a rare bird from the merchant's private aviary. Excited to be included and eager to show off her climbing, Mayve clambered through the Locks to the underside of the Arch, then scaled up to the manor. Hopping the yard's wall that bordered the cliff, she easily made it into the outdoor aviary without being spotted.

The bird itself was an enormous parrokip with rare pink plumage. Only native to the Noatara Jungle in the South Verdant, the merchant probably paid several chests' worth of teirs to have the bird brought all the way into the desert. The parrokip itself was so fat, it was almost a perfect circle of feathers, its feet and beak buried in the overwhelming plumage. Pampered and plump, it lacked any survival instincts, and Mayve caught it with ease. The bird was so rotund, young Mayve could barely wrap her arms around it.

That's when she realized there was absolutely no way she could climb back down the cliff with this creature in tow. Woefully ill-informed and unprepared, she attempted to sneak out down the Arch Road, where she was quickly apprehended when the blasted chicken started screaming. It took years before she realized that Ingo and Spotch probably just wanted to eat it.

Archtown did not have a jail of any sort. Building one up there would take away precious space that a merchant or guild could use to build a lavish mansion. The Merchatzi dragged her down every step of the Arch Road to throw her into a cell on the edge of Silt Row. She had languished the entire day away in that dry, sand-choked cell, and just as the horizon swallowed the sunset, Dreva found her by complete accident. Her poor mother had been scouring the city for her missing girl and had stopped at the guard post in a desperate attempt to see if the Merchatzi could aid her.

Since she was just a kid, the guards released her to her mother's care. Despite the destructive scolding that followed, Mayve had been ecstatic to see her mother. Dreva had rushed to the cell door, yelling at the guards to get the keys, tears of relief streaming down her cheeks. Mayve had leapt into her mother's shawl, basking in her love.

The dark hallway behind the cell door of her present jail remained silent and empty. She pushed herself off the floor and leaned against the wall. Would Eiklo or Srrith come for her? They didn't know she was here, and they probably wanted nothing to do with her anymore. Srrith had the Oasis Stone, Eiklo had his crew. They would soon forget about the strange girl they met on their travels, who disappeared into Port Wenstnor never to be seen again.

Srrith has the stone, Eiklo has his crew, and I have no one. Mayve had burned the meager bridges she had built, only to discover there was nothing on the other side. She could have used Eiklo's logical thinking earlier. If she had just opened up to him about what she wanted to do.

He would have talked me out of it, and I thought I could not live with myself if I didn't try. How could I? What kind of person accidentally kills their mother with their own recklessness and then walks away?

Suddenly, the walls of her cell shook violently. The metallic crash of a bell reverberated through her skull. One boom, signaling an hour past noon, rattled every bone in Mayve's body. *They built the cells into the walls of a bell tower. Vent-cursed Merchatzi, that's cruel.* She reached for her shawl to wrap it around her head, and found they had taken all her belongings.

Thank Phovus I had the foresight to return the Oasis Stone, at the very least. It was one thing she got right. At least Srrith could continue her adventure, wherever that led her, and maybe Eiklo would get a kick out of whatever research Srrith let him do on the artifact.

Both of them were good friends who'd saved her life, and she had tossed them away.

Another small part of her was glad her dagger was gone. It only reminded her of her follies. If she had spent Dreva's hard-earned coin on sandpeppers like she was supposed to, maybe she'd still be alive. *No, she'd certainly be alive.*

She missed her shawl and canteen, though. The canteen she had stolen from a drunk patron at The Skewered Barge—a pickpocket job she was especially proud of—but the shawl had been handwoven by her mother. It had been months of work, as Dreva bought each bit of cloth only when she could afford it. Mayve would have stolen what she needed, if she had known, but Dreva had kept it secret until her birthday, weaving in the light of the garden or by the dim light of their dwelling's oven whenever Mayve was gone.

By habit now, she reached for her mother's ring on her finger, only to find empty space. *Excuse me? Taking my dagger I understand, but fleecing me of my jewelry? Maybe it slipped off my finger during the fight.*

The gong of the bell resided, and Mayve heard a pained groan from the cell next door. As the ringing faded, the groan fell into a seething hiss, accompanied by the unmistakable sounds of large scales sliding against stone as the occupant shifted. *It can't be.*

"Srrith?" Mayve called out. "Srrith, is that you?" A faint flame of hope reignited as she realized she wasn't alone.

A voice returned through the iron grate in the door, faint but recognizable. "....Mayve..." Srrith's low voice was steeped in exhaustion. *Fucking depths, that bell rings every hour. Her poor hearing.*

Mayve felt some life return to her numb limbs at the sound of the tauninaga's voice, and leapt up to the door grate. "Srrith! Yes, it's me! How are you here? Why are you here?"

The snake's faint voice hissed through the dark hallway. "Mayve... can you hear them, Mayve?"

Mayve felt sick hearing the weakness in Srrith's voice. The tauninaga was not well. "Are you okay? We'll get you out of here, I promise."

Adrenaline surged as she finally found purpose again. She had to get Srrith out.

"I can hear them. Can you?" Srrith muttered. "Can you hear the screaming?"

A shiver shot down Mayve's spine. "What screaming? I don't hear anything. Where is the screaming?"

The sound of scraping scales drifted through the hallway as the tauninaga shifted in her cell. "The screaming beneath the floor, Mayve. He has grown them in the basement. They scream just like they did in Devar." The tauninaga sounded dazed, as if she were struggling to stitch her thoughts together.

Phovus, no, please no. The memory of the eldritch brambles' horrific screams cut through her mind. Mayve dropped her ear to the floor, the cold stone pressed against her cheek. She heard nothing but her own heart beating and blood rushing. Still, her hearing was completely outclassed by Srrith's. Perhaps the tauninaga was delirious, her hearing destroyed by the bell.

All concerns about her own fate were gone, replaced with one singular purpose. Mayve had to get Srrith out of here.

The door was too sturdy, and she had nothing to pick the lock with. Jumping up to catch the iron bars of the ceiling, she threw her weight down. Nothing budged. Trying to calm herself, she tried to trap the Du'ul, but the thought of the brambles writhing beneath her was too overwhelming. Any second, she expected them to erupt from the ground like they did in Dreva's garden.

The hallway door opened and several sets of footsteps entered. Mayve paused her investigation of the cell and calmed her nerves. If the guards had arrived earlier, she would have submitted willingly. Now that she knew Srrith was next door, potentially gravely ill, she could not be taken away to her fate just yet. Mayve balled her fists. Could she take the guards? Maybe two. Three or four, less likely.

A mask appeared in the door window, dark eyes staring in. Mayve's breath caught in her chest and her muscles froze.

Face-to-face with the dreaded masked volcomancer, wielder of shadows, creator of the monstrous seeds, Mayve failed to find a single word. The mask hid all the emotions of its mysterious wearer, allowing Mayve to interpret his gaze however she wanted. The dark eyes seemed to regard her with a sinister curiosity. Behind him stood two guards, and a third man dressed in brown leather armor with white fur padding, two scimitars sheathed on his back, eerily similar to how Srrith wore her sickles.

The memories of the mask, burned into her mind weeks ago, did not compare to seeing it again. It was made of smooth onyx, cut so perfectly, it must have been crafted by a master jeweler. It conformed to the man's face with a flawless fit, carved with a firm jaw and an unassuming nose, with small slits for breathing. The mask's mouth was a thin line, almost imperceivable on the black onyx, and showed as much emotion as a sleeping corpse. A large black hood, attached to the pauldrons of his ornate, black leather armor, was pulled far up to obscure the sides of his head. The hood and the mask's strong brow cast shadows over the eyes of it, completely hiding the one identifying feature of his face that the mask did not cover.

Above all else, the most striking aspect of the mask were the trails of glittering amethyst gemstones, embedded in the onyx as if they grew there naturally. They traveled from beneath the eyes all the way to the bottom of the mask like rivers of purple tears.

The moment of stunned silence passed. Before Mayve could speak, the door opened. As the Merchatzi stepped in to grab her, the masked man spoke in a silky, golden voice. "Please, no need to be so rough with our guest. She is quite capable of grasping the consequences of resistance." He placed his words gracefully, like a noble standing in a Citadel court, with a tiny hint of an accent that Mayve did not recognize.

The guards stepped back without a word to either side of the cell door, raising their purple-and-blue shields in a salute. The masked man stepped into the cell and stopped a few paces before Mayve, standing calmly with his hands clasped behind his back.

The man with the scimitars waved his hands, which flashed with magenta light, then the door vanished in an instant, replaced with a solid brick wall.

"How fortunate for us to cross paths again. Our first meeting was so brief, we did not get the chance to introduce ourselves." He placed a gloved hand on his chest and gave a short bow. The mask's eyes pointed toward the ground, but Mayve just barely perceived the white glint of his pupils still locked on her. "You may call me Zeteph. And you are?"

Zeteph's silky voice made Mayve feel sick. She held her tongue and stared defiantly into the mask's eyes. His question hung tentatively in the air, stifling the room. *Why did he come to me? He can kill me at any second, so why wait?*

"You don't keep the best manners, it seems." Zeteph clasped his hands behind his back again. "I understand that in your current situation, silence is your only way of fighting back. I do hope we can establish *some* rapport, without resorting to more barbaric methods." The light in the room dimmed for a brief second as he finished his sentence. "I don't need to know your name, I'm merely curious. Now, how about you ask a question? You might be dying of curiosity yourself."

The playful intelligence and aloof nobility of Zeteph's voice was especially off-putting coming from behind the crying eyes and emotionless mouth of his mask. *He wants me to ask a question? I refuse to let this monster toy with me.*

"You killed my mother," Mayve stated, trying but failing to conceal the fury that dripped from her words. "I'm not playing whatever game you think you're winning."

"Tsk, tsk." Zeteph shook his head. "That's not a question, so I have no answer for you. But I suppose that might be the answer to my next question. Why did you attack our merchant today? Revenge for a lost soul, perhaps?"

"Perhaps," Mayve said coldly.

"Nothing more?" Zeteph asked. Mayve could tell he knew something more, although she had no idea what about. There was an air of smugness in his voice, taunting her.

"Just say what you want to say already," Mayve spat. "If you're going to kill me, just do it already."

"Frankly, I'm quite undecided on that. Whether or not you die depends on the answers you give," Zeteph said. "I'm not in the business of indiscriminate killing."

Mayve almost laughed. "But if the killing is done by your monstrosities, then it's *fine*? You left so many dead around Devar. *Phovus*, you've already tried to kill me before!"

Zeteph shook his head. "I said *indiscriminate* killing, young human, please listen. Unfortunately, killing with purpose is a necessity sometimes, for those with grand plans and lofty ambitions."

"What purpose does unleashing a horde of monsters on Devar serve, exactly?"

"It sated my curiosity." Zeteph shrugged. "I thought about hunting you down and reclaiming our wares, that day we first met, but I'll admit my intrigue got the better of me."

"You could have stopped it. You could have warned everyone," Mayve seethed.

"I should tell everyone that I made those monsters, *and* let them get stolen? Of course not." He seemed offended that Mayve would propose such a stupid idea. "I wasn't planning to release them in Devar—that was all *your* fault."

I know. Mayve boiled in rage, condensing her anger into an ice-cold stare. "Then where are you going to attack? Is it here? I know you're hiding more of those creatures in the basement."

"Ah," Zeteph taunted. "And how do you know that?"

Mayve realized her tongue slip too late. She could not let him know she knew Srrith. Panicking, she blurted out, "I know what those screams are. I could hear them through the floor when your guards threw me in here."

"You could hear them?" Zeteph asked, that same taunting tone dripping from his voice. "Are you sure it wasn't your friend in the next cell over?"

Mayve froze.

"Yes, I know you too are working together. I know quite a lot, actually." Zeteph laughed. "We'll get to that later, of course. Are you sure you don't want to tell me your name? That's one of the few things I don't know, and it seems so rude to keep calling you 'human' or 'girl.'"

How does he know Srrith and I traveled together? Did he talk with someone on the Ferry? The possibility that he had tortured Srrith for that information churned Mayve's stomach in fury. *Everyone that comes in contact with me suffers some horrible fate. Srrith saved your life three times and look how you've repaid her.* She held her tongue.

Zeteph paced around the perimeter of the small cell, forcing Mayve to swivel in place to keep her eyes locked on him. He tapped the onyx chin of his mask with a gloved finger, pondering out loud. "There is something I don't know, though, and what I can't quite figure out. Are you a worthless nobody from the gutters of Devar, swept into chaotic, foolish vengeance? Or are you far more troublesome than that? Care to enlighten me?"

Mayve stared daggers at the weeping violet eye holes. "I'm not quite sure what you mean, but I'm glad you see me as a threat."

"Please, don't flatter yourself." Zeteph snorted. "See, on one hand, you clearly look like a distraught little ruffian who steals to survive. On the other hand, you manage to befriend a *tauninagan hunter,* of all folks, and you stroll around flaunting a *stamp ring*? Did one of the Citadels send you? Teirmond? Waldheath?" He placed a hand over the mask's mouth in a mock gasp. "*Ashfell?* The Coalition has not had any fair dealings with them in years."

"What on Phovus's green earth is a stamp ring?" Mayve snapped.

Zeteph stopped his circuitous walking and simply stared at her. "You're telling me you don't even know what you've been wearing on your hand this whole time? I don't believe it."

My mother's ring? She always thought it could be worth a few teirs if she tried to sell it, but Zeteph was talking about it as if it was worth as much as the Oasis Stone.

"So you stole that ring from some noble and just decided to keep it?" Zeteph asked. This question seemed real, not the fake rhetorical garbage that he had been throwing at her where he clearly already knew the answer. She decided to hold her tongue. He did not need to know it was her mother's.

"Well," Zeteph remarked. "Maybe you'll find out what a stamp ring is one day. I'll be keeping that one, though. Can't have you find your way onto a Citadel now, can we?"

Mayve kept her stoic glare, but her mind was racing. Did Dreva have a connection to a Citadel somehow? *Then why in the depths did we spend our lives in a literal hole in the ground, scrounging for food?*

Zeteph stopped circling her, silently watching from behind the dark eyes of his mask. A shiver ran down her spine. It dawned on her that as she had turned to face him, she forgot which wall the door had been on.

Looking up, the barred ceiling was gone too, replaced by more bricks. She was completely trapped in a room with no exits, alongside a psychotic volcomancer.

Shadows seemed to coalesce and leak from the seams where the walls touched. Breaking out into a cold sweat, she clenched her fists and prepared to launch at Zeteph if he showed any signs of volcomancy. Chances were he'd kill her instantly, but hopefully she'd at least get a punch in. Maybe break a rib or smash that silly mask to pieces.

Why does it seem like he knows everything? How does he know Srrith and I traveled together? Mayve was fighting her fear, trying to maintain her composure as the shadows leaked down the walls. *We're in the Verdant, where manifestations are weaker. I don't know what he can and can't do. Just breathe.*

Zeteph uncorked a flash from his belt. A glass bottle filled with bright cyan fluid. A sweet stench filled the room, leaving a metallic aftertaste in Mayve's mouth. He turned his head away to hide his face, removing the mask and drinking deeply from the mysterious fluid.

This is my chance. Depths below, Mayve, move! Kill him while he's turned! Her body refused to listen. The shadows leaking from the walls pooled at her feet, melding into her boots, worming up her ankles and into the skin. She felt nothing but pure fear, her heart pounding in her chest, her skin freezing cold. *He doesn't care if he turns his back. He knows I'm too scared to move.*

Finishing his drink, Zeteph turned back, raised his hands, and clapped twice. As he did, the room returned to normal, the door appearing to her right. To her horror, it was not the wall she would have chosen if she had to guess.

Zeteph spoke in an eerily cheery voice. "This went well. I think we both learned a lot, and you'll be pleased to hear that I'm inclined to let you live at the end of this, so you can go back to your life of picking pockets and cutting purses."

He left the cell, heading for the hallway door. "Depends on how the negotiations go, however. Come along. You two, grab the snake, and our other guest."

Mayve stood still, confused and terrified. "Negotiations?"

"That's what I said. Please listen better," he called back as he exited the hallway. "Vrato, if you will."

The man with the sheathed scimitars nodded, grinning, and tried to grab Mayve's arm. "Come on, girl." His voice was slimy, his eyes staring too intently as he looked her up and down. Mayve felt like she had already met this man a thousand times in every tavern she'd ever walked in. However, most idiots in the drinking holes could not make doors disappear with a wave of their hand. She slapped his hand away and strode out of the cell on her own. Behind her, she heard the other guards unlock the door to Srrith's cell, along with a door to a third cell with an unknown occupant. As she turned to look, Vrato was already behind her, hurrying her out of the room.

Exiting the hallway of cells, Vrato pushed her through a guardroom, outfitted with a large table for eating meals, playing cards strewn across it. The brick walls were equipped with weapon racks, holding up the adorned shields and assorted weaponry that the Merchatzi used. Hurried through the room, Mayve had just enough time to spot her shawl hanging from one of the hooks, right next to Srrith's sickles. She wondered if, given the chance, she should dash for their gear, or the exit.

The only other door from the guardroom led into the great hall of the Coalition building. Brick walls stretched three stories high, with brick arches and wooden rafters holding up a vaulted ceiling. On one end of the hall stood a set of study dark oak doors that led to freedom.

The hall was divided into two floors. The ground floor was a large expanse with a gray stone floor, with plenty of room to accommodate all the business of a merchant guild. Side doors led away into other rooms and offices, all stemming from the grand hall. The upper floor was one story higher, and ringed the perimeter like a large balcony. Merchatzi in Coalition purple, blue, and gold looked down onto the ground floor, keeping a watchful eye on Mayve.

The hall was well lit by staggering glass windows, almost floor to ceiling, allowing the noonday sun to flood everything with natural light. Crafting and installing those windows must have cost a small fortune— another subtle display of wealth for the guild. This hall should have been an epicenter of guild activity, but as Mayve walked in, everything was silent. Zeteph stood on the upper floor, looking down on an assembly of guards and merchants on the main floor. Despite the well-lit room, Zeteph's mask still seemed wreathed in shadow underneath the hood. Vrato pushed her in front of the assembly, directly below the upper floor balcony that Zeteph was on.

Mayve had no idea what to expect. The Tyrak-Wenstnor Coalition was an exceptionally influential guild along the Devaros. Yet everything was halted for this one man. How much power did Zeteph wield in the guild?

Vrato stepped aside, leaving her alone before the audience. Right beside her, the guards dragged Srrith out of the jail quarters, along with one other disheveled person Mayve did not recognize.

Srrith had seen better days. Her pristine black scales did not hold their usual sheen, shedding from stress in many places. Her cobra hood was flared, but drooping on the edges as if she knew she was in danger but had no energy left to fight. The worst part was her arm, wrapped in dust-covered bandages and hanging limp. Mayve's heart dropped as she remembered how Srrith got that injury; being pushed out of harm's way from the Vent beast's maw. As the guards dragged her in front of the audience, her head remained lowered and her eyes closed.

The other prisoner was a regular human man. He was dressed in grubby Coalition robes, and his blond hair was wildly unkempt. Unlike Srrith, he was frantically looking around at the people who used to be his colleagues, hopelessly pleading with the guards or anyone that caught his gaze. As he got closer, his terrified eyes locked with Mayve and a spark of recognition hit her. *Faldmor!*

The disgraced merchant babbled frantically at her, the recognition hitting him at the same time. "*You.* You! This is your fault. All of this is your fault! Look what you've done to me! What you've done to us!"

To her own surprise, Mayve held her tongue. *It is all my fault. But he doesn't mean the attack on Devar. He doesn't mean the lives that were lost. He's only concerned with his own losses.* This man had haunted her waking moments since Devar, but seeing him again lacked the same gravitas that seeing Zeteph carried. Right now, he was nothing more than a pitiful rat, hoping for gods to answer his screams at the sky. *A greedy pawn in Zeteph's game.* To think that she had been so devoted to ending this man's life. Mayve shuddered at her own callousness.

Zeteph interrupted Faldmor's ramblings, waving to one of the guards. "Could you shut him up, please?"

The guard stepped forward and slammed the edge of his shield into Faldmor's stomach, sending him to his knees gasping for air. Zeteph then raised his hands in welcome, addressing the crowd before him, his golden voice flowing through the hall with the slightest echo.

"Merchants of the Tyrak-Wenstnor Coalition, today is a day for celebration, for today we rectify the mistakes that have plagued us since Devar. A random act of thievery forced our...*special*...crops to make an unpleasant, but spectacular, first impression." An excited murmur flitted through the small crowd. *These people cheer for destruction. Why?*

Zeteph continued, "Not only that, but our dear allies were also the victims of thievery, the centerpiece of our ambitions wrenched from their Oaken hands! We feared it lost into the sprawls of Devar or the sands of the desert. Do not fret, my companions. The ebb and flow of fortune has favored us once again. As fate would have it"—Zeteph looked down directly at Mayve—"both robberies were the work of only one thief. That very burglar sits before us now. Surely I'm not mistaken. The description they gave me matches perfectly. Green eyes, dark hair, olive skin, a common thief? That is you, isn't it?"

I only stole the seeds from him, what else did I take? Mayve's eyes widened and the numbness returned. *His Oaken allies...the centerpiece.*

Looming over her like a dark silhouette, Zeteph shouted to the crowd. "Tell me, thief. Tell *us*!" The orator's boom disappeared from his voice, and he spoke next as if he whispered a question into Mayve's ear alone, a question that made Mayve's heart sink in her chest.

"What did you do with the Oasis Stone?"

Chapter 36

Negotiations

All eyes were on her, but the only ones that truly mattered were the dark eyes of Zeteph's mask, waiting for her answer. *I might be the most abysmally unlucky person in Ralvera. Phovus, you must have abandoned me.* To accidentally rob monstrous seeds from this madman, then the next day head across town and steal a powerful artifact from his allies?

At least she gave away the Oasis Stone before embarking on her naive quest for vengeance. It would be safe in the skeletal grasp of the Ferrymen.

Srrith let out a pained hiss, and Mayve glanced over at her. The poor tauninaga looked delirious, propped up limply by two guards like a scaly cloak. With her eyes shut, her forked tongue tasted the air at irregular intervals. *I did one thing right, Srrith. The Oasis Stone is in good hands.* As Mayve looked at her, Srrith's eyes groggily opened. In a flash of a moment, the snake's yellow iris locked onto Mayve, instantly finding eye contact with her. Without a doubt, Mayve knew it was a swift, deliberate action. Srrith's gaze was intensely alert, not the unfocused stare of a sick creature.

The tauninaga was not delirious—she was lying in wait. The two guards holding her looked borderline frustrated they had been saddled with lugging around the massive snake. Unbeknownst to them, they were carrying a deadly hunter, waiting to strike. When she did, it would be their necks first.

Knowing Srrith was by her side, Mayve's confidence grew tenfold. Their situation was still dire, but if they had to break for it then it was extremely comforting to know that Srrith would be fighting alongside her.

"Don't make me repeat myself, human. The Oasis Stone? I know you're the strong, silent type, so let me take this opportunity for a demonstration, one that should hopefully loosen your tongue and open up negotiations." Zeteph paced back and forth along the railing of the upper level, staring down at his prisoners. "You mentioned in the cell that I killed your mother. I find that accusation to be baseless, and it shows you lack any sort of self-reflection. You killed your mother."

Deep down, Mayve knew that was true, but hearing Zeteph say it out loud was all the worse. Tears welled in the corners of her eyes, and she clenched her teeth trying to quell them. Zeteph clapped his hands together. "But there is no need to fret. You're not solely responsible for the tragic loss of life that evening. There is one other—Faldmor."

At the sound of his name, Faldmor snapped to frightened attention. "No, Zeteph, please!" he begged. "I can do better, I need another chance!"

Zeteph shook his head solemnly. "I'm so sorry, Faldmor. I entrusted you with critical items, and you let them get pilfered from under your nose in broad daylight. If you had taken proper precautions, perhaps this mess would be completely avoided."

"It was a freak occurrence, Zeteph! A freak occurrence by a moronic girl!" Faldmor thrashed against the guards holding him. "My usefulness is not over, you need my connections to get onto Citadel Waldheath! You *need* me—" His breath was knocked away by another swift punch to the gut.

Zeteph sighed. "Faldmor, you are embarrassing yourself. The only useful thing you can do right now is serve as an example. Do our memory of you a favor and have a shred of dignity as you pass." As he said that, Zeteph raised his hand and unleashed a torrent of writhing shadows.

Tendrils of purple-and-black darkness spiraled at Faldmor. The guard holding Faldmor leapt aside as the tendrils pierced Faldmor's chest, burrowing into him like eels into a waterlogged carcass. Faldmor spasmed in a silent gasp, back arched, eyes peeled open. As he rolled on the ground, his skin faded to a sick gray, then dark brown as it decayed off his body. In his twisting agony, he locked eyes with Mayve for just a few seconds before his eyeballs collapsed to dust, draining from his head like sand from an hourglass. His dead skin shriveled, lips peeled back to reveal yellowing teeth, his final breath wheezing out from shrinking lungs. The decaying muscles tightened, curling him into a fetal ball until he finally lay still, mummified in his own robes.

No one in the guild hall moved, everyone holding a collective breath. There were many disturbed faces, but not many surprised ones. *They've all seen this happen before.* Srrith hung limp with her eyes closed, likely watching everything through her hearing.

Faldmor's body sat untouched as a grim reminder. Zeteph leaned his elbows against the railing, mask staring at Mayve. He sounded regretful as he spoke. "Dreadful that things must happen this way sometimes. I find it truly sickening how only a few careless decisions from two simple folk like yourself and Faldmor can plunge a city as magnificent as Devar into such bloodshed."

He pointed at Faldmor's body. "Take a good look at him, girl. The very same will happen to your tauninagan friend here if you do not reveal the precise location of the Oasis Stone."

I can't endanger Eiklo. But if he catches me lying, then... Her imagination ran wild with the image of Srrith twisting and decaying on the floor, yellow eyes turning to dust and scales shriveling. Could she doom the Ferrymen to such a fate? Another image haunted her of Eiklo decaying away, the vibrant blue lights of his eyes wide with terror before fading. *Eiklo will be fine, he has the entire Ferry at his disposal. Srrith and I only have each other.*

Faced with an impossible decision, she had to know more. Mayve stared at the eyes behind the onyx-amethyst mask. Beneath the shadows, they shone with excitement. Zeteph wanted more than the Oasis Stone, and it was so tantalizingly close.

"What do you want with the Stone?" Mayve asked.

"Enlighten me as to why that matters?" Zeteph replied

"I think you're a madman," Mayve spat. "Maybe I'd rather die like Faldmor than hand over the artifact."

"As I told you before, I am not here to kill indiscriminately. Only those who stand in my way," Zeteph said. "My pursuits are quite noble, grander than wanton chaos."

"That doesn't convince me."

"This is so far beyond your stature, girl. You don't have to suffer for this. Tell me what you did with the Stone, then scurry back to Devar. Return to your days as a nobody, and thrive in the meaningless, unburdened freedom of an unassuming life."

Part of Mayve craved that. The other half knew Srrith and Eiklo would never forgive her. "Perhaps I'd rather die a meaningful death than live a meaningless life. Especially if it saves more folk from you. Maybe I'll die just to spite you."

"It's not just your life on the line, girl." Shadows spun across Zeteph's fingers, reaching toward Srrith. Mayve grinned, taking small pleasure in the brief hint of anger she saw in Zeteph's eyes.

He paused in what looked like contemplation, or perhaps to calm himself. After a moment, he spoke. "Were you born in the desert?"

Mayve was taken aback by the shift in conversation. She nodded.

"Then this must be your first time seeing nature in such abundance. Trees swaying in a cool breeze by a rushing river, leafy shade protecting even the smallest creatures from the sun. More water than a thousand cities could ever drink." Zeteph gazed out the large windows at the green Azrak foothills surrounding the town. "All of Ralvera used to be like this, until the Vents erupted. One day, it could *all* be like this again."

"What does this have to do with the Vents?"

Zeteph's voice seeped with contempt. If his rigid mask could scowl, it would have. "It saddens me that you cannot conceive of a world without them. They were not always here. You used to be able to stare at any horizon without seeing a putrid column of ash. How complacent we have grown in their wretched shadow. I intend for that to change. The Vents are a fatal disease upon these lands. A disease we have suffered for so long, we have forgotten how it feels to be healthy."

He gestured to himself. "I know the cure, human. I can set us on a path of healing, and all I need is that Stone. Is this really something you want to obstruct? Everything I do, the seeds, the death, this is how it has to be done. When the Vents first burst from the ground, all those centuries ago, they fractured the land through its very soul, and they *will* erupt again. Even now, they rumble in their sleep, spewing their monstrosities and their nature-killing aura. When the Vents erupt again, will you be glad you died a *meaningful* death?"

Mayve had no idea what to think. Her instincts screamed not to trust him, but the passion in Zeteph's voice was oddly convincing. Gone was his mocking, aloof voice that had taunted Mayve earlier. Feeling overwhelmed, she pressed forward with her intended questions. "The Oaken Legion, then, they're part of this plan?"

"They are very interested in the extinction of the Vents, as everyone should be," Zeteph said. "Surprisingly, there are many who are content to live under clouds of ash and blood. Are you one of those people?"

"I suppose I'm not," Mayve said. His golden voice was starting to make sense. *Am I about to hand over the Oasis Stone willingly? If he's honest about not needlessly killing, then maybe I can save both Srrith and Eiklo.* Srrith might be displeased, but it was the only way she'd survive. "If I tell you where it is, can you promise safety to the people who hold it?"

"If they are agreeable to selling it, I'll match any price named. I'll only turn to more nefarious means if I have no other choice," Zeteph said.

Why am I doing this? Zeteph's golden voice seemed to gush through her mind itself. Mayve took a deep breath, and was cut off by a muffled crash behind her, from the other side of the huge oaken doors.

Guards shouted from outside. Another loud boom echoed through the building. The doors shook, and the crowd shuffled nervously. Another crash hit the door, and the heavy fixtures gave way with a violent snap of wood, flying open on their hinges.

Captain Vulinor strode confidently in, flanked by Oribori and Drai. Behind them followed Kinglor and Vanite, with Eiklo sheltered safely in the center of the formation. The Ul'Varins' eyes burned brightly, weapons gleaming in their skeletal hands, the crowd parting from their path.

Zeteph looked on from his vantage point, mask obscuring whatever he thought of this intrusion. Mayve saw Faldmor's corpse get hurriedly dragged away before the Ul'Varin could push through the crowd to see. The other guards formed a defensive line between her and the Ferrymen, while any merchants in the crowd quickly scurried into other rooms.

The Ferrymen looked furious. She had never seen the Ul'Varin-Rak burn so brightly. Pulsing with fiery elemental energy, their bones were almost luminescent. In stark contrast to his Rak brethren, Eiklo studied Mayve from across the room, his deep blue lights wide with worry. She wanted to call out and reassure him, but Zeteph's presence loomed above her.

They shouldn't be here. Eiklo, you need to go. Zeteph would not let her go under any threat; he *needed* the Oasis Stone.

One of the guards tried to stop Vulinor, planting himself in the skeleton's path. Vulinor effortlessly pushed the man aside with what looked like a gentle shove, but the man crumbled like parchment in a strong wind, skidding across the floor with a flaming handprint on his chest. The hall rang with steel as every guard drew their weapons, and Vulinor raised his hands in a gesture of peace. A tense silence gripped the hall until Vulinor finally spoke.

"My apologies for the rude intrusion. My crew and I are normally quite respectful of a guild's private affairs," Vulinor boomed. "We heard through the grapevine that one of our crew had been arrested, on rather surprising charges, and we had to investigate the troubling news for ourselves."

Zeteph clasped his hands behind his back, tilting his head in mock confusion. "Captain Vulinor of the Ferry, your reputation precedes you. I unfortunately cannot accept your apology at the moment. You're interrupting official guild business, not to mention the rather expensive damage you've delivered to our doors." He waved his hands, and a few guards cautiously skirted the perimeter of the room to shut the doors. The strong hinges had held against Vulinor's assault, but cracks through the wood were visible even from where Mayve stood at the other end of the hall. "Those were both carved from the same Cenoreth oak. Truly pricey."

"Cenoreth oak? You don't say." Vulinor looked at the door, but

Mayve knew he was really checking his exit. The guards who shut the doors remained there, blocking the Ferryman's escape. "The Tyrak-Wenstnor Coalition has never been short on coin—has trade been slow?"

"Make your claim already, Vulinor. We don't have time for your antics," Zeteph hissed.

"Let me start by asking why you've detained our friend Imayva here."

Zeteph took a second to look down, directly at Mayve. She could almost hear his golden voice in her head, whispering, *So that's your name. Nice to meet you, Imayva.* He addressed Vulinor. "Your crew member, Imayva, was apprehended trying to murder one of our merchants."

"I wonder why she would do that," Vulinor said.

Zeteph pondered out loud, "Perhaps it was a thievery gone wrong, or perhaps—"

"Oh, I wasn't asking you." Vulinor cut him off with a booming voice and a flare of fire from his eyes. "Imayva, can you explain yourself?"

Mayve suppressed a grin, but said nothing as a nearby guard gripped her shoulder. A subtle threat. Zeteph tried to wrest back control. "Excuse yourself, Vulinor. You have no power to question our guild's prisoners."

As they spoke, Mayve glanced at Srrith, still motionless. As faint as possible, nothing more than a wisp of breath passing over the silent forming of words, Mayve whispered, "Srrith, can you hear me? Once for no, twice for yes." Her words were completely inaudible, except, of course, for those with the sharpest hearing.

Fwhik, fwhik. The tip of Srrith's tail flicked twice, just in the corner of Mayve's vision.

"Thank Phovus's luck," Mayve whispered again. "Are you okay?"

...*Fwhik, fwhik.* A hesitant two flicks. Not great, but acceptable given their circumstances.

"Eiklo has the Stone. Do we give it up to Zeteph if it means we all make it out of here?"

Srrith paused for the longest time. *Fwhik.*

Mayve was worried she'd say that. That only left them with two very poor options. She whispered, "But the Ferrymen. They might die alongside us if fighting breaks out."

Fwhik.

"No? But if we don't fight, we die at Zeteph's hand. He'll do to us what we did to Faldmor. Do we tell the Ferrymen to leave?"

Fwhik.

Srrith *had* to know something she didn't. "Those are our only options. We fight our way out, or we take the Oasis Stone's location to our grave."

Fwhik, fwhik, fwhik, fwhik. Mayve furrowed her brow. The tip of Srrith's tail was flicking in the same direction repeatedly, upward toward the second floor. *Ah, she's pointing! At what? At the windows?*

Through the huge windows upstairs, all she saw was a panoramic view of the mountains and the tops of other buildings. There was no way to access them easily. To climb up there and break the glass while evading Zeteph and the guards would be impossible. *What is she talking about? Maybe she actually is delirious.*

Vulinor's booming voice echoed through the hall. "If I can't hear Imayva's own version of events, I'll have to take your account with healthy skepticism."

"As I said, it's official guild business," Zeteph said. "You are overstaying your intrusive welcome, Captain."

"Was attacking Devar also part of your official guild business? My men and I killed one of your plant creatures. They burned quite spectacularly." Vulinor's red orbs flared. The air was sucked out of the room as everyone collectively held their breath.

Zeteph shifted uncomfortably, the first time Mayve had ever seen him caught off guard. Vulinor had that effect easily, even on men like Zeteph. He continued, "Imayva told us everything. It seemed like a tall tale for quite a minute. A fanciful story made up by a Devarian urchin. Hard to dispute its credibility however, staring at the mask itself."

"Well, then," Zeteph said, "I suppose I should release the girl and in return you'll keep this little secret safe?"

"Took the words right out of my mouth."

Zeteph shrugged. "I get the same result if none of you leave alive."

The entire crew burst out laughing, and Vulinor said, "Five Rak against a room of Merchatzi? We've taken down Vent beasts that could kill everyone I see here with a flick of their claws."

Zeteph planted his hands on the railing and leaned forward, almost excited. "I think I'll take my chances. You don't want a fight either, otherwise you would have burst through that door swinging."

He stood up straight, clasping his hands behind his back, staring down Vulinor with giddy confidence. "Who will be found at fault for an attack here? Did the Ferrymen bravely rescue a prisoner from the clutches of a merchant guild? Or, perhaps, was our fine, reputable establishment brutally attacked by the monstrous Ventwalkers in order to save a murderer? Tell me, Vulinor, which one will the public believe? What will the guilds believe? Many want your Ferry gone. Your prices often undercut the market."

The guards around Mayve shifted nervously, adjusting the grip of their weapons. If fighting erupted, they would be the ones facing the Rak in open combat. They would become the martyrs that Zeteph would leverage. Mayve watched helplessly. She wondered if she should yell at the Ul'Varin to run, to leave her and Srrith behind. *Srrith said not to. Trust Srrith.*

The rest of the crew watched Vulinor with grim anticipation. Their weapons were still sheathed, but they didn't need them. A single punch from any of them could turn a human's chest inside out.

Pointing at Srrith, Vulinor asked, "What crime is the tauninaga here for?"

"More questions that aren't any of your business, Captain. My patience has worn thin." The tips of his fingers were suddenly cloaked in inky shadow, invisible to anyone who did not know what he was about to do.

"All I know is that the tauninaga was on my ship yesterday, and never returned that night," Vulinor pondered. "Seems unlikely that two of my crew would commit crimes against the same guild by chance. Perhaps there is something else you need from them?"

Lowering his hand, Zeteph asked, "And that would be?"

"You already know," Vulinor said.

"No!" Mayve shouted. "Don't give it—" A guard clamped her

mouth shut with a gauntleted hand. The shadows beneath Zeteph's hood twisted slightly, just enough to make the emotionless obsidian mask look like it was grinning. Eiklo looked at Vulinor with deep concern and asked, "Are you sure?"

Vulinor turned and brought Eiklo in close. They exchanged a few heated whispers. To her side, Mayve saw Srrith's head tilt inconspicuously. Eiklo retreated from Vulinor, frost spreading in claw-like branches from his temples across his skull. A grim expression.

Stepping forward, Vulinor announced, "Imayva entrusted the Oasis Stone to us. Are you interested in negotiating now?"

"Perhaps you could persuade me," Zeteph said. "Your terms?"

"The immediate release of Mayve and Srrith, and no further harm to anyone in this room."

"Agreed. As soon as the Stone is in my possession."

Vulinor shook his head. "No, they'll be released first."

"They most certainly will not," Zeteph hissed. "I'm skeptical you even have the Stone in your possession. Care to prove me wrong?"

Vulinor and Eiklo exchanged quick glances. The rest of the Ferrymen stood tall and strong, eying the circle of guards that outnumbered them seven to one. The guards bristled, spears and swords leveled at the Ul'Varin, and armor clinking like sparse raindrops. Eiklo reached into his cloak and pulled out a familiar object; Mayve's old leather pouch that carried the Stone all the way from Devar. The bottom of the pouch bulged in a perfectly spherical shape from the artifact within.

"We have it right here, masked man," Vulinor boomed. "It's all yours once our friends are safe."

"Forgive my distrust," Zeteph said. "Nothing about your reputation suggests that you are a fool, Vulinor. So you must know I have to see *inside* that pouch before these negotiations can move forward."

"I expect nothing less." Vulinor said. "Eiklo, if you will."

Eiklo reached into the bag and Zeteph raised a hand, signaling him to halt. "Please hold on, Zul." The mask fixated on Vulinor. "I like to believe your reputation as a shrewd captain is well-founded, Vulinor. But reputations are easily exaggerated."

Zeteph's golden voice dripped with malice. "I take it there is a slim chance that you do not actually have the Stone in your possession, and have been utterly wasting my time. I do not suffer the antics of fools. So, if you don't have the Stone in your possession here, this is your last chance to leave. I will ask no questions, and never pursue you. You can return to your simple life on the open river, and we will both never speak of this day."

He raised his deadly hand, shadows forming along the creases of his glove. "If you remove anything from that pouch that isn't the Oasis Stone, I will slaughter you here and now, and then I'll pry the information I need from the weakest among you. Deal?"

Eiklo's eyes were wide in terror. The guard on Mayve tightened his grip, while the other guards shifted on the balls of their feet, ready to charge toward the skeletons. None of the Ul'Varin-Rak reached for their weapons, standing stoic and unwavering. Vulinor nodded to Eiklo. "Go ahead, lad. Raise it so the room can see."

Reaching into the bag, Eiklo removed the Oasis Stone. The glittering blue color was unmistakable. Mayve shuddered. The Ul'Varin had no idea what they were doing. Whatever Zeteph was planning, he was about to have the Stone, for better or for worse.

The Coalition guards looked at Zeteph. Shadows twisted down his arms and around his hands, ready to burrow into Srrith at a flick of his wrist. His hand raised toward the tauninaga.

The grand windows shattered. Glass rained down as a horde of screaming raptors fell upon the Coalition hall, and everything descended to chaos.

Chapter 37

Chaos

Before the hail of shattered glass hit the floor, Srrith struck. Her long tail, hanging limp on the ground, sprang to life, wrapping itself under the arms and around the neck of the guard on her left. Using him as leverage, Srrith exploded off the ground while wrenching him downward. Before he even knew what was happening, she grabbed the shoulder and face of the guard on her right and sank her fangs deep into his neck. It only took one swift twist of her body to simultaneously rip out the throat of one guard and snap the neck of the other.

The glass fell like daggers, followed by seven snarling raptors, pouncing from all directions. She closed her hearing—there was no point trying to echolocate in this raging chaos. The raptors charged at Eiklo, clearly intent on snatching the Oasis Stone as fast as possible, but were quickly intercepted by the Rak. The first raptor to reach them—an ambitious lizard with blue scales and brown feathers, carrying a bone spear—took a firmly planted kick to the chest from Kinglor, sending him flying backward into a squadron of guards with a sickening crunch and clattering of metal.

The moment of surprise disappeared, and the Coalition guards joined the fray with a roar. All semblance of order evaporated as skeleton fought raptor fought human, each side trying to run for the Stone and stop the others from reaching it. A gray-feathered raptor dropped a guard with a brutal slash of his sword, then launched off his falling body to sail through the air with a snarl onto the back of Oribori, who promptly grabbed the raptor and hurled him into an advancing pink-feathered raptor. Oribori was then tackled by five or six Coalition guards and pinned to the ground. Elsewhere, Kinglor drew his axe and cut through a swath of guards before ducking for cover as a raptor threw an axe at his skull. Before the raptor could follow with another swing, they were attacked by another two guards and forced back to the outskirts of the room, savagely fighting tooth and claw to break through the Coalition shields.

Beside her, Mayve also used the moment of chaos to her advantage, smashing her head backward into the guard's jaw, then spinning around and launching her knee into the guard's jaw again, sending him crashing to the ground, unconscious. *No surprise—the girl has fought the Merchatzi before.* As Mayve looked at Srrith, her eyes grew wide as she spotted something behind her, and Srrith knew she had to move.

Leaping sideways, Srrith felt the vicious wind of two axes slices through the air where her head had been a moment prior. She spun to face a green-scaled raptor with blood-red feathers flared in rage, eyes crazed and maw foaming. This raptor looked strangely familiar. *The Devar dockyard...*

"I thought I killed you—" Srrith barely finished her sentence before the raptor flung himself at her. Without her sickles, she was practically defenseless. The next axe blows never fell as Mayve grabbed his arms at the peak of their swing. "Ingo, stop! We all need to run!"

Ingo roared and slammed his scaled elbow into her nose, sending Mayve reeling back. He launched again at Srrith, every attack blindingly fast, every swing a deadly near miss. Her injured arm burned from all the sudden movement—she knew she could not keep this going for long. She needed her weapons.

As Ingo snarled and leapt, Srrith uncoiled and wrapped herself around the raptor's torso, locking one of his arms in a coil of her tail and knocking the axe in the other hand away. "Mayve, get our gear, we need to go—*ahhiiisss!*" Pain shot up her tail as Ingo clamped his maw onto her coil, teeth piercing her scales. Mayve wiped away blood that was pouring from her nose and sprinted toward the guardroom door, weaving through the battlefield as if it were empty.

Ingo and Srrith fell to the ground, locked in a writhing mass of fang and scale, each wrestling to get their fangs on the other's throat. In the corner of her eye, Srrith saw Zeteph, wreathed in terrifying shadows. *The same shadows I used to control. They obey him, not me.* A spike of terror shot through her. The masked man raised his hand, pointing death at her.

With a roar and a blast of flame, Vulinor launched himself from across the hall, leaping over the entire battlefield and up to the second floor. Zeteph saw this and tried to readjust his aim but it was too late, and the gigantic Ul'Varin-Rak fell upon him, smashing through the railing. Zeteph sidestepped at the last possible second, Vulinor's white-hot gauntlet missing his mask by a mere hairsbreadth, and the two of them disappeared from view.

Ingo clamped his jaws deeper into flesh, forcing Srrith to break her coil. The tauninaga and the raptor slid apart, Srrith grabbing one of Ingo's axes as Ingo dove for the other one, barely snatching it before Srrith's tail could sweep it away. He rolled to his feet and snarled, "This is for Spotch, you filthy snake."

Srrith flared her hood, brandished Spotch's axe, and hissed through bared fangs, "You shall reunite soon." The two leapt at each other's throats.

* * *

Eiklo was completely lost. *Get Mayve and Srrith, and get out. Pay no heed to anything else and don't look back. That's an order.* He hated what Vulinor had whispered to him, but he had little choice now. That was the only plan that made sense. Any other had been immediately abandoned when a *raiding party of raptors* burst through the windows.

Stuck in the middle of his crew, Eiklo stowed the Oasis Stone pouch beneath his cloak, holding his new mace awkwardly with the other hand. Without thinking, he formed a shield of ice around the forearm of his off hand. Overwhelmed, he spun in circles trying to see where he could help. The Ferrymen defended every angle, each keeping a close eye on him. Then suddenly, Oribori went down, and Eiklo started whaling on the back of the nearest guard with his mace. It felt weak and ineffective on the guard's chainmail, but after a moment Oribori burst from beneath the pile in a superheated blaze, throwing the guards away and igniting the clothing of the nearest one.

Get Mayve. He could not even see Mayve. Next to him, Vulinor roared and leapt at the masked volcomancer. Guards tumbled backward as the skeleton flew over the battlefield in an enraged leap. In that moment, Eiklo finally caught a glimpse of Srrith, locked in combat with a raptor, and glanced Mayve ducking into a side room.

He chased after her, shouldering aside a guard with his ice shield. Just as he reached the side door, a raptor leapt out of the fray at him, spear raised and fangs bared in a snarl. As the spearhead fell toward him, Eiklo raised his ice shield, bracing for impact. Like a charging bull, Kinglor caught the raptor mid-leap with his shoulder and smashed the lizard into the wall with enough force to leave a bloody crater in the bricks.

As Kinglor turned, a Coalition guard cut through a joint in his armor. Kinglor yelled in pain, and fiery red light burst from where his bones were damaged. He turned to engage the guards collapsing in from all sides, and Drai marched over to help, also leaking red light from several places underneath his armor, crushing guards in his wake like a mammoth crushing the underbrush.

Drai saw Eiklo pause, torn between helping them and pursuing Mayve, and pointed solemnly at the door. Another raptor cut through a guard with a spray of blood and lunged at Eiklo, only just grabbing his cloak before Drai grabbed the raptor's tail and dragged the poor lizard away, clawing and snarling. Seizing the opportunity, Eiklo rushed for the door, wrenching it open and throwing himself inside.

* * *

Mayve remembered she had seen their gear in the guardroom, but her mad dash for the weapons came to an abrupt halt. Someone was already in the room. Once again, she found herself face-to-face with an Oaken Legion soldier. A very familiar-looking soldier.

The tree leveled a sword at her. A Coalition blade, grabbed from a nearby weapon rack. "Imayva. Remember me? It's been a long chase."

Last time Mayve had seen this soldier, he was outfitted in full timbersteel plate, with a head of neatly trimmed branches. Now, he looked disheveled and overgrown, with too many leaves in some places and not enough in others. A dirt-smeared bandage was wrapped around his forehead, and his fine Legion clothes were ratty and torn. She didn't know his story, but she guessed it had all been downhill for this soldier after she stole the artifact from his guard.

Mayve held up her hands in peace. "I'm just here for my gear. We don't need to fight."

The tree stepped toward her. "You ruined so much. Everything I've been through is your fault."

"I don't care, I don't even know your name. Are you going to be trouble? 'Cause I don't have the artifact anymore; it's out there with the Ventwalkers."

The tree scowled. His eyes darted back and forth between her and the door. Mayve saw panic in his eyes—he had no plan at all. He came in here for a weapon just like her. She took a step to the side to give him a clear path out of the room. "Your master is waiting. He'll be furious if he doesn't get the Stone."

"Ingo is not my master," the tree spat.

"Ingo? I'm talking about Zeteph."

"Who's Zeteph?"

"You don't even know who you're working for?"

They both stared at each other, dumbfounded, then both jumped as something slammed into the wall between the guardroom and the great hall. The sounds of battle intensified outside as steel rang against steel and raptors howled in bloodlust.

The tree took a step toward the door just as Eiklo burst through it, slamming it behind him. The three stared at each other for only a brief second before all eyes darted to Eiklo's belt, where the pouch with the Oasis Stone hung clear as day. The very same pouch that the Oaken Legion stored the Stone in while it was in their possession.

The tree charged Eiklo, who tried to raise his ice shield and new mace in shaky defense. Despite his ragged looks, the tree clearly had training from the way he held and swung the blade, a swift blow aimed at Eiklo's neck. Luckily, the chair Mayve threw hit him first, breaking against the tree and sending him tumbling to the floor in a clatter of wooden shrapnel.

She was overjoyed at the sight of Eiklo. They had no time to exchange pleasantries or apologies, but just his presence gave Mayve a burst of energy. They had survived worse together. Sheathing his mace, Eiklo froze the tree's hand to the floor in a block of ice with one flick of his wrist. Grunting in frustration, the tree battered the icy manacle with the hilt of his sword, crunching away at the bluish-white casing around his wrist. Mayve ran for her gear.

The tree had obviously searched the room already. The open chest in the corner was partially ransacked, but luckily Mayve found her shawl and canteen, and secured them to her belt. Unfortunately, her mother's ring was nowhere in sight. Zeteph had been very interested in it, so it made sense the ring wasn't here. That masked bastard probably had it in his pocket. *Oh well. At least I have my shawl.* It was a far more sentimental memento of her mother than some ring her father left behind.

On the weapon rack, she grabbed Srrith's sickles, easily carried in their dual sheath, then saw her dagger tossed on the floor nearby. *All of this. It's all because I bought that dagger.* She had enough of it. Leaving it on the ground, she grabbed a Coalition sword instead. The weight felt terrible—it was a far heavier weapon than she had ever used. *If that dumb tree can use one, then I can too.*

"Mayve, we have to go!" The anxiety in Eiklo's voice was strangely comforting. A reminder that she was no longer alone—she had a very nervous skeleton to look out for.

Ice shattered as the Oaken Legion soldier wrenched his hand free and scrambled for his sword. Eiklo whirled around, hand ready to manifest, but then the guardroom door opened and they all caught a brief glimpse of the chaos outside.

The Coalition guards had suffered heavy losses, but they had an immense numbers advantage. The Ul'Varin-Rak were still fighting strong, stopping the raptors and Coalition from barging through the door after Eiklo and the Stone, but almost all of them were injured, red light pouring from the cracked and broken bones beneath their armor. Two of the seven raptors lay dead, strewn around like birds fallen from the sky after a volley of arrows, but the remaining five fought with the ferocity of Vent beasts, savaging their way across the battlefield. Srrith and Ingo were just out of view, and Vulinor and Zeteph were nowhere to be seen. In the fray of battle, no one seemed to notice the guardroom door open.

The open door swung shut as quickly as it opened, with no one walking through. Mayve wondered how it even opened in the first place. Then the door disappeared, replaced with a blank wall.

Vrato materialized from thin air, a malicious grin plastered across his pale face and his twin scimitars drawn. He strode forward, slow and confident, dancing his scimitars through the air in a flashy display. Mayve and Eiklo raised their weapons, but something felt deeply wrong to her.

An illusion volcomancer...why would he show himself? Isn't it better to fight invisible? Mayve realized the trick at the last second and dove toward Eiklo, tackling him to the ground and hoping she'd timed it right.

An invisible blade slashed down behind the Ul'Varin-Zul. What would have been a killing blow instead cut across Eiklo's shoulder, unleashing a burst of freezing blue energy. Eiklo yelled as he and Mayve tumbled out of the way, blue light leaking from the slice on his bone. The illusionary Vrato continued its mindless march forward, spinning its scimitars and grinning as if Eiklo were still standing in front of it, while the real assassin stalked the room, completely invisible.

Realizing what was happening, the tree grabbed a purple-gold Coalition cloak from a nearby peg and threw it wide through the air like a net, hoping to reveal the invisible assailant. The cloak ripped in two as an unseen scimitar carved through it, and Mayve saw a shimmer of light refract from where Vrato was hidden. She and Eiklo scrambled up and spread out, circling the spot of the room where they thought the assassin stood.

A disembodied laugh echoed from thin air, then a dark magenta silhouette of a man materialized. From the glowing form sprang three

Vratos, each one sprinting at Mayve, Eiklo and the tree, their scimitars raised.

Mayve's mind raced, trying to make sense of it all in a split second. *Any of them could be the real assassin, or none of them!* As Srrith had taught, it was always better to evade. She timed her leap backward to evade the curved sword at the last second. To her sides, the tree retreated with a broad parry, aiming to catch the blade while keeping himself at a safe distance. Eiklo raised his ice shield, feet planted. He was going to get hit...

The scimitars cleaved down and passed right through him, the illusions harmlessly bisecting him. The tree also parried nothing, the scimitar passing through as if made of mist. Mere inches from her face, Mayve felt a slice of wind as she ducked underneath a very real scimitar. Spinning away, she brought up her sword to catch the second scimitar as it swept in a horizontal arc. Steel on steel clashed as she made contact with an actual blade.

Vrato spun away and glowed purple again, the two illusionary Vratos blinking away in an instant. Immediately, three more Vratos leapt from the purple silhouette. Again, two illusions and one real. Or even three illusions, and the real assassin was invisible, hidden in thin air.

Eiklo had exposed himself as the one with the worst defense. He was in the most danger. Mayve brandished her sword and leapt at the illusion in front of Eiklo, ignoring the one coming at her.

If she had guessed wrong, she was dead. The assassin cleaved down with both scimitars, the steel making contact with her skin and passing right through with nothing more than a tingle of Du'ul. The assassin before Eiklo raised his swords and brought them down—but his eyes snapped to Mayve charging at him, not something an illusion could do. He scowled and spun his swords mid-swing in quick reversal to parry Mayve's blow.

Steel clashed against steel, but Vrato was too close to Eiklo, who smashed his shield into the assassin's chest. The ice shattered, and the assassin went tumbling backward. The tree leapt at the falling assassin, but the assassin disappeared into invisibility the instant he hit the ground, and the tree's sword clanged off the stone floor as the assassin twisted away, disappearing into the room again.

Purple silhouettes shimmered from all around the room as eight Vratos appeared and charged. Each one could be the real one. None of them could be. There were too many to guess. Mayve knew that someone was about to die, and she had no idea where the Vent-cursed door was. She knew which wall, but where was the handle? The illusions circled them, pressing her and Eiklo back-to-back with the tree. The illusions closed in, sixteen scimitars slicing toward them.

With a pitiful war cry, Eiklo charged, brandishing his mace. Frantically, Mayve scanned the eyes of the illusions, looking for a cognitive glance that would betray the real Vrato. Nothing. Eiklo was too far forward, all illusionary blades descending on the skeleton.

Eiklo's mace passed through the illusion and slammed into the stone floor. As it did, the iridescent iron glowed with radiant fire as it passed through, a shower of blue sparks flying off the weapon. The illusion twisted, contorting and ripping apart in purple strands, and the other illusions followed, unraveling into nothing. Screaming in pain, the real Vrato unveiled himself behind Mayve, crumbling to his knees, scimitars clattering to the ground. He had not been one of the eight illusions, and was moments away from slicing her neck clean through. Blood poured from his nose as he was spasmed uncontrollably.

Mayve kicked him in the face as hard as she could. With a whiplash snap, Vrato crumbled onto the floor, unconscious. She was suddenly very aware of the sword in her hand, and the helpless man at her feet.

The tree yelled at Eiklo, "You were carrying *Cavotros iron* this entire time?!"

Eiklo threw his arms wide in protest, still holding the mace. "It was all happening so fast. I'm not a soldier."

"Thank Phovus's luck you had it, or we'd all be dead." Mayve looked at the assassin twitching on the ground, blood still pouring from his nose and a few specks from his eyes. *This is what happens when Cavotros iron touches a manifestation. All the Du'ul in his body, evaporated in an instant.*

The three took deep breaths, reveling in their victory. But the fight was far from over yet, and everyone realized that at the same time. With sudden ferocity, the Oaken Legion soldier swung his sword at Mayve, who stepped in and caught his arm before he swung. Eiklo quickly clubbed the tree with his mace, which elicited a grunt of pain from the tree but mostly bounced harmlessly off his thick bark. The tree's root-like feet dug into the ground, hurling them back, then he leapt in front of the door, sword raised.

The sounds of battle still raged outside. The tree leveled the sword at them. "Give me the Stone, now, before all your friends are dead outside this door."

Mayve had no idea how Srrith was faring, weaponless against Ingo, but she needed to get to her as soon as possible. The worried frost creeping across Eiklo's brow showed that he too was deeply concerned about his crewmates, suffering an assault from both the raptors and the Coalition. But the Stone...could they just give it up after all this?

She readied to fight the Oaken Legion soldier, but it was not up to her. Eiklo pulled the pouch off his belt and tossed it to the back of the room, far from the door. "Here. Now get out of our way."

I hope that was the right idea, Eiklo. She felt defeated, but also relieved. The Legion and their strange merchant ally had the Stone again, but at least her friends might make it out alive. That was all that mattered. The sand-cursed Stone had done nothing for her but cause trouble. The tree sprinted for the pouch, and Eiklo and Mayve sprinted for the door.

Bursting back into the main hall, Eiklo shouted, "They have the Stone, run!" The Ul'Varin-Rak needed no further incentive. All of them were bleeding vast amounts of red light, a stark contrast to Eiklo's one cut leaking blue. The area around them was lit up deep crimson like a Vent on a sunset horizon. Oribori was crumpled motionless on the ground, the others defending her body and the door in a tight half circle. The ground around them was littered with broken guards and a couple raptors.

On the upper floor, Vulinor roared, "Ferrymen, retreat!" He appeared from out of view and vaulted over the railing, cracking the stone floor as he landed hard. He appeared uninjured, and there was no sign of Zeteph. Drai hoisted Oribori over his shoulder, and the Ferrymen pushed for the door, trampling any guards who got in their way. The remaining Coalition guards turned from the retreating skeletons to engage the raptors, who buckled as the new reinforcements surged against them.

Mayve spotted Ingo and Srrith from across the room. Srrith had wrangled one of Ingo's axes out of his hands, and was using it to defend herself. Both of them looked exhausted, but barely injured, locked in ferocious combat. Srrith had been trying to stall as long as possible, wrapping Ingo in her coils and dodging away from his strikes. On the other hand, Ingo looked rabid, blood and foam leaking from his maw, his eyes bulging with rage.

Srrith spotted Mayve approaching and twisted her coils to fling Ingo into her path. Mayve leapt and kneed Ingo in the chest, sending him sprawling to the ground. Rolling quickly to her feet, she tossed Srrith her sickles. The tauninaga flung Ingo's stolen axe far away into the sea of battle, then donned her weapons, unsheathing one of the sickles comfortably with her good arm. The tauninaga pointed at the retreating Ul'Varin. "With them. I'll be right behind you." Mayve shook her head and readied her sword. She refused to abandon Srrith again.

Ingo, frothing bloody foam, howled and charged the tauninaga. Caught in the thrall of a blind rage, he was a tornado of axe, fang, and feather.

But he was reckless. With a flourish of her sickle, Srrith caught his axe and whipped his legs out from under him with her tail. Mayve looked for an opportunity to step in, but found none. She did not want to get in Srrith's way unless absolutely necessary. Ingo rolled backward in a fit of unhinged snarling.

"Ingo!" a gray raptor, fighting off two Coalition guards, screamed across the room. He parried a sword swing, but got knocked backward by the other guard. "Ingo! Defend your tribe!" he screamed again, louder and more frantic.

The other raptors were getting overwhelmed, and the gray raptor's pleas fell on deaf ears. Ingo flew at Srrith, blind to everything else. He rained blow after blow down on the tauninaga, who twisted, spun, and parried her way backward, retreating defensively toward the door.

A blue-scaled, brown-feathered raptor emerged from the guard-room, holding the Oasis Stone's pouch. The Oaken Legion soldier was nowhere to be seen. The raptor snarled a victory cry, and the other raptors echoed it, reinvigorated by the capture of the Stone. Ingo saw nothing, locking weapons with Srrith and snapping his jaws like a starving crocodile, inches from Srrith's face.

The raptor who held the Oasis Stone collapsed to the ground as shadows burrowed into their neck. Within seconds, they decayed to a shriveled corpse. The victory cries of the raptors fell away as the Oasis Stone pouch rolled from the raptor's mummified hand.

Zeteph stood on the upper-level balcony, hand outstretched. His fine black armor was torn and singed, his mask ajar. As the shadows uncoiled from his fingers, he adjusted his mask so it was just right, then surveyed the great hall, callously glancing over the raptors but pausing with curiosity on Ingo. The void eyes of the obsidian mask rested on Mayve, and he pointed at her.

Mayve's stomach dropped, and she fell onto the balls of her feet, ready to leap for cover, away from Zeteph's erupting shadows. However, nothing came. He was not manifesting, he was *commanding*.

An earsplitting, sickening scream pulled Mayve's heart into her throat. Three eldritch brambles charged out from behind Zeteph and threw themselves off the balcony in a writing mass of thorns.

Every one of Mayve's muscles screamed at her to run, but she could not abandon Srrith, even as the bramble eldritches careened down the great hall toward them. Stepping backward, she almost tripped on the round helmet of a fallen guard. An idea came to mind, and she kicked the helmet into Srrith's tail, which instinctively wrapped around it. As Ingo leapt, Srrith parried the axe away and spun, the momentum sending the tip of her tail—and the helmet—at a violent speed right for Ingo's head. With a crack of bone and clang of steel, Ingo collapsed.

They ran for their lives. The raptors were right behind them, but it was too late. Zeteph executed the gray-feathered raptor with a flick of his wrist, the gray feathers falling off stark white as their scales stretched and decayed, shadows bleeding through every pore. A bramble eldritch savaged the pink-feathered raptor, thorny vines ripping them apart limb from limb. The other raptors fell one by one to Coalition swords and bramble screams. In a matter of seconds, the raptor war party was extinct.

Vulinor's eyes roared with fire, smoke pouring from his skeletal jaw, as he punched the great doors of the hall so hard they snapped outward and crashed into the street. Eiklo was at the entrance, yelling at Mayve and Srrith to hurry. They burst into daylight, eldritch screams at their heels. Passing denizens screamed and fled as the skeletons flooded out to the street, weapons drawn. Vulinor let out a piercing whistle, answered by a shriek from the sky.

Screech brushed the rooftops and landed on the cobblestone in a blustery heatwave. The phoenix looked extremely agitated, feathers flattened in anger at the commotion and the injured Ul'Varin. Eiklo climbed aboard, but Mayve and Srrith both looked at Vulinor.

Vulinor waved them toward the bird. "Screech will take you where you need to go, and Eiklo's going along. His journey on the Ferry has ended, just as yours has. I fear this might be the end of the Ferry for some time, but don't worry about us."

He turned to his crew and started booming orders. "Drai, get Oribori back to the ship, directly to Bolios. Tell them to shove off, full oars downriver. Kinglor, Vanite, form on me if you can still stand. We help them escape, then we sprint for the river."

A chorus of "Aye!" resounded through the Ferrymen, and Drai took off down the streets with the limp Oribori on his shoulders.

"What do you mean? We can all escape to the river!" Mayve shouted. "They won't pursue us, they have the Stone."

"I wish it were that simple," Vulinor said, flames grinning across his skeletal jaw. Atop Screech, Eiklo reached into a saddlebag and pulled out the Oasis Stone, unmistakable in its brilliance.

Mayve gasped, and Srrith hissed in surprise, hood flaring. Eiklo grinned a frosty smile. "All that chaos in there over a ball of ice in a soggy leather pouch. Poor tree. He really thought he had it." He patted Screech's back. "Now get on, please. Quickly."

The sapphire artifact was so resplendent, shimmering in the afternoon sun, that Mayve could not believe she had been tricked by a glittery ball of ice. Plucking the artifact from Eiklo's outstretched hand and attaching it to her belt again felt so gratifying. This was the path she should have chosen, instead of putting her friends in harm's way for vengeance. Relief flooded through her knowing she had a second chance to do what she should have done in the first place. *Even though I'm skep-*

tical of prophecies, I do want to carry it. It feels like I should, and I should have never given it away.

Clambering into the saddle, she said, "You're all insane. Zeteph would have killed you for that instantly."

"You can thank the raptors for their well-timed interruption," Srrith remarked, sliding awkwardly into what was left of the saddle. "Zeteph was not fooled."

Vulinor laughed and said, "We had to try. Persistent monster, that one. I broke him over my knee and he seems to be walking around fine. His manifestation did nothing to me, though. He cannot decay what is already dead, it seems."

The banshee screams of the bramble monsters grew louder as the writhing mass of thorns rushed toward the open doorway, done feasting on raptor and Coalition guard alike. Vulinor turned to Screech, stroking his bird's feathers. Blue flames formed in the corners of his eye sockets like molten tears as he bid his companion another farewell. Then he pointed at the guild hall and said, "Screech, the door?"

Screech reared back and let loose a cannon of flame, catching the first bramble eldritch as it leaped out of the building. Its engorged blood boiled into steam, then the flames caught, turning the creature into a flailing bonfire. As the fire raged, Vulinor said, "Best of luck, friends! May Varin keep your minds and your swords equally sharp! Now fly!"

A few wingbeats later, Screech was in the air, screaming one last solemn caw to Vulinor. The phoenix climbed slowly, burdened by the extra weight of three people.

The two remaining bramble eldritches screamed into the sunlight, one partially ablaze, and fell upon the weary Ul'Varin-Rak. As the flames licked up the brambles' twisted bodies, blood steamed off their thorns, and petals from the wilting black flowers smoldered to ash.

From their bird's-eye view above the city, Mayve saw regiments of Merchatzi collapsing down every alleyway toward the Coalition hall. Mayve looked at Eiklo, who appeared grimly ill, pale ice melting down his skull. She laid a hand on his cold shoulder, but did not know what to say. He was leaving behind all his friends to an unknown fate.

Port Wenstnor's wall passed underneath them, the ground below transforming from cityscape to forest. Green mountains loomed on either side as Screech banked south toward the Azraks. Looking behind, Srrith hissed, "Eiklo, dive for the forest. Right now." The rushing wind took her words away before they reached Eiklo.

Black shadows curled up the guild hall's bell tower like a kraken wrapping its tentacles around the mast of a ship. The tentacles all coalesced into a single point—the palm of one man, standing in the bell tower. Zeteph, gathering an immense amount of energy. Srrith yelled, "Eiklo! Get out of sight, now!"

This time, Eiklo heard, spurring Screech toward the nearest peak as shadows engulfed the entire bell tower. Mayve gripped Screech's saddle as she stared aghast at Zeteph's volcomantic strength. *We're in the Verdant, there's barely any Du'ul! How in the depths is he this powerful?*

Screech dove. The ground hurtled toward them, the mountainside rapidly approaching. Eiklo pulled on Screech's reins, trying to control her descent. Mayve and Srrith clung to the saddle for dear life, wind screaming past them. The sun itself seemed to dim as Zeteph launched the tendrils of shadow, the darkness hurtling through the air over the town, then over the forest, twisting toward them.

Tucking her wings, Screech rolled in midair, sheltering her riders from the shadows as they slammed into her feathered chest. The shadows pierced her, and the phoenix's scream faltered into a gasp as she plummeted from the sky.

Mayve gripped the saddle, bracing for impact into the forest. Screech flapped her wings as hard as she could, using the last of her strength to slow their fall just enough to save them all one last time. Bit by bit, her feathers burned away into ash, drifting into the wind. They crashed into the canopy of the forest, branches snapping and igniting. All three of them were thrown from the saddle as Screech slammed into the ground, stumbling into the dirt as her feathers turned white, then ashen. Then she was gone.

Mayve hit the ground hard and rolled, shifting her momentum as far forward as she could. Eiklo crashed down next to her, bones bursting with injured blue light. Srrith took the impact in the worst way, hitting the ground in a sharp hiss of pain as she landed on her bad arm. Mayve ran over and helped her upright, then checked on Eiklo. "Is everyone okay?"

"No time to check," Srrith hissed. The sound of alarm bells ringing in Port Wenstnor drifted through the trees.

"Don't go anywhere!" Eiklo shouted. "Find the saddlebag, and Screech's feather!"

Mayve saw the saddlebag crumpled on the ground nearby. She checked that the Oasis Stone was safely secure, then slung it over her shoulder. Inside, the Ferrymen had also packed several days' worth of food for her and Srrith. A huge wave of guilt overtook her. Many had suffered for the Stone, and likely even more would.

"I have the feather!" Srrith hissed, holding a fiery red feather by its stem.

Eiklo grabbed the saddlebag from Mayve, unbuckling different straps and reattaching them elsewhere, discarding certain parts as he did, until the entire bag was converted into a wearable backpack. It was an ingenious design, made for phoenixes who frequently died on their missions to fight Vent beasts. Then he pulled out a slim metal container, perfectly sized for a phoenix feather, and stowed Screech's inside. As he did, he whispered, "There you go, Screech. This will keep you safe and dry until we can get you back."

There was no time to celebrate. Zeteph would not wait, so they could not either. Fear chasing their every step, the trio took off in the direction of the Azrak Mountains, toward Srrith's home of Savin Actai, and the Great Seer.

Chapter 38

Cries in the Dark

Raudius ran like wildfire through Old Wenstnor. Muffled alarm bells rang through the sunken halls, echoing through the earth from above. After turning over the false Oasis Stone to the raptors, he used the chaos of the battlefield to flee through the guild hall and escape through a side door.

Everything was a complete and utter failure. A raid on a prominent guild, for a ball of ice. A fucking *ball of ice*. Once again, he was made a fool by Imayva. Not only that, but the blasted tauninaga was there as well! With the Oasis Stone and the snake in one place, he had no more leverage against the raptors.

He chased the twinkling quartz chips that marked the way back to Cindri, catching their glint in the dim light. The torch in his hand sputtered, threatening to extinguish and abandon him to the darkness. Maybe he should have stayed to fight. Show the raptors he was on their side. Surely they would not take well to him fleeing, but he had nothing more to offer them. Tash, Ingo, any of them would gladly plant an axe between his eyes. The poison rotting away in his stomach spurred him onward. He just had to reach Cindri before the others. They were surely retreating now.

They should not have attacked. Even the worst strategists could see they were outnumbered. There were three dozen Merchatzi in that hall, not counting the Ventwalkers. The damned *Ventwalkers.* Ingo's eyes, though, looking in the window at the tauninaga, were pure malice. There was nothing stopping him. It was all over as soon as that icy Ventwalker revealed "the artifact."

Farther ahead was the sound of rushing water—the fallen tower over the underground chasm. He followed the quartz pathway through an old tavern taproom, bounding up a rotting flight of stairs and through the window of an old inn bedroom, which led through the ceiling of a collapsed townhouse. His footsteps echoed off the empty ruins, as if someone ran after him.

Imayva. Sand-cursed fucking Imayva. *Your master is waiting.* What in the depths did she mean by that? She thought he was working for that masked man? Why?

His footsteps hit stone as he stepped into the fallen tower. Slowing his pace just a fraction, he hurried through, carefully avoiding the holes that used to be windows and were now deadly drops into the void. The rushing water almost masked the echo of his footsteps on the cold stone, clicking off the walls around him.

Clicking? His boots were in rough shape, but the padding was fine enough that nothing should be tapping on the stone. To make that clicking sound on stone, he would need to have claws.

Those were not his footsteps.

He turned just as Tash leapt from the darkness. He dropped the torch to the ground, precariously close to a hole through the tower floor, and brought his sword up to catch her axe. Blade met blade, but the weight of the leaping raptor knocked him down onto the cold stone. Beneath him, he heard a crunch as the old stones shifted.

In the torchlight, Tash's maroon feathers were black. She threw her weight onto the axe, pushing the blade down toward Raudius's head. His back on the stone, he supported the flat of his sword with his palm, keeping the axe blade from landing between his eyes.

Tash snarled, "Thought you could escape, barkscum? Want to leave us so soon?" She planted a scaly foot on his chest and pushed down on the axe harder, the blade kissing the bark of Raudius's forehead. The bark of his forearms creaked, straining against Tash.

"Let me go! I did my duty. You have the Stone, the snake, and the girl," Raudius sputtered. He tilted his blade enough to dig the point into a gap between tower stones, then used it as a lever to throw Tash off. She twisted and landed on all fours, pouncing back at him with teeth bared. He steadied himself into a well-practiced dueling stance.

The dim torch, lying on the ground, barely illuminated the pitfalls in the floor. The old tower windows, now deathtraps in the fallen building, at least followed a pattern. Two wide, then one in the middle, then back to two. He knew where one was, therefore he might be able to guess where the others were. One wrong step, however, and it was certain death.

Tash snarled, "Let you go? Let *you* go?" Torchlight dripped from her fangs like blood. "I'm protecting our tribe!"

Raudius spat back, "You abandoned your tribe in a room of Merchatzi and Ventwalkers. I hope they make short work of all you pathetic savages."

Tash screamed and leaped at him. He carefully stepped backward with a sweeping parry. The crude human steel was much heavier than timbersteel, but the motions were the same. Axe clashed against sword over and over as Tash's onslaught pushed him backward, and he knew he couldn't retreat much farther, at risk of falling through a window. The river rushing below filled his head, or was it the roar of the Oakfire in his chest?

He would *not* die today.

The poison tablet in his stomach was minutes from breaking, if not seconds, releasing the Verdant's Bane and melting his innards into sludge. *Tash doesn't need to kill me, she only needs to stop me from reaching Cindri.* With a roar and a rush of Oakfire, leaves and veins glowing green, Raudius parried an axe blow and launched into the offensive, raining down blow after blow onto the raptor, stepping with precise footwork and swinging precise slashes of his blade. They arrived next to the dropped torch, balanced on a window's edge. *That means there's another window to my right, one behind Tash and one behind me.*

The raptor had to know this as well. He saw she was relying far more on blocking his blade rather than keeping her distance—a sign she was hesitant to back up. Fighting in close quarters like these, every strike had to be calculated. There were no second chances if your opponent outmaneuvered you. The fight became as mental as it was physical.

Raudius pressed his advantage, switching to a defensive two-handed grip on the sword to keep his guard strong while driving the raptor backward. Her axe was not built for parrying; any swing could sunder the axe's handle if she caught his weapon at the wrong angle. She gnashed her teeth at him, footwork inching backward, each step closer to the inevitable drop to her death.

On the next parry, her axe deflected from the blade poorly, dropping her guard wide open. The window had to be behind her—he had driven her backward for some time, but the darkness hid the drop from sight. Raudius lunged, left foot planted firm and right foot reaching, sword point aimed for Tash's exposed throat. Tash's maw twisted into a grin.

His forward foot slipped into thin air. The window was right in front of him, Tash standing on the other side. How had she stepped around it? As he fell forward, he saw her tail, swishing side to side. Not keeping her balance, but instead searching. *She knew exactly where it was and stepped around it as she retreated.* And now he was dead.

Raudius dropped his sword and caught the rim of the window with both hands, wedging himself in the window frame before they slipped over the edge. His blade fell silently through the window, swallowed whole by the void. Suspended, he was at Tash's mercy.

Tash broke into victorious laughter, echoing off the cold stone. Muscles on fire, Raudius desperately fought the pull of gravity. Above him, the raptor placed her clawed foot lightly between his shoulder blades and said, "Why we ever dragged a sorry, pathetic excuse for a soldier like you along is beyond me. This is a fitting end for an exile like you. Swept away into the bowels of the earth, alone and forgotten." She slowly shifted weight onto his back, pushing him toward the abyss, savoring every creak as the sinews in his bark screamed in protest.

"Tash! What are you doing?" A second torch blazed into view. Cindri rushed over, picking his way around the open windows of the floor. He looked around in frantic confusion. "Where are the others? Get your foot off him!"

Tash snarled, "Your brother told you to stay behind. Hurry along."

She kept her foot firmly pressed on Raudius, ready to send him screaming into the abyss.

"I heard the sounds of combat and thought I could help. Yet here I find you, murdering our prisoner! Get *off* him!"

Tash brandished her axe at Cindri. "You naive whelp. He fled the battle, coming here to kill you and take the antidote. You should be thanking me."

Cindri brandished his fangs. "It looks like you abandoned them too, all to kill a prisoner. Now let him go."

"Listen here, you sheltered runt, I'm *saving* you! This is how things *are*! Grow the fuck up!" Tash gnashed her teeth at Cindri, threatening him to keep his distance. She raised her foot to stomp Raudius into his watery grave.

"No!" Cindri leapt forward and grabbed her arm, yanking her backward. The force of her foot pulled back and he knew she was off-balance. The Oakfire surged through his veins, blazing vitality into every fiber of his body. His eyes and mouth, every leaf on his head, and every vein in his body blazed Verdant green with the strength of the Oaken Legion.

As Tash fell backward, he rose. Seeing Raudius's face, Cindri dropped Tash's arm in fright. Snarling wildly, Tash raised her axe at Raudius.

It was too late. With an Oaken war cry that boomed through Old Wenstnor, Raudius caught her axe in his hand and kicked Tash square in the chest. She crashed backward, tumbling over the hard stone, and disappeared through the floor. No screams. No curses. Nothing. In an instant, the darkness swallowed her whole, and she ceased to exist.

Stunned, Raudius and Cindri stared at each other, one furious, one horrified. Oakfire still raging through his veins, Raudius leapt for Tash's dropped axe and Cindri sprinted for the end of the tower. He had a matter of seconds to get that antidote before his insides sizzled into a puddle. Cindri scrambled for the mazes of tunnels, where he might lose the tree. But he had to step very carefully to avoid Tash's fate, and Raudius only had to follow his footsteps.

He caught Cindri right at the end of the tower tunnel, tackling him to the ground. Planting his knee on Cindri's back, he pinned the lizard's shoulder with one arm and placed the blade of the axe against the back of his neck. An inferno of Oakfire burning his chest, Raudius screamed, "Give me the antidote! *Give it!*"

Beneath him, Cindri was a blubbering mess, struggling to form words between the sobs and gasps for air. "Raudius...please...it's not..."

"I have seconds, Cindri. *Seconds! Where is it!*"

"I did...it's..." Cindri sobbed louder.

His old wound ached underneath the bandage, where the slice of Oaganshi pine grafted in his forehead hid. The wound that Cindri healed for him. The Oakfire dwindled. "I don't want to kill you, Cindri. Just give me the antidote! Please!"

The raptor gasped for air and shouted amidst tears, "I didn't...I never poisoned you!"

His words echoed off the walls, screaming at Raudius from a thousand angles. He dropped the axe and stumbled backward. Cindri scrambled away into the shadows outside the range of the torch. Hidden, he whimpered from the dark ruins, "I never poisoned you. There was no Verdant's Bane in that pellet. I wanted you to have a chance."

The Oakfire snuffed out to a mere candle's flame, leaving his chest cold and hollow. He stared into the shadows, into the yellow eyes staring back, wide and terrified. He whispered, "Why?"

Cindri's eyes blinked away, disappearing into the ruins as he fled without a sound. Tash's axe grew heavy in Raudius's hand, and it slipped from his grasp onto the stone.

Finally alone, Raudius fled.

Chapter 39

Toward the Azraks

The dawn, like every morning in the deep Azraks, was draped in chilly fog that drifted down from the jungle mountaintops. Srrith wrapped her cloak tightly against her scales, knowing the mist would burn away within the half hour once the sun peeked above the mountains. They had survived the night, though she could not guarantee the next one.

She had marched Mayve and Eiklo through the forest until the sun disappeared behind the horizon, and then a few hours more, guided by echolocation. Putting distance between them and Port Wenstnor was essential to their survival. As far away as possible from Vrato and Zeteph.

A shiver ran up her spine. Was it the mist, or the thought of their pursuers? Srrith did not scare easily. She was supposed to be the one that folks feared. Despite her scattered thoughts, she took the time to carefully check her tunnelsleeve and inspect her sickles. Dire circumstances are where habits die, and she intended to stay prepared. It would give the others an extra minute or two of sleep as well.

Any Merchatzi would deem Srrith's weapons fit for battle. To her, they were in pitiful shape. Since she had last tended to them, she had clashed blades with both Vrato and Ingo. It was just her luck, truly, that

Zeteph had a cavern-cursed *Dreaming Blade* at his beck and call. And the *one raptor* she killed in Devar had a vengeful twin. Perhaps there *was* a good reason the other tauninaga feared her.

"Wake up," she hissed. Mayve grumbled and pushed upright on weary arms. Blue lights awoke in Eiklo's empty eye sockets like sapphire matches struck against rock. They had slept only for a few hours, and if it was anything like Srrith's sleep, their slumber had been interrupted often, adrenaline snapping them awake at every small noise.

Despite their dogged looks, no one complained. Srrith had made the stakes perfectly clear as they marched yesterday. They put distance between them and Port Wenstnor, or they die.

Mayve and Eiklo hurried about their business, packing their meager belongings into Screech's converted saddlebag. The Ferrymen had been kind, leaving ample supplies with the phoenix in case they had to flee. Excellent foresight by Vulinor. Srrith hoped he was okay.

Packed, the others looked to Srrith for directions, and Srrith started off without a word. She wanted to hack the underbrush away, but that would only make their trail even clearer for pursuers. For now, they would stick to the sheltered valleys between the Azrak foothills, then intersect the Tithe Road later, or perhaps cut straight through to the Way of Waterfalls.

As the sun rose, the forest warmed. The shade of the leaves and shadowed valleys provided cool respite from the golden daylight heat simmering through the canopy. Srrith found some peace in familiar scenery as she slithered along. These mountains were home to her. Many at Savin Actai would say otherwise, that her real home was her old clan's hunting grounds, buried deep beneath the Crimson Tors. Those were harsher mountains, caked in red clay and cloaked in the scents of salt and brimstone. Many said that's where *she* belonged, not up here with the blue sky and greenery.

Those tauninaga would be displeased to see Srrith return, but she had weathered worse. The cold stares in Savin Actai were more welcoming than the treatment her old family gave her.

Mayve and Eiklo trailed behind her, still shaken quiet by yesterday's trials. Despite their gloom, Srrith had higher hopes. Mayve was safe, and while she was as determined as ever, she was now focused on bringing the Stone to the Great Seer rather than on her shady past. Srrith could not blame her for what she did, though. Mayve was a thief, and thieves often stumble headfirst into the consequences of their own actions. However, the girl's poor misfortune to steal both the bramble seeds and the Oasis Stone from the same murderous man and his allies—perhaps Mayve was just as cursed as Srrith was. They were kindred spirits in that regard.

On top of that, Srrith was beyond pleased to have Eiklo along for the journey. He was a bright young lad, or at least acted like one, considering his undeath. Not to mention, having a volcomancer was always invaluable.

The Ul'Varin-Zul seemed lost, though, his mind elsewhere. Srrith could not listen to his heartbeat or his breathing, but she did not need those signs to know what he was thinking about. Eiklo was worried about his crew, left behind in the heat of combat. Srrith had high hopes that the Ferrymen would escape downriver or into the mountains. No prison existed that could hold the skeletons of the Scorch Vents, in all their fiery strength.

That also meant they were far more likely to be executed if captured. At best, they escaped and Zeteph was pulling strings to drag their reputation through the mud. At worst...Srrith did not wish to think about that sacrifice. The Ferrymen had risked everything for them, and she had a lot to repay them for. She would start by keeping Eiklo safe. Along with Mayve, she had a lot to look out for now.

The snap of a twig cut through the underbrush, and all three froze, hands leaping to the hilts of their weapons. Srrith slithered forward, hissing through the foliage for any sign of life. Something moved between the trees—and a plump brush pig waddled into view, snout buried in the dirt. Srrith relaxed only a little, still on edge, and motioned Mayve and Eiklo to come look.

The pair crept up and visibly let down their guard when they saw the little round beast snuffling through the leaves. Mayve exhaled a held breath and whispered, "I got all riled up over dinner."

Eiklo whispered, "I read that you can spot where they dig and collect any truffles left once they move on. It's less effort and often faster."

"All I'm hearing is that we can eat truffles *and* a pig."

Eiklo protested, "We already have plenty of supplies."

"You don't even eat, you have no say in this."

"Stop," Srrith hissed. "Hunting the pig or digging for mushrooms will both take too much time. Instead, enjoy that we're not under attack, and let's move on."

She slithered away. Mayve and Eiklo lingered just a bit longer to watch the creature go about its business, then trudged behind her. The silence of the morning was broken, though, and conversation started to circulate as the rising sun eased their fears.

"I saw you manifesting ice from nothing during the battle," Mayve mentioned to Eiklo. "I remember you saying that's hard to do."

"The first time I did that was fending off that gorgonwolf." Eiklo sounded almost embarrassed talking about his volcomancy. "It's coming to me easier now. I think being in several life-and-death moments has helped make it more instinctual."

"Do it now, then," Mayve goaded him into a friendly challenge.

Eiklo flicked his wrist at a nearby tree. A dagger of ice crackled from his hand and embedded itself in the trunk.

Omaea's coils, those fools! Srrith hissed angrily, "Cease! You are leaving a trail. We are lucky that will melt."

Eiklo hung his head. "My apologies, Srrith, I was not thinking."

They were shushed into silence again, and Srrith suddenly felt guilty for killing the conversation. Mayve, still curious about the volcomancy, eventually spoke again. "What changed then?"

"I'm not entirely sure. I've always trapped the Du'ul, and then manifested it out of my hands. But when I threw that hailstone at the gorgonwolf, I didn't just manifest it. I *thought* about how I'd like it to manifest, and it worked?" He shrugged. "That's a terrible way of putting it. I always think about what I'm trying to do, but this time, it's like the Du'ul actually responded to my thoughts, and not just my actions."

They fought gorgonwolves? More happened in the desert than I thought. Srrith made a note to ask them about it later, around the campfire.

Mayve nodded silently, mulling over what Eiklo said. Then she asked, "How do you use volcomancy in the middle of combat? I tried and found it completely impossible."

"It's no simple task," Eiklo said. "It gets easier as you get better at trapping, but it never comes without struggle. Now that we're traveling together again, we can resume our training. I'll have you try to trap the Du'ul while I throw hailstones at you."

Srrith heard Mayve's heartbeat jump excitedly at the thought. She hissed, "You are learning volcomancy?"

The human nodded. "Eiklo showed me the basics while we were in the desert. I am getting quite good at trapping the Du'ul, but every time I manifest it, nothing happens."

Srrith let out a long hiss and said nothing more. She knew very little about volcomancy, but she knew it was a task that some studied for years to master. From teaching Mayve herself, she knew the girl was a fast learner, perhaps against her own good.

Eiklo chimed in, "The man with the illusion manifestation and the scimitars, what did you say his name was?"

"Vrato."

"Right, Vrato. Intentions aside, he was a skilled volcomancer. I'd be lying if I said I wasn't impressed."

Srrith cut in, "You fought Vrato?"

Mayve nodded, "We did, while you were tangling with Ingo. He ambushed us in the guardroom."

"How did you survive?"

"We weren't going to, but Eiklo was carrying Cavotros iron."

Srrith could not hide her surprise, hood flaring slightly. Eiklo spoke softly, his voice laced with worry. "A parting gift from Vulinor."

"An excellent gift indeed. We will have to give him proper thanks when we see him again," Srrith said, aiming to instill a little bit of hope into Eiklo. She did not dwell on the topic of the Ferrymen. "Very adept of you both, to defeat a Dreaming Blade."

Eiklo's eyes grew wide. "*Varin's sword...*"

"Who are they?" Mayve asked.

"The Dreaming Blades were a clan of swamp tauninaga, all elite assassins," Srrith said, "As they grew from clan to organization, they started to accept other folk into their ranks, as long as they could

Naturally Manifest illusions. The swamp tauninagan sfa-zrueen is nearly identical to illusionary volcomancy. What do you know about them, Eiklo?"

"Only that they're extremely dangerous, and their headquarters are hidden in Gloomwall. I heard whispers of them as I traveled through the North Verdant."

"Dangerous is an understatement. I'm honestly surprised you survived against Vrato. Luckily for us, he is likely no longer a member, and is merely selling his swords to the highest bidder. True Dreaming Blades do not work as mercenaries."

"They just let him leave?" Mayve said.

"Unlikely. Joining the Dreaming Blades is a lifelong commitment. I bet Vrato is a hunted man as well, but I wouldn't expect them to catch him before he catches us."

Lazy birdsong drifted through the trees, comforting Srrith. If there was danger nearby, the birds were always the first to know.

"Do you think Vrato is the one pursuing us?" Mayve asked.

"Zeteph will send his best, if he doesn't give chase himself," Srrith said. "Which is why we cannot trust anything we see. He knows who we are, the weapons we carry, and every trick we hold up our sleeves. He'll use all that knowledge to his advantage. That is partially why I did not want to hunt that brush pig earlier."

"Because it could have been an illusion?" Eiklo asked, surprised frost arcing across his forehead.

"Exactly." Srrith looked at Eiklo. "You are well-read—do you know how the second jarl of Fjordhearth died?"

The skeleton tapped his jaw with a clack, trying to remember. "He disappeared on a hunt."

Srrith hissed, "It is far worse. He was constructing ships for the Oaken Legion, which caught the attention of the Dreaming Blades. While he was hunting, they manifested an illusionary boar. As he gave chase, they manifested an illusionary forest off the edge of a cliff. The fake boar ran into the fake forest, with the jarl close on its heels, and the hunt ended then and there. All while the tauninaga watched, cloaked in sfa-zrueen."

Mayve and Eiklo tensed up, glancing suspiciously at the trees around them and the ground beneath their feet, wondering what they could trust. Srrith added, "Do not worry. Illusions have no substance, which means I cannot see them when I echolocate. The ground beneath your feet is safe as long as you walk where I walk."

"So you knew the brush pig was real and did not want to hunt it?" Mayve asked.

"Yes, but that is because I have something that you don't."

"Your echolocation?"

"No. An abundance of caution," Srrith hissed, amused.

Her words offered little reassurance, and the conversation died as Mayve and Eiklo nervously marched behind her, far more aware of the potential danger that chased them.

All you do is leave people unsettled and ill, Srrith's conscious whispered to her. *Why return home when you should be living alone, like all cursed tauninaga do?*

If not for the Great Seer, I likely would be. She grimaced and pushed forward.

* * *

They marched in tense silence until darkness fell. The fair weather held all day—a blessing Srrith hoped would stay until they made it up the Way of Waterfalls. Even a short rainfall and the pathway would become completely impassable. There was only one other route to Savin Actai, and Srrith wanted to avoid it at all costs.

Feasting on smoked fish did little for their morale, and soon the others fell asleep, with Srrith taking first watch. She now had two wards, and it was quickly weighing on her shoulders. *It will be another sleepless night for me, so might as well be alert and ready.* As the night smothered the forest and shadows crept long across the moonlit underbrush, she could only think of the one person she had pushed out of her mind all day. Zeteph.

Not much scared Srrith, and she was mortified by the masked volcomancer. Putting aside his influential connections through the Tyrak-Wenstnor Trade Coalition, he seemed to be one of the most skilled volcomancers in Ralvera. If they were to fight, she had no idea how to defeat his shadows. None.

Not to mention his ability to twist the shadows into pure fear, just like her own sfa-zrueen. Perhaps even better. *His shadows create terror and decay flesh. I cannot strike him down unseen if he rips the shadows away from me.*

That night in the alleyway, he had *sensed* her somehow, while cloaked in shadow. When she used her sfa-zrueen, it alerted him to her very position. He looked *right at her.* The shadows that she had long considered her allies had turned against her in a second. *How did he sense my sfa-zrueen like that? What is his manifestation?* She shuddered, remembering how his shadows wrapped around her, filling her with terror, just like how she used them on others.

His lack of heartbeat or breathing meant that he was completely unreadable behind that mask of his, and he was somehow always one step ahead. Perhaps he had an extensive network of contacts; he knew far more about Mayve and Srrith then he let on. He could have killed Srrith in that alleyway, but he didn't. *I thought, at the time, that he wanted to interrogate me, to see why I was spying.* That would have made sense.

But he never did. He never spoke to her once in that cell, because he already knew who she was. He needed nothing from Srrith, except to use her as a bargaining chip against Mayve. That's what terrified Srrith the most. Because that meant someone close to them was a traitor, or he had vastly more power than she thought.

A twig snapped in the forest. The smallest noise to most, but an exploding firecracker to Srrith. Adrenaline heightened her senses to an apex, and suddenly she heard the muffled crunch of footsteps on dirt and the crackle of torches. So far away that she couldn't even see the light yet.

Four pairs of footsteps. Chainmail clinking like gentle wind chimes. Vrato and Zeteph wore leather armor—this was just a search party. Such hubris, to venture into the night like this. Her night.

She unsheathed one of her sickles with her good arm. She used to think she owned the shadows. The darkness used to comfort her. Now, it felt like she was surrounded by enemies. Wordlessly, she slithered into the night.

When she returned, Mayve's eyes flitted open, and she murmured, "Is everything alright, Srrith?"

"Everything is fine. I'll wake you for the next watch soon." In the darkness, the human did not see the blood dripping from her sickle. Mayve rolled over and fell back into slumber, her beating heart slowing to a drowsy thump.

The shadows were hers. They had to be. She struck so swiftly, the search party never even knew they were dying. She was at home in the dark, whether it was the blackest of nights or the most lightless caves. But if that was true, why did she feel as if she was merely borrowing the shadows?

Srrith did not wake Mayve or Eiklo for any watches. Too many thoughts screamed through her mind, and she spent the night hissing into the shadows. She knew if she slept, the nightmares would find her.

Chapter 40

Feathers and Bones

Cindri huddled alone, deep in the belly of Old Wenstnor. Raudius had taken his torch, and the other torch, dropped in the center of the fallen tower, had long dwindled to nothing. To cross without light would be a death wish. Maybe if he crawled at a snail's pace, feeling the path in front of him? He could end up like Tash, gobbled by the void in an instant. Her death was just as much his fault as it was Raudius's.

He waited. The other raptors would find him on their way back. Tash said they would arrive any moment, but far too many moments had passed. Minutes churned into hours. The echoes of his sobs taunted him, like he was being mocked by the very walls. Eventually, his tears dried up, and he curled into a feathered ball, waiting to be discovered.

For what seemed like an eternity, he waited in the darkness. Drops of fetid water splashed onto his scales from the decaying ceiling, while the dirt beneath him leached his heat into the wet earth.

Then, over the sounds of rushing water, he heard the solitary click of claws on stone, and the light of a torch danced across his closed eyelids.

A hulking shape lurched through the door, stopping when the torchlight hit Cindri. "What are you doing *here?*" Ingo snarled.

With a sob, Cindri leapt to his feet and scurried over to embrace his older brother, but stopped short as he saw his appearance. It wasn't Ingo's feathers, matted together with blood and dirt, that gave him pause, or the dried blood coating his dark green scales. Neither was it Ingo's glaring head injury—dried blood oozing from a purple-black bruise on the side of his skull. It was his eyes. Something was not right in his eyes. He stared at Cindri with crazed but obscured intensity, as if he was focused with all his willpower on something that wasn't there.

He glanced behind him; there was no one there. Just him and Ingo, in the depths of Old Wenstnor. Cindri cautiously asked, dreading the answer, "Where are the others?"

Ingo ripped in a sharp intake of breath, eyes focused elsewhere. He snarled again, "Why are you here? And where is Tash?" He held up Tash's axe, which had been lying untouched where Raudius dropped it.

"The Oaken Legion soldier," Cindri whimpered, afraid of Ingo's reaction. "She tried to kill him, and he won."

Ingo bared his fangs, feathers flaring. "Where is the tree? Dead from Verdant's Bane?"

Cindri lied. "I don't know...he threatened me for the antidote, I had to give it to him, then he ran."

The older raptor's breaths grew more raspy as his rage grew. "Where is Tash's body?"

Cindri pointed a shaky finger to the fallen tower. Ingo slunk over to a window and dropped the axe through, returning Tash's weapon to her. He stood there for some time, head bowed, his shoulders rising in jagged breaths. Cindri dared not interrupt him. Should he pay his respects? Would Tash accept them? He had gotten her killed.

Ingo growled, "Are you okay? Are you hurt?" For the first time, his eyes were focused on Cindri, not trapped somewhere else. Ingo looked like the brother he knew and loved. Cindri nodded. "I'm okay, I promise. Where are the others, Ingo?"

The crazed, faraway look swamped Ingo's gaze again, and he turned away, toward the fallen tower. "It's just me and you. Come. We have somewhere to be." He started slinking back the way he came from, expecting Cindri to follow.

Cindri didn't follow. He already knew the answer, but asked anyway. "Just us?"

Ingo snapped around and gnashed his jaws, eyes bloodshot. "They're dead! Lairro, Haro, Baritri, everyone is dead! And do you know who is alive? The tauninaga. Imayva. That Vent-cursed fucking tree! They're all fucking alive. Now shut your maw and follow me. We have someone to see."

Cindri held back a sob. It was easy, he had very little tears left to cry. Something horrible had happened up there, and he had no idea what. Did Tash chase Raudius before or after everyone died?

She'd thought they'd be right behind her. She had abandoned the others. *Why does that make me feel better about her death? It shouldn't. Oh Taru, what is going on?*

Cindri rarely felt angry—he did not carry his older brother's temper —but for once it burned in his chest. "Did you even find out where that *precious artifact* is? The one you dragged Lairro and the others out here for?"

"It doesn't matter anymore."

"It *doesn't matter*? So what did our tribe die for!"

"Shut up!" Ingo snapped his jaws at Cindri. "Shut up and follow!"

Pacing away into the darkness, Ingo kept muttering under his breath. Cindri hurried to stay in the light of the torch as they crossed the fallen tower. They were heading back into the city? As he neared, he heard the words Ingo was muttering. Not sentences, just names, over and over. *"Snake. Mayve. Raudius."* He did not even know the tauninaga's name still.

On his heels, Cindri pleaded with his brother, "Why not return to Presh? We should be leaving, back to the desert. The animals must be worried sick." Ingo slunk onward, still muttering.

In deep silence, they picked their way through the underbelly of the city, Cindri trailing Ingo like a frightened dog. Somewhere in the woods, Presh was waiting with the bonds. Why were they not returning to him? *Taru's bow,* so many bonds left alone. Borgo, Lairro's kuwraku, Haro's gorgonwolf—they would all be devastated. They might already feel that their bonds were dead.

They crawled into an old cobbler shop, tiled at a precarious angle.

Rotten leather shoes lay discarded around the main floor, while a cascade of rank water splashed through a hole in the ceiling. A pathway of wet claw prints cut through the dust—the raptors had been this way, but there were far fewer footprints returning the other direction. The stairway to the second floor was turned into an ascent of jagged wooden edges by the odd angle of the shop, and they carefully picked their way up.

The hole in the ceiling opened into a well-cut stone tunnel. *A sewer tunnel. Explains the smell.* They must be close to the surface. Ingo climbed through the hole, then offered Cindri his tail as a handhold, pulling his brother through after him. They sloshed through the tunnel for only twenty feet or so before Ingo stopped at a loose grate, streaks of evening light filtering through the bars.

"Here," he growled, and pushed it open, stepping out into the fading orange twilight. Cindri poked his head up and recoiled in fright. Ingo had walked right into a crowded street! He tried to duck back down but Ingo grabbed him by the feathers on his neck and hauled him into view.

Merchatzi were everywhere, dressed in purple and blue, adorned in gold livery. There were no other pedestrians in sight, or Merchatzi from other guilds. Down the street, Cindri spotted a blockade stopping all foot traffic through the area.

All around them, the Merchatzi turned and saw Ingo emerge from the sewer—and let him pass with a simple nod. Cindri tailed his brother like a shadow. He had never been in a Verdant town before—it was dangerous enough for him to travel to desert cities with his orange plumage. How were they able to walk down the street with no troubles?

The signs of battle were everywhere. Cracked cobblestones, discarded weapons, piles of ashes? Cindri eyed a burning lump of brambles with confusion. *That's graveyard briar. It's not even native to the Azraks, why is it burning in the street?* Distracted by the plants, he wracked his brain trying to remember where they were commonly grown.

Ingo slunk through a set of massive oak doors, hanging precariously on smashed hinges. They had been slammed open from within by an immense force. Above the doors, iron letters spelled out a jumble of words: *T rak Wen nor Tr e Co litio*. Looking down, Cindri saw the missing letters scattered about, knocked loose by whatever had happened here.

Inside was even more disastrous than outside. Servants were hard at work scraping blood from the stone floor, erasing the signs of battle. There were no bodies to be seen, but Cindri knew they had to be somewhere. People died here. His tribe died here.

On the ground, trapped in a pool of dried blood, was one of Lairro's gray feathers. Cindri almost threw up, his heart pounding in his chest, and he quickly pulled a dollop of mashed sandroot from a vial on his bandolier to calm his nerves. Why had Ingo brought him here?

Two guards approached, stopping them in the middle of the hall. Cindri tensed, but instead of attacking, one of the guards grunted, "This way."

He walked toward a side door out of the main hall. Ingo slunk behind him and Cindri followed, deeply confused. *I don't like this. We should be heading back to Presh and leaving for the desert. We should be mourning.* The second guard fell in line behind Cindri in a rigid lockstep.

They were escorted farther into the guild hall, through several doors and up a flight of stairs, stopping at a plain wooden door. The front guard knocked politely before opening, and the rear guard herded Ingo and Cindri through.

"Ingo, you've returned. Excellent." A refined, golden voice filled the room. A tall, hooded man dressed in brand-new black leather armor and a fresh cloak stood in front of a large window, watching the sunset. He fixed something to his face, then turned to greet them. An onyx mask, crying tears of embedded amethysts over an emotionless mouth. The rest of the room was a tidy office, with a sturdy desk and plush chairs, lit generously by several lanterns. "You may go." He waved the guards out the door.

On the desk, a strange device started humming, emitting small bird-like trills from punctured holes in its metal shell. The masked man raised a finger and said, "Excuse me just one moment, this is important."

He sat down at his desk, pressed a small button on the oval contraption, and said, "Ready." The contraption buzzed and trilled along with his voice, then he set it down and dipped a quill into some ink. As the contraption started humming again, he seemed to translate the hums and trills into words, recording a message onto the parchment.

Cindri had never seen anything like that before, but he knew it was of Citadel origin. The humans crafted many marvels up on their floating islands. Living in the sands outside Devar, it was impossible not to notice their other newest invention, the coreskiffs, slicing through the clouds.

When the contraption stopped humming, the masked man returned the quill to ink, placed the paper aside, and fixed his gaze on Cindri. "This must be your brother. Cindri, right? Ingo has already told me about you. It is a pleasure to make your acquaintance." He extended a hand in welcome, and Cindri cautiously shook it. "You may call me Zeteph. Take a seat, if you can."

Ingo and Cindri remained standing. Human chairs were not usually crafted with tails in mind, and Cindri wanted to stand regardless. The feathers on the scruff of his neck were slick with fear, his nerves on high alert.

Zeteph paced behind his desk, eyes fixed on Cindri. "First, let me offer my condolences not just for Spotch, but for all of your tribefolk lost in pursuit of bringing his name to peace. It is a shame that those who seek justice often meet their gods early. I am no stranger to fighting for what is right, so I must commend your family."

Cindri nodded and stammered out, "Thank you...sir." He had no idea how to address the masked man, but did not want to offend him. He clearly had station and power. Cindri took a deep breath. "If I may ask, what happened to my tribe?"

"Ingo did not tell you? I'm afraid my perspective might be biased toward my own soldiers, so please take my recounting with a grain of salt." Zeteph said, shooting a glance at Ingo before focusing the mask's void eyes on Cindri. "As a merchant, I am accustomed to dealing with raptor tribes along the Devaros. In my experience, it is usually better to reach an agreement and capitulate to some demands, for the safety of my merchants and the guild's profits. Imagine my surprise, Cindri, when a war party of raptors bursts through the windows of my humble guild hall, so far in the Verdant. In Port Wenstnor, no less! No tribe would ever do this for money alone. I must say, my curiosity was piqued."

He's in love with the sound of his own voice. Cindri had to admit, it flowed with such golden timbre, like sinking in a pool of nectar.

"It is with grave misfortune, however, that your tribe attacked at the same time a group of Ventwalker thugs were trying to intimidate my guild into relinquishing some prisoners—the tauninaga who murdered your brother, and a thief who assaulted our merchant. When your tribe arrived, the monstrosities seized upon the chaos and attacked. Realizing their mistake, your tribe quickly sided with my Merchatzi against the monsters, but were overwhelmed. Your brother is extremely lucky to escape with simply a blow to head. Imagine that as 'lucky.'"

Ventwalkers! That explains the scorch marks on the battlefield. The rest of the story seemed hard to believe, but Ingo was nodding along with solemn agreement. *Lairro let them attack while Ventwalkers were in the room. Was the artifact even here?* If the tauninaga was here, Cindri suspected Ingo was to blame and shifted uncomfortably. He asked Ingo, "Sorry, but why are we here, then? We failed."

Ingo snarled, "Listen to what Zeteph has to say."

"We should go home." Cindri pleaded with his brother.

"*Listen.*"

The void eyes of the mask looked at Cindri. "All is not lost, Cindri. The tauninaga who killed your brother is gone from this city. Srrith, her name is." Zeteph took a seat behind his desk and leaned forward, "But I know where they're going."

Ingo growled and smiled at Cindri. He sounded almost giddy at the chance to continue the hunt.

Cindri's jaw dropped. "You can't be serious..." He glanced at Zeteph to see his reaction, but the mask hid everything. Ingo, however, hid nothing. The bloodlust in his eyes dissolved into furious confusion, as if Cindri had suggested jumping into a Scorch Vent.

"What do you mean, *brother*?" Ingo spat. "Do you want Spotch's killer to *live*?"

"Our chief is dead, Ingo. Many of our finest warriors, dead! The rest of our tribe needs us, we can't just leave them."

"All the more reason to hunt down Imayva and that snake!" Ingo's fury swelled. "Our tribes' blood is on their hands!"

"That's not a reason!" Cindri yelled. "Why is this merchant even helping us? How does he know where they are?"

Zeteph cut in. "They have something I want, and no one likes loose ends. You and Ingo seem like the perfect folk to tie them for me."

That's what this is about. He wants the artifact, and I bet my life that Imayva and Srrith still have it. It doesn't matter to me anymore, I just want to go home.

Zeteph continued, "As for how I know where they are, I don't. I have Vrato following their trail now, into the Azrak Mountains. Savin Actai, if I had to guess. Tauninaga are so predictable."

He tapped a gloved finger on the desk. "What I do know is this. Vrato will have some successes, but he will also have some failures. You will finish what he cannot. As I said, I don't know where they are, but I know where they *will be*. That's where you will go...*if* you are still interested?"

"Of course," Ingo snarled, and elbowed Cindri in the ribs when he did not show the same enthusiasm. Zeteph's mask looked at Cindri with cold, knowing eyes. He seemed callously disappointed, as if Ingo had brought a liability instead of a second raptor.

Zeteph paused, holding a gloved hand around the side of his mask as if massaging away a migraine. "Excuse me." He opened a desk drawer and pulled out a round glass bottle, filled with swirling cyan fluid. He unstopped the bottle, then turned away from the raptors to tilt his mask up and drink.

Ingo seemed to think nothing of it. Cindri tried to catch a glimpse of what was under Zeteph's hood by looking in the faint reflection of the window behind him, but saw nothing. Zeteph had clearly kept that angle in mind when he turned. Then the smell hit. A sickly sweet stench like rotten fruit, then a metallic aftertaste that crept through Cindri's nose and throat. His eyes widened as he recognized that smell.

Wekavan Whisper. Made of three parts cerulean branchknot, one part poretree leaf, with a pinch of kingrot, boiled together in fermented cadaver blood. Their mother had kept a small vial of it, and had uncorked it only once to let Cindri learn the smell.

It was one of the deadliest poisons ever made. Even a full-grown mammoth would succumb to an agonizing death in minutes from just a few drops, and Zeteph was drinking a whole flask like a desert nomad reaching an oasis.

He had to run. There was something so grossly unnatural about this man, it froze Cindri in place with terror. To his side, Ingo sat seething in rage, glaring at Cindri with unknown eyes. He barely recognized his older brother. He only had until Zeteph stopped drinking to act, in this moment of brief distraction.

A grim realization set in. *If I don't run now, Zeteph is going to kill me, and Ingo is going to let him.*

Adrenaline burst through him, loosening his muscles like hot water over a frozen wheel. Cindri leapt for the door and threw it open. Ingo shouted and leapt after him, Zeteph dropped the bottle and turned, hand raised. The two guards on the other side of the door were unprepared, and Cindri spun through their fumbling attempts to grab him. As he did, he pulled a vial from his bandolier and poured a pile of red dust into his hand. When the guards turned, he closed his eyes and blew a massive cloud directly into their faces, then raced down the hallway.

The guards sputtered, tears welling in their swollen red eyes as they coughed up the sandpepper dust burning their throats. Doubled over, they blocked the door as Ingo tried to force himself though, screaming after Cindri.

Down the stairs. Right. Second door down, then through. As he ran, he pulled vials from his bandolier, mixing them together and tossing the empty ones. Thank Taru that Ingo had forced him to train like this, mixing concoctions under pressure. He never thought he'd have to use them against his own kin.

Cindri burst into the guild hall and sprinted for the door, gathering bewildered looks from the Merchatzi. Would they stop him? He was there by Zeteph's permission. Using the momentary confusion, he sprinted for the unhinged great doors. A yell from the hallway behind him spurred the guards into action, but he was already into the street.

I'm alone in a Verdant city, where folk will scream at the sight of me. Where in the depths do I go? He looked for the sewer entrance they used before. Merchatzi were closing in, chainmail rattling. With no luxury of choice, he bolted for the emptiest alleyway, the guards' fingers scraping the scales on his tail.

With complete abandon, he barreled out the other side of the alleyway, right onto a busy street filled with Port Wenstnor denizens returning home with the setting sun. Someone screamed, the crowd parted, and he took whatever opening he could. The sun was well below the buildings now, casting long shadows over the streets. More shouts reached his ears over the rushing wind.

The alleyways twisted around him as he raced past street after street, claws gripping the cobblestones, tail flicking as he slid around sharp corners. As he ran south, the buildings shrank and compacted, and the alleyways became longer and more maze-like. Even so, he could not shake the guards, who were pointed in his direction by every passerby, urging them to catch that *sand-cursed raptor.*

Armor clanked behind him. Cindri whipped around another tight corner and screeched to a halt in front of a stone wall. A dead end. He was flanked by two decrepit warehouses, their dirty, faded windows looking into the alley. Several stacks of long-forgotten crates were pushed against the walls.

There was no escape now. Cindri fumbled with his bandolier, pulled out and struck a match on the stone wall, then dropped it into the vial with everything he had mixed while running. The Merchatzi rounded the corner, trapping him. Cindri muttered quick thanks to Taru that Ingo and Zeteph were not among them.

The guards advanced, drawing their swords. One raised their hand in warning. "Just come with us, raptor. We're not supposed to kill you, but accidents happen. Don't give us a reason to cause any."

The vial grew hot in Cindri's hands, and he smashed it into the ground. Thick gray smoke exploded through the alley, choking the air blind. The guards shouted and ran forward, hoping to locate him just by running into him in the narrow alley. Scrounging on the ground, Cindri found a loose cobblestone and threw it through one of the nearby windows.

One of the guards yelled, "He's going through the warehouse!" Cindri leapt onto a stack of crates nearby and narrowly avoided collision with a guard, sensing the passing wind on his neck feathers. Feeling his way blindly upward, he clambered atop the crate pile, then fell inside the topmost box, which was missing a lid.

Down below, he heard the clink of shattered glass as some guards climbed through the window in hot pursuit of the raptor they thought was heading that way. "Go around, cut him off!" one of the guards yelled, and footsteps thundered away. Breath held tight in his chest, Cindri waited for someone to check the crates, to drag him back to Ingo and that terrible masked man. The sounds of the guards only drew more and more distant, until silence took the alley.

Cindri peeked over the lip of the crate. The alley was empty. Inside the warehouse, he heard footsteps and shouts. Afraid to move, he curled into a feathered ball at the bottom of the crate and prayed they'd never find him. As the sounds of the guards faded, so did his adrenaline, exhaustion overwhelming him. He once again found himself frozen in fear, curled up alone in a dark, unfamiliar place.

Utterly crushed by the day's events, he wondered whether sleep or the authorities would find him first. Hours passed as Port Wenstnor quieted for the night, and soon he soon heard nothing but the lap of the Devaros waters, and strange sounds drifting on the wind. Somewhere in the woods, a chorus of animals howled into the mountains, calling for their family to return.

"Branches prevent the Oaken Legion from wearing traditional helmets. Instead, the helmets are made of two pieces that cleverly lock together around the front and back of the soldier's head. In my humble opinion, it's more like two masks fitted back-to-back than a helmet, but the timbersteel smith did not appreciate that observation."
—from the journal of Oswal Briggin, cavernfolk explorer

Chapter 41

Shields

Raudius awoke to the screams of a hawk, circling above the canopy. Through drowsy eyes, he saw the lone bird harassed by a murder of crows protecting their nests, swooping at the hawk through the light blue morning sky. The Felled soldier groaned and sat up. The bark on his fingers creaked as he unclenched them from a stick—the most club-like stick he could find the night before. His back ached as if he had slept on the cobblestone streets of Port Wenstnor. The truth was nearly as bad—he had fallen asleep with his back leaned against a birch tree, clutching his makeshift club for when the raptors would set upon him in the night.

To his relief, and surprise, he had survived. Green Verdants, he had survived! What an amazing tale he'd have to tell when he returned to the Bastion of Growth. He stretched away the aches of the night. His tale was not over yet, of course. Raudius was still a Felled soldier. And once again, Imayva had bested him and escaped.

Looking at the pathetic stick in his hand, he grumbled and hurled it away, where it snapped in two against a tree trunk, the *thwack* resounding through the woods. How did he ever think it would protect against a raptor axe or spear? He was a fool for leaving behind Tash's axe. What was he thinking?

Cindri's face flashed through his mind's eye. The overwhelming sorrow painted across his maw. Raudius had never seen those emotions in a raptor before. It was never talked about in any of his Legion training. They were savages, hellbent on raiding and killing. What was that sand-cursed creature doing? Cindri had *saved* his life. He had never even poisoned him.

What a dumb thing to do.

It wasn't dumb. It was kind.

It did not matter. The raptors were behind him now. Raudius did not know how many survived, but at least Tash got what she deserved. It was time to head into town to pick up Imayva's trail. As he ran through the chaos, he saw her escape with the Ul'Varin, who assuredly had the real artifact. Not the ball of glittery ice that he tripped over himself chasing after. He would have to leave that part out of his heroic tale.

Before heading off, Raudius took stock of his meager belongings. No weapon, of course. His clothing was little more than rags now, the last vestiges of nobility scraped away in the dirt of Old Wenstnor. His old pack, along with his remaining rations, was still down there as well. He patted his pockets and felt a small lump, then remembered with a jolt what he had found in the Coalition guardroom.

A thick iron ring, with a hefty signet inlaid with an intricately unique pattern of iron bumps and curling grooves—some so minuscule, it would be impossible for a normal jeweler to make. Except with volcomancy.

Out of all the chaos of the prior day, from all the fighting and trickery and death, he had somehow walked away with a *stamp ring*. By Verdancias's great roots, he hoped it was not a forgery—it was just sitting in the guardroom after all, perhaps stolen from a common thief. He had to try it, though.

His family, the Fenmors, had a stamp ring from Citadel Ashfell—an offering of goodwill after the Wildfire Siege. They would use it on occasion when they traveled to Gloomwall or Fjordhearth. The ability to purchase anything you wanted at the expense of a Citadel was a powerful gift. Even if it was a forgery, maybe he could fake his way through if he simply looked the part.

Remembering a secret of his family's stamp ring, Raudius tilted the ring to catch the dappled forest sunlight. Hoping this ring had the same details, he found what he was looking for on the bottom of the iron band—a pinprick of light. To an untrained eye, it simply looked like the curve of the iron was catching a glare. In truth, near-invisible veins of crystal implanted in the metal formed the Citadel's symbol—another impossible detail left by the volcomancers who forged it. Holding it as close to his eye as it would focus, Raudius angled the ring slowly until he could see the tiny symbol without blinding himself. Two hands, overflowing with coin, set against a mountain backdrop. *Citadel Teirmond! Depths below, my luck has turned.*

If this ring was real, he could buy anything he desired.

A bath would have to come first, then laundry. Anyone dressed in filth like he was would be slapped in irons immediately for presenting a stamp ring. He set off toward the Devaros.

It was only a short walk down the slope and through the thicketed valley, skirting the outside of the town. Soon, Raudius was floating on his back in the frigid river waters, cleansing the grime from his body, layer by layer. The sweat of battle, followed by the filth of the underground. Then the sands of the cursed desert. He even picked a few hairs out of his bark that looked suspiciously like Borgo's fur.

Borgo is probably waiting for Tash right now. He shoved the thought away. That disgusting animal would be better off for it. Hanging his shirt to dry on a nearby rock, he sat and watched a ship rowing upriver toward town, small figures scurrying like ants across the deck, preparing to dock.

Waves lapped at the riverbank and the sun warmed his bark, catching in his leaves. He basked in the moment of peace, waiting for his clothes to dry. Imayva still had the artifact, and he was still Felled, but at least he was done with the raptors. He was done with the desert. He was free, and he clung to that thought as he breathed in the vibrant tranquility of the South Verdant.

Leaning down to wash his face, he finally recognized himself. With the grime scrubbed away, he saw the soldier underneath once again. But the bandage had washed away too, showing the red scar of Oaganshi pine embedded above his right eye. Gingerly, he touched the grafted bark. There was no numbness—it was simply part of him. Smooth, almost soft, unlike the rough oaken bark on the rest of his body. A slice of desert permanently stuck in his skull. Another reminder of Cindri's kindness.

Raudius grabbed his clothes, now dry, and took another look at his reflection. A fraction of the noble soldier he used to be, but a small step closer. It would have to do. He patted his pocket to double-check the stamp ring was safe, and set off into town.

* * *

The obelisk market was bustling with shoppers, but the atmosphere was muted compared to the day before. Every conversation Raudius passed swirled with rumors. Raptors had attacked the town? Or was it the Ventwalkers? The Ferrymen had allied with Raptoran bandits and attacked a prominent guild? The Merchatzi were out in force as well, which did not ease worries.

Raudius took care to keep a low profile, in case anyone was looking for him, particularly the purple-and-blue Merchatzi of the Tyrak-Wenstnor Trade Coalition. As he wondered what to do first with his stamp ring, his stomach growled. Food. He could not chase down a thief and restore his stripped titles on an empty stomach.

He ambled through the market, until his senses were suddenly entranced by the aroma of grilled vegetables, drifting from a nearby storefront. It was time to put on his best show. Raudius adjusted the collar of his tunic and hoped he looked like a dashing officer returning from sparring practice, rather than a slimy urchin trying a quick con.

A small line led to the counter, which faced the street. Raudius strode past everyone up to the counter, chin held high. There were plenty of quiet grumbles, and he saw a beefy Oemorg with pale gray arms the size of ship masts start to take a step out of line toward him, but think better of it at the last second. No one interfered in Legion business, no matter how mundane.

Rapping on the counter with his bark knuckles, Raudius stared daggers at a human in a flour-soaked apron until she approached. She spoke in a Reath accent. "The line starts over there."

"Not for me," Raudius snorted. "I'll have a skewer of those vegetables."

"Wait in line and I'll think about it."

"I'm hungry now." He straightened up tall and laid a hand on the counter, surreptitiously tapping the stamp ring against the wood where only she would see it. "You do take these, yes?"

She eyed him suspiciously. "I might have a few blank tablets in the back. What Citadel is that from?"

"Citadel Teirmond." Raudius was overjoyed to have the richest Citadel's coffers at his disposal. Even if it were fake, merchants would be far less likely to question the ring's legitimacy. Citadel Teirmond was always good for it.

A massive gray hand clamped on his shoulder, and Raudius winced. The Oemorg behind him grunted, "Is this tree bothering you, Wygrid?"

"Get off me, you oaf!" Raudius slapped the hand away. "How dare you lay a hand on a Fenmor! Do it again and you'll lose both."

The Oemorg cracked his knuckles. "He's certainly bothering me."

Wygrid held up her hands. "Enough, Rorgros. Don't want trouble today." She looked at Raudius. "An order of spiced vegetables, then."

"Absolutely. I don't want any trouble either." Raudius leaned over the counter, closer to Wygrid. "How about we say you're feeding my whole quindecis. Twenty-five orders, out of Citadel Teirmond's vault?" Raudius gave an exaggerated wink. "And add whatever Rorgros here wants as well. How does that sound, Rorgros?"

Rorgros grumbled, "The usual, please."

Wygrid glared at Raudius, then at his stamp ring, then nodded and left for the back of the shop.

Raudius and Rorgros stood awkwardly at the counter, receiving angry glares from the customers held up in line. In a haughty voice, Raudius asked, "Quite the grip you have there, Rorgros. How'd you get so strong?"

"Building your roads," the Oemorg muttered.

"Ah." Raudius decided it was best to not speak to him anymore.

Wygrid returned with a soft clay tablet, a few inches by a few inches large. The details of the transaction were etched around the perimeter— the cost of each item, quantity bought, date purchased. On the bottom was a physical description of Raudius. A common inclusion if the shop-keeper believed the ring was stolen or fraudulent. Then she could at least claim a small reimbursement of the purchase by providing his information to the Citadel. If it did work, though, she'd receive twenty-five times the coin for one meal. A worthwhile risk.

He pressed the stamp ring's signet into the soft clay, leaving a complex impression of lines and dots. Hopefully Citadel Teirmond would not fly past this town for a while. Wygrid carefully placed the tablet into the oven to bake, and passed Raudius and Rorgros their dishes.

"Many thanks," Raudius said, and marched out of the store, disappearing into the flow of the crowd. The more distance he put between him and Rorgros, the better. He bit into the spiced vegetables and almost cried at the first bite of real food he'd had in weeks. After the first bite, there was no holding back, and he completely ravished the vegetables as he walked. He probably looked like a madman, scarfing down his food so fast, but at that point he didn't care. *Depths below*, he should have asked for more, and maybe some rations for the next leg of his journey. He did pay for twenty-five servings, after all. *Well, Citadel Teirmond paid. My thanks to the Flying Lords.*

Now what to use the stamp ring for? To the blacksmith for a sword? A tailor for some traveling clothes? Perhaps a general store for some rations and a pack? He had so much to prepare for and unlimited money to do so, as long as he played his lies correctly and no one checked if the ring was stolen. Some merchants certainly had the means to do so.

Hunger sated, Raudius decided that he should try to get a lead on Imayva first, then prepare for the chase after. It would be best for his appearances if he knew everything he had to buy beforehand.

Raudius started toward the docks, swagger in his step. Asking around there was a good place to start. If Imayva left by river, there would be countless witnesses, and perhaps even someone who would know a general direction. Traveling with Ventwalkers and a tauninaga, people *must* have seen her. Then he could use the stamp ring to charter a boat. A reputable ship, devoid of nasty cavernfolk who would sell him to the raptors.

While the marketplace had been bustling, the dockyard was pure tumult. Folks of all shapes and sizes scurried to load and unload the docked ships, especially the recent arrival that Raudius had seen while relaxing on the riverside. Rows of merchant stalls sold everything—seaworthy rations, repairs, fishing supplies, everything a boat would need—and each vendor had to shout louder than their competitors to attract business, constantly adjusting their prices based on whatever their neighbors were screaming.

Raudius strode along the street that ran parallel to the water, with the merchants set up along one side and the dockworkers on the other. He decided to approach a stall hosting a Torn merchant selling rope. The little insectoid was unable to shout louder than the other merchants in its neighboring stalls, so it held a handful of signs with different prices on it, raising whichever one had its latest price.

As Raudius approached, the Torn dropped the sign it was holding and rubbed its chitinous hands together with excitement. In the bug's orange-brown fractal eyes, Raudius saw his own disjointed reflection and the street behind him, multiplied into a thousand images. Already feeling bad about taking up this Torn's time, Raudius held up his hands in apology and asked, "Sorry, I'm not here for rope, but I'll pay for information. Have you seen any Ventwalkers or a tauninaga?"

The Torn's antenna drooped in annoyance, then his eyes went wide. In the bug's fractal eyes, Raudius saw the reflection of figures approaching behind him. The Torn curled into a chitinous ball and rolled behind his stall as a gruff voice called out, "Raudius fucking Fenmor?"

Grenner. Raudius spun to find himself face-to-face with an old nightmare. Oakfire flared in his eyes.

"What in the ice and sands happened to your head? You look like elk dung." Grenner smirked.

Flanked by twelve other Oaken Legion soldiers, his old quindecis obstructed the entire street, bristling with timbersteel armor. The din of the street faded as nearby merchants huddled down, and the stream of passersby scurried around them like waves around an island. No one dared interfere. This was Legion business.

In the excitement of his freedom, Raudius had forgotten his old quindecis was due to arrive, and here they were. After being ambushed on their journey north, they were forced back to Devar, and then surprisingly ventured south.

There's only thirteen. Half of them died in that attack? Raudius tried to look through to see who was missing, but Grenner crowded his vision. "What on the Verdant earth are you doing here? You get on a boat going the wrong direction? The Bastion of Growth is in the *North* Verdant, in case you're lost."

Even though he hated the vile tree with all his oaken heart, Raudius still found himself standing at attention. "I thought your orders were to travel north as well," He said, meeting Grenner's gaze.

"Don't you dare speak about Legion business, Felled!" Grenner yelled. "Things have changed since *you* let a gutter rat human steal from right under our branches!"

Raudius stood firm. "I'm working to right my wrongs and restore my place in the Legion. I have the right to try."

"That's why you're here?" Grenner laughed. "You're trying to recover the artifact in hopes that we restore your position!" The soldiers laughed with him, then Grenner's face grew deadly serious. "That means you're interfering with Legion business."

"You don't need to do this, Grenner," Raudius said. "We can work together. I'm on the trail. Unfell me now, or wait until we recover it. I'll pass all the credit to you, but I swear I can help. I've been ahead of you this whole time."

"No chance. You already botched everything. This is what we get for including greenling noble boys on important expeditions." Grenner turned and marched back to the quindecis. "You'll have better luck crawling back to the Bastion and begging the Praetor to Unfell you than convincing me. Go home."

Raudius looked at his old comrades, staring at him with a mixture of pity and mockery. He caught a brief glimpse of Yuetrix in the back, looking on with sad eyes. The old tree gave a small nod in greeting, then averted his eyes. *Thank the green earth he survived. But what about Claud? Traticus? Batia?* He saw no other friends of his in the ranks.

Something was eerily wrong about the soldiers standing before him. Their armor...they all wore the symbol of Hope's Gauntlet.

A pit of raging Oakfire ignited like hot coals in his chest. Raudius shouted after Grenner, "How did you know to travel south? What brought you to Port Wenstnor?"

"That's Legion business, Felled," Grenner called back, still marching away. Imayva's strange words rang in Raudius's mind.

Your master is waiting. He'll be furious if he doesn't get the Stone.

You don't even know who you're working for.

Zeteph.

He thought she was insane, but she knew more than he did. *Of course she did, she's sand-cursed Imayva. She shouted the answers right at me and I refused to listen.*

Oakfire coursed up his veins, raging from deep within his heart, and he shouted at Grenner, "Swords! I challenge you to swords!"

Grenner halted in his tracks. "Are you mad, Felled?"

Raudius spat back, "Are you a coward as well as a traitor? Or just the latter?"

Grenner stomped back toward him, hand on the hilt of his timber-steel sword. "Speak plainly. They will be your last words before I cut out your tongue."

"Quite miraculous that only Hope's Gauntlet soldiers survived that ambush up north," Raudius said. "Must have been easy for Zeteph's men to identify which soldiers to kill. Just aim for the ones without this symbol." He tapped his shoulder, where the Hope's Gauntlet symbol would be if he was wearing timbersteel. "And no one asks any questions when you return, because you didn't kill those soldiers. Bandits did."

His accusation was a complete shot in the dark, but the shock on Grenner's face all but confirmed it. His old leader's eyes burned with recognition at the name Zeteph. Several of the soldiers behind him, Yuetrix included, seemed confused. Others—Grenner's closest—looked grim. *They knew as well.*

"Watch yourself, Raudius," Grenner warned.

"I assume you traveled south because Zeteph told you to? Do you not serve the Legion anymore? You serve some masked merchant?"

"Everything we do is *for* the Legion!" Grenner shouted.

"Is that why you *murdered* good soldiers under your command?"

Grenner unsheathed his sword. Raudius kept shouting, "Do you have no *fucking* honor? Cut me down here, at least you'll have the decency to swing the sword yourself this time!"

Grenner paused. Calling a soldier's honor into question was as good as driving a knife into their eye. That was one thing Raudius's noble upbringing taught him well. Raudius's Oakfire swelled to a Verdant inferno, his eyes and leaves glowing green, then he spat, "Like I said. Swords, you fucking traitor."

"You don't even have a sword."

"He has mine!" Yuetrix yelled. The quindecis parted as the old tree rushed to Raudius's side. He drew his sword and unbuckled his armor, fitting each piece onto Raudius one by one. Grenner stood by and watched, looking like he was about to snap with rage.

Yuetrix's armor did not fit perfectly, but it was more than adequate. Yuetrix quickly tore off strips of a shirt from his pack to use as extra padding in spots where the armor scraped incorrectly. Finally, he clamped the two-part timbersteel helmet around Raudius's face. *Green Verdants*, it felt good to wear timbersteel again.

Yuetrix's sword felt light and deadly. A standard-issue Legion sword of well-forged timbersteel. Not the heavy iron trash that the Merchatzi carried. Raudius leveled it at Grenner.

Grenner raised his own sword and snarled, "What are your terms?"

"If I lose, I live out the rest of my days as a beggar in Reath and you never hear from me again. If I win, I am no longer Felled, and you turn in your armor to be escorted as prisoner to the nearest Bastion, where you will stand trial before the Praetor and the Elders for conspiring against the Legion!" The Oakfire burned the inside of his chest as he yelled.

"Deal," Grenner said. "But I have an additional term." And he unlatched his shield from his back, locking it in place on his left arm.

The gravity of the situation struck Raudius like a hammer. "I said swords, Grenner. Drop the shield."

"No, Raudius, pick yours up. This is how it will be. You want to be brave? You want to stand against Hope's Gauntlet? Then pick up your fucking shield and fight me!" Grenner's eyes glowed with Oakfire, and Yuetrix held out his shield with worried eyes.

Raudius slid his timbersteel arm against the shield, locking it in place and hoisting it from Yuetrix. Was he truly ready to die for this cause? His stomach felt numb with worry. *My friends are dead, and they didn't get a choice. I will march the same path.* He dropped into dueling stance. "Shields, then."

"Shields," Grenner replied, and raised his.

The rest of the Oaken Legion soldiers fanned into a circle around them, forming an arena of timbersteel in the middle of the street. Grenner and Raudius circled each other, shields raised and swords ready. *I can't trust him.* Raudius looked around at the watching soldiers. *I can't trust any of them. Even if I win and Grenner falls, then what? They won't give up their quest so easily.*

He had no more time to doubt, as Grenner launched forward with a war cry. Raudius matched his ferocity, and their shields crashed together, sounding the funeral bell for one of them. Immediately reeling backward from the impact, Raudius just managed to get his sword up to block a vicious downward swing from Grenner. He turned the parry into another blow, but Grenner's shield deflected it away.

Back and forth they went, locking shields and swords together, each trying to overpower the other. Sword duels were about true skill. They required strategy to outsmart the opponent's blade and scratch their bark. Shield duels were about strength and brute force—smash your opponent to pieces as violently as you can, before they can do the same to you. This was why swords was to the yield, and shields was to the death.

The onlooking soldiers leered at Raudius, throwing insults toward him and praise toward Grenner. Raudius stepped backward with impeccable footwork, avoiding Grenner's strikes while keeping his distance from the ring of Oaken Legion soldiers. Soldiers with real honor would never interfere with a duel. Raudius was hesitant to believe they had any.

He dropped his center of gravity as Grenner charged again. The shields clashed, the jagged timbersteel locking together. Timbersteel was meant to do that—it kept a shield on a soldier's arm, and kept a shield wall strong against a horde of raptors. In a fight of Oaken Legion versus Oaken Legion, though, it turned lifesaving design into a deadly contest of strength.

Raudius felt his legs slide backward, his arm aching, and he barely twisted his head as Grenner stabbed, aiming for his eyes. It sounded like his face was being dragged across shattered bricks as the sword scraped against the side of his helmet. A stab like that, however, meant Grenner's balance was compromised.

Shields still locked together, Raudius wrenched his to the side, spinning Grenner so his back was exposed. He stabbed at the exposed joint in Grenner's armor underneath the arm, blade scraping as it forced its way through the timbersteel. Grenner yelled as the sharp point found purchase in his bark, and he dropped his own sword to grab Raudius by the branches. Shields still locked, Grenner slammed Raudius's skull onto the top of his shield like cracking an egg, then headbutted Raudius so hard his own helmet cracked.

Raudius tumbled backward onto the street, shield luckily unlocking from Grenner's. Unluckily, Yuetrix's sword clattered away, only the tip covered in green blood. Not even close to a mortal wound, and now he was disarmed. Through his spinning double vision, he saw Grenner stalking toward him, cracked helmet awkwardly dangling.

"Everything I do is for the good of the Legion!" Grenner screamed, ripping his broken helmet off. "Dying will be the only useful thing you've done!" He lunged at Raudius.

Grenner's sword hit cobblestone as Raudius rolled backward, right to the edge of the fighting circle. The ring of soldiers jeered and kicked at him, forcing him to his feet to avoid the blows, only pushing him closer to Grenner. *They're all traitors. Every single one. They killed their fellow soldiers, for what? Why?* Amidst the crowd, the lone voice of Yuetrix yelled out, "For the Legion, Raudius! For the Legion!"

For the Legion. Not for these vile pretenders. The Oakfire burned away the fog in his head. Roaring like a wildfire, Raudius slammed the edge of his shield onto Grenner's incoming stab, using the jagged timbersteel to catch the blade and smash it into the street, pinning the blade to the cobblestones. Grenner tried to bash him with his shield, but Raudius caught the shield on his free sword arm and wrenched Grenner off-balance. As the tree stumbled, Raudius grabbed Grenner's branches and slammed Grenner's skull into his armored knee with a resounding crack that echoed through the docks like a bullwhip.

Green blood splattered the cobblestones. Raudius crunched Grenner's face into his knee again and again and again until Grenner's branches snapped off in his hands. His leaves glowing with Oakfire, every seam in his bark ignited with green light, Raudius wrenched his shield from the ground and held it over Grenner's head like a guillotine. Through fiery eyes, he looked down at his old commander and screamed, "Yield. Or. Die!"

His face mangled beyond recognition, Grenner spat a wad of blood into Raudius's eyes. Raudius slammed the shield down, but suddenly his balance gave out as someone kicked him in the back of the knee. The shield glanced harmlessly off the cobblestones as Raudius lost balance and fell, all hope vanishing. Grenner rolled on top of him, grabbed his sword, and raised it above Raudius's heart. *This is where my story ends. Felled at the hand of the honorless traitors.*

Grenner's weight evaporated off his chest as Yuetrix tackled him away. They tumbled and landed near Yuetrix's sword, which the old tree grabbed and threw to Raudius. Yuetrix was completely defenseless —Raudius had his armor and weapon.

"Yuetrix!" Raudius picked up the sword and charged. Yuetrix grappled with Grenner as best he could, the sharp timbersteel gouging into his bark, and he screamed back, "Run, Raudius! You have to live!" Raudius stopped frozen in his tracks, and Yuetrix screamed again, "They have no honor! They made their choice, you have to live to make them regret it!"

Shouting erupted from the ring of soldiers, followed by the scraping of timbersteel swords unsheathing. *Run where?* He was completely surrounded by Hope's Gauntlet.

Suddenly, someone shouted, "Traitors, all of you!" From the back ranks, the massive tree named Adarias smashed his shield into a fellow Hope's Gauntlet soldier, knocking him away and opening a gap in the timbersteel wall. His comrades shouted in surprise and turned on him, followed by more shouts as another brawl broke out.

Oakfire burning away his hesitation, Raudius sprinted through the gap as Adarias was run through by a sword, green blood spilling down his armor. With his dying breath, he cried, "Redeem us, please."

As the Legion fell to infighting, the dockyard's populace scattered, only adding to the chaos. Hope's Gauntlet soldiers charged after him, and Raudius looked over his shoulder just once. Behind him, Yuetrix was roughly pulled away from Grenner. The old tree was bloodied, but looked strangely at peace. He gave Raudius one last weak salute before Grenner ran him through.

His Oakfire died with Yuetrix, his will crushed, and Raudius almost faltered. But now was not the time to grieve. He charged south through the town, denizens and Merchatzi alike scurrying out of his way to avoid interfering in Legion business. Hope's Gauntlet soldiers thundered after him.

Twisting and turning through alleyways and across streets, Raudius tried in vain to lose the soldiers. He just had to lose them in the streets and get out of town. But then where? Back to Old Wenstnor?

Something grabbed him, pulling him into a nearby building. The door slammed behind him, shutting out the daylight, except for a few meager rays casting trails of dust through the air. Raudius spun wildly, pointing his sword at his assailant, and shouted, "Unhand me!"

Cindri whispered back, "Shut up and follow me!"

Chapter 42

Oil and Water

A hailstone the size of Mayve's fist flew over her head, exploding into powdery snow against a nearby tree. Ducking underneath, she trapped the Du'ul, feeling a burst of energy. Her senses heightened, the next hailstone Eiklo threw was vividly outlined in the twilight of the forest, the gleaming ice sparkling in the light of the campfire. She caught the glint of another hailstone forming in Eiklo's other hand, already seeing where his third attack would fly.

Spinning underneath the first hailstone, she sensed the Du'ul all around her. *My skin is iron. Strong and unbreakable. Even the rage of the Vents cannot crack me.* She transferred the momentum of her spin into a sideways flip, tumbling over the second hailstone. Midair, she trapped the Du'ul.

Landing like a quiet breeze, she felt awake. *Alive.* Every bone in her body sang with the Vent's energy. Eiklo must have seen the fire in her eyes, shouting, "Yes! Now manifest! Channel everything out!"

She channeled every ounce of Du'ul in her body through her hands, feeling the energy rush away into thin air. Nothing happened.

Eiklo's excitement died away. He asked a question he knew the answer to already. "Still nothing?"

Mayve sighed and sat down next to the campfire, exhausted. She had been practicing her volcomancy for the past hour. She could trap the Du'ul on command now, even under pressure, which was difficult enough in the Verdant. Then she'd manifest while flailing her arms, twisting her fingers, scrunching her face—anything and everything to try and get *something* to happen. No matter what she did, nothing.

Vrato and Zeteph are coming for the Stone, and I am ill-equipped to fight back. That blast of shadow Zeteph manifested was such powerful volcomancy, and he's in the middle of the green-cursed Verdant. I can't even make a spark with all the Du'ul I'm trapping. Mayve needed to get the Stone to the Great Seer, not just to satisfy her own curiosity now, but to also keep it out of Zeteph's grasp, whatever his plan was. If it involved the Vents, no good could come of it. *This is how I will honor my mother's memory. By making sure Zeteph never gets what he wants. That's what she really would have wanted, not for me to repay her death with more death.*

She saw Eiklo growing frustrated also. His advice only got more and more cryptic as each idea failed. Srrith did little to bolster her confidence, coiled nearby, looking very amused.

They had tried everything Eiklo could think of. Any hope she had of throwing fire or hurling lightning was gone. Those were *easy* manifestations to discover, according to Eiklo. The skeleton paced around their small forest clearing, tapping his forehead.

"I'm dumbfounded," Eiklo muttered, defeated. "I'm no scholar or instructor, but how can *nothing* happen? I have two conclusions. First, your Natural Manifestation is so complicated, it requires you to channel the Du'ul in such a specific way, you may never discover it without months of extensive testing. The bright side of that is, it might be very powerful if you can master it."

Mayve grabbed a handful of berries and a slab of smoked fish from the saddlebag, the food pleasantly warm from sitting next to Screech's feather container. Between bites, she grunted, "What's the other option?"

"You're a special anomaly with no Natural Manifestation. Well, I should say, you *do* have a Natural Manifestation. You manifest the

Du'ul into nothing. It's very unique; the Northern Ice raptors would love to study you."

Srrith hissed, "This is good. I do not need more to worry about." She had a piece of fish hooked on her sickle, held over the campfire. The tauninaga looked relaxed, but Mayve saw her eyes often glancing away into the woods.

Eiklo took a seat next to the fire and asked, "Srrith, your sfa-zrueen is quite complicated, yes? Very similar to more complex manifestations. How do you use it? More precisely, what do you *think* about as you use it?"

The tauninaga let out a long hiss, and propped her sickle up against a log, waiting for her fish to cool. "It is not the same. As I understand, volcomancy comes from the Vent's power that pervades all the land. The *Du'ul*, the *Ventix Stratus*, whatever you choose to call it. It is unnatural power, created from the unnatural cataclysm. Sfa-zrueen comes from the natural world around us. They are opposites. Just like how the Du'ul is strongest at the Vents, sfa-zrueen is strongest in the Verdant."

"Surely there are some commonalities?" Eiklo pondered out loud. "Both are powers that can shape reality."

"Sfa-zrueen is ancient, unlike your Du'ul. It was here before the Vents, and if they ever fall dormant, it will be here after."

Curious as always, Mayve chimed in, "If it comes from the natural world, like the Verdants, does that mean you gather it from the environment around you, just like how we 'trap' the Du'ul?"

Srrith let out an annoyed hiss, as if she did not want to find similarities between the two forces. "I suppose so...the processes are nothing alike, though."

"Right. You have to be asleep," Eiklo said.

"No, we have to be *dreaming*," Srrith hissed. "An important distinction. Tauninagan dreams are powerful. They are how we gather sfa-zrueen. Once it is gathered and woven from dream into reality, we can use it how we wish. Only the Fae were able to use sfa-zrueen without dreaming. Since they're gone, it is only the tauninaga's gift now."

"Where'd they go?" Mayve asked.

Eiklo shrugged and Srrith shook her head, hissing, "They are gone, simple as that. All that is left is ruins and tombs, reclaimed by nature."

"Maybe this is a strange question, but what do the tauninaga and the Fae have in common that allows them to wield *sfa-zrueen*?"

Eiklo jumped in, excited to share what history he knew. "The Fae and the tauninaga were close allies during the Paroxysm. They helped each other survive, and in return, the Fae shared their power."

He looked at Srrith and she nodded. "The Fae gave each of the six tauninagan races a portion of their power. Cave tauninaga were given the shadows. We were given fear." The tauninaga flashed her fangs as she hissed the last word, and a chill ran up Mayve's spine. As her friend, it was easy to forget that Srrith was akin to an apex predator. *That's how she likes it.*

"What were the other tauninagas given? You've mentioned the mountain tauninaga can heal," Mayve wondered.

"Eiklo enjoys lists, perhaps he can answer," Srrith hissed, wanting to eat her food without speaking.

Eiklo leapt at the chance. "Cave tauninaga were given fear and shadows. Swamp tauninaga were given illusions, hence the Dreaming Blades. Mountain tauninaga do indeed have the healing sfa-zrueen, oasis tauninaga were given sanctuary, forest tauninaga got divination, and the jungle tauninaga can speak with the nature around them."

Gulping down her fish, Srrith hissed, "What about the seventh sfa-zrueen?"

"Excuse me?" Eiklo sounded offended. "There are only six tauninagan species; there is no seventh."

"There are six tauninaga, but seven sfa-zrueen. The Fae chose not to teach it."

"How intriguing. What does it do?"

"No idea, no one knows. It is as lost as the Fae. You got the rest of them correct, though, well done. Good thing too—you will meet mountain and jungle tauninaga soon. Savin Actai is their city."

Mayve noted how Srrith hissed about the other tauninaga. *She speaks like it's not her home as well.* She chewed her fish in silence, her curiosity about sfa-zrueen sated, but her curiosity about her tauninaga friend growing.

They all sat and watched the fire crackle away, sparks flying up through the smoke into the forest canopy. Then Srrith uncoiled and hissed, "Everyone get up."

Mayve and Eiklo scrambled to their feet, reaching for their weapons. Mayve whispered, "What do you hear?"

"Nothing. You had fun hurling ice and punching air, now it is time for real training. Pick up your blades."

Chapter 43

A Strange Pair

S taying low and out of sight from the windows, Cindri slunk on all fours through the abandoned warehouse, tail skimming the dusty floor. Behind him, Raudius crawled along through the maze of crates, following close behind. Outfitted in timbersteel, he looked like a proper Oaken Legion soldier—much to Cindri's discomfort. It seemed much had happened while he was hiding.

They crept up a cobwebbed stairway, avoiding the windows. Cindri made it to the landing, then froze as boots thundered by outside. His head snapped to Raudius, who was frozen wide-eyed at the bottom of the stairs.

The thunder of the soldiers faded down a street, followed by muffled shouts. Cindri hissed, *"Hurry!"*

The pair ran to the second floor, down a hallway that spanned the length of the building, and into a storage room stuffed with even more crates. In the center, however, was a pull-down attic ladder leading through a trapdoor in the ceiling. Cindri scampered up and the tree followed closely behind.

The attic was coated in dust—save for a wandering trail of raptor footprints—and exposed to the elements by a gaping hole in the slanted roof. Just before dawn, Cindri had decided to find a better hiding spot and risked sneaking through the warehouse. The attic was slightly safer than the lidless crate he'd slept in, and it looked like the Merchatzi had completely overlooked it in their search. The low, slanted ceiling was cozy for Cindri, but Raudius could only stand in the very center of the room. Even then, his leaves brushed against the ceiling.

Cindri pulled the attic ladder up behind them and wedged a rotten plank through the bars of the ladder, piling pieces of fallen roof on either end to create a makeshift lock.

"We should be safe here." He turned to see Raudius looking out the hole in the roof. It had a perfect view of the docks, where the Oaken Legion had cordoned off the area to take care of their fallen. *Rumors of this will spread like sand on the wind,* Cindri thought. *Infighting amongst the Legion...it's unheard of.* Raudius sank to the floor with a clank, looking utterly crushed.

Cindri slunk over and took a seat across from Raudius on a rafter beam. The tree sighed and grunted, "You saw everything from up here."

He nodded. "I don't understand what I saw, but I did see it."

The tree stared at the slate gray timbersteel figures barking distant orders. "Why did you help me?"

"You looked like you needed help."

"Must be a busy raptor if that's your only criteria," Raudius murmured.

Cindri scratched awkwardly at the wooden floor with his claws. "We're both cut off from the rest of our people. It seemed right, I don't know."

Raudius looked at him with morbid curiosity, his green eyes dull. "I'm...so sorry, Cindri." There was real empathy in his voice. "If I may ask, who survived?"

"Ingo. And Presh, of course. As far as I know."

He saw Raudius tense up at the mention of Ingo's name, and he quickly added, "But Ingo isn't here. I'm hiding from him myself, actually."

Raudius didn't say anything, stewing in this new information and his own thoughts. Cindri was content to sit and watch the town, with the Devaros flowing gently past. Far, far downriver, his tribe wandered the sands, waiting for their return. He wondered if Raudius had anyone waiting for him back home.

Shifting uncomfortably, Raudius opened his mouth like he was going to say something, paused to mull on his feelings, then spoke. "I could not see it at the time, but Lairro was a good chief. I have respect for him, in hindsight. I'm sorry to hear of his passing."

Cindri was stunned by the tree's reverence. Raudius continued, "I'd be proud to serve under him if he were an Oaken Legion soldier. Good leaders can be hard to come by." His voice trailed off.

"He would have hated to hear you say that."

Raudius cracked a sad smile and said, "Such is the path we march."

They fell into silence again, Cindri watching the river and Raudius staring at the passing clouds. He unclasped his helmet and held the front half, staring at the empty timbersteel. With the armor removed, Cindri saw the bright red slice of Oaganshi pine sitting in his bark, perfectly healed.

"They treated you poorly."

"Who? The Legion?"

"No, my tribe."

Raudius sighed and shrugged. "I expected nothing less. Our people are not allies."

"The line has to be drawn somewhere," Cindri said.

"Let me know when someone draws it."

Cindri fell into sullen silence, but Raudius chimed in again, "Not everyone was cruel. Lairro even stood up for me. And you kept me in good health."

"I still do." Cindri smirked.

On the streets below, the sound of scraping timbersteel and the thunder of boots passed by. Raudius closed his eyes and held perfectly still until the sounds faded, hand on the hilt of his sword. When he opened his eyes, he spoke with sudden defiance in his voice. "I am not apologizing for Tash."

Cindri had hoped they wouldn't talk about her. He simply muttered, "Okay. I don't think I expected you to."

"But I will apologize for how I treated you down there, when I thought I needed the antidote. You saved my life yet again, going against your own tribe, and I am forever in your debt." He spoke to Cindri with as much respect as if he were addressing a commanding officer.

"It was not anything special," Cindri deflected. "It was just the right thing to do."

"Nevertheless, you've proved to me that you're a raptor of honor and integrity." Raudius climbed to his feet and stood as high as he could with the low ceiling. "For that, you have my trust." He snapped to attention and gave Cindri a proper salute.

Confused and abashed, Cindri stood up and returned a haphazard salute. It felt somewhat ridiculous, but Raudius seemed to really appreciate it, and sat back down gruffly, looking sullen but content that he got that off his chest.

Cindri sat as well and said, "What's your plan now?"

"It's time to figure that out. I suppose I'll wait here until the Legion clears away, then I need to resume my search for that girl who has the artifact." Raudius huffed. "I was trying to find her trail by the docks when I was waylaid."

"Ah, Imayva? Ingo told me about her. She's heading into the Azraks to Savin Actai."

Raudius could have cracked the floorboards with how hard his jaw dropped. "How in the ice-rotten, sand-cursed earth do you know that?"

Cindri pictured Zeteph's dark mask and a chill shot up his spine. "I found out when Ingo took me to meet Zeteph, who wanted us to hunt them down."

"I keep hearing that name. I assume it's the masked man?"

"That's the one."

"I only saw him briefly during the fight," Raudius said. "He held an audience with raptors? I thought he was allied with Hope's Gauntlet."

Cindri shivered, internally recounting his encounter with the insidious masked creature. "I'm sure he allies with whoever will help him accomplish his goals. He's a merchant, after all."

"What did he want with you and Ingo?" Raudius asked.

"He wanted us to chase down Imayva, but he spoke so vaguely about it, I'm not sure," Cindri recalled. "He spoke like he was sending us to where they would be, instead of where they were going." The raptor ran back over his words in his head. "That doesn't make any sense, but it's the best I got."

"Strange. Ingo was fine with this? He is quite overprotective of you. And this Zeteph, was he not partly responsible for the death of your tribesmen?"

Cindri nodded sadly. "My brother is not himself right now." He found himself recounting the entire experience to Raudius—Ingo's strange behavior, Zeteph drinking lethal poison like a mug of refreshing ale, and his escape from the guards. As he remembered the events of yesterday, Cindri grew more and more grim, the reality of his situation burying him like a tent in a sandstorm. At the end, Raudius wore the most disturbed look.

"That monster is who Hope's Gauntlet has allied themselves with?" Raudius growled. "Scum attracts more scum. What do you plan to do?"

"*Taru's bow*, I have no idea." Cindri said. "I wish I could help Ingo, but seeking him out sounds like a death sentence if Zeteph is involved. My best bet is to escape town and hope that Presh is still waiting in the woods."

"You still want to help your brother?" Raudius asked. "Then come with me."

"To follow Imayva?"

"Why not? Zeteph is sending Ingo to where Imayva *will be*, apparently. If his knowledge is to be trusted, then if we follow Imayva, we'll eventually run across your brother."

"And then what?" Cindri asked.

"At least you'll have a chance to talk to him without Zeteph whispering over his shoulder."

Cindri ran his claws through his feathers. *If I leave with the soldier, there's no going home. I have no money, no food, no supplies. Scraping together a way home is going to be near impossible. I'll be a raptor stranded in the South Verdant. A fugitive, hiding in the mountains until the Legion comes for me.*

But if I leave for home, I abandon my brother to the same fate. He took a deep breath and looked at the Oaken Legion soldier standing in front of him. *What does Raudius want from all this?*

The clank of armor rang from the street as a group of soldiers marched past. *Merchatzi.* Cindri could tell by the metallic shuffling of their chainmail rather than the wooden scrape of timbersteel. The pair sat in silence until the thuds disappeared, a calming breeze from the river wafting through the room.

"What happened at the docks?" Cindri asked. "All I know is that you were exiled, if that's even true. If we're traveling together, I want to know why you're doing what you do."

Raudius nodded. "I was the one guarding the artifact when Imayva and your brothers stole it. For that, I was Felled. Exiled from the military and told to return home. The greatest dishonor an Oaken Legion soldier can suffer." He looked at Cindri with sad eyes. "By traveling south, I hoped to restore my status by recovering the artifact before my old quindecis. That's when I was handed over to your tribe by those miserable cavernfolk."

"Wuilge and Oraine are pests," Cindri said. "I'm surprised they've survived as long as they have."

"*Pests* is an apt description," Raudius agreed. "Anyhow, you know all about the deal I made with Ingo and Lairro to survive the capture and continue my journey south. I lied through my teeth the whole time. Not once did I know where the tauninaga was. This is my first time in the South Verdant."

"You did what you had to do to survive," Cindri agreed, and Raudius nodded solemnly.

"My fellow soldiers were supposed to return home to the Bastion of Growth, to the north. When you passed along the news that they were ambushed, then suddenly heading south, I was beyond confused."

The tree grimaced. "In the fight at the Coalition guild hall, Imayva yelled at me to go follow my master, Zeteph, which I did not understand at the time. But seeing my soldiers after, it became clear. The ambush was a ploy to remove all the soldiers not aligned with Zeteph, then travel here."

"So in a way, it was lucky you were Felled," Cindri pointed out.

"Perhaps," Raudius said. "It may be egotistical of me to say, but..."

"From the Oaken Legion? Never," Cindri scoffed.

Raudius glared at him. "I believe I was Felled before the ambush because of my social standing back home, and the undue attention it would attract if I was killed. Grenner was never pleased that I was added to the expedition."

Cindri pondered out loud, "Makes me think that the plan was for Grenner to bring the artifact to Zeteph all along."

"Precisely."

"Who is Hope's Gauntlet? Surely the Oaken Legion has no tolerance for traitors," Cindri asked.

"We don't, because they're not. Until now. Hope's Gauntlet used to be more of an ideal than an actual union of soldiers, but it's changed as the decades passed. They've grown in prominence following the Ashen Century." Raudius said. "While most of the Oaken Legion is content to sit in our Bastions and defend the Verdant, soldiers who pledge themselves to Hope's Gauntlet believe more in expansionism—increasing our influence and defending our borders by growing them."

"You already hold the best land in Ralvera. There's nothing left for you to capture other than desert and ice," Cindri said, incredulous.

"Usually, a mix of ideals is welcome in the army. A defensive army can grow complacent, while a conquering army will overstep its reach and fall to ruin. Besides that, no Hope's Gauntlet soldier has ever done anything even close to as treacherous in all the Legion's history. It's perplexing, and troubling."

All of Raudius's words gave Cindri the same feeling as poking a sleeping bear. He knew all the tales of the Legion forces, marching into the sands, slaughtering every tribe in their path. *If this Hope's Gauntlet grows in power, if the Legion marches again...will they ever stop?*

He shook the thought from his mind. "So, you're going to get the artifact from Imayva and give it back to Hope's Gauntlet?"

Raudius looked taken aback. "No, of course not. That was the plan, but now, I'll..." He trailed off, reassessing his plans. "...I'll take it back to the Bastion of Growth on my own."

"Will it be safe from Zeteph and Hope's Gauntlet there?"

Raudius again fell deep into thought, looking troubled. "I don't know."

"What if they control your Bastion—"

"Cindri, please." Raudius held up a hand to stop the raptor's incessant questions. He scratched at some dried blood on the helmet, lost in his own mind. Cindri guessed what he was thinking about. Every Hope's Gauntlet soldier that Raudius had ever met, now a potential traitor. Leading armies, sitting in positions of power, consorting with dark merchants...

They sat in silence again, with only the chatter of the street below and the warm river breeze as company. Finally, Raudius said, "I don't know what I'll do."

Cindri felt a pang of empathy for the tree. *He can't return home without that artifact, and I can't return home without Ingo.* He mustered as much enthusiasm as he could. "Why worry about what you'll do with the artifact when you don't even have it yet? Let's get the sand-cursed thing and find my brother, then decide."

The tree mulled it over further, then nodded. He still looked worried, but content to have a direction. "Alright, that's what we'll do, then," Raudius said, removing his gauntlet and extending a hand.

Cindri nodded back and shook on it, Raudius's oaken bark coarse against his scales. Raudius stood and looked out the window, studying the town. "We'll wait until closer to sunset, when the town has died down, then we'll find transport. The merchants will have some idea where Savin Actai is."

"Sure," Cindri said, "I'll lie low while you buy what we need."

Raudius thought for a moment, then said, "Actually, I could use your help. You're not going to like it, though."

* * *

Raudius pushed Cindri through the shadowed streets of Port Wenstnor, heading for the eastern edge of town. The raptor's hands were bound by rope scavenged from the warehouse, or at least they appeared to be. Cindri held the ropes in place, able to free himself at a moment's notice. The sun had long set below the mountains on the other side of the Devaros. The sky above was still light blue, but fading quickly into oranges and pinks. It might as well have been night already underneath the shadows of the Azrak peaks.

Sticking to the edge of the city, Raudius tried to put on a grand show of marching the "captured" raptor past any denizens they saw.

"Keep moving, sandscum!" Raudius barked, giving Cindri a light push forward. A group of passersby gave them a wide berth, eying them with curiosity and caution. There was no need to interfere. It was Legion business.

Thank Yuetrix for this armor, it helps me look the part. He had a lot to thank Yuetrix for, and he'd never get the chance to say it. *One thing at a time, Raudius. You may grieve on the road.* Reaching a crossroads, he veered Cindri right with a gentle push, eyes peeled for Merchatzi or other Legion.

Avoiding the main roads, they cut through the shoddy townhouses of the south side toward the eastern outskirts of the city. There, they would hopefully find a transport merchant who accepted stamp rings. Bolstered by the morning's encounter at the bakery where he had been dressed in little but rags, Raudius had confidence he could secure transport. Now he had full timbersteel to hide his rags and a hostage as a convincing prop.

As they cut through an alley, Cindri hissed, "I'm having second thoughts about this *great* plan." He looked nervously over his shoulder at a lamplighter holding a flame up to a lantern. When the wick caught and light roared to life, the illumination caught the man staring after them suspiciously. "Escaped raptors and Oaken Legion infighting have to be the talk of the town by now," he whispered.

"There's nothing to worry about." Raudius replied, "I've already captured the raptor, so the town is safe."

"Then you tell me you have a ring that buys anything you want, and I just go along with it. You've really taken me for a fool."

"Have some trust, won't you?" Raudius whispered, then loudly exclaimed, "Eyes down, shit-feathers!" A party of young nobles, heading to a seedier tavern for cheaper drinks, hurried past, sneaking glances at the captured raptor.

Cindri snarled, "Shit-feathers? I should have poisoned you."

Up ahead, they heard the telltale thud of boots and clinking of chainmail from around a corner. Quickly, they ducked into an alleyway and hurried silently to the parallel street, dropping their prisoner facade while no eyes were on them. Raudius was not sure which Merchatzi were looking for them other than the Coalition, but it was not worth finding out.

The townhouses were looking nicer, which told Raudius they were nearing the center of town, almost parallel to the obelisk marketplace. On their right, the blocks of townhouses were sparser, broken up by uneven mountain cliffs and encroaching forests. They had reached the edge of town—now they had to find a merchant that would accommodate them.

"Come on, we can hop the wall and run into the woods right now, let's go," Cindri hissed.

"We have nothing to eat. We need these rations."

"I can scavenge, I know which plants are edible."

"You know which plants are edible *for you.*"

"You don't know which plants you can eat?" Cindri sounded aghast.

Raudius grumbled, "I know which ones, I just don't want to look for them."

A horde of grubby children ran past them on the left, sprinting home as night fell. Seeing Raudius, they broke into a unified chant as if on cue.

Stomp, stomp, romp, romp,
The Legion goes to war,
That's all they know, it goes to show,
The Legion's such a bore!

The hivemind of children kept the chant on repeat as they frolicked out of view. Disgruntled, Raudius quickened their pace, while Cindri chuckled out loud.

Raudius whispered, "I'm sure they have songs about raptors that are just as scathing." The raptor hummed the tune under his breath as Raudius seethed.

Some shops ahead showed promise. Past an arched stone gate, a cobblestone road jutted into the forest, the stones fading into a well-trodden dirt road that curved away into the trees. Lining the street here were several buildings marked with horseshoes, wagon wheels, and other guild symbols, each with an accompanying stable. The smell of hay and horse dung drifted across the street, mixed with the brisk scent of falling night. On the outskirts of the city, a few Merchatzi stood watch, gazing into the forest, their backs turned to the town.

Keeping an eye on the guards, Raudius and Cindri ducked into the nearest shop. From the counter, a human looked up from the book he was poring over, finalizing the numbers of the day's business. Clearly apprehensive at the sight of a Legion soldier and a raptor, he asked, "Can I help you, sir?"

Raudius held out Cindri by the scruff of his neck like prized game and flashed the stamp ring. "Can you help *me?*" he asked.

The merchant stammered, "No, sir, we don't accept those here." His face grew a shade of sweaty red. "But we happily accept teirs, and I can assure the quality of our—"

Raudius turned heel and stormed out, cutting the flustered merchant off with a slam of the door. He hurriedly pushed Cindri across the intersection to the next stable, keeping the Merchatzi in the corner of his vision. Pushing through the wooden door, they were greeted by a Twelian, shimmering behind the shop's counter.

Dark green energy with jagged streaks of turquoise formed a human-like shape, as if a silhouette was struck by lightning and granted life. The creature wore a robe of intricately woven strands of metals, and it hovered just above the ground like a ghost. Its wispy feet left trails of turquoise Ventish energy along the ground that lingered as briefly as candles in a strong wind. More woven metal strands curled up its crackling energy arms, blossoming into expertly crafted prostheses that worked just as well as the most delicate fingers, if not better.

The Twelian's shimmering head turned toward them, featureless. It saw them with no eyes and heard them with no ears. As it spoke, streaks of turquoise lightning arced through its green head with every word, illuminating the dark green silhouette. "A curious sight, raptor and Legion. We are about to close, so do hurry." Its voice hummed, with crackling inflections at the beginning and end of each sentence.

Raudius dragged Cindri forward and placed the stamp ring on the table. "I'm looking for transport, leaving tonight. Two horses minimum, but I'll take whatever is fastest. Rations for the trip as well."

"Curious. Your destination?" The shape's "head" flashed with turquoise lights like floating lanterns in a green fog.

"Reath," Raudius said, remembering the lie that he and Cindri concocted.

"Excellent, it can be done." The Twelian leaned forward and inspected the stamp ring. "An Oaken Legion with a stamp ring. How did you come by this, perhaps?"

"That's Citadel business," Raudius gruffly stated.

"Ah, of course, my apologies," The Twelian said. "May I ask which Citadel?" Raudius noted that the Twelian was tilting the ring to catch the light of his glowing body, no doubt looking at the Citadel's symbol to see if it matched what Raudius said.

He's prying for information, not just to see if the stamp ring is stolen. Information can be bought and sold just like his horses. I'll humor him, it's all lies anyway.

"Citadel Teirmond," Raudius said. Hopefully it would ease this merchant's fears of not getting its reimbursement. The Teirmonds had more gold than the rest of the Citadels combined, so much so that the gold coin of Ralvera bore their name.

"Poor luck," the Twelian said. "Our only coreskiff was taken yesterday; it could have flown you right to Reath, or the Citadel. Horses will have to do. Please wait." It floated away from the counter to a back room. Cindri hissed and spat on the counter as the Twelian left, then turned and shrugged at Raudius.

The merchant returned shortly, carrying a set of clay stamp tablets and a roll of parchment. "You are aware that Citadel Teirmond will not be in Reath for many months? If you wait here a few days, you can rent our coreskiff to go directly to the Citadel."

Raudius feigned outrage. "*Months?* A few months?" He wracked his brain for the name of Citadel Teirmond's ruler. *We reviewed these in last year's lessons, you dumb tree. Think.* "That is not what Lord Berin promised. Show me their route."

Raudius had no idea if the Twelian was suspicious of them or not. It *did* have body language, but none that Raudius was familiar with. Angry nobles usually got their way, however.

The Twelian unfurled the parchment, which turned out to be a map of Ralvera. Over the city of Carve, the symbol of Citadel Teirmond was marked—cupped hands overflowing with coin, set against a gray mountain.

A dotted line of dark ink meandered from Carve across the South Verdant to the Ysera Vent, which was also marked with another symbol —a blade of wheat crossed with a blade of steel. *That has to be Citadel Waldheath.* The symbols were so difficult to remember. All Raudius wanted to do was study swordplay and strategies, and he often confused the Citadel emblems with the merchant guild emblems. Citadel Teirmond's dotted line then took a sharp bend, traversing the desert toward Obsidian Leap and the Unfalreth Vent

Pretending to study the map in disbelief for a moment, Raudius threw up a hand, keeping the other clamped on Cindri's bindings, and cursed under his breath. The merchant calmly interjected and said, "Again, if you wait just a few days, we will have a coreskiff available."

"No, no, I have other business in Reath as well. The horses will do fine, I'll find a coreskiff there." Raudius feigned exasperated defeat.

"Do I get my own horse?" Cindri mocked.

"Of course, scalescum. You'll be thrown over the back of one of them."

The Twelian crackled noisily to grab Raudius's attention. "If you don't mind."

It held out its metal fingers for the stamp ring. Raudius handed over the ring, but instead of pressing it into a fresh tablet, the merchant started pressing the ring through a series of already used tablets, one by one. "This is standard practice, you should have nothing to worry about."

What is he doing that for? It hit Raudius like a flash of lightning. *Those are molds of stolen rings!* The merchant pressed the ring into each indentation while Raudius tried to maintain his composure. Any second now, the ring would fit perfectly into one of the molds and they'd have to run for it.

The merchant pressed the stamp ring to the last mold, paused as if surprised at the imperfect fit, then placed the set of tablets aside and pressed the ring into a soft fresh tablet before handing it back to Raudius. "Not stolen. Forgive me for checking, it is unusual for the human lords to part with their stamp rings. You must be *quite* important. My congratulations."

It's not in Teirmond's records of stolen stamp rings? Depths below, I cannot believe this was just sitting in the Coalition's guardroom. Raudius breathed an internal sigh of relief, the Oakfire in his chest settling. "You don't know the half of it. Do you remember that I'm in a rush?"

"I do recall." The Twelian hooked a thin metal finger through the handle of a small bell and gave it a tiny ring, then returned to scrawling the details of the transaction into the tablet. "Your horses and rations will be waiting for you outside."

"Appreciated." Raudius turned to the door, then Cindri nudged him in the shins. Just a gentle tap, meant as a reminder. *He's trying to hint at something, did I forget—ah, right.* He turned back to the merchant and asked, "I've heard there's a snake city somewhere in the mountains here. Is it something I need to be wary of?"

The merchant looked up, processing the question. Raudius kept talking. "I'm from the North Verdant, not too familiar with these parts. The snakes aren't very friendly in the north. "

"There is a city in the mountains, yes. Savin Actai." The Twelian seemed amused at the tree's overt, yet expected, xenophobia. "You will be fine as long as you stick to the Eight Kings' Way."

"Are you sure? I have one of their scaled friends under my care." He jostled Cindri, who snarled under his breath.

"I am sure. The city is far off-road, up the mountains. The closest you'll get is a crossroad with a trail that the tauninaga call the Way of Waterfalls. Merchatzi that patrol the road usually mark the trailhead with a stone cairn, although the tauninagan knock it down whenever they pass. It's not even a road, just a less steep section of mountain. Quite impossible to accidentally stumble upon." The Twelian waved them out the door. "Your horses are waiting and the light is fading. Go, we are past closing."

Raudius hurried Cindri out the door, where an attendant was holding two steeds, one gray and one speckled beige. Raudius threw Cindri over the back of the gray one and tied the reins to the other horse before swinging into his own saddle. Checking the saddlebags, he found them full of ample supplies for both him and the raptor. The attendant, a round, balding human, handed him a torch and said, "Safe travels, sir."

Raudius nodded and spurred the horse forward. He had ridden many elk before, but never a horse. *They should behave similar enough. I hope.* Luckily, his prodding worked, the horse trotting forward toward the town gate. The guards turned and watched him approach, and he kept an aloof stare ahead into the forest, holding his breath. *They don't wear Coalition colors, they might not care.* As he passed, one guard grunted, "Safe travels."

Good soldiers. They know it's Legion business. Raudius gave him a curt nod, then he and Cindri disappeared into the valleys of the Azraks.

Chapter 44

The Way of Waterfalls

E iklo hauled himself up a boulder and collapsed, drained of energy. Trapping the Du'ul, he basked in the sharp jolt of Vent energy, then manifested a cloud of freezing air around him to cool off. Snowflakes collected on his cloak like tiny diamonds.

The path ahead only grew steeper. If Eiklo could breathe, he'd be winded. *Anyone who calls this a "path" is taking some extreme liberties with their definitions.*

According to Srrith, however, this was a well-traveled route up to Savin Actai, although Eiklo failed to see how these cliffs were *well-traveled*. The climb so far had been mostly clambering up boulder after boulder, weaving up and around steep cliffs, and slicing through the occasional grove of lush rainforest that clung greedily to the rock. Not to mention jumping over countless ice-cold mountain streams that dribbled from the high peaks, cutting down the cliffs like crystalline worms.

Looking up, the peaks were shrouded in fog, drifting off the rainforest cliffs. These were the tallest peaks in the Azraks, dominating the skyline, but Eiklo was barely impressed. They barely held a torch to the height of the Scorch Vents, which, in turn, were utterly dwarfed by the two Frost Vents—one of which Eiklo called home. Up on the slopes of the Rulnevrin Vent, the world looked impossibly tiny.

Mayve came into view, scrambling up a boulder and leaping onto a sheer rock face. Sticking herself to the cliff with unmatched grace, she scaled upward at a blinding pace then leapt backward to catch the edge of a second cliff, pulling herself up and disappearing. With that short-cut, she had skipped what would be a ten-minute climb for Eiklo.

"*Varin's sword,*" the skeleton muttered. "She better slow down or I'll be left for a second death on these slopes."

Somewhere on the rocks above him, Srrith called down, "I will keep her from getting too far ahead, Eiklo. Focus on the climb."

"Ugh, I forgot you can hear me," Eiklo whispered, even quieter. When they started, he thought that he and Srrith would be evenly paced on their ascent, but the tauninaga quickly unveiled her skills as an expert climber. Not as skilled as Mayve—who seemed to be part mountain goat—but Srrith still far outclassed Eiklo, even with an injured arm. Having no legs did not slow her down for a second, as she used her specialized sickles as deft extensions of the two limbs she had, and her tail wormed around rocks, finding tricky handholds in some places and supporting her weight in others.

Turning his attention back to the climb, he tackled the boulders one by one, inching slowly after his companions. *If only I had died on a Scorch Vent.* Never had he envied the Ul'Varin-Raks' strength more. He'd be leagues ahead of Mayve if he could leap up the mountain. The thought of the fiery skeletons pulled his mind back to Port Wenstnor. What had become of the Ferry? Was it sailing the Devaros as a crew of outlaws? Or was it rotting on the bed of the Devaros River, the crew scattered to the wind?

Guilt pooled in his chest, lines of ice forming down his skull like claw marks. *They risked everything for me, and the consequences struck fast.* Eiklo would have risked everything for them, just like they did for him. That's the kind of crew they were. Captain Vulinor made his decisions, and Eiklo had to trust them. Everything was still so unclear. *We must keep the Oasis Stone away from Zeteph. Other than that, we have no answers.*

What does the Stone do? What would Zeteph use it for? These questions burned in the back of his mind. If Eiklo didn't find the answers, then Vulinor's sacrifice would be for naught.

As he heaved up a particular steep cliff, fatigue caught up with him. If only he could resurrect Screech from her feather in his pack. It was impossible to make a fire hot enough without the help of a Scorch Vent or a crew of Ul'Varin-Rak. Eiklo called up to Srrith, "I need a few minutes!"

Up the slope, Srrith yelled, "Mayve, we're stopping!" From even farther ahead, Mayve's distant voice yelled back something that Eiklo could not quite decipher. He wondered if she'd climb back down to meet them or just stay up there. She would not dare trek farther ahead, would she? *Of course she would. But she's also insane enough that she'd love to climb down and climb back up again.*

At the beginning of the climb, Mayve was visibly bristling with anticipation. She had said, "Don't turn around until we're at the top, you'll spoil the view." However, the boulder Eiklo stood on faced a sheer ledge, and he'd be damned if he spent his brief respite staring at more rocks. "Spoil the view, *Varin's scroll,* I was reborn on the Rulnevrin Frost Vent. I've seen views that would make her skull crack."

If Eiklo could breathe, his breath would have been ripped from his chest. Far below, Lake Nawai glistened in the sun like the Oasis Stone itself, stretching out to the horizon. The glorious Azraks, formed of whitish-gray stone and covered with lush rainforests, encircled the dazzling mountain sea like a stoic marble wall. Waterfalls poured from the cliffs down to the lake, some so high they never reached the bottom, falling to mist in the sky. A singular ship meandered across the lake, almost lost in the reflection of the sun off the water. At the bottom of the mountains, the forest swept through the valleys like luscious moss clinging to gargantuan rocks.

"Beautiful, yes?" Srrith said. She was coiled on the ledge above, her tail dangling over the edge, sickles wedged in a nearby cliff. Eiklo's slack-jawed awe must have been noticeable—the cobra looked quite amused, tongue flicking in and out.

Eiklo collected himself, still taking in the view, and said, "It has redeemed the climb, somewhat."

Srrith scoffed, "Were you not reborn on the tallest peak in all Ralvera?"

"The view is otherworldly, when the blizzards clear. But it's all snow and ice. Not like this." He breathed in the view, then asked the snake, "You're quite excellent at climbing. Did you learn that here or in the caves?" Eiklo asked.

"The caves," Srrith hissed. "Climbing through the tunnels is as necessary as walking or swimming. The path forward will twist in every direction, up or down. If you are not prepared, you will easily find yourself trapped beneath the earth."

"That makes sense," Eiklo said, morbidly curious. "Are your home caves in this area?"

"In the South Verdant, yes, but far to the west, in the Crimson Tors," Srrith said. There was a distant look in her eyes, almost melancholy.

How did a cave tauninaga end up so high in the mountains? Eiklo wanted nothing more than to pry Srrith's story out of her, but the tauninaga's cagey demeanor made him think twice. He decided not to push it. "I suspect the view from up here is leagues better than the caves."

Srrith smiled, and tasted the fresh air with her tongue. "Yes, far better." Eiklo suspected she meant more than the view.

A cold southerly wind blew from Lake Nawai up across the rock face, rustling the small outcrop of jungle below and infiltrating Eiklo's cloak. The chill was refreshing until he turned his face into the wind, where it rushed through his empty eye sockets and rattled through his skull. *I've never gotten used to the feeling of being so empty. Like a discarded snail shell, brought to life.*

As the sun's warmth returned, Eiklo saw the wind had drawn Srrith's attention east. Dark rain clouds hovered over the distant peaks, almost like the flying islands of the Citadels. Srrith had mentioned that any amount of rainfall made this journey impassable, and worry grew in Eiklo's ribcage. He asked, "Do you think that weather will come our way?"

"Hard to say," Srrith said, studying the horizon. She tasted the wind with a hiss. "If the wind holds like this, it will miss us, but barely. Any easterly winds will be just the start of our bad luck."

Eiklo hated the vagueness of her statement. "If it *does* shift, can we avoid the flooding?"

"I know of several safe places to camp along the Way of Waterfalls; as long as it does not hit soon we will be safe."

"That is good—"

"However," Srrith interrupted, "the rest of the pathway up will be completely inaccessible. If our enemy is as close as I think they are, then we will have to seek an alternate route. One I would rather avoid."

"We haven't seen a sign of any pursuers," Eiklo stated. "Not to mention they don't know where we're going."

Srrith shook her head. "We have not seen any because I've led us through the woods instead of taking the Eight King's Way. I have no doubt they have scoured its entire length and back on horseback." She hissed in disdain. "Zeteph, as well, seems to be an unnatural font of knowledge. If he knows where we're heading, then they may be lying in wait already on the slopes above."

Eiklo looked up at the crags, his awe at the mountain's grandeur replaced with ominous anxiety. Who might be hiding in the lush undergrowth of the rainforest groves, or lying in wait amidst the rocks? Intently studying the landscape for hidden danger, he nearly jumped out of his cloak when Mayve's face suddenly poked over the edge above.

The human's tan skin glistened with a few beads of sweat, but there was no sign she was even close to tired. Her smooth, dark hair was held up in a ponytail, and the reflection of the lake and rainforest in her green eyes made them glisten like perfectly cut emeralds.

Mayve leapt down next to Srrith and playfully asked, "What's with the grim looks? This climb is amazing, just look at that view!"

"We're looking at *that* view," Srrith hissed, pointing at the nefarious dark clouds far on the horizon.

Mayve laughed. "We wouldn't have to worry if you two would pick up the pace. I'd be at Savin Actai by now if it wasn't for you all."

"Shut up and enjoy the view for a minute, won't you?" Eiklo said.

"If you insist." Mayve dropped to Eiklo's ledge and sat next to him, fishing around in her pack for her food. Srrith did the same, producing thin slices of dried fish from her tunnelsleeve. Not needing to eat, Eiklo decided to practice a Du'ul meditation he learned at Thaumaturn Six. *Breathe in, trap, breathe out, manifest.* Each exhale, a cloud of snowflakes rushed out his mouth into the air and drifted away in the wind.

"How much farther?" Mayve asked.

Srrith gulped down her food whole, wiped her mouth, and said, "After sunset, luck permitting."

"Tell me again why we're worried about a little rain?"

Srrith sighed and started telling Mayve what she just told Eiklo. Half-listening, Eiklo was staring out at the sparkling waters of Lake Nawai again. He almost heard the waves, gently lapping on the rocks. But how? They were so far from the shore. *It's like I'm remembering it. But that's impossible.* It was the same familiarity he felt when he looked at the Oasis Stone, like his memories were chained deep inside his head. *I've never seen the Stone before. I've never been here before. Why do they feel familiar?*

Srrith cut off mid-sentence, perking up from her coils with her hood half-flared. The movement made Mayve freeze, and snapped Eiklo out of his thoughts. He strained to hear what Srrith heard, even though he knew it was impossible. She could be hearing the bated breath of an ambusher, hiding up the slope, or the scrape of a sword in its leather sheath from someone scaling up from below. All he heard was the wind.

Head on a swivel, the tauninaga scanned the surrounding mountains, clearly confused. Still, Eiklo only heard the wind. But maybe that was it. The wind sounded...strange. Almost like it was rushing toward them in a hurried crescendo.

Srrith uncoiled herself, ready to spring into action. Mayve and Eiklo both scrambled to their feet, Mayve placing her hand on the hilt of her sword while Eiklo trapped the Du'ul. *What am I going to do? Fight the wind?* The rushing wind was closing in, growing louder by the second.

A coreskiff ripped around the side of the mountain, tilting at a sharp angle to make the turn. Huge wings and a tail fin made of fibrous sailcloth sprouted from the hull, held in shape by metal frames. At the front, a cockpit encased in glass and metal reflected the landscape as it rushed by, and in the center were two concentric rings of Cavotros iron, revolving around the heated core—a steaming rock swept in red, orange, and purple flames. The sound that Eiklo mistook for the wind was actu-

ally the great wings of this vessel, carving through the air like twin guil-
lotines.

Srrith jolted upright and shouted, "Hide!" as she ripped her sickles
from the rock, but it was too late. Caught on the slope, they were
completely exposed to the sky. Eiklo watched in dismay—and awe—as
the coreskiff sliced by. On the deck of the vessel, he saw small figures tied
to the deck's railings, distant faces locked on the three travelers. He saw
from their vague shapes that some pointed directly at them, calling out
their discovery. They had been found.

In the wake of the coreskiff, their ledge was hit with a staggering
gust of wind. As the noise died down, Srrith hissed, "They'll circle back
and look for a landing spot. We need to disappear."

Without another word, they returned to their climb, this time with
anxious fervor. Mayve still took the lead, but now she stayed just ahead
of Eiklo. Srrith took up the rear, keeping her sharp ears tuned for the
distinctive avalanche of wind that the coreskiff generated.

After only a few minutes of climbing, Srrith called a halt. Eiklo and
Mayve looked at her nervously, expecting the order to run and hide. The
tauninaga scanned the horizon and hissed, "They should be back by
now, and I don't hear them."

"That could be just a scout," Mayve thought out loud. "Maybe
they're off to report on our location."

"If that's the case, they'll be picking up their main fighting force and
bringing them right to us," Srrith hissed. "Likely Vrato. Maybe even
Zeteph."

"Then let's hurry while we have the chance," Mayve said, and
turned back toward the climb.

Srrith's tail blocked her. "Speed is good, but it's more important
that we remain hidden. That coreskiff is blindingly fast. I know what it
sounds like now, but that still only gives us a couple seconds to hide. We
have to stay close to cover at all times, or they'll drop down right on us."

Eiklo saw the anxiety in Mayve's eyes. *She could be long gone up the
mountain, to safety. I'm slowing them down. Both of them.*

They pushed onward and upward, no one straying far. At each
boulder scramble and patch of jungle, Srrith would listen to the air, then
give them the go-ahead. Then they'd scurry upward to the next cover,

whether that was a small rocky cave, a field of boulders, or a patch of trees. It was far slower, but it gave Eiklo much-needed respite between climbs. He was painfully aware of how much he slowed down Mayve and Srrith, who he bet would be at Savin Actai by now if it weren't for him.

It was in a jungle grove, farther up the mountain, that Srrith called a halt. "It's coming, everyone down." She coiled low into the leafy underbrush, Mayve and Eiklo mimicking her movements.

Sure enough, Eiklo heard the rush of the coreskiff seconds later. Despite the dreadful people it carried, Eiklo could not help but marvel over the engineering. The concentric Cavotros iron rings, coupled with a small Citadel core, allowed the ship to hover and propel itself forward. *Ingenious. I need to get a closer look, next time the people piloting one aren't trying to kill me.*

A shadow passed across the face of the mountain as the coreskiff cut through the clouds. The gust of wind ripped at the foliage around them, then the noise died away as the coreskiff slowed down somewhere in their vicinity.

Srrith stalked to the edge of the grove, her dark scales melding with the underbrush. Even though she was not using her shadowy sfa-zrueen, she clearly knew how to position herself in the best way to avoid being seen. Mayve crept behind her, silent as a ghost, and Eiklo reluctantly followed, unsuccessfully trying to match the grace with which both of them moved.

Following them was well rewarded, though, because the view of the coreskiff was phenomenal. The ship hovered farther down the slope, putting them high enough to look down onto the deck. The glowing core—much smaller than the enormous cores that flew the Citadel islands—sat in a metal basin, impaled by several metal staves to keep it in place, while the crew ran about carefully maintaining the temperature of the rock with coal and water. Too hot, and the vessel would rise too high for its crew to disembark. Too cold, and the vessel would sink dangerously close to the slope of the mountain.

Around the core were two concentric rings, fitted with huge Cavotros iron plates that swiveled depending on where the pilot wanted to fly. Because the craft was hovering, both plates were rotated to be underneath the core, keeping it afloat. The massive, sail-like wings were folded up like a nesting bird's, mitigating the chance that a sudden gust would tip the vessel. But even folded they were an impressive sight.

Lost in the spectacle, Eiklo remembered back to what the Northern Ice raptors taught him about Citadel cores. *The great rocks that carry the human strongholds, created through complex volcomancy, are repelled by Cavotros iron with excessive force. The hotter the core, the greater the repulsion. One might think of this as similar to how magnetic lodestones repel each other, but no!* In his memory, the white-scaled, blue-feathered raptor snapped his maw, emphasizing his point. *The core exerts no returning force back onto the Cavotros iron, an entirely one-sided reaction. Thus, it is more akin to blowing air into a sail.*

The blue orbs in his skull were wide. *Only a Citadel has the resources to create such a mechanism. All that Cavotros iron and a Citadel core, to build one vessel! It is incredible what they create.* The coreskiff was such a recent invention, Eiklo had never seen one for himself, and he doubted Srrith had either. *She must have had no idea what sound it made. I'm sure she remembers now.*

Enthralled by the craftsmanship of the coreskiff, Eiklo finally looked at what Mayve and Srrith were staring at. Ropes hung from the deck of the coreskiff, depositing small dots of people and supplies on the slope below. One particular human stood out from the rest, with distinctive leather armor lined with white fur, and twin scimitars. Vrato.

The Dreaming Blade assassin was in the midst of ordering around a cohort of soldiers, dressed for wilderness trekking in leather armor and cloaks, carrying bundles of supplies. They were only an hour or less down the slope from them. If they climbed faster, they'd catch them by the day's end.

Mayve and Srrith could easily outrun them, if not for me. Eiklo felt a knot of shame in his ribcage. If they got caught, it would be because of him. He tapped both Srrith and Mayve on the shoulder and pointed to the slope. Srrith nodded and led them away from the coreskiff, back toward the mountain.

The rest of the day was a nerve-wracking climb, filled with glances over their shoulders and cautious searching of the rocks above and below. After dropping off Vrato, the coreskiff had risen and flown higher up the mountain. Eiklo theorized that they were dropping off soldiers up there as well, to catch them as they climbed. Srrith muttered that it would be foolish of them. The higher they climbed, the greater chance they encountered the tauninaga of Savin Actai. But she looked worried just the same, so Eiklo remained worried as well. The rainclouds from the north were steadily creeping closer as well, only adding to their stress. Dreaming Blade assassins and Merchatzi aside, it would all be made worse if the slope beneath their feet turned into a river.

At one point, a particularly steep cliff brought them to a grand vista. There was no time to appreciate the glorious view as they had last time, but Eiklo saw Mayve pause and look down the slope. The trail snaked back and forth as it hugged the cliff, crossing over a tiny stream each time. In the rain, this entire pathway would be transformed from a dribbling creek into a cascading waterfall.

At the very bottom of the cliff was the search party, where Vrato stood, staring up the slope. The assassin gave them a taunting wave like he'd just spotted a good friend across the street. Mayve lobbed an angry ball of spit over the edge and muttered, "I hope that hits him in the eye."

Eiklo picked up a rock, tossed it off the cliff, and said, "I hope *that* hits him in the eye."

Mayve laughed, and for a moment the gravity of the situation lifted away. But it was hard to remain hopeful. Vrato and his forces were gaining on them. They would have to run through the night to Savin Actai or they would be killed.

That all changed when the first raindrops fell.

As Eiklo felt the first plink of water on his skull, he shuddered. Already, rivulets of water traced familiar paths down the cliffs, trickling down from the mountains above. Somewhere over the peaks, a boom of thunder rolled down the slopes.

The drops grew into a drizzle, and Eiklo learned firsthand how dangerously quick the Way of Waterfalls could transform. Even though the rain had just started, water was pouring down the cliffside with disturbing force. *The brunt of the storm must be overhead, the wind must have carried it south over the mountains, then west over us.* Looking into the sky, Eiklo saw flashes of lightning just behind the peaks, followed by rolling thunder. The storm was moving so quickly that Lake Nawai and the westward mountains were still basking in afternoon sunlight.

He turned to the tauninaga, hoping she would say everything was fine. The tauninaga stared at the sky with a deciphering look, her hood flaring. *She's trying to find any excuse to not take her alternate path.* He could hardly imagine the other path was any worse than being trapped in a flash flood.

Mayve unwrapped her shawl from her belt and pulled it tight over her head, covering her already wet hair. The rivulets were swelling to rivers, washing around their boots, then over them, until they were ankle deep in water. The human, looking pale, leapt to a higher rock and said, "Srrith, we have to get to safety."

The tauninaga scowled, baring her fangs at the sky, and muttered, *"Akthoru take us."* Thunder boomed and water poured down her scales as the rain became a torrent. "Follow. We must take the Way of Echoes."

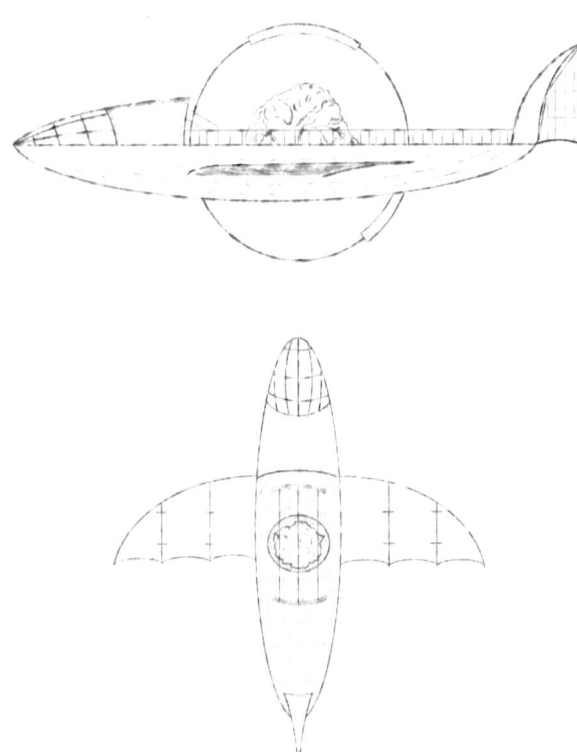

"I've had the utmost privilege of traveling by coreskiff only once on my journey, heading from Citadel Marcrest to Citadel Waldheath to present my work to the Lords. What would have been a perilous, weeklong journey turned into a few days of relative comfort and splendid views! Oh, what more would I have discovered? What adventures would I have undertaken if I had one at my permanent disposal? I consider the coreskiff the pinnacle of human ingenuity. It is marvelous what is created when brilliant thought meets endless gold."

—Oswal Briggin, cavernfolk explorer, 56 SR

Chapter 45

The Way of Echoes

This was only the third rainfall Mayve had ever experienced. The first two had been celebrated as miracles in Devar—indisputable signs of good luck, for only a raincloud blessed by Arcus and Tyberia could survive in the land of the Scorch Vents. The Devarians did not lack water, with the greatest river in Ralvera running through their city. Instead, the rainclouds brought hope. Hope that the power of the Vents was waning. Now, as the Verdant deluge soaked through her shawl, Mayve did not feel as lucky.

Thoughts of Vrato were washed away as the rainfall rushed down the cliffs and underneath their feet. All Mayve thought about was the abyss beneath the Devaros, where she had almost drowned twice in the past weeks. The smallest comfort she felt was that if she was swept away, she'd be killed by the fall instead of the water. *At least that's always how I assumed I'd die. Tumbling from a great height.*

Srrith was no longer leading them up the cliffs, but parallel to them. The dry boulders they had been scrambling over were now islands jutting from white-capped rapids, all growing stronger by the second, forcing them to leap from rock to rock over the rushing water. With each step, the rocks felt more and more slippery, turning every leap into potentially their last.

To Mayve's immense relief, the slope angled upward and away from the Way of Waterfalls, up into a rainforest grove tucked against a sheer cliff face. The canopy offered meager protection from the storm, but the ground was solid. She pulled her soaked shawl tightly around her and huddled in the underbrush, shivering.

Unaffected by the cold, Eiklo removed a glove and scratched away frozen rainwater from his skull carvings. His blue orbs were wide and faded, though, an emotion Mayve knew as intense worry. The Ul'Varin looked at her and said, "That wet shawl will only make you colder."

She peeled the cloth off her skin and said, "Thanks. I don't have much experience with being cold."

"I'm somewhat of an expert," Eiklo said, picking at the carvings on his forehead.

"You're not an expert on having skin, though, so how do you know about this?"

Eiklo paused, stuck in a thought. "I'm not sure. I used to have skin, maybe that knowledge stuck with me."

With the afternoon sun obscured by dark clouds, their grove of trees fell to a gloomy gray. Srrith appeared next to them as if made of shadows, yellow eyes piercing the dark underbrush. She had not even realized the tauninaga had disappeared. Srrith hissed, "It has been years since I walked the Way of Echoes. I found the entrance over there."

Mayve and Eiklo followed Srrith through the underbrush toward the cliff face. At the base of the cliff, Srrith unsheathed a sickle and cut away the leafy ferns, revealing a dark entrance into the rock.

Mayve shared a skeptical look with Eiklo, then they both turned toward Srrith, silently demanding a better explanation. Instead, Srrith opened her tunnelsleeve and removed her climbing rope. She tossed it to them and hissed, "Tie yourselves together at the waist while I explain."

As they started on the knots, Srrith spoke. "The Way of Echoes is named so because you cannot traverse it without a cave tauninaga. You have me, but that does not lessen the danger."

The tauninaga tied her end of the rope around her waist. "This tunnel cuts upward, through the mountains to the peak, very close to Savin Actai. If all goes well, we will reach the city just after sundown. Listen closely, because our safe passage depends on it.

"You will not know when, you will not know where, but at some point in this tunnel, we will not be alone."

A shiver ran up Mayve's spine, colder than anything the rainstorm could bring. Srrith hissed, "This tunnel is infested with glint butchers, creatures of voracious appetite that cannot stand even specks of light. We will carry no torches and we will swing no weapons, lest the metal hits a rock and sparks fly. Eiklo, your glowing eyes will earn you a swift and violent death. You will keep them closed for the journey. It will not matter because you will not be able to see anyway."

Mayve finished knotting the rope around her waist. It felt as if she was tightening a noose. She asked, "Won't the tunnels be flooded? I always had to find new paths home through Darkmist whenever the Devaros flooded." She wanted any excuse to not enter the tunnel.

Srrith shook her head. "The path is safe from the water, trust me. Now, the glint butchers are deaf, so we can speak freely. Follow my directions *exactly*, the moment you hear them. Understood?"

Mayve and Eiklo nodded grimly. Eiklo asked, "What *is* a glint butcher? An animal?"

Of course he had to ask. Even situations like this could not sate Eiklo's curiosity.

Srrith bared her fangs. "No one knows exactly, but they used to be cavernfolk, or maybe humans. The more scholarly cavernfolk believe it to be a disease contracted from deep caves. The more superstitious ones believe it to be the dark twistings of Nol."

"Who or what is Nol?" Mayve asked, staring into the darkness of the cave.

"A myth of the Caverns," Srrith hissed. "The leader of a vast necropolis, buried so deep in the earth that it will never be found, by light or living soul."

"It's the deity of the cavernfolk. Nol, Goddess of the Caves and Lady of Death," Eiklo said. "They only believe in one god, and it's not a kind one. Legend says, she steals away anyone who gets lost in the Caverns, living or dead, then she forces them into her servitude, doing her bidding and tending to her empty city. Some even say they'll find their family crypts empty, then catch glimpses of them wandering the tunnels, brought back to life."

Mayve stared into the cave, wishing Eiklo had kept his mouth shut. She was no stranger to the Ralveran Caverns. *Phovus,* she grew up on their outskirts. She had heard plenty of tales of what lurked deeper, but never gave it a second thought.

Srrith cinched a knot around her waist and sliced the remaining rope away, spooling it meticulously back into the tunnelsleeve. "Remember, whatever commands I order must be followed without hesitation. The terrain will be unsteady, so step with caution."

Mayve wanted nothing to do with the cave before her. The fissure in the mountain wall felt nothing like her home of Darkmist. It seemed to leak shadows like dark blood, devouring the meager light around it.

"Are we sure that this is our best option?" Eiklo said, looking over his shoulder at the water-cloaked cliffs outside the grove.

"The Way of Waterfalls will be impassable for the entire day after this weather clears, if not several days," Srrith said. "We will be trapped, and Vrato will dive upon us from his coreskiff like a hawk to a mouse in an open field."

With frost furrowing across his brow, the Ul'Varin's eyes widened with fear. He tugged the knot around his waist for the sixth time, checking its security. Mayve double-checked her own knot, the rope connecting her to Srrith up front and Eiklo behind.

"Come now," Srrith hissed. "We must be off." She offered her tail for Mayve to hold, who in turn grabbed Eiklo's hand. With that, the tauninaga slithered into the cave entrance, her black-as-night scales melding with the shadows, leaving only a rope that trailed taut into the darkness. Gulping a last breath of fresh air like she was diving underwater, Mayve followed behind. The last sources of light she saw were Eiklo's blue eyes, which winked away as he closed them.

Travel through the tunnel was beyond tedious. They moved at a snail's pace, feeling blindly for rocks and uneven terrain at each step. Just earlier today, Mayve had leapt across the mountain slopes with the jewel of Lake Nawai beneath her. Now, she wormed her way through a cavern so devoid of light, she could not see her hand in front of her face.

At times, the tunnel flattened, and they were able to pick up the pace. At others, it collapsed into nothing more than a crack in the earth, where Mayve felt the weight of the mountain on both sides, threatening to crush the air from her lungs. Some sections were completely vertical, forcing Mayve to feel her way, handhold by handhold, up a sheer wall, climbing the mountain from within.

It was after a particularly tight fissure—so narrow that Mayve had to lie on her back and claw against the low ceiling to move—that Srrith called a halt. "We are entering glint butcher territory. Stay close, move slowly, and follow my *exact commands.*"

Mayve's heart felt like it was trying to escape her chest. She flailed an arm in the cold air behind her until she grabbed Eiklo's arm, and gave the cloth-wrapped bone a reassuring squeeze, for his sake and her own.

As they crept forward behind Srrith, her senses screamed at her, searching frantically for any sign of the danger. Light-starved hallucinations danced on the peripherals of her vision, forming shapeless creatures leaping out of the dark, while her hearing strained to catch anything in between Srrith's searching hisses.

"There's a hole in the floor, five strides to our left," Srrith whispered, "and a glint butcher seven strides to our right. Walk as straight as you can."

It went against everything Mayve knew about staying hidden, talking so openly with a threat lurking so close. She just had to trust Srrith that the monsters were as deaf as she was blind. Every footstep was placed with utmost care, all her muscles on edge in case Srrith hissed a sudden command.

Her boots made gentle taps on the rock, tiny rocks shifting and crunching underfoot, as she meticulously trailed the smooth rasp of Srrith's scales. Mayve strained to hear even the quietest scrap of noise from the glint butcher's direction.

There was the unmistakable sound of footsteps. Three taps on the stone, eerily close to her right side. A lone creature, wandering aimlessly through the shadow, unaware of its next meal mere feet away. Mayve froze in her tracks. Eiklo bumped into her from behind and the rope to Srrith went taut as the snake continued forward. *"Keep moving,"* Srrith hissed. "It's not coming this way, so *do not stop.*"

Mayve swallowed her breath and searched for her next steps forward. In the darkness, she heard several more erratic steps as the hidden glint butcher shuffled away.

"Two on the left," Srrith said. She directed them in a wide circle away from the creatures. Mayve heard more disjointed footsteps tapping across the stone. Something groaned, rasping at the air as it stumbled on uneasy legs.

Mayve's heart beat on her chest like a man buried alive, pounding on a coffin lid. The raspy breaths and tapping footsteps grew more frequent, coming from every direction, and Srrith hissed more and more urgent orders, stopping and starting them, guiding them almost in circles as the glint butchers walked mindless paths.

With a pit of terror in her chest, Mayve realized they were surrounded, and her sense of direction was shattered. She had no idea which way they were supposed to be traveling, and she clung even tighter to Srrith and Eiklo.

Without warning, tapping footsteps accelerated toward her, the ragged panting gaining. Steel rang as Srrith unsheathed a sickle, pulled from Mayve's grasp, and sliced the rope between them. "Stay there and *don't move!*" With the rope limp, there was no trace left of Srrith's existence other than her voice.

The glint butcher, oblivious to the feast in front of it, limped by within arm's reach. For what felt like eternity, Mayve and Eiklo were frozen in the dark, alone and cut off from Srrith. The rope between her and Srrith would have snagged the creature if Srrith had not severed it.

The panting faded to their right, and Srrith's grabbed her arm. She hissed, "There are more here than the last time I took this path." She pulled them along through the tunnel, forcibly redirecting them out of reach from wandering glint butchers every few strides. Then she stopped and her voice dropped to the smallest whisper. "*Akthoru take us,* why are *they* here? They shouldn't be here."

"Who are *they?*" Eiklo whispered back.

Srrith replied, "No more talking above a whisper. There are lumitails on the ceiling ahead. They normally don't sleep this far in; the storm must have driven them deeper."

Mayve remembered lumitails from Darkmist. Tiny creatures that flew from the caves at night and danced across the waters of Darkmist Pool, attracting insects to eat with luminescent bulbs on their heads and tails. She used to sit on the docks with Dreva and watch the swarms twirl through the darkness like clouds of fireflies. If they accidentally startled the swarm...

"They probably drew more glint butchers here," Eiklo whispered, "That's why there's so many?"

Srrith's voice hissed from the shadows, "Stay as close to me as possible. There are many holes and side passages up ahead. No more noise until I say so."

They crept forward, and soon Mayve heard a new noise. Small high-pitched chirps and the rustle of leathery wings far above, from the tiny creatures clinging to the ceiling.

Srrith sped up. Glint butchers wandered on either side of them, waiting to leap at the first sign of light. A retched gasp sounded in her ear, and hot breath blew on her neck. Srrith yanked her and Eiklo backward and hissed, "*Do. Not. Move.*"

The footsteps tapped directly in front of her, completely invisible but inches away. One step closer and it would touch her. The butcher's gasps grew louder, and Mayve instinctively stepped backward.

Her foot slipped on the edge of a drop she didn't know was there. Her body pitched backward and her head spun, trying to make sense of the sudden movement without any help from her sight. Eiklo and Srrith pulled hard on her arms, trying to keep her from tumbling over the edge without pulling her back into the glint butcher. Mayve scrambled for footing, and she felt a large rock drag underfoot and slip into the chasm.

Bang! The rock smashed into the unseen depths, and the ceiling exploded in light.

The lumitails dropped into the air like a thousand stars falling from the sky, the pinpricks of light on their tails barely scratching the overwhelming darkness. But it was enough to illuminate the creature mere inches away from Mayve's face. She stared into two dinner plate-sized eyes, bulging from gaunt gray skin, and an unhinged human-like jaw bristling with dagger-sized teeth.

The glint butcher unleashed a blood-curdling howl, snapped its head around, and bit a lumitail out of the air, devouring it in seconds.

Guttural howls rang through the tunnel as the entire horde of glint butchers flung themselves at the swarm of lumitails, consumed with violent rage. Mayve thought she heard Srrith yell something, but it was drowned in the screaming pandemonium. The tauninaga pulled Mayve forward, hacking her way through with a sickle, and Mayve pulled Eiklo, hanging onto her friend with white knuckles.

The glowing bats illuminated flashes of gnashing teeth and twisted, pained faces, hellbent on extinguishing the light that seared their massive eyes. The glint butchers sprinted with inhuman speed at the swarm of glowing bats, which Mayve was caught in the middle of. One glint butcher leapt out over a chasm, grabbing several lumitails from the air as it plummeted into the depths, shredding the bats as it fell to its death.

They had to get out of the swarm. It took all of Mayve's concentration to dodge through the leaping glint butchers, who were throwing themselves with complete abandon at the lumitails. Ahead, Srrith sliced in every direction with both sickles, the wounds of her injured arm reopening. *She doesn't know where she's going either. The howls are blocking her echolocation.* Despite the light, they were blinder than before.

Claws raked across her back as a glint butcher slashed through the swarm. It stood right in front of Eiklo, but the Ul'Varin didn't react, still running forward.

He can't see. Even though there's light, he can't open his eyes. Mayve let go of Srrith's tail and kicked the glint butcher away. She screamed at Eiklo to follow but her voice made no sound amidst the howls, and when she reached for Srrith, the snake was gone. Dragging Eiklo behind her, she ran as fast as she could through the flashing light and gnashing teeth. Srrith was nowhere to be seen, lost in the chaos, but the glint butchers were everywhere, ripping the lumitails, and anything amongst them, to pieces.

A lumitail was knocked out of the air onto the ground where it spasmed, injured and flickering, before a glint butcher threw itself onto the creature in a headlong dive, right between Mayve and Eiklo. She shouted at Eiklo to jump and tried to pull him over the thrashing monster, but there was nothing she could do.

The Ul'Varin tripped on a glint butcher and was wrenched out of her grasp. He stumbled, then was knocked by another glint butcher into the darkness, just outside the light of the lumitail swarm. There was a sharp crack of bone as he hit the cave wall. Freezing blue elemental light burst from where he collided, and dark howling shapes fell upon him.

Lost in shock, Mayve stood alone, lights snuffing out around her as glint butchers eviscerated the swarm. Teeth ripped into her thigh. Claws raked down her back. A hand grabbed her arm. Srrith's hand, pulling her onward. She numbly ran behind the tauninaga, eyes over her shoulder, fixated at the point in the darkness where she had seen Eiklo's burst of light. She tried to scream for Srrith to stop, but Srrith could not hear, and neither of them could see. She had to go back. They were leaving Eiklo.

But if she stayed, she would die too. So she ran. They ran through the gauntlet of claws and howls until the last lights around them winked out. Until they felt fresh wind and smelled the earthy scent of rain. As they burst from the tunnel, Mayve collapsed onto the jungle floor, staring at the yawning cave mouth. Eiklo would be right behind them. She waited for the blue lights of his eyes to emerge from the darkness.

They did not, leaving Mayve crying in the underbrush, pelted with rain from the dying storm. Beside her, Srrith coiled up and buried her head in her scales.

For the first time in a while, she felt the Oasis Stone weigh on her belt. Only one thought coursed through her mind: *How many more of my friends and family will die for this Stone?*

Chapter 46

Savin Actai

In the aftermath of the storm, life crept back to the rainforest of the Azraks. Insects hummed and birds chirped from the mist, reveling in their hidden shelters as water dripped like a second rainfall from the canopy. They called out to the others, to let them know they survived the storm. To Srrith, it sounded as if they were mocking her.

Vulinor had sacrificed so much for their quest, so much for Eiklo, and she led him to his death. They should have turned around, faced Vrato and his soldiers. At least they would all be dead and she would not have to feel this guilt.

Something stung on her back. Rainwater seeped into a deep bite mark from a glint butcher. As the shock faded, pain rushed back. She uncoiled and looked for Mayve. The human was sitting on the jungle floor with her knees pulled to her chest, blankly staring back into the Way of Echoes. As Srrith slithered over, she could see the rainwater was running red down her arms as it mixed with blood from nasty slashes across her arms and back.

Using the last of the bandages in her tunnelsleeve, Srrith dressed the worst of Mayve's wounds, then laid a hand on her shoulder. "Come. Savin Actai is near."

Mayve did not stir, and Srrith tried to gently lift her, which she allowed. "The mountain tauninaga will treat your wounds. Please. It is not far, and you are losing blood." Srrith was losing blood as well, but she did not want to worry Mayve any further.

"What is all this for?" Mayve asked, her voice a pained whisper.

"That is what we are here to find out," Srrith hissed. She slithered away through the underbrush, the ferns brushing against her like grasping hands. The Great Seer would have answers for them, but would those answers be worth the price of Eiklo's life?

They shambled through the moonless night to Savin Actai, not far now. Sheltered between mountain peaks, the jungle grew to unfathomable heights, the thick trunks punching through the lower canopy. They arrived in a steep canyon between two mountain cliffs, wide enough to accommodate a thin strip of jungle with a river winding between the gargantuan trees. Besides the river, the trees, and the sheer mountain walls enclosing them, there was nothing here.

Srrith slid into the river, the refreshing mountain water rushing over her scales. Mayve tentatively waded in behind her, blood dripping from her wounds fogging the clear waters. Srrith stopped in the middle of the river and hissed, "We are here."

Mayve looked around in confusion, searching for any sign of light or civilization. The human was too weary to be curious, too numb to question anything. Meanwhile, Srrith strained to hear over the gurgle of the water and crash of hidden waterfalls. *Someone has to be here. Their breathing will betray them.* Suddenly, she snapped her gaze into the darkness of the canopy and called out, "I see you, Hssov. Lower the lift."

A torch flared to life, revealing a vibrant green jungle tauninaga in a nearby tree, coiled like a vine around a sturdy branch. His snake head was bulkier than Srrith's, with large ridges over the eyes, more reminiscent of a viper than a cobra, but he still wore the traditional dual sickles, sheathed on his back. Hssov partially uncoiled to rear up on the branch, revealing his green leather armor, adorned with jungle leaves. "Nineteen heartbeats before you noticed me. Thought I almost had you."

"Call the lift, Hssov," Srrith growled.

"I already sent the signal up. Who else approaches Savin Actai in the black of night?" He hissed in amusement, then leaned out of the tree, squinting at Mayve. "Is that a human with you? The one who the Great Seer sent you to find?"

"Tell them to hurry. We are injured." As if to drive home Srrith's point, Mayve staggered to the left and tripped on a rock, almost crashing into the water if not for Srrith catching her. She hissed, "Now!"

Hssov's amusement melted away and he leapt from the tree, arms outstretched. Scaled flaps unfurled underneath his arms and his body flattened, curling into an undulating shape designed to catch the air beneath him. Torch sputtering, Hssov whipped through the trees in a breakneck glide, latching onto a different trunk with his sickles. Placing his forehead against the tree's bark, he whispered to the giant plant, asking it to carry a message to those above.

Srrith steadied Mayve on her own feet, feeling that her bandages were completely soaked through. A creak of wood from above signaled the lift was falling, and soon a platform of rough planks suspended on a myriad of ropes touched down into the river. As soon as Srrith helped Mayve aboard, Hssov spoke to the tree again, the ropes snapped taut, and they were lifted from the water, swiftly rising toward the canopy.

Like a cloud of leaves, the canopy enveloped them. Twigs snapped away as the dense branches gave way to the lift. Srrith had been waiting for this moment since the journey began, to show Mayve and Eiklo the grandeur of Savin Actai, for them to feel the same awe that she did when she first arrived. Now Mayve was pale and shaking, and Eiklo was lost.

Branches snapping, the lift broke through the lower canopy and the city of Savin Actai stretched before them. The two cliff walls of the chasm were dotted with the lights of pagoda-style dwellings, stretching up both mountain slopes. Stone bridges spanned the crevice at different heights, jutting over the sea of leaves from the lower canopy and intersecting with the massive goliath trees, which were covered in wooden platforms and dwellings, clinging to the trunks like lichen. Waterfalls tumbled from the mountain heights into carved pools, their water collected and then diverted into thin canals that flowed adjacent to the streets before finally tumbling down into the canopy.

The lift stopped at a wooden platform, secured to the trunk of a goliath tree. Hssov was waiting there, along with two mountain tauni-naga. They were dressed in identical white robes that draped over their tails, one with light blue scales and the other with slate gray, each with a white stripe that ran from the tip of their nose to the tip of their tail. Their most distinctive feature was their dagger-like claws, razor-sharp and long enough to almost be cumbersome. Tressis and Lusa were their names, if Srrith remembered correctly. Lusa was already glaring at Srrith with animosity. She was used to it. Some people did not care about her history. Others did.

As soon as the lift ground to a halt, the two mountain tauninaga hurried them off and herded them toward the western cliff. Srrith yelled to Hssov, "Inform Alactashi Sen that I've returned."

"As if she doesn't already know." Hssov chuckled, but there was real concern in his eyes. Srrith saw him looking at the bloody droplets trailing down Mayve's shoulder. He leapt off the platform and glided away toward the western cliff.

Srrith and Mayve were led across one of the bridges and up a set of stone steps, climbing the eastern side of the chasm. The town was quiet at night, to everyone but Srrith. She heard the creak of doors cracking open for residents to glance at them, the scrape of scales sneaking to the windows and the hushed whispers within the dwellings. Some cared, some did not, but Srrith only ever noticed the former.

The healer's dwelling was a two-story pagoda made of dark wood, overlooking the jungle chasm from the top of the eastern cliff. Mayve was laid on a square reed mat, large enough for a coiled tauninaga, and Srrith coiled herself on an adjacent one. The human looked like she was barely present in her own mind, dazed and weak. Lusa applied fresh bandages and some poultice to Mayve's wounds to ensure she was at least stable. Tressis inspected Srrith's cuts and hissed to Lusa, "This one is in better shape. I will begin the sfa-zrueen." He coiled on a mat next to Srrith, settling into a comfortable sleeping position.

Within a minute, Tressis's heartbeat slowed and his breaths drew deeper as he slumbered. All at once, the exhaustion of the day finally crashed into Srrith, as if she was smacked in the head by a falling rock. Struggling to stay awake, she curled into a sleeping coil while Lusa did the same. As she drifted away, Lusa hissed, "Can you not stay awake for now?"

Srrith's eyes snapped open and stared daggers at the healer. "I am tired, so I will rest. If the human dies, my nightmares will be the least of your worries."

Lusa scowled and hissed, "How can I dream when I am in danger?"

"You are a fool to fear me only while I am sleeping, and not while I'm awake," Srrith snarled.

Tressis snapped awake. "Hush, or I cannot heal you. Lusa, please." He nodded urgently at Mayve.

Lusa glared at Srrith, who met her gaze with shadowy animosity, then settled into a sleeping coil. Srrith stayed awake for a little longer, long enough to see the white stripes on the mountain tauninagas glow in the torchlight. As if tended to by ghosts, Mayve's cuts started to stitch themselves back together, and the human's breathing relaxed. Srrith used that fleeting comfort to drift to sleep.

* * *

Srrith awoke to sunlight pouring in through the paper screen door. Uncoiling with a disgruntled hiss, she hoped she did not keep Alactashi Sen waiting.

"Relax." Tressis slithered over with a plate of seared fish and Srrith's canteen, brimming with chilly mountain water. "They want to see you, but only when you are ready."

Srrith accepted the food, then raised the canteen to her mouth before she realized she had grabbed it with her injured arm. The movement was fluid and painless, the stiffness gone. Even the pockmarked scars where the Vent beast's fangs sank into her flesh were erased. Srrith rolled her shoulder and flexed her fingers painlessly, marveling at the potency of the mountain sfa-zrueen.

The Fae must have truly favored the mountain tauninaga, to gift them the power to heal. Their sfa-zrueen only produces miracles. For the first time since the Devaros Cataracts, nothing ached.

Someone appeared at the door, framed in morning light, and Mayve stepped inside. Her hair was matted wet against her shoulders, and her clothes were clean, even if they were still in partial tatters from the glint butcher's claws. Behind the rips in the linen, Srrith saw only bare, unmarked skin, not the bloody gashes that were there last night. It was as if someone else had worn that shirt when the glint butchers attacked, and Mayve was now simply borrowing it. The Oasis Stone hung from her belt in its oval leather pouch.

The human sat down cross-legged next to Srrith, accepting some more food from Tressis. Srrith gulped down the rest of her fish, then asked, "How are you feeling?"

"Better than I have in a while," Mayve replied between bites. "Every ache and pain is gone, and they didn't even leave scars."

Tressis hissed deep with gratitude. "I am glad to hear. We take great pride in the gift the Fae left us." He turned to Srrith. "I apologize for Lusa's behavior last night. It is unbecoming of a healer to put their fears before treatment."

Srrith nodded. "It is nothing I am not used to. Regardless, we thank you for your aid."

"It is our duty, and our honor," Tressis said. "Nevertheless, I've assigned her to scrape algae from the eastern canal for the day. She will take it as a learning experience, I hope."

"That pleases me," Srrith hissed with a smile.

"Is there anything you can't heal?" Mayve asked.

"We cannot regrow limbs, and many times cannot even save ones that have been severed. Fast-acting poisons are dangerous, killing far too quickly for the sfa-zrueen to begin, so we try to rely on natural antidotes for those. Sometimes, the body is far too mangled to heal, like with a fall from a great height or a particularly savage beast attack. In those cases, you'll live, but it won't be the same life as before," Tressis hissed. "I would recommend not getting injured if you can avoid it. The healing sfa-zrueen is as close to a miracle as we can get, but it's not perfect."

"It looks like a miracle to me. I think I was one step away from death yesterday—I barely remember arriving here."

"We thank you for your kind words, human," Tressis hissed, then turned to the door. "Please excuse me. We used the last of our coagulation salve last night, so I must collect more burn-blossom before the day goes long." He slithered through the open entrance and disappeared from view.

They ate in silence until the last of the food was gone. With each bite, the knot of guilt Srrith's chest grew, as if she was feeding it like a ravenous tapeworm. As Mayve finished her breakfast, Srrith hissed, "I am sorry, Mayve, for leading you through the Way of Echoes. I thought we could make it safely, and I failed."

Mayve looked a little paler, and said, "I understand why we had to. It was that, or die fighting Vrato and his soldiers."

"Maybe we could have hid on the mountainside until the Way of Waterfalls cleared. Or perhaps tried to hijack the coreskiff," Srrith hissed. "There was no easy way, but I made the decision and failed."

"You weren't counting on the lumitails flocking there."

"That's no excuse to me."

Mayve's heartbeat was calm, and the human took a deep breath before saying, "I should feel sadder, no? Last night, I was overwhelmed, and now, it feels muted. Is that wrong?"

"The mountain sfa-zrueen heals all wounds, physically and emotionally," Srrith said. "Your grief is sealed for now, but it is only temporary. Physical and emotional wounds are not too different. Ours will reopen the more we tear at them."

"It feels strange. This was the first morning in a long while that I did not think of my mother." The human mulled over her thoughts, and Srrith only let out a solemn hiss.

Hesitantly, Mayve asked, "With our wounds healed, can we return to Eiklo?"

The mention of the skeleton's name sent only a weak pulse of guilt through Srrith's chest, her sadness muted by the mountain sfa-zrueen. She shook her head. "As much as it pains me to say so, it is unsafe to travel back down with Vrato so close behind."

"But what if he's alive? What about Screech?"

"His bones glow when he is injured. If he is somehow alive in a tunnel of glint butchers, then only fate can save him. Screech's feather, perhaps, will last longer if her container is secure." Even through the mountain sfa-zrueen's-dampened grief, Srrith felt awful saying it out loud. "Even so, I promise I will return after Vrato is dealt with."

Mayve looked like she was dealing with the same thoughts, staring distantly at the hut's wall. Finally she asked, "Is the Great Seer ready for us?"

"She is." Srrith nodded. "It is time to seek answers."

"Good. If all this was for nothing, my emotional wounds will be ripped open pretty quickly."

They climbed down the eastern cliff, a babbling creek flowing down a gully next to the stone stairs. The steps joined with a large road at the same time the creek joined with the canal of crystal clear water, both running perpendicular to the stone bridges spanning the chasm.

Savin Actai was alive with activity. Jungle tauninaga swooped through the air, jumping from the cliffs to the goliath trees nestled in the middle. Mountain tauninaga scaled the cliffs, using their long claws to glide up the rock as easily as walking, and tauninagas of both kinds swam through the crystal clear canals, graceful as ribbons drifting in the wind. The sun, rising in a perfect arc over the chasm, made the undergrowth canopy glisten like a sea of molten emeralds.

At the first chance, Srrith slipped into the canal, swimming alongside the path as Mayve walked. She twisted through the water, letting her long journey wash away, basking in the purifying cold. As homeless as she felt, Savin Actai was the closest place to home she had.

Passing through the mist of a small waterfall, they crossed a bridge to the western cliff. The bridge was half canal, half stone walkway, and angled slightly so the water still flowed. Thanks to the system of canals, the tauninaga could swim practically anywhere. Water was more than a staple of tauninagan cities—most Ralverans did not know they were semiaquatic creatures. Even her birthplace, deep beneath the Crimson Tors, sat at the edge of a sunless lake.

She surfaced onto the road next to Mayve as they approached Alactashi Sen's dwelling, a one-story stone pagoda, partially buried into the cliffside it was carved from. It was surrounded by a luscious garden of trimmed jungle foliage and crystal clear pools, fed the rivulets running down the cliffs.

As they entered, they saw the one-room dwelling was far more spacious than it appeared outside, with substantial space carved out of the rock. The grotto was lit by paper lanterns floating amongst lily pads in pools of water. Tapestries depicting Savin Actai's history covered the walls, and vines covered the tapestries, tangling around the old artwork. On the far side, a huge platform of stone covered in a reed mat rose from the floor, and coiled upon it was Alactashi Sen.

A forest tauninaga, the Great Seer was covered in dark green scales patterned with brown stripes, and wore a gown of gray silk that draped over her scales, covering her completely when she was coiled up. Her thin, patterned head perked up at the sound of Srrith's scales sliding across the rock floor, and she stared in the direction of the door with milky, blind eyes.

Two other tauninaga flanked Alactashi, bickering amongst themselves. A jungle tauninaga with vibrant yellow-green scales, clad in leather armor decorated with leafy pauldrons and curling metal vines, and a mountain tauninaga with sky blue scales and the signature white stripe, clad in nondescript gray platemail. *Ressi and Zaatal. Unchanged, of course.*

Srrith and Mayve approached the trio. She gave both Ressi and Zaatal respectful nods, which were returned in kind, then coiled into a bow before Alactashi Sen. Mayve remained standing a little ways behind, wanting to remain unnoticed for as long as possible.

Alactashi Sen spoke first. Her hiss was soft, weakened by age, her heartbeat slow. "Welcome home, my dearest Srrith." She beckoned for Srrith to rise, her cloud eyes seeming to stare right into Srrith's mind, calming her worries. *I will have to tell her about the nightmares returning. She will know what to do, as she did before.*

Srrith uncoiled to stand eye level with Ressi and Zaatal. At full height, Srrith was a full head taller than Ressi, but was absolutely dwarfed by Zaatal. As they were all equals, they all stayed at Ressi's height.

"It is good to return," Srrith hissed. She extended a hand toward the human behind her. "This is Imayva, the human who carries the Oasis Stone. Mayve, this is Ressi and Zaatal, the leaders of the two clans that call Savin Actai home, and this is Alactashi Sen, the Great Seer."

Ressi and Zaatal gave Mayve two curt nods, and Alactashi Sen extended her hand to Mayve. The human, with what Srrith considered to be a disrespectful amount of skepticism, cautiously stepped forward and placed the Oasis Stone in Alactashi's outstretched palm.

"What is this?" Sen hissed, then her milky eyes grew wide. "Oh, the Stone! No, dear human, I was asking for your palm. You are the one who carries the Stone, not I."

"My apologies, Great Seer," Mayve said, taking the Stone back and giving Sen her palm. The Great Seer spent a silent moment tracing the lines on Mayve's palm, humming to herself under her breath. Seeming satisfied, she released Mayve's hand and said, "Welcome to Savin Actai, Imayva. It has been many years since we welcomed a human into our valley, but you do not owe us thanks. You have shown much courage and no shortage of trust to follow Srrith on such a long journey."

Mayve bowed, trying her best to match the tauninagan customs, and said, "Thank you for welcoming me here, and thanks to your sfa-zrueen for saving my life."

"Thank Zaatal and his mountain clan for that, dear. I was informed late last night that you two arrived, bloodied and delirious. Would you care to inform us why?"

Zaatal spoke, gruff and concise, in a low hiss. "Tressis reported claw marks, and glint butcher bite patterns. They took the Way of Echoes."

"It was a regretful decision on my part," Srrith hissed. "Merchatzi pursuing the Oasis Stone were within a stone's throw, and the Way of Waterfalls was overwhelmed by yesterday's storm. We were lucky enough to make it here, and unlucky enough to lose a friend in the caves."

"My scouts have reported sightings of soldiers scouring the mountains," Ressi said. Her voice hissed like a gentle summer breeze rustling through the canopy. "As well as unconfirmed sightings of some sort of flying vessel. Can you confirm these rumors?"

"I can confirm the craft exists, but I am unfamiliar with its details."

"It's called a coreskiff," Mayve said. "Invented by Citadel engineers within the last year or two. How it works is beyond me. I didn't get the chance to ask Eiklo about it..." She trailed off, but Ressi wasted no time in voicing her concerns.

"So if they're determined to find our city, they can do it with ease."

Zaatal hissed back, "Then the question is not whether they can find us, but whether they will attack us."

"If the Oasis Stone is that important to them, then they very well might."

"They'd have to be fools, or madmen!"

"They're led by a madman," Mayve said. "I'd bet a purse of teirs that they're more afraid of him than they are of you."

Ressi and Zaatal looked curious, shifting in their coils, their thin pupils narrowing even further. "A madman, you say?" Ressi hissed. "Tell us more."

Srrith heard Mayve's heartbeat increase as the two tauninagan leaders turned their eyes on her. The human took a deep breath, recalling the uncomfortable details about the masked man.

"He calls himself 'Zeteph' and holds some power in the Tyrak-Wenstnor Trade Coalition. A merchant guild that operates on the Devaros, if you are unfamiliar." Zaatal and Ressi nodded. "He is a skilled volcomancer, able to kill people with shadows that spring from his fingertips, and he desperately wants the Oasis Stone."

"You have talked with this Zeteph?" Ressi asked.

"Briefly. We were both captured in Port Wenstnor by his guild."

Srrith hissed, "He is seemingly unkillable. I'm also not able to deduce who or what he is, as he lacks a heartbeat and wears a mask at all times. Considering he survived hand-to-hand combat with Captain Vulinor of the Ferrymen, I'm inclined to think that he too is an Ul'Varin-Rak."

Mayve furrowed her brow. "Eiklo said that Ul'Varin-Rak always make fire when they manifest, and Ul'Varin-Zul always make ice. That would mean he's not Ul'Varin, or he is so talented at volcomancy that he can Innaturally Manifest."

"This creature is coming to Savin Actai?" Zaatal hissed.

"Not that we know of, but I would prepare regardless," Srrith said. "Although, we have confirmed that the Merchatzi are led by an exiled Dreaming Blade."

"A *traitor*?" The two tauninaga leaders hissed angrily, and Ressi spat on the ground. Srrith hastily added, "Not a tauninaga, simply a human with an illusion manifestation."

"Trained by the swamp, no doubt," Zaatal hissed.

"Yes, unfortunately," Srrith agreed. "Assassin aside, if Zeteph is coming, then your scouts must take caution. He will kill them with a glance, and they must not use their sfa-zrueen in his presence. I stalked him through the streets of Port Wenstnor, hidden from view, but when I called the shadows to wreath around me, it *alerted* him to my presence. Perhaps it is because my cave sfa-zrueen shares many similarities with his manifestations, but you must be cautious." Srrith shuddered at the memory of Zeteph's masked eyes staring into her soul, hidden from all others in the darkness but him.

Alactashi Sen hissed softly. She had yet to speak, but at the slightest hint of noise, Srrith and the other tauninaga held their tongues immediately.

With a raspy flick of her forked tongue, the Great Seer spoke, "Great leaders, if you wish to discuss the defense of our people, I ask that you step outside. No doubt, you have many preparations should the enemy fall from the sky upon us. Our friend Imayva has traveled a great distance to join us here, not to defend our city but to seek answers. I intend to use this time to answer those questions."

Judging by the heartbeats of the two tauninaga leaders, Srrith knew they still had many questions for both of them. She would take the time after to sate their knowledge, but Alactashi was right. Mayve had more than earned a right to know why she carried such a sought-after artifact all the way into the heart of the South Verdant.

"Akthoru take me," Zaatal whispered under his breath, then shot a glance at Srrith. He muttered, "Forgot you can hear me like that. Welcome back." Srrith hissed in amusement as he slithered away.

Ressi hissed out loudly, "Come join us when you are done, Srrith. The only way to defend against illusions is with someone who can see through them." With that, the two leaders exited the Great Seer's hall, bickering with one another.

As the stone door swung shut, Alactashi Sen hissed, "Before you speak, Imayva, know that you have earned the right to every question that I have answers for. I hope that you will feel enlightened by the end of our conversation."

"I hope so too," Mayve said. "This Stone has already cost me the lives of friends and family. If the journey is not worth that steep price, then I am not sure what I'll do."

Srrith agreed. If anyone had ever earned the right to talk to the Great Seer with such callousness, it was Mayve. The tauninaga remembered the flash of blue light as Eiklo slammed into the cave wall, the silhouette's of the butchers falling upon him. That emotional wound, sealed by the mountain sfa-zrueen, peeled open. She could not fathom how deep Mayve's wounds were. *First her mother, then Eiklo. Did I truly succeed on my quest to bring the Oasis Stone safely here? So many have suffered under my care.*

The Great Seer hissed in agreement with Mayve, blind eyes staring at nothing, then waved her withered hands, indicating for Mayve to proceed. The human upturned the Oasis Stone pouch into her palm, cradling the magnificent gem. With defiant purpose, she spoke. "What *is* the Oasis Stone?"

Alactashi Sen held out her hand again, this time for the Stone, and Mayve dropped it into her waiting palm. The Great Seer hissed, "When I was young, growing up in the Wekavan Meadowlands, with the energy of youth and working eyes, I would explore the abandoned palaces of the Fae, overgrown and crumbling in the furthest recesses of the woods. Many thought it was foolish to do so, believing anyone who sets foot inside to become deeply cursed, but I was not deterred. They are not cursed, simply hollow. The vibrant, empty towers sit patiently, waiting for their beloved inhabitants, who will never return."

She took a deep breath. "Of course, here I am, blind as a bat and cursed with the terrible gift of foresight, so perhaps they are as the legend says." Alactashi let out a wheezy chuckle. "There was little treasure to be found. The Fae took a great deal when they left, then the remains were picked clean by the Oemorgs, then the Legion, then by tomb robbers and bandits. But, the Fae were experts at keeping their secrets, and in my searches I discovered a great deal of hidden passages and rooms, inside which sat this book."

The Great Seer unwound, procuring a faded tome hidden in her coils. She handed it to Srrith with the same care as passing a sick baby. Srrith held it open between her and Mayve.

After flipping through a few pages, Mayve exclaimed, "It looks like a book of recipes?"

"That's exactly what it is, dear Imayva. A book of *alchemical* recipes. With all their innate sfa-zrueen, the Fae turned the natural world around them into miracles. Creations so powerful, they make the mixtures of the raptor herbalists look like a fresh hatchling threw garden clippings in their morning breakfast."

Alactashi's tail reached out, feeling for the book. Srrith held it up, and the Seer's tail flipped through the crumbling pages. She knew exactly what she wanted, turning to the page by memory alone. As the stiff parchment folded over, both Mayve and Srrith stared wide-eyed at the book.

"That's an Oasis Stone!" Mayve exclaimed. She held up the real Oasis Stone to the page, where the huge sapphire with its golden-etched runes was mimicked perfectly in ancient ink. "So it's not a weapon or a useless treasure, it's—"

"An ingredient, yes." Alactashi Sen hissed. "I have held this book for nearly all my years, and I haven't been able to read it for almost as long. But imagine my surprise when I had a vision about this very object, clutched in your hands."

All the strife over this Oasis Stone. Humans killing raptors killing Legion, just for an object that the Fae considered an ingredient. Srrith was taken aback. Why was everyone fighting for this if they had no idea what it was? Deep down, she had a grim suspicion that Zeteph knew what it was. So far, he seemed to know everything.

Mayve stared at the page, trying to decipher the description. "I can't read Fae. What about you, Srrith?"

"Unfortunately, no."

Alactashi hissed, amused, "Lucky for you, I am fluent, and I memorized the readings long ago out of fascination." She turned a few more pages gently with her tail, to the very last page of the book. Even though she was not fluent, Srrith could tell that this page was covered in mindless writings, with many iterations of the recipe crossed out and rewritten.

"This particular recipe right here—" She tapped the page delicately with the tip of her tail. "That is a recipe on how to quell a Scorch Vent."

The pair sat in silence, balancing the book between them, stunned with disbelief. Mayve spoke first. "Quell a Vent? To stop it from erupting?"

"According to the notes, it's more than that. The Vent would be silenced forever. No more monsters, no more lava or blizzards, no more Ventix Stratus. It would turn the Vent into a dormant obsidian mountain, nothing more."

Mayve gingerly flipped between the two pages. "Those words look similar enough. The Oasis Stone must be one of the ingredients to do this?"

"Precisely. Thank goodness the Oasis Stone fell into the hands of someone clever," Alactashi hissed. "The Oasis Stone is an amplifier. It can be added to almost any alchemical creation, boosting the effects to unparalleled powers. Without it, no concoction would be strong enough to quell a Vent."

"Why have you never mentioned this before?" Srrith almost shouted, raising her volume to a sharp hiss. "Scholars need to know about this. We could have had people searching for the Stone, for more information!"

"In my better days, I continued my search. But what would become of it? The recipe to quell a Vent is incredibly simple. The difficult part is *making* an Oasis Stone, which has never been detailed in any book I've found. It's the most complicated ingredient. Not to mention, this book only mentions Scorch Vents, it holds no promises of quelling a Frost Vent, which might be an even mightier task." She threw up her hands, the most movement Srrith had seen her make in years. It was evident the Great Seer was energized by this topic. "On top of all that, we would need eight Oasis Stones, one for each Scorch Vent. *Eight!* It took decades just for *one* to surface."

"It's not just that," Mayve said. "There are many out there who would not want the Vents destroyed. The Scorch Vents power the Citadels. If you're worried about Vrato coming here, those prissy nobles in their flying cities would send so many assassins for that book, you might as well just burn it now and save your own life."

"Mayve makes an excellent point," Alactashi hissed. "Not to

mention the Northern Ice raptors, who have built their lives studying the Ventix Stratus."

"And the Twelians, who might immediately die if the Ventix Stratus disappears," Srrith hissed, the ramifications becoming clear as day.

"At the very least, the Ul'Varin-Rak would be on our side," Alactashi said. "Every one of those skeletons would die again if it meant that the Vents would stop spewing cursed monsters into the air." She hissed softly.

Srrith saw Mayve freeze at the mention of the skeletons, and she patted her on the back with her tail. *She might need more sfa-zrueen from Tressis to help her sleep tonight.* She changed the topic. "Why was this recipe never tested?

"The date marked is in the eighty-ninth year of the Ashen Century. Do you remember your history well enough to remind me what happened then?"

Srrith grimaced. "The Wekavan Massacre. The Fae never got the chance."

The Seer nodded, and the room fell silent as everyone soaked in the new information they had. *All this time, we've carried something that can stop a Vent, and we're not even sure if we should use it. Should we not? The Vents are nothing but apocalyptic evil, but after all these years, many depend on them to survive. Do we change life as we know it to prevent a future apocalypse? They will erupt again. It is only a matter of time before the Paroxysm returns.*

Breaking the silence, Mayve asked, "What are the other ingredients, then?"

"There's only three, each one quite difficult to get. First, of course, is an Oasis Stone. So rare, this is the only one I've ever seen, and the recipe to make one is completely unknown to me, or perhaps anyone. It may be lost forever. It's like we have a recipe for making cake with icing, and the first ingredient is to already have a cake." The Great Seer hissed, her papery scales curling into a soft smile. "Lucky for us, we have one now."

"Second, you need rainthistle. This one is particularly aggravating. It used to grow in abundance in the Wekavan Meadowlands after each rainfall. It's a unique plant that absorbs sfa-zrueen, the only plant we know to do so." Her amused smile faded. "It's extinct now, except for one specimen on Citadel Waldheath, locked away in their greenhouses.

"The third and final ingredient is impossible to get. The blood of a Fae. You will have to find and raid a Fae tomb, of those buried before they left, and hope that there is something remaining in those bodies. Or, find where the Fae disappeared to." She chuckled as she hissed.

Srrith flicked her tongue, frustrated. *The power to stop a Vent in our hands, and we're simply too late. The Fae are gone. They were so close to saving us all, and instead they left us behind.*

She coiled up tighter, taking in all the information. "Forgive my forwardness, Alactashi, but if the task is impossible, why send me to retrieve Mayve and the Stone?"

Alactashi hissed, "You remember my vision, yes?"

"*A green-eyed girl drifts through an ocean of sand. Gallows swing from an arch of sandstone overhead. The green-eyed girl holds a stone as blue as the deep sea. Without it, we are all lost, for it is worth life itself.* Your heartbeat told me there was more, but I trusted your guidance. It led me to the Hangman's Swing in Devar, which was enough."

"I knew a lie would never work on you, but then again, you understand more than anyone that it is good to be in the dark sometimes," Alactashi Sen hissed. She turned her head in the direction of Mayve's voice. "You see, Imayva, my divination sfa-zrueen is stronger than most forest tauninagas, barring an exceptional few in the Forest of Twilight Waters. However, ever since I learned how to weave my sfa-zrueen, I have only been able to predict disasters."

Mayve's expression grew deadly serious. "Srrith told me that you foresaw me carrying the Stone. Does that lead to disaster or prevent it?"

"I withhold information from my visions because there would be panic if I did not, and in the work of preventing disasters, panic only hinders. In your case, however, we simply did not know you. All we had was a face and a location. It very well might have been that you would love to see the world burn."

Srrith caught Mayve's eyes. "Fortunately for us, you have proved yourself to be a worthy and caring ally, despite all the hardships you've been through." Mayve averted her eyes toward one of the floating lanterns drifting by.

Alactashi turned her blind gaze toward the dim, rocky ceiling, and let out a long, low hiss as she gathered her thoughts before speaking. *"A green-eyed girl drifts through an ocean of sand. Nine gallows swing from an arch of sandstone overhead. Each carries a different folk of Ralvera. Human and Ul'Varin. Raptor and Oaken Legion. Oemorg and Cavernfolk. Twelian and Torn and Tauninaga. We hang together, silent and dead. Our skin is charred black and our faces covered in frost, eyes encased in ice and mouths frozen open in an eternal scream. The green-eyed girl holds a stone as blue as the deep sea. Without it, we are all lost, for it is worth life itself. She stands on the precipice of an erupting Scorch Vent, nothing more than a silhouette amidst the fire and ash."*

The room fell silent. Srrith's mouth felt bone-dry. No stranger to Alactashi's visions, she had seen the Great Seer predict many disasters. A landslide that carried several dwellings off the western cliffside. Hurricane winds that brought down a goliath tree. A heavy rainfall that caused a flash flood over the lower bridges. A Vent erupting...that was destruction of a different kind. If even just one Vent erupted, the death toll would be insurmountable. It had been centuries since the Paroxysm, when the Vents last erupted. If it were possible to even *cause* that to happen, who would commit such a heinous act?

Zeteph.

She bared her fangs. "If an Oasis Stone can quell a Vent, then we can only assume it can erupt one as well. That *must* be what Zeteph wants."

Mayve's eyes grew wide and she leapt up. "The second ingredient, rainthistle? Found only on Citadel Waldheath?"

"Yes, that's right," Sen hissed.

"When I stole the monstrous seeds from Zeteph, back in Devar, the seed packets were marked with a blade of wheat crossed with a sword. The symbol of Citadel Waldheath!"

Srrith flared her hood, arriving at the same conclusion. "They're going to bring the monstrous seeds to Citadel Waldheath! In a single blow, he'll take down a Citadel and destroy the only plant that can quell a Vent, or claim it for himself!"

"Exactly!" Mayve paced back and forth. "That explains the Oaken Legion involvement. The Citadels are the only power in Ralvera that can contest the Legion—it would be a victory for them as well. If the

Vents erupt, the Legion will be safe in their Verdant bastions while the raptors of the ice and sand perish."

Srrith hissed, "But Zeteph spoke about the Vents with such hatred. Why would he erupt them? Are we sure that silhouette is Zeteph?" Her thoughts crashed together. They were still missing important information. Information that Zeteph likely already had.

Mayve shrugged. "Erupt or quell, either way it hurts the Citadels, and it helps the Legion."

"I understand why the Legion is involved, but what does *Zeteph* want from all this? More power for the Coalition?" Srrith hissed. "We still do not know his intentions."

"And do you know if he wants to destroy the rainthistle, or use it himself? It is a powerful plant in its own right," Alactashi hissed, "Knowing this, what do you two intend to do about it?"

Srrith and Mayve looked at each other for answers. *What can we do about it? Hide the Oasis Stone and hope it's never found? Zeteph may never get the Stone, but if he gets the rainthistle, we have no hope of quelling any Vent. As long as we have the Oasis Stone and the rainthistle safe, we could work on finding Fae's blood, or substituting it.* She saw the same questions reverberate through Mayve's mind. *Does Mayve even want to carry the Stone anymore? She's gone through so much.*

The moment of contemplation lasted long enough for Alactashi to intervene. "I think it is wise for everyone to consider what it is *they* want, before we arrive at something hasty. Mayve, dear, how about you take the Oasis Stone up to the Peak of Blossoms and meditate with it, perhaps camp there for the night? You have had such a long journey with such little time to yourself. You need solitude, and I would prefer you and the Stone to be safely hidden should the Merchatzi attack."

Mayve thought it over. "I think I would like that."

Srrith was surprised. She thought Mayve would want to stay and fight, but looking at the human more closely, she saw why. She was exhausted and numb. *Savin Actai is not her city. If she no longer wants to carry the Stone, then she should not die for it. Her part in this prophecy is already over; it is up to her if she wishes to continue.*

Alactashi Sen hissed, "Excellent. Zaatal will show you the trailhead. It's a hard climb, I hope that's alright for you." Srrith heard Mayve's heartbeat perk up at the mention of climbing. The Seer turned to her. "Srrith, as you already know, the leaders need your help with preparations for the Dreaming Blade."

"It is already on my mind, Great Seer. We thank you for your time."

"No, I thank both of you for your trust and your tribulations. Mayve, Zaatal should be just outside. Hopefully he has not wandered far. Srrith, may I speak with you privately for just a moment?"

Mayve, understanding her dismissal, bid them farewell and left. Once the door to the dwelling closed, Srrith coiled next to Alactashi, happy to once again be in the presence of the one tauninaga who never thought ill of her.

Alactashi hissed, "Your journey has ailed you, my dear. I am sorry, I knew the vision was of importance, but I never saw how wrought with peril it would truly be. I never thought I could be more proud of you, yet you surprise me every time."

Srrith coiled low, bringing her eye level below Alactashi's. "Your vision was dire. I could not fail."

"We are lucky Mayve is strong. But I can tell she has been through more than most. Enough to break a weaker human," the Seer hissed.

"She lost her mother to Zeteph's monstrosities, the night our journey began," Srrith said. "Then the Way of Echoes claimed another of our friends. That was my own fault."

"Does she blame you?"

"She might, in time."

"Are you okay, my dear Srrith?"

"No. I do not think so."

"Have the nightmares returned?"

"They come closer every night."

"You are stronger than them." Alactashi placed a hand on Srrith's smooth forehead.

"I used to think so. Then I fought Zeteph, and he turned my fear sfa-zrueen against me. I am afraid again, Great Seer. I am afraid to dream. I still practice everything you've taught me, yet the nightmares still chase me."

Sen placed her hands on Srrith's shoulders and touched their foreheads together. "No matter how prepared you are, your mind can always wander down the darkest paths. That is *never* your fault," she hissed. "Have your dreams hurt anyone?"

"Not yet."

"Then you are still stronger," Alactashi said, reassuringly. "Remember everything I've taught you. I will be gone soon, and you'll need to protect those you love."

Gone? Srrith looked into the milky eyes of the Great Seer, hood flared. "What have you seen?"

"The forest sfa-zrueen gave me another vision as I dreamed last night. One I knew that I would eventually have. Today is my last day, Srrith. Vrato is coming for me."

Chapter 47

Eight Kings' Way

Raudius did not expect riding a horse to be so pleasant. Elk riding was a requirement of his training at the Bastion of Growth, and both beasts handled in a similar fashion, but the horse seemed so much studier, and was so much more maneuverable without antlers.

His horse was named Rhino—courtesy of Cindri—who named it for its gray coat and several white dots along its snout that *could* represent horns if viewed from a very creative perspective. Raudius had never seen a rhino, but Cindri assured him it was an apt name. Down the road behind him, Cindri rode on the speckled beige horse, who he named Sandy, for obvious reasons.

Eight Kings' Way was a well-traveled road, and they passed a few travelers every day heading toward Port Wenstnor, mostly merchants. A raptor and a Legion soldier traveling together invoked the strangest of stares, but Raudius did not care as long as they did not encounter the Legion or the Merchatzi. The mountains grew taller and taller as they wound their way deeper into the heart of the Azraks. Around every bend, he hoped to see the rock cairn that marked the trailhead to the Way of Waterfalls, but they had no luck so far.

Hooves clopped against the worn stones as Cindri gained on him, pulling Sandy alongside Rhino. The raptor's orange plumage blazed like a wildfire amid the sea of green leaves, and he was attentively pouring small vials of crushed leaves and drops of extract into a spherical wooden casing while he rode.

"Can we switch horses?" The raptor asked.

"We can, but why?"

"I'm worried I'm starting to bond with Sandy."

"Excuse me?"

"Bond. I haven't bonded with an animal yet, and next year would be the year if I were with the tribe."

"I've heard that word many times. Bonding is why all those animals followed your war party?"

"Yessir, those were all their bonds. Every raptor can bond, but for us desert raptors it's a part of our culture. We need the animals to survive, far more than the ice raptors, Northern or Southern."

"And when the bonded animal dies, do you bond with another one?"

"They don't! Bonding grants the creature an extended lifespan. They usually live as long as their bond. Don't ask me how, I don't know. You'll have to ask the Northern Ice raptors, they've done studies on it."

Raudius opened his mouth, then held his tongue. He wanted to ask about all the bonded animals that the slaughtered war party left behind, but then he remembered Spotch's lone sabertooth that prowled around their camp before disappearing into the desert. *Cindri won't want to think about that and neither do I.* He thought about Borgo. *I hope that stinky oaf is too dumb to be sad.*

He drew in the reins and pulled Rhino to a stop, dismounting onto the road. "Alright, get off, then. No bonding with our horses, they can't follow us into the mountains."

"My worries exactly." Cindri dismounted. Sandy shook her mane, and Rhino let out a comfortable whinny as the raptor climbed into his saddle. *The animals do seem far more comfortable with Cindri than me. The raptors have a strange connection to the animals around them.* The Oaken Legion touted itself as being the protectors of nature, the last bastions of defense from the Vent's scourge. But, the more he traveled with Cindri, the more clear it was that they were not the only ones who revered the land they lived on.

Remounted, they set off side by side down the road at a brisk trot, looking to gain some ground on Imayva and her companions. He still had no idea how they were to get into Savin Actai itself, but hopefully the promise of information and aid would convince the human to accept them. If they arrived at the city too late, Mayve might already have left, and he doubted the tauninaga would point them in the right direction.

"Do you like the South Verdant?" Cindri asked, grinding some herbs with a mortar and pestle that he pulled from his satchel.

"Hmm?" Raudius barely heard the question, pulled from his thoughts.

"The South Verdant. Is it different from the North?"

"It's warmer," Raudius said, thinking of his homeland. "Different trees."

"Ah. I'd like to be cold in the daytime some day, like in the snowy forests up north. Seems so strange to have the sun shining down and still be freezing."

"It would quickly grow old for a desert native like you."

"Maybe." Cindri mixed a few more vials together, then steered Rhino closer and smeared a dollop of the purple paste onto the back of Raudius's neck.

"Vent-cursed fucking raptor, what are you doing?" Raudius tried to wipe it off and Cindri yelled, "Don't let it touch the horse!"

"What is this shit?" Raudius carefully wiped the paste onto the leaves of a passing branch, overhanging the road.

"Does it burn?"

Raudius sat there, focusing on his bark. "No."

"What about up here?" Cindri tapped his skull. "Any dizziness, slowed thoughts?"

"No?"

"Fantastic results." Cindri tossed Raudius a rag from his saddlebag.

This Vent-cursed lizard is using me for experiments! Raudius growled, "You *cannot* test your concoctions on me."

"It will help later! I was very confident you'd have minimal side effects."

Raudius wiped the remaining paste into the rag, then handed it back to Cindri. "Minimal." He snorted.

"It's a good thing you hurt yourself so much, I think I'm getting a solid grasp on what plants I can and can't use on a Legion soldier."

Raudius grunted his displeasure and turned his attention to the road. Underneath dappled, sunlit leaves, the road curved between the Azraks' sharp foothills like a dirt river. Warblers chirped away the afternoon, hidden in the green underbrush, and a breeze rustled his branches along with those of the passing trees. He was deep in the Verdant now. Deep in Oaken Legion territory.

He never thought he would feel so uneasy in a forest. A Legion soldier in full timbersteel, eying the tree line like a common bandit. As if touching an old scar, he reached up and brushed the Hope's Gauntlet symbol etched into the pauldron of Yuetrix's armor and wondered if he should remove it. *If I come across more Hope's Gauntlet soldiers, it might help. Maybe they'll think I'm one of them.*

He steeled his gaze, glaring at no one but the forest. *That's a coward's choice. I'd rather die cutting them down than pretend to be one.* He looked at Cindri riding next to him and asked, "Do you have anything that can eat away at timbersteel? Nothing that would truly damage my armor, just enough to wipe away this etching?"

Cindri leaned over in his saddle and scratched at the pauldron with a claw. "Perhaps. Will need to mix some things. I say this respectfully, raptors usually try to melt timbersteel, not clean it."

The raptor rummaged through his satchel, dropping pinches of herbs and rocks into vials of liquid. Satisfied, he wet a cloth and draped it over the Hope's Gauntlet emblem. "Let that sit for a bit and don't touch it. Unlike the paste, I'm certain this one will sting you."

"Thank you for the warning this time." Raudius took a deep breath of the Verdant air, trying to get the familiar smell of the forest to calm him. A sharp, acrid scent from the rag bit at his nose and coated the top of his mouth.

"Is that your tribe's symbol?" Cindri asked.

Without looking over, Raudius grunted, "Not quite. Some soldiers choose to wear it, like the one who gave me this armor."

"Ah." Beneath them, the horses' hooves clopped against soft dirt. "Do you have a tribe? Or a family? Whatever you call them."

"Yes."

"What's their name?"

"We're the Fenmors. It's not a tribe, just a family. A grove, as we call it back home."

Cindri snarled, "The Fenmors? Like that old general?"

"Exactly like him. That was my grandfather."

"The one who massacred all the raptors in the Daro Sands?"

"There was no massacre. Raiders were threatening Gloomwall and he led a successful campaign to drive them out." Raudius trotted a few more yards before realizing that Cindri had pulled in Rhino's reins and halted in the middle of the road. Turning Sandy around, he yelled back, "I'm not debating history. Come on, we have to keep moving."

Cindri looked furious. "You can't argue about history if you don't know it. The Daro tribe were peaceful. General Fenmor drove them into the Quicksand Sea and slaughtered everyone who did not drown."

"This is why I don't want to argue, I knew from the start we have different versions of history."

"One of them has to be true, right?"

"Whichever one is true, I doubt we'll figure it out here. Neither of us were alive for it."

"There were no 'raiders' trying to reach Gloomwall. They were looking for asylum from your marauding army."

Raudius grimaced. "A horde of raptors was descending on our city, so we fought back."

"You must mean a horde of refugees was descending on a tauni-nagan city! What was the name of Gloomwall before you occupied it? Do you even know?" Cindri's voice was rising, and Raudius felt the Oakfire flare deep in his chest.

"We were in Gloomwall *because* you were invading," he seethed. "You expect us to not defend our territory?"

"Oh! I see! You were just occupying it for your own defense. Well, every raptor in the Daro Sands is dead. We're done invading! Surely that means you left that city, right?"

Raudius snorted and wheeled Sandy around. Cindri urged Rhino forward, cantering up next to him. "No! Your Legion is *still* there, all these decades later. That's why we're talking about the Legion outpost of Gloomwall, and not the tauninagan city of *Savin Vesso!*"

He snapped at Cindri, "That's not what I was taught. If we want to talk about atrocities committed during the war, let's make camp right now and I'll talk all night about your *refugees.*"

Cindri's feathers flared like a lion's mane and he growled, "Who do you think you should believe? My people, who have passed down the stories word for word? Or your people, whose symbol you're trying to wipe off your fucking armor." He kicked his heels into Rhino, who galloped up the road in a cloud of dust.

Oakfire ripping up his veins, Raudius clenched the reins so tightly that the bark on his knuckles cracked. Cindri already out of earshot, he caught his words in his throat and swallowed them, trying to calm down.

You're not angry at Cindri. You're angry that he might be right. He took a deep breath of Verdant air and tried to quell the Oakfire.

Gingerly, Raudius peeled the acidic rag off his armor and chucked it into the woods. Running his fingers across the pauldron, the Hope's Gauntlet symbol was gone, leaving a smooth patch in the middle of the rough timbersteel.

He wanted to sit back and enjoy his travel in silence, but a knot in his chest forced him, almost against his will, to spur Sandy into a canter, gaining on Cindri. The raptor didn't turn as Raudius rode up alongside. They rode quietly for even longer, with only the plod of hooves and chirp of birds breaking the silence.

Finally, Raudius forced out a grunt. "It worked."

Cindri glanced at his armor, the symbol gone. "I knew it would."

A familiar sound of eerie rushing wind pricked Raudius's ears, and he snapped his eyes to the sky, searching. His sudden movement startled Cindri, who followed Raudius's gaze.

A coreskiff ripped overhead, following the Eight Kings' Way from the sky. Wide-eyed, Cindri exclaimed, "What in the depths was that? It looked like a mechanical Vent beast!"

"A coreskiff," Raudius said. "I got to ride in one of the first ones, invented at Citadel Ashfell two years ago."

"It was so fast!"

"It's an impressive piece of technology. Citadel engineers are the best there are."

The sound of roaring wind started growing again, and Raudius realized too late that the coreskiff had turned around. Before he could even shout to Cindri to run, the vessel was hovering overhead, huge wings blotting out the sun.

Raudius reached for his helmet, and Cindri tossed him a fresh cloth rag. "Cover your nose and mouth this, I was making these for this exact moment." He palmed one of the wooden casings he had been filling with different plants, a small rope fuse dangling from the top.

"We cannot run for it, the coreskiff is too fast." Raudius said.

"Sandy and Rhino won't be doing much running after this anyway."

"Cindri, what are you going to do?"

"What if we take the coreskiff? Did Citadel Ashfell teach you how to fly it?"

"Not exactly. We need to run." Raudius knew they could not. *The coreskiff can follow us until our horses tire, unless we lose them in the woods.* The thought of galloping at breakneck pace through the dense forest was just as much a deathtrap as staying.

Cindri snarled, partially nervous and partially excited. "You know we can't, so trust me on this."

A metallic buzzing sounded from above the trees like a swarm of angry bees, then a full cohort of Coalition Merchatzi, armor glittering in steel, golds, and purples, rappelled down from the coreskiff on ropes attached to their belts. Raudius wrapped the cloth tightly around his nose and mouth, then clicked the two halves of his timbersteel helmet around his head. In the corner of his eye, he saw Cindri light a fuse, and whisper an apology to Rhino.

In a chorus of thuds and clanks, the Merchatzi surrounded them. One of them strode forward and shouted, "A raptor with orange plumage and a lone Oaken Legion soldier. Lucky us, two bounties traveling together. Both of you are wanted by the Tyrak-Wenstnor Coalition. Dismount and surrender, or we will take you by force."

Raudius looked at Cindri, waiting for his signal, and Cindri shrugged back. "Looks like they got us, nothing else to do but turn ourselves in." They grabbed their gear and swung out of their saddles. The guards converged on them, bringing them all comfortably into the blast zone.

There was a muffled boom from Rhino's saddle, and a purplish-brown cloud of thick smoke burst out, blanketing the road and mushrooming up toward the coreskiff. Shouts erupted from all directions, and Raudius sprinted for the nearest guard. The commanding soldier drew his sword, then slumped forward, dangling from the rope on his belt like a limp puppet. One guard managed to grab Cindri, then his eyes rolled in his head and he collapsed backward, spinning on his rope.

Raudius held his breath and drew his own sword, grabbed the rope, and cut the guard away, who slumped onto the ground with the rest of his troop. Through the smoke, he saw Cindri leap onto a sleeping guard like a step stool and give the rope a sharp tug. With the buzz of a pulley, the raptor and the unconscious guard started to ascend to the coreskiff. Raudius did the same, and immediately was zipped into the air.

They rose from the smoke like two birds bursting through a cloud, wisps of purple haze following their wake. The deck of the coreskiff rapidly approached, and once it was within reach, Raudius grabbed the railing and swung over, sword in hand.

Just over the railing was a crewman, winch in hand, clearly expecting the Coalition guard he had lowered, not an Oaken Legion soldier. Raudius threw his momentum into a swift punch to the skull that knocked the crewman to the deck, timbersteel gauntlet lacerating the man's cheek.

From the other side of the coreskiff, Cindri vaulted over the railing and onto the shoulders of another unsuspecting crewman who was winching him up. Riding the human's shoulders, he stuffed a rag over his mouth and nose, and the human fell limp after a brief, pathetic struggle. Another crewman rushed Cindri, who dodged under the man's clumsy attempts to catch him, grabbed one of the nearby ropes, clipped it to the man's belt, and drop-kicked him over the railing. With a scream, the man swung overboard and into the purple cloud below.

Looking around, Raudius and Cindri saw the remaining crew was only several humans strong, and pitifully unarmed. Raudius leveled his sword and shouted, "Everyone overboard, now!"

The terrified crew looked down at the purple haze, the silhouettes of crumbled bodies littering the road, and froze. Cindri shouted, "Don't worry, you'll live. Just listen to the Legion tree with the sword, and you'll have a pleasant four- to sixteen-hour nap."

Raudius unlatched his shield from his back and locked it into his gauntlet, slamming his blade against it. "The sleep cloud or the blade, you have three seconds to choose. Three! Two—"

The remaining crew scrambled for the ropes, not bothering to secure themselves safely. The pulleys whirred, followed by a smattering of thumps as the crew members collapsed into the fog. Shield and sword raised, Raudius approached the door of the coreskiff's enclosed cabin, smashing it open with the heel of his boot. Another human, dressed in a plain linen tunic, charged Raudius with a scream, knife drawn. A pathetic attempt against his timbersteel. Raudius snapped the blade with one swipe of his shield and sprawled the man flat on his back.

Raudius planted a heavy timbersteel boot on the man's chest and lifted his chin with the flat of his blade, drawing a prick of blood on his neck. Cindri slunk in and knelt beside the man, flashing his maw of sharp teeth. Raudius spoke, plainly and coldly. "Are you the man who flies this vessel?"

The human beneath him gave the tiniest nod he could without drawing more blood onto the sword. Cindri snarled with a toothy grin, "There's been a change in the crew, but no need to worry about that. You get to stay!"

Stammering for breath under the crushing weight of the Oaken Legion soldier, the man gasped, "Where...where do you want to go?"

"You know this area well?"

The man nodded.

"Then we'll go to Savin Actai."

Chapter 48

The Peak of Blossoms

"Halfway up the slope you will come to a crossroad, marked by a cairn. Take the left path, and you will summit around sunset. Only mountain tauninaga take the right path, it is impassable for all other folk."

Zaatal had no idea he was goading Mayve into taking the right path, especially when he clicked his long mountain tauninagan claws together, as if reinforcing his point. Razor-sharp and hard as stone, they were evolved for scaling any vertical wall with perfect grace.

When Mayve had reached the cairn, she remembered thinking, *If it's difficult, I'll turn around.*

That is how she found herself clinging to a sheer rock wall yet again, the wind ripping through her clothes, plastering her hair to her face. Her green eyes studied the rock intently, searching for her next hand-hold. Long crimson-and-gray ribbons, used to mark the trail, streamed in the wind from pitons hammered into the rock. They showed the safest path up the cliff, *for mountain tauninaga.*

The view up there was maybe the most spectacular Mayve had seen yet. The gray mountain peaks towered above the jungle below, covered in bare rock and alpine shrubs. Above, a layer of white clouds blocked sight of the summit and the path ahead. Zaatal said the Peak of

Blossoms was the highest point in the Azrak Mountains, and she was determined to see it all from the top.

She took the right path partially for the challenge, and partially to stick it to the mountain tauninaga, but there was a third reason she was frightened to admit. The adrenaline and the focus required to not plummet to her death—it all distracted her from thinking about Eiklo. From thinking about the Ferrymen, and her mother. She felt the wounds reopening in her mind—flashes of their faces, glimpses of the last time she saw them.

Mayve dug her fingers into the rock and shook the images from her mind. *Focus, or you'll join them.*

All along the rock were tiny, needle-sized pinpricks in the rock, as if a woodpecker got lost and decided to hunt for bugs on the cliffside. It occurred to Mayve dangerously late that those were marks left by mountain tauninaga claws, as they climbed paths completely inaccessible to humans. The tauninaga often crawled across smooth, windswept surfaces using their claws alone, forcing Mayve to find creative new pathways between the ribbon trail markers.

A few careful steps later, Mayve pulled herself into the layer of clouds. The moisture cooled her burning muscles, and she took a second to support herself by her feet, resting her arms one by one. She relished in the numb feeling that crept up her spine whenever she dangled hundreds of feet above the ground.

For peace of mind, she checked that everything on her belt was still with her, including the Oasis Stone. A gemstone powerful enough to kill a Vent, and the Great Seer wanted her to carry it wherever she went, even up a mountain. She shook that thought from her mind as well. Another distraction she could not afford to think about.

Fully engulfed in the clouds, she noticed something dark looming above her. It was the pathway itself, arching into a sharp overhang. The telltale marks of mountain tauninaga covered the underside, and she saw a crimson-gray ribbon snapping in the wind at the edge of the overhang.

It was becoming all too obvious why Zaatal told her to take the left path. She had climbed the underside of the Devar Arch many times, but she relied heavily on the anchored ropes of the Locks dangling underneath. There was nothing on this overhang to help her. Just a ceiling of bare rock.

If it's difficult, I'll turn around. What a lie that was. Slowly but surely, the tilt of the overhang grew treacherously steep. Gravity shifted from pulling on her feet to pulling on her back, threatening to rip her from the rock like brushing a spider off the ceiling.

She dug her boots into the rock, wedging them against whatever surfaces she could find. Her legs no longer supported her—at this angle she just needed to wedge them somewhere so her arms were not carrying the whole weight of her body. Arm by arm, foothold by foothold, she crawled upside down into open air.

It was halfway up, when she was horizontal against the rocky ceiling, that her right foot slipped, and just like that, she swung into open air.

Instantly, her arms lit on fire, her grip almost tearing away. Her entire body weight hung on her fingers, dug into the rock above her. She tried to swing her legs back to the rock, her shoulders burning, but the wind caught her like a sail and wrenched her away from the rock face each time. She reached for another handhold to try and reposition herself, but the rock crumbled as she applied weight, falling past her and vanishing into the clouds. Mayve dangled by one hand over the mist, her grip on the verge of failing.

Seemingly on instinct, she trapped the Du'ul, feeling the warmth of her Darkmist dwelling, envisioning her skin as the iron of Dreva's stove, strong enough to hold the power of the Vents inside. As the energy rushed through her, her grip returned, and she moved hand over fist toward the edge, legs dangling uselessly in the clouds. She reached the edge of the overhang, the pathway curving back into a vertical climb, and her boots found purchase in the rock. With a heave, she pulled herself up and onto the ledge above, collapsing to the mist-covered stone.

Quickly, she manifested the Du'ul through her hands, half expecting something to happen after that ordeal, but just like all the other times, she simply felt the energy drain away. Catching her breath, she looked for the next trail marker, fluttering in the wind, and resumed her climb, her recent scare already forgotten. If she paused longer, her thoughts would catch up with her.

The air grew brighter with every step as the cloud layer thinned and sunlight filtered through. Then the sky was clear, and Mayve heaved herself onto the summit.

The Peak of Blossoms was an island in the clouds, just tall enough to break through the cloud layer. Warm afternoon sunlight fought bravely against the chill of the high-altitude winds, burning away the moisture of the fog that clung to Mayve's skin. The summit itself was no more than a collection of boulders, balanced atop the sharp cliffs, and a crimson-gray ribbon whipped atop a metal spear, driven into the highest rock.

At the center of the summit, clinging to the crags and shrouded by large boulders on three sides, was a small, gnarled tree. It was a bent spiral of gray bark, never breaching the height of the boulders that sheltered it from the battering winds. The gray branches split into many reaching tendrils, each adorned with red, orange, and pink blossoms.

Sure-footed, Mayve crossed the boulders with the ease of walking down a flat road, then dropped into the tree's recess. She found it surprisingly warmer, with the wind's assault blocked and the sun beating down above. The tree itself looked pitiful, clinging to life in a place it should not be, and barely grew above four or five feet tall. At its base, a pool of crystal clear water bubbled up from within the mountain, emptying into a tiny stream that wandered underneath the boulders to the edge, where the wind caught it and swiftly dispersed it into the clouds. Petals drifted across the surface of the water like colorful boats, sailing with the current until they were sent floating into the wind.

Eager to rest, Mayve crawled underneath the tree, finding a tauninaga-sized reed mat underneath a blanket of old petals. She splayed out on her back, looking up through the radiant branches into the blue sky beyond. The colorful canopy almost reminded her of the Silt Row Market, and how the sun would filter through the fabric of the tents. The very first time she went, Dreva held her hand through the crowd and they wove between the rainbow ocean until they found a tent that sold sweets. Years later, Mayve realized her mother would stash coins for weeks before the trips to make sure she could always buy something for Mayve.

She remembered scrambling across the nearby rooftops with Spotch and Ingo, each with their pockets full of whatever caught their eye. They'd all crash through the door of an abandoned Outer Sands dwelling and divide their haul amongst them, sharing the pilfered food with their sabertooth cubs and laughing amongst themselves. The raptors joined the Coinclaws later that year, drifting away from her. Changing into what they were, when Spotch died.

Mayve sat up cross-legged and looked at her reflection in the pool. She was surprised she could recognize herself. Her dark hair was longer than she usually wore it. Dreva was the one who would cut it when it got too long. Her smooth olive skin was untouched by the journey, but her piercing green eyes seemed darkened. The wind rushed over the hideaway, catching a burst of petals from the tree. For the first time since she stole the Oasis Stone, she was alone.

With no more distractions, Mayve's thoughts finally flooded in, and her tears flowed freely. Wrapping the shawl around herself, she huddled underneath the blossoms, her mind drifting from her mother, to Eiklo, to the Ferrymen and the raptors. There had been so much loss, and no moments to grieve until now. When she descended the mountain, she would have to be strong again. She hoped Srrith was okay. The tauni-naga had her people to protect her. Mayve only had Srrith now.

Her tears flowed faster between deep, shaky breaths. She thought of Eiklo, bones lost in the darkness below. He deserved so much more. It should have been her that was taken by the glint butchers. Did she even care about the Oasis Stone? Eiklo did. She felt a blaze of energy as she inadvertently trapped the Du'ul between breaths.

Mayve let it manifest from every pore, trapping and manifesting with each breath, letting the Du'ul fade back into the world. *Eiklo joined us, wishing to uncover the truth of the Stone and help us wherever that path led, and we led him to die in a cave.* Tears poured in rivers down her cheeks. *If I can quell at least one Vent, then he won't have died for nothing.* The Du'ul swelled within her, and she mouthed the words, "I'll quell the Vents, for Eiklo and for Dreva." The Du'ul roared within her. Even in the middle of the Verdant, she was absorbing more than she thought she could.

Instead of punching the air, or trying to breathe fire, she simply sat and waited, meditating in the Ventix Stratus. *Eiklo always preached the virtues of patience, and I finally have nowhere to go. I'll only get in Srrith's way if Vrato appears.*

As the sun dipped toward the horizon, Mayve fell into a cycle. Breathe in, trap, breathe out, manifest. She focused on trapping just enough Du'ul that she could manifest it all in one breath. When she found that balance, each breath in felt like a rush of fire, and each breath out felt like the calm exhaustion just before drifting off to sleep. She trapped more and more Du'ul with each breath, until the energy of the Vents within her felt like a roaring inferno, barely contained by her mortal skin.

Suddenly, she was trapping so much Du'ul with each inhale, she had to force it out of her when she exhaled. Her senses were screaming, her heart pounding in her ears, her vision sharpened to grating clarity. She rolled from beneath the tree and ran up to the summit, the sunset painting the sea of clouds orange.

I'm manifesting more Du'ul than I ever have, something should be happening. Why is nothing happening! She threw a punch. Nothing. She screamed into the wind. Still nothing. She *felt* herself manifesting this energy, where was it *going*? She tried to throw a rock with her mind, twist the air into an illusion, whip the sea of clouds into a raging tornado. Nothing.

Her arms fell limp at her sides in defeat. With each pant, she still trapped and manifested, afraid to let the energy disappear. The power of the Vents twisted her stomach into sickening rage, and she yelled into the wind, "What am I good for! Why does everyone around me die! What can I *do*?"

The wind did not respond. In her frustration, she picked up a rock and hurled it off the summit. With a shrieking whistle, the stone whipped into the sky like a cannonball, puncturing a hole in a cloud drifting by.

Mayve stumbled backward, almost falling off the boulder she was standing on. Her arm vibrated like an enraged beehive. She manifested through her arm again, and threw another rock. It shrieked away into the sunset like a roaring coreskiff. Her eyes grew wide, and she grabbed a larger rock, this one twice the size of her head. For a second, it weighed nothing in her hand, then her Du'ul ran out and it nearly pulled her arm from its socket as it fell. She manifested again, picking the boulder back up like a piece of parchment.

What in the depths is happening? This isn't like any manifestation that Eiklo described.

She chucked the rock as if tossing a pebble into a pond, watching it arc away into the cloud layers. Clenching her fist, she curiously eyed a boulder three times her size.

It's good that the mountain tauninaga are healers, because this will really hurt if I'm wrong. She manifested all the Du'ul into her fist and punched the boulder. With a momentous *crack*, the massive rock exploded into dust and rubble.

Holy gods, Phovus, anyone! She planted her foot on another boulder and manifested through her leg, shoving the boulder. It shot forward and crashed over the edge of the mountain, no harder than kicking tumbleweed.

All the training Eiklo put her through to grow her capacity for the Du'ul was paying off. She still had plenty of power to keep trapping and manifesting. Caught in her own curiosity, Mayve pushed the Du'ul through her legs and jumped. In an instant, the Peak of Blossoms shrank beneath her as she soared up through the sunset air, the blossoming tree nothing more than a red dot. At the peak of her jump, gravity caught her, then tugged with full force, ripping her back toward the mountain.

Realizing the danger far too late, as usual, Mayve plummeted toward the mountain. By instinct, she trapped the Du'ul and manifested it through her whole body, hoping her newfound strength would lessen the fall.

She landed directly on the metal spear that the mountain tauninaga used to mark the summit, bouncing off it with a sharp metal snap. Unclenching her eyes, she saw the rock she landed on was cracked down the center from the impact, and the metal spear was bent in half. The point on her back where she should have been impaled was gently throbbing, and she pushed her fingers through a new hole in her shirt, feeling only smooth, unmarked skin.

That was all the proof she needed to know she was indestructible. "Holy shit. Eiklo would love this. He'd demand so many tests. Of all the experiments he ran, he never had me just *punch* something." She stared at the bent spear with a sad smile. It turned into a real smile as she said, "Srrith is going to *hate* this."

Srrith could be in danger right now. Vrato was coming. He could *be* there, fighting Srrith, *killing* Srrith, and she finally had the strength to save someone she cared about.

With a deep breath, she trapped the Du'ul and leapt off the Peak of Blossoms.

Chapter 49

Fighting Fate

With Mayve stashed safely on the Peak of Blossoms, Srrith set to work aiding the leaders in Savin Actai's defense. Ressi's scouts confirmed that the coreskiff had been sighted the evening after the storm, flying several trips up and down the mountain to deposit soldiers on both sides of the city's gorges. The coreskiff was especially troubling to Zaatal—Srrith had heard a rare shudder of anxiety in the mountain tauninaga's chest. A vessel that could easily deposit soldiers directly into their high-altitude homes was a real nightmare for his people.

Ressi had one of her scouts follow Mayve at distance to make sure the human arrived at the trailhead safely. Once she was up the mountain, the clouds would hide her if the coreskiff returned. Assuming Zeteph did not already know she was heading that way.

How they knew we made it past the Way of Waterfalls into the city is beyond me. We were both trapped on those slopes, and now they assault the city as if they're so sure we're here. Srrith knew the answer even as she thought it. Zeteph, in some unnatural way, knew everything.

He could know that Mayve is up there, all alone with the Oasis Stone. Srrith had to assume he did not, otherwise they had already lost. If he knew everything, then every path they chose would lead to failure.

At least she knew where Vrato would be. The Great Seer had fore-seen herself dying on his blades.

Srrith almost considered traveling back to the Way of Echoes to get Eiklo's mace. The Cavotros iron would prove invaluable against Vrato—and Zeteph, if he were to appear—but she could not bring herself to face whatever was left of his corpse. *Mayve would skin me alive if she found out I went back and looted his grave.* She would rather join Eiklo in death than return to that wretched hole.

Srrith emerged from the canal and slithered onto the stone path, water trailing behind her. *Tonight is the night that Alactashi Sen dies.* The Great Seer always said that no prophecy was set in stone, that the fates can always be twisted in your favor. But, how do you know if your actions are subverting fate, or merely playing right into its hands?

Alactashi explained it well to Srrith, one night while they were sitting amongst the lanterns. "If I predict that the mountain will break and a landslide will take the eastern cliff, crushing half the town while they sleep, what part of that prophecy are you able to take into your own hands? Do you stand in the mountain's path and try to hold back the onslaught, or do you evacuate the villagers before the sun sets and let the mountain run its course? The latter, of course, but was my vision wrong? It was, partially, but that is because we focus on what we *can* change, and accept what we cannot."

Srrith did not accept that this was Alactashi Sen's last night alive, so she focused on what she could change. She pored over every detail of the vision that Great Seer was kind enough to share. Alactashi recounted that everything was bathed in red, then she was stabbed from behind, twin scimitars sprouting from her chest.

The twin swords pointed to Vrato, so Srrith prepared the tauni-nagan forces for such. Each fighter was told a codeword and a subtle sign to use as a greeting, in case Vrato was impersonating one of them. Zaatal chose the words *nighttime spear*, which Ressi vehemently disagreed with. She pointed out that both of those words were likely to be used during an actual nighttime battle, to which Zaatal replied, "That's what makes a good codeword."

Srrith had interrupted their bickering to point out that the words did not matter as much as the accompanying sign—flick your tongue twice before and after the sentence. She had hissed at the soldiers, "Only trust someone who does both, otherwise attack on sight. Do not forget, because you will find yourself under attack from your fellow soldiers."

Entering into the Great Seer's dwelling, she was met with seven tauninaga—Zaatal, Ressi, four of their best fighters, and Alactashi Sen herself, who was coiled on her sleeping mat. Everyone greeted Srrith with a hiss.

Srrith took a spot next to Alactashi, who reached out and held her hand in a motherly grasp. She turned to the two generals and hissed, "Is everything ready?"

"My forces are spread on hidden lookouts throughout the upper cliffs," Ressi said. "They'll alert us at the first sign, using the alpine grass to carry their messages home. If they attack from the west, we will have to glide back. There is not enough foliage to use our sfa-zrueen on that side. If they dare try to scale the trees from the forest floor, we will pick them off like mites clinging to a corpse."

Zaatal spoke in his gruff hiss. "My forces are split onto both cliffs. I'll be commanding from the middle, using Ressi's scouts to communicate."

"Remember, they're here for the Oasis Stone, which is safely secure on the Peak of Blossoms," Srrith hissed. "Do *not* divulge that information, in case the coreskiff is nearby with more troops. Bear in the mind, the real threat is Vrato. He will pass by your troops without second thought, and can impersonate anyone. The only one who can see him is me, which is the only reason we know he's not watching us from the corner right now."

There were solemn nods around the room. A knot of anxiety ate at Srrith's heart. Alactashi was no longer alone in her dwelling, like the vision dictated. Ressi and Zaatal would leave them, but the four other fighters would stay. Fassisa and Savat, two of Ressi's best fighters, each wielding the traditional sickles in foliage-adorned leather armor, alongside two of Zaatal's best—Iessei and Urris, armored in slate gray plate and wielding a broadsword and glaive, respectively.

Srrith also planned on extinguishing the lanterns, keeping each fighter hidden in the shadows with flint and tinder. If she could not immediately slay Vrato in the dark, where he was just as blind as any other human, then the other four would ignite their lanterns and join the ambush. She hoped this would also counter Alactashi's prophecy. The room could not be bathed in red if there was no light to begin with. Srrith was hellbent on changing any minor details she could of the Great Seer's vision, even wanting to move Alactashi from her dwelling, but there was nowhere more defensible. Who knew what details might be crucial in swaying fate's decision.

No matter the precautions, only one thing truly mattered. Could Srrith defeat Vrato? With no illusions, Vrato was just a skilled swordsman. Better than Srrith? If anyone asked, she'd confidently say no, but still she was troubled. He knew he could not use his illusions against her, but he still dared show his face.

It does not matter. Srrith ran her tongue over her fangs, her gaze as strong as iron. *I bested him before, with ease. I will do it again, regardless if fate is with me or against me.*

"Shall we dream?" Alactashi hissed. The seven other snakes nodded, coiling in a large circle throughout the room. The mountain tauninaga would use their sfa-zrueen to focus their minds and heal their ailments before the upcoming fight. The jungle tauninaga would soak the essence of nature through their scales, gaining the ability to communicate with the plants they called home. Srrith would call the shadows, wrapping fear itself through her scales. Alactashi Sen, the only forest tauninaga, would open her dreams to see if the future had anything to tell her.

Soon, the eight thumping heartbeats calmed one by one, the tauninagas' breathing slowing as they drifted into dream. Srrith's waking mind receded, and her dreaming mind took control. She awoke in the middle of the dark forest clearing that she knew so well. Her personal sanctuary against the nightmares that roamed her subconscious. There she began weaving her cave sfa-zrueen, tenderly spinning the shadows into tangible threads. Then one thread snagged, like a fishing line stuck at the bottom of the pond.

The stuck thread of shadow trailed from the spool in her hand, across the meadow and into the trees, where it held taut. The thin trunks seemed to multiply by the hundreds, and the meadow's grass dried and sank flat, dead. Her waking mind screamed not to pull thread, but it was not in control, muffled by her subconscious. She pulled, harder and harder, begging the thread to unlatch, then Zeteph stepped into the clearing.

The other end of her thread was wrapped tightly around his wrist, clasped in his gloved hand. His mask dripped with shadows, cascading down the amethyst tears like fog pouring down a cliffside, and although his mask was emotionless, her dreaming mind knew he was grinning. He pulled the thread, and Srrith lifted off the ground toward him, flying at breakneck speed.

The moment before her throat flew into his gloved hands, the forest and meadow disappeared in an instant, and she was left floating in a void. Behind her, Alactashi Sen hissed, "You have not dreamed like this in many years, Srrith. Why have the nightmares returned?"

Srrith caught her breath and quelled the fear in her chest. "I do not know."

"Because you are not used to being afraid."

Srrith remained silent.

"It is okay to be afraid, Srrith. Even the mightiest huntress is allowed to fear. Only fools have no fear."

"I am the one who uses fear. Fear is *my* weapon."

"A master swordsman knows how to strike, and also how to parry. How can you use fear as a weapon, yet not know how to defend when it is used against you?"

Srrith thought about all of Savin Actai's leaders and greatest fighters, blissfully asleep around her. "Is the waking world okay?"

"Your nightmares have not bled into reality. But they will, just like they used to, if you do not control your fear."

Relief rushed through Srrith. "Thank you for saving me. Again."

The Great Seer asked, "Do you know what you'll do when I'm gone, Srrith?"

Srrith flared her hood and hissed, "You *will not* die tonight."

"When I'm gone, you will continue to be strong, just like you always have been."

The muted sound of a distant horn, blown from the peak of a goliath tree, shook Srrith from her sleep. One blast, signaling enemies from the west. She looked for the shadows around her, and saw nothing.

The nightmare had interrupted her sfa-zrueen. She had no shadows under her control.

One less weapon to use against Vrato. She cursed Akthoru's coils under her breath, and caught a concerned glance from Alactashi Sen. The other tauninaga awoke, shaking off the dreariness of sleep and grabbing their weapons, focused and ready from the mountain's healing sfa-zrueen. Srrith felt that same calm for only a few seconds before she fell into troubled thoughts again.

Ressi and Zaatal turned and bowed to everyone in the room. Zaatal hissed, "Fight with the strength of the mountain and the veracity of the jungle, brethren." They all returned the bow, then the two leaders hurried out the door. Srrith and the other fighters slithered to their chosen positions, and at Srrith's command, the lanterns were extinguished.

There was nothing to do but wait. They were too far away to hear the sounds of battle. Once more they heard a horn blast through the valley, two distinct notes signaling enemies from the east. Even in the pitch-black, she felt exposed without her sfa-zrueen shadows wreathed around her. Without her control, the shadows were indifferent, aiding whoever wanted to hide amongst them. Opening her hearing, she heard the thumping hearts of her fighting companions, the ragged hisses of the Great Seer, and the constant trickle of water.

Then the door creaked open.

Torchlight created a thin alley of dim illumination down the center of the room. Vrato called out, "Come now, Srrith. Do you expect me to stroll into a dark room with a lurking cave tauninaga?"

With a swoosh of fire, Vrato tossed a torch inside, where it clattered on the floor and rolled idly, turning the alley of light into a circle. From the doorway, the scrape of unsheathing blades jarred her hearing.

She remained silent, dipping her sickle into a pool of water. With a flick of her wrist, water extinguished the torch, drenching the room in darkness once again. Sliding across the room into a silent coil, she repositioned herself to avoid detection. "I knew you were waiting," Vrato barely whispered, knowing she'd hear. Then with a loud, malicious laugh, he charged into the room.

Srrith rushed to meet him. Opening her hearing, she hissed and the room painted itself in her mind. Vrato, scimitars drawn, rushing in with a smile plastered across his face. He had no idea where she was, his face staring blindly into the darkness. She uncoiled to strike, her sickles carving through the shadows for his unsuspecting throat. Something broke against the stone floor, dropped by Vrato as he ran. The crack of ceramic shattering...

BOOM. Whatever Vrato dropped exploded in a harmless shower of sparks and a puff of smoke. But the sound smashed Srrith in the head like a hammer, the painting in her mind shattering to static. Her head rang like a gong, echolocation utterly ruined. In the meager light of the sparks, Vrato saw her shape and lunged. She tried to raise her sickles in defense, but it felt like someone was driving glass shards into her ears.

Muffled shouts forced through the ringing, and lanterns bloomed to light. A green shape crashed into Vrato, blocking his downward strike with a clang of steel and forcing him away with a flurry of spinning strikes. Through blurry vision, Srrith saw Fassisa and Vrato exchange blows, then Vrato leapt backward, manifesting illusions and disappearing into invisibility with a hideous cackle.

Akthoru take me, what was that! Does he have more? Srrith tried to hiss, the image in her mind rife with static. The four other tauninaga turned back and forth, searching for the invisible assassin. The knot in Srrith's chest tightened. Without her echolocation, the fight was suddenly even.

Like a ghost in fog, her echolocation caught a blurry abnormality behind Urris, and she shouted, her voice making muffled words she couldn't hear. Urris leapt forward and spun his glaive in a savage arc. Vrato flickered into view, twisting in an acrobatic tumble over the blade. Savat struck like lightning, sickles flying, but as Vrato landed, his body glowed a sick violet, and when the somersault ended, five Vratos leapt in different directions. Savat cleaved through one of them, which flickered harmlessly. Each Vrato ran at a different tauninaga.

Srrith hissed, fighting through the agony to see which Vrato was real. *BOOM.* Another explosion of sparks and thunder rocked the room, and Srrith collapsed with a scream. The Vrato in front of her plunged his swords down, the blades wavering through Srrith's chest without pain. Through her ringing vision, she saw the other four tauninaga dodge away from the illusionary blades, yelling at her for aid. She watched helplessly as Fassisa's throat opened as if pulled apart by thin air, spraying crimson blood.

If she closed her hearing, Vrato would slaughter them. She had to see through his illusions. She shouted, "Form up, back-to-back!"

She barely heard her own words through the earsplitting ringing in her head. The tauninaga ran for each other, then Iessei collapsed, his head lifting from his shoulders in a clean cut, decapitated body writhing.

The static in her mind blurred her real vision. Urris and Savat flanked her, weapons ready. She could not hear their heartbeats, but she knew they were racing. She hissed, and from the corner of her eye she saw a shard of ceramic ping against the stone. In an instant, she shut her hearing just before another explosion of sparks. With her hearing closed, the explosion was manageable, but now she was blind to Vrato's tricks. "Over there!" Savat shouted, words barely legible, pointing at the sparks. Urris swept his glaive through the nearby water pool, sending a wave toward that direction.

A perfect outline of a human appeared in the spray and Vrato laughed. Srrith leapt forward, focusing with all her concentration on the wet footprints appearing from nothing. Vrato dropped his invisibility as their blades met, sickle ringing against scimitar. She drove him back toward the other side of the hall, Urris and Savat flanking on either side. Vrato had to twist and turn, blades spinning, dodging every strike and parrying where he could.

The assassin disappeared, and Urris swept his glaive in another arc, trying to catch the invisible assailant with the weapon's immense reach. Srrith tried to follow Vrato's wet footsteps, then she realized there were two sets of boots. Then four, then eight, then the entire floor was criss-crossed in soaked boot prints. Then the boot prints turned red as they walked through the blood of the fallen tauninagas. Something gurgled, and Savat dropped to the ground, blood pouring from her mouth as a blade pushed through her skull from behind.

Alactashi would have died alone. Now you've twisted fate so five more die with her. Srrith opened her hearing and *BOOM*, Vrato timed another noise bomb perfectly. She collapsed on the ground, spine arched in pain. Two dozen Vratos formed around them, all laughing. Urris sprinted for her, shouting something about running. Alactashi sat silent, weeping through closed eyes, not for her own inevitable demise, but for those who died trying to stop fate.

Dozens of Vratos rushed at Urris, who spun his glaive in deadly arcs, carving through the illusions. The mountain tauninaga twisted and spun like a hurricane, defending every angle. Srrith clawed herself upright, trying to hiss. Nothing broke through the static in her mind.

Zaatal crashed through the door, spear drawn. "To me! Form up!" Urris adjusted his stance, retreating toward the door. As he formed up with Zaatal, the mountain tauninaga chief stabbed his spear into Urris's head. The illusion dropped away, revealing Vrato with his twin scimitars embedded in between Urris's eyes.

As Urris fell, Vrato disappeared once again. Srrith clawed her way toward Alactashi. She tried to stand, but her balance was destroyed. The incessant, agonizing ringing in her ears would not end. Lakes of blood spread across the floor, clouding the lantern pools. *A room bathed in red. Alactashi all alone. I am once again the center of a living nightmare.*

Alactashi Sen opened her eyes, looking at Srrith with all the kindness and sadness in the world. "This is not your fault," the Great Seer hissed. "You are strong."

She closed her eyes as twin blades erupted from her chest, blood spraying across the floor. With a rasping breath, Alactashi Sen slid off the blades and crumpled lifeless to her crimson-soaked mat.

Hands materialized around the hilts of the scimitars, followed by the rest of Vrato. He was soaked in tauninagan blood, pale skin smeared red, a bloodthirsty grin plastered on his face.

"You are *strong*?" Vrato chuckled as he nudged Alactashi's corpse with his boot. "To think that Zeteph was worried enough about you to send me, all for you to squirm on the floor at some loud noises."

He stepped down from Alactashi's mat, blood dripping from his blades. Srrith tried to push herself up, and Vrato chuckled. "Here, I have one more, you can have it." He tossed another ceramic ball from his belt onto the ground near Srrith. *BOOM.* She covered her head in her hands, trying to soften the ringing.

The assassin kicked her blades away, and she watched them skitter off into the blood. He leveled his scimitar at her throat. "I was given three tasks from the masked man himself, in no particular order. First, kill the Seer. It's problematic having an enemy with so much knowledge. Second, recover the Oasis Stone, and third, kill everyone who dared escape Port Wenstnor. I've searched high and low for the girl and the Ventwalker with no trace, so now I have to cut the information out of you."

Pain pulsing behind her eyes, she managed to whisper, "Just kill me."

She hoped Mayve stayed far away, never to be seen again. Everyone she ever met with, fought with, talked with, they all met their end too soon.

A blade sliced across her ribs, the pain barely registering amidst the agony in her head. Vrato screamed at her, voice muffled by her ringing ears. "Where *is* Imayva?" His grin widened. "Where is the *Stone?*"

His second blade opened a long cut down her spine. "What will it be, Srrith? Death by a thousand cuts? You can die quickly, just tell me where *they are!*"

"Vrato!" a figure called from the doorway. A human? Dark hair, green eyes, olive skin. *No. Please, no more deaths. Run, Mayve. You have to run.* She screamed at the human, unsure if her mouth was making noise. Vrato muttered, "I guess I don't need you anymore. I can torture this one now." He raised his blades above her.

Srrith did not care for her own demise. She looked at Mayve, eyes pleading with her to run. Pleading with her to forgive her.

Mayve looked calm. There was something else in her verdant eyes. Not rage or resentment, only fierce determination.

In one motion, Mayve grabbed the huge stone door, ripped it from its hinges, and hurled it at Vrato.

There was no time for the smug look to disappear from the assassin's face before the heavy stone crunched into his ribs, picking him off Srrith like a bug and smashing him into the wall in a blast of stone rubble. His body crumpled into a blood-soaked pool, red waves washing over the lily pads.

Srrith's numb mind could not process what she saw. Mayve was suddenly by her side, as if she drifted across the floor in two steps. The human slid to Srrith and picked the tauninaga to her feet with *surprising* ease, stammering "Come on, let's get you to Tressis."

Still dazed, Srrith hissed, "How are you..."

"Later. You're not allowed to die. We've both had enough of that."

A gasp sounded, and Vrato pulled himself from the pool. His chest was crushed, and his legs dragged limply behind him. Bloody water clung to his body, painting him a fetid vermilion hue. Violet shreds of illusions flitted around him like spirits. His eyes, crazed with hatred, locked onto them, and he screamed, "You will all burn!"

Mayve balanced Srrith on her own coils and asked, "Can you stand?"

Srrith nodded, and Mayve left her, walking toward Vrato. Srrith felt like she should stop her, but she didn't. Mayve had returned from the Peak of Blossoms with the confidence of someone completely unbreakable.

The human shouted as she walked toward the crawling assassin, "You're already dead, Vrato, sent to your death by a masked madman. Spit out your last words before I crush them out of you."

"Zeteph is no madman." Vrato grinned, blood dribbling from his lower lip. "He is a visionary. He knows how to save us, how to save *everyone!*"

"Zeteph wants to erupt the Vents!" Mayve grabbed Vrato by the scruff of his blood-soaked shirt and pulled him up to her face. "He's a raving lunatic who tricked you with golden words."

"He will put our world through fire, where the strong and loyal will rebuild under a new Ralvera, free from the Vents! Why do you wish to live underneath the icy, ashen shadows of our monstrous oppressors? Zeteph knows how to end it once and for all, no matter the cost."

"We know what the Oasis Stone is for. We know how to stop the Vents, to quell them forever."

"No you don't," Vrato rasped. "You don't know the consequences. Zeteph does. His way is the only way."

"What is his plan? What is he going to do to Citadel Waldheath?" Mayve shook the assassin's limp body.

"You and he want the same thing. You want the Vents gone. But... only he knows how to do it *right*. Your ignorance...will doom *everyone*."

Vrato scowled between dying breaths. Then a smile crept over his face. "For Zeteph, and his glorious vision!" A hidden dagger flashed into his palm and he slammed it into Mayve's throat.

The blade snapped off Mayve's skin as if he stabbed a rock. She stared into Vrato's pitiful eyes, unbent and unflinching. Vrato looked at the hilt of his broken blade, then cracked into hysterical laughter. Mayve tossed him aside, his paralyzed body crumpling to the floor, and turned her back without another word.

She grabbed Srrith, supporting her on her shoulder. Srrith leaned onto the human, feeling limp in Mayve's immense strength. As they stumbled out of Alactashi's dwelling, Vrato's echoing laughter crescendoed to a howling, manic fit, peaking in one final, rasping breath.

Chapter 50

Healing

Heading toward the eastern cliff face, Mayve strode across one of the stone bridges that spanned the Savin Actai gorge. The canopy sea beneath rustled in the wind, stirring up remnants of the morning fog that still lingered in the leaves, safe from the morning sun. Colorful dots of exotic birds flitted through the air, diving from the branches of the goliath trees into the lower canopy.

A new confidence filled her steps. Before, she carried herself with a reckless confidence, assured she could wrench her own survival from the jaws of death. Now, she could turn indestructible on a whim. A mere thought, and blades would snap against her skin. Mayve walked with the confidence of someone who knew they could not die.

Mayve wanted nothing more than to run into the mountains and test the limits of her manifestation. First, however, she had to visit Srrith in the infirmary. The mountain tauninaga had assured her that the snake would survive and make a full recovery before hurrying her out of the room. That had eased most of her worries, but still she fretted about Srrith's emotional state.

She had spent some time with the serpentine soldiers of Savin Actai last night. It was impossible to not catch the whispers, the rumors of the nightmare that lived among them. A nightmare whose very presence brought misfortune to those around them. A nightmare who was there when their best fighters and beloved Seer died.

Now that the Great Seer was slain, there was no one left to warn them of what the nightmare tauninaga might bring.

I don't care about their silly rumors. Srrith has saved my life many times over, she deserves to live wherever she damn well pleases.

There was a rush of wind and two bright green jungle tauninaga whipped overhead, scaled flaps outstretched and tails undulating. Ahead of her, a scaled gray head peeked from a canal like a lurking crocodile, then Zaatal emerged onto the stone path. Instead of his plate armor from yesterday, he wore more the traditional robes of the mountain healers. He did not seem to mind the sodden fabric, and bowed as Mayve approached. She returned the gesture.

"Good morning, Mayve, I was just on my way to fetch you. Srrith is awake and in good health."

"That's so good to hear, thank you, Zaatal. I was heading over now myself."

The mountain tauninaga adjusted his height as he walked to match her eye level, something Mayve had figured out was a sign of respect. Srrith did it all the time, but she thought it was just to make conversation more comfortable.

He hissed as they walked together, "It has been many years since I practiced my people's sfa-zrueen, but I oversaw her recovery personally. The other healers were...reluctant...to care for her."

"Why does she carry this legacy?" Mayve asked. "She does not speak of it—do you know what happened?"

"Have you asked her?"

"I did not want to intrude."

"I don't believe it is my place to say. She will talk if you ask. Srrith is private but not secretive," Zaatal hissed. "I will say this about tauninagas in general. Because our sfa-zrueen creates reality from dream, nightmares can be dangerous in the wrong minds. Srrith has struggled in the past with keeping her nightmares contained, and although no one in this town has ever been harmed by her, our people can be suspicious at best, and fearful at worst."

Mayve narrowed her eyes. "You said nothing has happened in *this town*, does that mean—"

Zaatal interrupted, "Again, not my place to say. She is a cave tauninaga living in the mountains, draw your own conclusions or ask her yourself."

They walked in silence until they were up on the eastern ledge, walking through the clifftop dwellings. There were no signs of battle, thankfully. Fighting had been contained on the outskirts of town, out in the alpine and jungle wilds where the Merchatzi stood little chance against the snakes. Apparently, their only plan had been to draw forces away from town so Vrato could infiltrate.

All sacrificial lambs for Zeteph's plan. The tauninaga had dispatched the Merchatzi so efficiently, there were few tauninagan injuries. The only casualties that Savin Actai suffered were the five snakes in the Great Seer's dwelling.

"The Peak of Blossoms was beautiful," Mayve said, changing the subject to something lighter. Zaatal remained stoic-faced, but his voice betrayed a hint of pride, "I am glad you made it there safely. It is a strenuous climb, but quite worth it."

"Definitely strenuous. That overhang was tougher than anything I've climbed before."

He looked at her with deep concern. "There is no overhang on the left path..."

Mayve grinned back.

"Did you—?" Zaatal took an exasperated breath. "You are an enigma of a human, Mayve."

She almost mentioned how she broke the spear that was marking the summit, but decided to hold her tongue. *They'll find out eventually. No need for me to still be in town when they do.*

They approached the healer's hut, her first time back there since escaping the glint butchers. Mayve forced Eiklo out of her mind—Srrith needed her to be strong right now, not misty-eyed at her lost friend. Following Zaatal through the open door, they saw Srrith coiled on the same mat, alone with a small meal of fish.

The cave tauninaga uncoiled and reared to match their eye level, no wounds or scars visible. The only evidence of injury was the dried blood soaked into the healing mat, which had not been washed yet. Her leather armor was laid in the corner, and she wore a mountain tauninagan robe. Her eyes were the worst though, locked in faraway gaze that told Mayve the healing sfa-zrueen had done little to take the edge off last night's losses.

It occurred to Mayve that Srrith may have lost her mother-figure last night, and she was likely blaming herself. Mayve knew exactly how that felt, and tears welled in her eyes.

The two tauninagas bowed to each other, then Mayve pushed through and embraced Srrith in a hug. Surprised, it took Srrith a few seconds to return the embrace. As Mayve stepped back, she whispered, "I'm sorry."

The faraway gaze receded from Srrith's eyes as she saw Mayve. "Thank you, friend."

"As long as there is someone to hold you in their sleeping thoughts, you are not truly dead," Mayve said, recalling the tauninagan words. "I hope you dream of them."

The pain in Srrith's eyes did not leave, but a faint smile fought across her face. "This time, I owe you my life."

"You've saved my life a few times now. One day I'll get even."

"Hopefully not."

"It only gets more dangerous from here. We've been running from Zeteph this whole time, now we have to run right at him."

Srrith coiled up uncomfortably, inviting Mayve and Zaatal to sit. "You have made a decision, then?"

"On the mountain, I thought about how we have an opportunity to change Ralvera for the better, even if it's quelling just one Vent," Mayve said "That would be an accomplishment worthy of all the friends we've lost on the way."

"Yes." Srrith nodded, a fierce gaze in her eyes. "We will honor the dead and their sacrifice, and take down a Vent while we do it."

"Maybe even more, if we can find how to make more Oasis Stones."

"One task at a time," Srrith said. "Zeteph has plans for Citadel Waldheath, and we need the rainthistle kept there. We can talk about quelling Vents and crafting Oasis Stones once that is done with."

Zaatal, silent until now, hissed, "This quest of yours. It is noble, and Savin Actai will aid however it can."

"The less everyone knows the better," Srrith said. "We'll take some food and some coin, nothing more."

Mayve looked at Zaatal with concern. "Zeteph had Oaken Legion allies in Devar. I don't know how far his reach into the Legion goes, but Savin Actai might be in danger if he decides to call in some favors."

Zaatal let out a half-hearted hiss. "We have always laughed at the notion of the Legion climbing our mountains. Now with these coreskiffs flying higher than our peaks, we may have to rethink our defenses."

"The Citadels wouldn't sell coreskiffs to the Legion, would they?" Mayve pondered.

"The Citadels will do anything for coin as long as it doesn't bite them in the tail within a couple moons," Zaatal hissed. He uncoiled. "I will make preparations for your departure. I see it best that you leave immediately."

"Is my presence that discomforting?" Srrith asked.

Zaatal was taken aback by the directness of the question. He looked stunned that someone had seen through his stone-faced emotional facade, but then must have remembered he was talking to a cave tauni-naga. Srrith was dissecting his very breathing. "People are talking, Srrith. I'm sorry. It's best if you leave. Ressi and I will calm things down in your absence."

"Right," Srrith said. "It is good I was leaving anyway."

"Srrith..."

"It's fine, Zaatal. Make the preparations."

Zaatal bowed and left. Mayve shifted nervously, wanting to ask about Srrith's past. Instead, she said, "I don't think you're bad luck. I'd be dead if you weren't around."

Srrith looked appreciative. "Thank you, but there are many that disagree with you."

"Zaatal said the tauninagas are afraid of nightmares becoming reality when they dream. Do you have nightmares?"

Srrith hissed, "I used to. Alactashi Sen helped me dispel them, for many years." She looked worried. "I have had a few recently. None have escaped my sleeping mind, but I worry it is only a matter of time."

"Have they—?"

"They've escaped before, when I was young. It is why I am no longer welcome in my home caves," Srrith said. It was the first time outside of the heat of battle that Mayve saw a hint of anger flash through her eyes.

"I'm not afraid."

"I find you rarely are, especially in times when a little fear would be good for you."

Mayve shrugged. "I have other things to be afraid of. As he was dying, Vrato laughed at us, called us fools. He said Zeteph wants the same thing as us, but knows how to do it right. What are we missing? Does Zeteph also want to quell the Vents?"

Srrith grimaced. "Zeteph has a gift for knowing things that he shouldn't. I doubt his goals are as amiable as that. There is nothing for us to do but learn as we travel, and make our decisions as they come." She uncoiled and reared slightly above Mayve's eye level. A height she often took during their training sessions on the Ferry. "Speaking of Vrato, perhaps you can take this time to explain to me your newfound gift of strength? Unless I was so delirious that I was hallucinating."

Mayve grinned. She had been secretly itching to show Srrith what she could do. "On the Peak of Blossoms, I finally found out what my Natural Manifestation does." She looked around for something to smash or break in half, and Srrith held up her hand. "Words will suffice. I already saw you throw a stone door like skipping a rock across a pond."

They were interrupted by a rustling of scales and wind as Ressi landed in the doorway, folding away her gliding-scales and slithering inside. "Greetings, both of you. Srrith, I am glad to see the healing was a success. My deepest condolences to you. I know you and the Great Seer were close."

"I appreciate it, Ressi. I am sorry I could not protect her or your warriors. They were brave until the end."

Ressi bowed her thanks. "I will see them in my dreams. Mayve, are you well?"

Mayve nodded, and Ressi said, "I thought I would deliver this report personally, to check in on you. Zaatal said you two were leaving shortly, but this is interesting."

Mayve and Srrith looked at each other, and Mayve asked, "Has something happened?"

"My scouts came across a coreskiff, flying low over the alpine fields. They boarded it, captured the occupants, and grounded the coreskiff."

"That's excellent news." Srrith said.

"Are you taking us to look at it? Do you think we can fly it when we leave?"

Ressi laughed. "It will never fly again. My warriors acted too quickly, capturing the occupants and shredding the wings. We will salvage it later to see how it works and aid in our defenses. It's the occupants that I'm here to discuss. They are unusual, and they're asking for you by name."

"Me?" Mayve asked. She looked at Srrith, who appeared just as confused. Turning to Ressi, she said, "Who are they?"

"If you can believe it, a desert raptor and a Legion soldier."

Chapter 51

Beneath the Azraks

Something tapped on the stone cave floor next to Eiklo's head, pulling his senses back to him. He was lying face-down on the cold rock, with something jabbed into his ribs. The breath of a glint butcher rasped above him, mindlessly waiting for the next hint of light to appear, unaware that Eiklo lay motionless at its feet.

His skull throbbed, and he knew light was leaking from where he had cracked his head on the cave wall. *Praise Varin, the cloth on my hood must be covering it. If I shift at all, I'm dead.* He was beyond lucky that he had bounced off the wall, and the glint butchers had attacked the point of impact instead of his actual body.

Keeping his eyes squeezed tightly shut, he felt something scrape against his ribs. A sharp rock had punctured his robes and was lodged between his ribs. It had narrowly missed direct impact with his spine. He fought down a swell of panic. *If I lift myself at all, it will be impossible to hide the light of my injured bones. Focus only on what I can move.*

He rotated his ankles, feeling his boots drag across the stone. Slowly, he bent each knee, then inch by inch scraped his right arm in a wide arc, keeping his left pinned at his side to avoid touching the glint butcher.

Okay, Eiklo. If you stand up, you die. But let's pretend that's not the case. Say you stand up and miraculously don't get ripped to shreds. Then what? The tunnel was swarming with glint butchers and he was completely blind. He didn't even know which direction to run. *If I open my eyes, I'm dead. If I touch a glint butcher, I'm dead.* His skull throbbed, and he knew beneath the thick cloth of his hood, he was bleeding blue light, his own body becoming a deadly target for the deaf monsters.

I don't need to eat or sleep. I could lie here for an eternity, until another cave tauninaga comes through. Eiklo decided he would rather be ripped to pieces than wait for that. *Maybe Srrith and Mayve will come back soon? They have not already, so they must think I'm dead. Let's solve the first problem. Stand up without being torn to shreds. What do I have on me?*

Vulinor's mace hung at his side, and his pack was still secured on his back, but he could not reach either without disturbing the glint butchers. Lying on his stomach, he scavenged his immediate area until his palm wrapped around a loose stone. *That's a start. I have a rock.* He froze as the glint butcher took a few steps, tapping along the floor, inches away from stepping on him.

Forcing the pain from his mind, he trapped the Du'ul. The surge of energy was muted, almost meager. He *was* in the heart of a Verdant— there was little Du'ul to use. Still, he manifested it around him, leaking it across the surface of his bones. A layer of ice encased his skull and the outside of his robes, blocking the leaking light and hopefully adding enough armor to survive a few impacts from an enraged glint butcher.

Above the rasping breaths, he heard a different sound. A gentle chattering, and a rustle of leathery wings. *The lumitails are still here.* He had no idea how long it had been since he'd smashed his head. Perhaps they had left and returned. Perhaps they never left, and only minutes had passed since Mayve and Srrith were forced to run. *I hope they're okay.* The thought of tripping over their mutilated bodies on his way out crossed his mind.

The more he thought about his predicament, the more the panic grew. There was no rational course of action. None. Every option was far-fetched, and led to a visceral death. He lay there alone, panicking in the darkness, the glint butchers rasping and tapping around him, until realization dawned on him.

Right now, Eiklo, you are a dead man, for the second time in your existence. But, you have a rock. You can do whatever you want with that rock. One final choice, then the rest is in Varin's hands. A glint butcher will find you, whether you throw the rock or not. It's inevitable. So just throw the rock and pray.

He manifested the Du'ul through him, ice cracking as he grew a suit of frozen armor around him. As it grew, he whispered under his breath, "For Varin, for Vulinor, for Srrith and for Mayve." Then he pushed himself off the ground, and threw the rock at the ceiling.

Blue light from his cracked ribs poured from the hole in his robes, but it was lost in the explosion of light as the lumitails took flight. Eiklo opened his eyes for the first time since entering this godforsaken cavern, and the dim bulbs of the luminescent bats looked like star-fire to his light-starved vision.

Then, the howls erupted and he fled in a blind sprint, following the chaotic constellation of lumitails, praying they were flying for the outside.

Teeth gnashed around him and bodies flew as the glint butchers leapt with enraged abandon at the lights, trying to violently extinguish every last trace. His icy armor cracked and shattered as glint butchers slammed into it, claws splintering the ice. Eiklo pushed forward, swinging his mace at anything that moved in front of him. His armor crunched but held and his speed picked up, the light leaking from his bones, lost in the ocean of dancing stars.

The ground beneath his feet disappeared.

He watched the lumitails rapidly disappear out of reach, flying over the chasm that he had run into at full speed. Ice crunched, shattering to fragments, as he slammed hard onto a ledge below. His vision spun, the stream of lumitails blurring into a river of zipping lights, and he steadied himself against the cliff wall. He realized too late that everything around him was blue. Sapphire light shone from every injured bone in his body.

A silhouette blocked out the lumitails above as a howling glint butcher launched itself into the chasm with no self-regard. The wiry mass crashed into Eiklo, claws tearing at his bones, opening more wounds. The light, pouring forth, only enraged it further. Grappling the ravenous monster, there was only one thing Eiklo could do before more glint butchers saw him. He threw himself off the ledge with the screaming creature, tumbling farther into the mountain.

Slamming into rock after rock, ledge after ledge, they crashed deeper down the gorge, Eiklo doing everything in his power to stay conscious and keep the creature's claws from pulling his skull from his spine. The raw strength of the monster never seemed to waver, no matter how hard it was hit, as it tried to snuff out the light pouring from Eiklo. Crunching into one last ledge, they separated mid-fall and crashed into a pool of water.

They had hit too many ledges on the way down to build up any deadly momentum, and the water saved them from the worst impact. Still, Eiklo shakily pulled himself to his feet in the rushing current, scrambling for a foothold. The entire cavern was illuminated in blue, his bones burning like a cerulean sun. The glint butcher burst from the water, mere feet away, like a spindly gray corpse pushing up from a grave.

One of its arms was snapped clean at the elbow, and it stood with an awkward limp from a twisted ankle. One of its large eyes was crushed shut, but the other locked on Eiklo immediately, its jet-black, iris-less pupil fixating on the glowing skeleton with more malice than Eiklo ever thought possible in a living creature. The slits of its nostrils flared, its gulping jaw unhinged, and it screamed, charging Eiklo as if it were not injured at all.

Eiklo howled back, his scream reverberating up the chasm. Every bone in his body erupted in freezing blue light as he trapped the Du'ul and exploded it from his body. Stalagmites of ice speared up from the water, eviscerating the glint butcher as it leapt for his throat. Eiklo collapsed to his knees, grabbed his mace, and dragged it to the creature, who hung impaled upon the spears of ice—it still rasped for air, still reached for Eiklo with the last muscles it could move.

With a yell, Eiklo heaved the mace over his head and crushed the creature's skull. The glint butcher finally fell limp, limbs twitching and black blood dribbling down the ice it was impaled on.

Eiklo barely managed to secure the mace on his belt before collapsing into the river. With no energy left to fight the current, he let it sweep him away, deep into the caves of Ralvera.

Enjoy *The Oasis Stone*? Leave a rating or review wherever you found the book, and visit *teirmondpublishing.com* for more from Ralvera.

The adventure continues in *The Onyx Mask*, available now!

Art by John Spencer

- Cover Illustration
- Map of Ralvera
- Devar
- Cave Tauninaga
- Oaken Legion Soldier
- Raptors
- Ul'Varin on Phoenix
- The Torn

Art by Jack Davidson

- The Ferry
- Tauninagan Sickle
- Oaken Legion Helmet
- Coreskiff

Acknowledgments

It feels odd to share my writing with others. I am an introvert at heart, quick to flee, and this book is where I would escape to. To me, it's a cozy nook hidden behind a locked door that I've decorated just the way I like. Now, I've unlocked the door and nudged it open, waiting nervously for others to wander in and see what they think of the space. Everyone has, so far, found a comfortable seat and admired the view, and for that I'm forever grateful.

Thank you for my dad for my love of storytelling. You showed me how vast the world is, and inspired me to make my own.

Thank you to my mom for believing wholeheartedly in everything I do. Where I have doubts on if I can succeed, you have none. I aspire to be the person you see in me.

Thank you to my lifelong friend John, for turning my incoherent ramblings into real art.

Thank you to my D&D group, for toughing out my days as a beginner storyteller. Sorry that you had to play with the bad ideas so I could put the good ones in here.

Thank you to my editor, Shawna, and my beta readers. Your helpful insights and inspiring words helped a new author keep moving forward.

Thank you to anyone who looks inside this book and decides to stay.